NIMPONIN

SHINGAKUSHA HOSEKI TRILOGY - BOOK I

Robert C. Foley

NIMPONIN
SHINGAKUSHA HOSEKI TRILOGY - BOOK I

Copyright © 2022 Robert C. Foley.

All rights reserved. No part of this book may be used or reproduced by any means, graphic, electronic, or mechanical, including photocopying, recording, taping or by any information storage retrieval system without the written permission of the author except in the case of brief quotations embodied in critical articles and reviews.

This is a work of fiction. All of the characters, names, incidents, organizations, and dialogue in this novel are either the products of the author's imagination or are used fictitiously.

iUniverse books may be ordered through booksellers or by contacting:

iUniverse
1663 Liberty Drive
Bloomington, IN 47403
www.iuniverse.com
844-349-9409

Because of the dynamic nature of the Internet, any web addresses or links contained in this book may have changed since publication and may no longer be valid. The views expressed in this work are solely those of the author and do not necessarily reflect the views of the publisher, and the publisher hereby disclaims any responsibility for them.

Any people depicted in stock imagery provided by Getty Images are models, and such images are being used for illustrative purposes only.
Certain stock imagery © Getty Images.

ISBN: 978-1-6632-3458-2 (sc)
ISBN: 978-1-6632-3457-5 (e)

Library of Congress Control Number: 2022901023

Print information available on the last page.

iUniverse rev. date: 07/05/2022

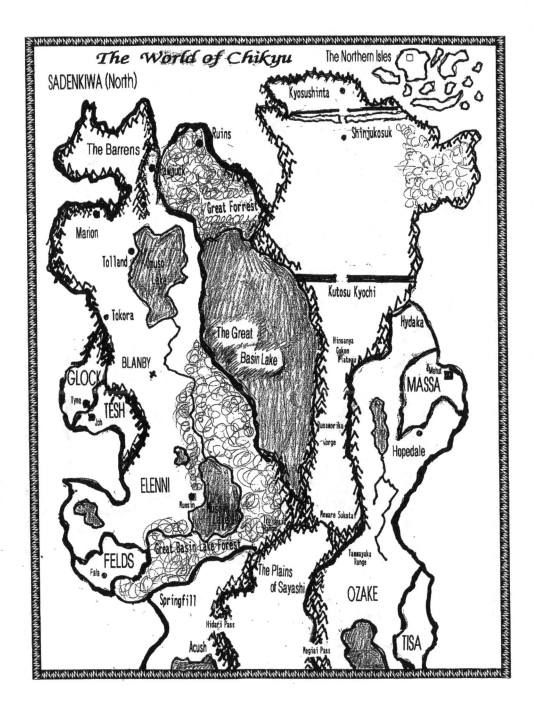

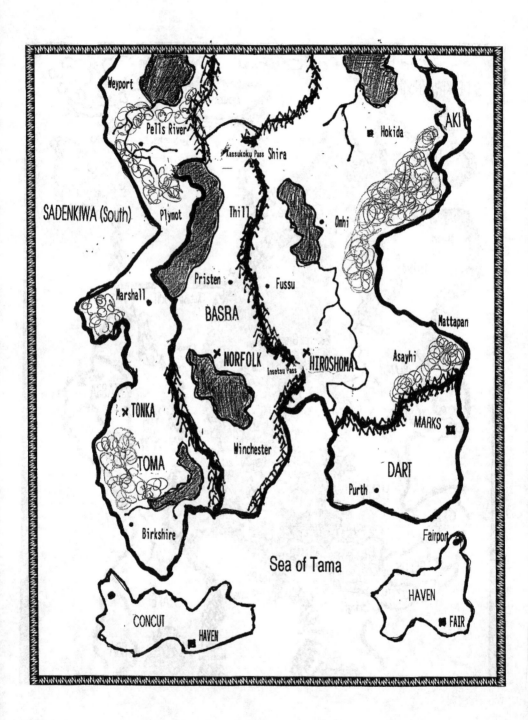

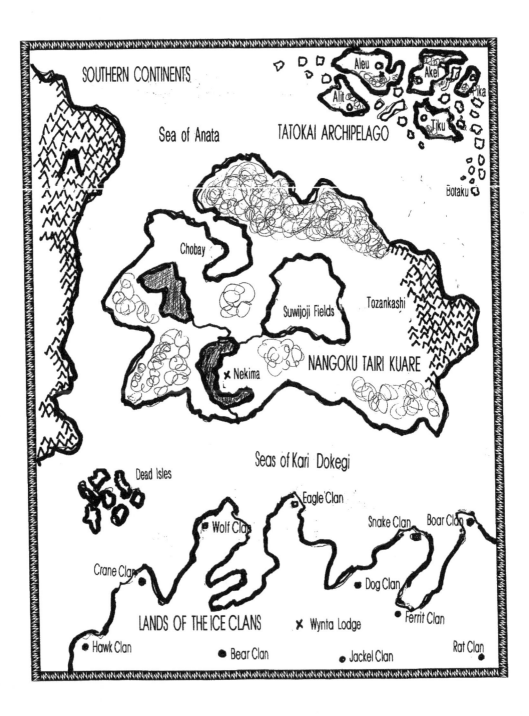

THE SHINGAKUSHA
HOSEKI TRILOGY

NIMPONIN
BOOK I

Contents

Prologue	The Beginning..	xiii
Chapter 1	Chikyu and the Sacred Artifacts................................	1
Chapter 2	The Tendaishi...	24
Chapter 3	The Blessing	40
Chapter 4	The James Clan	55
Chapter 5	Sarah Priscilla Novasta...	71
Chapter 6	Samuel Miro..	87
Chapter 7	William James	102
Chapter 8	The Dark Twins	113
Chapter 9	The Chiraka Blossoms..	132
Chapter 10	Loved Ones Lost...	149
Chapter 11	The Kaisoshosuko..	159
Chapter 12	Revenge Is Bitter Sweet...	175
Chapter 13	A Special Guest...	191
Chapter 14	Reaper of Souls	201
Chapter 15	Rebirth	214
Chapter 16	Tokora	232
Chapter 17	Imprisonment	248
Chapter 18	Nova Meets Mia and Mae...	255
Chapter 19	Nova's Training	266
Chapter 20	Gustavo Heinz...	277
Chapter 21	Tolland	289
Chapter 22	The Traitor	307
Chapter 23	The Keep	319
Chapter 24	The Battle of Shira..	336
Chapter 25	William Meets Laki..	350
Chapter 26	Defeating the Enemy	363
Chapter 27	The Investigation	375
Chapter 28	Carrie Ann Barnes	391
Chapter 29	The Mission To Hokida..	402
Chapter 30	The First Chosen	414

Chapter 31	Exiled	427
Chapter 32	Jutsuk Finds Samuel	442
Chapter 33	William Meets Samuel	458
Chapter 34	The Sacred Valley	474
Chapter 35	Gifts from the Goddesses	486
Chapter 36	The Temple and the City	498
Chapter 37	Alivia Ruth Casrone	514
Chapter 38	Failure is Not an Option	527
Chapter 39	The Gifted	541
Chapter 40	Pawjuck	552
Chapter 41	Mijikuna Inkinjo	566
Chapter 42	Reunion	577

Prologue

The Beginning

A faint pulsation is felt once, then twice in a vast expanse of blackness beyond the imagination. Just before a third takes place, an infinitesimal pinpoint of brilliant white light bursts onto the expanse of darkness. Within a heartbeat of appearing, the single point of bright white light separates into two distinct points. They immediately begin to revolve around one another, and soon they rotate faster and faster; until they appear to be one continuous circular blur. They gradually start to slow, and as they slow, they take on the characteristics of two different entities, one female and the other male. The two newly formed celestial beings slowly begin to move and gently caress and fondle each other ever so tenderly and seductively. Then without reason, the tenderness is replaced by a raging maelstrom of sexual aggression that displays an erotic form of dance. Their lips barely touch as their bodies press against each other, and their limbs intertwine, and once they do, they release themselves from each other's grasp, only to smash their bodies together again and again. Every time their bodies touch, energy slowly builds, and this energy begins to expand, and it expands to the point of being nearly uncontainable. Their bodies touch one last time, and just before the built-up energy erupts like a climactic orgasm, they push themselves away from each other, forcing them in opposite directions through the vast blackness.

The distance they travel from one another is inconceivable, but like a rubber band stretched just before its breaking point, the newly formed entities gradually slow and then come to a complete stop. They maintain the connection, and one collective thought passes between them. An undeniable love immediately starts to pull the two entities back towards each other. Slowly at first, and then it steadily builds to a high velocity, almost a thousand times faster than when they pushed themselves away from each other. Seconds pass, and their speed intensifies as they steadily pick up so much momentum that the two celestial beings are again two indistinct blurs racing through space. Neither one is slowing, and they seem to be on a collision course with each other, in the exact spot where they came into being. Their paths do not falter as they continue heading toward each other. They are within a heartbeat of crashing into each other when they abruptly stop., The tailwinds they created crash into them, and their bodies absorb most of it, but some spills out around them. These ripples of energy saturate the darkness, and unknowingly these same ripples of energy somehow pierce the very fabric of the darkness.

The energy that their bodies have absorbed pulses and continue to build. They both feel it, and each takes a deep breath, and with unspoken words, they lock eyes and smile. They each raise their hands, with their palms facing each other, and move them together slowly until they are just a hair's breadth from touching. Small surges of pure energy and light dance and jump between their palms and fingertips. A crescendo of energy builds, and they ever so slowly touch the heels of their palms and then their fingers, and as they do, a surge of infinite power passes between them. They perceive a unification of an enormous magnitude and create a nexus between them that is so strong that it can never be broken as they interlock their fingers. They pull their bodies close and press their lips together in a seductive kiss. The kiss seals their fate, allowing them total fulfillment and enlightenment in becoming Eternal Gods.

Their bond is complete, their bodies begin to glow, and their combined radiance builds. A massive paroxysm occurs when it reaches its zenith, as billions upon billions of glittering orbs of white light and energy shoot out in every direction from their glowing bodies. Glittering orbs quickly spread throughout the expanse that was once a vast unimaginable blackness only seconds ago. What was once dark is now a spectacle of bright shimmering lights.

They watch as galactic bodies clash and merge, creating millions of spirals, barred spirals, lenticular, elliptical, and irregular galaxies. Galaxies, large and small, start forming in the blackness's far reaches. Solar systems spin within these galaxies, stars blaze with life-giving energy; planets begin to cool with small satellites orbiting around them.

The very fabric in space that separates many realms now has a flaw as a microscopic pinpoint of vacuity has manifested itself in the expanse of the darkness. The pinpoint appears to be slightly darker than the vast blackness surrounding it. It would be hard to discern, even if one were looking for it. The vacuity expands just enough to establish a rift of sorts, and then it pulses only once and is silent, leaving a discernible void, an impurity of darkness on this side of the cosmic veil. The female feels something, like a passing thought, and she also feels a slight pull at her very being, and then nothing, and like the thought, she forgets it.

Millennia pass while traversing through the cosmos, admiring the energies of light and life. They are elated as they gaze upon their newly created universe.

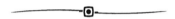

Millennia continue to pass, and the Gods stop momentarily here and there to view their beautiful new worlds. While they pass through one of several galaxies, she stops just long enough to gaze at a single star with nine satellites rotating around it. She notices a spiraling blue and white sphere, unlike any previously seen. She thinks it is pretty and remembers where it is as the two of them continue their travels.

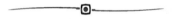

The microscopic vacuity that manifested itself in the cosmic veil of their creation pulses for a second time. As it does, a rift appears, similar to a door, and slowly grows more prominent. When it is large enough, a black tendril from the other side of the cosmic veil enters the Realm created by the Eternal Gods. The tendril continues to move through the rift, and as it does, it seeks out and consumes the very worlds that the Gods created. With every world devoured, it gains power, and from this power, it brings forth evil from the other side of the cosmic veil, from a Dark Realm.

The female feels a definite pull, which is more assertive this time than when she first felt it many millennia past. She informs her mate that they need to go. They race through the cosmos to return to their point of origin, not realizing that this darkness that has made its way into their worlds is devouring small pieces of their creation and is slowly growing stronger in power.

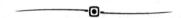

They return to the point of their creation, and as they arrive, they sense something is wrong. Galaxies and stars that were once brilliant with light and life are gone, and in their place are floating debris of crushed rock, and the residue of rock now floats in a cold dead void. Together they sense a deformity in the blackness, which gives off an unsettling feeling deep within their souls. The male cautiously reaches out and discovers vile darkness, and in that darkness, he feels a persona of pure evil, an evil, unlike anything he or his mate could have imagined. The female feels something more profound, and then she feels something similar to a barrier or veil that hangs in the shadows. She reaches out but cannot touch it, as the veil seems to float precariously. Then she senses the rift, and her mate tells her that something is moving in the shadows when she sees it.

She is the first to feel it, as it caresses her ever so lightly on her cheek. The slithering blackness quickly recoils when it touches her, leaving a disgusting taste in her mouth. Her mate tries to draw her away, telling her to go, but she is unwilling to move. She tells him that she cannot allow this evil to consume any more of their creations and that they need to confront it, whatever it is that has entered their Realm. He bends to her will and agrees that they must either eradicate this blackness or send it back from whence it came. He takes her hand, and together they concentrate and focus as one.

A form begins to take shape, and they see a shadow, and the shadow slowly transforms into a black tendril that pulses with evil. The two watch as the tendril starts to manifest into something discernible, and with each pulse, it grows larger. Just moments ago, what was once a pulsating thin slithering black tendril, has now taken o the concept of black liquid that expands and contracts even more rapidly with every pulse. They hear strange garbled thoughts, and though they cannot understand, they are determined to drive whatever this may be back to where it has originated.

The black liquid moves toward them, and they feel something opposite of themselves, whereas the Eternal Gods are the epitome of beauty, pure, clean, love, harmony, and full of life. The pulsing black liquid, which now resembles a throbbing Stain, feels filthy, dirty, impure, vile, evil, and dead. They watch as this Stain reaches out and wraps itself around some of their creations, and within seconds, the once brightly life-giving stars and planets turn a cold black and are sucked of all life by this vileness. The Gods sense that this vileness, this evil, will instill depravity, perversion, corruption, wickedness, and evil into anything it touches.

A second tendril approaches them from the Stain, and it reaches out and is about to touch the male when the female lashes out with a ball of pure energy that she has drawn from a sun that is close by, that hits the Stain directly in its mass. The Stain screams in excruciating pain and swiftly withdraws back through the rift to what they assume is its place of origin.

The female reaches out and grabs her mate's hand, and as they interlock their fingers, they look at each other and nod. Together they draw on the essences from the surrounding stars and planets, careful not to draw too much and manipulate these essences into balls of pure multicolored energy and throw them at the rift, hoping to seal it. When the balls of energy strike the rift, they hear screams of pain and then realize that nothing has changed.

The rift is still as it was, and then suddenly, multiple smoking tendrils burst forth from the rift, and as the Gods retaliate with orbs of energy, the tendrils are quickly extinguished, but in their wake is a curled-up shape lying before them. The shape slowly uncurls itself and stretches. They see that it is another male, and he is entirely different from her mate, whereas her mate is tall, slender, has a toned muscular body, light-colored hair just above his shoulders, blue eyes, a defined nose, a set of full lips, and a smooth complexion.

In this other male, she sees a tall but broad-shouldered figure with black hair that hangs past his shoulders and is held back with what looks like a leather cord. He has a rugged, chiseled face with dark brown, almost black eyes, thick eyebrows, an intense nose, slightly plump lips, and a chin with a small dimple. He looks somewhat taller than her mate, and his chest is solid muscle that gradually tapers down to a slim waist, only to continue to well-formed muscular thighs and calves. She then looks at his hands and can tell they have power. She also notices that his fingernails are black and almost smoldering as if emitting something that she cannot quite place.

The female moves forward and asks, "Who are you?" He stares back at them, not saying anything, and all he does is smile and send impure thoughts to the female. The male also feels these thoughts and moves forward when the female places her hand on his shoulder, smiles at him to let him know that she is alright, and waits for him to relax though he does only slightly. She ignores the man's thoughts and asks again, a little more forcefully, "Who are you?" and then she notices something on his chest and sees that it is a blood-red pentacle, and in its center is a single glyph that seems to drip blood, depicting the word "Evil."

Her tone piques his interest, and in a guttural voice, he says, "I am *Nimponin*. I am you and not you. I destroy what you create; what you love, I hate." He laughs and lunges at the two of them with what are now four-inch-long talons where his fingernails used to be. The Gods are but a blur, as Nimponin is surprised that they could move with a speed he had not thought possible.

Surprised, Nimponin watches the two of them draw on the life energies from some suns and planets around them and soon hold what seem to be multicolored orbs, and then without warning, they throw them at him. When they hit him, he finds himself screaming in excruciating pain, and the two Gods are surprised to hear a roar that sounds beast-like.

Gashes, burns, and lacerations appear on his chest and body, and though they can see that Nimponin is hurt, they watch as the wounds inflicted on him slowly begin to heal, as if miraculously. Nimponin smiles, and like them, he conjures orbs of a black-like substance from the throbbing tendrils around him, and he quickly throws them at the two of them. The Gods are agile and use multicolored orbs to deflect the black orbs, and the black orbs disintegrate when they are touched. The battle continues, and they slowly push Nimponin back towards the rift. Then when they think they are about to defeat him and send him back through the rift, he counters their attacks with his own, and as he regains his strength, his attacks are more potent than the previous ones.

The female senses something strange and asks her mate to keep him occupied as she focuses her thoughts on the actual rift itself. She now sees several smaller, almost invisible black tendrils protruding through the rift. She concentrates a little harder and now sees that these smaller, nearly invisible tendrils keep him connected to his Realm. She delves even deeper, and though she feels nauseous, she watches as the smaller, almost invisible black tendrils throb and pumps into his body the very lifeblood he requires to heal and maintain his strength and power. She sees that trying too severe is impossible and rejoins her mate.

The battle rages on as the struggle for power and dominance continues. Millennia pass and the battle is more aggressive than ever. The Eternal Gods know that this vile, evil abnormality that has entered their world through this rift needs to be destroyed or sent back to whence it came. The rift continues to slowly expand, allowing more tendrils to seep through, empowering Nimponin with even greater strength. Still, the constant battling seems to be taking its toll on all three of them, and like the ebb and flow of a storm tide, the attacks continue with neither side giving way.

The fighting suddenly stops, as all three hear a whisper at the exact moment in time, though what they hear is different. Nimponin hears, "You will fail," and he roars with rage, while the male God hears, "I am sorry," and he looks towards his mate, and the female hears, "Come to me," and is overwhelmed with a strange feeling deep in her loins, as a vision invades her mind, and then in a blinding flash, she is gone.

The flash blinds Nimponin, and before his vision returns, he is struck by orbs of pure energy that drive him backward. He regains his sight and sees that the female is gone. He now sees an opportunity to possess this Realm and immediately throws black orbs at the male and watches him deflect or absorb his attacks.

Nimponin roars with rage, and with a wave of his hand, he commands multiple black tendrils to come out of the rift and head straight for him. The male sees more of them coming at him and throws several orbs to deflect or destroy them. He turns to escape when he suddenly feels something grab his ankle; he looks down and sees that a black tendril has locked itself around his ankle.

He begins to conjure an energy orb from a nearby sun when he is suddenly pulled towards the Dark God. The sudden pull disengages him from the elements of the sun, which only allows him to harness a small portion of its essence. He knows it is not powerful enough to break the tendril locked around his ankle, so he hides it in the palm of his hand.

He sees several new black tendrils come through the rift, aiming directly at him. He encases his body with his essence, and the black tendrils wrap around him, forcing him to stretch his arms out from his sides, pinning his legs together as if crucified.

Nimponin sees his prey coming toward him and realizes that his feral side would have enjoyed the hunt and the slow kill, but now he will have to satisfy himself with the slow kill. He feels confident that he can destroy this Realm's male God, this lesser being. He thinks of the female, knowing she is somewhere out there in the expanse of this universe, and he smiles as he relishes the idea of finding her and showing her the tortured and mutilated body of her beloved mate. His thoughts return to his prey as the tendril pulls him within his grasp. He revels in the sheer enjoyment of stripping his flesh from his bones while still alive. Nimponin starts to drool as his prey is now a prisoner stretched out before him.

Nimponin begins to pummel the male, but try as he may, he cannot break through the essence that encases him. Frustrated, Nimponin draws more of the darkness through the rift, and as it fills his body, a new power grows within, and he punches the male's essence with mighty blows while slashing at it with his talons. He continues to draw more darkness, and his attacks become even stronger until finally, he sees a tiny flaw, and as he strikes at this flaw with one mighty blow, the flaw becomes a crack, and soon the crack spreads, and then it shatters.

How long he has endured Nimponin's attacks, he does not know, but with every strike, he feels his essence waiver and struggles to keep it in place, but the attacks become stronger and stronger as Nimponin draws more of the darkness through the rift. The male senses a tiny flaw in his shield of essence and watches it turn into a tiny crack and slowly expand until it finally shatters, exposing him to Nimponin's full wraith. His essence is gone; the tendrils wrap themselves tighter around his body, but he is able to keep one arm free, and then he feels Nimponin's hand on his throat.

Nimponin starts to squeeze, and he cannot fight back as bound as he is. The pressure on his throat is too much, and he is on the brink of losing consciousness; and then feels the pressure on his neck ease and is snapped out of his semi-consciousness state as he feels a very sharp object puncture his flesh just below his collar bone. He sees something black ripping open his skin as he watches as Nimponin drags his razor-sharp talon across his chest and ends it by cutting deep into his side. The male is overwhelmed with searing, burning pain from where the talon has sliced him, and he feels his energy rapidly depleting. Nimponin laughs and begins to pummel and thrash him with its fists. The beatings continued; he could not say how long, but the beating stopped. Broken, beaten, and in terrible pain, the male does not surrender as his inner core stays intact, and as long as that is there, he will survive. Nimponin stares at the male God, who hangs limply in his grasp, then pulls him in close and says in a rasping voice, "You thought you could defeat me; even your pathetic female fled with fear. I am the one true God of Darkness, and soon your insignificant worlds will be basking in the very darkness that I thrive to attain," and then he laughs.

He stops laughing, imagines the female, and explains to the pathetic male God that he has in his grasp how he will have his way with her, and then she will become his pet. Unknowingly, to Nimponin, the male God still has the small orb of energy in the palm of his hand and squeezes it tightly in his fist.

Nimponin holds him by his throat at arm's length, and for a second time, he drags one of his black talons down across his chest. The male screams with the unbearable pain as he feels the skin on his body being slowly ripped open and peeled back. He cannot take anymore and starts to sob and says something incoherent. Nimponin pulls him close and asks him to repeat what he just said. The male repeats himself and says, "You cannot have her," He quickly jerks on the black tendril holding his hand with the small orb of energy. The tendril snaps, and he shoves the orb directly into his right eye. Nimponin screams with pain as he grabs for his right eye, and by doing so, he releases the male. Severely beaten and weak, he moves away and is shocked as he watches the Dark God Nimponin transform into something unimaginable.

The creature takes a deep breath as if, for the first time, and releases a beast-like roar with rage. The male sees that his body is just about healed through its eye is still missing, and his presence is more than it was previously. He sees calves and thighs that are more muscular and well defined and a stomach that is rippling with muscle that continues up to enormous pectorals. Its arms are massive, with solid biceps and triceps that continue down to its forearms, chiseled and tight as taut steel cables.

Its hands are huge and look like they could crush stone. At the end of its fingers are now eight-inch talons shiny and black. Its sinews of neck muscles support its head, as its hair is now a long black mane, with streaks of silver running through it. His once defined nose is almost the same, only slightly larger. Its ears are just somewhat pointed, and a prominent brow slightly shades its eyes that are now a piercing blood-red. His lips are thin, and when he opens his mouth, they pull back to display three-inch-long canine teeth that now protrude below his bottom lip, and the smile sends a shiver down his back.

Nimponin is now in his true form, and he lunges at the male, locks his fangs into his shoulder, drives his talons into his side, cutting deep into his flesh, and comes very close to his inner core. The creature withdraws his talons, and when it does, one of his talons nicks his inner core, causing him to be overwhelmed with searing, burning pain from where the talon has sliced him, and he feels his energy slowly depleting.

Nimponin goes to grab the male when he sees a flash of bright light and is unexpectedly struck broadside by an unseen force so great that he is thrown backward away from the male. Every nerve in his body emanates with pain, and he is on the verge of passing out but somehow holds onto consciousness. Though the vision in his one eye is blurry, he sees the female rush to her mate, and though he is bloody and severely beaten, he smiles at her, and then as she feels his pain.

He can see her rage building, and as she looks at Nimponin, she sees that his right eye is now just a hollow socket. She calmly draws a massive amount of energy, and before he can react, she releases a very powerful blast that hits him directly in his chest, and he roars in great pain. Doubled over and shuddering from her attack, he senses his ties with the dark Realm are severed and feels his body returning to his earlier form. Still, with only one eye, he sees that she has something in her hands, which looks like a clear crystal. She holds it out in front of her, and says, *"Nitto Tikki Min Harko Lesko."* His ties to the Dark Realm are gone, and he feels thin threads of energy wrap around him, and within seconds, he feels bound in a finely woven mesh of energy.

He struggles to try and break his bonds, but to no avail, and lets out a yell of frustration as the strands of intricately woven energy begin to tighten around him with every movement of his body. He is trapped inside this intricately woven web that the female has somehow brought forth from the crystal that she now holds in her hand. He then sees the female bring forth another crystal, and it is also a multi-faceted flawless crystal, buffed to a high sheen. She whispers to her mate, and though he cannot hear what she is saying, he sees her hand him the second crystal and watches the wounds he gave him are mending and slowly disappearing, except for the bite mark on his shoulder.

She tells Nimponin, "What you see in my hand is called the *"Shingakusha Hoseki Crystal,"* and though this crystal cannot destroy you, it can imprison you." He immediately starts to struggle, and as he struggles, the woven mesh tightens around his body, and the strands start to cut into his being, and he screams.

She approaches Nimponin and says, "You should have never entered this Realm, fore where you are going now is a place that is so dire that you will wish for death, even though you and I both know that will never happen.

Nimponin does not say anything but stares at her with pure hate. She stares him down and then raises the Shingakusha Hoseki and holds it very close to the mesh but does not touch it. She begins chanting *"Senyo Ori Mukashi Kenyokyu Koeta."* The male, now almost healed, approaches, places his hand on hers, and follows her lead. The crystal starts to glow, and the effects are instantaneous; as she watches, tiny wisps of this being begin to transfer into the crystal. Nimponin's essence is slowly drawn into the crystal, and the woven mesh shrinks to keep a tight bind around him. Tiny wisps of his essence break away and float out into space, but they ignore these and concentrate on the larger mass of evil trapped before them. Nimponin starts to feel his black soul dissolve and then starts shouting and protesting. They ignore him and continue to chant, *"Senyo Ori Mukashi Kenyokyu Koeta,"* as more of him continues to be drawn into the crystal. When the last remnant of Nimponin is encased inside the crystal, the tightly woven mesh continues to shrink until it is gone. They hear a feral roar, and the female quickly chants, *"Manaketi Shimuka Hontai,"* and seals the crystal.

After millennia of fighting and great pain, they have finally captured Nimponin and sealed him in the crystal. The two admire the pure, flawless beauty, a personification of perfection when they notice an epitome of dark essence swirling inside. They watch as it starts to swirl faster and faster until the evil within the crystal transforms it into a soleless, vile piece of retched darkness and horror. She looks at the crystal in her hands with revulsion and watches the swirling cold blackness begins to liquefy and take on the appearance of the Stain. As it continues to liquefy, blood-red veins appear pulsing and throbbing under the surface of the crystal. She feels the coldness in her hands, and then the black crystal is torn from her hands as if something has savagely grabbed it. They watch as the crystal suspends itself in front of the rift. They feel the rift pulse several times, and as it beats, a rancid smell of death and decay emerges into their Realm, quickly followed by several black pulsing tendrils. The tendrils reach out as if trying to caress the crystal, and they feel the crystal begin to throb and pulse louder. Suddenly, more black tendrils come crashing through the rift, as if the throbbing of the crystal is calling out to them. Like the first tendrils, these new ones immediately wrap themselves around the once beautiful crystal and seem to be applying pressure to try and break the very crystal itself.

The Gods conjure orbs of raw energy and throw them at the tendrils encompassing the crystal. The crystal is released when the orbs strike the tendrils, and they swiftly withdraw back through the rift.

The Shingakusha Hoseki, now unencumbered by the black tendrils, begins to pulse slowly at first and then gradually faster and louder. With every pulse, the veins that run through the crystal pump their dark red blood faster and faster.

The Gods see a hairline crack manifest in the crystal, and then the hairline crack branches out and run the crystal's length. A catastrophic influx of energy expands outward and then draws itself swiftly back towards its center. When this happens, an implosion takes place, and a portion of the veil's very fabric and a portion of their creation collapse in on itself, creating a massive black hole, and inside the black hole is a swirling vortex. The vortex begins to pull everything within its reach toward its center. Planets, suns, whole galaxies, and even light cannot escape the wrath of the black hole's devouring, swirling vortex.

The rift that started as a tiny insignificant pinpoint in the fabric of the veil that separated the two realms has now become an abortion of nature, and there is nothing they can do to stop it. The female stares at the abomination before her, and she does not notice several black tendrils trying to circumvent the immense vacuum caused by the swirling center of the black hole vortex. Most are sucked back into the void, but one is able to break free and races toward the two of them. The tendril rears back to strike the female; when the male throws himself in front of her. The black tendril hits him in his shoulder in the exact spot where the creature bit him. She sees it penetrate deep into his shoulder, and just as it rears to attack again, she throws a blast of pure energy into the center of the vortex. The blast severs the tendril from its source, and then there is nothing as the tendril dissolves, and its remnants are pulled back into the swirling vortex.

She rushes to her mate and sees tiny black spider web-like veins slowly spreading out and working their way down his arm and across his shoulder, and she watches as part of his shoulder begins to turn black. She draws forth the elements and energy from some of the surrounding planets. She then weaves a binding and places it around him to try and stop the spread of this corruption that is now trying to spread through his body.

She turns back to her mate, hears a whisper, *"I will destroy everything you love!"* and sees several pieces of the once beautiful Shingakusha Hoseki fly past her into space to merge themselves with other remnants of dust, rock, and debris. She sighs heavily and then smiles at her mate as she sees that the binding is working and the black spider-like veins have stopped spreading.

She now stares at the spiraling horror before her, and then she hears the same voice that instructed her to create the Shingakusha Hoseki Crystal. It tells her that if this abomination did not exist, the worlds they created would die, and she and her mate would not become.

She senses that one cannot exist without the other and that if the Dark God did not exist, then everything she and her mate have created would become unbalanced or unraveled. She now knows that the Light needs the Dark, the Good needs the Evil, and in the end, the Hinashi above needs its Tusukam below.

Chapter I

Chikyu and the Sacred Artifacts

She places her arm around her mate, and they leave the horrendous abomination behind. She carries him through the cosmos and stops to ensure that the corruption has stopped spreading. She is uncertain where to go, remembering a small, insignificant solar system with nine orbiting planets and a brilliant little star. The planets vary in size, but the one had beautiful blue waters.

They arrive, and she sees the swirling deep blue mass that revolves slowly around a small star. The rich blueness of the planet draws her in, and she sees that within the deep blue, there are patches of browns, greens, and other colors of the spectrum spread throughout the planet. She senses something in the swirling blue waters and sees microscopic organisms swimming within its depths. She scours the world, passing volcanic eruptions in some parts with ice caps in another while the lands seem to vibrate and shake. She helps her mate down to the ground and brings forth the remnants of the five elements of other planets. She enchants them, and with the five of them in her hand, she turns her palm over and slaps the ground, driving them into the planet's core to flourish and meld with the existing natural elements of the planet. She feels them coursing throughout, and almost immediately, the lands begin to settle, the oceans slowly recede, and calmness flows around the planet. She grabs her mate, scours the world, and discovers an isolated valley. The two of them make their way to the surface; she notices a large crop of trees with a clearing located on its eastern edge. She guides her mate to the clearing, places him delicately on the grass, and checks his bindings.

Satisfied, she bends down and kisses his forehead, and when she looks back at him, she sees a calmness come into his eyes. She smiles, and he smiles back. She can sense his internal struggle and can only imagine the pain he is going through as he tries to fight the corruption that is trying to spread itself in his body. He raises his right hand, and she reaches out and intertwines her fingers with his, and in unspoken words, she leans forward and allows their lips to touch. Though she cannot feel the blackness, she knows it is there, and tears form in her eyes. She pulls her lips away from his, and her tears fall on his cheeks; when they do, a small glowing sphere appears above them and begins to grow slowly, and as it grows, it becomes brighter. At first, they hear muffled beats, then the sphere splits in two, and they can now hear and feel four distinct heartbeats. Both spheres slowly descend to the ground, and just before they touch, the second sphere seems to shimmer just slightly, and a faint shadow seems to pass.

They touch the ground, and she sees that one sphere contains a pair of females who are identical twins, and the second sphere has a pair of boys who are also twins and are opposite of the girls. She helps her mate to sit up and sees the look of adoration for the girls, but not as much for the boys, and then a small frown creases his forehead, but he smiles. She waves her hand over the two spheres and places them into a deep sleep. She looks back at her mate and kisses him, and then like the twins, she puts him into a deep sleep. She stares at the five of them and, feeling content, soars upward into the sky, and is about to soar out into the heavens when she gradually slows. She descends back down and hovers just above the surface of a narrow canyon that leads to the valley, just before the valley's opening. She chants, "*Katarume Mokararuse Gusefu*," and the ground starts to rubble, and then slowly, a black obsidian wall rises out of the earth in one fluid motion. It expands and molds itself to the canyon's width filling all penetrations and crevasses along the valley's walls, making the valley impenetrable. The wall rises to over twenty meters high and ten meters wide, blocking all access to the valley. When the wall is complete, she waves her hand, and the wall becomes smooth as glass with no blemishes. She then invokes an invisible shell over the valley so that nothing may enter from the land or the Air. Satisfied that her mate will be safe, as well as her children, she soars into the sky at a high-velocity speed and races back into the heavens to look for a cure to save her beloved.

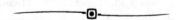

She travels farther and farther out through the heavens, not knowing that the planet she has left her mate and children on has begun to evolve. The vast oceans that once covered a large portion of the landmasses slowly recede, exposing even more significant landmasses. Ocean creatures make their way onto land, and like the planet, the creatures evolve. While changes are happening globally, a significant threat is streaming toward the blue sphere.

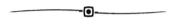

Three pieces of the blood-veined dark crystal that harness some of the most potent essences of Dark God are hurtling through space in the wake of a large chunk of asteroid. The asteroid is from the epic battle between the Eternal Gods and the Dark God Nimponin. The large rock hurtling through space seems to be on a collision course with several planets but somehow misses many of them as it continues to make its way through the dark reaches of space. The asteroid continues to ignore many worlds except one, and that planet of large land masses and swirling blue waters takes the blunt force as the asteroid crashes into it. The three dark crystals trailing in its wake are cast-off in different directions from the impact, and the shockwave emitted after the rock strikes the planet.

Of the three dark crystals, the smallest one plummets into an area in the northwestern part of a large continent. The velocity of the dark crystal is so incredible that it shears off the tops of mountains, and when it hits the base of another mountain range on the far side of the valley, the heat and pressure turn stone into black diamonds. The rock and gravel do not deter the path of the crystal as it continues to bore ever deeper into the mountain's base. It continues its course, creating large caverns and tunnels ever deeper into almost the planet's core, and finally comes to a stop, embedded in the wall of a small desolate cave.

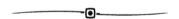

A second piece hits a small mass of land south of a large continent in the western hemisphere. The force of the impact of the dark crystals cracks the mass into several smaller pieces, allowing the surrounding sea to flood into the open crevasses, creating several islands. On the surface, the islands are separate, but far below the surface, the land mass is still as one, and the crystal buries itself into that land mass far below the water's surface.

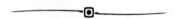

The most significant and last piece of the three crashes into the base of an active volcano, and the impact causes the volcano to erupt. The volcano spews ash and smoke into the Air, and the prevailing winds soon carry the smoke and ash throughout the planet, to eventually shroud the planet in darkness. The dark crystal burrows ever deeper into the bowels of the volcano and finally comes to rest on a precarious ledge just above a river of flowing molten lava. All three dark crystals pulse once, then twice, and then emit an aura, while the lush rich lands around the impact area become barren of most life.

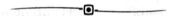

The force at which the asteroid has struck the planet causes the planet to tilt slightly off its axis, and it causes a drastic climate change that, within a few weeks, all cold-blooded creatures, as with all flora and fauna, perish. Within a month, ninety-five percent of the planet is covered in ice and snow. The new ice age consumes a collective portion of the planet except for a tiny area unaffected by the asteroid strike, the misalignment of the planet's axis, or the change in climate conditions. The tiny area of the planet houses a valley filled with windswept luscious green grasses and blooming flowers. Ancient trees that do not exist anywhere else in the world. In the valley is also a large crop of trees, and in the southeastern part of the trees is a clearing, and in that clearing is a prone body of a man, wrapped in an intricately woven binding, and beside him are two spheres that house two sets of twins, one of female and the other male.

Unknowing what has happened on the planet, the female God continues searching the heavens, hoping to discover an antidote or something to save her beloved.

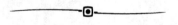

Millennia continue to pass, and the warm-blooded creatures that somehow survived the blast from the asteroid and the ice age start to recover and evolve. Some make their way out of the water onto dry land, while others remain in the life-giving waters. Some transitioned from the water to land and learned to climb and swing through the trees, while others stayed on the ground and learned to walk upright. Either way, evolution takes its course as the new life cycle begins, and with new life comes two classes...

"One of the Predator and One of Prey."

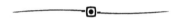

Millenia quickly pass as the female travels throughout the cosmos, searching for anything. She has visited millions of galaxies, and in those galaxies, she has scoured ten times that many solar systems, always looking or reaching out for anything that could help her cure her mate to get rid of the corruption that has invaded his body. She listens for the voice that came to her on what she needed to do, to defeat and capture Nimponin. Now, after all these millennia of searching, the only voice that she hears is her own, and she accepts that the voice no longer exists. She presses on in her travels and, as time passes, sees planets evolving, new ones forming, and others consumed to end up dead.

She is leaving one galaxy and heading to another when she stops, and the realization comes to her. She now knows there is no remedy or cure for her beloved and decides that she needs to go back and see her mate before it is too late. She streaks through the cosmos with a heavy heart, thinking about how she wasted valuable time searching for something that does not exist when she could have spent this time with her loved ones. Anger sets in, and the anger brings her to one conclusion: that there never was a whispered voice that guided her to find and create the *Shingakusha Hoseki*. She now knows that the voice she heard was her own and that it remained dormant and deep in her subconscious until the Dark God known as Nimponin appeared and threatened their worlds.

She thinks that as they matured and formed, the very act of what brought them into existence could have created the rift that brought Nimponin into their Realm. She also believes that when she and her mate created the heavens, the Dark Realm already existed, and the thought of something so pure and innocent like their Realm caused the rift to expand and allowed Nimponin into their Realm. She remembers the voice telling her after Nimponin was captured, and after the black hole allowed the void to come into being, that Light needed the Dark, that Good needs Evil, and in all things, that Hinashi above needs its Tusukam below.

She passes close to the very spot where the abortion of their creation, the black hole, fluctuates and pulses. She feels the pull of the swirling vortex in its center and the stench of evil that it omits. She slows and stops to stare at the blemish on their creation. She remembers how they captured the Dark God Nimponin inside the *Shingakusha Hoseki* crystal and how it imploded, shattering into pieces. She observes a spiraling vortex reaching out to pull anything and everything into its gaping maw. She remains just out of its reach, and the longer she stares into the darkness of the vortex, the more she becomes infuriated. She reaches out and grabs the elements of a planet being drawn into its vacuum, knowing that there is nothing she can do to stop this from happening, so she takes the elements of the world and conjures an orb of pure raw power. She does not hesitate and propels the orb of raw power into its swirling center, and as with everything, the vortex draws in the orb, and it disappears. She feels the orb being propelled through the Dark Realm, and then she feels it explode deep within the vortex and then feels something, but she is not sure what it is until she hears the muffled screams and what sounds like bestial roars of pain, suffering, and death as it erupts deep within the vortex.

She leaves the black hole with its spiraling vortex and continues on her journey back to the planet where she has laid her loved ones to rest. She vows to herself that she will return to investigate the source of these sensations and the faint screams that she has felt and heard later if the opportunity arises.

Several millennia pass, and as she approaches the planet where she had left her loved ones, she senses a difference in the lands and the life on the planet. She finds that the vast oceans have receded and are now exposing more significant landmasses. She sees that the world has evolved, and she also notices some creatures that did not exist before, who are now walking upright and roaming the lands. She by-passes them and proceeds back to the patch of woods in the secluded valley surrounded by high peaks and blocked off by a black obsidian wall. She floats down, kneels beside her mate, and bends over to kiss his forehead. He opens his eyes, and she feels something different. She kneels beside him and starts to release his bindings, and when his arm is free, he lashes out at her with a look of hatred in his eyes. She knows that the corruption of the Stain is coursing through his body, and she can only imagine the depth of his pain and how excruciating it must be. She continues to hold his arms down at his sides and stares at the man she has loved since they came into existence.

She sees that his whole left arm and most of his upper left side are now almost entirely black due to the corruption that is trying to run rampant through his body. She looks at him and sees the hate in his eyes that he had just moments ago is gone. She sees her beloved as he was and knows he is not long for this world. In a whisper, he asks her to come close, and as she leans in, he tells her, "Thank you," and a single tear slides down his cheek. She leans in closer, tells him, "I love you," and places a long, loving kiss on his lips. He reaches up, puts his hand on the sides of her head, and holds her there while they kiss. She feels his body go stiff and continue kissing, and then she feels the core of his being pulsing in his chest. She senses the corruption of the Stain that has invaded his body and watches as it slowly tries to reach his center of being. She places her hand over his core and reaches out with her center of being, and when she does this, the corruption retreats.

He nods, and she brings forth a small white crystal and goes to place it over his core. She is hesitant and does not move when her mate reaches out, gently places his hand on hers, and helps her lower the crystal to his chest, right above his core. She looks at him with tear-filled eyes, and he smiles and then gently pushes on her hand to allow the crystal to touch his chest. Once the crystal comes in contact with his body, it slowly draws his inner essence, a center of being, and life's existence. When the last of him is consumed, there is a bright flash, and he is gone. She screams aloud with pain and sorrow as her beloved mate is now gone, and he leaves her feeling empty. She feels nothing, and as troubled as she is, she does not sense the vile blackness that gradually destroyed him, lying on the ground's surface in a black puddle. The essence of the Stain and its gross corruption burrow deep into the ground. She wipes her eyes and goes to stand when she hears a menacing laugh that suddenly changes to a bestial roar resonating with anger and infuriation.

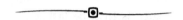

The essence of the Stain that carried the corruption that destroyed the male God burrows deep into the ground to escape any revenge from the female. It intertwines its very being with what small remnants of the essence of the male God it was able to consume while it had corrupted his body. The Stain remembers what they did to him when he was in his true form and can only imagine the pain it will inflict on the remnants of the male's essence once it feels safe. It has burrowed far enough and placed a barrier to hide its true nature. It begins to exact its revenge when it senses that the male's core has somehow anchored itself into the very essence of Stain's being, and it now seems to try and corrupt it. The Stain does not understand how this could be, and then it somehow feels a small, almost non-existence spec of bright light. The sinister laugh roars its infuriation as the once pure black Stain of the Dark God is now tainted with the male God and cannot rid itself of it.

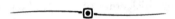

She feels the loss of her mate deep into her core of being and realizes a large portion of her inner self is gone. She also senses something very small, almost unrecognizable, and it brings a smile to her face as she realizes it has corrupted the same Stain that consumed and destroyed her mate. Suddenly, she loses breath as she feels her mate's presence. Then she hears the laugh turn into a feral roar. She feels his presence like a passing thought and smiles.

She looks down and sees six rough light blue diamonds, about the size of qual's eggs, laying in the grass. With a heavy heart, she reaches down to pick one up, and just as her fingers take hold of it, her mind is saturated with images and visions of death and destruction. Excruciating pain surges through her body, and she falls to her knees, unable to move.

She sees vile creatures killing and slaughtering men, women, and children. She witnesses small and large battles, decimating massive areas of some unknown world. She shakes her head to try and stop the images, but to no avail, as they continue. Then suddenly, the images stop. She remains kneeling, and though she is shaking, she takes deep breaths to calm herself. She remains kneeling and does not entirely understand what she has just witnessed. She is uncertain if these are memories of another world or Realm or are they visions of this world.

She remains kneeling and now thinks that what she has just witnessed is the aftermath of what the Dark God has done to its Dark Realm. She now realizes that this Dark God, the very essence of evil that is known as Nimponin, cannot be allowed to escape his prison. Still, she is not so naïve as to believe it could not happen. If that day were to come, something would need to be done to stop him from doing so.

She cannot and will not allow this to happen to her Chikyu or any of her worlds. She looks down at the blue diamonds and hesitates before touching them. She is relieved when nothing happens but cautiously picks up the other five. She notices the scorched patch of grass, and though she cannot feel the corruption of the Stain, she can feel the tiny essence of her mate. She places a wall around the black patch and then walks out of the crop of trees. She is now standing in the valley, and she knows she needs to come up with something to prevent the visions she has just witnessed from coming true.

She decides to walk to try to come up with a plan or something that will battle and hopefully defeat this evil that has destroyed its world. She finds herself standing at the base of the tallest mountain in the valley and senses a cave near its top. She soars upward and steps into the cave, and immediately the two spheres appear at her feet. She checks on the girls, sees that they are embracing each other, and feels their bond. They are developing quickly and seem content, bringing a smile to her face. She looks down at the boys and sees they are also growing, but they stay apart and are restless. She stands there, staring, and wonders why they are so opposite. She puts the thought away and knows work to do.

She is The Eternal God Mother, who created this world and the billions of galaxies, solar systems, and other worlds in the cosmos with her mate. She knows her one true mate is gone, and she does not have the power alone to defeat Nimponin. She is uncertain what to do, and as she looks at her children, an idea starts to form. She sits down, begins thinking, and plays out scenarios in her mind, and with each plan, Chikyu ends up shrouded in darkness and filled with evil. She is worried that whatever she tries to do, Chikyu will suffer. She walks to the cave's opening and takes a deep breath, and as she slowly exhales, a thought occurs to her, and she turns to look at the two spheres. She asks herself, could her children possibly defeat the Darkness and imprison Nimponin if he ever escaped.

She decides to take the name Kamiyobo and walks over to the cave wall, raises her hand, and says, *"Eera no Gasasu."* A large hollow appears in the solid stone wall. She encases the hollow with seals on all sides, creating an undetectable vault. She then waves her hand, and a large crystal materializes in her hand. She takes the flawless crystal, wraps it in soft cloth, and places it inside the newly created vault. She then takes the six light blue diamonds, puts them in the vault beside the crystal, and closes it. Once done, she chants *"Nimeto Ranasai Shingakusha Hoseki Hotesska,"* and the seams of the vault disappear as though they never existed. She then says, *"Kokashukin,"* and binds the seals. She then reaches out, and she feels nothing of its contents, and the vault is now completely sealed off from anyone or anything.

She sits down and closes her eyes. She touches the world and watches as time passes, and she observes the humans of Chikyu evolve over the next several millennia. Time moves on as small clusters of mud and grass huts slowly grow into villages of stone and brick, and then towns and elaborate structures rise in the skies to decorate the vast cities. Kingdoms fight amongst themselves, as lives are lost, and lands are torched and burned, leaving death and destruction. The wars and battles eventually stop, peace prospers as treaties are signed, and the evil across the lands is suppressed.

Conflicts have ended, and the lands are at peace, other than small outbreaks or skirmishes. Kamiyobo is content with how this creature, Man, has developed. She continues to view the world at a steady but quick pace when out of nowhere, she feels three tiny pulses scattered throughout Chikyu. Though the pulses are faint, she immediately knows what they are, as a shiver runs down her spine as she tries to locate them. The visions return, but this time they are different than when she first picked up one of the light blue diamonds.

They are weak, and she can block them with little effort. She lets only the smallest amount of the visions into her mind for her to witness while keeping most of them at bay. The ones she allows try to run rampant, but this time she controls them and then shuts them out. Surprisingly, she hears a voice, the same voice she desperately spent millennia searching for. She sits there unthinking as the voice guides her hands as they move across a piece of parchment as if possessed. She continues to write in explicit detail as the voice guides her hands. Suddenly she stops writing and sees lying before her a stack of papers. Then again, she hears the voice, and her hands begin to sketch finely detailed pictures to coincide with the explicitly worded papers. She knows it is her voice, but she allows it to fulfill her desires, and she looks down and now sees a stack of completed drawings beside the notes. Satisfied with what she has accomplished, the voice slowly fades away. She has achieved what she set out to do, and now she must find artisans in this world to assist her with the next level of her plan. She feels that the artifacts she has sketched should come from the very hands of the men of this world.

She takes a deep breath and allows her mind to reach out into the world, to search for artisans who can fulfill her needs and complete another part of her plan. She searches and finds an old woodcarver in the small town of Mattapan, a quaint village in southern Basra, and then discovers a purveyor and master gem cutter of rare and fine stones in Blanby in the capital of Elenni. She continues searching and finds a Cutter of Crystal in the Inuona people, a nomadic tribe from the Great Plains of the southern continent. She finds a renowned bladesmith in Hiroshima, the capital of Ozake in the Far East Empire, and finally a metalsmith in the small town of Hopedale, on the border of the Massa and Ozake.

Satisfied, she visits them in their dreams and whispers that she is Kamiyobo, the Eternal God Mother, and explains what she requires and leaves the ingredients as she has asked. She leaves the Purveyor of Gems a bag of rough gems consisting of rubies, emeralds, sapphires, and pink diamonds. Next to the bag, she places the six light blue diamonds and a small stack of drawings. She moves on to the Bladesmith and places ingots of tungsten, chromium, titanium, all precious and rare metals, and drawings like the purveyor. She stops by the Woodworker and sets several chords of Quebracho wood from an ancient tree that can grow only in one spot on Chikyu and a stack of sketches with measurements and dimensions. Finally, she reaches out to the Cutter of Crystals of the Inuona tribe on the Southern Continent and does the same but leaves behind a flawless piece of crystal along with detailed sketches. She moves up to Hopedale and places ingots of platinum, gold, rhodium, and iridium on the metalsmith's table with all the sketches.

She gives the Purveyor of Gems, the Bladesmith, the Cutter of Crystal, and the Woodworker twenty-four full moons to complete what she asks. She provides the metalsmith with an additional twelve moons because she knows that he cannot complete his tasks until the purveyor of gems and crystal cutter has completed theirs. However, she has left him duplicate drawings of all the others he will need and disappears.

Twelve full moons have passed, and Kamiyobo decides to visit her artisans. She first stops at the gem cutters and finds the gems on his table beside his tools. Some are already cut and polished, while others are still in the final stages of being cut. She picks up a completed gem, and as she looks at it, she notices several rolled-up clothes stacked on the counter and picks one of them up. It is a little heavy, and she carefully unrolls it and discovers various cutting and carving tools. Satisfied, she leaves a note and two solid gold ingots on the counter. She visits the Bladesmith and sees that he has created the blade and is working on the handle. She heads to Mattapan, and when she arrives, she finds the older man sitting at his workbench, hunched over and working on something. It is late, and she stands near his workbench and watches him put the final touches on a delicately hand-carved figurine. The figurine is of a woman with her hair blowing in the wind. She is surprised by the detail, and as he blows gently on the figure to remove any dust, she sees that it is a replica of her; and he places the small statue on the side of his bench and covers it with a cloth. The older man leaves his workshop, and she hears him walking down the hall. She looks for the crates and sees several half-completed pieces around his workshop and other components in different stages of being assembled on the other tables.

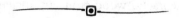

She is content with the way her plan is coming together. She stands in the cave and holds out her hand, and a large black onyx stone appears in her palm. She sits down, reaches out with her mind, and taps into the memories of the Purveyor of Gems. She observes his training from a young boy who swept and cleaned to becoming an apprentice, journeyman, and Master. She has memorized his technique, unfurls the cloth with the tools, and starts practicing on smaller stones. She then moves onto the Cutter of Crystal and performs the same feat. Once satisfied, she takes the black onyx stone, carefully cuts off one-third, and places it off to the side. She takes the larger piece and carefully begins to trim and shape the stone with her acquired tools. The days pass as she gives it her full attention, ignoring everything else, until one day, she finds herself holding a multifaceted black onyx stone. She turns it in her hands, and as she admires it, she now must start the daunting task of etching every stone facet with a rune, a glyph, or the ancient words.

Time passes, and she looks at the stone and sees it is finished. She gets up, stretches, wraps the stone in a white linen cloth, and places the stone inside the vault with the other objects. She closes the vault and seals it.

The twenty-three full moons have passed, and it is the night of the twenty-fourth moon and time to visit her artisans. Her first stop is the Master gem cutter, the purveyor of gems, and she finds two sturdy silk bags on the counter. She opens the first bag, and one by one, she takes out the blue diamonds and lays them side by side on the counter. She sees that her six light blue diamonds are no longer rough-looking pieces of rock but are exquisitely multifaceted fragments of beauty. She carefully examines all six of them and sees four blue diamonds are etched with one prominent glyph of each element of Earth, Fire, water, and Air in its center. The remaining four elements are set like a compass around the prominent glyph in the center. They are connected to the prominent glyph with small runes, interlocking them altogether. The last two diamonds are different; with one of them, she sees in the middle the glyph for *"Sukaimohotai,"* and it has all five elements evenly spaced and sized etched around the edges of the stone. She picks up the last blue diamond, and she sees in the middle a different glyph depicting a single word, *"Genkakuna,"* this glyph, like the other has all five elements etched around the edge of the stone, but these are slightly smaller. She places them back in their bag and closes the ties.

She opens up the second silk bag, pours a multitude of cut gems into her hand, and immediately sees two beautifully cut pink diamonds. She picks up each one, holds it up to the full moon's light, and sees that the two rose-colored diamonds, like the jewels, are exquisitely cut. The Purveyor of Gems has outdone himself and fulfilled his obligation, and after she gathers the two bags, and leaves a bag of gold and a simple note that says, "Thank you."

Next, she travels to the Bladesmith, sees that he has also completed his work, and finds a cotton cloth lying on the counter secured with a leather cord. She unties the cord and removes the cloth to discover a detailed engraved metal sheath with ancient glyphs etched into the metal sheath on both sides. She draws the blade to find a finely honed blade approximately six inches long, with an ivory handle inlaid with gold. Though she barely touches it, she runs her thumb along its edge and feels its sharpness. She places the blade on her finger and sees that it is perfectly balanced. She puts the blade back in its sheath, rewraps it in the fabric, and ties the cord.

She is pleased with the craftsmanship and finds it exquisite, and then she sees a folded piece of parchment. She puts the box down, picks up the parchment, and sees it is sealed with wax and stamped with the Bladesmith's initials. She opens it, smiles, and leaves a large bag of gold on the counter and leaves.

> *Dear Benefactor,*
>
> The metal you left me to make your blade was exquisite, and in all my years of being a bladesmith, I have never experienced anything like that type of metal before. If you need anything, please allow me to create what you need.
>
> *The Bladesmith*

Kamiyobo heads south to the Great Plains of the southern continent to find her cutter of crystal in the Inuona tribe. She finds them camped near some fields and watches them harvest the strange-looking *Suwiitpia* plants. She searches out her artist of fine crystal and finds him buffing the crystal goblet with a soft cloth and then wraps the crystal in a thick but soft cloth. He leaves to help the others with the harvest, and she carefully unfolds the cloth to see an exquisitely flawless hand-cut crystal goblet with ancient glyphs and runes delicately engraved throughout the outer bowl of the goblet. Satisfied, she wraps the goblet and places a bag of gold on his table, and just before she leaves, she takes a couple of the cloths that he had used for buffing the crystal.

She travels back north to the woodcarver's shop, and when she arrives, she finds him reaching under his workbench, pulling out an array of different size boxes, and placing them on top of his workbench; he then leaves the room. She quickly looks at them and is impressed with the details on every box. She counts nine, not eight, boxes on his workbench. She removes the lid from the largest box and sees runes engraved all around the insides. She moves to the next box, picks it up, and reads the glyphs inscribed on the top. The glyphs read, *"Shingakusha Hoseki."* She moves on to the next one and sees that it is perfectly square. She takes the crystal goblet and places it inside, seeing that it slides in almost perfectly. She puts the sheathed blade in a thin rectangle box. She opens the next box and sees eight small individual compartments and places one blue diamond in each compartment and the rose-colored diamonds in the last two spots. There are four boxes left, two rectangular-shaped boxes with one more prominent than the other and one small square box, all of which have removable lids. She notices that one of them is a plain ordinary wooden box with no markings. She picks up the last three engraved boxes and places them in the larger box. She picks up the simple box, finds a note, and reads it.

Thank you. You have made an old man very happy. I enjoyed the challenge of making you these boxes.

Arlo the Wood Maker

She then opens the plain box and finds something wrapped in a soft cotton cloth inside. She lifts it out, unwraps it, and sees that it is the figurine she saw him carving during her previous visit. She sees that the facial features are more defined and resemble her even more.

On the same note, she writes "Thank you" and places a small, perfectly cut flawless yellow diamond, about five carats in size, on top of the note.

She heads out to visit the last artisan, the metalsmith, and when she arrives, she leaves the bag of cut gems, the two boxes containing six perfectly cut and faceted blue diamonds, two rose-colored diamonds, and the crystal goblet. She reminds him that he has twelve full moons to complete his tasks.

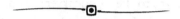

She makes her way back to the cave, and when she gets back, she places the large box on a low table, opens it, removes the smaller boxes, and places them on the table beside the larger box. She opens the sealed vault and takes out the perfectly flawless "*Shingakusha Hoseki*" crystal wrapped in lambskin and the black onyx stone wrapped in a cotton cloth. She places the "*Shingakusha Hoseki*" inside its rectangular boxes inscribed with its name and places the black onyx crystal in the larger of the two empty rectangular boxes. She returns the box with the "*Shingakusha Hoseki*" crystal and the box with the sheathed knife back into the vault. She then places the box with the black onyx stone inside the largest of the boxes, closes the lid, and seals it.

She places the boxes inside the vault and seals it. She assumes a comfortable position on some pillows and reaches out to the world. She sits there enjoying the sights and sounds of the land, the people, and the planet. She enjoys these little excursions over Chikyu and has the same feeling as before, but it is a little stronger this time. Something or someone is stirring, and she tries to concentrate and sense where they are originating from, and all she can feel is that they are on Chikyu. She cannot determine their locations because they are shrouded and indiscernible. She concentrates harder, and then quite unexpectedly, visions of horror and death overwhelm her. The darkness she experienced once before is spreading. Still, this time, the darkness is different, as she sees two men embrace the darkness and encourages it to spread out and consume anything in its path, as she witnesses this evil encompassing and corrupting her beautiful world. She watches as cities, towns, and villages are put to flame or razed to the ground. She sees men, women, and children strung up on wooden sacrificial x-bracing along the roads. She tries to force the images from her mind, but try as she might, she is forced to watch. Then she gasps as she watches Nimponin in his true form rip and tears the hearts out of his victims. His hands bloody from his kills, he devours their hearts along with their souls.

Kamiyobo is exhausted, and she can take no more. She musters her strength, pushes back with all her might, and bocks the visions from continuing, and as they stop, they slowly fade. She remains seated, as she is uncertain if she can stand. She tries to stay calm, but with the images comes anger, and with the anger comes something that she had not felt since that day when he ceased to exist, and that is pure unadulterated hate, and not just hate but hate with a vengeance. She remains seated and allows the day to pass, and though she is wary, she finally has the strength to rise from the pillows, and she slowly begins to pace the cave floor.

She has a plan, and now she needs to complete it. She removes the large black onyx stone and polishes it with the cloth she took from the cutter of crystals. She continues with the engravings, and then she is done. She diligently buffs the stone once more to a high mirror-like sheen. Satisfied, she places the black onyx stone back in its designated box. She now takes the one-third piece of stone she had cut previously and cuts that into nine smaller pieces, all the same size except for one. She takes one of the smaller pieces and starts cutting, shaping, and etching the stone with ancient runes and glyphs. She then gives it a high sheen, and when satisfied, she grabs another one. She finds the task slightly more time-consuming than the larger stone because the smaller stones have to be a perfect matching pair with no flaws. She finishes the etchings on the one pair and scrutinizes them for any discrepancies. When she finds none, she buffs the stone to a high sheen. Satisfied, she moves on to the next pair and does this for the other two pairs. She is on her stone, the seventh larger stone, and carefully etches runes and glyphs in the very center of the stone. She places the stone on its edge and scribes' ancient words around the stone, and like the others, she buffs it to a high sheen. She sits back and looks at the seven highly polished black onyx stones. She has one large one and three pairs of smaller stones, all etched with ancient glyphs and runes. The three pairs of small stones are identical and etched with the words *Piptu, Sefugu, Koda, Gichu,* and the larger stone with *Mashin Rita Toko.*

She takes the seven black stones, places them in the carved rectangular box, places that box along with the larger box with the etched black onyx stone already inside, and puts both of them in the largest box. Now she has two small stones left and engraves them with ancient glyphs and runes, buffs them like the others, then places the pair in a smaller square box by themselves, and then puts it in the large box with the others. Soon the days and nights pass without notice, and she loses all track of time. She now realizes that eleven new moons have passed, and the twelfth new moon is about to reach its zenith.

She arrives at the metalsmith's shop and finds the objects covered with a large cloth sitting on his workbench. She opens the square box and sees that each of the six blue diamonds that are now attached to a finely handcrafted platinum chain. She also sees that the two small rose-colored diamonds have a braided leather cord and are also in the box. She then picks up the larger square box, removes the crystal goblet, and sees that the inside is covered with a thin layer of highly polished gold. She sees that precious gems are inlaid around its stem and base. The moonlight dances across the goblet, and she lightly touches it feeling its exquisite design. She feels the runes and the glyphs filled with silver. She then sees a blue sapphire attached to a delicate handcrafted necklace and a note that says, "For you." She smiles and places it around her neck. She picks up the box with the six light blue diamonds, the two pink diamonds, and the box with the crystal goblet and she is gone, leaving a bag of gold on the counter.

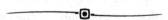

She is back in the cave and takes everything from the vault except the one box holding the "*Shingakusha Hoseki* crystal." She lays them out on the floor in front of her. She looks down and sees six light blue diamonds, a crystal goblet inlaid with gems and silver glyphs and runes, the blade and sheath, seven etched black onyx stones, along with two other small black stones, two small rose-colored diamonds on leather cords, and one larger black onyx stone engraved with runes and glyphs.

She takes a deep breath and starts chanting. The chant echoes in the cave as she repeatedly says, "*Sojaraniti Karen Shensai Koshawit Kani Arata.*" Kamiyobo finds herself glowing, and several flowing, sparkling delicate-looking filaments reach out from her glowing body and softly caress each object on the floor. As beautiful as they are, the filaments finish their caressing of the artifacts and are slowly absorbed.

Kamiyobo keeps repeating the chant, and once she feels that the filaments have embedded themselves and have a firm grasp on the objects, she holds out her hand, and a small white crystal materializes in her palm. She looks at the crystal and can feel the last of her mate's core of being inside. She continues chanting, and more beautiful glowing filaments reach out from her body and caress the crystal's core. When they do, instantaneously, the crystal begins to glow, and small filaments reach out and intertwine with hers. A tear runs down her cheek as she knows she is embracing her beloved mate for the last time. The filaments merge to become one, and the objects seem to reach up and absorb them just as quickly. Then she feels it as she stops chanting, and looks in the palm of her hand and sees a dull, lifeless crystal, then she crushes it in the palm of her hand. She waves her other hand slowly over the pieces and feels his essence combined with hers inside each piece. Her hand is over the blue sapphire, and she reaches down to pick it up. When she does, she feels a very small resonance of his core, then she holds the gem against her heart and softly cries.

Unknown to her, one fragment of Dark Crystals begins vibrating and gives off a very subtle, almost undetectable essence of its own that is carried throughout Chikyu on prevailing winds.

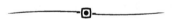

Though lightheaded, Kamiyobo carefully places all the artifacts in their boxes, except for the blue sapphire, and then puts them inside the vault and seals it. Now that she has completed the enchantments of the artifacts and closed them away, she must do one more thing before her plan comes to fruition.

She is tired and no sooner falls asleep when she feels two of the dark crystals vibrating and dark visions invade her dreams. She sees a massive horde of men and women with strange tattoos and piercings, robed ones throwing balls of flames from their hands, heavily armed soldiers, and strange-looking creatures mauling and butchering anything in their paths. The horde is unstoppable as it smashes its way through cities, towns, and villages, leaving nothing in their wake. Kingdoms topple as these forces continue to wreak havoc throughout the lands. She continues to watch as victims of the horde are tortured, or crucified, while others are brutally slain and then eaten by the beasts that show no mercy for their victims.

The horde is constantly moving and throws the greater kingdoms into chaos. Kamiyobo sees the approaching horde suddenly stop its advance, and she notices a swirling of the Air, and a gateway of some sort appears. Next, she sees a powerful stream of elemental power come out of the swirling Air and decimate the front lines of the advancing army. She then sees two men appear through the swirling gateway, and one of them has an array of colors swirling through his fingers and over his hands, and right next to him stands a man who wields a sword that seems to scream for blood. What surprises her the most is the force behind them entering the battlefield, through other gateways behind them. She guesses what looks to be over forty-five thousand well-disciplined soldiers who wear the same uniform as the man with the sword, and just behind them are about twenty thousand men and women wearing white robes with runes running down their sleeves.

Kamiyobo tosses and turns as she watches the advancing horde part its ranks, and she sees a single person in a hooded robe walk to the front of the army. She can see that words are exchanged between the two but do not know what they are saying. Then she sees the hooded figure in its hands, the same black orbs she has experienced. The hooded one throws the black orbs of the Dark Realm at the man with the elements coursing through his hands, and he blocks the orbs with the elemental forces that she now feels are drawn from Chikyu.

The two juggernauts face off and throw attacks at each other that are blocked by both. They seem to be testing each other to feel what each can do when suddenly it happens; the one harnessing the power of the Dark Realm throws the full force of the Dark Realm just as the man throws the full force of Chikyu. There is a tremendous explosion, and anything within the blast zone is immediately incinerated. The man with the sword seemed to know what would happen and kept his men back. The enemy is unsure, and as they try to overrun their opponent just as the two powers collide, they pay the price for being too close to the blasts.

The man with the sword takes advantage and charges directly into the battle with his forces behind him.

Another blast, but both armies feel the devastation, as losses are felt on both sides, but the battle continues.

As she watches it happens, one of the two juggernauts falters and loses ground. The slight loss allows the other to draw on vital powers and throw more attacks, never letting up and continually pushing the other further back. Massive energy is drawn from both the Dark Realm and Chikyu. The two armies collide around them, and with the powers now being drawn, Kamiyobo feels this will be the final showdown between the two juggernauts that will declare a winner and a loser. Suddenly a blinding flash erupts and saturates the battlefield.

Kamiyobo can see bodies being thrown into the Air on both sides, and then the smoke begins to clear, she looks to see the outcome, and then she awakes from her dream, and she is drenched in sweat. She sits there and tries to remember the outcome, but she cannot, but she knows enough that her dreams do not dictate a destiny, and what she dreamt can be changed. She knows that she must do everything in her power as an Eternal God Mother not to allow whatever evil that might invade this world does not reach that point that she has just witnessed.

She does not know how long she has been asleep, but she casts her thoughts over Chikyu to see what she can find. She starts slow, covering heavily populated areas and surrounding lands. The people of Chikyu seem to be lost. She does not sense the evil but knows it is out there because it is like an itch that she cannot scratch.

She remembers when they first encountered the Dark God calling itself Nimponin when she and her mate had the power to stop him. Now that her beloved is gone, she is only half what she used to be. She is still an Eternal God, and she knows with the objects imbued with her and her beloved's essences; she can defeat Nimponin if it were to happen and he escaped. Also, with help, she can beat this evil and change the destiny if need be that she saw in the dream, even though she is not sure of its outcome. entrap it once again.

She senses it and knows it is coming at her fast, and before it can manifest itself in her mind, she throws up a wall and keeps the darkness out, and then it is gone. She relaxes slightly, and she now knows what she must do. She has created what she thinks is needed to confront this evil if and when it returns. She takes a deep breath, lets it out, readies herself for the next step in her plan, and thinks.

"It is time to wake the children."

Chapter 2

The Tendaishi

Kamiyobo now sits at a table scribing and transferring sketches of what she is now calling the Sacred Artifacts that she and the masters of their crafts made in a leather-bound book. The instructions are explicit in the procedures for using and activating them. She finishes and sits there thinking, knowing deep down that she must follow through with what she has planned. She looks at the two spheres and is saddened by what she is about to do but knows it needs to be done. She is even saddened by what she will put her children through to save Chikyu and possibly the universe.

She walks over, kneels beside the two spheres, and sees that their bodies are grown and matured while sleeping. Though they are many millennia old, the four look to be in their early to mid-twenties. She reaches out to them with love while they are in deep slumber. As she looks at the girls, she sees that they resemble her in many ways, tall, with slim toned bodies, full breasts, though not enormous, long flowing blond hair that reaches down to their waists, almond-shaped eyes, sensual lips, slender noses, and flawless completions. She remembers when they came into being as babes, they both had deep emerald green eyes with tiny flecks of gold.

She looks at the boys and sees they are slightly shorter than the girls and stocky in build. They are more muscular than toned, with straight dark hair, like their sisters though not as long. Their faces are broad, with square chins, thin lips, and slightly bulbous noses. She remembers that they had dark brown, almost black eyes, and they only slightly resemble their father and do not seem to have any of her features. She does not feel the same connection with them as with her daughters. Deep down, she senses something is wrong but suppresses it and ignores it. She needs to wake them to complete the final phase of her plans.

She spreads her arms and softly speaks, *"Kashiwa Dumoko Musama To Koroyubo,"* and the thin walls of the spheres begin to dissolve. The twins start to stir, and the girls stretch and smile while the boys stare at her, showing no motion. She gestures to the pillows, and the four of them sit down.

She says, "Welcome my children to Chikyu, a beautiful world that you will go out and explore very soon, but first, we will need to begin your lessons." She explains to them that they should believe in what is right, especially with all the good virtues in the world.

She speaks of the creation, the beauty in the stars and planets, the billions of galaxies, the solar systems, and other forms of life on distant planets that she and her mate, their father, created. The girls listen and ask questions while the boys remain quiet. She emphasizes the brilliance and magnitude of the skies above, and still, the boys show no emotion or interest. The lessons continue, time passes, and she sees that the four seem eager to discover this world. One morning as the sun fills the cave with its light, she feels that they are ready and decides it is time to send them out into the world of Chikyu to see for themselves and explore. The girls squeal softly with delight as the boys remain silent though they look eager to venture into the world.

She sees the two of them whispering between themselves and thinks she hears one of them say, "I wish she would shut up!" She ignores what she thinks she just heard and continues with the lesson. She tells them that not everything in the world is good and that evil hides in the shadows, and when she says this, the boys seem to perk up and listen more intently. She tells them about the rift and how it came into being when they created the heavens. She teaches them about the Stain to help guide them and explains how it manifested into an entity of great evil. The Twins need to embrace the good in the world and avoid evil because it will corrupt their minds. She looks at the four of them and sees in their faces two emotions. In the girls, she sees worry, while the boys smile. She looks away but continues the lesson and tells them to listen carefully. She takes a deep breath and describes the creature calling itself Nimponin and how he came into this realm through the same rift mentioned earlier. She talks about the battle that took place millions of millennia ago and how they had to destroy millions of other life forms to entrap the Dark Lord Nimponin. Once they subdued him, they took the *"Shingakusha Hoseki"* crystal and imprisoned the very essence of his vileness and evil inside the crystal.

She tells them how he corrupted the crystal and turned it into a hideous dark object and how the crystal ended up imploding on itself. When this happened, it created a massive Black Hole in the fabric of their creation, and the vacuum of the swirling Black hole vortex sucked all the fragments of the crystal into its center.

She tells how several black tendrils had tried to escape the swirling vortex. Still, none could escape the pull of vacuum, except for one, and this one in particular somehow stayed hidden in the outer edges of the vortex and was able to break free. It was about to strike her when their father threw his body in the way, and it struck him instead and injected its black essence into his body instantly, causing the corruption to spread through the wound. She explains how she placed a binding on the wound to stop the flow of corruption and keep it from spreading through his body. She does not tell them what she saw through the Black Hole or that the black hole with its swirling vortex is somehow a gateway or portal to another Realm, a Dark Realm that reeked of evil.

She notices that the two boys are enthralled and display a deep interest, and like their sisters before, they now ask many questions. Finally, all questions are answered, and there is silence.

Kamiyobo tells them it is time to venture out into the world and see for themselves the wonders of Chikyu. The twins look eager to venture forth into the world. She steps forward to embrace the girls, and when she lets go, they are gone, and when she goes to embrace the boys, they just leave. Kamiyobo bites her lower lip as the feeling returns that something is wrong, the same feeling she felt just before she woke them.

The sun feels good on their faces as the girls scour Chikyu admiring the tranquility and beauty of the planet. They think they should seek out those special ones that display a combination of honesty, morality, virtue, and hope in their hearts but decide to enjoy the wonders a while longer. The girls float down to the outskirts of a large town and somehow materialize into the same forms as the humans. They acquire clothes to match the locals and walk arm-in-arm into town. While the girls walk through town, they notice many humans bow and place their hands over their hearts, bow, and nod their heads. They arrive in the central marketplace and are overwhelmed by the exotic aromas of spices and other delicacies filling the Air. Merchants offer them samples, and they accept them willingly. Sweet jams and jellies, fruits, bread, and roasted meats are all offered as they walk around the market. One man approaches them, and they ask him, "Why is everyone giving us these things? We have done nothing to give in return." The man looks at them and says, "My ladies, you two are the epitome of beauty. Did you know that your presence somehow brings joy to those who have the opportunity to gaze upon you? May I ask where you are from?" One of the sisters tells him, "Far away."

The man smiles and asks, "I see. If the two of you do not mind, I would like to sketch your portrait?" The sisters look at each other and say, "Ok!" The man takes them to his studio and places two high-backed chairs outside his studio. The sisters look at him, and he tells them it is for the natural light and asks them to sit. The man places a new canvas on his easel and begins sketching. As he sketches, a crowd gathers behind him. An hour later, the artist puts his charcoals down and steps back to admire his work. The sisters hear the gathered crowds ahhs! They walk over to stand beside the artist to see what all the noise is about, and when the artist shows them, they are happy with his work and tell him, "Thank you" They walk through the crowd, and they feel that something is missing. The humans they meet seem to desire something. Whether it be guidance or enlightenment, they are not sure. The sun is setting, and the girls are walking towards the outskirts of town when the artist that sketched them earlier approaches them and hands them a rolled-up piece of canvas. He tells them, "Thank you, "bows, and heads back into town. They unroll the canvas and see it is an exact copy of what he sketched earlier. They agree that it has been a pleasant day with the sights, sounds, and meeting the different people, but now they need to find the special ones.

Night settles across the lands, and they begin to visit the dreams with the ones they feel they should choose and encourage them to fulfill their destiny. The girls hold their hands and take turns lightly touching their fingertips to the ones that will hopefully be their future. A blue flame cradled in the curve of a crescent moon is tattooed on their chests just above their right breast. The blue flame disappears, and as the girls depart, the moon fades along with it, but they leave behind a thought, and that thought is "*Soon.*"

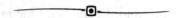

The boys do not care about the festivities in the marketplaces or meeting people. They venture into the dark recesses of the cities and towns. The back alleys and the sewers differ because of their sisters' beliefs. Their sisters talk about love, *Spirit*uality, hope, and honesty in their Chosen dreams, whereas the boys speak openly of hate, debauchery, lies, cheats, deception, and above all, power. They seek out the oppressed, the cutthroats, murderers, whores, and thieves who want more and will do anything to get it. They also seek out the corrupt in the hierarchy of the towns and cities. When they find them, they burn a symbol of devotion consisting of a small blood-red teardrop surrounded by a pentacle. The boys do not lightly touch their selected with their fingers; they brand their mark on the ones they choose and enjoy inflicting pain as they burn their stigma into the skin of their future followers. They place the stigma on their backs between the shoulder blades below the base of their necks. They perform this satanic ritual many times in their visit throughout Chikyu, and after every branding, they tell them to be patient because change is coming.

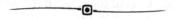

It has been five years since the twins ventured out into the world to select their Chosen and spread their words. When the boys return, they find their sisters have already returned and heard them telling Kamiyobo about their exploits, what they saw and ate, and the artist that sketched their portraits. The two of them are bubbling with excitement, and they almost end up finishing each other's sentences and start laughing when they do, which causes Kamiyobo to *s*mile.

Kamiyobo looks at the boys, and they say nothing, only that it was interesting to see these creatures roaming around like cattle, lost and with no guidance.

Kamiyobo softly sighs and tells the four of them, "What the four of you have experienced is all well and good, but what I want to know is what you learned over these past five years when you were out a meeting; the denizens of this world?"

The girls look at each other, and one of them says, "Mother, what we saw out in the world, is these humans want, no better yet, need something and be able to ask for guidance. The people need something to look up to, something to worship. Her sister chimes in and say, "What my dear sister is saying is correct." The people want something to guide them Spiritually and tell them that there is something out there that truly loves them. Someone or something that can help them tell the difference between good and bad, something they can look up to and worship." We think it would benefit them and us if we were to become the Spiritual existences they seek."

The two boys nod their heads in agreement and say, "It was different for us, but we have visited many, and we agree that they need guidance."

Kamiyobo tells the four of them what they will need to do and smiles. The girls smile, and when the boys smile, it looks almost sinister, and she tries to remember where she has seen that smile before.

A few days later, the two girls are talking, and they tell Kamiyobo that they have decided to take the names of Laki and Jutsuk. She tells them they are beautiful names, and then the boys tell her they will take the names of Guichi and Tanin. She looks at the two and hesitates slightly before giving them her blessing.

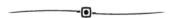

Many leagues away and shrouded in a cloak of impenetrable darkness are three pieces of the dark crystal lying dormant in different locations throughout Chikyu. One-piece stirs as the two names of Guichi and Tanin are spoken for the first time. Moments later, it is dormant once again but emits a faint, barely audible whisper, and like before, is carried on the winds for the selected one or ones to hear.

She embraces them, and as they pull away, she feels it, now even more, and it breaks her heart, but it answers so many questions that she thought of as to why they were so interested in the teachings and stories of the

Stain, the battle, the creature known as Nimponin, and the dark crystals. She senses the darkness or, like her mate, the corruption that she has not felt for a very, very, long time. She sees a look on their faces, which sends a shiver down her spine because she can now see the resemblance, not of her mate, but the monster she and her mate fought millenniums ago. She sees the Dark God, Nimponin, in them.

The four of them venture out again into the world of Chikyu, and before they come back, she thinks back to their creation and that the boy's sphere did not seem to glow as bright as their sisters, and she vaguely recalls seeing a shadow cross over their sphere. She remembers the look on her mate's face and the feeling deep down just before she woke them. The sense of dread for her children and that feeling returned just now when she embraced them.

They soon return, and Kamiyobo tells them their lessons are complete, except for one, possibly the most important. She tells the four of them to listen carefully and heed her words. She tells them, "When your father and I created the four of you, the corruption had infested his body. We could not pass onto you the power that we had hoped, which is why the four of you can never become actual Gods but will probably be revered as such.

"What does that mean, Mother?" Laki asks,

She clears her throat and tells the four of them, "You are *"Tendaishi"* celestial beings that can pass between the Spiritual and Earthly Domains, which I know the four of you have already accomplished while you were out into the world of Chikyu. In the Spiritual Domain or Spiritual form, mankind will feel your presence and hear your whispers. When you enter the Earthly Domain or take on your Earthly form, you will physically place yourselves on Chikyu and may be susceptible to man's ways. You could feel and experience love, hate, joy, pain, and sorrow. Whether in the Spiritual or Earthly Domains, you, as *"Tendaishi,"* are immortal. Remember, until your powers mature, you will only be able to maintain yourself in the Spiritual Domain for short periods, so be wary of the world around you and your surroundings.

Kamiyobo tells them that this is their final lesson and is about to give her blessing; when Guichi and Tanin quickly stand up and say, "We are going!" just like that, they are gone. The girls are as surprised as their Mother, but they walk up to her and hug her tightly. She asks them to stay a moment longer. She moves to the pillows, sits down, and gestures to the girls to join her. She tells them that what she just spoke of was not their final lesson but what she is about to say to them.

Laki and Jutsuk ask her, "What about Guichi and Tanin? and, shouldn't they be here for this final lesson?" She quietly tells them, "No, this is only for the two of you."

"What I am about to tell you, your brothers must not find out about this in any way, and this must be kept in the utmost secrecy. Do I make myself clear!" The girls tell her, "Yes, Mother." She tells them, "I believe that the corruption from the Stain has somehow infected your brothers. The corruption now courses through their bodies and has slowly grown stronger daily. You two must try to convince them to fight the darkness and let it go, or the corruption will consume them.

Jutsuk asks, "How can this be?" and Kamiyobo tells them, "I can only guess that when your father had the corruption of the Stain in his body, and even with my bindings, he was constantly fighting for control. At one point, he seemed he could subdue it, and when he did, we created the four of you and created you two girls first, and I think that within that heartbeat just before your brothers were created, a small portion of the Stain seeped into your brother's sphere and became part of them. The amount was so small that your father nor I could detect it. When I told you and your brothers that you were to venture out into the world to spread your Spiritual beliefs, I think that right before they left, the corruption awoke, and over the past five years, it has become stronger, more powerful.

She takes a deep breath, slowly lets it out, and then says, "I know through visions that three pieces of the Dark Crystal, that is contaminated essence of the Dark God Nimponin, have landed somewhere on Chikyu. I have seen and felt they are somewhere in this world through my dreams. I do not know how big or small these three pieces are, nor can I discern their whereabouts, but I do know these three pieces are very powerful. If your brothers were to discover that the crystals are somewhere on Chikyu, and with the corruption plaguing their insides, they would stop at nothing to try to find them.

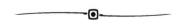

When Guichi and Tanin had been traveling around Chikyu and initiating their followers, they heard a voice explaining how to cloak their essences; they could only hold it for a short time before it would fade. When they left the cave to venture out into the world, something told them to cloak themselves and hide in the shadows of the entrance to the cave. They listened as they heard Kamiyobo explaining to their sisters how they could have the corruption of the Stain coursing through their bodies and that three pieces of the Dark Crystal had landed somewhere on Chikyu. Guichi feels the cloak fading, and they step away from the shadows of the cave entrance. Once they are clear, they are elated by what they have just heard and know they need to find these fragments or pieces of the Dark Crystal. They enter the Spiritual Domain and leave the valley, never looking back.

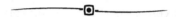

Kamiyobo feels the cloak fade, and then she senses them. She curses softly to herself, but what is done is done. She now looks at her girls and tells them, "Your brothers know about the dark crystals," and leaves it at that.

She says to Laki and Jutsuk, "My daughters, you two have true virtues of love, harmony, and enlightenment in your hearts, but before you go out into this world. I must tell you one more thing. You must know that at some point, the four of you will each come to a crossroads, and that crossroads will present you with a choice. You must decide then and there whether to accept this birthright and be Reborn, or you can deny it. If you choose to accept it, you will also be accepting sin, hate, and other things that you have not felt yet or are innocent to them. These new feelings may go against everything you believe or have preached, but you must accept them. They will enter your hearts and minds and try to control you, but it will be up to you to with them as you see it.

If you turn away from your chance to be reborn, the opportunity will never present itself again. You will remain as you are at this very moment; you will be immortal, but you will deprive yourself of power and fortitude. You will need to reflect on your Rebirths and choose wisely. Remember, when the time comes, I cannot tell you when it will happen, only that it will, but you must consider all aspects. In choosing your Rebirth, you will have to take on a great responsibility, but it will also enable you to draw forth tremendous power, and with this power, you will be able to stand against a Great Evil that will try to destroy this world. I cannot tell you if the humans will welcome this evil or turn it away, nor do I know when it will come. I have already mentioned this evil in your lessons, and when the evil returns, it will be the Dark Lord and will go by the name of Nimponin, and it will be evil incarnate and try to destroy everything good in this world.

When your father and I created this universe and everything you see in the heavens above, we knew we did a good thing. Kamiyobo walks over to the wall and waves her hand. The wall opens, and the girls are surprised to see this for the first time. She reaches inside and pulls out a rectangular-shaped box. The girls notice that the box is an ornately decorated wooden box with etched glyphs and runes all along the outside of the box. She places the box on the table, and they see the words "*Shingakusha Hoseki*" engraved on top of the lid. They look at their Mother, and she tells them to open it, and as they do, they see a lambskin wrapped around what looks like a cylindrical-shaped object tied with a leather cord. Laki undoes the leather cord, and when Jutsuk unfolds the lambskin, they see that they are holding a beautiful, flawless multifaceted clear crystal in her hands. Kamiyobo tells them, "You are holding in your hands the one object that will allow the both of you to stop the spread of this great evil. You are holding a "*Shingakusha Hoseki*" crystal, similar to the one used to imprison Nimponin millions of millennia ago."

She sees the confusion on their faces and says, "I'm sorry, let me explain; what you are holding in your hands is the other half of the original "*Shingakusha Hoseki,*" but this crystal is stronger twice as powerful. The "*Shingakusha Hoseki*" cannot destroy the evil; it can only entrap it. I have told you of the great battle and how your father and I were able to entrap this evil, but the cost was tremendous, as the crystal seems to have created a black hole into what I think is the Dark Realm. Corruption through the Stain is just one of the horrors that can infest itself into this world, but the biggest threat is the Dark God Nimponin himself, especially if he is released."

Kamiyobo pauses, takes a drink of water, and then continues, "The broken pieces of the dark crystals have the evil and corruption of the Stain embedded in them. If any pieces of the Dark Crystal came in contact with one another, the unknown horrors that could be released would allow a foothold for evil into this world. If three pieces were to come in contact with each other, the corruption of the Stain would cause havoc and begin to spread its evil. If four pieces were to be reunited, then the Stain could break free of its entrapment, and this would set the stage for Nimponin to reanimate himself into our world. If Nimponin were ever to be released, know that the two of you must perform a ritual together so that one can draw on the other's strengths to beat this evil. You must combine your powers to weaken it enough so the vile evil can be incarcerated back inside the crystal you hold in your hands."

The girls rewrap the crystal and hand it back to Kamiyobo, and she places it back in the box, walks back over to the wall, and puts the box with *"Shingakusha Hoseki"* back inside the vault. She pulls out a square box, but larger, and the girls see that it too is an ornately decorated wooden box, etched with strange markings all along the outside of the box. She places the box on the table between them. She tells them to open it, and as they do, they see four boxes of different sizes, intricately packed so that there is no wasted space, and on top of the boxes is a small linen-wrapped object tied with a leather cord.

Guichi and Tanin are walking along and scouring the planet, trying to sense anything that will lead them to any of the fragments of Dark Crystals that they heard Kamiyobo mention to their sisters when they feel something reaching out to them, pulling at them. However, it is very faint, almost nonexistent. They hear the whisper of two words floating on the winds: "The Barrens." They do not understand the Barrens nor know where they are, but they find themselves following a very light pull.

Laki and Jutsuk take out the four boxes and place them on the table in front of them. The girls unwrap the first two boxes and see that they are of the same type of wood and ornately engraved with the same symbols, but they also notice that the lettering is slightly different. Jutsuk opens a box and finds herself looking at a multifaceted black onyx stone, smooth like polished glass and etched with ancient glyphs and runes. At the same time, Laki holds a small rectangular box containing seven highly polished black onyx stones engraved with different runes and glyphs. Kamiyobo explains the purposes of the onyx stones, and the girls put them back in their boxes. Jutsuk opens another box, and Laki unwraps the linen cloth to find a leather-bound book. Jutsuk stares at six beautifully flawless blue diamonds attached to platinum chains and sees two rose-colored diamonds on leather cords in the box. Kamiyobo tells them to take the two rose-colored diamonds and place them on their necks. Laki is turning the pages of the leather-bound book with its writings and sketches. Kamiyobo places two more boxes on the table. When they open them, they see a beautiful hand-crafted blade and an elaborately decorated crystal goblet with cut gems and finely threaded strands of gold and silver. Kamiyobo says, "I have written down everything in the small leather-bound book.

They put all the smaller boxes inside the larger box, and then Laki places the linen-wrapped book on top of the boxes. Kamiyobo leaves the larger box on the table, looks at the two of them, and says, "My beautiful girls, there is one other thing that you will need to do, and that is for the both of you to go forth into this world and find your Champions." She sees their faces and tells them that she will explain. "Laki and Jutsuk, I need to tell you that the evil that will come across this land is inevitable. I have seen this in my visions, and there is nothing you or I can do to prevent it from happening. The best I can do is try to prepare you for what is to come." She pauses and takes a sip of water. "The both of you will need to go out in the world and find your Champions. These Champions will do your bidding when the time comes. If you think you have found them, be wary, and choose wisely, for they will be a Spiritual leader, and the other will be his sword and shield to defend him, the two of you, this world and its people. They will fight for you unconditionally and assist you in defeating the evil that will eventually come to this world and sweep across its lands. They will be your weapons and shields when the time comes to activate the *"Shingakusha Hoseki"* crystal so that you can imprison the Dark God Nimponin once more."

"When the time comes, and you have found your Champions, you will give each of them one of the rose-colored diamonds you now wear.

There are certain fates in this world that you cannot interfere with, and one of those is allowing your Champions to find each other on their own. These two rose-colored diamonds will assist them in finding each other."

Kamiyobo sees the looks of worry on their faces but knows they need to hear this and understand everything. She continues, "When you come to those crossroads, and the opportunity for Rebirth presents itself, do not hesitate to accept it. You will know it is near because you will feel a craving called *"Mijikuna Inkinjo."* I cannot tell you when, where, or how your Rebirth will take place, but the powers you will receive will be unbelievable.

You will gain an almost God-like status that will allow you to break the chains that shackle you to this world. Remember, with these great powers come even greater responsibilities, and the girls nod in understanding. "I have told you and your brothers that you are *Tendaishi*. You can travel throughout this world in the Spiritual Domain unseen and unheard, or you can walk among the peoples, but remember, while you are in the Earthly Domain or form, and though you might be immortal, you can still feel pain, sorrow, joy, and happiness.

They nod and say, "Yes, Mother, we understand; we will be careful and wary of our surroundings and brothers."

They rise and embrace Kamiyobo, and she sees the worry in their eyes. The girls get ready to go out into the world of Chikyu, and she gives each of them a light kiss on the forehead, whispers *"Wasasaru,"* and then snaps her fingers. The lines of worry are gone, and the girls are smiling. Seconds before they descend to the valley floor, Kamiyobo says, so that the girls do not hear, "When it is time, and you are Reborn, you will remember and do not worry, I will be with you," the girls take the larger box with them and step out of the cave to land on the soft grass below.

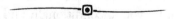

Laki and Jutsuk walk into the valley carrying the large box between them. They enjoy the feel of the grass on their feet and eventually arrive at a spot that feels right to them. They place the box on the ground and chant, *"Ana O Akeri Hori Sa Tegu,"* and several black obsidian flat stones appear, and a hole that is perfectly square as it is deep manifests itself. They place the large box inside the ground and position the flat obsidian stones on top of the box. They finish stacking the stones and then chant, "*Kokashukin,*" which seals them, and now they can only be unlocked when the right words are spoken.

Done, they look towards the mountains and watch the morning sun's rays slowly work up the side of the tallest peak in the valley. They know what is going to happen and are saddened as they watch the rays of the morning sun slowly make their way up the face of the tallest peak to the cave's entrance.

Kamiyobo sits in the cave on her pillows and patiently waits as she watches the sun's morning rays clear the mountain peaks on the opposite side of the valley. The morning sun rays slowly make their way across the isolated valley floor and gradually work their way up the side of the mountain. The sun's rays touch the lip of the cave, and they seem to hesitate for a brief moment. Then the morning light floods the cave, and as rays of the sun illuminate the cave's interior, there is a brighter flash, and the Eternal God Mother, Kamiyobo, is gone.

The Twins stand there watching the sun's rays illuminate the cave entrance. They see the flash and immediately feel a loss, knowing that their God Mother is gone and that they are on their own, with the possibility of having corrupt brothers out in the world doing who knows what.

They remain in their Earthly forms and walk through the valley, admiring the natural beauty around them. They reach the wall their Mother created millennia ago and stop and say, "*Kotaku to Kumataseru,*" and the massive black obsidian stone wall erupts higher and broader out of the ground to finally stand over thirty meters high and over twenty meters wide. They look at each other, and Laki says to Jutsuk, "Shall we go find our Champions?" Jutsuk replies, "Yes," and enters the Spiritual Domain and vanishes.

Laki and Jutsuk travel throughout the lands and reach out to the selected they had touched many years ago. They are pleased with the way of this world and watch their religion slowly spread across the lands of Chikyu.

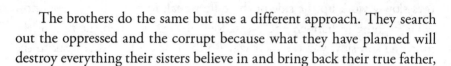

The brothers do the same but use a different approach. They search out the oppressed and the corrupt because what they have planned will destroy everything their sisters believe in and bring back their true father, Nimponin.

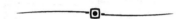

Millions of light-years away, Kamiyobo floats before the portal to the Dark Realm. She stays just out of its reach so as not to be drawn in and periodically hurls essences of energy into the swirling vortex of the black hole. She has no concern for the inhabitants, as she hears countless screams of pain. She hovers before the rift, and a thought enters her mind, and she becomes even more furious about why it did not come to her before. She now knows her boys, their emotions, their questions, and now she feels the same corruption, and her eyes tear. Her boys are tainted, and she manipulates an enormous amount of energy that she can muster and hurls it into the portal. When it explodes, she can see and feel the essence of all the evil creatures she has just slaughtered in the Dark Realm. A smile crosses her face as she senses the pain of many lost souls.

Chapter 3

The Blessing

Laki and Jutsuk have been traveling throughout the kingdoms of Sadenkiwa, the largest Continent on Chikyu, to recruit followers for their religion. They decide to take a break from being in the Spiritual Domain and enter the Earthly Doman to sit casually on the roof of the Royal Palace of the Ozake Empire, located in the eastern part of Sadenkiwa. The one thing that the two decided when they first ventured out into the world was that they would not interfere with man's actions unless it were specifically for the greater good of their plans or if it were to be severely detrimental to said methods. They have witnessed injustices but would not entirely interfere, though they have allowed themselves to assist specific individuals.

The summer evening is warm, and they enjoy the evening breeze and admire the city while waiting patiently for the news of the Royal Prince or Princess's birth. He or she will play a key factor in their plans in the future. Jutsuk notices a peregrine falcon flying toward the Palace, and she sees a message tied to its back. They sense something is wrong and invoke a shield around the Empress to protect her. Moments later, there is a loud commotion inside the Palace as they hear the Emperor storm into the nursery and start shouting orders and for guards to surround the Empress. They listen to him, ordering all the midwives and maids to lower their clothes and expose their backs. The women immediately do as they are told, except for one, who refuses and starts to protest and claims she has done nothing wrong. The Emperor gestures to two of his guards, and they seize her. A third guard walks up behind her, grabs her robe, slits it open with a knife, and pulls the material apart. The guard exposes her back, and the Emperor sees a symbol burned into her flesh, consisting of a small blood-red teardrop surrounded by a pentacle. The Emperor orders that the woman be locked up and held for questioning.

The guards go to take her away to the dungeons when suddenly she kicks one of them in the groin, and as he lets her go, she breaks free from the other and runs out of the nursery towards the balcony. There is shouting, and then the woman starts shouting something indiscernible about the Dark Scriptures and that the Dark Gods will prevail. The woman jumps onto the balcony's railing, and before she can escape, one of the guards raises a bow and releases an arrow; the arrow pierces her right between her shoulder blades, dead center of the pentacle. The woman topples forward without making a sound. The guards and the Emperor run to the balcony and see two other men in the royal household attire waiting below. The two on the street watch the woman's body hit the street with a thud and realize that their accomplice is dead and their plans foiled; they mount two horses and try to escape but find their escape route blocked by a platoon of the palace guard and are quickly surrounded. The Emperor watches from the balcony and sees the two of them drink something out of what looks to be small glass bottles; then, the two men start choking and foaming at the mouth and then fall from their horses dead. The Emperor orders everyone other than Old Magami, the Empress's midwife, from the room. She is the only one he trusts because she had been there when he was born. He tells the guards to secure the door. Everyone quickly leaves, and then the Emperor writes something on a small piece of paper, hands it to one of his guards, and the guard leaves the room immediately. After everything is quiet, the Emperor sees the same peregrine falcon fly from the Palace and watches it head west towards the Tammayaku Mountains.

Jutsuk tells Laki that she is curious and will follow the falcon to see where it goes and asks Laki to watch over the unborn Prince or Princess. Laki nods, and in a flash, Jutsuk is gone; and as she follows the falcon in her Spiritual form, she hears Laki's thoughts telling her that they discovered some papers on the woman, telling her to kidnap the baby after it was born, and the papers are unsigned.

Jutsuk sees the falcon circling a remote outpost and watches it slowly descend to perch set up in the shade in the outpost corral on the backside of the building. She then sees men dressed in ordinary attire coming out of the Insetsu Pass and riding towards the outpost. She remains in the Spiritual Domain, watches from above, and patiently waits for the riders to approach and enter the corral. They dismount from their horses, give them water and feed, and then head towards the building, talking amongst themselves.

She watches a big sturdy man walk over to the perch and gives the falcon some meat from a pouch, and he strokes the falcon affectionately. He then unties and removes a rolled paper from the falcon's back harness, heads to the outpost's back door, and goes inside. A minute or so passes when she hears a voice say, "Dammit!" and then sees another man who carries himself with authority exit the building, walk over to a brazier with some smoldering coals, and place the parchment on top of the coals and watches it burn. He then walks over to the corral fence, leans on it, and again she hears him say, "Dammit." She sees that he has changed his previous clothes to a lightweight black military attire. The big sturdy man walks over to him, and she sees that he has also changed his attire, and they converse between themselves. The others come out of the building carrying small bundles, and she sees they are now wearing the Emperor's household clothing.

Curiosity once again piqued her interest, and she slowly descends into the corral of the outpost to land beside the falcon's perch. She remains in her Spiritual form, and she gently strokes the falcon's head and watches the men walking across the corral towards their mounts. They are all standing beside their mounts and seem to be waiting, and when she sees the two men walk over to the horses, and is about to mount up. She knows that the tall man who came out first is the leader of these men, and the others are waiting for him to mount his horse before they do. She snaps her fingers, and all the men and horses seem to freeze, except the man she now knows is the leader.

He looks around and notices that his men and their horses are standing still as if frozen. He then looks closer and sees that they are not frozen but moving very slowly, as if at a snail's pace. He steps back from his mount and places his hand on a small dagger at his waist. When he hears, "Do not worry," only to turn and see the most beautiful woman he has ever laid eyes on standing in the middle of the small corral wearing a thin sheer material that flutters around her body at the slightest breeze. He walks up to her, immediately drops to one knee, and places an open hand over his heart, and she recognizes the pledge of devotion to her and her sister. She tells him to stand, and when he does, He tells her that he has seen their portrait and it does not do her justice. She smiles and tells him not to worry for his men, for she will not harm them unless he gives her a reason. She asks him if he is the leader of these men, and he steps toward her and says, "Yes, my Goddess, I am their leader."

Jutsuk looks at him and sees that he is a handsome man, and she asks, "Who are you?"

The man says, "I am Hakimi Hideo Miro, the Emperor Hisa Hojiko, General Advisor, my Goddess."

Then she asks, "Why, do you change your clothing and smell of tainted black death?"

Hakimi responds, "My Goddess, we were on a mission on the other side of the Tammayaku Mountains to stop a threat of a planned kidnapping of the yet-to-be-born Prince or Princess of the Empire. We could not allow this to happen, so we acted to stop the kidnapping before it could take place. We also discovered that one of the maids hired to assist in the caring and well-being of the new royal heir was in cohorts with the conspiracy group we crossed paths with. We captured one of the conspirators with a little "friendly persuasion." Jutsuk notices a sly smile as he says, "friendly persuasion." He told us that an accomplice worked in the nursery and that after the baby was born, and sometime during the night, when everyone was sleeping, she was to kidnap the baby and bring it to the group we encountered. The prisoner told us that the infant would be sacrificed to the Dark Gods, whoever they might be."

Jutsuk immediately thinks of Guichi and Tanin but shakes her head.

Hakimi politely asks her, "Are you okay? Can I do anything for you?" Jutsuk tells him, "I am fine; please continue."

"We had decided to make camp on the summit, and the prisoner needed to relieve himself. We let him, and he broke free of his guards and jumped off the cliff at the summit. I sent a message to the Emperor to tell him of the woman and how to find her.

Jutsuk tells him not to worry that the Emperor received his message, and the maid who was in with the conspirators was exposed. In an attempt to capture her, she tried to escape, and one of the guards shot her with an arrow, and she plummeted to her death if she was not already dead. They also discovered that she had two accomplices that took their own lives before they could be apprehended. She hears the Emperor's Advisor again say, "Dammit!"

She asks him why he is mad, because he stopped the kidnapping, and the Empress and unborn child are safe.

Hakimi tells her, "She could have been a key witness in bringing charges of kidnapping against the Emperor's brother, Lord Tao, the presiding Governor of Hokida. When we uncovered the plot to kidnap the baby, we also discovered that the kidnappers were to plant evidence that would blame the Chancellor of Basra. I reached out to him and unknowing to the conspirators, Sir Herbert Soan, the Chancellor of Basra, and I are close friends. I contacted him to let him know, and he permitted us to enter Basra under a covert operation. The Chancellor found out through his sources that the fanatics planning the kidnapping had close ties with the Emperor's brother, Lord Tao, the Governor of Hokida, and that they were going to plant evidence to incriminate him and possibly start a war between our two countries. He also found two conspirators in the King's court and had them arrested. That is when he found out that the fanatics were following something called the Dark Scriptures."

He tells her that the band of men and women they encountered were fanatics of these Dark Scriptures. Instead of surrendering and allowing themselves to be captured, they took their own lives by swallowing a kind of poison that killed them almost instantaneously.

Hakimi asks Jutsuk if he can ask something of her. She nods her head, yes, and he shows her a sketch of a teardrop surrounded by a pentacle and tells her that the teardrop is blood red and that these fanatics had this symbol branded on their backs between their shoulder blades. In his message, he told the Emperor about the brand and where to find it. Any individuals who had the brand were to be immediately arrested and incarcerated in the dungeons of the capital. Jutsuk approaches Hakimi Miro and places her hand on the side of his face. She reaches deep into his mind to see if he is telling the truth.

She releases him and tells him, "Hakimi, you and your men have done both the Goddesses and the Royal family true. The newborn will be important to us and must survive at all costs." In her mind, she hears Laki say. "It's a girl, and her name is Asami."

Jutsuk smiles and says, "We can give you our thanks, but now I must go to welcome and bless Princess Asami. She smiles and then is gone. The moment she is gone, his men move at a normal pace, and a few of them are bewildered how Hakimi ended up standing in the middle of the corral when they saw him just about to mount his horse.

Hakimi Miro orders his men to mount up and ride ahead to the Palace. His men do as they are told and head out at a slow trot. Only one man remains beside Hakimi, and he sits atop his mount and waits patiently for Hakimi to head out with him. Hakimi sits there for a few minutes and thinks to himself, smiling, "A Royal Princess, this is going to send the Imperial Court and its advisors in a whirlwind." then he smiles. Hakimi Miro, Advisor General to the Royal Emperor of the Ozake Empire, looks at his friend and Second in Command, Master-at-Arms Sargent Vernon Higgs, and tells him, "It's a girl; we have a new Princess."

Higgs whistles through his teeth and says, "This is not going to go well with the Emperor's Advisors!"

Hakimi Miro looks at him and says, "I know," and spurs his horse forward to catch up with the rest of his men and thinks about his son, Samuel, and what he was planning for him, but now that a Princess has been born, this changes everything, and it will be up to Samuel to make that choice.

Sargent Vernon Higgs asks, "How do you know it is a girl?"

Higgs leans slightly towards the Hakimi as they ride towards the Palace and asks again, "How did you know?"

Hakimi says, "Let's just say I got it from a reliable source," and then smiles, only to ride a little faster towards the Palace, and his men are soon keeping pace.

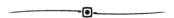

Jutsuk sits next to Laki and explains the disturbance and plot to kidnap Princess Asami. They both agree that something must be done to ensure the Princess reaches adulthood.

The Palace is quiet, and they drop down to the balcony outside the nursery. The scent of lavender fills the room, though it is not overbearing. Jutsuk walks over to the Empress and can see the stress on her face as she sleeps. Laki lightly touches her temple, and the Empress's face relaxes as if a heavy burden were removed.

They walk over to a bassinet draped with a sheer soft cloth, and Laki pulls back the fabric and finds an adorable baby girl cooing softly in her sleep. They say, "*Ishodotanaka Ina to Akajarema Princess Asami,*" and touch her chest above her heart. Three small blue stars cradled in the curve of a crescent moon appears just above her heart, and it slowly fades. The Princess opens her eyes, stares at the two Goddesses, smiles, and then quickly goes back to sleep. They look at each other, nod their heads, and then depart, leaving a scent of lavender in the room.

After they are gone, the Empress awakens and goes to the bassinet to check on her new little Princess. She sees that the baby is sleeping and also seems to be smiling. She then smells the soft fragrance of lavender and says, "Thank you."

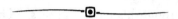

They have given their blessing upon the Princess and now need to find the "coveted three," who will protect her and be willing to sacrifice themselves for her should the need arise. They decide to cast a spell that will blanket the Empire, allowing all those eligible to be blessed with the seed of the *Chiraka*.

The *Chiraka* will implant many with its seed but will choose only three to fulfill the destinies required of the blessing. The seeds will plant their roots, and the *Chikara* will begin to encompass the very being of that selected one's mind and body when they blossom. The *Chiraka* will raise the selected ones' levels of expertise in many ways. The inducement will allow the Chosen ones to achieve a level of enlightenment so great that whatever they strive to accomplish will be on a far more superior level than anyone will ever achieve.

The *Chiraka* will Spiritually strengthen the relationship between the three, and as that relationship grows, so will a bond between them that can never be broken. When this is complete, the three selected will be so refined in their skills that the flow of the *Chiraka* will saturate their body, mind, and soul when summoned, and the *Chiraka* will come forth and be a force to be reckoned with.

Three are to be selected, but only one will have a bond with the Princess though all three will feel the connection. That bond will manifest itself in creating a link between the coveted one and the Princess, which will allow a Spiritual strengthening between the two. The coveted one will be the ward's protector and harbor a love that cannot be altered or swayed, a love that is not only from the heart but the very depths of one's soul. The other two coveted will create an intricately braided weave around that union and create a bond to make it even stronger.

That night, the Goddesses maintain their Spiritual forms high above the Imperial Empire's lands and take each other's hands, and they control their breathing to mimic each other. When their breaths are in rhythm and they sound like one, they softly chant, *"Chiraka Shotanso Zukuki Sharazita."* Silver flakes appear in the sky and start to fall, spiraling down, blanketing the lands of the Empire, not on the ground but to individuals, while they sleep. The silver flakes touch many bodies, and who they touch might feel a tiny tickle in the night as the seeds of *Chiraka* implant themselves in their bodies.

The *Chiraka* will touch all eligible, though the *Chiraka* is selective on who will have its sees planted, and the Goddesses know that the *Chiraka* will only embed itself on young boys and girls not more than nine or ten years of age.

The Goddesses depart and travel to other areas on Chikyu.

Hopedale, a quiet little town in the northern part of the Empire, lives a boy named Hikaru Sato, who works in a blacksmith shop, along with his father. He is known for his knack for fixing broken pieces, and though he loves tinkering and fixing these broken things, he keeps to himself because the other boys constantly make fun of him for being big and awkward. One day, just after he turned nine, an older boy called him names. Hikaru tried to walk away, but the older boy pushed him from the back and knocked him down in the mud. All the other boys started laughing and calling him piggy boy. They didn't realize how strong Hikaru was, and he had enough. He gets up, faces the older boy who pushed him, and decided to walk away. The boy says, "Hey, piggy boy, don't you turn your back on me, and reaches out and spins Hikaru around. Hikaru faces him, and then the boy tries to punch him; Hikaru raises his hand and catches the older boy's fist. The older boy tries to pull his fist back, but Hikaru doesn't let it go, and then he slowly squeezes. The older boy pulls a knife and goes to slash him, but Hikaru grabs the boy's wrist and then squeezes his wrist just enough to make him drop the knife. When the knife falls to the ground, Hikaru bends the boy's wrist making him scream even louder in pain. Soon the older boy is on his knees, screaming in pain, and his friends go to make a move when they hear the bones in the older boy's hand that Hikaru was squeezing break. He lets go of the boy's broken hand and punches him in the face. The older boy feels his nose break and finds himself lying on the ground holding his hand and whimpering in pain. Hikaru squats down and says, "Sorry."

The older boy remains on the ground while the boy's friends are hesitant to step in after what Hikaru did to their friend. They do not move until the older boy, still lying on the ground, shouts, "Kill that Fucker!" They come at him all at once, and a few minutes later, they end up no better than the older boy with the broken hand. The fighting stops, and Hikaru looks around and sees that one of the boys has a fractured nose, lost some teeth, and two others have broken arms. Hikaru has a few scratches and bruises but walks away, leaving the others crying in the street. That night while he sleeps, a silver flake lands on his cheek, and he feels a slight tickle as warmth fills his body, and seconds later, the feeling is gone. Hikaru wakes up from the strange sensation but does not recall what just happened and goes back to sleep.

The following day, all the parents are banging on the door of the blacksmith's home, demanding that he do something about his boy because he is a menace and a bully. The blacksmith knows the truth because he has seen it for himself and always has told Hikaru to be the better man. Later that day, the town elders stop by and have a long discussion with the blacksmith, and they also know that the boys probably deserved it. Still, the parents are prominent pillars of the community, and they are demanding some justice. That night the blacksmith tells his son that he knows he didn't start anything and was only defending himself, but the town elders have decided to send him off to join the Imperial Army as a steward. The young boy does not challenge his father because he thinks it would be for the best. The following morning Hikaru Sato is put on a caravan heading to the capital of the Empire with a letter of introduction from the town elders to join the Imperial Army as a steward.

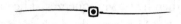

The Blossom Inn, located in a small village on the east coast of the Empire, is known for a rare seasonal dish that many consider one of the most delicate dishes in the Empire to be found only at this specific Inn a delicacy. A good family consisting of a husband, wife, and three daughters, owns the Inn, and people come from all over to taste this rare delicacy.

Reiko Takahashi is the oldest of the three girls and is about to turn nine, as her two younger sisters are five and three. She is a slender girl, cute in a tomboyish way, and has been helping at Blossom Inn since she was old enough to walk. She is up every morning at dawn to help her parents prepare the morning meals for the visitors staying at her family's Inn. When in season, travelers come from all over to try the Inn's most famous delicacy, a tender combination of whitefish and vegetables. The vegetables are not unusual, but the whitefish migrates up the coast in the colder months and spawn. Reiko's parents know the secret seasonings to enhance the flavor of the fish, which allows it to be a delicacy.

One morning, right after dawn, and as the sun is just starting to rise, Reiko is in the garden picking some vegetables when one of the patrons staying at the Inn comes outside to smoke his pipe. He observes the young girl going about her business and inside with the vegetables. A few moments later, she returns, and the man smoking the pipe asks her if she wouldn't mind helping him with his horse. She says, "Okay," and she follows him into the barn; and he turns quickly and places his hand over her mouth to stifle any screams. Reiko struggles to break free, but the man has a knife pressed to her throat and threatens her. He tells her not to scream or he will cut her. She doesn't yell but remains very calm.

The man tells her to unbutton her blouse, but she refuses. He starts to reach for her, and they hear her father calling for her. The man grabs her and covers her mouth with his hand to stop her from calling out, and as he does, she pulls out her small vegetable knife and jabs the small blade into the man's thigh. He screams, dropping his knife, as the doors are pulled open, and her father and several guests are standing there, and they find the man holding his thigh, screaming that the girl just stabbed him. A couple of the guests help the man and take him back to the house to care for his wound.

That day and into the night, she stays in her room and cries because no one would believe her. She is lying awake in her bed and sees a small silver lake float through her window, and ever so softly lands on the back of her hand. The tiny silver flake melts when it touches her skin, and warmth fills her body. Seconds later, the sensation is gone, and she doesn't give it another thought and then drifts off to sleep.

The following day, at the crack of dawn, her father and mother ask her to sit with them before the guests wake up. Her father tells her he and her mother believe her, but she must leave the village. Reiko asks, "Why?" Her mother tells her that the guests are complaining without further explanation. Her father then slides an envelope across the table and tells her that she called in a favor from an old friend and that this morning she will depart for the capital of the Empire to join the Imperial Army as a steward. Like Hikaru Sato, Reiko Takahashi rides with a local merchant to the capital to join the Imperial Army the following day.

A single flake floats along on a light breeze through the capital as if with a purpose. It is floating by an open window when it stops and seems to hover. Kneeling on a pillow at a low table is a young boy about nine years old, and he is studying and writing down his lessons from earlier in the day. He finishes when the door opens, and an older man steps into the room. The cross draft from the door opening pulls the flake into the room, and it continues to hover high in the corner of the room. The young boy puts down his writing utensil, stands, bows to the older man who is his teacher, hands the man his papers, and waits. The teacher starts to review what the young boy has just given him. The boy sits motionless as he watches his teacher raise his eyebrows as if surprised. He puts the papers back on the boy's table, sits across from him, and asks him to explain.

The boy stands up, bows, and explains his answers to the lessons. The teacher sits quietly, and when the boy finishes, he nods in approval and is just about to critique the boys' lesson when the bells start ringing throughout the city to inform the capital that the Empress has given birth.

The older man takes the papers from the writing table and tells the young boy that he has completed his assignment though his summarization is a little unorthodox. There is a knock on the door, and the older man tells whoever it is to enter. A girl steps into the room, bows and whispers something in the teacher's ear, bows again, and leaves the room. The old man's tone changes, and he says to the young boy, "You have mastered your lessons, but I need to tell you that the Empress has given birth to a baby girl."

The older man stands, walks over to a bookshelf, and looks at the books until he finds the book he is looking for; and grabs it off the shelf, but before he turns around, the flake floats down and lands on the young boy's forearm. The boy sees the flash of silver and feels the warmth spread through his body; then, moments later, just like the others, he has no recollection of it happening.

The older man brings over a sizeable leather-bound book and places it in front of him on his writing table. The young boy opens the leather-bound book and starts reading. The city celebrates the news of the Empress giving birth. The young boy pays no attention to thanking the Goddesses for a healthy heir and returns to the book to continue reading its contents.

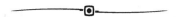

It has been a month since the Goddesses created the *Chiraka*; now that the seeds have been planted, they depart the Empire's lands and head west over the Tammayaku Mountains. They soon settle onto the Great Plains and walk in silence through the wind-swept grasses, billowing fields of wildflowers, and clusters of trees.

Jutsuk brings up the subject of the sketch that the Emperor's Advisor General Hakimi Hideo Miro had shown her, and she tells Laki that she believes that Guichi and Tanin are behind all of this.

Walking arm in arm, Laki says, "I have to agree with you, sister; we both know that they are up to something, and if Mother is right about the Dark Crystals being on this planet and the Stain has tainted them, then they can only be up to no good."

"What do you suggest we do?" asks Jutsuk

We need to find them and explain that whatever they have planned is wrong. Mother has said they might be infected and not thinking with clear minds, but that does not mean they are lost. If we can bring them to our way of thinking, then we have a chance to save them."

Jutsuk says, "What if we can't persuade them, and they continue to embrace the darkness inside them and try to connect with the Dark Realm? What are we going to do then?"

Laki looks at her and says, "I guess we will have to take that path and make a choice when the time comes." She says, "We know that when Mother brought father here, she helped quiet the planet and assisted it in its evolution and must have used something of this world."

Jutsuk says, "Didn't she say she used Chikyu's natural elements of *Spirit, Earth, Fire,* Air, *and Water.* If we can do the same and bring forth a "*Kachirano,*" then Laki finishes what she was going to say and says, "Then we could have it lay dormant until the time is right, but how would we do it?"

Jutsuk says, "We can place statues in honor of Mother throughout the Chikyu, and place the *Kachirano* inside the statues, and like the "*Chiraka,*" we let the *Kachirano* find their hosts and plant the seeds. Then as the hosts grow and mature, so should the element or elements that the *Kachirano* recognizes as their strongest potential."

Laki smiles and says, "Let's do it!"

They both sit in the middle of a patch of wildflowers, take each other's hands, and once again control their breathing to mimic each other. When their breaths are in rhythm and sound as one, when they chant, "*Kuziki Bahure Kachirano Sukureta.*"

Small stone statues of Kamiyobo, the Eternal God Mother, appear throughout the lands. The statues immediately start sending out pulses throughout the lands. The pulses are not felt or heard, but when people are near the statues, the *Kachirano* touches them and caresses them, and if they sense the ones, they will plant a seed, and the five manas will sleep until the time they are to be awoken. Upon awakening, they will release the kinship to the most powerful and fulfill their destiny of the "Gifted," They are content, rise from the patch of wildflowers, walk north towards the valley, and continue with small talk.

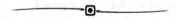

Four mothers in different parts of the world are carrying their newborn daughters, wrapped in swaddling, past the small statues of the Eternal God Mother, "Kamiyobo." at the exact moment in time. The four mothers stop near the statues simultaneously, and each takes a deep breath. They each feel something suddenly unique about their young daughters, as though a special blessing has touched them, though it is very faint. The mothers all exhale as one, and without realizing it, a bond is created that will link their four daughters together in the future. The bond that will establish a relationship to fulfill their destinies.

The four mothers return to their everyday lives, with none being the wiser at what has just happened inside their babies and between them. The "*Kachirano*" has touched many but has determined that these four newborns are its "Gifted." That night, all the God Mother statues crumble to dust and are blown away by a light breeze, and anyone who might have seen them cannot remember except the newborns.

Chapter 4

The James Clan

Patriarch Michael James is the leader of the James Clan and has led his people for over forty years and has attributed to the success of the Clans' exploring and trading qualities. The Clan has traveled to many lands from the Northern Isles to the Great Southern Continent to the Lands of the Ice Clans, where they have established many trade agreements with the indigenous natives from the Northern Isles to the Great Southern Continent to the Lands of the Ice Clans.

On one of their excursions, they had just traded wares down in the Lands of the Ice Clans, and as they were heading north, they got caught in a severe tropical storm off the east coast of the Southern Continent with severe gale winds. They rode out the storm, but their ships were heavily damaged and were taking on water, so Michel James through a maze of islands until they came to a harbor to repair their ships. It was the perfect harbor to carry out the necessary repairs.

While they were making their repairs, they befriended the local natives. As with others, they have befriended, they established a trade agreement with the indigenous natives for an island delicacy known as the Painapp fruit.

They completed their repairs a few months later, left the harbor, and sailed back to Sadenkiwa in the north. They did not realize that the demand for the Painapp fruit would be so great, and soon the Clan found themselves trading primarily in the fruit of the Tatokai islands.

They discovered that the Archipelago consisted of six main islands, with Aleu being the largest of the six. The five other islands were Pika, Tiku, Akel, Alit, and Pilka, and many smaller islands, with Botaku as one of the chain's last inhabitable islands. The Tatokai Archipelago is situated approximately eleven hundred kilometers off the southern coast of the island kingdom of Haven.

Over time, Michel James, the Patriarch of the Clan, bonded with Chief Magee, the leader of the largest tribe in the island chain, and they became true friends. Though the Clan continued with their other trades, the most profitable was the Painapp fruit, and the demand quickly became greater than the supply.

Michel was talking with Chief Magee one day, and he asked about the possibility of supplying more of the fruit. Magee explained to Michel that that would be impossible to do with the present inter-island situations. Chief Magee explained how he was trying to unite the islands under one ruler, but there was resistance, especially from two larger tribes, with one residing on Pika and the other on Botaku.

Chief Magee tells Michel that the islands are already at war because some of the tribesmen in the outer islands did not want the unification to happen. They wanted to remain independent so that they could keep practicing cannibalism, and if the islands were united, they would have to give up their way of life and beliefs. They were also kidnapping natives from the smaller islands for sacrifices and food. Chief Magee had told Michel that this was not his fight, and he will continue with their agreements.

That night after the meeting with the Chief, Michel met with the Clan, and after he explained the situation, everyone thought this was atrocious. The Clan agrees to help their friends in the war, to help put a stop to cannibalism, and to unify the islands.

After the Clan joined with the Tatokai and taught them how to use the many weapons in their arsenal, the tides of war started to turn. The small tribes controlled by the larger cannibalistic tribes were soon freed from the tyranny and joined the unification. Any tribes who practiced cannibalism were either forced to flee to smaller islands or were killed. Many of these smaller islands wanted unification. Still, they feared the repercussions if they went against the two brothers who were Chiefs of the two largest cannibal tribes in the Archipelago. Chief Bukuso resided on the island of Pika, while his brother Chief Madisuke lived on the island of Botaku. Both Chiefs fought against the unification of the islands and stopping cannibalism.

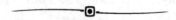

One night there was a lull in the fighting, and it was a peaceful night in the main village on Akel, the closest island to Pika. The Clan leaders and the Tatokai Chiefs were discussing the final assault on the island of Pika.

Suddenly a runner barges into the room and tells Chief Magee that a war party of cannibals had somehow made their way into the main village on Akel, kidnapped the Chief's daughter, Mima, and took Michel's daughter Camille.

Chief Magee became furious and knew that if they did not hurry and try to save the two girls, they would become human sacrifices and be eaten. Michel told Chief Magee that he would not let that happen and called together the Clan and a large portion of Tatokai warriors and that they would rescue the girls and end this war against cannibals on Pika. They were getting ready to go after the two girls and their kidnappers when Michel and Chief Magee were told that two warriors and one Clansman were missing, and they found some of their gear hidden in bushes down on the beach.

The Clan and the Tatokai warriors head out under a full moon that is just beginning to rise when they are just about to make their way around the first island, where Pika would come into view but also show the cannibals that they were coming. It is as if the island Gods were watching over them because just as they were making it past the first island, clouds moved in and blocked the full moon's radiance, reaching the island undetected. Michel immediately sent a couple of his Clansmen, and Chief Magee sees that his warriors are nervous but tells them to follow them and scout the area. They are gathering on the beach when out of nowhere, one of the cannibals steps out of the bush. He sees them, but before he can shout out a warning, one of the Clansmen is behind him, covers his mouth, and drives a long knife into his lower back, killing him. The others return shortly, reporting nothing but a large clearing in front of a cave, and in the clearing is a large stone slab. One of the warriors tells Chief Magee that it looks like fresh blood is on the slab. The Chief is worried as he explains to Michel that they might be too late. When the Shaman Taku tells Michel and Chief Magee that the full moon has not fully reached its zenith and that the moon needs to come out from behind the clouds before any sacrifices take place. Even Chief Bukuso does not want to anger the island Gods and fears retribution.

Michel directs some of his men to make their way to the village and remove any threats. Chief Magee sends some of his men with them. The remaining Clansmen and warriors start moving towards the clearing when they hear voices and a girl's scream. They follow the voices and discover several warriors with spears positioned around the edges of the clearing standing guard, luckily with their backs to the jungle. The Tatokai warriors take them out quickly and without a sound. They don their headdresses and assume their positions. The rest stay quiet as they move up to the edge of a clearing and ready their bows. Michel passes the word for the men to wait for his signal.

Michel sees Mima, just to the right of the stone slab, naked and tied to a large wooden post in the ground. He also sees that she is crying and has several minor cuts on her body. Michel looks for Camille, and when he doesn't see her, he starts to worry and is about to signal when he hears a girl's scream coming from inside the cave and then sees a group of females coming out of the cave and dragging Camille, and like Mima, she is naked and has several minor cuts on her body. They carry her over to the stone slab and place her on top. She lies there crying when a man with an elaborate necklace made from small bones steps out of the cave. Taku whispers to Michel that he is Chief Bukuso, leader of the cannibals. The Chief then walks over to stand near Camille's head, and a woman holds her down, and she seems to be chanting. Tato tells Michel that she is the Chief's wife and the tribe's Shaman. Michel sees that both the Chief and the woman are wearing necklaces made from small bones, and their noses and earlobes are pierced with the same type of bones. The Chief speaks a different dialect, raises the blade, and stands there waiting for the moon to bask the altar in its glow. Suddenly the clouds part and the altar is basking in the glow of the moon. Camille screams, as does Mima, as Chief Bukuso starts to bring the knife down towards Camille's chest.

Michel lets out a high-pitched whistle, which causes the Chief to hesitate, and as he turns to see where the noise has come from, several arrows come flying through the Air and hit the Chief in his upper chest. The Chief looks down and is surprised as the knife falls from his hands. He drops to his knees, clutching his chest as if trying to pull the arrows out. The woman is also hit with arrows, though her wounds are not life-threatening like her husband's. The woman reaches out to catch him as he crumbles to the ground. She lays over his body, covering him, protecting him, though she knows he is already dead. Within seconds she sees that the clearing is suddenly in turmoil as the Tatokai warriors and other men as white as their young captive on the altar attack and slaughter anyone who defies them. She hears the screams of the dying, and then she sees the sacrificial knife lying in the dirt next to the altar. She reaches out, grabs it, and then hides it under her body. The woman remains to lie over her husband's body.

Soon it is over, and the screams of the wounded are quickly silenced as the Clansmen stay back, and the Tatokai warriors show no mercy as they go around and kill any survivors. The Chief's wife watches in silence as she sees her tribe's warriors and young men lying in the clearing with their throats cut, knowing they are dead. She glances up and sees a tall man walking over to the head of the altar, and he starts cutting at the young girl's bindings, and she also sees Chief Magee of the Tatokai doing the same to the other young captive tied to the pole.

Unknowing that she has grabbed the knife and is hiding it underneath her, she lies there, remaining perfectly still, as she watches the white leader cut one of her bindings and move onto the second one. She waits patiently for her chance, and then she sees it, as the white-skinned warrior turns his back to her to cut the young girl's last set of bindings, and she gets ready to move when she sees movement out of the corner of her eye.

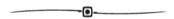

One of Michel's men starts walking towards the cave, and before he enters, he grabs a lit torch to the left of the cave entrance. He immediately sees another stone slab, dark red, but this one is smaller. He looks closer and realizes that the red tint is some old blood, and he also sees some fresh blood and assumes it belongs to Camille and Mima. Disgusted, he turns to leave, but something peculiar catches his eye. He raises the torch a little higher, and as it illuminates the back of the cave, he sees some bones. He raises the torch for a better look and sees three bodies stacked on the pile of bones, and that is when he realizes that the three bodies stacked on the bones are the two Tatokai warriors and the Clansman that disappeared from the beach. He throws up and staggers out of the cave, and when the others see him, they run over to see what is wrong.

They gather around him and ask questions when suddenly there are several war cries, and five of the tribe's younger men, who are not much older than teenagers, come running into the clearing, yelling war cries, and some are brandishing war clubs, and some have knives. The Clansmen already have their swords drawn and swiftly deal with the young boys. Like the others, most are run through by a sword, and one is decapitated.

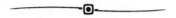

The woman sees the five young men enter the clearing, brandishing war clubs and knives and yelling war cries. She sees the one leading the others is her only son, and she is proud of him until she sees his head leave his shoulders. Her husband and son are dead; she has nothing to live for and sees her chance. She quickly stands, almost jumping, and keeps the knife hidden by her side.

Michel is now standing with Camille and watches his men check the young boys for any signs of life. The woman is slightly behind Michel; when she starts yelling something incoherent. Michel pushes Camille behind him and brings his sword, swinging it towards the woman trying to plunge a blade into his chest. He realizes he is just a bit too slow as the woman plunges the sacrificial knife into his chest, pulls it out, and tries to plunge the knife again. When Michel feels his blade strike the woman's neck and sees that he has almost completely taken her head off, he looks down, sees the blade sticking out of his chest, and watches as his shirt turns a bloody red.

Camille shouts, "Father!" but it is too late. Michel knows she has ruptured vital organs and knows he is not long for this world. He feels his sword slip from his fingers and then drops to his knees as Camille rushes to him and tries to hold him up. He smiles at her and says, "I am glad that the two of you are safe," and falls forward only to take his last breath before he lies prone face down on the ground. Camille kneels beside him and cries, and then the other Clan members are beside the two of them.

It has been a month since Camille and Mima's rescue, and the Patriarch of the Clan, Michel James, was placed beside other Clan members of the war in a family tomb. Another two weeks pass as Thomas James and the other Clan members discuss the appointment of a new Patriarch for the Clan. Soon word arrives that the last of the cannibals have joined Chief Madisuke and have taken refuge on the island of Botaku.

After the kidnapping and return of Camille, Thomas James, Michel's oldest son and Camille's uncle seemed to be always at the forefront of the campaign to unite the islands. He always had the best-laid plans for leading the war on the remaining tribes that resisted the unification under one Chief. Thomas seemed to have an uncanny knack for identifying strategies and contingencies, which enabled the campaign to continue with little and sometimes no losses. Though he never actually fought in any battles, being a superior strategist, the war with the natives was finally in their favor. This final battle that will take place between the two Chiefs will either make or break the islands.

The last report stated that the remaining tribes against the unification had sided with Chief Madisuke, who was notorious for ripping out the victim's hearts while they were still breathing. The tribes were gathering back on the largest island of Botaku.

Within a few days, several Tatokai boats loaded with Clansmen and the Tatokai warriors arrived on the island; as they disembarked, they were confronted by an enormous force of over three hundred warriors. The disembarking party led by Thomas shouts out to Chief Madisuke to surrender and become one with the unification. If he denies the offer, he alone will be responsible for the deaths of his warriors.

Chief Madisuke laughs and orders his warriors to attack. They advance, thinking they have the numbers as the Clan and Tatokai fall back and make their way to the pits. They reach the pits and begin shooting arrows into the advancing group of warriors. Chief Madisuke continues shouting for his warriors to advance and push the enemy into the pits. Suddenly, a war cry is heard behind them, and Madisuke stops screaming long enough to turn and sees two larger forces of Tatokai warriors and Clansmen approaching from behind him and flanking him on both sides. He commands that his warriors keep fighting and to the death if need be. They continue to fight even though the odds are against them. A spear pierces Thomas's leg, but he remains standing at the precipice of the pits, with his men, with their swords drawn. He sees Chief Madisuke disappear and then sees him again and realizes that his warriors brought him down. When he sees the Chief's head skewed on the end of a spear, and as it is raised in the Air, most of the remaining warriors start dropping their weapons and kneel in surrender, and the ones who continue to fight are quickly killed by either their tribes. The war for the unification of the Archipelago is over, and the warriors erupt in celebration and start chanting Chief Magee's name.

Once the chanting dies, Chief Magee tells the surviving warriors under Chief Madisuke that they have a choice: to live here on Botaku or be banished from the islands. The survivors decide to stay on the island and mine the salt pits. Though the Botaku cluster of islands is slightly isolated from the other islands, there are smaller islands that are inhabitable. The warriors are permitted to make excursions to the other isolated islands in the cluster to establish homes for their families. Before he leaves them, the Chief warns them that if any surviving members resort back to cannibalism, it would be a death penalty for the individual and their families.

Word has spread that the war against the last tribes has finally ended, and the islands are united as one nation. Over the following few weeks, supplies are taken to Botaku to help the new occupants build a new life and equipment to work the salt pits.

After a week-long celebration, the Clan and Chiefs called a meeting to discuss the appointment of a new Patriarch for the Clan. Many Clan members still wanted Thomas to take the position, but he politely declined, stating that he could not adequately fulfill his duties as Patriarch. He decided it was time for the truth to come out, and it was not him who came up with the battle plans and strategies.

The Clan members asked him, "Then who was laying out the plans and strategies because whoever was doing it should be appointed as the new Clan Patriarch."

Thomas clears his throat and tells them that Camille's master planning and strategies turned the war in their favor. After a week-long discussion between the Clan members, they agreed Camille was young, but her planning led to the unification of all the islands in the Archipelago. Three days later, Camille James became the Matriarch of the James Clan, and the locals immediately started calling her *"Choobachi,"* which meant Tamil of the Islands. Celebrations erupted throughout the islands, as the natives were delighted to have her Chosen as their Choobachi. The people of the Tatokai Archipelago swore their allegiance to her. They changed their name from Tatokai to the old language to Seishin in honor of Camille for unifying the Archipelago islands to become one nation.

The Tatokai shows the family how to grow and cultivate the Painapp fruit, indigenous to the islands. They explain that it takes the fruit five years to mature, and once it does, it will never rot or go bad. Camille recognizes the potential of this delicious, sweet fruit and realizes that exporting the fruit to the continents could be very profitable. She discusses her ideas with the island Chiefs and Shamans, who agree that more islands will be cultivated to grow the fruit.

A large seaport is built in the largest harbor on the main island of Aleu for the sailing ships of what is now the Tatokai Isle fleet. Members of the Clan travel to the continent to set up brokerage firms to sell the fruit. Within another ten years, forty-five percent of the islands flourish in cultivating the delicious Painapp fruit.

The Clan elders, the Chiefs, and the Shamans govern the allotted fruit exported to other nations. Any dealings that include the Painapp fruit must go through the island of Aleu and the newly established Tatokai-James Trading Company.

The only thing the islands have that no others can seem to copy is the ability to grow the fruit and maintain its sweet texture. Others have tried, but the fruit grown off-island might start out having a sweet taste, but if the texture of the fruit becomes too soft, and changes to a sour taste; and also tends to rot once it matures. When the island's fruit reaches a specific size, it stops growing and develops, making them sweeter and juicier.

Camille has been the Matriarch of the Clan and the Choobachi of the Islands for several years. She has grown into a lovely young woman with a good head. At the end of a harvest festival, she announces and proclaims that a cluster of islands in the Archipelago is now off-limits to anyone other than full-blooded Tatokai Archipelago natives. These islands are now considered holy ground and can only be visited with permission from the tribal Chiefs. Anyone caught on the islands without authorization will be sent to the "Pits." The Chiefs and Shamans are surprised by this proclamation, and a great rejoice is felt in the crowd.

Every six months, Camille travels with Thomas to Kaji, the largest of the Sacred Islands, and holds a meeting with all the Chiefs and Shamans. She would explain in great detail everything involved in selling and exporting the fruit through the company brokers or trading vessels that provide services to the islands. Whenever Camille goes to the islands, there is always a chest filled with gold bars. Over the past few visits, she has been bringing two chests because the islands prosper.

It has now been_twenty-five years since the James Clan received permission from the Tatokai Chiefs and Shamans and be allowed to settle on the main island of Aleu. Over the years, they grew and soon populated the other large and small islands.

Camille is just about to make her journey to Kaji and thinks back to the last time she made this trip six months ago; the Tribal Chiefs wanted her to become the true leader of the islands' people, and they wanted to make her a Queen. Camille did not wish the title of Queen and politely turned it down. She is just about to leave Aleu for Kaji when she receives a request to come to the island of Toke', an island that she has never been to.

The boat carrying her and the donations soon arrives at a small island of Toke', and she sees that it is dense in plant life and also what looks like a freshly cut path through the jungle. The five Tribal Chiefs and five Shamans meet her at the boat pier and say, "Welcome to Toke'," They ask her to accompany them and leave chests where they are in the boat. She follows them up a hill, and before long, she finds herself standing in front of two massive wooden doors inscribed in a very ancient language. Without realizing it, Camille says. out loud, "May only the true Choobachi enter through these gates." She stops reading and looks at the Chiefs and Shaman, who all have a look surprise on their faces.

Take the lead and oldest Shaman in the group, very politely asks Camille how did she know what was written on the doors. She tells him that she can read the words as if she were reading her native language or the Seishin-Tatokai language, which she has learned since settling on the islands, especially after becoming their *"Choobachi"*.

The other Shaman talk among themselves, and when done, they smile at Camille and bow. She is slightly concerned, but Taki tells her not to worry and tells her that the cavern and the doors have only just recently been found, and that was because a scroll describing the location somehow miraculously appeared in the temple on *Kanji*. It appeared right after you declared this small cluster of islands sacred. We were able to decipher the scroll, up to the cavern, and find the massive doors. It took several weeks to clear the vegetation to the doors, and they did not know how to open them. They can only assume that the one true Choobachi can only open the doors.

They follow her as she walks up to the two massive wooden doors and sees two indentations that look like a hand print. Taki asks her to place her hands on the door, and when she does, her hands fit perfectly, and then she feels a slight prick. She pulls back her hands and sees a tiny smear of blood left on the wood and a hole about the size of a pinprick in her palm. She watches the wood absorb her blood, then hears noises behind the door as if something were turning. The noise stops, and the large wooden doors slowly swing in. The eleven of them enter, and she is surprised to see a long cave with walls smooth as glass. She walks with them, pointing out finely detailed carvings on the cave walls, and like her, the Chiefs and Shamans see these carvings for the first time as she continues walking with them. They show the Seishin coming to the islands and flourishing as one people. Words in the ancient language are etched into the wall under the carvings, and, ironically, Camille has to translate the ancient writings on the wall to the Chiefs and Shaman. Then the carvings display fighting between the tribes, and as the conflicts grow, the one people separate and become many, isolating themselves and forming independent nations. Taki tries to explain what he can of the history of the Seishin people, but Camille reads it differently than what Taki is telling her, and it does not correspond with what she is seeing and reading. The words etched throughout the wall in the ancient language tell a different story, but she does not tell them that.

Camille looks at the images on the wall and pauses when she recognizes a taller figure than the others around him. The scene depicts a bloody battle, with the next scene showing the tall figure lying on the ground and a young female weeping over his body. There is no mistaking it as Camille stares at her father's killing, and she kneels beside his body. She sees the funeral procession and the body being placed inside a tomb, and above the tomb is written "James." Camille is more surprised to see that the same female stands before the people. In front are chests filled with riches, and she sees the Painapp fruit growing and flourishing. The next scene depicts her above the islands, and it looks like streams of something are coming from the islands and entering her body. The odd thing about this etching is that it only shows colors of red, brown, blue, white, and something that is almost clear. The last images show the same woman standing before the people, wearing a necklace. She looks to the Chiefs and Shamans, and in their native tongue, she asks how this could be; they tell her that the carvings and images were here long before her Clan arrived on the islands, but they cannot explain the pictures or the writings on the wall. She departs Toke', and when she returns to Aleu, she has a long discussion with her brother, Thomas, and he agrees with the Chiefs and Shaman that she should become the island's "Tamal." Camille laughs and tells Thomas she will think about it and then reaches for a deck of stiletto cards, and Camille tells him that he still owes her, and all Thomas says is, "You're just as bad, Putra, and Camille laughs more.

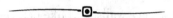

Camille James is preparing for her semi-annual visit when Taki sends her a note asking her to meet on the island of *Futa*. Camille is again surprised for the second time not meeting at Kaji, and when she arrives, she is greeted with open arms by the Elder women, and they ask her to join them in the communal sweat lodge. Camille feels honored because the only ones with true blood in their veins are allowed in the sacred sweat lodge. Camille follows protocol and is now sitting in a circle with twelve other tribal women, all wives to the Shamans or Chiefs. The steam is heavy and intoxicating in the lodge, and she detects the scent of lavender. The Elder woman starts singing a lovely melody, and Camille becomes light-headed. She closes her eyes, and then images begin to appear. She hears the whispered song from the women sitting with her in the sweat lodge and the Eldest Takiyu saying, "Be brave, be strong," repeatedly. Camille next finds herself soaring through the Air above the islands of the Archipelago.

Camille circles the first island of Kanejo (*Pika*), and she smells freshly turned soil rich and minerals, and she feels invigorated with power and strength. She then moves over to the next island of Kaji (*Tiku*) and feels the warmth from dozens of small fires that send heat throughout her body, and it is a heat of passion. She is now over Kawa (*Akel*) and feels a cleansing of her body and mind as if being washed in a soft rain shower. When she is over Kazi (*Alit*), she senses a gentle, delicate breeze move over her flesh as it dries her body and opens her mind to new things. She feels a purity, but then she feels a turmoil as the senses she has just felt seem to be battling each other for something, but she does not know what it is. Without realizing it, she finds herself hovering over Seishin (*Aleu*), and she looks down and sees a kaleidoscope of beiges, reds, blues, and soft whites flowing around the center of the island of Seishin (*Aleu*) and also feels the inner turmoil within these colors as if vying to be the first. She is not afraid and lands softly in a circle etched into a solid stone; she looks around and sees symbols depicting *Earth, Air, Fire, and Water* in the ancient language.

She calmly stands there as the four colors swirl around her ever so lightly, caressing her body, and the turmoil she felt before is completely gone. She sees that the colors represent the four natural elements in nature, and she also remembers seeing that each of the main islands was strong in each mana. She remains standing in the circle and feels something completely different. She has a feeling of euphoria, which saturates her body. Camille finds herself kneeling in the circle, and with tears in her eyes, she hears an ethereal voice say, "*Thank you, the prophecy is fulfilled, and the islands have their Tamil.*"

She then feels something delicately placed around her neck, from who or what she does not know, but when she looks down, she sees a necklace hanging from her neck. She also sees that the necklace is made from the purest of rare metals. She feels the warmth of the gem hanging between her breasts and sees a large dark blue, almost black, flawless sapphire. She crosses her hands and places her palms over the stone. Her heart skips a beat as she feels the essence of Seishin and the other four mana's saturate her body, and she feels power. She then gently grasps the stone in her hands and makes a fist, and then she feels as if her body has been possessed, but for the greater good. She can feel the power emanating from her body and herself rising into the Air. Camille is now directly above Archipelago, and she looks down and sees the other four main islands glowing and pulsing with life. Then each island explodes, and she feels the four elements ultimately give themselves to her and feel them wrapping themselves around her body, and a different type of euphoria builds. She calls forth each mana of *Earth*, then *Fire*, followed by *Air*, then *Water*, and she has the four stretching out from her hands. She brings them together to feel the inner turmoil that she felt before. Just as she somehow weaves them together, Seishin explodes, different mana saturates her body, and she hears the ethereal voice say, "*Spirit*," and her body absorbs it, as does the deep blue, almost black sapphire. She feels the other four manas suddenly settle down and are calm; compared to the turmoil she felt just seconds ago. She now feels like a harmonious union, and the euphoria returns. She blinks, opens her eyes, and is back in the lodge. She sits there drenched in sweat and looks at every face in the lodge, and they are all smiling. The Eldest of the women says in the ancient language, "*Da Aru Kuta Akata Shiru Chi Kara*," and she smiles. Camille sits up straighter and wonders if it was all a dream when she feels something around her neck and looks down to see a flawless dark blue, almost black sapphire hanging between her breasts. One of the women holds a mirror to her face, and she sees that her eyes are now a deep sapphire blue with tiny silver specks. she gazes around the room, and first, the Eldest of the women bows, and then the others call her "*Kinoumi Gotenku*."

The Eldest tells her how *Spirit* had disappeared when the tribes fought amongst themselves and divided the islands. The necklace, along with *Spirit*, had been lost for hundreds of years. The necklace she now wears symbolizes power among her people, that only a true *Tamil* is allowed to be the bearer of the necklace, and that *Tamil* will rule over the Tatokai Islands and its people. The Tamils' reign will be passed down from generation to generation, but only on the female side.

The women wrap themselves in blankets, and as they leave the sweat lodge when Taki approaches them and bows and tells them of what is happening throughout the islands. He tells them that the Painapp fruit has begun to change color to a beautiful deep purple and that the fruit itself has a different taste, and it is for the better if it could ever have seemed possible. He tells them that even the harvested fruits on the islands have changed color and are sweeter.

When word reaches the other islands about what is happening with the Painapp fruit, the natives know that "*Spirit*" has returned to the Seishin Islands. The natives praise Camille for reuniting the islands and bringing the five elements back to the islands. They wanted to do something special for her, so they decided that a Tamil needed a palace. Camille politely tells them that a palace is unnecessary and that she is content with living in the house she has occupied for many years. Three years later, a magnificent but modest palace with green grasses, vineyards, and winding paths overlooking the town and the harbor is complete.

Camille ruled the islands as Tamil for many years until her death at one hundred and eighteen. The catacombs underneath the Royal Palace are where she was placed, and the only markings were in the old script above the sealed door. The necklace became the symbol of royalty and power, and the line of succession was not by blood, lineage, or heritage, but the next Tamil who was to become ruler of the islands was and is always decided by the necklace, and over the subsequent years, the next in the line of succession has always been a female

Chapter 5

Sarah Priscilla Novasta

Mary Katherine Novasta was married to Duke Novasta, who resided in a small Dutchy of Marion in the northwestern region of Elenni, just south of the Barrens. He was a good and fAir man but sadly was killed in the Great War while Elenni supported Basra against the Empire. Lady Mary Novasta was devastated when she received word of her husband's demise. The Queen of Elenni, Priscilla Henrietta Montage, had met Mary on several occasions, and over time, they became close friends. When the Queen found out that Mary was with child, she could not bear her being alone at the family's Keep and brought her to the capital to live, and soon she became the Queen's trusted confidant. Mary Katherine was well-liked by all and wholly devoted to the Queen, dedicated so that she would have sacrificed her life to protect her Queen. When her time came, Mary Katherine gave birth to a beautiful little girl named Sarah Priscilla Novasta; her middle name was in honor of the Queen. Mary Katherine became the Queen's best friend and most trusted advisor and was awarded many accolades as the Queen's confidant. Sarah was four years old when the Queen was pregnant with the now-present King Theo II, and there were those in the court who did not care to have Mary Katherine being the Queen's most trusted confidant. They thought that she had too much influence over the Queen and would help sway her in court matters that were not beneficial to them or the Kingdom and could turn the Queen against them. They wanted her dishonored and banned from the Kingdom or entirely out of the way. Sarah was just over four years old when the present King Theo the II was born.

Right after the Prince was born, a plot was formulated and put into place to discredit Mary Katherine Novasta. The ones against her had to make it look like she was in league with a factor of undesirables to kidnap the King and Queen's son, Prince Theo II, and ransom him for a large amount of money.

One evening while Mary Katherine was in the nursery holding the young Prince and rocking him, Sarah was on the floor playing with her dolls. The doors to the nursery open, and the King's Chamberlain enters the room with four palace guards. Mary asked the Chamberlain to keep the noise down because Queen Priscilla was in the other room getting some rest. The Chamberlain asks Mary to place the Prince in the crib, and she does. Once she lays down the young Prince in his crib, she is struck from behind and falls to her knees. Two guards push her down and hold her down with her face on the floor as two other guards place shackles around her ankles and wrists. They pick her up by her arms and drag her from the nursery. Sarah comes running up to her mother, and one of the guards backhands her, and she falls to the floor crying and calls out, "Mommy" Mary is being forcefully escorted from the room when the Queen enters and demands, and asks "What is going on here?"

The King's chamberlain answers, "Your Majesty, it has been brought to our attention that this woman is in league with a faction against the Kingdom and is plotting with them to kidnap the young prince." He then holds out a paper with the other conspirators' names.

Mary calls out to the Queen, "My Queen, this is not true! I would never do anything to hurt you or the Prince!" One of the guards punches her in the stomach to silence her. The Queen reads the letter and says nothing as she watches her confidant and best friend Mary Kathrine Novasta being hauled away in shackles, leaving Sarah on the floor crying.

Mary Kathrine Novasta is beaten and shackled before the King the following day. She kneels in bloodied, torn clothes as the treason charges are read aloud before the court.

The high treason trial against Mary Kathrine starts right after hearing the charges. Mary is heartbroken as she realizes that her best friend, Queen Pricilla, is not there. Mary Katherine pleads innocent to all the charges saying that this was wrong and she would never hurt Prince Theo. She also asked the court to show evidence of these trumped-up charges against her. The Chamberlain brings witnesses saying that they saw Novasta talking with the collaborators. A Duke she knew had never liked her brought forth several people who told the King that it was her idea to kidnap the Prince. They even bring forth a handwritten letter supposedly stating in her own words that she was the mastermind behind the conspiracy. The

Duke demands the death sentence for a vile person who would even think about kidnapping the Royal Prince.

The King himself finds Mary Katherine Novasta guilty of high treason and plotting to kidnap the young Prince. The King rises from his throne, walks up to her, and backhands her across the mouth. He stands before the gathered court, announces that the penalty for her crimes is death, and says that the Kingdom will confiscate her estate and properties. The King commands everything in the Kingdom's records about her name be removed from the records. Mary Novasta, still in shackles, collapses to the floor and is dragged away sobbing and thrown into a cell to await her execution.

Sarah Priscilla Novasta is now known as Sarah Novasta and is an orphan. Queen Priscilla cannot believe that Mary, her closest confidant, would do any of these things. The courts were wrong in accusing her of treason, but her husband, King Theo, forbade her to attend or interfere with the trial. Priscilla might not have been privy to the trial, but she would be damn sure that nothing happened to little Sarah. The Queen sends for her chambermaid and tells her to arrange for Sarah to find a good home, and they would receive an allowance every month for the child's well-being.

The next day the chambermaid takes Sarah from the castle and puts her in a carriage with a note telling the driver to take Sarah to her sister's orphanage a few towns over. The carriage is trying to make its way out of the back courtyard when it starts to get bogged down by the crowds of people trying to make their way to the executioner's square. The carriage comes to a complete stop. Sarah is sitting in the carriage, unsure what is happening, when she hears a voice whisper to her, telling her to *"get out."* She jumps from the carriage and hears the driver yelling after her. Sarah soon finds herself swept through the crowd, and over the cheers, she hears a drum banging in the distance, but something inside her, tells her that she does not want to be here. Sarah tries to move back through the crowd, but the crowd is tightly packed, screaming insults and throwing things. She hears the drumbeat getting closer, and the people in mass start cheering and shouting louder. Somehow, in her attempt to move away, she now stands in front of the crowd, just below a large wooden block with leather straps. The voice tells her, *"Watch."*

She stands there, unable to move as the drumbeat gets ever louder. She can see the crowd begin to part to let the drummer through, and then he is followed by two palace guards, a woman in shackles who is bruised and battered, with her hair loped off, and is bleeding in places where they had no regard for how they cut her hair. She is wearing a dirty, torn dress that might have been beautiful at one time. Sarah watches the palace guard half drag the woman up the stairs, and just before she gets to the top of the stairs, she trips and falls. The two guards shout at her to get up, and one of them jams the butt of his spear into her side. She cannot stand, so the guards poke her and make her crawl over to a large wooden block. Then a priest, two more guards, and a big man wearing a black hood come up the stairs to the raised platform. The priest stands beside the woman and preaches from the book of Enlightenment as the four other guards stand behind the woman. One guard takes a step forward and unrolls a parchment. He proceeds to read the charges on the parchment. All Sarah hears is treason and something about a baby. She does not take her eyes off the woman through all of this. Sarah watches the hooded man walk over to the rack holding all types of axes and swords and watches him take a large ax from the rack. He then stands back and swings it a few times, and the crowd cheers with excitement. She hears a commotion, looks back to the woman, and watches as the guards remove the shackles, tie her hands behind her, and force her head down onto the wooden block. The two other guards secure her head to the wooden block with thick leather straps so she cannot move.

Sarah stands there staring at the woman secured to the block and slowly walks towards the raised platform where the woman is kneeling. The man in the black hood walks over to stand next to the large wooden block. Suddenly the crowd erupts into cheers, and some yell, "*Go to Tusukam BITCH!*" Some throw rotten vegetables at the woman kneeling, tied to the wooden block. One throws a rock, hitting the woman in the head, and one guard steps forward to stand in front of the woman, and the crowd stops throwing things. They step back as the man in the hood steps closer to the block, and she hears the priest say, "May the Goddesses have mercy on your soul." She sees the hooded man raise the ax with both arms above his head. Sarah stares at the familiar-looking woman and extends her hands to reach out to her. The woman looks at her and says, "I love you, and now look away."

Sarah does not look away and says, "Momma," just as the large blade comes down. She hears the thud from the ax hitting the wooden block, and she feels the splatter of something hit her face and clothes. She watches as her mother's head rolls off the wooden block into a basket. Sarah reaches up and wipes her face with her hand, looks at her fingers, sees they are red and knows it is her mother's blood. Something inside her snaps, and she wipes her hand on her dress. She shows no emotion as one of the guards reaches into the basket and pulls out her mother's head holding it high in the air to show the crowd. The crowd turns into a frenzy that is now cheering and yelling, "May the Bitch Rot in Tusukam, and She deserved it" Through all the shouting and screaming, Sarah hears a voice, and the voice says, "*Remember.*"

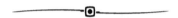

The coach driver somehow finds her, and though covered in blood, he drags her back to the coach, and she doesn't say a word. It is early evening when Sarah arrives at the orphanage. She is brought before the Headmistress and sees a tall, slender woman who seems to be frowning. Someone shoves Sarah into the office, and she stands there. The woman tells Sarah, "I am Miss Elenora Marbell, the orphanage's Headmistress. If you act up or cause trouble, you will be put in the closet however long as I see fit. Do I make myself clear?" Sarah just looks at her and says nothing. She orders Sarah to be taken to the baths, stripped of her blood-covered clothes, and rinsed off. An older girl, who goes by the name of Edith, drags Sarah to the baths and washes her with buckets of cold water. The girl then hands her some dry clothes and puts them on. She is back in Miss Marbell's office, and she tells the older girls Edith to show Sarah to her bed and that she will not get any supper.

That night, while in her bed, she has a dream, which is of the blade coming down and her mother's head falling into the basket. Every night after that, she dreams of the blade coming down and her mother's head falling into the basket. Every morning she awakes and finds herself curled up into a ball, and her pillow is wet with tears. One night as the tears wet her pillow, she hears the same voice as before, telling her, "*be strong,*" and she stops crying. Sarah does as the voice tells her and says, "Momma!" one last time. She falls asleep, but this night her dream is different. Sarah sees an older woman with red hair just like hers but cannot see her face in this dream. She notices her standing in front of a man wearing a black robe and a blood-stained white cloth covering his eyes. Sarah sees some hideous-looking beasts or creatures just behind him. Sarah is not scared, nor does she cry out. She cannot hear what they are saying, but she sees the robed one bow down before the redheaded woman.

In the morning, she awakens and feels strong. Every night after that, she falls asleep, and the same dream comes, and soon she is looking forward to the dream. She also realizes her pillow is dry when she awakes in the morning.

One month after coming to the orphanage, Sarah becomes the focal point for the older girl named Edith, who is constantly hitting and tripping her. The Headmistress always looks the other way when Sarah is pushed, hit, or tripped by Edith or the other girls.

When Sarah was about eight, they started calling her Nova not only because of her name but for the fire-red hair she had. Nova accepted her name and the beatings she regularly received from the older kids. Edith was three years older and the girls' leader at the orphanage. She knew all about Sarah and despised her for what her mother tried to do.

One day when Nova was ten, Edith was sneaking up behind her and was just about to push her when Nova heard, "*behind you.*" She turns around, looks Edith straight in the eye, and without saying a word, she punches Edith right in the face breaking her nose. Edith falls to the ground crying, and then Nova jumps on her; it seems that all the torment that Edith had put her through surfaces, and Nova begins beating her face to a bloody mess. Two adults had to pull Nova off of Edith before she killed her. They were dragging her away when Nova broke free, and as she ran back to Edith, and before they could grab her again, Nova bent over her and said to Edith, "This is for everything you have put me through, Bitch!" and swiftly kicks her in her side, and she hears ribs break. Nova then walks towards the Headmistresses office without being told. When she reaches the two adults that had dragged her, she says to them, "Let's go! we can't keep Miss Marbell waiting now, can we?

Minutes later, Nova is standing before Miss Elenora Marbell and receiving a lecture on violence and how it will not be tolerated here. After the rantings are done, and as predicted, Nova finds herself in the discipline closet. She spends one week in the closet and is allowed stale bread and water. After her release, she calmly walks into the yard and looks for Edith and cannot find her, and when she asks, a group of the girls, Zaja, tells her that she is still in the infirmary. Nova and Zaja are stilling on a stone wall when Nova asks Zaja if she wants to help her, and without hesitation, she says, "Yes."

Nova explains that she has a plan, and with Zaja's help, they can run this place. Within two weeks, Nova and Zaja have entirely controlled the orphanage. She seeks out Edith's friends and tells them that she runs the orphanage now. One of the older girls laughs and says, "Enjoy it while you can Bitch, because when Edith gets out, you will wish you were never born Traitor." Nova knows what she is referring to, looks around to see if there are any adults, and slaps the girl hard in the face when she doesn't see any. The older girl Lizzy is surprised and tries to say something when the other girls, to who Edith and her friends had always been mean, attack her and the others. Soon there is a small riot in the yard, and Nova remains sitting on the wall with Zaja pointing their fingers at Edith's friends as they are beaten and trampled by the other girls. The adults start breaking up the fights and ask who started this. No one says anything, and the adults say okay but stay in the yard watching to ensure no other fights break out.

Nova walks over to Lizzy, Edith's best friend, and tells her again, that she is in charge, and they will do as she says. Lizzy looks at the others and sees that they are afraid. Nova looks at her and asks, "Do I make myself clear Bitch!" Lizzy submissively nods her head yes, and tells her, "Now run along, little bitch and let everyone know that there is a new Queen in the courtyard." Zaja laughs, and she becomes Nova's enforcer, and the girls fall in line. Two weeks after taking control, Nova, Zaja, and a couple of the other girls are sitting at one of the outdoor tables when Nova sees Edith enter the yard. She gets up and tells the others to stay at the table. She then walks over to her and extends her hand. Edith flinches and then hesitantly takes it. Nova pulls her in close and whispers, "The orphanage is mine. you Fucking Bitch; if you fight me, you will die." She drops Edith's hand, looks at her, and sees what she did to her. Edith's nose is slightly askew from when she broke it, and she can also see that her right eye is discolored, there are some permanent scars on her face, and she lost a tooth. She then says, "Do we have an understanding?" and Edith nods her head, and all Nova says is, "Good! now get the fuck out of my face."

A few more years pass without incident, and Nova, now almost fifteen, is out in the yard one day, laughing and joking with Zaja when she is told to report to the Headmistress' office. When she gets there, Miss Marbell tells her to stand at her desk, and if she doesn't stop bullying and terrorizing the other girls, she will take action against her. Nova denies everything and tells her she does not know what she is talking about when the Headmistress smacks her across the face and calls her a lying little bitch. Nova turns red with anger, and after all the abuse from the Headmistress, Miss Elenora Marbell, Nova grabs the large piece of pink quartz that has always been on her desk and strikes her in the head with it. The Headmistress staggers back and then falls forward on her desk, and Nova proceeds to beat her severely on her head, screaming at her, calling her names, and demanding what was due.

Three adults hear the screaming and rush to the office, and they see Nova beating the Headmistress with the piece of quartz. Three of them pull her off and throw her in the disciplinary closet. Later that night, when all is quiet, Nova hears two people walking by and say that the Headmistress is very badly hurt, and if she dies, Nova will probably be charged with murder and meet the same fate as her mother. Nova sits in the dark closet, smiling.

Later that night, while she sits and waits to hear of her fate, she hears the door lock click. She tries the door and finds it unlocked. She opens it and quietly tiptoes down the corridor hugging the wall and staying in the shadows. She gets to the yard door and hears a voice in the dark. "The Headmistress died tonight, and they are saying you killed her and will be held accountable for her murder."

Nova recognizes Zaja's voice and sees her holding a metal box in the moonlight. Nova removes a small key from a string around her neck and unlocks the box. She opens it and sees two bags of small coins; she takes one of them and then closes the lid. She presses the key into Zaja's hand and closes her fist. "You're the boss now; everything I have is in that box, and it is now yours." Nova leans forward, kisses Zaja full on the lips, and says to her, "I am sorry and thank you for keeping me company at night, and I love you and will miss you." Nova opens the door, turns back to Zaja, and says, "If and when you get out of here, find me!" she looks back and sees that the courtyard is clear and runs to the far wall and squats down behind some bushes. She jumps up and pulls herself to the top of the wall, and before she drops down to the other side, she looks back and sees Zaja standing in the doorway, placing the key around her neck, and smiling. Nova gives her a quick smile back and disappears into the night.

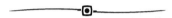

Nova carefully walks through the streets, staying in the back alleys and hiding in the shadows. She gets to the gates and finds them closed. She crouches down in the shadows of an alley and patiently waits.

Early the following day, she is woken by one of the criers yelling about the murder of the prestigious orphanage's owner, Miss Marbell, and how the authorities are looking for a young girl with hair the color of fire. It is early, and most of the shops are still closed. Nova stays in the shadows, grabs a dirty cloth off a drying line, and covers her hair. She carefully makes her way to the street, and she sees a double wagon filled with bales of hay pulled by two teams of horses making their way toward the gates. She looks around and sees that the coast is clear and quickly dashes to the back of the second wagon, jumps in and works her way through the bales to hide between them. The wagons stop at the gate, and she hears the men talking about a young girl and murder yesterday at the orphanage. The guard asks the driver if he has seen anything suspicious. She hears the man answer, "No," and then feels the wagon moving and prays that the guards do not search the wagons. After a few minutes, she peeks out and finds that she is outside the capital walls. She watches as the wagon takes a bend in the road, and when she can no longer see the city gates, she carefully climbs out of the wagon with the older man being none the wiser.

Nova travels the southern part of Elenni, begging and scrounging for food. A few more years pass, and in her travels, she has worked in slop houses, opium dens, tanneries, and restaurants and even tried thievery, from looking out for others to pickpocketing herself. When she had to work in the whorehouses, she cut her long red hair short and always had dirt and grime on her face and clothes to help hide her looks.

She is now seventeen and is walking through the Old Quarter in Fairlawn one afternoon eating an apple she stole when she sees an older woman sitting on some steps in front of a house smoking a pipe. The woman looks a little distressed, and as Nova walks by, the woman calls out to her, "Hey boy, come here!" At first, Nova does not realize that the woman is calling out to her, but when she tosses a small rock and hits her, she hears the woman say, "Yeah you!" Nova walks over, and the Madame asks her if she wants a job. Nova asks, "What do I have to do?" The Madame explains, and as she is telling her, she looks at Nova and turns to get the house ready for the night customers, and she says, "Don't let anyone get too close and find out that you're a girl." She follows the Madame inside her office and tosses Nova a large rolled-up bandage. She tells Nova to bind her chest. Nova does, and even though it is uncomfortable, it does what it is supposed to do by hiding her breasts.

Nova is content with what she has to do, whether running errands, changing sheets, cleaning up the vomit occasionally, or helping the girls with their customers.

One night one of the town's Commanders came into the whorehouse very drunk and looked for his regular girl, Penny. Penny was preoccupied and staggered to the bar and ordered a drink. Nova was walking by with a bucket of slop, and the Commander thought it would be funny if he tripped her. He did, and slop went all over the floor. The Madame of the establishment is furious and slaps Nova on the side of the head, calls her a stupid, clumsy bitch, and tells her to clean up her fucking mess. Nova was angry and just looked at the drunken Commander with hate. Just as she was cleaning up the last of the slop, Penny came downstairs and walked right over to the Commander and started rubbing her breasts all over him. Nova watched her reach down and could tell that he had had too much to drink, but nothing was going to stop her from getting his gracious coin. She grabs his hand and leads him upstairs to her room when she signals for Nova to come upstairs when she finishes cleaning up the mess. Moments later, Nova knocks on the door and hears enter. She does and sees Penny sitting at her table, brushing her hair, and her client lying on the bed. Penny tells Nova to fluff him. Nova looks at Penny, and Penny starts laughing and tells her, "What's the big deal? You have one. Pretend it's yours."

Disgusted, Nova walks over to the drunken Commander, reaches into his pants, and caresses his member until it is hard. Penny squeals with delight as she thanks Nova, places a silver coin in her hand, and then politely tells her to get out. Nova is leaving, and she sees Penny's head going up and down on the Commander's member and thinks, how could she do that, believing it's disgusting, and closes the door.

Her disguise in keeping her face slightly dirty, short hair, and loose unflattering clothes seem to be keeping up the premise of her being a boy. One or two girls in the house know the truth, but the clients are none the wiser. The clients look at Nova as a very feminine boy. The months pass, and with the premise that Nova is a boy, all is well and good. She does realize the ongoings under all her disguise and that she is developing in more ways than one. She looks in a mirror one day and sees under all the grime and dirt that she is turning into a young woman.

It is a quiet night, and most of the girls stay in their rooms, but this particular night, Nova is called to Mary's room to do her thing for one of Mary's very high-paying clients. She walks in to find Mary's client drunk and is leaning with his back against the wall near the bed, mumbling to himself. Mary is smiling and drinking a glass of wine. Nova approaches him and hears the voice say, *"Run,"* but it is too late as the big man grabs her shirt. Nova tries to step back, but he is a big man; he holds onto her shirt with one hand, and she loses some buttons. The man spins her quickly around and slams her against the wall. Stunned from being thrown against the wall and hitting her head, she feels the client grab her wrists to hold them above her head. Though dazed from her head hitting the wall, Nova struggles, but she cannot break his grip. He takes his free hand and rips the front of her shirt open to expose the tight bandage around her chest. The client tells Mary to give him something to cut the bandages, and she hands him a small knife. He takes the knife, places the tip just under the bottom of the bandage, and slowly slides it up, cutting away the bindings. Halfway up, they unravel, and he stares at a set of perfect breasts. Mary walks over, looks at Nova's breasts, and then her breasts mutters "Bitch" and slaps Nova. Nova tries to free herself, and the client slaps her and tells her to stop struggling.

Mary reaches over, grabs his crotch, and says, "See, I told you he was a girl and probably a virgin." The client says, "That you did, Mary and

I apologize for calling you a liar," They both start laughing. Standing beside Nova now, Mary says, "Well, isn't this a surprise? I never knew our little boy has been hiding these goodies!" and leans over and starts to suck on Nova's breast and nipple. Nova can see what he has in mind in the man's eyes as he reaches with his other hand to pull down her pants. Before he can undo her belt, she brings up her knee and catches him right between the legs. The man grunts and doubles over, releasing her hands. Nova then pushes him onto the bed holding his crotch. Mary backhands Nova across the face and tells her to get the fuck out and that she will tell everyone that she is a girl. Nova tries to cover herself as Mary is now climbing on top of her client and kissing him, trying to comfort him. Nova walks over to Mary's mirror and looks at herself in the mirror. She sees her lip swell when Mary and her client slap her. Mary screams at her again, "Wait until I tell everyone that you're a girl, "Now! Get the Fuck Out" Nova sees a small straight razor on Mary's makeup table and grabs it. She walks back over to Mary, grabs her by her hair, tilts her head back, whispers in her ear, "This is for slapping me bitch!" and runs the straight edge across her throat. Mary starts choking as Nova holds the razor in her hand and watches Mary reach up to grab her own throat and desperately try to stop her blood from spurting out of her throat. Mary falls forward, convulsing, and lies prone across the client's body. The big man struggles to get out from underneath Mary when he sees Nova beside him, and she places the razor at his throat. He stops struggling, stares at her, and asks her, "Do you know who I am? I am on the city council, and I will have you thrown in jail for what you have just done!" Nova hesitates as she watches Mary's body convulse, soaking her client with more blood, and then Nova pushes Mary's body forward, and she lies on his chest, keeping the big man trapped underneath her. Nova removes Mary's underpants, cutting them away with the straight edge, and the big man asks, "What are you going to do with those, keep them as a souvenir; then Nova smiles and shoves them in his mouth. He immediately starts to gag and cough and now has a look of fear in his eyes. She stands beside him, and with her breasts exposed, she leans forward and tells him, "This is the last time you or any man will ever see them unless I say so," and reaches down to pick up the blade that he used to cut her bandages and drives the knifer through his eye and into his brain, and leaves it there. She hears the voice telling her. *"Leave"*

She walks back over, covers the two of them with a blanket, and then steps into the hallway and closes the door. She is coming downstairs, and when the Madame sees her, she asks, "How is Mary doing with her friend?" Nova smiles and says, "They are a bloody happy couple!" I'm stepping out for some fresh Air." The Madame tells her, "When you come back in, go up and tell her that he is the last one and he needs to leave so we can call it a night." Nova says, "Okay," and heads to the back door.

She stops at her room and stuffs her belongings into a bag when she comes back in. She quietly makes her way into the Madame's room and walks quickly over to her desk. She breaks the lock on the desk drawer and slides it open to find the strongbox. She is just about to stuff the strongbox in her bag when she hears, "Why, you little bitch!" and looks up to see the Madame standing in the doorway. She walks over to Nova and lashes out at her. Nova sees it coming and ducks underneath her swing. She has the strongbox in her hands, and with both hands, she swings it and smashes it against the Madame's head. The Madame goes down, and Nova sees a significant dent in the corner of the strongbox. She looks down and sees a puddle of blood seeping onto the carpet. Nova opens the busted strongbox and quickly empties its contents into her pockets, then drops the box on the floor beside the Madame. She is in the hallway and closes the door when one of the girls comes down the hall, and Nova tells her that the Madame is busy counting the night's receipts and does not want to be disturbed. The girl says "Okay" and heads back to the parlor. Nova watches the girl walk away and then exit through the back door. She slides some boxes to block the exit in the back. Nova grabs a coal oil can and pours some of it on the back door, the boxes blocking the door and the porch. She splashes some on the windowsills as she walks by them and leaves a trail of coal oil between them. She gets to the front door, and like the back, she douses everything with the oil and then blocks the exit.

She walks out to the street, leaving a trail of oil behind her. She is standing across the road near one of the braziers and waits. Seconds go by, and then she hears a scream from the second floor, and then a minute later, she hears another one coming from the back of the first floor. She lifts a lump of burning coal from the brazier and drops it on the oil. The oil ignites, and she watches the flames race across the road towards whorehouse. Within minutes the front of the house is on fire, then the fire moves quickly around the windows, towards the back porch trapping everyone inside.

Soon the building is engulfed in flames, and the voices inside are quiet. Nova stands there and watches a light evening breeze carry some burning embers across the alleyway and land on the house's thatched roof next store. Within minutes the top of the second house is turning into a roaring blaze of flames, and new screams are coming from the second house. She hears a man shouting, a woman screaming, and a baby crying. She can feel the heat from the two blazing infernos and walks away when she hears a window breaking, and Nova turns to see the young girl she had talked to once or twice lowered to the street. Nova smiles at her and starts to walk away, then stops and looks back one last time to see the roofs of both buildings collapse, and the blaze begins to run rampant as more buildings start to smoke, while some are already on fire. She turns, throws the can of coal oil and tongs onto a pike of rubbish, and walks away, never looking back, and then she hears the voice tell her, "The Barrens."

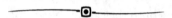

A window is smashed, and a young girl is lowered to the street by her father. He tells her to get back. She steps away and sees a movement off to her right and then sees a redheaded young woman throwing a can of some sort and a pair of tongs onto the rubbish. The young girl watches her standing and staring at the fires. She smiles at her, and then the woman disappears around a corner. The young girl remembers seeing her many times on the back porch of the house next door and has said hello to her several times. She looks back towards her home and calls out for her family, with no response. Her name is Erin, and she is quickly pulled back from the blaze as the house she and her family live in collapses. Soon other buildings and homes start to catch fire, and in no time, a third of the buildings in the Old Quarter are ablaze.

Erin looks back up the street and sees that the one she is sure had something to do with this is gone. She will never forget that woman because their paths crossed, and they always said hello. Erin remembers asking her one time why she dressed like a boy. The young woman just held a finger to her lips and said, "It's a secret," and got up and walked back into the house. She knows she started the fires; though young, Erin swears that she will exact her revenge. She stands there with tears in her eyes as she looks at the pile of burning rubble that was once her house, stares at the flames, and desperately tries to remember the older girl's name, she can feel it just on the tip of her tongue, but it does not come.

One of her mother's friends comes up to Erin crying, wraps a blanket around her, and tries to pull her away. Erin stands her ground and continues to stare at the flames. Soon other adults are standing around her, and she hears them talking. One woman asks if the Madame or any of her girls escaped, and another speaks up and says, "I don't think so, other than maybe that young boy who cleaned up the place." Another says, who! the one with the short red hair?" Yeah, that's him. What name did he go by, Neva, Nera, or something?"

Erin is holding her breath, just waiting for someone to say it, and then she remembers and says out loud, "Nova." One of the women says, "That's it, Nova."

Chapter 6

Samuel Miro

Samuel Miro was born into a very long line of military heritage. When Samuel was about five years old, word spread that Empress Machiko was with child, and Samuel was the firstborn of the Emperor's Advisor, Hakimi Hideo Miro, so he began his education in the finer points of becoming an advisor under Empire Law. His schooling consisted of court protocols, mannerisms, and diplomacies of becoming an Advisor General and included the military's fundamentals.

The royal bloodline was strong in Emperor Hisa Hojiko, and everyone was hoping for a boy to carry on the Hojiko Dynasty. Nine months later, the Empress gave birth to a beautiful baby girl, and she is named Asami. Turmoil erupted in the Emperor's court when a conspiracy in a kidnapping attempt on the new Princess was discovered and was foiled by the Emperor's Advisor General and his men. The perpetrators were killed or took their own lives. Everyone was expecting a Prince, and they got a Princess. Anyone who knew Hakimi Miro respected him and knew that he would order his son to reject the Princess and wait for a male heir to be born. Samuel's destiny, like his father, was to become an Emperor's Advisor General.

Samuel takes a break from his packing because, after today, he will enter the Stewards Corps and start training to become an officer in his Emperor's Royal Army. He sits there enjoying a cup of tea and thinks back to the day when he first met the Princess.

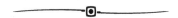

The Empress was sleeping, and a slight lavender smell filled the room. Moments later, the Empress wakes up and walks over to check on the Princess. She sees the Princess sleeping with a smile on her face and a crescent moon on her chest slowly fading away. She says, "Thank you, and goes back to bed, knowing the Goddesses have been there and blessed her daughter.

The nursery is bustling with maids and advisors attending to the Empress's and Princess's needs for the next week. They find Samuel in the library, usher him into the nursery, and tell him to sit on the bench against the wall. Sitting there, Samuel can see Empress Machiko and the newborn Princess. He watches both mother and daughter and is aware that the new Princess seems uncomfortable and agitated by the small crowd in the nursery. Samuel gets up and makes his way through the crowd towards the Princess. The Empress looks up to see Samuel coming toward them, and she notices that the closer he comes, the Princess is less agitated. He walks up to the Empress, bows, smiles, and looks down at the new Princess. The room becomes hushed as they notice the Princess no longer fussing. Samuel looks around the room and sees everyone staring at him. The Empress lies there holding the Princess and notices that the Princess is staring at Samuel.

Suddenly the nursery doors open, and the Emperor walks into the room with Samuel's father behind him. The Emperor calmly orders everyone to leave the room. Samuel starts to follow the others when he feels a hand on his shoulder gently restraining him. Samuel looks up to see that the Emperor has stopped him from leaving. The Emperor looks at him and kindly says, "Stay." He sees his father walking to the doors to lock them.

The Emperor then walks over to the bed, gently kisses his wife's forehead, and asks, "How is she?" She replies, "She is well, my love." He then picks up the baby and kisses her forehead, and when he does, the new Princess makes a soft cooing at her father. The Emperor smiles with love in his eyes, and then he looks at Samuel's father, and in a gentle voice, he says, "Hakimi would you be so kind?"

Hakimi walks over to Samuel, places his hand on Samuel's shoulder, and asks him to walk with him. They walk out to the balcony, and he gestures for Samuel to sit on a bench beside him.

"My son, I understand that you are excelling in your studies for becoming an Advisor General, and I am very proud of you. However, with the recent birth of the Princess, you need to make a decision tonight that only you can make. Let me explain your choices; if you bond with the

Princess and accept her, she will remain in the palace and live a healthy life. On the other hand, you will lose all chances of becoming an Advisor General, which you have been studying so hard for." Samuel's father pauses to look at him, "If you decide not to accept the Princess, she will be moved to a remote wing of the palace and raised by loyal servants of the Royal family. If you wait for a prince to be born, he will need to be born within two years. If not, you will have to withdraw from the Advisors training, and your younger brother will take on the role of becoming the next Advisor General when a son is born. Emperor will be required to choose another house to fulfill the obligations of raising an Advisor General to the Prince when he is born, and you will hopefully pursue a life in the services of the military."

Samuel looks at his father and asks, "Father, what should I do?

His father replies, "My son, I cannot make this choice for you. You must do what feels right in your heart, but know this, whatever choice you make, I will stand behind you and be proud of you." He gets up, leaves Samuel to his thoughts, and walks back into the room and over to the Emperor and Empress to take a closer look at the new Princess Asami.

Samuel sits there and remembers seeing his father dressed in his formal attire, standing beside the Emperor in the Emperor's court, and realizing then that he wanted to follow in his father's footsteps to protect and advise the Emperor.

Samuel loves his father and knows his father loves his family. He always seemed busy and knew his father's time was precious, but he never missed a special occasion that had to do with his family. He always put aside time for his family. His father taught him friends could change, but the family can't, so it should always be family first. Samuel sits there, contemplating what to do. He gets up and walks back into the nursery towards Empress Michiko's bed. He sees that she is holding Princess Asami, and the Princess is quiet.

His father and the Emperor are whispering when Samuel hears his father say, "Don't worry, Kazue, he will do the right thing." Samuel is almost to the bed when his father places a hand on the Emperor's arm. The Emperor turns to see Samuel slowly walk up to the Empress and Princess. Samuel is still undecided as he finds himself standing beside the bed. Samuel bows to the Empress and then to the baby Princess. Staring at the Princess, he looks deep into her eyes and sees blue-green eyes with what look to be swirling gold specks as she remains perfectly still as their eyes stay locked on each other. Samuel leans forward to place his forehead within inches of the baby and hears his father's words echoing in his head, "family cannot change." He thinks to himself that she is family, smiles and lightly touches the Princess's forehead with his own, and says, *"Boturoka Tomoni"* He then feels something pass between them and knows that he has bonded with the Princess. He pulls away, and he sees that she is smiling, and then she reaches up to touch Samuel's cheek, and when she does, he feels the bond fuse together, and it is even stronger, and he now knows that it is complete and everlasting.

Samuel steps back and bows first to the Princess and then to the Empress and notices tears in her eyes, and she says, "Thank you, Samuel," as she holds the Princess a little tighter. He steps back a little more and feels two hands on his shoulders. He looks to his right, sees the royal crest ring worn by the Emperor, and realizes that he has backed up into him. The Emperor leans forward, and as Samuel feels his breath near his ear, the Emperor says, "Thank you, Samuel."

The Emperor releases Samuel and then sits down beside his wife and daughter. He sees the Emperor lean forward to place his head against his wife's and sees a tear run down his cheek.

Samuel's father walks up to him, says, "Let's leave them be," and guides Samuel toward the doors. The door opens, and two guards come to attention. Hakimi tells the guards that the royal family will not be disturbed under any circumstances. If anything needs the Emperor's attention, you are to direct them to me, is that understood?

The two guards reply, "Yes, Advisor-General." Samuel's father says, "Good," and walks down the hallway with Samuel. Hakimi Miro takes hold of his son's hand as they continue down the hallway. Hakimi Miro, Advisor General to the Royal Emperor of the Imperial Hojiko Dynasty, says to Samuel with pride in his voice, "I am very proud of you, my son," and squeezes his hand.

For the next three years, Samuel took to his private studies with vigor and strived to be near perfect in every aspect, no matter how daunting or boring the classes might be, and through it all, he always made time to stop by and see the Princess at least once a day. It seemed no matter how bad a day she might have been having, she always perked up when Samuel showed up, and once the Princess could walk, she always knew when he was close and would run to the door to greet him. Their bond was unique; in the history of bonding with Royals, it has never been recorded that any two who bonded could sense each other when they were nearby.

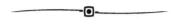

Samuel adjusts quickly to not becoming an Advisor General to the Emperor, even though Empress Machiko gave birth to a son just twenty-two months after Princess Asami was born. The Imperial laws state that if the General Advisors House's firstborn cannot bond with a Prince, then the duties would fall onto the next male in line. If there were no male heir to the Advisor General, then the Title of Advisor General would fall to the next house in line for succession. Samuel's younger brother started training to become the next Advisor General to the House of Miro. Samuel excelled in his private studies for the military, and with the Princess as his ward, he was happy.

Soon, Samuel would be turning ten years old and moving up as a steward in the military. Samuel's father was proud of his son and knew he would continue the Miro line of military service, and his brother would be the next Advisor General. Samuel would follow in his father's and grandfather's footsteps, enter the Officer's Academy, and receive his commission as an officer when he came of age.

Samuel had one worry and asked one day to speak to his father and the Emperor in the Emperor's anti-chamber. Samuel was in the Emperor's anti-chamber with his father when he told Samuel to ask his question. Samuel started with all the courtesies when the Emperor told him to stop and just say what he needed.

Samuel said, "Yes, Your Highness. I have concerns that when I begin my duties as a steward in the active military, I feel that the name of Miro may hinder my training". Samuel's father raises an eyebrow. Samuel takes a deep breath and explains, "Father, do not misunderstand, I am proud of my name, but I want to enter the military and the Academy on my own merits. If I enter under the name of Miro, there is a possibility of favoritism with me being the son of the Emperor's Advisor General."

The Emperor looks at him and asks, "What do you suggest, Samuel?"

"Sire, when I start my training, I would like to take my mother's maiden name Shinpo for the induction, and when I graduate, I will graduate under the name of Miro if it pleases his Highness and my father." The Emperor looks at Samuel's father and replies, "I agree. My daughter's Guardian will have to stand on his own merits." Samuel tells the Emperor, "Thank you," bows, and quickly hugs his father. He then resumes the protocols required in the Emperor's presence, and the Emperor tells him to go with a wave of his hand. Samuel bows and sees the Emperor smiling. Hakimi hugs his son a second time and tells him he will talk later. As Samuel leaves the room, he hears the Emperor say to Hakimi, "You should be very proud of him."

He then hears his father say, "I am."

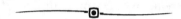

Samuel has finished his studies and duties for steward training and has just turned ten years old, and it is time to take on his duties as a steward in the Royal Steward Corps. Samuel Miro is now known as Samuel Shinpo, and only a selected few know who he is, and per the request of the Emperor, they will not show favoritism. During his studies after becoming a steward, Samuel tackled any endeavor head-on. He did his very best, whether it was the menial task of being an office runner or taking care of the horses and mucking out the stalls. Samuel loved to work in the stables and took pride in his care of the squad Captain's horse and the men's horses in his squad, a total of twenty-five in all, and he treated all the horses equally. Samuel did not show favoritism to anyone's horse.

The Colonel-in-Command of the squadrons of cavalrymen totaling over one-thousand horse soldiers noticed that when they did parades, one squad's horses always seemed to outshine the others in the parades. The horses assigned to Samuel always displayed a higher *Spirit* in the parades, as if hoping for Samuel's approval. Of all the stewards who worked in the stables, whether boys or girls, Samuel's horses always seemed to have glossier coats and combed-out manes and tails. The men in the squad were soon asking Samuel how he did it.

After five years of mucking out stalls, feeding the horses, combing out manes and tails, and throwing in a bit of competition between the squads, it was time to take the next step in his training.

On the day before his enrollment into the Military Academy as a squire, Samuel stops by the Princess's room to bid her farewell. She wrinkles her nose at him and says, "You were in the stables again." Samuel laughs and tells her yes. She hugs him, and he tells her he will move into the Squire Barracks tomorrow. Samuel notices all the open trunks scattered about the room and knows that The Princess is getting ready to be escorted to the royal summer palace. She will start her education and training to become a Royal Princess and be gone for eight years.

He is sorry to see her go, but he knows she has obligations to fulfill just as he does. He bends down and kisses her on the cheek, and just before he stands back up, she gives him a tight hug. She stands on her tiptoes and returns the kiss on his cheek. When her lips touch his cheek, he feels the same jolt as he did when he bonded with her right after she was born. She says, "My Protector, I will miss you." Samuel hugs her back and tells her to study hard and that he will miss her. He places his forehead against hers and says, "Be brave, be safe, my ward!" He turns to leave so he can start his future in the military and she can fulfill her destiny. He looks back to see her smile, and he smiles back.

Almost all the boys and girls of the Steward Corps are twelve years of age when they enter the Squires Corps.

Everyone is mustered in the training yard on the morning of assignments to see who they would get assigned to for a senior ranking non-commissioned officer. The worst fear for the new squires-to-be was to get assigned to Master-at-Arms, Sargent Vernon Higgs.

Everyone was aware of Sargent Higgs' reputation, and every squire-to-be who had moved up from Steward to squire was in the yard. Many hesitate to look at the roster board for their assignments, but Samuel is unconcerned. He pushes through the gathered crowd, walks up to the roster board, looks for his name, and sees two names below his and one above. He then runs his finger across the board and sees Master-at-Arms, Sargent Vernon Higgs.

He goes back to the three names, and though he is not familiar with them, Soon, three other bodies are pushing against him, and he sees a stocky boy with dark hair, a skinny girl with short-cropped light brown hair, and another fellow, who is taller than him, with brown hair. They are all reading the roster board and see Sargent Higgs across from their names.

Squires Asa Ami Abel, Hikaru Hito Sato, Samuel Shinpo, and Reiko Anzu Takahashi are listed alphabetically on the board. The four of them are standing away from the others waiting patiently for Higgs to appear. They hear one of the other non-com officers call out, "Hey Vernon, who are you going to eat for breakfast this morning?" followed by laughter. The stories tell how demanding he is and how he has had young stewards resign their commissions within the first week of being under his tutelage.

They hear a commotion and watch as the crowd of squires and other non-commissioned officers' part, and the biggest man that any of them had ever seen makes his way through the crowd stopping at the assignment board. He calls out the four names assigned to him, "Abel, Sato, Shinpo, and Takahashi."

Asa Ami Abe looks at Higgs and then at Samuel, Reiko, and Hikaru, says, "Screw this," and immediately walks over to the officer-in-charge of the roster and resigns his position as a steward. He is quickly escorted from the yard and taken to collect his things. Samuel and the others hear a "Dam!" and the words "Pay up."

Samuel sees this as a challenge, stands his ground, and notices the other two beside him. All three immediately snap to attention and salute Sargent Higgs. Higgs starts laughing and tells the three to drop their fucking salutes because they have not earned the right to show him that respect. "Now grab your gear, fall in and follow me, double time!"

The three of them are running to catch up to Higgs and hear the chatter of bets on who would ask to resign next or disappear. The favorite was Squire Reiko Takahashi with 5:1 because she was a girl, then Squire Hikaru Sato, because he was heavy, came in at 3:1, and it was even money on Squire Samuel Shinpo.

Samuel decides at that moment that he will do whatever it takes so that all three of them make it through training to become commissioned officers in the Empire's Royal Army. Higgs double-times them to their barracks, which was the farthest one from any part of the training fields. When they stop, they find themselves staring at an old, dilapidated barracks with broken windows, a broken door hanging by one hinge, and a roof needing serious rethatching.

Higgs looks at them and says, "Welcome to your new home for the next six years if you are so lucky" he then walks away but stops. He turns back to say, "That is your area and is the only place in this glorious Empire where you can escape my wraith for about eight hours a day; the other sixteen are mine. Do with it as you please but remember the winters are cold. I will see you in the sword yard bright and early tomorrow morning, and don't be late!" Higgs then walks away whistling.

They enter the rundown barracks and place their gear on the floor. Reiko introduces herself and asks the others, "Any suggestions?"

Hikaru says, "Yes, let's torch it and build a new one," Reiko and Samuel laugh.

Samuel introduces himself and says, "I noticed several things about this place, and it is livable."

Hikaru introduces himself and asks, "How so?" as he looks up through the hole in the roof.

"Good point," says Samuel, "I noticed a few bundles of thatch on the way here, and I think we might be able to find a thatcher among the ones we met in the Steward Corp who could fix the roof or at least tell us how to do it."

Reiko says, "That's right, come to think of it, I noticed several parts from old stoves scattered about on the walk up here. I think I can scrounge enough pieces to put this old stove back together so we would be able to boil some water at least."

Hikaru says, "I'll be back," and steps away into another room and comes back after a few minutes and says, "There is a pump in the kitchen, if you want to call it that, and if maybe the parts are about, I can scrounge them, I think I can get it working. Hikaru says, "I also noticed a large tub for bathing in a separate room off the kitchen."

Reiko says, "We might as well get started."

Samuel notices it is still quite early as Reiko heads out to scrounge through the piles of stove parts she had seen lying around. Hikaru goes into the kitchen, and Samuel hears banging and cursing, and then Hikaru walks past him and out the door. He listens to more cussing as Hikaru, like Reiko, goes scrounging through the piles of junk. Samuel tells them he is heading over to the stables and shouts that he will be back soon. Samuel heads down to the stables of his old squad because he remembers hearing that one of the soldiers in the squad was a thatcher in his hometown but decided to join the Imperial Army instead.

Samuel arrives at the stables and finds Corporal Sutton with his back to Samuel, grooming his mare. The mare immediately picks up its ears and snorts. Sutton doesn't turn around, and all he says is, "Hello Samuel, tired of being a squire and decided to come back here among loved ones?" Samuel starts laughing but reaches up to pet the mare and says, "No, Corporal Sutton, I did not get tired of being a squire and return to my friends, and he reaches up and pets the horse behind her ear, and she snorts again. Sutton laughs, he stops grooming the mare and gestures for Samuel to join him, and they sit down. "I heard you got stuck with Vernon Higgs. Is it true?"

"Yes, Corporal, it is true, but that is not why I am here."

Corporal Sutton listens to Samuel as he explains their living quarters' and emphasizes the hole in the thatched roof. Corporal Sutton places his hand on Samuel's shoulder and tells him not to worry; he will take care of it and asks, "What time does Higgs want you at the practice field in the morning?"

Samuel replied, "Probably at first light from what we have heard about, Sargent Higgs has any truth to it."

Corporal Sutton looks at Samuel and says, "Whatever you do, don't ever be late. I know that is one of Higgs's pet peeves, and you had better get back. Your roommates are probably worried about you and think you already quit like that, Abe fellow." and snickers. Samuel looks at him, and Sutton says, "News travels fast in the military!"

Samuel stands and says thank you, He walks back over to the mare and says, "Let me see your hand and takes Sutton's hand to place it just behind the ear of his mare and tells him, "She likes it here, and she prefers apples over sugar." Samuel then asks Sutton for a piece of paper, and he writes down all the little things about the other horses, their favorite spots, what they like and don't like, and hands it back to Sutton. Samuel tells Sutton to have a good day, then turns to head back when Sutton calls out, "Do not worry and thank you," holding up the piece of paper.

Twenty minutes later, Samuel walks into the barracks and sees that the stove is in a different location and is now in the center of the room. He sees Reiko on a ladder, applying a sealant on the stove's single vent pipe. She looks down at Samuel and climbs down. Samuel asks, "Why is the stove here?"

Reiko replies, "Because something did not feel right in the room, I decided to explore the ceiling and found the actual stovepipe exhaust hidden in the rafters, which puts the stove in the middle of the room for even heating in the colder months.

Hikaru comes into the room carrying a dented pot with water and asks, "Can we boil some water for tea?"

Reiko smiles and says, "Sure, but give the sealant a few minutes to set up."

They begin unpacking their gear, and after that, Reiko checks the sealant and then stokes a fire to boil the water. When done, the three of them sit on the floor and share a pot of tea. Samuel tells them about the roof, and someone should be stopping by to fix it. Reiko asked, "What should we do next?"

Hikaru suggests that they make a room divider so Reiko could have some privacy. Reiko immediately shoots down that idea, saying, "Samuel and Hikaru, we will be living together for the next six years. There should be no concessions because I am a girl, and if you even think about treating me like a girl, then I will have to kick your butts to show you that I am not a delicate little flower."

Samuel and Hikaru both hold their hands and say, "OK, you win, no divider!" Samuel and Hikaru start laughing because of the look on Reiko's face. She sticks out her tongue at them, making them laugh even harder, and soon all three are laughing. As the laughter dies down, Samuel picks up his tea and says, "To Sargent Higgs," Hikaru and Reiko do and say the same.

The following morning all three are waiting in the sword practice field at dawn. There is an early morning mist, and no one hears anything when three wooden practice swords fly out of the mist, landing at their feet. They look at the swords, then at each other, and when they pick them up, they are quickly and forcefully knocked from their hands. Each holds their hand from the stinging pain they received from the hit. They hear

Sargent Higgs saying, "Pathetic," as he steps out of the mist and stand in front of all three.

Sargent Higgs says, "If you three were in battle and you happen to lose your swords, are the three of you going just to stand there and think about whether to pick up a sword, or even better, look for someone to give you permission?" They stand there unsure what to do when Sargent Higgs says, "Just a little spoiler, that hesitation cost you your lives and probably some of the men under your command." While Sargent Higgs reprimands them, the morning mist has burned off, and the other squires and non-comms start coming into the sword practice yard. With a few snickers, most walk by as Sargent Higgs continues with his rampage toward the three of them. "Now pick up your fucking swords and defend yourselves!"

The onslaught was brutal as Higgs constantly attacked with overhanded strikes, sweeping his wooden sword and knocking each to the ground at any given time to have it end with each of them getting a blow from his sword to mark the kill. It was midafternoon when Sargent Higgs called a stop to today's training. He looks at all three of them and says, "Pitiful," and notes that there isn't a complaint or remark from any of them. All three are battered, bruised, and covered in sweat and dirt.

Sargent Higgs dismisses them and tells them to rest because tomorrow will be worse. Samuel, Hikaru, and Reiko say, "Yes, Sargent!" and know better than to salute him. They turn and start to walk away when Sargent Higgs calls out to Reiko, "Takahashi!" tossing her a can and saying, "All three of you, apply some of that on your bruises, and it will help with the pain" Now go get some rest." They walk past the other squires, and Samuel hears Gustavo Heinz, "Hey Takahashi, when will you quit? I have a silver coin on you by the end of this week." He starts laughing. Samuel never cared for Heinz because he always tried to take the easy way out of things and bragged about his father being a General. Samuel sees the look on Reiko's face, and before she can say anything, he walks close to her. He says to her, "Just walk away; he ain't worth it," as Hikaru steps to her other side, turns, and waves his middle finger at Heinz, and then he hears Takahashi yell back, "That's right, Heinz your number one," and the three of them start laughing. Higgs has watched the entire thing, and he has come to two conclusions, Heinz is a total ass, and his three recruits have something in them, what it is he does not know, but something, and as they walk away, he hears them laughing, and is determined to find out what it is.

They are walking up the path to their barracks, and Samuel notices that new thatch is in place, along with new lashings. Hikaru and Reiko also see it, and as they enter the main room, Hikaru goes straight to the kitchen, while Reiko walks over to the stove and sees that the chimney has been fixed and adequately sealed. They hear the squeaking of the pump and then the splash of water. Hikaru comes walking back out of the kitchen with a newer pot filled with water, and Reiko asks him to wait a moment as she places some wood and kindling in the stove and gets a fire going. Hikaru puts a newer pot on the stove to heat water and says, "I found this letter addressed to you in the kitchen." Hikaru hands Samuel the note; he recognizes Corporal Sutton's handwriting, breaks the seal, and opens up the letter to read it:

Dear Samuel,

I invited some of the guys from the squad to give me a hand. We got the holes fixed and replaced most of the lashings on the rest of the roof. Private Thurl noticed that the pump in the kitchen needed some work and, in the room, off of the kitchen, he found the old tub. He started tinkering with it. He was able to replace some parts on the heater for the tub. He filled the tub and started a small fire to heat the water. It should be hot enough when you get back after your training. You won't believe the morale of the squad and the horses.

Again, Thank you.

Corporal Sutton

PS. The Captain thanks you, as does the squad.

The three eat, clear, wash their plates and proceed to the tub off of the kitchen. All inhibitions are gone. Reiko is the first to disrobe and enter the tub and utters a sigh of relief. Samuel and Hikaru quickly follow her example and like her utter sighs of relief. The three are sitting in the tub soaking and relaxing when Samuel suggests showing each other their bruises. Hikaru is slightly hesitant, but Reiko says, "Sure, why not?"

Samuel goes first and stands up. All he heard was "Wow!" and "Jeez!" from Reiko and Hikaru.

Samuel looks down and sees bruises all over his body, from his thighs to his chest. He turned around for them to look, and he could tell by their silence that it was terrible, and he sat back down in the tub. Reiko stands up next and, as with Samuel, bruises cover the better part of her upper body and continue down to her lower calves. Then she turns, and it looks like one massive bruise, and all she hears is. "Wow!" from both of them, and she sits back in the water. Then it was Hikaru's turn, and when he stood up, both Samuel and Reiko remained silent because Hikaru was just one large bruise covering his torso from the front to his back. Hikaru asks, "Is it that bad?" Both Samuel and Reiko reply, "Yes!" and then he sits back down. They soak a little longer until the water starts to cool. They stand and then step out of the tub, dry themselves off, and after they are dry, Reiko pulls out the tin that Higgs had given her, and they apply the ointment to their bodies, helping each other with the areas they cannot reach. The cream smells horrible, but they immediately feel the soreness slowly fade away.

Chapter 7

William James

Every descendant of Camille James, female or male, is born with at least one affiliation of the natural elements or manas known in the ancient language, whether *Fire, Water, Earth, or Air.* The one stipulation is that the necklace can choose only the females to become the next Tamil. When they are Chosen, their main element usually expands three-fold, but in some instances, it could expand more, as it has done on several occasions.

The first stage of becoming the Tamil is that the necklace will need to accept you, and the acceptance needs to be witnessed and recorded by female court scribes. The scribes under island law must record all observations down to the smallest detail. The recordings are stored in the library of the history of the Royal court in a sub-vault underneath the palace. A member of the James Clan, and only a Senior Scribe for the Tamil herself, can open the vault and are allowed inside.

The *Spirit* itself is accepting the second stage, and that is the only thing that the scribes cannot witness is the acceptance and the bestowing of *Spirit* in the Chosen's mind and body. In all the successions of female descendants of Camille James, only two were not selected by the necklace and denied the virtues of "*Spirit.*"

The first female descendant denied by the necklace was distraught with grief, and no one could understand why the necklace rejected her because she was a good and sweet person. It was not until a later that some rare blood disease infected her, and though the *Spirit* can remedy many things, this was one it could not, and it was because of this rare disease that the necklace would not allow her to become Tamil. The young woman accepted the necklace's choice and supported her younger sister as the next Tamil until the disease ran its course, and the young woman died at the young age of twenty-five. She was interred next to the other Tamils in a small separate tomb.

The necklace denied the other one who everyone thought the necklace would pick, and when she refused to remove it, the necklace slowly choked her to death, and there was nothing anyone could do to save her. After her body fell to the throne room floor, it was immediately set ablaze by an unknown source of fire, and after the fire went out, all that was left was a small pile of ash swept away by a slight breeze in a room with no open windows.

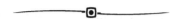

Roxanne James is a direct descendant of Camille James and was only twenty-three years old when her mother, Nicole James, died unexpectedly at the age of fifty-eight. After two weeks, of mourning of her passing, it came time for the necklace to choose the next Tamil. Roxanne has prepared herself to accept the duties of Tamil. When the necklace was placed around her neck, her eyes immediately changed to the acceptance of sapphire blue with silver specks like her mother, grandmother, and other female James before her. Her affiliation with the *Water* element expanded tenfold.

Once the necklace accepts, the Chosen Tamil is obligated to enter the sacred garden and be touched by the fifth mana of *Spirit*. The *Spirit* mana imbues a change in the bearer, both mentally and physically. Mentally, the Chosen Tamil can connect with the *Spirit* of the islands and feel what the islands feel. Physically it allows her to be one with the united islands and harness the power of *Spirit* to defend the islands at all costs. One other change takes place, which allows the appointed Tamil to read and write the ancient language, and the *Spirit* mana also imbues the wearer of the necklace with the truth behind the origins of the Seishin people. To this day, it is never spoken out loud or written down. In history, since the unification of the islands more than over nine hundred years ago, has the *Spirit* mana been called upon by a Tamil to defend the islands.

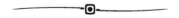

It was about the time the fourth Chosen Tamil was in reign. She was known as Laura James when a band of marauders landed in the harbor of Aleu and proclaimed that the islands were now theirs and that they were going to take over the Painapp fruit business, and if anyone tried to stop them, they would be dealt with severely. The leader of the marauders saw the palace on the hill and started making his way to the palace, and before he even got halfway up the hill, Laura met them and asked him very nicely, "Could you please leave the islands before someone gets hurt?" The marauder leader laughs, raises his sword, says, "I don't think so Bitch," and then says, "That is a mighty pretty necklace; maybe if you give it to me, I won't hurt you." Laura looks at him and says, "I asked you nicely, and before the leader can do anything, he and his men are drenched in a torrent of water, and knocked down, and they find themselves rolling back down the hill. Laura calmly follows them down the hill.

The leader, now drenched, gets up, and before he can say anything, Laura asks him, "Please take your men and leave these islands and never return.?" The leader, now angry, brings up his sword, and before he can even move, a very fine stream of water strikes his face; he screams in pain as he feels one of his eyeballs explode from the buildup of water inside it, and he falls to the ground screaming. Laura tells him, "I warned you, and you ignored my warning. Now! begone from these islands and never return."

The other marauders pick up their leader now with one eye, and he yells are her saying, "I'M GOING TO KILL YOU!"

Laura looks at him, and all she says is, "I don't think so," and shoots another fine stream of water at him and takes out his other eye, and the leader collapses continues screaming as his men take him back to his ship. Laura continues to follow the band of men back to their ships, and she stands on the docks and waits. A man comes to the rail of the ship and yells, "BITCH WE WILL BE BACK, AND GET OUR LEADERS REVENGE, AND WHEN WE RETURN, WE WILL BRING BACK A FORCE TEN TIMES THIS MANY, AND WE WILL RAZE THESE FUCKING ISLANDS AND KILL ANYONE WHO DEFIES US!" Laura says to herself, "Really!" and watches the ships pull away from the docks and slowly make their way out of the harbor. Right after they make it to open waters, Laura climbs to the tower of the shipping company that looks out over the harbor and open waters. She looks just beyond the harbor and can see the ships unfurling their sails.

She raises her hands and says, "*Con Tu Ja Dowa Rega To Hawa,*" She calls forth the mana of *Air*, and watches the winds suddenly die entirely out, and the sails of their ships hang lifeless. She can see the men running around on the deck, trying to figure out how to get the wind in their sails.

She then chants, *"Mora Gen Fae Boe Dar Von Sae,"* and just as suddenly as the winds die, she calls forth *Water*, and the waters around the two ships become choppy. As the water becomes more turbulent, she sees men thrown into the churning waters and watches them being pulled under the surface and drowned.

She is not enjoying this, but as Tamil of the Islands, she is obligated to protect these islands and their people, and in her last words, she says, *"Hir Nit Wa To Cin Sar Spirit Re Fore."* She feels the *Spirit* of the Islands roll out from the harbor and spread out over the open seas. She watches as a whirlpool slowly appears, and the two ships are drawn to its center and dragged below the surface. The whirlpool slowly stops, and the ships and men will never be seen again.

Laura does not feel remorse because these men came to her islands, and even after she asked them nicely to leave, they refused and threatened her people. She returns to her home, and the people around her bow slightly and smile. Laura smiles back, and when she returns to the palace, she is greeted by her children; when they ask her if the bad men are gone, Laura laughs, and all she says is, "Yes, they are gone," and then hugs them.

Years pass, and there are no more incidences where foreigners have come to the islands and made demands. Other merchants and traders who come to the islands hear the stories and spread the rumors. No one is willing to challenge the rumors, and life goes on.

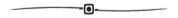

Once the necklace accepts you, one is required to enter the sacred garden and wait to see if the element of *Spirit* receives you. Roxanne remembers entering the garden, wearing only a floor-length robe and no slippers. She always enjoyed coming to this garden when she was a young girl. She always walked around smelling the different flowers, lying on the grass, and feeling the soft grass on her bare feet. When she entered the garden this time, she did not stop to smell the flowers or feel the soft grass under her feet, but she carefully removed the robe, folded it neatly, and placed it on a stone bench. She then removes the barrettes from her hair and puts them on the robe. She runs her fingers through her hair and allows it to lay as it falls. She is naked, besides the dark blue sapphire necklace around her neck, and moves to the middle of the circle. She sits down with her legs crossed and places her hands on her knees, palms up. She then takes a deep breath, holds it for a few seconds, lets it out slowly, closes her eyes, and waits.

Roxanne is a beautiful woman with curly dark brown hair that hangs just below her shoulders. Her complexion is nearly flawless other than a small beauty mark on the side of her neck below her ear. She is a slender girl, her breasts are slightly uplifting, and her stomach is trim without being muscular. She has always enjoyed walking; her legs are toned and firm. Roxanne sits there, thinking of her future and what it will be like when the *"Spirit"* of the Islands hopefully chooses her to become the next Tamil. She takes another breath, and like every Tamil, they ask themselves, "Will I be the next Camille James," She finishes that thought, and that is when she feels it, the rush of a breeze filled with warm air, the sweet smell of the freshness of morning dew on the grass. She sits there quietly and lets the *Spirit* of the Islands embrace her. Then she hears an ethereal voice, saying, *"The Prophecy is fulfilled, and the islands have their new Tamil."* Just as quickly as it came, it is gone, but Roxanne does not feel discouraged or sad; she feels alive. She stands and walks over to where she put down her robe and goes to slip it back on when she sees herself in the reflection of a pool and is astounded. She lets the robe slip from her hands, steps closer to the pool, and looks at herself. She sees the same face, but now the beauty mark on the side of her neck is gone. Her long curly hair is longer, fuller, and has a lovely sheen to it. She sees that her lips are a little fuller, and even her breasts are fuller, and the slight uplift is gone. She stands there admiring herself, and then she remembers that people are waiting for her to return. She knows she does not have all five manas, but she is eager to see which ones she can manifest. She knows that she can call upon *Spirit*, as all accepted Tamils can, but she is more curious to see what other elementals she can call forth.

Roxanne walks back into the throne room, and there are intakes of breaths throughout the room as they notice her changes. She walks over to the balcony, raises her hands in the air, and calls out, *"Sartu Domi To Spirit Hila Eka Carlon Ho Gemfa"* The element of *Spirit* goes out through the islands and touches every sole.

Once she became enriched with the mana of *Spirit*, the islands changed as they always did when a new Tamil was selected, and the change was always for the better. The Tatokai Archipelago was a wealthy sovereign, mainly to the export of the exotic Painapp fruits. The other export is the blue salt mined from the salt pits in the Botaku cluster of islands on the edge of the Tatokai Archipelago. Both are in great demand throughout the kingdoms.

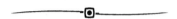

William James was Roxanne's second son to be born during her reign as Tamil on the island of Aleu, the largest island in the Tatokai Archipelago and the island nation's capital. William had an older brother Jeffrey and two younger sisters, Kendra and Jenna, who were still toddlers. When the time comes for Roxanne to pass on the necklace to an heir, and if the necklace allows it, his sister Kendra will be the one to accept the honors, and she will become ruler of the Tatokai Archipelago. Jeffery and William will be appointed to high offices to protect and guide their sister. Their youngest sister Kelli will support Kendra when she becomes Queen.

When Jefferey and William were younger, they had a habit of getting themselves in trouble and were always out exploring. One day they came across a broken old hatch, and after they pried it open, they went inside to explore. They soon found themselves in some dark tunnels, and after walking a bit, they realized they were in the catacombs beneath the palace. Unsure of where to go or how they would return, William pulls out a piece of chalk in his pocket. They learned on a previous excursion through some old caves that it was good to mark the walls so they could retrace their steps. They eventually found their way out but were grounded for two weeks on the palace grounds.

William starts placing marks on the walls as they go deeper into the catacombs. They are walking down a path when they come across a wall section that seems unnatural, strange, and out of place. They feel along the walls and find a stone seam different from the other seams. This particular seam ran vertically up the wall for about three meters and then turned ninety degrees to meet up with another seam running parallel with the first one. William also notices several strange-looking stones that are entirely different than the others. Curiosity getting the better of them, they both agree that they will come back to explore this strange wall section at another time, and William marks it with a symbol.

Two days after their studies, they are back at it again, trying to see if there is anything to make of these strange-looking stones. William feels along the seams and tells Jeffery that he thinks it's a door. William asks Jefferey to boost him up to see if anything is along the top edge. When William is high enough, he feels along the leading edge of the seam, finds some indentations, and realizes that this is some writing. A type of writing that he and Jefferey never learned in their studies. William wipes the stone's surface and lays a parchment over the letters. He then takes charcoal and rubs it on the parchment, copying the strange words.

They come out of the catacombs to see it better in the light, and neither one of them can discern what they are reading, but they know it is in the ancient writing.

Over the next week, they have looked through almost every book in the palace library yet found nothing. They decided to show their teacher, and he asked them, "Where did you find this? William and Jefferey replied, "We found it in a book and wanted to know what it said," The teacher looked at them and said, "I'm sorry, my young princes, but I cannot help you in this matter." The boys give him their "thanks." They hear the teacher shout something about tomorrow's lessons as they run off.

The two of them were sitting on a stone wall puzzling over the ancient script when Ole Hito. One of the Tatokai Shamans walks up to them and asks them, "Why so gloomy today, your Highnesses?"

Jefferey holds out the piece of parchment to show him the writing that William copied. Ole Hito is surprised at what he sees and asks, "Where did you find this? The boys are hesitant but finally tell him where they found the ancient script. Ole Hito asks, "Can you show me?" The boys know it's late, but they will meet him tomorrow right here after morning lessons. Ole Hito agrees and walks off.

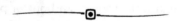

The next day the three of them are standing in front of the strange rock, and Ole Hito asks them to boost him up; when they do, he runs his fingers along the seam of the stone and feels the writings carved above the seam. He tells them to let him down, and then Ole Hito politely tells them that they must leave, and he will explain everything once they get outside. As soon as the three of them are out of the catacombs, Ole Hito invites Jeffery and William to sit down, and he will explain. Hito paces before them, and when he stops pacing, he faces the two of them. "What you two found is a gateway to something spectacular, like nothing you could ever imagine; what you found is the burial tomb of Camille James and where the manifestation of the five elements coexist. Legend has it that one must be pure of heart and a direct female descendant of Camille's, to enter the gateway and embrace the five manas. They must also have the seeds already planted inside them to be allowed to enter and must be able to coincide with the five manas, to be able to harness them. You see, when the four manas are in harmony, then, and only then, will *Spirit* show itself. Your grandmother knew of this, and to this day, they say she is part of the *Spirit* of the islands. The islands prosper and flourish when the *Spirit* is in harmony with the other, and *Spirit* protects the islands and their people.

The ancient legends also say, "That whoever controls these powers will have to one day fight a great evil that could destroy this world."

You two are of royal blood and direct descendants of Camille. Still, you are male descendants, and to witness the five manas in their natural form without being pure of heart, would destroy you. I came here today to confirm what you found and to warn you. You should never break the seal of this tomb."

Jefferey says to William, "Let's go; we do not need to break the seal on grandmother's tomb." William replied, "You are right; let's get out of here and never speak of this again. Do you agree, Hito?"

Ole Hito replied, "Yes, my Highnesses, never again."

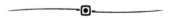

The weeks pass, and Jefferey and William continue their studies, though William always thinks about his grandmother's tomb. He has just celebrated his seventh birthday, and that night while William sleeps, he hears a voice in his dreams. "William come to me, do not be afraid; come to me." He puts on his robe and follows the voice. He soon finds himself standing in front of his grandmother's tomb door. He hears the voice again, is now awake, and does not feel afraid. She tells him of the sequence in which to press the strange-looking stones. He pushes the last stone, and suddenly, there is a hissing sound as what smells like fresh, clean Air escapes the once sealed room. The wall opens like a door, and William stares down a long staircase. The voice says, "Come, do not be afraid. I will guide you." William takes a step down and then another. The tomb door closes behind him, and the staircase becomes illuminated by what he does not know but continues downward.

When he gets to the bottom, a long corridor becomes illuminated, and when he reaches the end, he finds himself standing before another door. He reaches out to touch the door, hears a click, and the door opens by sliding into the recesses of the wall. He sees different colored beams of light dancing throughout the room on the walls and ceiling. William steps into the room and the rays of lights stop moving. He notices an attractive-looking older woman standing on the opposite side of a pedestal in the middle of the room. She steps toward him and says, "Hello, William." He knows that he is looking at his grandmother, the Matriarch of the James Clan, Camille James, the first Tamil, and the only one in history that could manipulate the five manas. He smiles at her as she continues around the pedestal and walks over to him, and then she embraces him, and he immediately feels love and enlightenment.

She tells him that there is not much time, and he must listen to her carefully. William goes to say something, and Camille places her finger against his lips and tells him to listen. She tells him, "William, my sweet child. When you are older, you will feel great pain and sorrow and need to leave these islands on your own accord. You will travel the lands on a quest only the Goddesses can show you. William looks at his grandmother and asks, "Grandmother, how can this be?" She tells him that is something only the Goddesses can answer, but know this; you will be the first male in the history of this Clan that will be able to manifest and control the five elementals of the islands and this world." William looks at her and says, "I thought only the woman of the James Clan were allowed to manipulate all five elements. His grandmother tells him, "That is true, but the women of the James Clan are tied to these islands and can only leave for short periods, and they will always need to return to the islands because the Tamils of the islands allow them to continue to flourish. You, William, will be Chosen as a Champion, and you will need to defend this world where we live. He gives Camille a worried look; she knows he has heard that any males who try to embrace the mana of *Spirit* go crazy. Camille smiles and says, "Do not despair; since I was the first to accept the necklace, you are the only one in our Clan history, other than myself, who has had the five seeds of mana bestowed upon them. William, your pure heart has allowed the five manas to lie within you.

Camille looks at him and says, "I will need to bestow my blessing upon you so that the seeds may grow and flourish. "Will you accept my blessing?" William looks her straight in the eyes, and without hesitation, he says, "Yes." With that, Camille takes William's hand, walks him over to the pedestal, and asks him to step onto it and stand in the middle. He steps onto the pedestal, and the multicolored rays of lights immediately return, but this time they do not dance around the room as they did before but land on his body. William feels each color entering his body and pulse through his veins. His grandmother steps closer, and William bends down as Camille kisses him on his forehead, and he feels those seeds that his grandmother mentioned begin to sprout and then start to grow. William looks at his grandmother and sees the deep blue sapphire of her eyes with the silver specs. He looks at his own eyes in the reflection of the mirrored walls and sees that they match his grandmother's, a deep sapphire blue with silver specks. Then William feels something completely different, the strongest feeling of them all, as the strength of *Spirit* courses through his body to touch the very end of his nerves, which is exhilarating. She sees the worried look on his face, and she then places a small, light kiss on his lips, and he feels the power continuing to energize and empower his body and mind. William now looks into the mirrored walls and sees in his reflection that his eyes are a shade darker than sapphire blue or his grandmother's, and the specks dancing in his eyes are not silver like hers but gold. He looks at his grandmother, and she smiles as she watches another change take place, as his eyes become a shade even darker, but blue nonetheless, and all she says is, "*Spirit*."

The following day William finds himself in his bed wearing his nightshirt. He gets up, looks in the mirror, and sees that his eyes are the same brown color as they were yesterday. He shrugs it off as a dream and gets dressed for breakfast.

Chapter 8

The Dark Twins

Guichi and Tanin hide in the shadows just outside the cave entrance and hear their Mother explain to Laki and Jutsuk about the pieces of Dark Crystal and that they have landed somewhere on Chikyu. They agree that they have listened enough and decide to leave the sacred valley. They look back once and see their sisters landing on the valley floor. Then watch the morning sun work its way up from the base of the mountain, and when it bathes the cave in sunlight, they see the bright flash and show no remorse that their Mother is gone. They decide to go forth into the world of Chikyu to search for these what their Mother called Dark Crystals and hopefully release their one true God.

They begin searching the lands laid out before them to try and feel for the crystals. They know they have a destiny to fulfill, and that destiny is to find the pieces of Dark Crystal and release the Dark God Nimponin. Once Nimponin is released, they can bring havoc onto this world, destroy their self-righteous sisters, and imprison them in the pieces of Dark Crystals as their Mother did to their father.

They are considered Gods in the world of Chikyu, and they are ominous in the eyes of the creatures that live here. As Gods, they do not require sleep, though they require breaks to re-energize themselves to travel in the Spiritual Domain. Guichi suggests a break, and the two enter the Earthly Domain to discuss what they have planned for the ones they previously sought out and branded with their mark. The true degenerates that they have Chosen will require words of guidance, and Guichi pulls out a large book from his satchel that he started writing in right after their journey began. Their words, beliefs, and thoughts are for their followers.

While the two of them are talking, Tanin asks Guichi, "What should we name this book?" Guichi thinks for a moment and says, "The Dark Scriptures," When he says that, they hear a distinct pop just a short distance from where they are sitting.

They get up and walk toward the direction of where the sound came from and are surprised to come face to face with a strange-looking beast standing before them. The beast stands just a little over one meter at the shoulders. The head is almost wolf-like, but its ears are more extended, and its snout is short with a large black nose. The canines are just under four inches long, while its legs are slightly longer in the front with six-inch claws that look able to rip and tear through anything. Its most noticeable feature is its eyes and how blood red they look. It sniffs the Air and cautiously approaches them, stopping a few meters from them, then it seems to lower its head as if in submission.

Guichi and Tanin approach the creature as it lowers its body even more, and Tanin reaches out with his hand to touch the beast when it rises off the ground, turns in the direction from which it came, and stops just long enough for them to follow. Guichi looks at Tanin, and they both shrug their shoulders and follow the creature.

They follow the strange beast and feel the pull of something but are unsure what it is. They continue walking, and then the beast stops. They find themselves standing at the entrance to a cave. They see a shimmer and then what looks like a rift their Mother taught them about in their lessons just inside the cave's opening. They step a little closer and feel the pull even more substantial. They step back as the tear flickers but continues to float just above the cave floor. They try to look inside but feel nothing, only a cold, deep blackness. The beast steps up to the rift, and as it does, the cold blackness begins to swirl and fade, and before them lies a world almost unrecognizable.

They see another world of once magnificent cities, towns, and villages. Some towns and villages seem to have been devastated by something and are now crumbling, while others are on fire, and still others are just smoldering piles of rubble. Throughout the cities, towns, and villages are dead bodies. The land itself seems to have been scorched by fire. Massive flocks of carrion birds circle the sky as other creatures, like the one that brought them here, are feasting on the bodies of what looks like dead men, women, and children.

A movement catches their attention as they see a robed figure walking through the carnage. Guichi and Tanin watch as it steps up to a person; though they cannot hear, they know that the person is begging for mercy.

The robed one pays him no heed and plunges what seems to be a long thin blade into his chest. The man screams, and as the blade is ripped free from his body, they watch as his body starts to convulse and contort and then see it begin to change. The man is now one of the beasts, similar to the one they followed to this cave, only larger.

Guichi says to him, "I think this is the Dark Realm she spoke of in her lessons. They continue to watch as the sky becomes bright, and a ball of energy comes out of the sky and strikes the surrounding lands. Still, they cannot hear but see the explosion and its aftermath. The beast steps into the rift and then turns off a path to join the carnage.

Tanin points to a river flowing with clean, clear water that seems to be feeding rice paddies in different growth stages and appears to encircle a temple-like structure. Then they feel the pull of a Dark Crystal, which is very strong. Tanin goes to step into it when Guichi stops him and tells him to wait because something doesn't feel right. Guichi conjures a small ball of his essence, holds it in his hand's palm, and allows the rift to draw it forth and float into it. The essence passes through the opening, drifting towards the robed one and the beast. It explodes before it reaches them, obliterating the robed one and the beast. They stand there watching and feel the draw of a dark crystal. The rift flickers, and just before it closes, they hear two female voices cry out, "Help us!" Once again, they hear a distinct pop as it suddenly closes, and they can no longer feel the draw of the Dark Crystal.

That night Guichi and Tanin are sitting, discussing what they think is the Dark Realm and what they heard after the explosion, and just before the rift closed. Tanin says, "If one of the Dark Crystals is actually in that world, then we need to go in there and get it, and who do those two female voices belong to?"

"Tanin, you saw with your own eyes what would happen if we were to step into that world. If it is in this other world, we will need to be patient and think of a way to get it". He walks over to where he left the large book and put it back in his pouch.

The next day, they continue their travels and soon find themselves in unexplored lands. They discuss their beliefs, what their teaching should include, and how to get their hands on the crystal. They continue to walk, and by midday, they've made their way through a series of valleys, continually feeling for another rift. They are just about to enter another valley with low hills when they hear the clash of steel in the distance, people screaming, and beasts snarling. They walk to the top of a large rock outcropping, and as they reach its crest, they overlook a large flat piece of land with a set of roads that cross each other just about in the middle. It is not the expanse of the land or the crossroads that catch their attention but the battle that is happening below them.

It looks like a combined force of two different armies surrounding two large tarps in the middle of the crossroads. The same beasts they encountered with their massive teeth and claws look like they are trying to get to the tarps. The soldiers defending the tarps are well-armed with swords, spears, and armor. Guichi and Tanin stand on the outcrop in their Earthly forms and watch the battle unfold. They assume that the robed figures on the opposite side of the valley control the beasts. There are four of them, and one seems to be the leader as he has three red stripes on the sleeves of his robe. The other three only have one or two. All four of them have their eyes wrapped in a red-stained white cloth.

The combined armies desperately fight to keep the creatures from reaching the covered tarps. Tanin looks at Guichi and says, "Shall we" and Tanin steps off the rocks and slides down to where the battle is happening. Guichi shrugs and follows him. While they slide down to the valley floor, clouds drift across the afternoon sky and partially block the sun. They reach the valley floor and walk towards the tarps. The human armies see the two appear out of nowhere and continue to fight to keep the creatures back. Just as they are about to reach the perimeter of the human forces, the robed ones call the beasts to return to them, and Tanin and Guichi see the human army also pull back to their defensive positions.

One creature lingers, sniffing the Air, then leaps at Tanin with its extended claws and mouth open. Tanin waves his hand and snaps the beast's neck killing it instantly. He looks over to see the robed one who ordered the attack, does the same to him, and watches him crumble to the ground. Guichi notices that the creatures have returned and are now circling the tarps and growling. He sees the robed leader wave his hand, and the beasts howl and roar with rage and attack. Guichi smiles and chants, *"Chirasa Shikamaru Wim"* half the creatures immediately drop dead from broken necks. Tanin stands and, without turning to face the impending threat, chants, *"Chirasa Shikamaru to Fiesta,"* and the remaining beasts fall to the ground and burst into flames. Suddenly a blinding flash encompasses the valley floor, and the only thing remaining of the creatures is charred places in the grass, where the beasts had fallen.

The two armies cheer and then look at the three remaining robed figures standing on the hill. Tanin looks at the leader and pinches his thumb and finger together. The leader reaches for his throat as if to pull something away. The other two robed ones suddenly burst into flames and fall to the ground withering in pain. With the three marks on his sleeve, the leader continues to grab his throat as Tanin forces him to walk toward them. They now see that the robed one is wearing a white cloth over his eyes, which is saturated in blood. Guichi asks him a question, and when the robed figure does not answer, Tanin snaps his neck, tosses the body to the side, and then sets it on fire, and soon there is only a smoldering pile of burnt ash.

Tanin removes the tarp, sees two heavily barred locked cages, and can smell the pungent aroma of skunk weed. When the afternoon sunlight breaks through the clouds, they are surprised to find what looks like two young girls cowering in separate cages. They are shackled to the cages' floors and wear thick leather masks covering their eyes, ears, and mouths. They are startled when they feel the warmth of the afternoon sun on their bodies, and what remains of their clothes are just tattered pieces of cloth that barely cover any parts of their bodies. Tanin can see that their hair is matted, unkempt, and a nest of tangled knots, and then the winds change, and Guichi can smell their bodies and see that they are filthy and covered with grime, mud, and what looks like feces.

Guichi and Tanin feel something for these two young women, though they are uncertain what it might be. Tanin is about to open the cages when he hears, "Wait!" He sees a small group of eight soldiers coming around the barricades and galloping towards them but keeping their distance.

The one that spoke first shouts again, almost demanding, "Don't open the cages."

Tanin looks at the man, and without saying a word, he scowls and waves his hand to watch the leader fall from his horse; he desperately struggles to catch his breath. Guichi watches as the leader starts to turn blue from lack of Air.

Guichi says, "Tanin, please." Then he asks, "Why do you have these two females bound and shackled inside these cages?" as Tanin releases him, the one in charge is on all fours gulping in large gasps of breath.

One of the others asks, "May I speak?" Guichi replies, "Yes."

The one who had asked to speak responds submissively, "My Lords, we had no choice. If we did not capture these two, bind them and shackle them to the cage floors, they would have brought devastation to both our lands".

"Why is that?" asks Guichi with a little less hostility in his voice, as Tanin allows the leader to breathe once again.

The soldier introduces himself as Captain Fitts of the Glock Army, comes to attention, and salutes them. He tells them, "Our two countries have been at peace as far back as anyone can remember, so we had a regular trade route established between our two countries, and life was good and prosperous for both our people."

A little over a week ago, one of the trade caravans was late in returning to the capital of Glock. We sent messages to the Kingdom of Tesh asking for any delays in the caravan departing. The Kingdom responded that the caravan departed on time without delays or issues. A couple more days passed, and the caravan still had not shown up in Glock. We started to worry because the daughter of one of our noblemen was on the caravan heading to Glock. We sent out a patrol from Glock, as did the Kingdom of Tesh.

Five days ago, at the borders of our two countries and this very crossroads, we discovered the caravan, or what was left of it, and within a couple of hours, the Tesh patrol arrived. The trade goods from the caravan were scattered all about the crossroads. We could not find any guards, soldiers, merchants, or the nobleman's daughter, and from what we found, we could only presume that everyone was dead. We searched the area when we came across these two women, seriously dehydrated and unconscious, underneath a half-demolished wagon. We continued searching, and one of the men from Tesh found a pouch that contained the trade manifests and the lead caravan's daily journal. We had our field mages check the girls while we set up camp and spent another four days searching, and we still had not found anything.

That night, I was leafing through the journal and saw what the caravan leader wrote regarding the two girls, how they appeared out of nowhere and seemed disoriented. I was finishing the last entry dated eight days ago, and the last words written in the journal were, "Beware of those fucking b....! I sat there contemplating what the journal was trying to say when one of the sentries sounded the alarm. One of my soldiers came barging into my tent and told me that strange-looking beasts were attacking the camp. I grabbed my sword and ran outside, which is when I heard the shouts and screams. The beasts were running rampant through the encampment and were attacking anything that moved. We killed most and drove the others away, but the losses were significant for both our countries. We pursued them, and as we were chasing them, we heard a distinct pop sound, and when we crested the hill that they ran up, the beasts seemed to have disappeared without a trace.

Captain Fitts stops and takes a drink of water.

Guichi, intrigued, motions for him to continue.

"We sent out search parties, and they all returned with the same reports. They found evidence of the presence of the beasts near some caves but could not see where they came from or where they went.

The next day, additional troops arrived from both countries, with emissaries from some of the more prominent houses to discuss the two young women's status and write an official report for both Kingdoms. The official report for the nobleman's daughter, merchants, and guard's disappearance is written as inconclusive. On the second day of talks with all parties present, an intense aroma of something swept through the tent, and then the delegates from both countries started arguing amongst themselves. The nobleman, whose daughter was missing, suddenly pulled a knife and stabbed a representative from Tesh. Word spread quickly of the stabbing, and the two armies from Glock and Tesh drew their weapons and were about to start fighting amongst themselves when the beasts came back in force and started attacking both of our armies. Their numbers were twice the size of the previous pack, and the hostilities between our two countries were quickly forgotten, and we joined forces to repel the beasts and defend the camp.

As I was defending myself against one of the beasts, I noticed the girls sitting on the grass outside the tent we supplied them with. They seemed to be smiling as they watched the fighting unfold. I had just rammed my sword through the beast upon me when I saw the two of them gesture with their hands, and the next thing we knew, another pack of these creatures came over one of the other hills, and they began to outflank us.

We thought we were dead until a large force of Tesha's military consisting of heavy cavalry, archers, and knights arrived. Their arrival turned the battle in our favor, but not before the delegations from both our countries were killed. The superior forces from Tesh helped us exterminate the beasts and those robed ones with the bloody white cloths over their eyes.

That night after the battle, I went back to my tent and picked up the journal again, and a torn folded page fell from the journal. After reading it, I realized that the "Beware of those fucking b...." warning was not about the beasts but the two girls. It was these two girls who caused the attack on the trade caravan. The caravan leader wrote how the two girls appeared, called forth the beasts, and heard them mention something about a Dark Realm. He also noted how he smelled the pungent aroma of something and how the smell would either dulls one's senses or causes severe anger in others of anyone who breathes.

We could not figure out where they were coming from, but we knew the two women were calling to them. We acted like we were none the wiser about what was going on, so we took drastic measures and placed some drugs in their food. When they were unconscious, we put the leather masks on them and shackled them in the cages. We think the beasts want the women, but we do not know if it is to help them or destroy them; we cannot take a chance either way.

Guichi tells the Captain they will take these two girls with them and not worry. He dismisses him and tells the soldiers to return to their troops. The soldiers fall back and wait patiently to see what Guichi and Tanin will do.

Guichi grabs the locks on the cages, and the girls start to tremble as they hear the locks snap. They then break the chains and shackles holding the two girls in the cages. Guichi takes their hands and helps them crawl out of the cages. Several soldiers grumble as Guichi reaches over and removes the thick leather hoods from one and the other. Guichi and Tanin smell the sickening aroma that would be beguiling to most, but it does not affect them. Tanin tells the two girls to stop it, or he will put them back in the cages and give them back to the two armies. The aroma quickly dissipates, but only to be replaced by billowing dark clouds, roaring thunder, and numerous lightning strikes in several places, which causes some of the horses to panic and a few riders to fall from their saddles. Guichi shouts, "ENOUGH!". The thunder and lightning quickly stop, but the dark clouds linger.

Guichi and Tanin are oblivious to their surroundings and stare at these two messy and filthy young women. Guichi chants *"Sentuka Sekuri,"* and a thick wet mist encircles them and begins swirling around them. When it clears, the dirt and grime are gone from their bodies, and they can see that they are identical Twins like themselves, except that one has a very tiny beauty mark on the right side near her temple, while the other doesn't have any. Both girls have a very light skin tone and flawless complexions. Their jet-black hair flows straight down the middle of their backs and ends just below the curves of their buttocks. Their eyes are almond-shaped, and their eyes color is deep emerald green. Their fingers are long and slender. Though the two of them are standing before them naked, it does not seem to bother either.

One of them says, *"Akappanisikata,"* and she is holding what looks like clothing and some other articles. They now wear dresses, and their hair is braided. Guichi and Tanin notice the dresses are of the same style but in different colors. One wears blue, and the other wears red, but both gowns hug their slender bodies and highlight their small, firm breasts. Buttons run from their throats diagonally across the chest and down the side to the waist. The lower portions of their dresses are midnight black with dark red and blue embroidery around the waist. The dress itself stops mid-thigh. Their boots are soft black leather with narrow three-inch heels, and the tops of the boots barely reach the dress's hem.

Though Guichi and Tanin are not compassionate types, they seem to like these two young ladies and want to see what they can do. Something about them feels the same as when they looked in that rift when they followed the beast to that cave.

After they are dressed and close the rift, one of the Twins lashes out at Guichi, and Tanin quickly catches her wrist before touching him. He tells her, "If you try anything like that again, you will die," he squeezes her wrist hard, and when she winces, he drops her wrist forcefully. The Twins are surprised at his speed and what this man tells them, "If you calm down and listen to us, I can promise you that Tanin will not kill you." says Guichi.

One of the Twins asks, "Did you say Tanin?

Guichi asks, "Yes, and I am Guichi."

The girls immediately fall to their knees, place their foreheads on the ground, and tell the two that they would understand if they were to strike them dead for their insolence. Guichi looks at Tanin and then tells them to stand up and asks them to explain.

The two girls say simultaneously, "Masters, please forgive us; we are sorry; we did not realize who you were."

Guichi looks at Tanin and asks, "Do you two have names?"

The Twin with the mole on the right-side temple says, "I'm Mia, and this is my sister Mae."

He then asks, "Why did you come here?"

Mae tells them, "The essence of our Master instructed us to come to this Realm and find you."

Tanin asks, "Who is your Master?"

Mia tells them, "Our Master is the Dark God who is known by all and goes by the name of Nimponin."

"How can the Dark God Nimponin be your Master? Tanin asks angrily, "He was trapped inside the crystal many millennia ago by the Eternal God Mother, Kamiyobo, and her mate.

Mia answers, "A voice told us that when you and your sisters came to be in this realm, we later came into existence in our realm, though we are not "*Tendaishi*" as you are, but are "*Chotan*," but unlike you, we learned."

"Who taught you?" Guichi asks.

Mae tells them, "The same voice who told us of our birth, and the same voice who we think is out Dark God Nimponin," and before either one of them can ask, Mae says, "We hear the voice through this piece of dark crystal that landed in our land right after the gateway came to be."

"What gateway?" Tanin asks.

"The gateway between our realms, you might know it as a Black Hole or Vortex in your universe."

Guichi and Tanin are both surprised that the black hole their Mother mentioned in their lessons was none other than a gateway to the Dark

Realm," and now they start thinking about what else their loving Mother might have left out in their lessons.

Tanin asks, "You mentioned a choice; what choice are you talking about?"

Mia says, "The choice was to either stay in our Realm and watch it slowly be destroyed or come to this Realm, find the two of you. We are to assist you in locating the Dark Crystals, release The Dark God Nimponin from his imprisonment, and create a new Dark Realm.

Guichi asks, "So, you came here unknowing what was going to happen when you came looking for us?".

"We entered your Realm in this very spot and were quite disoriented because we did not know what your world was like with the heaviness of your Air. Then the caravan they spoke of came to the crossroads, and after they found us, they tried to enslave us. We are no one's slaves, and we told them this. They became hostile towards us and tried to subdue us, so we fought back; the only way we knew how was to open a rift and call forth the creatures of our Realm.

Tanin smiles and asks, So, my two lovelies, what can you do to show your loyalty and devotion?"

Mia and Mae smile at each other and ask, "Would you like us to give you a sample of the Dark Realm?"

The two armies are standing in the distance and cannot hear anything spoken between the four but are getting restless. They see the girls bow for a second time, and the tension in the men seems to relax as the Commanders sigh in relief that the two strangers have them under control. It took many lives for the two Kingdoms to capture these two women and place them in restraints and cages. They hope that these newcomers take the women with them when they leave.

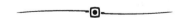

Guichi says, "Not just yet, please be patient," and walks between the two armies. He then calls the Commanders of both Kingdoms to approach, and when they reach him, he tells the Commanders, "Thank you, and that we will be leaving soon and taking the young ladies with us."

He can see the expressions of thanks on their faces and goes to walk back to his brother and the girls, and he hasn't taken but one step when one of the Commanders says, "May the righteousness and beauty of the Goddesses watch over you."

Guichi turns back, smiles, and says to the three of them, "Why did you have to go and spoil it?"

He turns to look at the Commander who spoke the blessing and sees that it is the same officer as before, and then he is on the ground screaming in pain. The other soldiers move to help their Commander when they are on the ground beside him, screaming in pain.

Guichi walks back to the Twins and says, "Show us!"

The Mae and Mia step around Guichi and chant *"Akappanisikata,"* and a small rift appears before them. The Twins draw forth an almost smoke-like substance from the rift, and they hold out their hands and let the dark smoke begin to swirl between them. They then pull two six-inch-long knives from their boots, and very carefully so as not to disturb the swirling dark smoke, they place the tips of the two knives at the bottom point of the swirling darkness. Guichi and Tanin watch as the blades absorb the swirling smoke and turn the blades themselves black. The Twins spin the knives in their hands, and as they touch the tips together, they look to Guichi and Tanin and say, "With our Master's permission, we will show you the Darkness."

The Twins move towards the fallen commanders and carefully pierce their skin. One of them is already dead, and they assume his heart just quit; as for the other two, the former Commanders of the two armies start to convulse, twist and contort. Seconds later, the commanders are now the same beasts that had previously attacked the caravan and the soldiers.

Mae says, "Go," and the creatures turn on their once fellow soldiers, clawing, biting, and slaughtering. The soldiers display no remorse for killing the beasts attacking them, even if they were their Commanders just a few minutes ago. Soon, both creatures are dead, and many soldiers are injured and mauled. Unbeknownst to them, small changes are taking place for some of them, as they are soon convulsing, and like their commanders, they begin to change, and as more change, the casualties continue to grow.

Then Mae and Mia find Captain Fitts, killing one of their creatures and possibly a former friend, the same Captain Fitts who ordered their drugging and imprisonment. The two approach him and say, "Hello, Captain, remember us?" He finds himself kneeling before them and is unable to move. The Twins take their blades and slowly cut the straps holding his breastplate, remove his remaining armor, cut away his clothes, and then force him to stand. The Twins laugh as he stands before them, helpless and naked. Mia and Mae each place a hand on his chest, and as they stand on their tiptoes, they tell Captain Fitts, "Goodbye." He looks bewildered, and then they both slowly pierce his skin with their blades and slowly imbed their knives almost halfway into his chest on both sides of his heart.

They remove their blades, and tiny wisps of black smoke escape through the cuts made by their blades. They release the bonds holding him, and he immediately falls to the ground screaming. As he screams, he starts convulsing, and a bloody foam trickles out of his mouth. A moment later, Guichi and Tanin watch as the man once known as Captain Fitt's eyes burst in their sockets, and then his nose and ears fall off. He releases a guttural scream, and they watch as his body continues to shake uncontrollably, and when they hear what sounds like the snapping of cartilage as its body seems to grow longer, until it is now almost two meters long. The shaking stops, and the transformation seems to end. Lying on the ground before the four of them is not a man but a monster with no facial features, and when he stands, Guichi and Tanin see that his genitals are also gone, and he does not move. Mae produces a folded robe with a white cloth lying on it. Mia walks up to him and orders him to kneel; she takes the white cloth, places it over his eyes, and then ties it. The cloth immediately becomes saturated with dark red, almost black blood.

Mae tells him to stand, and when he does, the two of them help him with his robe, and after they button it up, they say to Guichi and Tanin, "We give you a "Sutaraukaji or The Dead Eyes."

Tanin walks up to it, and the Sutaraukaji immediately recoils, and Tanin asks it, "Who do you want to serve?"

The Sutaraukaji replies, "The Darkness."

Tanin says, "Very good; show me what you can do for the Darkness?"

Mia steps forward and says, "From this day forth, you will be called Raspit and hands him a long slim blade swirling with the black smoke. Guichi notices that he has pointed black fingernails. The Twins tell him, "Now go and serve the Darkness," *Raspit* bows to them and moves very quickly, though he is not running into the battle. They watch him moving through the mayhem, stabbing some soldiers and passing on others. The ones he does stab drop to the ground and immediately start convulsing. Guichi and Tanin notice that some change into the ravenous beasts while others convulse and die. Few of the half-mangled soldiers lie bleeding to death, while others try and hold onto what little life they have left, and even others stare wide-eyed at the sky unmoving.

The four of them stand together as they watch the slaughter unfold, and Guichi and Tanin are impressed with the Twins. They watch as Raspit continues to move swiftly through the battle, converting men and women into savage beasts.

Tanin asks them, "What do you call these beasts?"

Mae tells him that they are called "Chizobutsu."

Guichi asks, "What else can you do?"

Mia tells them, "In the Dark Realm, we can teach many skills that would benefit anyone in this world, from all types of fighting, potions, ancient magics, and poisons. When the time comes, whoever you send to us will be above reproach in these skills and Dark Arts.

They watch the slaughter, and Guichi and Tanin both smile at the misfortune of others.

Mia says, "Excuse me, and joins Mae as they separate a group of five female soldiers from the fighting and force them to stand close. Mia binds them so they cannot move, and then they both casually walk up to the five women, slice and cut away their armor and clothing, and let everything fall to the ground and stand naked. Mae sees that the women range from eighteen to twenty and are all very pretty. Mia and Mae move among the five women and delicately touch each girl on their temples.

Mia releases the binding spell, and within seconds the five women are fighting ferociously amongst themselves, punching, biting, scratching, kicking, and pulling hair, and the fighting between them is ruthless.

Mae tosses a sharp blade among them and whispers, "Kill!" One of the youngest girls, around eighteen, sees the blade and quickly grabs it.

When the other girl tries to pull it from her hand, she lashes out and severs a couple of the girl's fingers. The girl clutches her bleeding hand to her chest as the young girl runs the blade across her throat. While the others are still fighting, she swiftly ends their lives with either a knife to the heart or a quick slice across the throat. The fighting is over, and the young girl stands among the dead, who were once her friends and sisters. The young girl just stands there drenched in blood, still holding the blade.

Mae walks up to her and asks her, "What is your name?"

The young girl responds, "Isa."

Mae says, "Look around you; look what you have done!"

Isa looks around, realizes what she has just done, and drops to her knees, completely devastated.

Mia whispers something in her ear, and she reaches up and touches Isa's temple again, and then Isa looks innocent as if nothing has happened, and Mia whispers to the two of them that Mae has taken away her memories. Then Mae opens the rift to the Dark Realm and tells Isa to walk through and wait for them in the temple to return. She steps through, and Mae closes the rift behind her.

Mia and Mae walk back to Guichi and Tanin and stand before them.

Guichi and Tanin are highly impressed with the Twins, and Tanin tells them, "Please come closer."

The Twins smile, and when they take a step closer, Tanin slaps them across their faces. The girls fall to their knees, ask what they have done wrong, and beg for forgiveness as they rub their cheeks.

Tanin says to them, "Now you will always remember who your Masters are!"

Guichi reaches out, helps them stand, and then asks, "Answer this for me; we are God's, so why can't we enter the rift and journey to the Dark Realm?"

Mia tells him, "My Lords, If either one of you were to enter the rift into the Dark Realm, you would become consumed by the darkness, and it would destroy your very essence. The rift thrives on the darkness, and the Dark Realm would destroy that side of you with your bodies being of half of the other essence."

Guichi turns to the Twins and tells them, "Go back to the Dark Realm and take your creatures with you. If what you say is true about training and fighting, we will send you a "Kaisoshosuko" who you will train. Train him in all skills that would benefit him in this Realm. Prove to us that you can do this without question,"

Mia says, *"Kaketa Hiriku Fetru Chusite,"* and the rift to the Dark Realm opens, larger than Guichi or Tanin had seen previously. Without being instructed, the creatures have just finished eradicating the last of the soldiers. They turn towards the rift and rush towards it, with some carrying human parts in their mouths, leaving many soldiers mangled, torn, mauled, dead, or dying.

Raspit walks up to Mae and Mia, bows, then turns to Guichi and Tanin and bows to them before stepping into the rift. Mia and Mae walk up to the rift, and Mia turns to the brothers and says, "We will be waiting to serve you, My Lords." Mae steps into the rift, and just before Mia steps through, Mae comes back out; Guichi and Tanin immediately feel its draw, and they see that Mae is holding a hefty leather-bound tome and a small wooden box. When Tanin takes hold of the box, he feels it. He opens the box, and inside are two pieces of Dark Crystal with blood-red veins running through them. One piece is slightly larger than a child's fist, while the other is a small chip no bigger than three carats.

Mae tells them, "This is but one piece of what you seek; use the smaller for whoever becomes your *"Kaisoshosuko,"* so that we will know the one you have picked. Once properly trained, it will heighten his dark powers tenfold. There are still more remnants scattered in your world, but alas, we cannot tell where they might be, fore we cannot touch them or sense them in your Realm. You will need at least four pieces of the Dark Crystal to release the Dark Lord Nimponin.

Mia tells them, "The Tome that you hold in your hands explains everything you need to know about the Dark Realm and how to use the Dark Crystals. There are pages of spells, potions, and other items, but one spell is crucial because it tells how to open a rift, so when the time comes and you need to send someone through, they will need to know how to do it. The Twins bow, and when they step into the rift, it closes behind them.

Guichi and Tanin can still hear the moans and whimpers of the dying as they walk through the blood bath while stepping over the maimed and mutilated. Guichi reaches into his pouch and pulls out the Tome that he started to write when their journey from the cave began. He hands it to

Tanin and asks him to open it to a blank page. Tanin does as requested, then watches Guichi take his hand and place his palm on one of the pages in the Tome that the Twins gave him, which has writings and sketches. Guichi glides his hand to all four corners of the page. He then does the same to their book on a blank page, and to Tanin's surprise, he sees the exact words and sketches appear on the blank page as Guichi moves his hand from one corner of the page to another. Together they transfer the writings from one Tome to the other. It is well into the night when they finish copying the pages. Guichi then takes the copied Tome and starts to erase words and diagrams from the Tome.

Tanin asks, "Why?"

Guichi tells him, "We must be careful," and he leaves it at that.

Guichi holds the augmented Tome and tells Tanin that this will be the Tome that will contain our beliefs and words and be known as the Dark Scriptures.

When it is time to bring our followers together and anoint a Priest, we can give him this copy to preach and speak our words to the masses. He holds up the one from the Dark Realm and asks Tanin what do you think; and Tanin looks at the book, and when he touches it, he says, "The Unholy Scriptures." Guichi agrees and says, "You, me, and who we choose to become our "Kaisoshosuko," will be the only ones who know that this Tome exists; the Dark Scriptures Tome will be given to who we appoint as our Kaisoshosuko and have her spread the word.

Tanin looks at Guichi, smiles, and says, "Seems another piece has fallen into place, and soon our beloved sisters will be in for a little surprise, and with the Twins training our army, and now that we have a piece of the Dark Crystal, we will be able to control this world."

Let us continue our search," and just as they are about to leave, Guichi waves his arm and says, "*Chirasa Shikamaru to Fiesta,*" and a blinding flash sweep through the valley, and when the flash is gone, so are the bodies of the maimed and dying. The only evidence they existed is scorched pieces of ground and abandoned armor. Guichi and Tanin step into the Spiritual Domain and are gone.

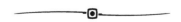

A week later, two large forces meet at the crossroads and immediately send out scouts, and when they all return, they all report the same thing. Pieces of metal armor from both man and animal lie throughout the crossroads, and everything shows the troops arriving, but nothing shows them leaving.

The commanders of both Glock and Tesh are on the top of one of the hills conferring. When they both notice the scorched patches of grass throughout the valley, they think it is peculiar but do not give it another thought and agree that the reports will state mass desertion.

Chapter 9

The Chiraka Blossoms

For the next sixteen weeks, Sargent Higgs batters them as he did that first morning, and every night they go back to their barracks to eat, soak in the tub, and apply ointment to each other.

One morning, they are in the same spot as they are every morning, waiting for Sargent Higgs to show up when they hear a taunting voice say, "What's wrong? Did your precious Sargent Higgs give up on you and find some real squires?" Samuel immediately recognizes that it's Gustav Heinz, one of the stewards that could never beat him in anything while they worked in the stables and always took the easy way out. He hated Samuel with a passion, and Samuel was just about to say something when he heard Sargent Higgs behind him say, "If you so much as utter a syllable back to that asshole, you will have a horrible day, and so will your two friends here." Samuel looks at Hikaru and Reiko and keeps his mouth shut. Sargent Higgs says. "Good, now follow me and be quiet," but before they leave, Higgs walks up to Heinz and says, "Little boy, if I ever fucking catch you talking to my recruits again, you will regret the day you were born. Do I make myself clear, you little Piss Pants?"

Heinz doesn't say anything when Higgs says, "Now go change your diaper because it looks like you wet yourself." Heinz looks down and sees that he has pissed himself. Embarrassed, he takes off and runs to his barracks, and as he runs through the training yard, the other squires start laughing, pointing at his wet spot. Soon everyone, even the training non-coms, started calling him Squire Piss Pants.

Higgs walks back to them, sees them smiling, and says, "Not a fucking word!" They follow him without question but refuse to stop smiling. They are out of the training yard and soon make their way through some woods and find themselves standing in front of a wall of briars with very sharp thorns. Sargent Higgs reaches out and pulls on a hidden rope, and the wall of briars opens up. Higgs tells them to go on through, and when they do, they find themselves in a secluded grove surrounded on both sides by trees and a very long pasture. Sargent Higgs tells them to remove all their clothing except their lower undergarments. When the three of them are standing semi-naked, Sargent Higgs walks up to each of them and hands them a wooden sword, and they immediately feel the weight of the wooden swords being lighter than what they had been training with.

Sargent Higgs tells them, "These are your swords, and you have probably felt the weight difference. These practice swords weigh the same as an Empire-issued katana but are lighter than the practice swords you have used. You will take care of them as if your life depended on it. You will carry your sword wherever you go. You will never lay your sword down under any circumstances unless I and only tell you to or when you are in your barracks, but you will always have it within arm's reach. You might be ridiculed or even given a direct order by others to put down your sword or forfeit it. Let me reiterate, under no circumstances are you to give up your sword no matter who asks for it unless it is the Emperor himself and addresses the three of them or the Emperor's Advisor General. He looks right at Samuel when he says it. You will never draw your sword unless I specifically tell you to do. Do I make myself clear?"

All three reply, "Yes, Sargent!"

Now for today's lesson, the three of them tense up slightly. Sargent Higgs chuckles and proceeds to instruct the three of them in the proper ways of holding a sword and using the blade for attacking and defending. The three now understood why he asked them to remove their clothes; it was so Higgs could show and point out what muscles and other parts of their bodies they could use to attack and defend with a sword and use little effort. The rest of the day consisted of this type of training, and for the next twelve weeks, Higgs instructs them this same way and teaches them "*Kata*," a form of maneuvers, almost like a dance, to demonstrate the principles of attacking and defending. While doing these, he carefully points out their strengths and weaknesses and adjusts an arm here or a leg and foot there.

On the morning of the twelfth week, when they enter the grove, they find Higgs is already there, and three other men are with him. They also notice that Higgs is holding three different shaped wooden swords.

Samuel, Reiko, or Hikaru had never seen them before, but with all inhibitions gone, they head over to the side of the grove to remove their clothing when Higgs says, "Keep your clothes on and line up there!" pointing to a spot in the grass. He introduces the three as fellow instructors, and when he does, they approach the three of them and stop in front of them. Each instructor carries one of the new swords, and the one standing in front of Reiko tells her, "Give me your sword so that we can give you this new one. Sargent Higgs says it is okay."

Reiko calls out to Sargent Higgs, "Is that okay with you, Sargent Higgs?" Higgs seems to ignore Reiko and the others and does not say anything. Reiko looks the man in front of her straight in the eyes and says, "Sorry Sir, but I cannot, and hears Samuel and Hikaru say, "Aye, sorry we cannot."

The one standing in front of Samuel shouts at him, "Why you sniveling little shit. How dare you question my authority?" and tries to strike Samuel with the wooden sword he is holding. On instinct, Samuel raises his sword and blocks the assault. The other two instructors attack Reiko and Hikaru, and like Samuel, they defend themselves. Sword hits click on both sides, but the two instructors get more hits on Reiko and Hikaru than they did on them. Samuel seems to take a few lesser hits and holds his own against his attacker.

After thirty minutes of sparring, Higgs observes three things: Reiko's sword falls slightly lower as the sparring continues, leaving herself open to attacks. Hikaru has stopped attacking and is only blocking, and he hesitates where he has opportunities to attack. He signals the two instructors to step back and motions Reiko and Hikaru to join him. Hikaru and Reiko take deep breaths to calm themselves and walk over to Higgs. Higgs motions for the four of them to join him. As Higgs and the rest watch, Samuel and the instructor keep at it with an onslaught of strikes, slashes, and stabbings against each other. If these had been real swords instead of practice swords, they would have amounted to more than a few minor non-threatening cuts. Samuel's opponent has fared better than Samuel, with probably fewer bruises.

Higgs senses something and pays very close attention to Samuel. Samuel steps back, and Higgs notices the change in his posture. Reiko starts to say something when Higgs holds up his hand for silence, never taking his eyes off Samuel. Reiko and Hikaru also sense the difference, and the three of them see it as a small silver flash crosses over Samuel's eyes.

His attacker does not notice the change, nor do the other two instructors, but he swings his sword at Samuel's torso. Samuels instinctively blocks the swing, and then Samuel takes the offensive and throws a series of thrusts, slashes, spins, and stabs at his attacker. His attacker can block most of them but receives a few more bruises than expected. After another fifteen minutes, the two end up about two meters apart, with the instructor breathing heavily and Samuel is only slightly winded. Higgs gets up, walks over, and places his sword between them as a signal to stop. The instructor lowers his sword, as does Samuel, and then walks up to Samuel with his hand out. Samuel takes it, and the instructor brings him in close so only Samuel can hear him and says, "Well done, my boy. I haven't had that much of a challenge or fun from one of Vernon's recruits for quite a while but next time, be ready to bring it on."

Samuel says, "Yes, Sir," and adds, "Anytime," and smiles. His opponent laughs and steps back. For the rest of the day, Higgs and his friends demonstrate what they observed while sparring with the three. At the end of the training day, Higgs tells the three of them to sit and relax.

Higgs begins with Reiko, "Takahashi, you did yourself justice, but being a girl, and I don't mean that in a derogatory way, you don't have the upper body mass and strength to maintain a prolonged sword fight with a katana. You must take out your attacker within the first few minutes of a fight, or it could cost you. Sargent Bills recommends using a rapier because it is lighter and allows you to deliver quick thrusts and cuts. He also suggests that maybe the sword isn't your weapon of choice. Don't get me wrong, you can still use a sword, but he thinks that should be your secondary weapon and not your primary. We will have to try different options." Reiko nods in understanding.

"Sato, you were able to defend yourself admirably, and your defensive stances and technique are exceptional, but you have massive upper body strength and need to be more assertive. My friend and I noticed that you tended to grab your sword with both hands. You did not follow through with your attacks on numerous opportunities, even after blocking his blows. You are the opposite of Takahashi. Sato, you have the upper body strength, but you don't have the finesse of using a one-handed sword. He thinks using a halberd for distance or a battleax would benefit you. As I said, you have the upper body strength. Why not put it to good use?" and Hikaru nods.

Higgs was just about to start in on Samuel, "Shinpo, where to?" when the instructor that sparred with Samuel politely interrupted Higgs and asked him if he could critique him. Higgs gestures for him to go ahead. Bruns stands and says, "Young man, Shinpo, is it?

"I told you earlier, this has been one of the better sparring's that I have endured for quite a while, and we, gesturing to his friends, have been helping out Sargent Higgs for quite a few years now, but now, however, I need to bring attention to your flaws. You might not notice, but you drop your shoulder a little when you counter a strike, and also, when you do that, your center core is out of alignment, which throws you off balance. If your center core is off, you might be over-extending without realizing it, as you were doing when we started sparring. You will need to correct these two things, and if you do, you will be a force to be reckoned with. The one thing that I don't understand is what came over you in the last part of our sparring. I can tell you this. If your balance was centered, I don't think I would have been able to block your attacks as well as I did."

Higgs thanks his friends and tells them they'll come back soon. They laugh, and as they leave the grove, he hears them say, "We look forward to it."

He tells Samuel, Reiko, and Hikaru that it is enough for the day and to rest up for tomorrow. Sargent Vernon Higgs smiles, which causes the three of them to roll their eyes.

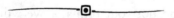

The three of them rise at the crack of dawn. Hikaru heats a pot of water for tea. When finished, they march to the grove with anticipation and some trepidation because they are eager to see what Sargent Vernon Higgs has in store for them. They enter the grove to see Higgs standing with two men. Higgs introduces them to Corporal Wiss and Corporal Nubbs and tells them that both men are masters in two-handed weaponry and archery, which is their next training phase.

Wiss walks up to Reiko and shakes her hand, as does Nubbs to Hikaru. They both look at Samuel to watch Sargent Higgs walk up to Samuel and say, "Shall we?" and brings an overhead strike at Samuel's head. Samuel brings up his sword in a defensive block, and the swords clash. Higgs is about to swing his sword to strike Samuel in the head, but Samuel does the unexpected. He brings his body in close, so Higg's downward swing is too far out to catch him, and Samuel brings his sword down to try and hit Higgs. Higgs shoves him back before connecting and follows through with multiple slashes, chops, and slices toward Samuel. Samuel is on the defensive but can defend himself and get a few attacks in, which again surprises Higgs, and they swap blow for blow. Samuel might have the age on his side, but Higgs has the experience, size, and brute force, and when he changes his tactics, Samuel finds himself struggling to defend himself. Higgs has shoved Samuel again and is waiting for the final knockdown blow when he feels a calmness overcome him. All outside noises are gone. He feels the weapon in his hand become an extension of his body, and a silver light flash crosses his eyes. His breathing immediately comes under control, and Higgs notices the change and sees the flash of silver but is unaware that Samuel's heart rate has become one with his breathing.

Samuel plants his foot in the dirt, takes the offensive, proceeds with a variation of everything taught, and combines it three-fold. Higgs can barely block what Samuel is throwing at him when like before, he jams up Higgs and goes to hit him again. Higgs feels the hit on his knee and cries out. He pushes Samuel back and immediately takes a defensive stance. Samuel is about to attack again when he sees Higgs lowers his sword. Samuel stops on cue and acts like nothing has happened as he casually sits down on the grass, not even winded.

Higgs walks over, puts out his hand to help Samuel, and tells him to follow him. Samuel looks at his two friends. Reiko has a longbow in her hands, and Samuel says to Higgs, "It looks natural," and Higgs responds, "That it does."

Higgs has Samuel sit down and offers him some water; just as Hikaru has taken up the battleax, he performs a smooth counter spin and blocks Nubb's attack, and they hear Nubbs say, "Dam!" Higgs smiles and then says, "Samuel, I just want to tell you that in all my years of training squires, you are the first to confuse me momentarily and the first to get a hit that caused me to cry out."

Samuel starts apologizing when Higgs cuts him off, "Don't apologize for a clean hit," then Higgs says, "I know who you are, who your father is, and about the connection you have with the Princess. Don't worry, I will not say anything, but I want you to know that what you did has all my respect." Now, to the point of our little conversation. I want you to concentrate on using the sword as your primary weapon. I have taught the three of you all weaponry aspects, but I want you to focus on the sword. You have a gift, and I watched it unfold as you were sparring with my friend yesterday and again today during our sparring match. Can I ask you why it showed up halfway through our sparring?

Samuel says, "I do not know why it appears when it does, but I do know that when I feel threatened, it seems to show itself. "Higgs stands and then says, "Let's try and figure it out, and walks over to see how the others are doing?"

They walk back over two of the other four, and as they get closer, they see Wiss moving Reiko's body to stand while holding a bow with an arrow drawn. They see Hikaru bashing and slashing with Nubbs. Higgs whistles, and the training stops. They gather in front of him. He tells Samuel, Hikaru, and Reiko that starting tomorrow. They will begin their extensive training in these three styles of fighting and other types of weapons that the Empire has in their arsenal. My associates and I will be instructing you for the next twelve months in all styles of weapons and how to use your bodies and hands to defend, maim, paralyze, and kill, if necessary, and then says, "That will be enough for today."

The weeks pass into months, and Samuel, Hikaru, and Reiko have become highly proficient in weaponry. Samuel continues with the Empires style of sword, the katana, as does Reiko with a rapier, but she favors the bow. Hikaru enjoys any two-handed weapons, but he prefers the short-handled battleax. Wiss places a longbow in her hands one morning, and Reiko feels invigorated. She has handled every type of bow, from a short bow to a crossbow, but the longbow feels right. Wiss has noticed that Reiko appears to have a sixth sense with Airs, drifts, and angles, and she has mastered the short bow quickly. She can throw a dagger, knife, or death star with deadly accuracy. Corporal Wiss considers her a natural and tells her that the longbow is challenging to master. Still, after only one month, she has perfected her skills with the bow. Wiss is highly impressed, and that afternoon after their break, Wiss starts walking out into the field, tossing an apple in the Air, and Reiko and Higgs see him place an apple in the split of a tree.

When he returns to Reiko, he says, "Shoot it."

Reiko looks at him, then she notches an arrow, takes a deep breath, and pulls the arrow and bowstring back as far as they can be drawn. She releases the arrow, and Higgs and Wiss watch as the arrow pierces the apple dead center. Higgs sees the bow as natural as breathing with her, but he does not see the flash of silver.

Higgs looks over at Sato and sees that he has found his specialty in the battleax and demonstrates that he is highly proficient with it, and it seems with any of the two-handed long-shafted weapons. Nubbs does not know how he does it, but Hikaru displays an uncanny skill that Nubbs or Higgs has never seen before, especially as long as Nubbs has been helping his recruits. Higgs is standing there, and as he is watching Hikaru swing, the battleax and his movements are smooth. Then Higgs sees the same silver flash across his eyes, and the smoothness is now fluid, and the ax, like Samuel's Katana, has become an extension of his arms.

Higgs is impressed with their training, and all three have become highly proficient in all the weapons in the Empire's arsenal and then some. Samuel has performed well beyond Higgs' expectations with the katana, Reiko and the longbow, and Hikaru with the battle-ax, and training continues as usual. Then, one day, Higgs sees that all three can adapt to just about any weapon placed in their hands and become proficient in using them. Samuel is skilled in the battleax and longbow and knows how to use them. He can hold his own when sparring with Hikaru, but he always ends up disarmed and, on the ground, making Hikaru smile. When it comes to the longbow, Reiko is the master. Samuel can shoot an arrow dead center on a target at two hundred meters. Reiko can do the same but at four hundred meters. He told her once that it would not be a good idea to piss her off and try to make a run for it. Reiko starts laughing and says, "Practice what you preach, Samuel, and don't piss me off." They both start laughing.

The following day Higgs is at the practice field early and starts thinking, He has seen Samuel and Hikaru's silver flash come across their eyes, and their movements become not just second nature, but the weapons they hold become one with them. He had not seen that same silver flash in

Takahashi's eyes when she was shooting the apple, and he begins to wonder if it is just Samuel and Hikaru who have this ability.

The following day, they arrive at the grove, and Higgs tells Samuel and Hikaru to go sit down on the log. He then walks up to Reiko and hands her a longbow and a quiver of arrows. She takes them, and Higgs points to ten clay pots hanging from a tree limb approximately one hundred meters away. Higgs then says to Reiko, "Takahashi, do you see those ten pots hanging from that tree?"

Reiko says, "Yes, Sargent Higgs."

Higgs continues, "Takahashi, I want you to pick ten arrows, and when you are ready, I am going to toss this coin into the Air, and I want you to shoot and break every one of those pots before the coin lands in the palm of my hand. If you cannot, then I will have to have you restart your training in the Squires.

Samuel and Hikaru start to protest when Higgs holds up his hand for silence and asks Reiko, "Do you understand Takahashi?"

Reiko looks at Sargent Higgs, and all she says is, "Yes."

Higgs stands to the side and says, "When you are ready?"

Reiko carefully examines the arrows in the quiver, pulls out the best ten, and hands the remaining arrows to Higgs. She then takes the quiver, straps it on over her right shoulder, reaches back with her right hand, and grabs an arrow. She notches it and draws the bowstring back, and holds it there.

Higgs says, "When you are ready?"

Reiko takes a deep breath, and Higgs sees her elbow shake just a bit, and then he waits for it.

He watches as her breathing slows, the shaking stops, and then she nods.

Higgs tosses the coin high into the Air, and as he watches it go up, he hears the first pot shatter, and when he looks at Reiko, all he sees is a blur as she reaches back, pulls the bowstring, and fires. The last pot shatters as he puts out his hand, and the coin lands in his palm.

He looks at her and notices that she is not even winded, and she stands there smiling.

All Higgs says is, "Well, Takahashi, it looks like you won't be restarting your training," and only gives her a slight smile that she can see. He tells the three of them that it is all for the day and dismisses them. Higgs leaves them, and he hears Samuel and Hikaru walk up to Reiko and tell her that what she just did was amazing. Higgs smiles again as he walks away when he hears Reiko say, "It was pretty amazing, wasn't it!"

The following day when the three of them get to the grove, Higgs is already there and instructs them to follow him. After a fifteen-minute hike, they arrive at a large open field, and hanging on a rack is a longbow with a quiver of arrows, two short-handled battle axes, and a pair of Royal Empire katanas consisting of one long and one short sword.

Higgs tells Reiko to pick up the longbow and quiver of arrows and bring them back to him. She does, and then Higgs asks, "Do you see that red clay pot hanging from that tree out there?" Reiko looks closely and nods her head, yes. Higgs tells her, "Shoot it." Samuel and Hikaru start to say something, but Higgs again holds his hand for silence. Reiko says incredulously, "Sargent Higgs, you can't be serious?" Higgs looks at her and says, "I am very serious. Now shoot it!" Reiko says, "Yes, Sargent," and proceeds to examine every arrow shaft in the quiver. She picks two of them, places one arrow in her mouth close to the feathers, and then notches the other one. Reiko slowly pulls back the string on the bow to its maximum tensile strength and raises the arrow's tip in the Air. She takes a deep breath, and while exhaling, she feels a calmness overcome her where all outside noise is gone, the weapon in her hand becomes an extension of her own body, and like Samuel, her heart rate becomes one with her breathing. Reiko can see the soft breeze blowing across the field, and then the Air around her becomes still. She then notices the leaves blowing in the wind seem to have slowed and just fluttering in the Air. Suddenly, the hanging pot stops swinging in the breeze, and she focuses on it as if it were a meter away. Her concentration is so acute that she pictures the arrow striking the pot and watches it explode. Then a flash of silver crosses her eyes, and Higgs now sees it, and she unconsciously adjusts her aim to the left of the target. Higgs knows the same flash of silver that he saw in Samuel's and Hikaru's eyes, and then she releases the arrow. All three hear the twang of the bow and a woosh as the arrow takes flight. Higgs watches it shoot upwards, and as it reaches its zenith, he sees it slightly veer to the right. Then seconds later, they see the pot disintegrate into pieces, and a second after that, they hear the clay pot exploding. Reiko lowers her bow and smiles.

Higgs looks at Reiko and says, "Takahashi, I knew from yesterday that you had it in you, but that was one hell of a shot. I have not known anyone in all my years, even a Master archer with twenty years of experience, capable of making that shot. He asks the three of them, "How far do you think that pot was?" Samuel guesses six hundred, and Hikaru says five-hundred-fifty. Reiko looks at Higgs and says, "One thousand meters." Higgs starts laughing. "Squire Takahashi, don't you dare get a big head, but you are exactly right, one thousand meters out!" Reiko is surprised not because she made the shot but because Sargent Vernon Higgs has finally called her Squire after four and a half years. She says, "Thank you, Sargent Higgs."

Higgs tells Sato to grab a battleax. Hikaru does and stands near Higgs. Seven men in light armor are standing in the field a few minutes later. Higgs informs Sato that he has to defeat all seven of them. Sato looks at Higgs, and all he says is, "Yes, Sargent," and nervously walks a little further out in the field, and just before he reaches the middle of the area, Higgs calls out, "Sato, you are not to take ant hits!" Hikaru calls back, "Yes, Sargent and a devious smile crosses his lips. Four men hold shields with swords drawn, while the other three have halberds and surround Hikaru. He hears Higgs say, "Defend yourself," and two of them attack, a swordsman and one with a halberd. Sato deflects the sword and brings up his battleax to stop the downward strike.

The other five see their opportunity and rush towards the fight. Higgs watches and sees Hikaru hold his own against the seven of them.

Hikaru somehow keeps them all back, then drops to one knee and takes a deep breath, and just like Reiko, as he exhales, the Air around him becomes still, and the outside noises of birds and insects stop. He senses the seven men charging at once, and then the silver flash crosses his eyes, and the battleax becomes an extension of his own body. Even before his attackers get close, Hikaru has already played the scenario in his mind. He drops down just enough to work his way under the first halberd and swings his ax to deflect it, so it ends up hitting the swordsman next to him in the face and knocking him out cold. He then spins the battleax and hits the one who attacked him with the halberd with the flat side of the ax to drop him to his knees. Sato then charges the two with halberds, which they were not expecting, and swings his ax with such force it snaps their halberds in half, and he follows through by hitting two of them with the handle of his ax, knocking them unconscious. He finds the three remaining swordsmen hesitant to move in. Sato smiles and picks up one of the broken halberd shafts, and because he is in the moment, he spins the battleax around in his hands and then tosses it up in the Air handle over the blade. The three swordsmen at that moment charge Sato. Right before they reach him, he takes out the first swordsman with the broken halberd shaft and then sweeps the feet out from under the second one. He puts his hand out, and the battleax comes back down, and he catches it perfectly, follows through with an unnatural swing, sweeps the legs out from under the last swordsmen, then runs the flat side of the battleax across their chests as if decapitating them. Higgs notices that Sato is not even winded.

Higgs stands there with his hands on his hips and says, "Well done, Squire Sato" He, like Reiko, says, "Thank you, Sargent Higgs."

Higgs calls for Samuel and tells him to grab the Katanas. He does, and as he stands beside Higgs, Higgs whistles, and Samuel sees his old sparring partner with two friends entering the field. Higgs says to Samuel, "You remember Sargent Bruns, don't you?"

Bruns walks up to Samuel and puts out his hand to shake, Samuel takes it, and Bruns says, "I enjoyed myself very much the last time we met, but this time I brought along a couple of friends. I hope you don't mind."

Samuel looks Sargent Bruns straight in the eyes, smiles, and says, "Let's dance!"

Bruns answers, "Shall we!"

Samuel walks out onto the field, places one hand on the handle of the longer katana, and holds the katana's blade cradled in his elbow. He has the short katana in his other hand, though still in its sheath. He plants his front foot on the ground. Reiko and Hikaru walk up to Higgs, and Reiko looks at him and asks him, "What is Samuel doing? He has opened himself to multiple attacks."

Higgs just watches and says, "I'm not sure. I have never seen this stance before." One swordsman attacks and charges without warning, thrusting his blade at Samuel's midsection. Samuel swiftly brings his short katana still in its sheath straight up, deflects the assault, and catches the attacker on his wrists. He then twists his short katana to make the attacker's sword fly out of his hands, then clips the attacker just behind the knee to drop him to the ground. Samuel has the blade tip at the man's throat and says, "Yield!". The man throws his hands up and says, "I yield," and gets up and walks over to Higgs, and says, "That was unbelievable, I have never been taken out with a katana still in its sheath before, and as for his blade, I never saw it move, but I felt it," and rubs his wrist.

The next attacker comes in cautiously, and the two of them place their blades together, and then the attacker moves swiftly to try to go under Samuel's blade. Samuel deflects the man's blade and smoothly but forcibly pushes the attacker and his blade back. The two of them are going back and forth, and all you hear is the blades clashing together. The attacker holds his sword like a true swordsman and comes at Samuel with everything he has. Higgs sees it, and a second later, so do Reiko and Hikaru as all three feel the silence and the stillness in the Air, and the flash crosses Samuel's eyes as the same feeling as the other two takes over. Samuel strikes once and then pulls his sword back to the side of his head with his arm crossing his chest, and his other elbow sticking straight out and holds the sword with two hands.

The attacker thinks this is crazy and assumes Samuel is leaving himself open. He lunges, and the next thing he sees is a blur as he feels Samuel's Katana strike his hips, his upper arms, and the tops of his shoulders, and then finds Samuel's blade on the side of his throat. He drops his sword, realizing that if they were fighting for real, he would be dead, and like his predecessor says, "Yield."

Sargent Bruns has been watching the entire encounter and then steps forward with his blade in his two hands and brings it to his forehead as a salute. Samuel does that same and then assumes a stance, and Higgs recognizes it as one of the katas that Higgs has taught them and notices that Samuel's feet are placed differently.

Bruns takes a step closer and raises his sword, then it happens. Samuels moves with incredible speed and strikes out at Bruns many times. Bruns feels them, but it is so quick that it feels like one long continuous blow to his body. Bruns puts up his sword to block Samuels but then realizes that it is not where he thought it should be and then feels the blade strike him three or four times. Bruns is frustrated because no matter how hard Bruns tries, he cannot even come close to defending himself against Samuel's attacks. He sees Samuel's katana coming straight at him and then realizes that his hands are empty, and he sees his sword sticking out of the ground just a meter away. Seconds later, Bruns is standing there trying to figure out what just happened, as Samuel is now standing back in the same spot as he started and is sheathing his katana.

He bows to Sargent Bruns and turns back to his friends when he notices the two other swordsmen standing there with their mouths open. Higgs starts laughing, walks over to Sargent Bruns, and slaps him on his back, which seems to bring him out of his stupor. He looks at Higgs and asks, "What happened?" Higgs laughs even harder as his two friends come over and try to explain what exactly happened.

Higgs thanks Sargent Bruns, Corporal Wise, and Corporal Francis for their time and training his recruits, and as they walk away, Wise and Francis are still trying to explain what happened to him. Higgs says, "Remember what happens in the grove, stays in the grove."

The three call out, "As always, Vernon, we will see you later for drinks," and wave.

After they leave the field, Higgs tells Samuel, Reiko, and Hikaru that they did exceptionally well, that it was getting late, and that he will see them tomorrow. The three of them are about to leave the field when they hear Higgs says, "Remember Squires, your training continues tomorrow."

The three of them are beaming with pride as they walk back to their barracks. When they get back, Hikaru puts on a pot of water for tea, as Reiko and Samuel start a fire to heat the tub water. After they finish bathing, they realize that neither one of them is sore and feel good. They are sitting on their bunks drinking tea and talking about today's events when there is a knock at the door. Reiko gets up to open the door and sees Sargent Higgs standing there. Reiko immediately calls attention to the room, and Higgs tells them to relax. Higgs enters the room and is impressed with what they did to the barracks to make it quite livable.

Hikaru offers Higgs some tea. He accepts and sits down.

Samuel asks, "Sargent Higgs, to what do we owe the pleasure of your visit?"

Higgs takes a sip of tea and says, "I want to talk to you three about what happened today in the training field. In my military years, I have never seen or heard anything of what you three did today. Reiko, that shot was physically and mentally impossible to make. I don't think the greatest bow master in all the lands could have made that shot, and Hikaru, how you handle that battleax is astonishing and, like Reiko's bow shot, impossible to do. The weight and style of the ax alone make it unbalanced and awkward, and I can't even try to guess how you timed it to catch that ax right in your hand. As for you, Samuel, the ebb and flow of the unorthodox kata you performed today and the swordsmanship you displayed with your blade have put you above any blade master I have heard of or seen. The three of you have surpassed any Master I have known in my lifetime. Samuel, so you know, Sargent Bruns is considered a fourth-tier blade master, and the other two are a third-tier. You made all three of them look like novices. I don't say this that often, but I am very proud of the three of you. I will give my highest recommendations that you three be assigned together. Individually, you are a force to be reckoned with, but together you would be unstoppable.

Higgs finishes his tea, stands, motioning for the three of them to remain seated, says, "I will see you at graduation tomorrow," and walks out of the barracks closing the door behind him. The three of them look at each other and say simultaneously, "Graduation."

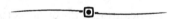

That night after graduation, they are relaxing in the hot tub. Samuel holds out his hand with his palm down and says, "My two best friends, no matter what happens in life or the future, I will always have your backs, "I swear." Hikaru places his hand on Samuel's and repeats the words. They both look at Reiko. She smiles, puts her hand on top of theirs, and repeats the oath. The moment she finishes, all three of them feel an unbreakable bond between them, a bond that is felt in their hearts and minds to the very bottom of their souls as it courses through their blood. They know that this bond is unique in a way that if anything were to happen to any one of them, the other two would feel it.

Many leagues away in the royal summer palace, a young girl is listening to her lessons when she feels a slight jolt and then the established bond between her Protector and two others. Their bond is powerful, and Princess Asami feels it, and she now knows she has three Guardians and is excited.

Samuel, Reiko, and Hikaru are all eighteen, graduated, and are gathering their belongings in the barracks when Sargent Vernon Higgs enters the room. Samuel calls the room to attention, and they salute Sargent Higgs. Higgs tells them to drop their gear and to stand before him. The three of them are standing in line when Higgs approaches Hikaru and hands him two letters, and on top of these are a set of silver second-lieutenant bars. He does this for the other two, takes a step backward, and comes to full attention.

He then says, "Congratulations, Hikaru Hito Sato, Reiko Anzu Takahashi, and Samuel Miro, on becoming Second-Lieutenants in the Emperor's Royal Imperial Army, "salutes them. Reiko and Hikaru look at Samuel, and Higgs starts laughing and says, "Second-Lieutenant Miro, I will leave it for you to explain." He then hands them their reporting papers, comes to attention, salutes the three of them, performs a perfect about-face, and exits the barracks. Just before he steps out, he stops at the doorway and tells them that it was a privilege to train them and is gone.

Reiko and Hikaru turn to Samuel, and all they say is. "Explain," and Samuel does, and when he finishes, they both bow to him, say, "Your Excellency," and start laughing. All Samuel says is, "Ha! Very funny." Then all three of them open their reporting orders and are relieved that they are reporting to the same office and need to report the next day. They do not open the second letter right away

Chapter 10

Loved Ones Lost

The years pass as William, and his siblings have grown. William is about to celebrate his eighteenth year when Jeffery, his older brother, returns home from his year of wanderlust and discovery. William's father, the Prince consort by marriage, believed that nothing should be handed for free, no matter your status. His children needed to establish themselves in the community upon graduation from any prestigious university on the mainland and spend one year traveling throughout the kingdoms.

Jeffery decided to pursue an interest in hospitality and open a restaurant. The restaurant featured exotic dishes specific to the islands and soon prospered, not because he was royalty but because the food was delicious. The locals enjoyed the Bistro, and everyone knew that you had to stop at the Bistro if you were to visit the islands. Jefferey was respected and loved by everyone, and everyone knew he would make an excellent advisor to the Queen someday. Though everyone knew who he was, he only had one rule when anyone walked through the Bistro doors, and all titles were left outside. He never allowed that to interfere with his customers and business dealings.

One afternoon a ship sails into port from the Northern Isles. The ship has sailed many days to arrive at the island of Aleu to establish trade agreements. Captain Alloysius Temple of the Horizon vessel wants to trade his goods for the island's Painapp fruit. Negotiations are completed as the customs officials sign and stamp the appropriate documents. Captain Temple of the vessel Horizon is now an authorized trader with the Sovereign of the Tatokai Archipelago.

The voyage seems very profitable for both the local merchants and the Captain and his crew. The profits from selling the northern islands' wares allow the Captain to hand out small bonuses to his men and tell them to enjoy themselves because they are sailing on the morning tide.

Several small groups of sailors come ashore and head into town to have a few drinks here and there. Some drink heavily after their lengthy voyage and become your typical drunken sailors, loud, obnoxious, and very touchy with the serving girls. They all decided they wanted to get something to eat, so they asked the locals in the tavern where the best place in town was for good food. All the locals said the same place, The Bistro. They finish their drinks, pay their bill, and leave the tavern to go to the Bistro.

A tall man greets them at the door as they enter the Bistro. He welcomes them and politely escorts the sailors to one of the private rooms, where the tall man introduces their serving girl, and she tells them that her name is Alexandria. They order the daily specials and mugs of ale. One sailor places a silver coin in her hand, tells her to keep the drinks coming, and winks at her. She smiles and says, "Yes, Sir."

The night is going well, and everyone is having a good time. The sailors realize how late it is, pay their bills, and call it a night. One of the sailors tells the others that he wants to finish his ale, will be with them in a few minutes, and ask them to wait for him outside. One of the other sailors said, "OK, we will wait but hurry up; you know how Mister Breen can be when we are not at our best when it comes time to sail. The one staying behind says, "Fuck Breen!" The others leave the room, and on their way, they thank the manager for a wonderful meal, and the next time they visit the islands, they will be sure to drop in. Jeffery thanks them and tells them to have a good night and safe sailing. The one sailor is sipping on his ale as Alexandria hustles around the table, clearing the dishes and empty mugs.

The sailor feels rambunctious and grabs her, causing her to drop a tray full of empty mugs. He has her tight around the waist and tries to force a kiss on her, and says, "Come on, darling, I've been at sea for a long time and will be back out to sea in a few hours, "Why don't you and I make my last night memorable." and tries to kiss her again. She asks him to let her go, but he says, "Come on now, I gave you a whole silver; why don't you show me your appreciation."

Alexandria tries desperately to break his grip and remove his hands from her waist. When she can't, she does not hesitate and grabs his mug and pours its contents on his head. The sailor releases her, jumps up, and screams, "Why! you, stupid little whore!" At that moment, Jefferey walks into the room and says, "Is everything alright in here?"

The serving girl says, Yes, Jeffery, everything is fine; this gentleman was leaving when he bumped into me, and I dropped the tray. Jeffery walks up to him, places his hand on his shoulder, and tells him nicely that he is sorry and will be happy to give him a free drink the next time he is in port. The sailor tells him, "Fuck off!" but Jeffery insists and starts to squeeze his shoulder, causing him to wince. And then says, "Now, Sir, if you would be so kind as to pay your bill and leave so the young lady can clean up the mess she made."

During the exchange between Jeffery and the sailor, the girl had picked up all the dropped mugs and stood up when she heard him call her a "stupid bitch!" He breaks free from Jefferey's grip and goes to take a swing at her. He feels a hand on his arm and realizes that the tall man has a hold of it, and then his arm is brought around to his back. He finds himself doubled over on the table and cannot move. Jefferey tells him, "There will be none of that here." and calls out "Sam."

Seconds later, another big brute of a man steps into the room and walks over to Jeffery and the sailor he has pinned on the table. Jeffery says, "Please remove this gentleman from here and make sure you get his name; we don't want to see him again." Sam takes hold of him, applies a little pressure to his arm, and asks him, "What is your name? When the sailor refuses, Sam pulls his arm a little more, and the man screams, "Wilkens!"

Sam ushes Wilkens through the Bistro and to the door by the scruff of his shirt. When they get to the door, Sam sees his friends standing outside. Sam tells them they are welcome back anytime but do not bring Wilkens.

Sam lightly throws Wilkens off the porch and lands in some slop on the ground. When he gets up, his shipmates take a few steps back and tell him that he smells like an old whore. His shipmates roar with laughter, and Wilkens says to himself, "No one laughs at me."

Jefferey stands by the door and politely says, "Gentlemen, have a wonderful evening and a safe voyage." Wilkins yells back as they walk away, "Fuck you and your restaurant!"

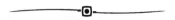

Later that night, Jefferey is in his office, checking and tallying the evening's receipts, when he hears a loud thud in the storeroom. He gets up and calls out. "Sam, are you alright?"

Jefferey comes out of the office and sees Sam lying on the floor. He rushes over to Sam, and he is struck from behind and falls to the floor unconscious. Wilkins is standing over Jefferey when he sees the serving girl from earlier this evening standing in the dining room doorway holding a tray of hot drinks.

She asks, "What is going on here?"

Wilkins asks her, "Alexandria is it; I came back to apologize for my behavior, and I found them like this."

Alexandria drops the tray of drinks and runs over to Jefferey and Sam, and as she kneels beside them, she smells an odor from Wilkens and tells him, "Why, don't you just go and let me get some help for my friends here?" She looks at Wilkins, sees the ship's belaying pin tucked in his belt, and notices the fresh blood on it. He sees her surprise and knows she doesn't believe him, that he just happened to find them like this.

Wilkins chuckles and says to her, "You and your two friends here embarrassed me tonight. All my friends just laughed at me because that big guy threw me into a pile of pig slop; all they did was tell me that I stank and should go live with the pigs. I am Wilkens, and no one ever laughs at me!"

Alexandria says, "I'm sorry, I didn't mean to embarrass you, but you shouldn't have grabbed me. I am the Second Heir's fian..." Wilkins slaps her, and tells her, "Shut the fuck up, Bitch. I don't care who you are!"

"You embarrassed me, and my friends don't respect me now; they keep saying I got beat up by a girl. After tonight they will respect me once I tell them how I fixed the bitch who started all this and humiliated me."

Wilkins pulls out a long knife and swipes it at her. She instinctively ducks under the swipe and thrusts her fist directly into Wilkin's crotch, and with her other hand, she shoves her palm into his nose. Wilkins lets out a grunt, and as he staggers backward, he drops the knife, and Alexandria seizes the opportunity and runs towards the door to escape and get help. She hears him say, "Bitch, you broke my nose!" and reaches for the belaying pin tucked in his belt. He throws it at her, and the pin hits her just behind her left ear, and she crumbles to the floor. Hobbling over to her, he grabs her by her ankles and starts dragging her back into the storeroom.

Alexandria feels herself being dragged across the floor, on her stomach, as she starts to regain her senses. She tries kicking herself free, but he drops her legs, steps over her, wraps her hair around his fist, and slams her face onto the floor. He grabs her ankles once again and continues to drag her. He pulls her near some crates and turns her over to straddle her upper thighs. He stares at this beautiful young woman and starts to drool and lick his lips.

He places his hand over her mouth as he reaches under her dress; she turns her head and bites his hand, drawing blood.

"Bitch!" he cries.

He reaches back and slaps her across the mouth, stifling her scream. She tastes blood from her split lip and feels it start to swell.

He smacks her across her face and tells her, "Don't try that again, bitch". He reaches down to find what he is looking for, and she tries to throw him off. He takes his knife and places the tip just below her chin. She remains still. He unties the lacings on her bodice, and as the bodice falls to her sides, he takes hold of her blouse and rips it open. Wilkins then grabs her by the throat and applies just enough pressure to cause her eyes to roll backward, passing out. He looks at her and cuts her remaining clothing down to her undergarments. Wilkens pulls her outer garments from under her and tosses them aside. He sits on her upper thighs and stares at her upper body through her silken undergarments. He starts fondling and groping her breasts.

Wilkins is so preoccupied with rubbing her breasts; that he does not see that Alexandria has regained consciousness. She is slightly disoriented until she remembers what had happened to her. Alexandria remains calm and slowly works her hands-free. She reaches up with one hand, and though disgusted, she places her hand on his thigh and squeezes. He responds by roughly groping her breasts. Distracted, she gets her hand on the belaying pin, and as she tries to throw him off, she removes the pin from his waist without him noticing. She then lays the pin on the floor, lets out a loud groan, and slides the belaying pin across the floor to end up between some crates. She has had enough and then brings her hand up, scratches him across his cheek and neck, and draws blood. He screams, sits straight up, and touches his neck with his hand. He pulls his hand away and sees blood on his fingers. Enraged, he punches her in the face breaking her nose and splitting her lip, and she nearly passes out from the punch. He cuts away her remaining undergarments and pulls down his pants. He gets off her thighs, spreads her legs apart, and forces himself between them, and within seconds, he has stolen her innocence.

She now lays on the floor, empty, lifeless, while he continues to thrust himself inside her. He finishes, and she feels his weight gone from her body, and she looks at him with pure hatred through slightly swollen eyes. He starts to button his pants, and a button pops off. He hears it hit the floor but doesn't see where it went, nor does he care. He has other things on his mind, leaves her lying where she is, and walks to the office. She hears him rummaging through the desk.

Wilkins finds the strongbox in the bottom drawer of the desk and places it on top of the desk. He forces the lock open and starts stuffing his pockets with coins. He then throws the strongbox to the floor.

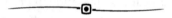

Alexandria lays there beaten and bloodied quietly on her back, sobbing. She reaches over to grab what remains of her torn clothing, pulling them towards her. Alexandria attempts to cover herself when she hears and sees the button fall from her clothes and roll on the floor. She picks it up and holds it in her hand.

Wilkins comes out of the office and sees her sitting against a crate. He steps over her, walks to the door, and then stops. He comes back and squats down beside her. She tries to move away, and he grabs her wrist so she cannot pull away. He leans forward and forcefully places a hard kiss on her smashed lips. When he pulls away, he takes hold of the small delicate gold medallion around her neck. Admiring it, she says, "Please no." he laughs and then snatches it from her neck, breaking the chain, and says to her, "Sorry Bitch! no witnesses," and runs a knife across her throat. Wilkins then walks over to where Jefferey and Sam are lying on the floor, lifts their heads, and runs his blade across their throats. He then walks over to the storeroom door, and before he steps into the ally, he turns back to look at

Alexandria and blows her a kiss. He then chuckles and steps into the alley to return to his ship.

Alexandria sits on the floor leaning against the crate, half-naked and feels her life slowly drain from her body. She sees Wilkens stop at the ally door, and through tear-filled eyes, she sees him blow her a kiss. She feels her heart slowing, and with her dying breath, and just before it stops, she softly speaks his name, "William," and dies still clutching a button in her hand.

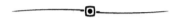

A few hours after it happened, a couple of the staff of the Bistro show up to start cleaning the place before the morning crowd, and as they head into the storeroom to get supplies, they discover the three bodies. They both scream as one tries to help, and the other runs outside to find help. Minutes later, the town militia has the Bistro closed and roped off. Soon a crowd is gathering and is asking what has happened. Rumors spread through the crowd that Jefferey, the eldest son of the Queen, Alexandria Platt, the fiancée' to Prince William, had been murdered. They found a third body, and they think it is Sam, the bouncer from the Bistro. Men and women pray that it isn't so, and others yell for the blood and who could have done this.

Ole Hito shows up, and the crowd parts to let him through, and then they see Prince William walking right behind him. The murmurs start, but all are for prayers for Prince William.

Ole Hito sees the bodies and asks everyone to leave the storeroom. No one argues or protests. William goes around to every window and closes the shutters. He then closes the two doors and seals them. The room is deathly quiet except for Ole Hito chanting softly and Williams breathing. Hito takes a couple of items from his bag and lays them on the floor. He continues chanting, and a blue smoke begins to rise from the objects on the floor and swirl around the three bodies. One tendril of smoke slithers across the floor to touch some crates. Ole Hito walks over to Alexandria first, lightly touching her face and then her head. He looks down and sees that she seems to be clutching something. He reaches down, pries open her fingers and removes a button from her hand. He then walks over to a small pile of stacked crates and asks William to help him move them. William does, and Ole Hito reaches down and grabs a heavy wooden pin off the floor. William recognizes it as a belaying pin from a ship and asks Hito if he can look at it. Ole Hito hands him the belaying pin, and as William turns it around in his hand, he can make out the initials carved into the wood. R.I.H. Hito goes over Jefferey, and Sam's bodies, lightly touch their heads, and turn them to examine the slashes to their throats. Ole Hito then stands and nods to William.

William then walks over to his brother's body, leans over, and places a kiss on his forehead; with tears in his eyes, he swears he will find out whoever did this. He does the same to Sam, who grew up with him and Jefferey. Both of them considered him family, and they loved him dearly.

William is hesitant, but he takes a deep breath and walks to his Alexandria. He kneels beside her and thanks whoever covered her body. William touches her hair and brushes it off her forehead. He sees the bruises and cuts and starts to get angry, and soon the beige, pink, blue, and white hues begin to materialize around his hands.

Hito is beside him and speaks softly, "William," as the four colors grow stronger and brighter. Hito just now realizes that William is manifesting the four sacred manas. In over nine hundred years, no one has ever been able to manifest all four manas since the Matriarch of the James Clan, Camille James.

Ole Hito is scared when he looks into Williams's eyes and sees that his eyes have changed to a dark sapphire blue with silver specks. William looks at him and calmly tells him, "Do not worry, my friend, as William brings forth the mana of *Spirit*. Hito sees William's eyes change from a sapphire blue with silver specks to a dark sapphire blue, almost black with gold specks. William brings forth the mana of *Spirit*, and Hito watches it wraps itself around the other four manas, and then a deathly quiet fill the room. William stands as Ole Hito kneels before him, saying, "*Kinoumi Gotenku.*"

William allows the five manas to reach out and encase the bodies of his brother Jefferey, his friend Sam, and his beloved Alexandria. Ole Hito watches as the slashes on their throats and Alexandria's cuts and bruises slowly disappear until it looks like the three of them are just sleeping. William releases the five manas, and his eyes are once again the color of brown. Hito remains kneeling when William walks over to him and says, "Get up, my friend, you are too old to be kneeling on a hard floor."

William reaches out his hand, Hito takes it, and as he helps him up to stand, Hito says, "Yes, you are right, my Prince. I am too old to be kneeling on hard floors.

At that moment, the bells start ringing, telling everyone that there has been a death in the royal family. White doves are released, informing others, and soon word spreads throughout the islands that a Royal Family member has died.

Chapter 11

The Kaisoshosuko

On the largest continent in the world of Chikyu, the Kingdom of Elenni refuses to lay claim to a portion of land, though it lies in the farthest northwestern part of their Kingdom. It is a barren region of land known appropriately as The Barrens. The oddity about the Barrens is that they have slowly been increasing their footprint on the land. Over thousands of years, the Barrens have reached out and swallowed up fertile lands that were once green and vibrant with life. These rich lands with thriving communities and villages are now abandoned and deteriorating.

No one knows how it came to be empty and desolate, but it is, and it is home to wild dogs, rodents, snakes, poisonous lizards, and other creatures that live among the stunted trees and coarse grasses that grow in the Barrens. The temperatures drop drastically from a severe, almost freezing at night to temperatures that rise well above scorching during the day. The animals that live in the Barrens have learned to cope and thrive in this forsaken land.

Caves and caverns are scattered throughout its many canyons, and deep gorges run through these canyons. On occasion, black diamonds can be found in these gorges. Small in size, they are a precious but very rare commodity. The most significant known piece was no larger than one's thumbnail. Many have traveled into the Barrens to explore the many caves looking for these rare diamonds; very few have found them. On several occasions, adventurers have gotten lost, only to have had parts of their bodies found by others. Usually, the features found are only pieces due to the scavengers that roam throughout the Barrens.

One of the utmost and unforgiving areas in the Barrens is a valley located in the northwestern part of the continent. Mountains surround the valley, with the highest peaks along the eastern border. These mountains continue north and gradually taper down to half the eastern ranges height at their most northern point. The mountains turn south and become just slightly lower as the range continues along the western border and gradually disappears into the upper highlands of the lands. As desolate as it is, the valley seems exempt from the harshness of the northern seas of wind and saltwater.

No one dares to venture into these upper parts of the Barrens due to some strange phenomenon that no one can explain. An imaginary line exists; when it is crossed, one is racked by headaches, nausea, and vomiting. If they persist, they would eventually become disoriented and possibly insane. Many have tried venturing north into the Barrens, hoping to find the elusive black diamonds scattered throughout the Barrens. These forsaken lands only exist north of several small plateaus that decorate the eastern mountain range. These plateaus only exist on the eastern mountains and look like something had come along and sheared off their peaks. The uniqueness is that only a couple of peaks seem to have been sheared off, and in their wake, plateaus with flat smooth surfaces remain. No one knows what could have caused this, but something had to have been traveling at an incredible speed and generating tremendous heat to do this to the mountains and continue on its projected path and strike the very base of the northern mountains. The ferociousness of the impact caused an eruption to blow out mass quantities of dirt and rock from the bottom of the mountain, causing the others in the range to shake and expose hidden riches. When the dust finally settled, an enormous cavern was exposed, and at the opening to this cavern was a ledge that jutted out over the valley floor. That ledge embodied riches, formed from the very substance that everyone desires and searches for. That embodiment is a massive black diamond precipice large enough for several people to stand on at once.

A full moon casts its glow over this desolate land, and the cavern's black diamond precipice seems to shimmer in its light. Though the nights are cold, the creatures of the night slowly venture out to hunt and scavenge for morsels of food. In the distance, one can hear the howls and screeches of the night creatures.

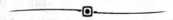

Guichi and Tanin have finally reached what they assume are the Barrens. They enter a large valley, and as they walk, they come upon an enormous black diamond precipice. They follow the path, and when they reach the top, they walk out to its edge and sit down. They both take a few deep breaths and then whisper very softly. It is almost indiscernible, but then it gradually grows louder. Soon, you can hear them whispering in the ancient language, *"Iku Hara Leku Komu Ket,"* The words flow outwards and latch onto the prevailing winds throughout the lands. Their whisperings touch the many who are branded and others who crave the same desires. People from all walks of life, from high-ranking individuals to murderers, thieves, cutthroats, prostitutes, and others of middle-class and poor standing throughout the lands, suddenly feel their brands pulse and grow warm.

Guichi and Tanin decide to leave than just wait, knowing they will come. Days turn into weeks, and then the first branded arrive, and they gaze upon the empty precipice, kneel and stare straight ahead as if in a catatonic state, with blank eyes in their eyes. Every day, more and more come to the northwestern valley in the Barrens. Every day they kneel and stare straight ahead, unmoving. In a few months, all the anointed have arrived to kneel before the empty precipice. The first branded have journeyed here from all over the lands, kneel, and wait patiently. These are the ones who Guichi and Tanin felt were the most devoted to believing in the Dark Scriptures. To go out and preach and spread their words. Thousands of others have been branded, but their time has not come yet.

The two brothers return and stand and look out over their congregation. They each raise one hand with their palms down and speak, *"Kagameru Arakajime Mokutekikaku,"* then pull back their hoods. The anointed see their Gods standing before them for the first time, and they immediately clasp their hands together and start chanting their names. Guichi, Tanin, Guichi, Tanin…The chanting continues as Guichi hands Tanin the piece of Dark Crystal and the leather-bound Tome of the Unholy Scriptures and then says, "Do not kill her!" Tanin smiles, then vanishes and returns to the cavern where his new congregation waits, along with his special guest.

Guichi raises his arms straight out in front of him with his hand made flat, he carefully sweeps it over the gathered anointed, and the chanting slowly dies out. He stops, points his finger at a single man in the crowd, and calls him forth. Guichi watches his approach and thinks he is the one to lead their congregation as he has all the characteristics of a person that others can look to for guidance.

He is pleased with the one he picked, tall, strong, and broad on the shoulders. The man climbs the slope to the precipice, drops to one knee in front of him, and casts his eyes down. Guichi tells him to rise and to follow him. The man does as he is told and follows Guichi into the cavern. They approach the stone altar, and then Guichi walks to the head of the altar and commands the man to remove his clothing and kneel on all fours upon the altar. The man removes his clothes and hesitates just the slightest before getting on the altar. Guichi sees the hesitation and knows that he has made a mistake. He waves his hand, and the man is thrown from the altar and lies crumbled on the cavern floor. Guichi approaches the man, and as he gets up, he throws a punch at Guichi. Guichi grabs the man by his throat with one hand and picks him up off the cavern floor with lightning speed. The man grabs at his throat, but to no avail. Guichi squeezes tighter until the man's eyes bulge out of their sockets, and his face turns purple. Soon, his tongue hangs out of his mouth, and every part of his body goes limp. His muscles relax, and bodily fluids spill out of his now dead body. He tosses the lifeless body to the side as if he were nothing.

Disgusted, he walks back out of the cave and again stands on the edge of the precipice. He chooses many candidates throughout the day, only to be disappointed repeatedly with the same results and cannot find one person to become their "Kaisoshosuko" for the leadership and teachings of Dark Scriptures. Guichi becomes more frustrated with every failure, and the bodies pile up.

He questions if he and Tanin were wrong in thinking that these branded anointed are the ones to help them fulfill their destiny, and he looks out over the gathered followers and is disgusted. He points his finger at one man, and the man begins screaming in agony as his body starts to burn and then crumble into a small, twisted ball. He is about to do it again when he stops and sees her kneeling in the crowd. He looks directly into her eyes, and she returns his stare unblinking. She removes her scarf and lets her hair fall free to cascade over her shoulders. He immediately notices her flaming red hair and how it hangs and compliments her features. He motions for her to come forward. She stands and walks up the path to stand almost defiantly before him and then gets down on one knee and bows before him, but not in a subservient manner.

Guichi stands there and thinks that maybe he has been wrong in their way of thinking, so why not choose a woman as a Kaisoshosuko? But he does not remember anointing many women with the brand, especially one so beautiful. He reaches out to Tanin, and all Tanin says is, "Kill her!"

Guichi thinks the same way, but curiosity has gotten the better of him, and he wants to see where this will go.

He takes her hand to help her stand and leads her into the cavern, and as they walk, he asks. "What is your name?"

She looks up at him and says, "Nova."

They stop just before the altar, he reaches over, brushes her hair back, and then pulls down her top to expose her shoulders and back, and he sees that she does not have the mark that he and Tanin have branded on so many. He steps back and quietly says, *"Moerutonoriko,"* conjures a ball of flame in his hand and asks her, "Who are you? Did my sisters send you here, and how did you come to the "Barrens" and not bear the sacred mark?"

She looks into his eyes and says, "I have told you, my name is Nova, and I do not require a mark to prove myself."

"How did you come to be here? Only the marked ones could hear the sacred words that my brother and I have spoken, so I ask you, how did you know to come here?" he asks.

"My Lord," she says, "All my life, I have heard a voice warn me of things or give me direction. The last time I heard the voice, it told me to go to the Barrens, so I made the journey here and saw others coming this way."

"What voice are you talking about"?

"My Lord, I cannot explain the voice I once heard. All I know is that it brought me here to the Barrens to pledge my allegiance to you and your brother and assist the two of you in your endeavors to rid the world of the Goddesses and fulfill my destiny."

Guichi says to her, "Tell me, Nova, What exactly is your destiny?"

Nova does not hesitate and tells him, "Why, to destroy your sisters of the light, to release the Dark God from his imprisonment, and most importantly to serve, my Gods Guichi and Tanin."

Guichi stands there for a moment and then says, "So be it, but I will tell you this, if you speak lies, you will die," he then tells her to remove her clothes and get on the altar.

She does as she is told without hesitation and sits on her heels with her hands folded in her lap. Guichi softly cups her chin and raises her face to his. He sees that her eyes are blue-green and cold. She has a delicate, slightly pointed nose with a dusting of freckles over the bridge and onto her cheekbones. Her cheeks are somewhat hollowed and slim to her smooth jawline, which ends in a small, rounded chin. Her complexion is flawless and smooth, accentuated by full sensual lips. His eyes travel downward to her two firm ample breasts. He gently grabs both sides of her face and stares deeply into her cold blue-green eyes. His eyes turn red, and Nova stares back at him without flinching. He projects the unimaginable horrors of murder, rape, slaughter, butchery, and unholy creatures as he did to the previous contestants. She does not shrink back as the others but looks back at him, smiling sexually with a hint of coldness. He lets one hand drop and keeps the one hand on her chin, and turns her face to the left and then back to the right, and he notices that her eyes never leave his. He lets go of her chin and tells her to remain as she is.

He steps to the side of the altar and runs his fingers along the length of her body. He stops in places that cause her to shiver. He moves around to the other side of the altar and continues the same ritual, stopping again in places with his fingers where she shivers even more. He slowly makes his way back to stand in front of her. He again cups her face in his hands tells her to kneel, and she does. He releases her face, and she looks down with her hands still folded in her lap, and her long flaming red hair drops to cover her breasts. She does not look up but feels something placed around her head. While still looking down, she sees a small chip of a Dark Crystal with blood-red veins running through it. Once the crystal touches the skin between her breasts, she hears the voice again, saying, "Kaisoshosuko" Guichi himself hears the voice and smiles, knowing now that he has Chosen correctly. Guichi bends down, takes her hands, and gently pulls her forward, so they are face to face.

He leans in close and presses his lips to her ear, "You will be my Kaisoshosuko, you will have the power to do my bidding, you tell me some voice told you to journey to the Barrens to fulfill a destiny, I have now heard that voice and believe you. I will tell you this: you have but one objective, and that is to obtain the *"Shingakusha Hoseki"* crystal, and if by chance the obliteration of the Laki-Jutsuk Religion and their beliefs were to unravel and my sisters should happen in the way, so be it. That, my sweet Nova, is your goal, or destiny if you want to call it that," and then pauses before he asks, "Do you understand?"

She nods her head in agreement.

He embraces her in a tight hug. "Good, he whispers, Nova," she tilts her head back to look into his now black eyes, "Mark or no mark, do not fail me!"

She leans forward, whispers in his ear, "I won't, my Lord," and kisses him on his cheek.

He helps her down from the altar, takes her hand, and places it on top of his. They walk side by side and proceed to exit the cavern. She realizes that she is wearing form-fitting garments to cover her nakedness. A white silk blouse covers her upper body and is open to display her cleavage and the dark crystal. Her hair is pulled back in a ponytail and is braided. She looks down and sees a black leather bodice that hugs her slim waist and pushes up her ample bosom to accentuate them but not in a whorish way. The leather is tight, and she likes how it hugs her body. She wears tight-fitting black leather pants that look almost painted on her and highlight her tight but curved bottom. She finds herself walking in thigh-high black stiletto-heeled boots. They walk out of the cavern to the edge of the black diamond precipice, and Guichi raises his hand for silence and speaks to the branded waiting below the precipice. "This is Nova; in the ancient language, she is now your Kaisoshosuko, and know that she has my blessing to create and destroy. You will assist her in fulfilling a destiny. Know this, that I have spoken, and this is the law. NOW! bow before your "Kaisoshosuko."

Everyone bows down by placing their hands on the ground and their heads on their hands.

He whispers in her ear, "Remember, do not fail me," and tells her, "I must go," and walks into the cavern.

Guichi leaves Nova and finds himself walking down a treacherous path as the pull leads him into the very bowels of the mountain. He is sometimes uncertain, but the draw is even greater than anticipated, so he continues deeper into the mountain. Rocks fall from above, and sections of path crumble beneath his feet. He does not know how long he has been walking, but the deeper he goes, the feeling gets stronger. He reaches a small insignificant cave and discovers it is a dead end, but he still feels the pull Guichi chants, *"Arakusa,"* and a light appears to cast a bright light causing shadows to flicker. He searches the small cave and finds nothing until he sees a shimmer of red underneath the caked-on dust on the walls. He approaches it and brushes away the caked-on dirt; he now sees what he and Tanin were searching for; embedded in the wall is a piece of Dark Crystal with blood-red veins running through it. He reaches out to remove it from the wall, and when his fingers touch the crystal, his mind is struck with visions of the battle that took place thousands of millenniums ago. Then he witnesses the entrapment of Nimponin, the implosion of the crystal, the creation of the vortex, the entrance to the Dark Realm, the attack on the gods, and finally, he sees several pieces of the dark crystal being cast out into space.

He drops to his knees, exhausted from the images that have impregnated his mind. Guichi is still shaking but stands and prepares himself for another onslaught of images. He takes a deep breath, again grabs the crystal, and tries to pry it from the wall. The visions start to overwhelm him, but he persists, and after a tremendous effort, and he is on the verge of passing out, something abruptly jolts him with a massive amount of energy, knocking him across the cave. Guichi tries to get up and feels the Dark Crystal in his hand. He now holds the very item that he and Tanin have been searching for, and he reaches out to his brother but gets no response.

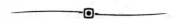

Just when Guichi disappears, Nova feels a slight tug on her finger. She looks down and sees a dark crystal about three carats in size, with blood-red veins wrapped in a delicate gold band on her finger. Nova is pleased with her actions and title of Kaisoshosuko and steps closer to the edge of the precipice.

She speaks loud and clear, "Rise my, Tashisans and hear me, go out into the world and spread the word of the Dark Scriptures and build our Gods and me an army."

They all start to leave except a few, who stand there defiantly.

Nova asks, "What of you, my Tashisans? Why do you not go out into the world as the others?"

One Tashisan, who seems to be the Leader of this small group, stands there silently, and when Nova demands that he speak up, the others standing around him start to shift their stances but remain defiant.

He shouts, "Why should we listen to you? You're a stupid bitch who fucked and manipulated her way into becoming our Kaisoshosuko. We all know that you are a whore, and weak, and like any good whore, you need to know your place. Why don't you come down here and let my friends and I put you on your back, where you belong. I demand you give up this farce and let us treat you like the whore you are?"

The others who stayed start grumbling, but Nova ignores them and looks at this one upstart and smiles. She is about to say something when she feels that Guichi has returned and walks out to the precipice to stand beside Nova and asks, "Why are they still here? Why have they not ventured out into the world? Have you already failed me, my Kaisoshosuko?"

My Lord, this is just a misunderstanding with a few Tashisans," answers Nova.

Under his breath, so only Nova can hear, he says, *"Moerutonoriko."*

Nova repeats the word, and a ball of flame starts to manifest in her hand. The Tashisans standing around the upstart fall to their knees, but the Leader ignores Nova completely and shouts out, "My Lord, we follow you and Tanin's beliefs; we think that a Priest needs to lead your Chosen and not some weak, stupid bitch!"

Guichi points his finger at the upstart and says, "How dare you to question my decision. You are nothing?" he forces the Leader to his knees, and before the Leader can say anything.

He whispers to Nova, "Show them!"

She bounces the ball of flame in her hand and then throws it at the upstart. The Leader and several others following him find themselves engulfed in flame. The heat is so intense that before anyone can scream, they are gone. The only remnants are piles of ash.

Guichi speaks again," Is there anyone else who wants to challenge my decision? "NOW GO!"

The remaining Tashisans are gone, and the area below the precipice is empty. Guichi feels something is wrong, turns to Nova, and says, "I must go. I have given you a gift, and Nova, and do not fail us," and remember I need an army that will dominate this world. Guichi vanishes, and Nova is alone.

She enters the cave, and as she comes to the altar, she sees the pile of dead bodies that her Lord deemed unworthy. Nova whispers, *"Moerutonoriko,"* and the flame materializes in her hand. She tosses it on the pile of dead bodies, and intense heat with a white flame engulfs the bodies, and soon there is nothing but ash. Nova notices something on the altar and sees a leather-bound tome. She picks up the Tome, opens it, and realizes she is holding the writings of Guichi and Tanin, the actual sacred Dark Scriptures, in her hands. Nova knows that this is the Sacred Tome that contains the words and beliefs of her Masters. She understands her destiny now and the other trials that she must bear to allow her Gods, Guichi and Tanin, to resurrect the one true God, to rain death and destruction throughout the world. She clutches the Tome close to her chest with tears in her eyes and says, "Thank you."

It has been over five years since the Tashisans have left the valley and traveled throughout the three kingdoms preaching the gospel of the Dark Scriptures. Some are branded as heretics and forced from villages and towns; others are stoned or thrown in jails; others are simply executed as evil worshippers.

The one thing that is for sure is that before these Tashisans are thrown in jail, stoned, or killed, their words have not fallen on deaf ears. Some want something better, something new, changes, and more.

Nova is sitting on the altar and leafing through the Tome', and a white silk cloth falls into her lap. She picks it up, sees writing on the fabric, and then places it back in the Tome'. She is pleased with the initial influx of followers who have come to the Barrens to pledge their allegiance to her Gods and preach the teachings of the Dark Scriptures.

While her Tashisans were out spreading the word, she had been researching and practicing enhancing her powers by working on the spells from the Tome'. She has learned to control her powers with just a whisper through the readings and teachings of the Dark Scriptures. She stands and walks out of the cavern to the edge of the black diamond precipice and gazes down upon her followers. She sees the numbers, and they have traveled near and far to the Barrens to bear witness upon hearing the words preached by the wandering Tashisans. She feels it is time for the second phase of her plan, with the first being sending the Tashisans out into the world. She stands on the black precipice and says, "Hear me," and over twenty-five thousand followers camped before her, consisting of a mix of murderers, vagabonds, mercenaries, cutthroats, molesters, fathers, mothers, brothers, and daughters, look to her.

She raises her arm straight out from her side and chants. *"Ikuto Jishin Chujitsuna Rinuki Imaguri."* She holds the Tome' with her other. A breeze is felt, carrying a taste of saltwater, followed by the pungent smell from the northern seas. A thick fog gradually comes over the top of the mountains and slowly works its way down the sides. When it reaches the base of the mountains, the fog starts to roll itself slowly outward to canvas the valley. A strange concurrence happens when the rolling fog brushes some of the followers. They start grabbing their heads, screaming and convulsing, and fall to the ground shaking, while others drop to one knee as though nothing has happened. Soon the breeze dissipates the fog, along with the pungent smell. Those who had fallen to the ground screaming and shaking are now quiet. She sees that they have transformed into something she was never sure of and had seen only briefly in a dream. She sees several lying on the ground below the precipice.

Nova senses a presence behind her and turns with a ball of flame in the palm of her hand. She is surprised to find herself facing a man in a hooded black robe. She cannot see his face because his hood is pulled forward, but he drops to one knee.

"Who are you?" she asks while still holding the ball of flame in her hand.

In a gravelly voice, he says, "My name is Raspit."

"Where did you come from? Who sent you? and Why are you here?

He pulls back his hood, and she sees that he is wearing a blood-soaked white cloth over his eyes. She remembers that this is the same man who had visited her in her dreams when she was younger, but he was standing beside a pair of young-looking twins in her dream.

Priestess, I cannot explain where I am from or who sent me, but I can tell you why I am here. I am here for them, and he points in the general direction of the followers that were also once the murderers and molesters that are now just lying on the ground shaking. Seconds pass, and then she hears the sound and several distinct pops as red-robed figures appear from nowhere and are helping the disfigured ones up off the ground and into red robes. She watches as they wrap white cloths around their heads to cover their eyes, and within seconds the white material is saturated with blood.

Raspit tells her that they are called "Sutaraukaji." She looks at him and realizes he has no eyes, nose, or ears. He steps up to her, bows, and says, "My Priestess." She releases the flame, opens the Tome' and pulls out the white silk cloth with the ancient writings. She reaches out her hand, holding the fabric from the Tome'. He removes the old material and takes the one she is offering. He has the cloth in his hand, and she says to him, "Know this, Raspit, as he wraps the new fabric over his eyes and ties it in the back, and, he says, "Yes, my Priestess'" She watches the new cloth immediately saturate itself with an even darker almost black blood.

She looks at him and tells him, "Raspit, know this. You will be the Leader of these Sutaraukaji, and it will be your responsibility to see to their needs, do you understand?"

"Yes, My High Priestess"

"And Raspit, one more thing."

"Yes, My High Priestess?"

"Raspit, "Know that I will not accept failure. Now go!"

Raspit bows and slowly steps back.

During her conversation with Raspit, she now sees that other cutthroats and mercenaries that did not change have dropped to their knees and immediately started defacing their bodies and faces by slicing marks on their bodies. She will call them her "*Zokotarumo*" and then notices two men standing among them, conversing, and she signals for them to approach. They come to her, kneel and bow.

What are your names?" Nova asks.

"Colonel Frank Tomas, formally of the Basra Army, and this is my friend Byron Sayle who held the rank of Colonel," they both tell her.

"Gentlemen, do you devote yourselves to me, this order, the Dark Scriptures, and the Gods Guichi and Tanin?"

They both kneel and say, "Yes, Our Priestess."

She tells them to rise, and as they do, she sees that the "Zokotarumo" are still defacing their bodies and faces with small knives leaving scars. The two men stand, and she sees that they have taken knives to their bodies, but not to the extent as the others. She hears and listens to the murmurings through the crowd by others and then tells her two commanders that the "Zokotarumo" is under their command. Colonel Tomas, you will lead the Zokotarumo, and Colonel Sayle, you will be his second now go and join your Zokotarumo!"

"We are honored, Priestess; we appreciate your trust" they both kiss the ring on her finger and bow to her. They walk backward a few steps before turning and continuing down the ramp. She watches them call the "Zokotarumo," and they gather around them.

Men and women alike stand still and stare at Nova. They have a look that she has not yet seen from any others. She looks at the ones who just stare and thinks to herself, "I have found my guard," and calls them forth. They are five hundred strong and drop to one knee, placing the back of their fists to their foreheads as saluting her. She stands before the cavern entrance, raises her hands into the Air, says, "*Matta Totic Zemhita Doeritik,*" and then directs them into the cavern. They pass her, and unbeknownst to them, as they march through the entrance, the magic takes hold, and the qualities of an elite fighting force engrained into them. They will now serve only her and forfeit their lives to protect her. She tells them to remain in the cavern as she walks back out to the precipice. Satisfied, she looks out to the others, and then she sees him, a large, solidly built man who carries himself with authority standing by himself and staring at her. She summons him up to the precipice, and as he arrives, he comes to attention and salutes her.

He apologizes and drops to one knee, and asks for her forgiveness.

She asks, "What is your name?"

He responds, "Former Officer of the Imperial Army, General Picard Harris, my Priestess."

"General Harris, I need an army. One who follows orders with no questions and a leader carries out those orders. Will you be the commander of my army, General Picard Harris?"

The General stays kneeling, then looks up at her, says, "Yes, My Priestess," and reaches up to kiss the ring on her hand.

She tells him, "Go now, General, find me the army and build me a war machine."

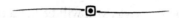

She stands there on the precipice and looks out over her army. She counts over one-thousand "Sutaraukaji," controlled by Raspit, four thousand Zokotarumo, or Freaks as they now like to be called, and Commanded by Colonel Tomas. Finally, a force of over sixteen thousand five-hundred regular army, commanded by General Picard Harris. Harris was a disgraced officer of the Empire who worshipped the Dark Scriptures in the Empire city of Fussu, and finally, five hundred Elite Guard. She has artisans from all makes of life blacksmiths, tanners, armorers, engineers, and weaponsmiths doing what they do best in equipping her army. Nova now has a large army but wants more, and she knows she needs one more faction: the Priests and Priestesses, to assist her in the magics. She knows they are out there somewhere, and she knows they will come.

She turns and goes back into the cavern and finds the five hundred men, sons, women, and daughters kneeling with all inhibitions gone, naked and incomplete submission. The five hundred kneel, and she can feel their acceptance and knows that they are hers.

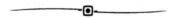

General Picard Harris is in his tent looking at the four kingdoms on the continent when he hears a knock on the tent's post. Harris tells whoever it is to enter and sees that it is his friend and comrade fellow General Buford T. Heath. He has known a man for many years and, like himself, was discharged from the Empire's military for worshipping the Dark Scriptures.

Harris and Heath, being top-ranking Generals in the Imperial Army, were disgraced and stripped of their ranks. Before being imprisoned for heresy, they fled the Empire and other devout followers. They were hiding north of Hokida when Picard heard the call. He and his men journeyed to "The Barrens."

Harris is looking over the map, and as Heath walks up to it, he tells him he has a mission. He proceeds to explain his plan, and Heath agrees with what he wants to do and tells him it is a good plan and it should not be difficult to recruit soldiers to establish a stronghold in the Empire. Picard pours two glasses of wine, and they toast to victory. General Buford T. Heath salutes General Picard Harris, turning and leaving the tent. The next thing Harris hears is Heath issuing orders to his subordinates.

Picard pours himself another glass of wine and stares at the map. He trusts his friend Heath and knows he will succeed in his plans. He knows that they will have to get the army to the northern pass of the Tammayaku Mountain Range undetected to succeed. If they can get there, then they can push through the pass and start to take control of the northern lands of the Empire. Harris finishes his wine and looks one more time at the area circled on the map, just east of the pass, and says the towns name, "Shira," and rolls up the map for safekeeping,

Chapter 12

Revenge Is Bitter Sweet

The sun is just breaking the horizon as Seaman Wilkins leans against the ship's railing, smoking his pipe and feeling proud. He only needs to wait another hour before the ship sets sail on the morning tide, and life is good. Captain Alloysius Temple has secured the rights to trade with the islands for the precious Painapp fruit. He hopes to be getting a big bonus when they return to their homeport in Ruxbury. The capital is on the main island in the Northern Isles chain, which lies just north of Massa mainland.

Wilkins believes that with the extra money he stole last night and stashed in his bunk and the bonus they will be receiving when they return to port, he should have enough money to marry that bar girl, Nala, who works at the local tavern where they dock. Wilkens remains leaning on the rail, thinking about his actions from last night and how he was able to get his revenge on the little whore that embarrassed him and on the other two for treating him like they did. The necklace with the gold locket he took from the little whore will look good on the neck of his girl Nala. The best thing was that he satisfied his urges after being at sea for a long time. He wonders if he should have just tied her up and then thinks, that bitch had to die because there should be no witnesses, and who will miss a lonely bar wench?

He snuffs out his pipe, dumps the ashes over the side into the water, and is about to head below deck when he hears bells ringing and wonders why so early in the morning. Then he hears some others in the distance. He thinks nothing of it and heads below deck to get some sleep, at least for an hour or so.

The crew is bustling around the ship to prepare for their cargo's arrival and get the ship ready to sail with the morning tide. The crew's *Spirit*s are high, knowing they will probably get a bonus when they dock in Ruxbury with the Painapp fruit. They know their Captain used his money to secure the trading rights for the fruit. Everything is almost ready as they wait for their cargo of Painapp fruit to arrive to take it home to their islands.

Captain Temple is on the quarter deck talking with his first mate Mister Breen when they see a squad of town militia marching up the docks towards his ship. The Captain and the first mate meet the Officer in Charge, a Lieutenant Welsh, to see what they can do for him, and the Lieutenant asks permission to come aboard. The Captain allows them to board, and The Lieutenant asks the Captain to join him off to the side. The crew watches the Lieutenant talking to the Captain, and the more he talks, the redder the Captain's face gets. Then they turn and see two other militiamen come on board, carrying a small chest, march up to Mr. Breen and place the chest at his feet. Then they hand him a small leather pouch, and the crew can hear coins jingling inside.

The Lieutenant stops talking, and the crew can see that the Captain is fuming and says, "That's preposterous!" and then calls Mr. Breen over, and the Captain explains what is happening. Breen steps away and blows the whistle to call all the sailors to line up on the deck. There is some grumbling because there is still work to do before the morning tide, but they follow orders. Breen reports to the Captain that all men are present and counted. The Lieutenant signals the squad of eight men to board the ship, and four of them follow Mr. Breen below deck.

A while later, Breen and the four militia appear back on deck, and Mr. Breen is holding an article of clothing and what looks to be other items in his hands. He walks up to the Captain and the Lieutenant and shows them. The three of them converse momentarily, and then Mr. Breen blows the whistle again to a different tune, and the men come to attention.

The Captain approaches the men and calls sailor Wilkins to step forward. Wilkins does as he is told and steps forward. Mr. Breen notices the fresh scratches on Wilkin's cheek and neck.

The Captain asks, "Sailor Wilkins, are these your trousers?"

Wilkins looks at the trousers and sees his name stenciled on the waistband. The Captain asks him again, "Sailor Wilkins are these your trousers?"

Wilkins says, "Yes, Sir, those are my trousers. Does there seem to be a problem?" Sailor Wilkins, can you tell me where the missing button to your trousers is?" Wilkins answers, "No, Sir, It must have fallen off on the ship somewhere.

Then the Captain asks, "Wilkins is this your gold locket and chain?" Wilkins responds, "No, Sir, I have never seen that before. May I ask where it came from?" The Captain doesn't answer.

"Wilkins, where did you acquire all this coin from the Sovereign of Aleu?" Before answering, the Captain asks, "Wilkins, how did you come about those scratches on your cheek and neck?"

"From a rambunctious bar girl, Captain," Wilkins replies.

Breen says, "Excuse me, Sir, and calls Sailor Wells. Wells takes three steps forward, saying, "Yes, Mr. Breen," and saluting.

"Sailor Wells, Can you please tell me what transpired last night after you left the ship, and who was with you?"

Wells looks at the Captain, Mr. Breen, and then at Wilkens and proceeds to tell them that Slips, Darno, and Wilkens were with him and everything that transpired last night until they got back to the ship.

Mr. Breen says, "Thank you, Sailor Wells," and then calls out Sailor Molt.

Molt steps forward and salutes.

Breen asks him, "Sailor Molt, you were on watch last night. Did anyone leave the ship, after hours, and everyone was accounted for?"

Molt is nervous and then says, "Sailor Wilkens left the ship about three bells and told me he would be right back because he thinks he left something at the restaurant they were at. When he returned around the fourth bell, I asked him if he had found what he had lost? And he said, "Yes, and much more."

Mr. Breen notices the bandage on his hand, asks him what happened to his hand, and asks to see it. Wilkens places his hand behind his back and tells Breen not to worry about it. He had a doctor in town look at it.

The Captain says, "Sailor Wilkens, remove that bandage, NOW!"

Wilkens does as he is ordered and removes the bandage; Mr. Breen looks at it and sees a distinct bite mark between his thumb and index finger.

The Lieutenant produces a belaying pin and asks if it belongs to this ship. Mr. Breen asks to take a look, then he hands it back and says, "Yes, it does have the markings for this ship, the Horizon." Then, Mr. Breen asks for a moment. He performs a quick walk around the ship's railings, and when he comes back, he reports that one of the pins is missing from Wilkins's station. The Captain clears his throat and says, "Sailor Wilkins, you are under arrest for the murder of a Royal family member and a citizen of the Tatokai Archipelago. You will also face charges of the murder and rape of a prestigious noblewoman who was the fiancée to the Queen's second son Prince William James.

"Lieutenant Welsh, you may take him away and tell the Royal family that I am sorry" Wilkins struggles as four militia place him in shackles and then drag him down the gangplank to take him off the ship.

As they drag him away, Wilkins starts screaming, "What did I do? Why are you doing this? I'm innocent, I tell you, I'm innocent!" Wilkens calls out to his friends, "Slips, Darko, help me, you know me, I'm innocent." The two of them turn their back on Wilkens.

The Captain approaches the crew and says, "Last night, a woman was murdered in town, and she was the daughter of a high nobleman from the Island of Pilka, and this woman was also betrothed to the second son to the present Queen of the throne, Prince William James of Aleu. The establishment's proprietor was the first son of the reigning Queen. The third person was a local native that worked for the establishment and was close to the Royal family. The restaurant in question was the one that Wilkins and a few of you ate at last night. Some workers found all three with their throats cut his morning; the two who found them said the woman looked beaten and raped. The Captain brings up the trousers, which belong to Wilkins that the first mate had brought up from below deck, and explains the missing button. He then tells the crew that Mr. Breen also found a locket in Wilkins' bunk, and he stole the locket from the young lady. I know this because Lieutenant Welsh told me it was a gift from the second son as a betrothal necklace. The Royals of the islands are the only ones who can possess such a necklace, and Wilkins probably assumed it was just another trinket, not knowing the island traditions when he stole it from the young lady.

The sailors start to grumble again, and the first mate steps forward. "Now listen up you, shit for brains, Wilkins screwed us all over; because of him, we have missed the morning tide. That means we must leave tonight on the evening tide when it is dark, and we all know how dangerous that can be. Just so you know, our trading rights for the Painapp fruit that the Captain worked so hard to negotiate for, have been canceled so that you can forget about any bonuses, and you can all thank Wilkens for that.

Breen shows the crew a handful of coins and then kicks the crate by his feet, and when he does, it tips over, and all the trinkets they brought from the Northern Isles spill onto the deck, and Breen tells them this is what we sailed all this way for, and again, you can thank Wilkins. Mr. Breen dismisses the men, grumbling; as they start to break up, Breen tells them, "Don't get any ideas about leaving the ship because we are all confined to the ship until this evening's tide. The men grumble even more, and Mr. Breen hears Wilkens's name taken in vain many times.

The Captain proceeds to his cabin to write his report.

That night just before the sun sets, Wilkens is in a cell beside the office of the Militia's Commander and can just make out the masts of the sailing ships in the harbor. He sees some movement in the harbor and the Northern Isles flag moving away from the docks. and he stands there and says, "Son of a bitch, those bastards left me," He thinks to himself, when I get out of here, I'm going to get every one of them." He then hears the cell door opening, and he sees standing in the doorway of his cell two of the biggest guards, and they are both smiling.

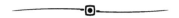

The following day, Wilkins is dragged before the Commander of the Royal Militia in shackles and forced to stand at the prisoner's podium. There are definite signs of a beating, with dried blood on his clothes, one of his eyes is swollen shut, and he seems to be missing a couple of teeth.

The Commander asks, "What has happened to this man?"

One of the guards holding him says, "He fell down the stairs, Sir."

The Commander clears his throat, reads the charges, then asks, "Sailor Wilkens, how do you plead?"

Wilkins stands there, and under his breath, he mutters, "Fucking Bitch," One of his guards hears this and forces him to the floor, saying, "Watch your language, you Bastard."

"Prisoner Wilkins, if you do not answer, I will presume you are guilty. "So, I will pass sentence; in two days, you will be transported to the Isle of Botaku to work in the "Pits" and will never see daylight again for the rest of your life."

He has heard the guards outside his cell talk about the "Pits" and how if it were either one of them, they would prefer death than having to go to the "Pits" Wilkins' knees start to buckle, but his guards hold him up.

Wilkens is escorted to the dungeon below to wait for transportation to "The Pits."

William James walks out of the Militia Hall where the sentencing occurred and does not believe that the punishment fits the crime. Life in the "Pits" is not a suitable punishment for what he did to his sweet and beautiful fiancée Alexandria, his brother Jeffrey, or his good friend Sam. William heads down to the docks and inquiries about what ships are sailing on the morning tide.

One of the dockworkers points to a ship bustling with activity. William sees sailors clambering all over the deck and sails. He walks up to the gangplank and asks permission from the Captain to come aboard. The Captain says "Yes," and William steps onboard. He briefly talks with the Captain, and William secures passage on the ship when it departs on the morning's first tide.

Just before he places a small bag of gold coins in the Captain's hand, he looks into the Captain's eyes and says, I hope this will cover the better part of discretion!"

The Captain tosses the bag in his palm and says, "Of course, completely, as long as it is not illegal!"

William assures the Captain that it is not and only buys him safe passage.

That night William stops by his sister's room and sees that she has been crying since it happened. Kendra is an emotional wreck because not only did she lose her older brother, but she also lost her best friend.

She and Alexandria grew up together until Alexandria's duties called her away, but that was only to her family's estate on one of the other islands. They constantly stayed in touch and always met up for special occasions. William sits in one of the chairs and asks Kendra to sit with him. When she does, he takes her hands in his and says, "Kendra, You are my sister, who I love most dearly, and I will tell you that I do not think that sending that bastard to the "Pits" to live out his life, is a punishment that fits the crime, especially for what he did to our family and friends.

Kendra looks at him and asks, "What are you thinking, William?"

"Kendra, my sweet, Whatever you hear, believe that I love you and my family most dearly. When the day comes and you are appointed Queen, I want you to know that I give you my blessing, and I believe you will make an excellent Queen."

Kendra sits dumbfounded and asks, "William, what do you mean when I am appointed Queen, and you give your blessing. Are you not going to be here?" Then she looks at William and sees why he is giving his blessing.

William stands, as does Kendra. She embraces him in a tight hug and whispers in William's ear, "I'll miss you" William can tell that Kendra understands completely. She asks him, "What do you have in mind?" William says, "The less you know, the better, and please tell everyone I'm sorry and that I love them." William embraces Kendra one last time, and just before he leaves the room, he stops at the door, turns and smiles, and then Kendra says, "Make him pay dearly for hurting our family and friends." William nods and then steps into the hallway and closes the door. Just before the door is closed, he hears Kendra break down again, knowing she has just lost another brother.

William makes his way to a different part of the manor to make one more stop before continuing with his plan. He knocks on a door, and it opens slightly. William hears a woman sobbing in the back. He speaks with the man at the door, saying, "Thank you, and be careful," and closes the door. William stands there feeling the pain and sorrow of losing Alexandria and says, "I will," to the closed door.

It is getting late as William walks through the catacombs to the prison cells. A selected few only know the catacombs that run throughout the Capital of Aleu. These catacombs were built for the Royal Family to escape if the islands ever came under attack. It is also where his grandmother Camille James is laid to rest as her final resting place.

William knows these catacombs very well from when he and Jefferey were younger. They explored and played inside them and had marked the tunnels in a secret code to avoid getting lost. They discovered their grandmother's tomb, and after, they agreed never to return. One night William was awoken and was called to the tomb of his grandmother, and when he entered the tomb, he was met by her essence and awarded the power of the five manas. William never told anyone, not even Jefferey, until Ole Hito witnessed him using the five manas to clean up the vicious attacks on Jefferey, Sam, and his beloved Alexandria. He keeps walking through the catacombs, and enthusiasm is replaced by hate as he thinks of what this lowlife did to his family. While he walks, he sees the five manas swirling around his hands as he gets closer to his quarry.

He approaches what looks like a dead-end and reaches over, and pushes on a stone. There is a soft click, and the wall slides open. William steps through and is in the corridor with prison cells on both sides. He quietly walks up to each cell and looks in. When he reaches the third cell on the right, he finds who he has been looking for and quietly slides the locking bolt open.

William steps inside and walks up to Wilkins and finds him shivering and sleeping under a threadbare blanket. William also sees more bruises from an additional beating that he probably received from the guards.

William quietly and quickly places a hood over Wilken's head, and before he can scream, William hits him in the head with the handle of his knife, and his body goes limp. William gets to work, and twenty minutes later, he throws a bucket of ice-cold water on Wilkins.

The cold water awakens Wilkins, and he coughs and sputters only to find it challenging to move. His vision is blocked, and he cannot see anything through the darkness. He is disoriented but knows he is hanging in the Air by his wrists, and his legs are in a spread-eagle position. He hears footsteps in the dark and senses that they have stopped before him. William reaches up, rips the hood from his head, and wipes the water from his eyes using a filthy rag. Wilkins then sees a young man standing in front of him, who appears to be no more than eighteen years old.

"Who are you?" Wilkins asks.

"Doesn't matter who I am. The only thing that matters is that you will give me answers to my questions, and I only have a couple."

"What questions?" asks Wilkins

"Why did you murder those three people and rape that young girl?" asks William.

Wilkins is defiant, ignores the question, and says, "Listen here, boy. You just cut me down, and I won't complain about this ungodly behavior."

William backhands Wilkens across the mouth and says, "I don't care about you complaining. I think you're a rabid animal that should be put down and not cut down." William then stuffs the same filthy rag in his mouth. Wilkins glares at him with hatred in his eyes.

William places the tip of a very sharp, slender blade against Wilkins' chest and draws it across his chest. Wilkins screams through the rag. When William stops with the knife, he removes the rag and asks him again, "Why did you do it? Wilkins doesn't say anything.

William looks at him and says, "I will give you one last chance to tell me the truth, and it is a simple yes or no answer. "Did you rape and murder that young girl?"

Wilkens hangs there, says nothing, and then spits in William's face.

William wipes the spit from his cheek and then says, "If you do not tell me the truth, we will have to take it to the next level."

Wilkins asks, "What do you mean next level? From what I understand is that I'm going to the Pits. What could be more next level than that? Now please, Fuck off."

"Let's just say it is a test, shall we?"

"A test, what kind of test?" he asks.

"Last time, did you kill that young girl and the two others?" he asks.

He looks William straight in the face and says, "No!

William shakes his head, places his fingertip on Wilkins' right ankle, and stands there as if nothing is happening.

Wilkins looks down and sees a blue mist slowly encompass the man's hand; and asks, "What are you doing?" and then feels his foot start to get very cold and soon numb. The cold starts to creep up his leg slowly. He can no longer feel his foot, and soon the same goes for his lower leg. Wilkins squirms and thrashes against his restraints, against the burning coldness.

Suddenly he has a sense of freedom as his foot comes free of its restraint.

William asks him again, "Why did you kill those three people?"

He again denies it, and William says, "So be it."

William touches his other ankle, and once again, Wilkins begins to squirm and thrash against the oncoming burning coldness. He senses that his leg has come free from the restraint and starts laughing and says, "What's wrong? Are you finally admitting I am an innocent man, so you cut my restraints to let me down?" Wilkins starts laughing.

William looks at him and says, "Cutting the restraints whatever gave you that idea? I am merely providing you a service by releasing the pressure on your legs, so why don't you take a look for yourself?"

Wilkins looks down at his legs to find that he is as he thought, free from his restraints, but he sees that his knees have turned into black stumps. He looks down on the cell floor and sees the lower parts of both legs have turned even blacker than the stumps and are on the floor beneath him. Before he can scream in disbelief, William shoves the filthy rag back in his mouth to stifle his screams and says, "That is a severe case of frostbite!"

He is screaming through the rag, and William very carefully takes his blade and cuts away his trousers, and with the tip of the blade, he lifts his manhood, allowing the same cold that he placed on his legs to travel over the blade encasing his scrotum. Wilkin feels the chill below, begins screaming through the rag in his mouth and then cries.

William tells him, "I am not a cruel man no matter how much you might deserve all of this because you violated my fiancée and murdered her, as well as murdering my older brother and our best friend, but I ask you, would you like me to stop the pain?"

Wilkins nods his head yes.

William reaches up, removes the rage from his mouth, and asks, "Well, should I continue?"

Wilkins begs, "Please, no more, I did it. I raped and killed that bitch along with those other two!"

William backhands him hard across his mouth and cautions him about using his language when referring to his beloved Alexandria. Then asks, "Why? You could have left them alone or tied them up and walked away. By morning you could have been on your ship sailing home with the precious cargo your Captain wanted before they probably could have escaped."

Wilkins says, "That bitch!" this time, William punches him right in the mouth, splitting his lip wide open and loosening some teeth. Wilkins spits out some blood and a tooth and says, "Because she saw me with the bloody belaying pin in my hand and realized what I had done to the two men."

William pulls over a stool, sits down, and then says, "Let's change the subject, shall we." William takes a sip of water and sees that Wilkens wants some. William ignores him and says, "Did you know that we as royals inherit a power associated with the natural elements of these islands? My brother Jefferey the man you murdered, was strong in the element of Earth. My sister Kendra, our next Queen, is powerful in Fire, but she also has an infinity with Air and is very good at both. My younger sister Kelli has not come into her powers yet, but we all think that water will be her element, but these powers do not usually appear until one's thirteenth birthday."

William then asks if he knows about the elements, and Wilkens nods.

William says, "Good," because we don't have that much time for a history lesson, and continues, "I am telling you this because these four elements are very powerful, individually, but bring them together, it would be a power beyond belief. The only problem is that bringing the four manas together will be wild and almost uncontrollable."

Wilkins remains still and silent. William asks him, "Do you understand?"

Wilkens asks, "Why are you telling me all this?

"Well, Mr. Wilkins, I am telling you this for one reason. There has never been a royal who could conjure all four elements simultaneously. Only once has this happened, and that was when my grandmother, who first came to these islands many generations ago, was able to unite the four manas, which magically united the islands. When that happened, the islands bestowed upon her the ability to call forth the fifth mana."

As if answering for him, William looks at him and says, "What do you mean five manas? Everyone knows that there are only four?" as Wilkins hangs there and continues to stare at him.

William ignores the look and continues, "As I was saying, "Since the unity of the islands, almost a thousand years ago, Tatokai Prophecy foretold that someone of royal blood would inherit the ability to manifest all four manas. The four manas would be wild and uncontrollable, and a catalyst would be needed to harness their power. Once the four manas are woven together, the fifth mana known as "*Spirit*." would be called upon to bind them together.

"Wilkins, you should feel honored because you will be the second person to witness and experience firsthand the powers of the five manas or elements, as I like to call them."

Wilkins starts swinging his arms as if to break free and starts to scream.

William shoves the rag back into his mouth, conjures the first element of *Fire*, and lets it flow from his hands to caress Wilkin's body. Wilkins starts screaming as the flames at first singe off all the hair on his body, and then it slowly begins to blister his skin. William then conjures *W*ater and a frigid *Air* and allows the two of them to flow over Wilkins' body, which is now oozing with blisters. He feels the relief, but it is short-lived, as William now brings forth the Earth mana. He watches as the very floor of the cell that he is hanging above reaches up to encase the stumps of his legs, and then he feels the very earth itself begin to tighten, and once that happens, he hears his bones begin to snap as the rag still in his mouth stifles his screams. With the *E*arth mana anchoring his body, William brings forth four tiny separate tendrils of mana and weaves them together in a finely twisted spiral. The four elements slowly tighten around each other, and when William feels the resistance, he brings forth a clear, pure feeling of *Spirit* and allows it to wrap itself around the four woven manas. The four immediately settle down, and then William says, "*Chikashinmizawa To Shi Ta Ko,*" and the now five manas blend as one into an intricately woven snake.

William wills the mana to wrap itself around Wilkins' body, and as Wilkens feels it slithering over his body, he spits the filthy rag from his mouth. He says to William, "I enjoyed every minute of fucking …, and that is all he can get out, as the *"Kinabi"* rears back and forcefully rams itself into his mouth, cutting off his last words.

William was going to leave him alive and a legless eunuch but changes his mind, after his last outburst. Wilkins sees the slithering mana serpent entering his mouth and sliding its way down his throat. William looks down to see his stomach start to pulse and become bloated. Wilkins feels the pressure in his stomach and tries to look down, but he can't and feels his stomach slowly expanding. The pain is excruciating as his insides continue to grow. Wilkens feels the tendrils slowly work from inside his organs to under his skin. He watches in disbelief as his skin begins to pulse and throb. He feels his blood vessels swelling just under the surface of his skin. William wills the Kinabi into smaller tendrils throughout his body and then manipulates them so that they break the surface of his skin in several places. Wilkin tries to scream, but the Kinabi in his throat stifles his scream. The tiny tendrils that have broken the surface of his skin begin to caress and encircle his body. William watches him hanging there like a piece of flayed meat and then walks up to him, lifts his chin, looks him straight in the eyes, and says, "For my Alexandria," and wills the tendrils to slowly constrict themselves. William watches as Wilkins' body is crushed by the coils of the *"Chikashinmizawa."* When done, the only thing remaining is a piece of burnt meat with broken bones hanging by two arms that are just as charred and broken. William steps right up to Wilkens's face, looks him in the eyes, and says, "That was for my Alexandria." William hears Wilkens moan.

William releases the manas, and as he looks at Wilkens, he says, "This is for my brother, my friend!" He then slowly pushes his blade with the family crest into what used to be his side, and as a reminder, he leaves it embedded in the hanging ball of flesh. William exits the cell and slides the locking bolt in place. He makes his way back down the hallway to the hidden passage. He steps through, and he hears the guards returning from their break. He secures the secret door and hurries through the catacombs. He knows that he hasn't much time before they find the body or what's left of it.

He makes his way through the catacombs, and he stops in front of Camille's tomb and places his palm on the door. He whispers, "I am sorry," and feels the embrace of forgiveness and love, then continues on his way.

William knows that he has just sealed his fate, even though being a royal, he is not exempt from the laws, and he could end up in the very Pits that Wilkens himself was being sent for the rest of his life. He knows he must leave the islands, and he also knows that he cannot put his family through what he just went through. Even though the guards have returned, hopefully, they won't check on Wilkins for another couple of hours when it is time to either feed him or prepare him to travel to the Pits.

He heads back to the citadel through the tunnels and comes out in one of the smaller rooms used for storage. He opens the storage room door, checks the hallway, and exits the room. He walks to another door, knocks four times, and hears, "Come in."

William walks in and says two words, "It's done," and walks up to an older gentleman wearing a royal crest himself and says to William, "I'm sorry that you had to do this."

William tells him not to worry about it, his daughter Alexandria was his betrothed and his beloved, and she deserved revenge, so hopefully, her *Spirit* can rest.

Sir Henry Platt shakes William's hand and embraces him. He hands William a small sack of gold and a rolled parchment and tells William that it is a line of credit to help him in his travels. William tries to give the gold back, but Sir Platt insists and tells William that if he ever needs anything, anything at all, all he has to do is reach out to him, and he will do everything in his power. William says, "Thank you." He shakes Henry's hand, walks over to Alexandria's mother, kisses her on top of her head, and says, "I'm sorry that I could not protect her." then turns and leaves the room quietly. He hurries to his room and packs a bag of essentials and a change of clothing. He sees the sun coming up and knows he needs to get to the docks before the morning tide. Having already paid for his passage, he hurries to the docks. The ship is ready to pull away as the last mooring lines are released and secured. William jumps to the ship's deck from the dock and asks the Captain, "Permission to come aboard!" The Captain laughs and says, "Of course, and then hands William a package wrapped in leather.

The Captain says, "From a friend on the dock."

William is standing at the ship's railing, looks back at the dock, and sees a lone hooded figure standing in the shadows. The figure steps out of the shadows and pulls back the hood just enough so that William can see that it is his sister Kendra. William sees her reach up and touch her temple, and he does the same. It was something that they came up with when they were younger to let each other know that things were good between them. The ship pulls farther away, and a small cross wave hits the ship as it catches the outgoing tide. William momentarily takes his eyes off the dock. When he looks back, he sees the end of a dark cape disappear around a corner, followed by several heavily armed militia, and his sister is gone.

He leans against the rail, looks down at the package, and unwraps it. Inside he finds the crafted blade with the royal crest that his brother Jefferey gave to him on his eighteenth birthday, and it is also the knife he left embedded in what was the remains of Wilkens's body. The blade is in a sheath that can be strapped to his arm or leg. Folded in the package is a note. He unfolds it and reads,

> "Dearest Brother, The guards are loyal to me. Take care, I love you, Kendra, *and he then sees at the very bottom,* "Thank you, Your Little Sister."

He remains leaning against the rail with his back to his homeland. The act is not treasonous, but he knows he can never return, even though his sister said he can. He thinks back to his grandmother's words and knows she was right, pain, sorrow, and leaving his home by his own hand.

Chapter 13

A Special Guest

Laki and Jutsuk are sitting on the grass in the Plains of Sayashi and discussing the rumors circulating throughout the Kingdoms about their brothers' religious beliefs and teachings. Fanatics gather to worship the evil and lack of morals through a book called the Dark Scriptures. The followers somehow justify the debauchery and human sacrifices that seem to be springing up in cities and towns.

The one rumor that concerns them the most is that Guichi and Tanin have gotten their hands on a piece of dark crystal, and they are desperately searching for another. Another rumor is that they somehow have opened up a doorway between our realm and the dark realm to bring strange-looking beasts and creatures into the world. Some witnesses say that caves in remote areas allow these creatures to enter our world.

The sisters hear of a strange phenomenon of two armies from two different countries have disappeared without a trace. They decide to check it out, and they head west over the Ishidosida Mountains to the two smaller kingdoms of Glock and Tesh. They both agree that if they separate and one goes to the Tyne, the Capital of Glock, and the other were to go the Joh, the Capital of Tesh, they would find out what they could and then meet where the incident took place. The following day, they meet at the crossroads and examine the remnants of the caravans' wagons. They are at a loss when the winds change slightly, and then they smell it, a very faint pungent smell of something that is not familiar. They notice some scattered dark patches in the grass and approach one of the dark patches, and out of nowhere, a nauseous feeling sweeps through them, and they feel that something massive has happened in this very spot.

They sense that something is wrong as they find a larger area of patches of the scorched grass and the residual essence of an enormous slaughter. They can feel the presence of two armies fighting for their lives at the crossroads between their borders. They search the area and discover the remnants of something vile, emitting its stench from a few of the surrounding caves.

They agree to go out and find their brothers and try to reason with them. They cannot just sit idly by and allow any of the dark crystals to be discovered or brought into this world and ultimately joined. They agree to reach out to each other when the time comes to confront them, and they will do it together. The Goddesses enter the Spiritual Domain and go their separate ways to look for Guichi and Tanin.

They both head east from the kingdoms of Glock and Tesh, and then Laki turns southeast as Jutsuk continues to the east, as they both reach out with their senses, trying to find their brothers. They both come across remnants of their brothers being here or there but still do not find them.

It is almost the end of the day, and Jutsuk is just about to reach out to Laki and tell her that she has found nothing when she hears a soft, bleating sound of distress. Jutsuk floats down to the surface, and just before her feet touch the grass, she enters the Earthly Domain and dons a sheer cloth shift tied at her waist. She walks through the lush green valley, feeling the warmth of the setting sun on her face and enjoying the smell of wildflowers. Then she hears bleating noise, and she walks a little farther, and when she comes across the source of the noise and finds a newborn fawn entangled in some thorny vines. She untangles the fawn and watches it run off to its mother. She then notices that the thorned vines seem to be concealing a large opening, and then she hears just above a whisper, many voices chanting as one. She removes the thorned vines and steps through the opening, and she finds herself in a small cave with a path leading downward. She can now make out the monotone hum of the voices chanting in an unfamiliar language. Jutsuk knows she should reach out to Laki, but she wants to see if her brothers are here. She also wants to see for herself before she reaches out to Laki and interferes with her search. She finds herself slowly walking a wide path that leads downward ever deeper into a series of small caves, and she sees several side passages. She remains on the main path, and she can hear the chanting growing louder, and then she feels something powerful and unnatural as she continues downward.

She arrives at the end and sees that she is on a cliff that overlooks an enormous cavern, and then she sees a path to her left that leads down to the cavern floor. Carefully, she approaches a crop of stalagmites and peers through a gap between them. The cavern is much larger than she first thought, and she sees about five hundred people below on the cavern floor, all standing and chanting. She then hears a deep, robust voice above all the others and looks about the cavern to see where it came from, and everyone starts to kneel.

She now sees notices the raised altar, and she sees a person whom she believes to be a man by his mannerisms, standing at the head of the altar, and she watches him climb onto the altar and then kneel. He remains kneeling as she then sees a woman in an almost sheer sleeveless robe that is tied at her waist climb onto the altar and crawls over to the man who remains kneeling, and he stares at the woman before him.

She sees him place his hands on the woman's shoulders, and she can tell that her body is shaking. The woman's sheer robe hides some of her features, but Jutsuk can see that she has long brown hair and a gorgeous figure the way the robe hugs her body. She cannot see her face as her hair hangs down and covers both sides of her face. Jutsuk then sees a second-robed figure climb up on the altar, and he stands behind her. The man standing raises his hand, and she sees that he has a leather whip in his hand, and for some reason when the followers see this, the undiscernible chanting starts to get louder.

Two other women approach the altar, and she watches them unbutton the woman's robe, who is still kneeling on all fours. They let the robe fall away from her upper body. The man kneeling in front of her reaches out and grabs her hair in his fist. Jutsuk sees that the woman is exceptionally beautiful both in her face and body, and she can also see that she is a woman of prominence, as she sees gold and silver bracelets adorning her upper arms.

Jutsuk has never witnessed anything like this before and is mesmerized by what is happening. The man standing behind the woman reaches over and grabs the bottom part of her sheer robe and throws it to one side, exposing her buttocks. His hand already holding the leather whip and having it raised, he brings the whip down and strikes the woman across her buttocks. Jutsuk cannot take her eyes off the woman and watches even more intensely when she hears the woman moan, and she sees that the woman seems to be enjoying it. The woman reaches up to open the man's robe kneeling in front of her, and she reaches in to release his manhood.

She takes it in her hands and opens her mouth. Jutsuk watches as the man has the woman's hair in one hand and places his other hand on her head to draw her in, as he begins to thrust his hips at the same time. She looks back to the man standing behind the woman and sees that he is not there.

Jutsuk is appalled and tries to turn away but finds herself staring more intently at what this man is doing to this woman. The woman seems to be enjoying every moment of what is happening to her, and then she sees the man let go of her hair and watches as his body shudders, and as he does, he throws his head back, and his hood slides back, and she sees that it is her brother Tanin. She looks again for the other, knowing it is Guichi but does not see him.

She knows she needs to find Laki with the utmost certainty and tries reaching out to her, but feels nothing, and then tries again, and the same thing, nothing. She panics and starts to back up, hoping to leave, when her senses tell her something is wrong, and then she feels a thin shroud begin to encapsulate her. She finds that she cannot enter the Spiritual Domain or form. She has never felt this way before, and she begins to panic even more as her mother's words come back to her about being trapped in the Earthly form. Then she hears a voice from behind, saying, "Hello Sister, are you looking for me, and did you enjoy our little performance?" and with the help of two big men, they grab her. Guichi steps around them and one of the men grabs her hair and pulls her head back. Guichi forces her mouth open and pours a warm liquid down her throat, and she is obligated to swallow.

She is forced to drink the liquid and almost chokes and starts coughing. She catches her breath and almost immediately feels nauseous. The onslaught of nausea causes her vision to start to fade in and out, and she feels her body begin to collapse. She then feels two sets of hands holding her up, then lift her in the Air, and then hears Guichi say, "Bring her." Jutsuk, now semi-conscious, realizes that she is being carried down one of the paths and through the crowd. She feels many hands groping her and ripping her clothes from her body. The liquid that Guichi forced down her throat is taking its full effect, and they lay her down on a cold hard surface, and she knows that it is the altar where she witnessed the sex acts with the woman take place just moments ago. She lays there and tries to reach out to Laki, but her thoughts are clouded, and before she passes out with the cold hardness of the stone altar, she looks over and sees the two women who helped the one woman to remove her robe, leaning against the cavern wall. She tries to focus, and just before she passes out, she can see deep slashes across her throat.

Guichi and Tanin leave the cavern and travel to the Barrens to find almost two thousand anointed followers that were branded by them kneeling in a catatonic state.

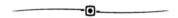

A soft moan escapes her lips, and she tries to open her eyes, but she feels dizzy, and her vision is blurry. She finally opens her eyes and tries to see where she is and what has happened to her. She has no idea how long she has been out, but it slowly starts to come back to her as she remembers seeing Guichi and Tanin forcing themselves on that young woman on the altar and remembers seeing that the woman seemed to be enjoying it.

She is still trying to collect her thoughts when she hears, "Hello, Sister: with a tone of contempt, and as her vision clears a little more, she sees Tanin standing beside her.

He then says, "Finally, you're awake. I thought that Guichi might have given you too much of the *Shikuzani*, and you wouldn't wake up for a very long time. The Twins told us to be careful because too much of it was not good. Well, we both know it wouldn't kill you, but it could do irreversible damage to who knows what, seeing that it came from the Dark Realm.

I want to say, "Do you know, sweet sister, it would probably have been better to have given you an overdose because what I have planned for you will only be satisfying to one of us, while the other will surely feel shall we say, uncomfortable," and then he laughs.

She tries to shake her head to help clear the grogginess and feels the pain in her throat from when it was forced done her throat. Jutsuk can't understand why she could not manifest into her *Spirit*ual form and then remembers a thin shroud or something that prevented her from changing.

Tanin sees the questions on her face and leans on the altar to rest on his elbows and tells her, "You could not enter the *Spirit*ual Domain or form because we learned from reading this, and holds up a leather Tome'. Jutsuk can barely read the words in the ancient language on the cover, and it seems to read "The Unholy Scriptures." Tanin then says, "It explains in great detail how to capture and trap one's being so that the shift from one Domain to the other is impossible." She tries frantically to reach into the *Spirit*ual Domain, and she feels herself hitting a solid wall; and then lies still on the stone altar and takes in deep breaths. Her vision clears a little more, and she can turn her head just enough; and watches Tanin walk over to a waist-high stone pillar, and he seems to be looking at something.

Tanin walks back over to Jutsuk and asks her. "Can you guess who is going to be the giver and who will be receiving? "Wait! Please don't tell me because that would take the fun out of it?" and Tanin starts laughing. She hears Tanin say, "Kill her!" Jutsuk realizes that they like her and that and are connected.

Jutsuk is lying there, unable to move, when she feels something on her lower legs and realizes that it is a pair of soft hands, and then she feels her legs slowly spread open. She can lift her head just enough to see the same prominent young woman she first saw on the altar, standing at the end of the altar, spreading her legs. Once they are open, she crawls onto the altar and kneels submissively between them. Jutsuk tries to close her legs, but she cannot because of the drug. She also sees that the woman is strong for her size as she runs her fingernails down the insides of her legs.

Tanin looks down at her and says, "I hope the *Shikuzani* has not given you too much of a headache. I want you to enjoy this because this is the last time you will feel anything, and he laughs again.

She tries to envision herself free of the restraints and reach out to her sister, but her thoughts are still jumbled as she feels the *Shikuzani* coursing through her body.

She looks at him and asks with a slight lisp in her voice, "Tanin, what is the meaning of this?" Why are you doing this? Where is Guichi? Tanin slaps her across the face and yells, "Shut the fuck up! You are asking too many questions, and it is none of your business where Guichi is?"

She sees others gathering around the altar, and then the young woman kneeling between her legs rips off the remnants of her tattered clothes and hands them to Tanin. He takes the material, places it near his nose, and smells her essence saturated with purity and good. It repulses him, and he tosses the cloth out to his followers, that have now gathered around the altar, and a frenzy erupts as they try to get a piece of the fabric.

The young woman sees what is happening, and she gets caught up in a frenzy and lowers herself to Jutsuk's now completely bare legs. Jutsuk feels the woman kissing her ever so lightly, at first near the back of her knees. Then she feels the young woman's hot breath working its way up her inner thighs, all the while as she continues licking and kissing and gently rakes her fingernails over her skin, and the sensation unexpectedly causes Jutsuk to let out a small moan.

Her soft moan seems to encourage the woman, and then she feels a flickering of the young woman's tongue near her womanhood. Slowly at first, and then the flickering becomes slightly more vigorous. Jutsuk tries to suppress the emotions and feelings when suddenly and without warning, she feels the woman penetrating her physically and orally. Jutsuk has never felt anything like this before, and though she is humiliated by her emotions, she cannot help herself. She wants to think it is the side effects of the *Shikuzani* because what this young woman is doing to her, she finds sexually stimulating.

The very idea of what this woman is doing to her and what is happening to her, she knows it is wrong, but she finds herself starting to squirm a little at first and then a little more with each flick of the woman's tongue or penetration of her fingers. Jutsuk suddenly finds herself trying to thrust her pelvis into the woman's face.

Tanin watches this and shouts out to his congregation, "Behold my followers, witness how little it takes for a Goddess to succumb to the physical pleasures of sex. What kind of Goddess enjoys this humility and does not fight back? I will tell you, "A weak, pathetic one, who does not signify being called a Goddess!" Tanin slaps her across the face, saying, "That is why the Dark Scriptures will overcome the teachings of the Goddesses and drive those beliefs and teachings from this world!"

Tanin raises his hand for silence and says to his congregation, "Look at her, a Goddess who is just a whore" then he backhands her and spits on her. Jutsuk lies there humiliated and crying; and runs her tongue along her lip and tastes blood in her mouth.

She hears the young woman moan as if the slap has somehow excited her, and then Jutsuk feels something slowly building, and she tries to resist, but the sensation is too great, and she hears the young woman's passion building more, and she feels herself doing the same. The young girl lifts her face, quickly moves forward and places her lips on Jutsuks, and forces her tongue into her mouth in her mouth. All inhibitions are gone; Jutsuk welcomes the woman's tongue, and they sexually explode together. They both stop shaking, and then the woman gets off her, sits back on her heels, licks her fingers, and then wipes her mouth and smiles at Jutsuk.

Tanin tells her, "You did well, but you were not supposed to enjoy it!" and backhands the young woman across the mouth and then commands her to get off the altar, or she will join her friends.

The others in the cavern start chanting softly, and Tanin turns back to face his followers.

Jutsuk raises her head just enough to see out over the crowd and can see the look of lust in their eyes, and she begins to panic. She slowly lays her head down and softly prays that Laki comes to save her.

Tanin sees that his congregation wants her, and he reaches over and grabs Jutsuk's breast and squeezes it hard enough to cause her to whimper in pain. He leans down, licks the side of her face, and leaves a smear of drool dripping off her chin down to her neck. Tanin goes to wipe away the spit, but instead, he slaps her with his hand. She cries out, and Tanin hits her again. He laughs, raises his fist, brings it down, and bashes her in the stomach, causing her to gasp for Air and start coughing.

Tanin turns to his followers and says, "Behold! The pathetic power of the Goddesses is nothing more than a weak little woman crying. How can people follow someone who lies before us whimpering, helplessly cowering?" Tanin turns and delivers a blow to the side of her head with his fist and looks out over the followers as she almost passes out. She cannot hear anything except for the ringing in her ears. Tanin turns back to Jutsuk, walks up to her, and whispers in her good ear. "Are you ready, my sweet dear sister?" and Tanin snaps his fingers.

She feels the bindings loosen just enough and feels a pair of hands groping her legs and inner thighs. She continues to lay spread eagle on the altar, and she feels the touch of three more sets of hands on her legs. She feels long, sharp fingernails raking her flesh on her legs and feels them penetrate her skin. Blood is now oozing from the scratches, and she tries to struggle. Her eyes fill with tears, and through those tears, she looks at Tanin and sees him smiling at her.

While he smiles at her, one woman, naked and filthy, climbs up onto the altar and starts rubbing her breasts and upper body up and down Jutsuk's legs smearing Jutsuk's blood on her own body. She can also feel the woman's piercings, made from small razor blades cut deep into her skin. The woman works her way up her legs to just below her waist. Then she feels a warm breath and small pointed teeth ever so delicately biting her inner thighs just below her womanhood, but this time there is no pleasure as before, but only pain and disgust.

Jutsuk starts crying as Tanin stands beside her and asks her, "What's the matter, Sister? Are you not enjoying this little game? Is this not the same feeling as you had before?" Tanin places the Book of Unholy Scriptures beside her on the altar.

Tears roll down her cheeks, and Tanin roughly wipes them away, leaving her cheeks red. He snaps his fingers, and one of the women walks around to stand behind him and helps him remove his robe. Tanin stands there watching his sister getting molested and almost raped by these women, and he starts to feel aroused and nods his head. The girl rises and stands near the other girl next to the altar. Tanin walks beside her, and as he runs his hand down her leg, Jutsuk shivers, and as he walks by, she sees that he is naked. She then watches him lick her blood from his fingers. He now stands at the far end of the stone altar and stares at her, and she sees him place a long slender blade on the altar. She sees the look in his eyes, and she starts to struggle even harder as he places both hands on the stone to climb up. Then she senses it, a pinhole in the drug-induced haze of the *Shikuzani*.

She reaches out and hopes it is enough for Laki to feel her and come to her before it is too late.

Chapter 14

Reaper of Souls

They have moved from the Squires barracks to the Officer's Barracks, and Samuel is in his room looking over his orders when there is a knock on his door. He says, "Enter," Reiko comes in, sits on his bed, and crosses her legs, and she smiles at Samuel and says, "I'll show you mine if you show me yours." Samuel laughs, and they exchange orders, and by coincidence, they find their orders are the same. Reiko tells him that Hikaru has orders to escort a royal family member to his remote estate and that they are to leave immediately.

Reiko asks, "Do you want to take the lead on this one?"

Samuel asks, "Are you sure?"

Reiko said, "Why not? It would probably be for the best, seeing that we are both new Second-Lieutenants, and the men would probably feel more comfortable with a man in charge."

Samuel protests and says, "You're just as good as any of us," when Reiko holds up her hand. Samuel knows the case is closed when she does that and will not waiver.

Samuel agrees, and the two of them go over their orders and start putting together a roster. They are to proceed to the northeastern border to stop a band of marauders terrorizing the Empire's territory along the border. The orders also state that under no circumstances are they to chase the marauders over the border into the neighboring country of Aki. The small country that the marauders come from is looking for any excuse to have a war. If a conflict with the marauders happens, it must stay inside the Empire's borders.

The next day, Samuel and Reiko are mounted on their horses, waiting for the troops to muster and fall in. Samuel and Reiko decided yesterday that Samuel would be in charge, and Reiko would be his second. They head out on their mission with fifty well-armed horse riders of twenty archers and thirty swordsmen. Behind them are three wagons, one carrying supplies, and two prison wagons. They travel for fifteen days, and a scout reports that they are getting close to the border of Aki. He also reports that they are close to where the marauders have been terrorizing the towns through extortion. They camp in a valley between two long hills, and Reiko orders the scouts to investigate the surrounding hills and valleys for any signs of the marauders and report anything they find.

After dinner, Samuel and Reiko are enjoying a fresh cup of tea when they see one of the scout's come galloping into the camp, quickly dismounts, and run over to where Samuel and Reiko are sitting. He salutes them, and before he can say anything, Samuel tells him to catch his breath and offers him a cup of water. He drinks it, says thank you, and Reiko sees that he has caught his breath; after he calms down, Reiko tells him to report his findings.

The scout tells them that the marauders are three valleys over and have made camp for the night. Samuel says, "Show us." The scout walks up to the map and points to a spot a few valleys away. Reiko asks, "How far and how long would it take to get there?" The scout says, one hour on a horse, and then Samuel asks, "How many marauders are there?" The scout reports as many as thirty marauders with eight lookouts on the surrounding ridges above the camp. There is a huge man who seems to be the Leader.

Reiko says, "Thank you," and tells him to get something to eat. He comes to attention, salutes them, and turns to get something to eat.

After the scout is gone, Samuel asks Reiko, "So what do you think?"

She answers, "I don't see a problem taking out the sentries; the marauders themselves concern me." We outnumber them by maybe thirty men, but to go against thirty marauders, I'm not too fond of the odds. I am worried more about our men getting hurt or killed than for them.

"How about if we do this?" Samuel explains his idea, and after he finishes, all Reiko says is, "I like it."

She musters the men and tells them to strip their mounts of anything that would make a noise and do the same thing with their gear. Some men start grumbling and muttering about why they should listen to a Second Lieutenant who is a woman. She tells the men to stop grumbling, and then she hears, "She is just a girl. I bet she doesn't even know how to shoot that thing," and then more mutterings with some laughter. Reiko has had enough and orders her men to stand down and then asks all of them who is the best with the bow. All the men say, "Corporal Stell is the best!"

Reiko orders Stell to step forward, and when he does, she sees that he is one of the biggest men and seems to be one of the instigators of the lot, and he has a smug look on his face.

Reiko says, "Corporal Stell, everyone is saying you're the best archer in the squad. I think that I am better. What do you say to a little challenge between us archers?"

Stell replies, "Anything you want, Lieutenant," with slight contempt.

Samuel is now standing close to Reiko, and she sees him taking a step forward and motions him to stay back and that she will deal with it.

She turns her attention back to Stell and asks, "Corporal Stell, what would you think to a little side wager, and in all fAirness, I'll even let you choose the target for you and me to have our little contest?"

Stell looks around, points to a tree that is probably thirty meters away, and says, "How about that tree there, pointing to it.

Reiko looks to where he is pointing and says, "Really, Corporal Stell, you can't think of anything a little more challenging, and you call yourself an archer."

She sees Stell turn red, she hears some snickering, and he starts to get mad; he then says, "Lieutenant, I was being nice because you are a female, but if you want a challenge, see that large oak out there about one hundred and fifty meters, with the large knot. Let's wager that whoever comes closest to the center of that knot is the winner and that if I beat you, you will hand your command over to Lieutenant Miro, and I take charge of the archers."

Reiko says, "Fine, but if I win, you, Stell, will apologize to me, listen to me as your commanding officer, and donate whatever coin you have in your pocket and every archer out here to the orphanage of my choice, do you agree to these terms?"

Stell looks at his fellow archers, and they all agree, and in his smug way, says, "Yes, Ma'am, and would you like to go first?"

"No, Stell, be my guest." She tells him.

There is some talk and wagering between the archers and Samuel's swordsmen. She sees Samuel talking to one of his men when she hears, "Are you sure, Lieutenant," and Samuel answers, "Yes, I'm sure, now go."

Reiko looks over at Samuel and sees that he brought over her chair, sits in his, and drinks some tea. She tells Stell to go ahead and shoot whenever he's ready. She sits next to Samuel and says, "What was that about?" as Samuel hands her a cup of tea.

Samuel replies, "I can't do it, but I had one of my men place a wager on you." Reiko almost chokes on her tea and says, "Really," and as Samuel told his man, "Yes, really"

All she says is "Jeez" and looks over to see Stell start to draw back his bow when she gets up, walks over to where Stell is standing, watches his aim, and sees that he is ready to release. Stell glances over at her, gives Reiko a smug look, draws back his bowstring just a bit more, exhales, and fires his arrow. The whole detachment is watching, and there is dead silence as they watch Stell pull back his bow just a little more and then release his arrow. The arrow takes flight with a woosh and then a faint thud as the arrow hits the tree. One of the other archers relays back to another, who shouts to the rest of the men that Stell's arrow is just a little down and to the right of the center of the knot. The archers cheer, and Reiko hears a comment, "How the hell is she going to beat that?"

Reiko walks up to where Corporal Stell shot from, checks her quiver, and pulls out two arrows. She then carefully strings her bow, places one arrow in her mouth near the feathers, and carefully notches the other. Reiko raises her bow and slowly pulls back on the string. When her bowstring is completely pulled back and tight, there is a deathly silence among the men, and then she hears Stell say, "Big deal, she can pull back a bow, but can the Lieutenant hit anything?" and hears that most of the wages are in Corporal Stell's favor, and someone else say, "She's just a girl." Reiko smiles slightly, takes a deep breath, and exhales slowly. As she does, she feels the calmness overcome her where all outside noise is gone, the weapon in her hand becomes an extension of her own body, and her breathing immediately comes under control and matches her heartbeat. The Air around her becomes still, and everything stops. The knot in the tree comes into focus as if she is standing a meter away. Her concentration is so acute that she pictures the arrow hitting the tree knot dead center.

Reiko stands perfectly still with her bowstring pulled back almost to the snapping point. She hears Samuel whisper, "Wait for it." and then it happens. Samuel sees the quicksilver flash across her eyes, and Reiko unconsciously adjusts her aim. Samuel says to himself, "Now!" As if she heard him, she releases her arrow; she takes the second arrow from her mouth, notches it, and lets it fly within a breath of each other. Reiko turns back to Samuel, walks over, and asks for some tea; and as she unstrings her bow, she hears wood splitting and then a second dull thud.

The men call out to the two archers and ask who won? The archer near the tree doesn't know how to say what just happened. The second archer who relayed Stell's shot runs up to the oak, and he cannot explain it either. Reiko is now sitting down and drinking her tea when she looks at Corporal Stell, and she sees his smug smile, thinking he beat her. She calls over to him and says, "Corporal Stell, why don't you go down there and come back and let me know if I even hit the tree, seeing that I am just a girl." Stell doesn't say anything but gives Reiko another smug look and heads to the oak, and when he gets there, he has to push his way through to see the target.

Then she looks at Samuel and asks, "Is there any more tea?" Samuel says, "Sure," and fills her cup, and he says, "Just a girl?" and she says, "Not my words theirs," and gestures towards her fellow archers.

No one is saying anything as Stell stands there looking at the Lieutenants' two arrows; one arrow sits dead center in the knot, while the other has split his arrow straight down the middle. He doesn't say anything, nor does anyone else, as he takes the three arrows and walks back to where Reiko and Samuel are sitting.

He is soon standing before her at full attention and salutes her. She returns his salute and asks, "Did I win?" Stell hands her the two arrows along with his split one. Reiko takes her two arrows and says, "Why don't you keep that one as a reminder," as he still holds the split arrow. "Yes, Ma'am," Stell answers, and then Reiko says, "Stell, you will be my lead. Please round up the archers; we move out in fifteen. Stell salutes her, says, "Yes, Ma'am," and then says, "Ma'am, I would like to apologize for disrespecting you in front of the men. I would understand if you want to take disciplinary actions when we return after this mission." Reiko looks at Stell and says, "Corporal Stell, let's call this little incident a lesson, and as long as you have learned from your lesson, then no other actions are required. Do I make myself clear?"

Stell stands a little straighter, salutes, and says, "Yes, Ma'am."

Reiko looks at him and says, "As I was saying, Sargent Stell, why don't you gather the men and have them ready to move out in fifteen minutes."

Stell salutes and starts walking away when Reiko hears him say, "Sargent Stell." She sees him walk a little straighter.

One of Samuels's swordsmen comes up to them, salutes the two of them, and then hands Samuel a medium size pouch. Samuel shakes it, and Reiko hears a good quantity of coins, and the Sargent says, "Sir, your winnings."

Samuel replies, "Sargent, not my winnings, but a donation to Lieutenant Takahashi's orphanage," Reiko laughs.

Fifteen minutes later, Reiko mounts up, she looks at Samuel, and he winks. He smiles as she heads out with her archers, and Samuel notices that the newly promoted Sargent Stell is at her side.

As discussed, Samuel waits fifteen minutes and instructs his men to mount up. He does the same with his thirty swordsmen and follows the same route Reiko and her archers took. Before he leaves, he tells the drivers of the prison wagons to head to the location on the maps in four hours just before the crack of dawn and that the supplies wagons to wait until they return. If they are not back by tomorrow night, they are to head back to the Capital at first light.

One hour later, they find the spot where Reiko and her archers secured their horses. He whispers for his men to dismount. He passes the word to be quiet and to follow him. They get to the beginning of the valley; Reiko is there waiting for them. She tells Samuel not to worry about the sentries. He asks her if there were any problems, and she replies, "No problems whatsoever." She adds, smiling, "Not after I took out three of them before they could get one."

"Show off, and then he smiles and says, "Shall we get on with this." and Reiko says, "Let's."

Reiko tells Sargent Stell to take the men, position them where the sentries were on the ridgelines, and keep watch, and if any of the marauders get up, they are to take them down quietly. Samuel hears Stell and the others whisper, "Yes, Ma'am." And then say, "You heard the Lieutenant, move out and be quiet," and they quietly move out and spread themselves along the tops of the valley's ridges. Once she sees her men are in position, she looks at Samuel and nods. Samuel quietly leads his men into the camp and begin to subdue and tie up any sleeping marauders. A couple of them get up to either get a drink or take a leak, and before they know what is happening, Reiko sees that her men are quick and quietly take them down. Each of them ends up with an arrow in their throat to not raise the alarm. After thirty minutes, every marauder still alive is bound and gagged and protesting behind a gag.

The sun is just beginning to rise as Samuel and Reiko go over to a small campfire near an outcrop of rock and are surprised to see a small pot staying warm by the coals. Reiko lifts the pot, removes the lid, and smells the aroma of tea. Samuel sees a cup, wipes it out, and Reiko pours some tea into it. They are sitting on the ground, leaning against some rocks watching the men keep guard and share a cup of tea.

Before long, they hear a commotion in the camp's only tent, and then the tent's flap is pulled back while discussing the tea they are drinking. A large, solidly built man steps out of the tent. He sees Samuel and Reiko sitting there and hears them talking about tea when he asks, "Who the fuck are you?"

Reiko holds up a finger to tell him to wait and finishes telling Samuel, "The aroma is rude, and I find it came off strong and bitter, like someone interrupting a conversation. What do you think, Samuel?"

The leader of the marauders sees the man Samuel roll his eyes, and the Leader now realizes that the woman was talking about him and not the tea they are drinking, and he asks again, "Who the fuck are you?"

Reiko looks at Samuel and asks, "Should I tell him, or do you want to tell him?"

Samuel says, "Second-Lieutenant Takahashi, as the expedition's Commander, don't make me...."

The marauder leader screams, "I demand to know who you are, and then shouts, "Men!" and when none of them respond, he asks, "What did you do to my men?" and walks towards the two of them. Samuel remains seated; as Reiko stands up, she hands Samuel the remaining tea in the cup and says, "Really." The big man towers over her, pulls a large knife from his belt, and swings at her. She blocks his arm, holding the long knife, and thrusts two fingers into his shoulder. The Leader's arm immediately goes numb and then hangs uselessly at his side. Just as the long knife drops from his fingers, Reiko snatches it before it hits the ground and then quickly lands a blow to the big man's neck, causing his knees to buckle, and he falls forward unconscious.

While the Leader lies unconscious on the ground, Samuel looks at Reiko, and all she says is, "Oh, all right, and she goes to give orders to the men when she sees all of them, her archers and Samuel's swordsmen alike just standing there, looking dumbfounded, with their mouths open.

Reiko shouts "Hey" to get their attention, and when they snap out of it, Reiko sees the prison wagons pulling up. She orders them to shackle the marauder leader and load the marauders into the prison wagons. She tells a few men to go up and retrieve the dead bodies, and when they return, she has their bodies searched and then placed on a funeral pyre.

Samuel orders fifteen of his swordmen to fetch the horses. He then enters the Leader's tent and, a few minutes later, comes out carrying a small chest under his arm and a leather book. He holds the chest in his arm while thumbing through the book and realizes that it is a ledger with the number of monies that were extorted or stolen from each town or village. Samuel walks over to Reiko with the chest under his arm and hands her the book. She quickly looks through it, and Samuel asks her how the numbers are, and everything seems to be going as planned.

She tells him that the final body count for the dead marauders is fifteen, who are placed on the funeral pyre and doused with alcohol from the marauder's stash. Samuel instructs two men to take the chest and ledger and return the extorted monies to the local towns and villages.

They are about to leave the valley when Samuel looks at Reiko and says, "Lieutenant Takahashi, if you please?" Still sitting on her mount, Reiko turns her horse, removes her longbow from its sheath, and attaches her bowstring. She asks Stell to wrap one arrow just behind the head in an alcohol-soaked rag. Her bow restrung, Reiko stands up in her stirrups, takes the arrow, notches it, brings it down, and asks Stell to do the honors. He lights the alcohol-soaked rag, and once it catches, she draws back on the string, holds it, and points the arrow in the direction of the funeral pyre. She calculates the Air and the distance and slightly adjusts her aim, releasing the flaming arrow. Everyone is watching as the arrow streaks through the sky. She hears the Leader of the marauders say, "There is no fucking way she can shoot an arrow that far and make it!" Reiko smiles and goes to turn her mount when she hears a marauder say, "No fucking way, how could that bitch make a shot like that." Samuel watches as the flaming arrow plummets to the ground and hits the pile dead center. Samuel, like everyone else, waits, and then there is a flare-up as the alcohol-soaked bodies ignite. She is about to ride up and join Samuel when she hears the Leader say, "You Bitch!" She flicks her hand and then hears a howl as the Leader finds a small throwing dart sticking out of his right shoulder. She asks Stell to retrieve her dart, and just as she gets up beside Samuel, she sees him sitting on his mount, shaking his head, and all Reiko says is, "What?" and looks innocent. A minute later, Stell rides up and hands her the throwing dart.

Samuel nudges his horse forward, and with Reiko by his side, they lead the men back to base camp. They move along at a good pace, and they hear the chatter among the men on how Second Lieutenant Takahashi was able to fire three arrows in quick succession and down three sentries without a scream from any of them. Samuel leans in close to Reiko and says, "I think you have some admirers" Reiko politely tells Samuel to shut up, and then Samuel notices her smiling. The detail reaches their base camp, and they secure the Leader to a tree and shackle his men to another. They are fed military rations and water. Samuel brings the Leader of the marauders some food, and he angrily knocks the food away and says, "Screw you and that Bitch for what you did to my men. The two of you had no right to kill my men without allowing them to defend themselves." Samuel looks at the Leader and says, "So you think it was wrong to kill your men while standing guard or sleeping, but it is okay for you to extort money and rape helpless villagers of the Empire.

The Leader says nothing, but Samuel looks directly at him, and in an icy tone of voice, which makes the man uneasy, Samuel asks him, "What is your name?" the Leader answers, "Barnaby Cook." Samuel looks at the marauder leader and says, "I'll tell you what, Barnaby Cook, I'll give you my word to let you and your men return to whatever country you call home under three conditions. The Leader looks into Samuel's eyes and sees an iciness that he has never seen before, and then it is gone, and asks, "What are your three conditions?" Samuel replies, "First, You have to give me your word never to attack, plunder, or pillage any Empire towns or Empire properties again. Second, you and your men will work for me, Lieutenant Takahashi, and a third person, who is not here but is known as Lieutenant Sato, who just so happens to be on another mission. You will work directly for us as long as we see fit and will be compensated for your time and efforts."

Cook looks at Samuel and asks, "What is the third condition?"

Samuel looks at him and says, "I am glad you asked because this condition is probably the most important of all three of them."

Cook is hesitant to ask but does, "What is that?"

Samuel gives him an icier stare than before and says, "You will apologize to Lieutenant Takahashi; you know her; she is the young Lieutenant who I heard you say that the shot was impossible, and then when she made it, you called her a "Bitch."

A look crosses his face, and Samuel continues, "As I said, you will apologize for calling her a "Bitch" and mean it, and another thing, if you go back on your word, there will not be a place on this continent for you to hide, Now! Do we have an agreement or not?"

Barnaby Cook looks Samuel straight in the eyes, and he sees a small flash of what he thinks is silver and then takes a big swallow. He has seen death dormant in this young Lieutenant's eyes, and it scares him. Barnaby Cook says, "Yes, I give you my word, and I agree to this verbal contract."

Samuel says, "Good." and calls one of his men over to unlock his shackles. Samuel escorts Barnaby Cook to where Reiko sits outside her tent, writing a report. When Samuel walks up to Reiko with the marauder leader by his side and says, "Lieutenant Takahashi, this fine gentleman who goes by the name of Barnaby Cook has something to say to you."

Reiko looks at the Leader and very casually says, "Yes. Mr. Cook?"

Barnaby Cook tries to avoid looking at her because he sees the same thing in her eyes that he saw in the Lieutenant's eyes. Barnaby Cook, one of the toughest marauder leaders in these parts, lowers his head. He slightly stutters and says, "Ma'am, I mean Lieutenant Takahashi, I am truly sorry for calling you a Bit..." then catches himself, "the B-word earlier today. Can you forgive me for my rudeness and stupidity?

Reiko stands and walks up to Barnaby Cook and asks, "Do you have a verbal contract with Lieutenant Miro? The look in Barnaby's eyes tells her that he recognizes Miro's name. "Yes, Ma'am," he says.

"Good, then you are free to go, and Mister Cook, if you think Lieutenant Miro here is Death, then remember this "I am his Reaper of Souls!" Cook bows and steps back, never taking his eyes off them. They watch Barnaby Cook as he finds his men already unshackled. They quickly walk from the camp, and Samuel tells a couple of his men to escort them to their horses. Ten minutes later, he watches Barnaby Cook and his men ride out of camp and head north towards the border.

Samuel looks at Reiko, chuckles, and says, "Reaper of Souls, are you?" Reiko punches Samuel in the arm and smiles, and then she says, "It sounded better in my head," and they start laughing.

They get back to the Capital and immediately go to Headquarters to report. Colonel Bilson sits behind his desk as Samuel and Reiko hand their reports and give him a verbal briefing of their actions. The Colonel asks them if they can trust this Barnaby Cook, and they both answer, "Yes, Sir," and he says, "Good work, now go get something to eat," and dismisses them. They salute, do an about-face, and leave headquarters. They are heading to the Officer's mess when they see Hikaru walking across the compound, they call out to him, and he quickens his step.

He meets them in the parade field and says, "Hey, how are you doing?" He quickly adds, "Let's get something to eat. I'm starving."

Reiko looks at him and says, "You are always starving."

Hikaru smiles at her and says, "What do you expect? I'm a growing boy."

The three of them laugh and head to the Officers Dining Hall.

After dinner, the three of them are relaxing and talking when Hikaru gets a serious tone but is smiling and asks, "So, which one of you is the "Reaper of Souls," then he says, wait, don't tell me, let me guess. Could it be our very own sweet little apricot Anzu?" Samuel starts laughing, and Reiko says, "Oh Jeeez!" and punches Hikaru in the arm, and soon all three are laughing. They explain to Hikaru how it all came about. After the laughter subsides, Hikaru takes on a serious tone and asks, "Can you trust this Barnaby Cook?" Samuel says, "I think so, I gave him a choice of adhering to a verbal contract with the three of us or face imprisonment, and if all else fails, we can always send the "Reaper of Souls" after him. Reiko chokes on her tea as Hikaru bursts out laughing.

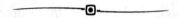

Over the next few months, all three are assigned tasks around the Capital or ordered to escort small caravans between the Capital and the surrounding towns and villages.

Life in the military is quiet.

Chapter 15

Rebirth

Laki is starting to worry because she has not had any contact or felt anything from Jutsuk. She continues scouring the mountains and valleys, looking for not only her brothers and now her sister. She hopes Jutsuk had not, by chance, found them, and she was overpowered by the two of them. She projects her essence, and suddenly and unexpectedly, she feels her sister's emotions explode inside her as she feels the pain, suffering, and torture that she is subjected to, and she also knows where she is.

Laki travels at an unheard-of-speed in the *Spirit*ual Domain and is just a blur streaking through the night sky. She finds herself hovering over a valley, and the air feels heavy. She senses a barrier as if it is trying to keep her out, and as she approaches, she feels slightly lethargic, but she also senses that Jutsuk is close and ignores it.

She hurries down into the valley and soon finds herself partially covered with thorny bushes at a cave opening. She takes on her Earthly form, brushes the thorned bushes aside, and rushes down a path to eventually arrive at a ledge with some stalagmites and is overlooking a large cavern. She sees a man with his back to her, standing at the end of a stone altar, and she sees that he is naked. It looks as if he is going to climb onto it. She then feels something dirty about the man, something vile, evil, and then she realizes that what she is feeling is the corruption of the Stain, and that means that the man standing near the altar must be...and at that moment, he turns around, and Laki can see that it is her brother Tanin. She hears chanting and notices a congregation of people kneeling in the cavern.

Her thoughts are a little hazy as she reaches out to Jutsuk to find where she is and hears a faint "Here."

Laki asks, "Where."

Jutsuk is just about to say, Here...." When Tanin slams his fist down onto her stomach, and as she cries out in pain, Tanin says out loud, "Here Laki, I'm here!" and Laki feels the pain from her sister coursing through her body and releases a terrifying scream. She watches Tanin walk back to a stone pillar, and she sees him pick up something, and she can feel the evilness ten-fold as she realizes that the rumors are accurate and that her brothers have a piece of Dark Crystal. She watches as Tanin opens a large book and leans it against Jutsuk's body. He stands there reading as the two women approach him and help him back into his robe. The women step away, and as they do, Tanin looks up from the book and looks right at her and says, "Hello Laki, did you come to join in the festivities?" He then closes the book and waves his hand, and Laki tries to take on her *Spirit*ual being, but she feels lethargic; and her head seems to be in a fog, and she cannot think straight

"Welcome to my little family reunion," Tanin starts laughing, and without provocation, he lashes out with a bolt of energy, throwing it directly at her. She leaps out of the way, but just barely, as the stalagmites catch the brunt of the strike and immediately disintegrate. Laki finds herself covered with bits of stone and dust, and when most of the dust has settled, she reaches up to touch her cheek, and she feels wetness; when she pulls her fingers away, she sees blood on them.

The followers see what is happening and begin to panic and stop chanting. Tanin throws another energy ball at Laki, and this causes them to scatter and try and make their way to the cavern's exit but find it blocked. The two women kneeling to his right remain where they are but stop chanting like the others. Tanin looks at the two of them and yells, "Did I tell you to stop?" he grabs the long slender blade from the altar and slashes their throats. Their blood sprays all over him and Jutsuk, and when Tanin wipes their blood from his face, he licks the women's blood from his fingers.

He stands, and with his robe covered in blood, he shouts for all of his followers to stop, and as they do. He says in a loud voice while walking towards the stone pillar and placing the Tome' and crystal on it, "Do you not believe in the powers of the Dark Scriptures, or are you all just mindless beings? If you are, so be it!" he raises his hand and then makes a fist. The followers in the cavern start grabbing their heads and start screaming. He brings his fist down hard into the palm of his other hand, and their heads immediately explode, showering the walls and cavern floor with sinew and gore. Tanin starts laughing like a maniac, and as Laki watches, she knows her brother is very dangerous.

Laki is now standing on the cavern floor and has just witnessed the butchering of two women and the aimless slaughter of over five hundred people, and she asks him, "Why are you doing this? We are your sisters?"

We want to help you!" Tanin ignores her questions and lashes out with more energy bolts to keep Laki off balance and away from her sister. He sees that Jutsuk is not moving and smiles confidently, thinking he has broken her. Now, it is time to finish off this other bitch.

He knows that the preaching of the Laki-Jutsuk Religion does not even come close to being as strong as the Dark Religion and that Laki is weak just as Jutsuk was. He knows they cannot defend themselves or fight back effectively because of their beliefs, teachings, and preaching about love and harmony. He yells, "You are weak," and continues to blast Laki with energy bolts causing her to dodge and move constantly; and hide behind large rocks when she can. Tanin sees that he is slowly wearing her down as she keeps getting pelted by the splintered rock from the blasts, and he can see small rivulets of blood drip where the chips and pieces of stone have lacerated her skin.

Laki realizes she is slowly succumbing to his continuous onslaughts, and she cannot get closer to Jutsuk. She sees that Tanin gives her an evil smile as he fires a massive bolt of energy at her. Waiting until the last moment, she turns her body so that it passes by her but does not see the smaller energy bolt in its wake, which hits her. She is thrown back against the cavern wall, and then she sees that the first blast of energy has hit several stalagmites. She sees that one is teetering on falling over, and she tries to move, but she is not quick enough as it topples and falls across her upper legs and waist, pinning her to the floor. She hears Tanin yelling, "You Bitch! You thought you could defeat me. Laki is hurting and too exhausted to escape the fallen stalagmite. She sees Tanin walking toward her, and she struggles to get free. She is cut, battered, and bleeding, and when he reaches her, he doesn't say anything but kicks her in her side, and she collapses to the floor. Jutsuk feels Laki getting kicked and screams "Noooo!" and then completely loses consciousness.

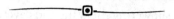

Tanin stands there staring at Laki as she lies on the cavern floor and sees that she is bruised, cut, and bleeding. He grabs her by her hair, lifts her head, slaps her across the face, and says, "My two loving sisters, my two favorite bitches. It's a shame that our brother Guichi had to miss this, but he had other matters to attend to."

Tanin easily removes the rock, picks Laki up, throws her over his shoulder, and walks back towards the altar. He unceremoniously drops her to the cavern floor, causing her to grunt in pain. She lies there on her stomach, unable to breathe, when he kicks her hard in the side for a second time, causing her to roll over this time, he hears bones crack, and he smiles. She is lying on her back and can only take shallow breaths. He places a binding spell on her like he did Jutsuk and then lifts her head off the floor by her hair, and as she softly stifles a cry, he slaps her across the face once and then backhands her. He lets go of her hair, allowing her head to hit the stone floor, and then spits on her. Laki lies there helpless; she doesn't cry or say anything. She can only think of one thing: and that is to save her sister no matter what it takes.

She is lying there hurt, bleeding, and finding it very hard to breathe; then she feels something, like a tiny tickle, and it is something she has never felt before. She feels it deep down in her loins, and it slowly begins to stir, and the sensation is intoxicating. She wants more and then thinks to herself, no, that is not it, she craves more, and the more she craves, the stronger she feels.

Tanin leaves her where she lies and walks back over to the altar. He grabs Jutsuk by her hair and pulls her limp body off the altar, not caring as her body crashes to the floor. He shows no concern for her well-being and drags her body across the rocks and dirt to where Laki is lying on the floor. Laki stares at Tanin, her eyes filled with loathing and hate.

Tanin looks at her and says, "Sister, why that look, aren't you supposed to be filled with love and harmony," and starts laughing. While still holding Jutsuk by her hair, he drops her unceremoniously to the floor near Laki and then squats down beside Laki and says, "Will you look at you two? I just want to tell the two of you that you two look like shit?" laughs, and then stands. Laki ignores him and looks at her sister, and when she sees the welts, cuts, bloody scratches, bruising, and the swelling on her beautiful face and body, a fury begins to fill her mind and body.

Tanin is still laughing as he walks over to the stone pillar where he placed the Tome and Dark Crystal just before attacking Laki. He is unaware that their hands were close to each other when he dragged Jutsuk over to Laki and dropped her on the floor.

Tanin pays them no mind, as he is overconfident that with both of them bound as they are, they are no threat, so he stands with his back to them as he continues looking through and reading the Tome'. He says over his shoulder to the both of them, "Did you know that a Dark Crystal can absorb one's essence." Then he says, "If you don't believe me, then read the incantation written in this Tome' it's fascinating." and continues reading the book paying neither one of them any mind.

Jutsuk is lying very still, and though it is shallow, Laki sees the rise and fall of her chest, knowing that her loving sister is still alive, if just barely. Laki painstakingly tries to force her hand and fingers closer to Jutsuk's hand. She is so close to touching Jutsuk's fingers that she collapses and is exhausted trying to fight against the bindings. She gasps with shallow breaths and sees that she is mere millimeters from her sister's touch. She looks at Jutsuk and sees that her eyes are open, and tears form and run down her cheeks. Laki watches as Jutsuk moves her hand and fingers towards Laki's painstakingly. Jutsuk closes her eyes, takes a deep breath, and extends her fingers ever closer to Laki's, and then Jutsuk passes out, and Laki sees that her fingertips are a hair's breadth from touching. Laki has no more and bows her head in defeat. She lies there with her head on her extended arm, and she starts to cry, and all she says is, "I'm sorry." Then she has a very soft, delicate feeling of a butterfly landing on her fingertips, and she looks over and sees that Jutsuks fingers have relaxed and uncurled, and when they did, it allowed the two of them to touch. She feels Jutsuk's fingertips brush her own, and the stirring she craved earlier returns. Now, she can feel the craving, giving her strength, and she intertwines her fingers with Jutsuk's.

Suddenly, the stirring stops, and she now feels a beat from within, and the craving morphs into something new, Laki now feels it deep in her loins, and she looks at Jutsuk, knowing she feels the same. Their strength slowly returns, and they can now hold each other's hands. Their injuries fade as Laki feels her broken bones mending and her cuts and scratches slowly healing. She looks at Jutsuk and sees the same thing. The cuts, bruises, scrapes, and swelling from being beaten slowly disappear. Jutsuk looks at Laki, and with their connection, they both feel hatred, an emotion neither of them has ever felt or confronted. The hate continues to grow to the point of it being almost unbearable as the churning in their loins becomes more aggressive, and like twin explosions, they feel something snap, and they realize that it is the bindings that Tanin placed on them. The two of them slowly sit up, and as the last of their cuts, bruises, and swelling disappear, they look at each other and see themselves again. They find themselves kneeling on all fours and see that Tanin has not realized what has happened. They find themselves kneeling, with their fingertips spread out, and an exploding feeling in their loins slowly begins to radiate through their bodies. Their core of *Spirit* merges with their core of Earth, arching their backs as they both feel the melding between them. Then they both feel two minor points on their backs begin to pulse, slow at first, and then slightly more rapid then it happens, a set of beautiful ultra-pure white feathered wings burst from their backs, and they find themselves being lifted off of the cavern floor and into the air. They watch Tanin, who is still none the wiser about what is happening behind his back. The hostility they felt before returns ten-fold, which has now turned into unadulterated hate. They know this hate is wrong and goes against everything they genuinely believe in, but they also know that what their brother did to them and what he could have possibly had planned is unforgivable, and it fuels the raw hate that is coursing through their bodies. They also know that what they feel in their bodies also engulfs their minds and souls, and they know this is real.

 They feel their hearts racing, and at the moment both of them are entirely in sync with one another, when untapped energy emerges, the same power that has been coursing through their bodies has reached a climax. They hear a voice asking them, "Do you accept your rebirth? Do you accept the *Mijikuna Inkinjo*?" Laki and Jutsuk both say, "Yes," and the voice says, "So be it!"

 They hold hands, floating ever higher, as heated energy radiates from their bodies, and a gentle breeze swirls around them, caressing them. They hover above the canyon floor, and any remnants of clothing disappear. They feel matching silver metallic paillette tops fabricated from a delicate silver mesh wrapping their upper bodies, with plunging necklines that cascade over her breasts that leave little to the imagination. Thin, intricately woven metal straps beaten to a softness secures the tops around their necks, and bottom straps made from the same metal secure the lower parts of the paillette around their lower torso, which keeps their backs exposed. They see that they wear skin-tight white leather pants that hug their bodies in the right places and display their more delicate curves. The leather pants are tucked into white knee-high leather boots with four-inch stiletto heels. Their hair is braided in fashion to a thick braid and is secured with a simple white leather cord. The air around them shimmers, and raw, untapped energy that they never felt before pulses through their bodies. Jutsuk snaps her fingers, and a shield encases the cavern and traps the essences of the three of them, locking them inside.

They find themselves doubled over, and then they feel something happening, though it is not painful, and then seconds later, they feel apertures or something opening on their backs. Then the unbelievable happens as they both see that each of them is now adorning a set of pure white feathered wings. They are elated as they unfurl them and spread them to their fullest. They beat them once to cause the pages of the Tome' that Tanin is reading to flutter the pages, and they are now hovering above the cavern floor, and Laki calls out and says, "Oh, Brother!"

Tanin is so caught up in his reading that when Laki calls his name, he turns, and it does not register that either of the girls should be able to talk, and then he sees that his sisters are no longer bound and they are not where he left them. He hears one of them say, "Up here, Brother." Tanin looks up and is shocked to see them hovering high above the cavern floor and flapping enormous pure white feathered wings. He shakes his head, thinking that what he sees is an illusion, but he sees that they have changed and looks closely. Their eyes are now a dark sapphire blue, their skin seems to glow, and all cuts, bruises, and every other mark and blemish are gone. He then hears Laki ask, "Well, brother, what do you think aren't they beautiful?" They both flap their wings. Tanin cannot understand how this could have happened, he performed the ritual flawlessly, and they should not have been able to escape, let alone break free from their restraints, and then he asks himself, where did they get those fucking wings.

Tanin pulls himself out of his stupor and screams, "Noooo!" He conjures a ball of energy and hurls it with tremendous force at the two of them. He is shocked to see Jutsuk catch it, and she somehow absorbs it. She holds out her palm, and the crackling of energy now appears in the palm of her hand, and he watches it gradually grow. Seconds later, she is holding a ball of energy about the size of a child's ball and flicks her wrist. The ball is fired directly at him. He feels the intensity of the explosion on his back; then, pieces of sharp rock strike him in several places, and the wetness of blood oozing from the cuts. Tanin is determined to end this and launches three energy balls directly at Laki. Laki does not move, and the three energy balls are extinguished before they come close to her. Tanin stands there frustrated and does not understand how this can be.

Laki and Jutsuk bring their hands up, almost touching, and Tanin can see the energy building between them. He watches as coils of energy appear in their other hands, and when they unfurl the coils, he sees that each of them is now holding a long slender whip of pure energy. Tanin cannot understand what has happened and knows he must escape. He tries to enter the *Spirit*ual Domain, but as he had done to his sisters, he finds himself barred from entering the domain. Out of sheer panic, he runs to the entrance to try and escape.

Laki nods to Jutsuk, bringing her arm straight up and releasing the energy coil. The energy coil makes a crackling sound as it unfurls. She brings her arm down quickly, and the uncoiled whip strikes out, making the crackling sound followed by a severe clap.

Tanin hears the crackling of the energy whip and then the clap as the whip is released, and then he feels excruciating pain in the middle of his back and stumbles forward and starts to fall to the floor. He catches himself from falling and thinks he might make it. He is about to reach the cavern entrance and runs into the same type of invisible barrier, smashing his face into it. Stunned, he falls backward and finds himself lying on his back. He hears one of his sisters giggling, and he rolls onto his stomach and tries to stand when he hears and feels the energy whip wrap around his ankles, and his feet are pulled out from underneath him, causing him to fall and smash his face on the cavern floor. He is dragged across the cavern floor on his stomach, and he realizes that Laki is dragging him as he looks over and sees Jutsuk standing near the pillar and reaching for the Tome' of Unholy Scriptures. He needs to stop her, and that is when he sees her wings are gone. He musters the strength and somehow fires an energy ball at Jutsuk just as her hands are about to touch the Tome'.

Laki sees what will happen and calls out, but it is too late, and just as Jutsuk looks up from the Tome, the ball of energy hits her, throwing her back against the cavern wall. She hits the wall, slides to the floor, and is semi-unconscious. Tanin hears Laki scream out, and then he is hauled up into the air, and like the crack of the whip, his body is slammed straight down onto the stone altar, and she sees that he cracks his head on the stone, and she also somehow feels a break in his essence as if it did not exist. Tanin is knocked unconscious and lays crumpled on the stone altar. Laki rushes to Jutsuk, kneels beside her, places her hand on the side of her face, whispers, "I am here," and kisses her deeply. Jutsuk's eyes flutter open, and she looks up at her sister with tears in her own eyes and softly whispers, "I'm sorry."

Laki has Jutsuk in her arms and walks over to Tanin, lying unconscious on the altar. She still cannot sense his essence, and then she binds him and hears Jutsuk say, "Don't kill him." She looks down at her, smiles, and says, "Don't worry, I won't, then holds her tightly against her chest and steps into Spiritual Domain, and just before she vanishes, she senses Tanin's essence before the two of them disappear. She leaves the bindings in place to keep Tanin from escaping if he wakes.

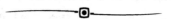

Guichi reaches out to Tanin to inform him that he has found a piece of Dark Crystal but does not feel his essence. He tells the young woman Nova, their new Kaisoshosuko, that he must go and steps into the cavern. Nova watches him and sees a look of concern on his face.

Guichi is about to leave when he feels Tanin's essence once again and decides to stay.

Seconds later, Laki stands in the cave and lays Jutsuk on the pillows. Laki leans over, kisses Jutsuk on the forehead, and tells her, "Sleep, my love. I will be back soon." And Laki just now realizes that Jutsuks wings are gone, and she is back to wearing the sheer material they usually wear. Jutsuk awakens and says, "Sorry."

Laki kneels on the pillows beside her, tells her there is nothing to be sorry for, and kisses her forehead. Laki stands and says, "Rest!" Before she disappears completely, she hears Jutsuk say, "Please, no matter what he has done to us, he is still our brother, so do not kill him," and then she closes her eyes.

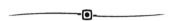

Laki is back in the cavern and finds Tanin, as she left him bound, unconscious, and still breathing. She felt a little remorse that she might have killed him when he hit his head on the stone altar, and then she remembered that they are immortal, and a blow to the head would not kill them, and she laughed. Though he is her brother, she hates him for what he did to the both of them, but more because of what he did to Jutsuk than herself. He violated her in ways that no one should have had to experience. She did not quite understand what he was talking about when he mentioned that the Dark Crystal could absorb one's body, and then she remembered her Mothers lesson. She remembered telling them how they captured Nimponin by absorbing his being, his core, into the crystal.

Laki immediately grabs the Tome' and starts flipping through the pages until she finds the earmarked page and starts reading. The Tome' falls from her hands as she realizes what Tanin had planned for her and Jutsuk. She looks down at the unconscious Tanin, and the hate fills her, and she says to no one in particular, "So, brother. You were going to place Jutsuk and me into this piece of Dark Crystal."

She picks up the leather-bound Tome' off the floor and reads through it. She comes across the earmarked page, and as she rereads the passage, she decides what she will do, but she will get some answers before she does. If his answers are not to her satisfaction, she can probably think of ways of getting what she wants.

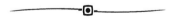

Tanin slowly awakens and tries to comprehend where he is and what has happened. He looks over, sees his robe on the cavern floor, and realizes he is naked and lying on something cold. His senses slowly return, and he realizes two things: first, he is lying on the stone altar in the cavern, and second, he feels discomfort on his back near his shoulders. Panic starts to set in, but he quickly subdues it.

He hears "Welcome back, brother!" and turns his head to see his sister Laki coming towards him, holding something in her hands.

She reaches the altar, "So you're finally awake. I thought that maybe you were going to sleep forever. Do you know how long I have been waiting for you to wake up?"

Through gritted teeth, Tanin replies, "No."

"One day, sweet brother!"

Tanin looks at her with hate in his eyes.

"Do you know what I thought about while you were lying on this stone slab?"

Tanin looks at her with no emotion whatsoever.

"How would I get my revenge for what you did to our sweet sister? No! let me rephrase that what you did to my sister?"

"But before I begin, I would like to know a couple of things,

Tanin turns his head away from her.

Laki ignores this and asks her question. "What are you and Guichi up to, and where is he?

Tanin continues to look away from her and doesn't say anything.

Laki chuckles softly and applies pressure to his bindings, then screams. She releases the tension, and Tanin lies there sweating and breathing heavily.

Laki is bending over Tanin with her elbows on the altar with her chin resting on her hands. She says, "Tanin, my sweet brother, I could do this all day, and there is absolutely nothing you can do about it."

"Now, I will ask you, what are you and Guichi up to?" She applies just a little pressure.

"Tanin says, "Guichi has gone to the Barrens to build an army, with the help from the Twins, you stupid B....and Laki applies pressure to his bindings to stop the word that was going to come off his lips.

She says, "Now, now, language brother," and then asks, "Who are these Twins that you mention, and what is this we are hearing rumors about rifts and the Dark Realm?"

Again, Tanin doesn't say anything, but Laki slowly tightens the binding, and Tanin lets out another horrific scream and then begins to cry and plead for mercy.

She releases the pressure just enough, and as he lies there trying to catch his breath, he looks at her and is about to say something when Laki tightens the bond again, and he screams. When she releases the pressure, she sees that he has wet himself and starts laughing.

Laki bends close to his ear and says, "Oh! Tanin, just so you know that while you were unconscious, I read your vile little copy of the Unholy Scriptures," and then places the Tome on his stomach. This Tome' you and Guichi received from who were they "The Twins" fascinating reading, and you will never guess what else I found, and don't worry, I will tell you."

"While you were lying there so innocent looking, I started to wonder if Jutsuk and I had these?" and she displays her wings for him to see, "What would be the possibility that you and Guichi could have them? Do you know what I discovered, Tanin, "I discovered that you do have wings like ours, and probably so doesn't Guichi. Oh! I'm sorry, did I say have? I meant to say had," and motions for him to look over at the floor. Tanin does, and he sees a pair of dull gray wings with bloody stumps slowly putrefying against the cavern wall.

Tanin looks back at her and sees that she is holding up a piece of jagged-looking Dark Crystal with blood-red veins running through it. He sees that she has the crystal encased in something so that she does not have to come in contact with it directly and holds it between her thumb and index finger.

Tanin starts to sweat, and his body begins shaking and asks, "What are you going to do?"

"Probably what you had planned for your two loving sisters," Laki smiles and says, "Tell me if I am wrong in guessing what you had planned., if you answer my questions truthfully, maybe I won't do what you had in mind for Jutsuk and me?"

Before Tanin can reply, she says, "Now, I will ask you one more time, and you had better tell me the truth. What are you and Guichi up to?" and applies pressure to his bonds.

Tanin screams and starts telling Laki everything she wants to know in more detail, especially about the Twins, the Dark Realm, and the High

Priestess. He goes on about the Army, the Sutaraukaji, and the Chizobutsu, and the thing that Laki finds the most horrifying is he and Guichi want to seek out the other pieces of Dark Crystal so that they can release the Dark God Nimponin. He tells her anything and everything she wants to know, anything to stop the pain.

Laki bends over near his ear and says, "Thank you, sweet brother, for being very informative."

Tanin starts to sweat as he sees the look in her eyes and watches her place the piece of dark crystal on his chest, and he struggles more against his restraints."

"Hmm, now, what was I going to do? Oh yes! Now let's see, how does that passage go?" She opens the Tome' of Unholy Scriptures and turns to the earmarked page. "Oh! Yes, here it is"

Laki brushes the hair from his forehead and places a kiss there. She reads the passage, *"Tisha Tae Da Jidai Wa Ma Rue,"* and sets the Dark Crystal near his leg. She continues with the passage, and the crystal begins to glow and pulse. She can see the blood-red veins pumping through the crystal, watching Tanin's leg slowly shimmer and then watching his foot and lower leg dissolve into a wisp of smoke and migrate into the Dark Crystal.

She hesitates and asks herself if this is right because this goes against everything, she and Jutsuk truly believe in, especially if the Dark God Nimponin is in the crystal. Then she places the dark crystal on his chest, looks down at Tanin, and now sees the hate in his eyes, and thinks, "Fuck it!" so she continues chanting, *"Tisha Tae Da Jidai Wa Ma Rue."* She takes hold of his arm and raises it so that he can watch the Dark Crystal slowly absorb his essence, beginning with his fingers and then his hand.

Tanin sees this happening and begs Laki to stop, and Laki says, "Why Tanin, my sweet dear brother, isn't this what you wanted to do to us, and, to tell you the truth, this is so much fun," and laughs.

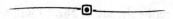

Guichi has dealt with the upstarts because he has appointed a woman as the new Kaisoshosuko when he senses something is wrong. He feels his brother's essence slowly begin to fade and says to her, "Do not fail me!" and disappears. He races back to the cavern, and when he gets there, he feels something stopping him from entering the cavern, almost like they captured Jutsuk. He sees Laki standing beside Tanin with the Tome' of the Unholy Scriptures open and is momentarily transfixed as he watches Tanin's upper body transform into a wisp of smoke and then watch it absorbed into a piece of the Dark Crystal.

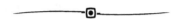

Laki smiles at him and says, "I thought this is what you wanted, to be closer to your God, or should I say to your father, Nimponin!" and gradually moves the crystal up his arm as more of his arm is absorbed. Tanin lies there bound as he watches his fingers hand, and now his arm turns to whisps and then absorbed into the crystal. She looks at him and sees that he has turned deathly white and has wet himself again. Whimpering, he begs her, "Please stop! You can't do this! I am your brother!"

Laki laughs and says, "Brother! Please tell me, what kind of brother would do those evil things to his sisters or even his half-sisters? I promised Jutsuk that I would not kill you, but I never promised her that I would not make you suffer!"

Tanin starts to watch his upper torso transform when he hears, "Stop!" He looks to see Guichi standing just outside Laki's shield and hears him yell, "You don't know what you are doing!"

"Sweet Guichi, but I know what I'm doing because I read your fucking vile book, and she looks at Guichi and says, "Who is going to stop me... YOU?" She laughs, "Now where were we, as Tanin's upper torso is absorbed, and soon the last of his essence is gone.

Tanin feels a strange sensation of nothingness as the last of his being is absorbed into the Dark Crystal.

Guichi yells, Noooo! and begins pounding madly on the barrier, and after several massive strikes, he falls to his hands and knees, gasping for breath. He feels the last of Tanin's essence disappear and a strange sensation on his back. He yells and arches his back as two appendages rip his back open, and he sees a pair of dark grey wings. He stands, feels strong, and strikes the shield again; this time, he feels it crack.

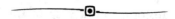

Laki hears Guichi yell, and she looks up to see that he now has wings like hers, but they are dark grey. She watches him strike the barrier again, and this time she can sense that her barrier begins to crack. She ignores him and works frantically, hoping that she has time.

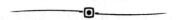

The Stain senses a change within the crystal and makes its way into where the difference is taking place; it finds an insignificant impurity and a means of escape. It tries to fight against the strong pull that seems only to allow one way, and that way is into the crystal. Then it hears the exact words that had initially trapped in here. The Stain releases a savage roar of anger and frustration, only to fall on deaf ears.

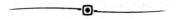

She sees that Tanin is no longer here on the altar and knows that if she doesn't seal the crystal, according to the Tome' the dark entity inside known as the Stain could escape. Then she feels as if something is rushing to the very opening, she created to entrap Tanin. She continues chanting the transfer spell; and quickly scans down the page and sees the sealing ritual for the crystal at the bottom. She quickly speaks the words in the Unholy Scriptures, and just before she feels the crystal seal itself, she faintly hears a savage roar, feels a chill, and is momentarily confused.

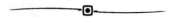

Laki hears the pounding, and she is back to reality. She then feels her shield shatter, and she sees Guichi immediately conjuring some sort of fireball, and then he throws it at her. She holds onto the Tome', and the ball of fire hits the altar. She reaches to grab the Dark Crystal and realizes it has been knocked off the altar onto the cavern floor from the explosion. She knows she has used too much energy to fight Tanin, set the barrier, and finally imprison Tanin in the Dark Crystal, and Laki is exhausted. She also knows that she cannot leave without the Dark Crystal and quickly goes around the altar to look for it. She looks up and sees Guichi conjuring another fireball, and this one is bigger. He has his wings and is thankful that he has not realized how to use them. She is about to give up when she feels something under her boot and bends down to find the Dark Crystal covered in dirt and dust. She encases it with essence and picks it up. Laki sees the fireball strike the altar and hears the stone altar crack. She knows it is dangerous to stay any longer. She has the crystal in her hand, the Tome' of the Unholy Scriptures, tight against her chest, and before Guichi can throw another fireball, she is gone in a blinding flash.

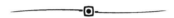

Guichi rushes to the altar where he had last seen Tanin. He feels the remnants of his essence, and he screams, "Damn you, BITCH! I will kill you" and quickly walks around the cavern, searching everywhere, when he comes across the remnants of a pair of dull ashen gray wings, with the feathers drying up and falling off, and a bloody knife on the floor near the wings.

Reality sets in, and he knows that the Tome of Unholy Scriptures and the piece of Dark Crystal with Tanin trapped inside are gone. Angry, he conjures an energy blast and shoots it at the cavern ceiling in frustration. Guichi screams for a second time, "You Fucking Bitch!" and knows that she has the piece of Dark Crystal and the Tome' given to them by the Twins. That is the only copy with the rites and rituals for joining the crystals and the sacred words to release the Dark God, Nimponin, from imprisonment. He must get both of them back, no matter what it takes. He needs the Tome' if not for anything else but to release his brother from the crystal. He swears to avenge his brother and destroy his sisters, especially Laki, that Bitch!

Laki returns to the cave in the mountain, and when she enters, Jutsuk is sitting on the pillows and looking much better. Jutsuk looks at her and says, "Nice attire." Laki smiles, walks over, kisses Jutsuk on the cheek, and then walks over to the hidden space in the wall and opens it. She places the Dark Crystal with the essence of Tanin imprisoned inside and the Book of Unholy Scriptures in the vault and then seals it. She sits on the pillows beside Jutsuk and explains what happened between her and Tanin and everything he said, from the Twins, the Dark Realm, a High Priestess, and finding the other Dark Crystals releasing Nimponin.

Then how Guichi showed up, gained his wings, and broke the barrier, and how she was able to grab the Dark Crystal and the Tome' and come back here.

Jutsuk looks at her and says, "Guichi discovered he has wings?"

Laki says, "Yes, and it is good that he did not know how to use them. I saw that when his wings manifested themselves, he looked in a lot of pain. When you and I discovered ours, it was more of a discomfort. We have the Tome' of Unholy Scriptures and a piece of the Dark Crystal with our brother inside. she smiles at Jutsuk and says, "Hopefully, that will buy us some time."

Jutsuk says, "While you were gone, I was thinking about what Mother told us, and we will need to work fast from what you have just told me. First, we will need three things: a *Spirit*ual leader with some connection to at least two of the five manas to counter this High Priestess's Dark Realm magic, along with her "Chosen." Second, we will need to build an army, a large army, and find someone to lead them," and finally we will need a temple, and once it is complete, we will have to find the "Gifted" that will battle these "Chosen that Tanin told you about."

Laki asks, "Do you think there might be another way?"

Jutsuk smiles and says, "No, I think this is the only way!"

Laki says, "Well then, I think we need to get started, but we cannot let anyone know what we did. It could ruin everything in what we have preached and built our beliefs. If it were to become known that what I did was completely out of hate, it could crush everything we have already built. Wouldn't you agree?"

Jutsuk looks at Laki and says, "Yes, I agree; we must not mention this to anyone." Now, shall we go out into this beautiful world and find our Champions?" Laki smiles and says, "Yes."

Chapter 16

Tokora

It has been five years since William left the Tatokai Islands, and he has been wandering through the lands of the Eight Kingdoms, searching for something but not exactly sure of what that something is, but something. William has passed through many towns and villages and has heard the stories of strange creatures and beasts terrorizing the towns and villages throughout the kingdoms.

William first started hearing the stories of these creatures just after he arrived on the mainland and had been traveling a little over a year and still had not encountered or seen them firsthand. He has made inquiries in the towns and has heard stories of people disappearing at night. Some are never seen again, while others are found mangled and mauled. The discoveries are usually in the morning, after the first light. Some victims were lucky, if you wanted to call it that, and received a decent burial. No matter what town or village William might pass through in his travels, the stories are always the same, robed demons with no facial features control beast-like monsters walking the lands.

Every time William hears the stories, he stays for a few days to see if these creatures or demons return. One night, William is in the local tavern sipping on a cold ale when the serving girl brings him some cheese and cold meats on a platter that he ordered, smiles at him, says, "Enjoy," and walks away to care for some other customers. William feels something different about the girl but does not dwell on it. He is sitting against a wall, eating some cheese and meat, and as he washes down his food, he thinks back to when he had encountered the robed demons and the strange beasts for the first time a little over three years ago. He remembers that he had just made camp and was sitting by his fire drinking some tea when he heard distinct a popping noise not far from where he was camping. He leaves his campsite to investigate the peculiar noise. He was getting close to where he thought the sound came from when he saw movement near an opening in a cluster of large boulders. He hid behind a tree, and that is when he saw one of the robed ones for the first time. It seemed to be muttering something, and then William sees a shimmering or something in the blackness inside the large gap between the boulders; the robed one has his arms raised. William is surprised to see the robed one face when his hood falls back, and that's when William sees why they say it's a demon, because the thing standing before him has no ears, nose, or lips, and over his eyes was a blood-soaked white cloth. Suddenly, he mutters something when a strange-looking beast steps through the shimmering gap between the boulders.

William decides that he has seen enough and goes to step away from the tree and does not realize it, but he steps on a small tree branch creating a loud snap in the stillness of the night. The robed figure hears the noise and instinctively turns and throws a fireball at the tree that William was hiding behind. William falls and watches the tree go up in flames. Unsure of what to do, William panics, and gets up to run, when he hears his grandmother's words, "William, the power of *Tatokai* is yours; call forth their power, release that power, destroy this vile evil!"

Williams's hands start to tremble. He looks down at them to find that they first glow a soft blue, then a bright red, followed by a pure white, and finally a light brown. William thinks of his grandmother, the islands, his family, and Alexandria. The bright red becomes a dark red, and the dark red extends from his hands; he is now holding two coiled whips in his hands and feels the power coming off them.

The robed one lets out a ferocious growl and charges William with a black sword in his hand. William instinctively lashes out with the two whips of fire mana, and they connect and wrap themselves around the demon's body, and the robed one immediately bursts into flames. Before its body hits the ground, its ashes are blown away by a slight breeze. William is surprised at what just happened, and then he catches movement out of the corner of his eye. He sees that the beast has somehow made its way behind him while was fighting the robed one.

Like the robed one, the beast charges with its claws, fully extended and its gaping mouth with sharp pointed teeth wide open, and then it leaps, and William realizes that he does not have time to bring the whips into effect, so he throws up his hands, and a white cloud shoots from his palms, and he feels a bitter cold. Moments later, the white cloud dissipates, and William stares at the beast mid-leap, just a meter from him. He calls forth the mana of earth, and a slim, almost spear-like rod of stone erupts from the ground and smashes into the frozen beast, and the beast shatters into hundreds of tiny ice crystals.

William cautiously approaches the cave, and as he stands in front of it and looks at the shimmering tear, he says one word, "*Chikashinmizawa*," and looks down and sees that his hands are glowing with a swirling array of colors. William holds his hand's side by side, with his palms facing each other. He slowly brings them together and has many vibrant colors swirling in a sphere between his hands. William feels more mana drawn into his hands and can now see the power in the sphere flowing from the four elemental mana's and watches it pulse as if trying to break free. He summons *Spirit*, and the Air around him turns thick, and then a pure, clear mist wraps itself around the four manas. The glowing, swirling sphere in his hands immediately calms down, and he admires the sphere as a creation of beauty. He knows it is a very powerful force to be reckoned with, so he releases the sphere into the blackness of the tear and then feels the explosion, followed by several agonizing screams of pain, and then the tear ceases to exist. He knows he must seal the cave's opening and call upon the *Spirit* and Earth manas. The ground trembles, and the entrance fills with a black obsidian stone, and once filled, he seals it with the five manas. He is walking back to his camp when he hears, "Sir, would you like another ale," William returns to the present and sees the serving girl standing there asking him if he would like another ale.

He looks at her and says, "Sorry, lost in thought, and yes, I would like another, please,"

William finishes his second ale, places some coins on the table, says thank you to the girl, and walks out. A couple of days later, he is walking through a large meadow, and comes across a crop of trees, and decides to make camp, That night, while drinking a cup of tea, he decides that he will need to practice to call forth the manas, and hone his skills. William knows he cannot depend on memories to bring them forth because he also knows that a split second of trying to remember could be his downfall. He remains in the meadow, without anyone around, and practices, and every day he gets better, quicker, and stronger. He hears his grandmother's voice and thoughts as she gives instructions and encouragement. After a month or so, he can now draw upon anyone of the five manas, and hopefully, by the time he encounters another robed one or a beast, he can call forth the manas to defeat these vile things as though he has been doing it his whole life. He breaks camp and continues with his journey.

William has been walking for a while, and though it is early, he decides to stop and rest for the night, he finds a good location, and when he opens his pack, the aroma of fresh venison stew floats along on an evening breeze. William decides to continue walking and follows the delicious aroma lingering in the Air. A small town appears at the base of a large rock outcropping, and he notices several caves along its base. The sun is just going behind a range of hills when he reaches the outskirts of the town. William knows something is wrong in this town, as he smells fear and death. He sees the town's name on the signpost, which says Tokora. He brings forth *Spirit* as he walks down the main street, and when he enters the town square, four men approach him. He sees two carrying swords and shields while the other two have long spears.

They meet William in the town square, and the group leader, "Can we help you, stranger?"

William says, "Yes, Sir. I am looking to get something to eat and a place to rest for the night."

The leader tells William, "Sir, these are trying times!"

William asks him, "Lieutenant, is it? Why is that?"

The Lieutenant looks at his men and says, "It would be better to tell you inside where it is safe," and asks William to follow them. The five of them head to the only tavern in town, and even before they reach the doors, they open. William enters and notices a prominent, heavy crossbar on a pivot, anchored to the wall, tied up against the wall just to the right of the door. William follows the four of them over to one of the larger tables in the tavern, and they all sit down. The barmaid, who introduces herself as Freya, comes to their table, smiles at William, and asks, "What would you like, Sir?" William tells her he will have a pot of hot water and asks the men sitting with him if they would like anything. The Lieutenant orders four glasses of water with fruit.

Moments later, Freya returns with four glasses of water, fruit inside, and a small ceramic teapot steaming with hot water. William has a small pouch in his hand, looks at the five of them, and says, "Tea, and is just about to pour some into the pot when Freya asks him to wait. She leaves, comes back, hands William a small envelope, and tells him it is a unique blend of tea. He says thank you, pours her tea into the pot, and carefully swirls the water. Seconds later, a sweet earthy aroma with a hint of mint erupts from the pot, but the aroma is not overpowering. William takes a sip, is overwhelmed by its taste, and smiles at her. He then hands her a small gold coin. She is quite surprised and tries to give it back to him, telling him it is way too much for four glasses of water with fruit and a pot of hot water. William tells her not to worry and think of it as an investment for future pots of hot water and her exquisite tea. She walks away with a smile on her face. William turns back to the four men, and they are staring at him. They tell William that it has been a while since they saw Freya smile, since her fiancé went missing just over two weeks ago, and something is terrorizing the town at night. William asks them what exactly is happening.

The Lieutenant says, "Sir, a little over three weeks ago, we started hearing strange noises at night. The following morning, we would find blood smeared on the roads; when we followed the blood trails, we would find the remains of animals, half-eaten and mutilated, usually in the fields north of town. Then about two weeks ago, one of the townsfolk disappeared and looked towards Freya, saying, "Her fiancé, and we have not been unable to find any trace of him" He pauses to take a sip of his water and then continues. "Some townsfolk have stated that they have seen strange beasts roaming the outskirts of the town at night. We are not sure exactly what we are dealing with."

William listens intently and asks, "Do you know where it might come from?"

The Lieutenant says, "We think from the fields north of town."

"How many victims since this beast or whatever has come to your town?"

The Lieutenant and his men confer for a moment, then he says, "There is only one still missing, but we found the others. Two elderly folks, a brother and sister, were discovered about a week ago after a routine home check. When this started, we tried to bring them into town until this was over, but the brother refused, telling us that they were born in this house and if so, be it, they will die in this house, and slammed the door. The next day, my men went back to try and convince them one more time, and that is when we found the two of them, and they were all mangled and mauled. We found a mother and daughter two days after completing our morning rounds."

William tells the four of them that he will be joining them tonight on their rounds. They start to protest, telling him that it's not good for a civilian to be out and that it would be safer for him to stay indoors.

William says, "Please do not worry, I have dealt with these creatures before, and if I can help this town get rid of them, I will!"

The four of them look at William, bewildered, trying to determine what could this one man with no weapons possibly do to help them resolve this nightmare. William waves Freya over and asks her, "Is the venison stew as good as it smells?" She smiles and says, "Better." William orders dinner for the five of them. During dinner, William learns that the Lieutenant's name is Joshua Pike and that he is in charge of the Town's Guard and the other three are Sargent Phillip Ross, Corporal Jonas Broth, and Corporal Peter Soon. They are just finishing dinner when the church bells start ringing to warn everyone to go home and secure their windows and doors. Everyone seems to leave the tavern at once, and within minutes the only people left in the bar are Freya, the barmaid, who William finds out that she and her fiancé are the owners and the five of them.

They remain at the table as William asks for more details on the attacks. They tell him what they know, the beasts always enter the town from the north, and it is swift to attack. William asks Freya for some parchment and a writing pencil. She brings it over, and William asks Joshua to draw a town map on the parchment. After he does, William takes the parchment, leans back in his chair, and taps his finger, thinking. He then asks, "As you know, the creatures always come from the north. Lieutenant Pike says, "Yes" Then William leans forward and tells them, "I have a plan, and this is what we will do!"

When William finishes laying out the plan's details, Joshua stands and asks William, "Are you sure you want to do this?"

William replies, "Yes!" and calls Freya over and asks, "Freya would you mind keeping an eye on my things? I don't want anything to happen to my tanbur." She agrees and puts his belongings behind the bar to keep them safe.

William places some coins on the table, looks at the four men, and all he says is, "Shall we?"

They hear the wooden cross beam lowering to secure the doors after leaving. William quickly tells the four of them to hand him their weapons. William takes the two swords and shields and chants, "*Kenryoku Hirata Bu,*" His hands start to glow soft blue, and he touches the swords and shields to enchant their weapons. William then takes the two spears and performs a slightly different chant, "*Kenryoku Hiratai Re,*" and his hands begin to glow a vibrant red. He then lays his hands on the spearheads, which glow the same rich red.

Joshua sees Williams's hands glow with the different colors and asks, "Can I ask why your hands are glowing different colors and exactly what have you done to our weapons?"

William looks at the four of them and says, "I have enchanted your weapons with the different manas or elements as you might know them to help you fight these creatures that are terrorizing your town and killing innocent people.

Joshua looks at William, knows he can trust him, and says, "Okay, what now?"

William asks if they have any netting, and a few minutes later, Philip and Jonas return with a large net. William takes the net and enchants it with a dark blue hue. He tells them to hang the net between the two buildings on each side of the road leading north out of town and be ready to cut the ropes with their long knives. He then tells Joshua and Peter to be prepared with their swords.

William stands in the square listening when he faintly hears the distinctive pop north of the town and says, "It's here," and he allows the mana of *Spirit* slowly make its way up the street to the outskirts of town and then draws it back leaving a faint residue in its wake. A few minutes later, a large beast enters the outskirts of town, and it is exactly like the others and does not resemble any known species on Chikyu. The beast stops just at the edge of the town and raises its snout to sniff the Air. It smells the scent, growls, and moves forward cautiously. The mentality of the predatory beast takes over when it sees the three of them and charges.

He stands there waiting, and as the creature is just about to enter under the net, he calls out, "Now!".

Joshua and Phillip simultaneously cut the ropes, and the net falls and lands on the top of the beast. The five of them see that the more the beast struggles to break free, the more it becomes entangled. William's enchantment on the net holds, preventing the creature's claws from ripping it apart.

When William tells them to stop, Jonas and Peter approach the beast with their spears raised. Joshua and Phillip quickly join them, and all four stand there looking at this hideous-looking beast and then at William.

William hears two low mitten growls, then looks at the four of them and tells them that two more of these creatures have just arrived on the outskirts of town. The four seem worried, but William assures them everything will be okay.

Jonas and Peter go to raise their spears to kill the beast when William tells them to wait. William sees the questioning look on their faces and says, "Trust me. We can use this as a distraction" and instructs Jonas and Peter to move to each side of the road and stay hidden, and then tells Joshua and Phillip to line up on each side of him with their bucklers and swords at the ready.

They no sooner get situated when two beasts enter the square, one about the same size as the one caught in the net and the other a bit larger. William hears Joshua say, "Geezus, will you look at the size of that one!" The larger one stops looking at the three of them and concentrates on the creature trapped in the net. It approaches the net, extends its claws, and swipes at the net, there are some sparks as if flint were striking stone, but the net holds. Its gaze returns to the three of them, and it seems that it is trying to determine which one is the biggest threat; then it notices William standing between the other two, and it somehow senses that he is the more significant threat.

The large one leaps, with its teeth bared and claws out, directly at William while the smaller one races to the one still entangled in the net. William raises his hands, glowing a deeper blue than before, casts them straight out in front of him, and hits the creature with a blast of ice. The beast falls to the ground, landing on its side, and William tells Phillip and Jonas to strike the beast to its exposed areas that are not encased in ice and to be careful of its teeth and claws. Phillip stabs the creature's front leg and watches it turn black, and then the leg shatters. Phillip is in awe of the effects of the sword. Jonas stabs the beast in the shoulder and watches as the creature's shoulder seems to melt from intense heat. A few more stabs by them, and the beast is still.

The smaller beast sees what is happening to its companion and charges Phillip and Jonas,

but William raises his hands, and the beast is caught by swirling Air and becomes bound by the bands of Air. William slams the beast to the ground with great force and breaks its neck. Joshua and Peter attack the creature with the same effects and then realize it is already dead.

They hear the one entangled in the net screaming in pain and watch as it struggles madly in the net, trying to break free. The five men approach it, and William tells Joshua to slice off one of the creature's front paws and then tells Peter to touch the severed limb with the tip of his spear. They do just as he says, and when done, William tells them to stand back because he will release the beast. All four of them look at him, and he says again, "Trust me." Then William removes the enchantments from the net, and the beast tears it to shreds. The beast instinctively goes to turn on them, but Jonas and Peter bring up their spears, and it recoils in fear, then turns and heads north out of the town at a slow limping gait.

William tells the four of them to come with him as they all keep pace with the beast as it continues to head north. Joshua tells William that it is heading towards Snyder's Field. The creature struggles to jump over the stone wall and enters the field. William tells them to stay low and to follow him. William peers over the wall, and he sees an outcropping of large rocks with an opening, and the Air is shimmering in the blackness; William sees the tear in the middle of the cave entrance and that it is about two meters high.

William continues to watch the beast limp back to the cave when he spots a robed figure standing in the shadows about three meters from the cave opening. He stares at him and sees the blood-soaked white cloth covering his eyes. He ducks down behind the wall and tells the four of them that the robed figure is deadlier than the beasts, but they need to kill him because he is the one who controls them and can bring more through the tear. They look at him bewildered, and William says, "I will explain later. William whispers to Jonas and Peter, "Can you throw those the spears and hit your target?" They both nod their heads. William tells them to make their way around the stone wall until they are opposite each other and then wait for his signal. They say, "Yes, sir," and move out in opposite directions keeping low behind the wall, and are soon in position. William tells Joshua and Phillip to charge the robed figure once Jonas and Peter hit it with their spears.

The creature they were following approaches the gap in the rocks, into a shimmering tear, and disappears. William starts to chant, and the ground begins to shake, and without warning, a wall of earth erupts from the ground blocking the cave entrance and preventing the robed figure from going back through. The robed one shouts out a scream, turns to look out over the field, and shoots red balls of flame blindly across the area. William shouts, "NOW!"

Jonas and Peter throw their spears. Peter hits the robed figure first, just below his chest on the side, and it lets out a loud shriek, and smoke starts to emanate from where the spear penetrated his side. The robed one's hands glow red as he turns towards Peter. Jonas' spear catches him in the back right between its shoulder blades, and smoke starts emanating from this second wound. The robed figure shrieks in agony, and its hands stop glowing. It reaches for the spear in its side, and as it tries to pull the spear tip out, it pulls back its hand in pain, as the spear's shaft and steel tip enchantments cause its hand to turn black. The robed one drops to its knees as black blood pours from its wounds and then tumbles forward, shaking and convulsing white foam pours from its mouth.

William approaches, and as it stops convulsing, he sees that it is not quite dead. William squats beside it to examine it. He pulls back its hood and sees that it has neither nose nor ears, and when William lifts the blindfold from its eyes, he sees that the sockets are empty. William undoes its robe and sees for the first time that the creature has no genitals. The two men gasp in shock as the Lieutenant points at a mark or tattoo on the chest of the robed one, and Phillip asks aloud, "How could this be? What could have done this to him? What could have changed him into this?" William is uncertain of what is happening and tells Joshua and Phillip to drive their swords into its body to finish it. Joshua tells William he can't, and Phillip shakes his head no. Jonas and Peter arrive, and what they see is too much for them, and they turn away, repulsed. William finds himself staring at what he knows was once human and places his hand on its chest and chants, "*Ite To Hidaku No Sensi*" William stands and tells them that it is dead and Joshua and Phillip to pierce the corpse. Hesitantly, they take their swords and drive them into its body. The body begins to smoke, and William tells them to stand back when suddenly the body erupts in flames, and just as quickly, there is only ash left.

William walks up to the earth wall and waves his hands, and the wall slowly dissolves, returning to the earth from whence it came.

William looks into the shimmering tear and sees the blackness. He politely asks the four of them to cover their eyes, and when they do, he summons the four elements of Air, Earth, water, and Fire. He weaves them together and then calls forth the fifth element of *Spirit*, and once it intertwines with the other four, he says, "*Chikashinmizawa*," and sends the sphere directly into the blackness. They all hear agonizing screams, and the tear closes. William immediately seals the cave with the *Spirit*, Earth, and black obsidian stone and binds the opening with the five manas. William tells the four of them that they can remove their hands. They remove their hands from their eyes, and Joshua asks him if it is over. William asks them if there are other caves close. They say yes, and give him a quizzical look.

William looks at the four of them and says, "Let's go back to the tavern, and I will try to explain over a cold ale." As they walk back, they explain to William that the robed one they just killed was Freya's fiancé. He asks them how they know, and Joshua tells him about the betrothal tattoo the robed one had on his chest.

William remains silent for a few and then says, "Let's not tell Freya about this; she has gone through enough. They all agree, and then Phillip asks William why he wants to know about other caves in the area.

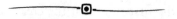

When they return to the tavern, they are surprised that somehow word has spread that the monsters are gone, and the tavern is full of locals, drinking and in great *Spirit*s, hearing that the monsters are gone. While William is waiting for his hot water, Joshua asks, "What were those things?" William tells them that he thinks the robed one is called a Sutaraukaji. The four make the sign of the Laki-Jutsuk and praise the

Goddesses. He also tells them that he does not know those beasts because he has only encountered them once before tonight, and no one knows anything about them.

Freya brings William his hot water, kisses him on the cheek, and says, "Thank you," then walks away. The four of them stare at William and tell him that Freya has never shown any display of affection to anyone since you know. William drinks his tea and asks them if there are other large caves or mine shafts near the town. Joshua mentions several caves that the townsfolk use as a shelter in an emergency. William tells them that they will need to look at them tomorrow. He finishes his tea, stands up, and says goodnight. The four also stand and tell William they will see him tomorrow.

That night William is lying in bed with just a sheet because the night is warm. He hears a light tap on his door and says, "Come in." The door opens, and Freya is standing in the doorway. She enters, closes the door, and walks up to William to stand beside his bed. Freya lets her robe fall to the floor, and William stares at this beautiful woman standing before him. She sees movement under the sheet and then lifts the sheet to slide in beside him. It has been a long time since he has felt a woman beside him, and he feels her warm body next to him, and she starts to place delicate kisses along his neck. He goes to hold her, but she does not allow it and forces his hands out from his sides. He tries to say something, but Freya places her finger to his lips and says, Shhh!

She leans over and whispers, "Tonight is for you; all you have to do is be here." She reaches out, runs her fingernails on his manhood, and then slowly works her way down his chest, kissing softly. When she reaches it, she gently holds it and starts stroking it. She slowly opens her mouth and starts moving her head up and down. William has never had this sensation before, and he becomes more aroused. Freya is a little surprised and becomes more energetic and enthusiastic in her endeavors. She feels him about to erupt when she stops and runs her tongue back up his chest to kiss him, wantonly on the lips. She moves to straddle him and guides him in gently, and as she takes all of him, she feels something new and realizes it is a complete raw ecstasy that she has never felt before. Her senses reach out to grasp the warm sensations, the cold chills, and a gentle breeze that causes her nipples to become more erect. Freya starts to ride him hard, and then she has a sensation of the very earth itself reaching up and taking hold of her, and then she feels it, the very pinnacle of pleasure. When she feels she can take no more, William reaches up to brush her hair out of the way, and that is when he sees the small betrothal tattoo above her left breast. He gently rubs his thumb over the tattoo, and then Freya gasps, takes a deep breath, throws her head back, and places her hand over her mouth to stifle the oncoming moans of ecstasy. An explosion she has never experienced causes her to arch her back, and her body spasms uncontrollably as a wave of orgasms ripples through her body. The spasms begin to slow, and Freya falls onto William's chest, gulping in deep breaths, desperately trying to catch her breath, and she is completely exhausted. Slowly, her breathing returns to normal, and she places a long kiss on his lips, says, "Thank you," and carefully moves off him, and as she does, she softly moans. Freya goes to stand, and as William steadies her, she wonders if her legs will support her. Shakily, she grasps the headboard, cautiously leans over, gives William another long sensual kiss, and says, "Thank you, and I know," as a tear rolls down her cheek.

In the morning, Joshua, Peter, Philip, and Jonas go with William to check on the cave they mentioned yesterday as an emergency shelter, and William asks the four of them to please wait outside. William enters the cave and begins to chant. A blue glow saturates the cave inside, and the four of them see it. William walks back out, and he tells them that everything is good.

They walk back to town and are in the tavern, and William thanks Joshua, Phillip, Peter, and Jonas for their assistance and tells them everything should be fine, and they should not have any more problems. Jonas asks to go with him as his bodyguard and traveling companion, but William tells him that it won't be necessary. He knows something is out there calling to him, and he is not sure what it might be, but he knows he has to be by himself when he finds it. Jonas, Phillip, and Peter shake William's hand and say, Thank you," then Sargent Ross says, "Duty Calls," Corporals Soon and Broth salute the Lieutenant and William then the three of them leave the tavern.

Joshua remains, and as he sits across from William, he reaches into his pocket and pulls out an old folded paper. He unfolds it, lays it down on the table, and slides it towards William.

William looks down at it, and it is an old poster inquiring if anyone has seen this man and to report him. William stares at the picture and can tell it resembles him. He looks up at the Lieutenant, and all the Lieutenant says is, "Just wanted to show you and let you know that these are out there." He then grabs the poster, crumbles it up, and tosses it in the fire. William looks at him, and the Lieutenant says, "Fuck em!" and then smiles.

William stays in the town another four days, and once the smell of fear dissipates, William knows it is time for him to leave. That night after the tavern is quiet, William grabs his gear, leaves his room, and stops behind the bar to fill up his canteen from the pump and to take some meat from the bar, when he hears a voice behind him say, "What do you think you are doing? William stands up and turns to find Freya standing in the middle of the tavern with her hands on her hips. The moonlight streams through the tavern windows and highlights her figure through her night shift. He sees that she is wearing no undergarments under her gown and sees her breasts as they were the past couple of nights, full and firm, while her waist travels down to her slender hips. She anticipated another night of lovemaking, but she sees him dressed in his traveling clothes and now knew those nights would be no more.

William tells her that he has to leave, secures the top of his canteen, and leaves some coin on the bar for the meat he is taking. He walks over to her, raises her chin with his finger, and as she stares at him, he kisses her forehead and whispers, "When the time comes."

He then steps around her and closes the door behind him, leaving her alone with tears in her eyes when he hears, "Wait." William turns, and Freya quickly walks up to him, embraces him, places a piece of paper in his hand, and says, "To remember me." She then kisses him on the cheek, and as William exits the tavern, he hears the crossbar being lowered and "Thank you. For everything"

William heads northeast out of town, and just as the sun begins to rise, he comes to a crossroad with a weathered sign. He looks at the sign, and the town names are faded, but he can just make out a town called Tolland to the north, Blanby to the south, and the sign pointing straight ahead is too faded to read. William adjusts his gear on his back, says, "Why not," and starts walking along the road with unreadable markings. While walking, he pulls out the paper that Freya gave him, and when he looks at it and smiles, and then puts the piece of paper with her tea recipe safely away.

Chapter 17

Imprisonment

Tanin's senses slowly return, and he remembers seeing his sister, Laki, looking down at him with hatred in her eyes. He was shocked that she and her sister Jutsuk have always preached love and harmony. Then he remembers her battering him with questions about, Guichi and what he is doing, the Twins, the High Priestess, the pain, and he told her everything she asked. He also remembers her showing him a pair of rotting dark gray wings, and he shivers to realize they were his wings. Then he recalls that she had the Tome' of Unholy Scriptures, and he hears the chanting of the words written in the Tome,' *"Senyo Ori Mukashi Kenyokyu Koeta,"* and he sees the Dark Crystal start to glow and pulse. He feels no pain but can see small smoke-like wisps of his Spiritual essence floating, which were pulled towards something Laki has placed on his chest. Tanin feels something; what it is, he is uncertain, but there is no pain as Tanin lies there immobile, and then it dawns on him what is happening. He feels Laki lift his arm and show him his hand and fingers as she continues chanting the same spell repeatedly. Tanin starts screaming as he watches his hand change into the wisps of smoke, and the Dark Crystal draws his Spiritual essence into it. He now realizes that, like the Dark God Nimponin, he will be trapped in one of the pieces of Dark Crystal. The pull of the crystal is too great as he continues to feel parts of himself dissolve. He has lost all feeling in most of his body, and what feeling remains begins to follow and go numb.

He is himself, but it does not feel like a physical presence. It feels more flowing, and just before he loses even that feeling, he hears a voice shout, "Stop," but it is too late as the last of his mental and physical being is now in a different place from where he was.

His mind is blank, and his memory is gone, and all he knows is that somehow, he is floating precariously through something, what it could be, he does not know or comprehend, and only knows that he is scared of wherever this might be. He concentrates, trying to remember when flashes of images appear, images that are familiar but are also unfamiliar.

The visions start to last longer and begin to meld together, and soon he sees what has happened to him. Anger and hatred fill his presence, and when that happens, he feels something more substantial occupying the same space he is floating in, though he is not exactly sure what it is. Then he senses it, and it immediately saturates his mind. The sensation he feels is evil, a hatred, an impurity, so deplorable that the fear he is now experiencing is so vile and terrifying and Tanin screams, or at least in his mind because he cannot fathom the horrors. Somehow, and though he cannot explain it, he now knows that his sister was the one who entrapped him in this piece of the Dark Crystal.

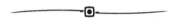

 The Stain is furious and lashes out at this new lesser being that now shares the same space as it does and watches as a searing pain pierces its essence. Tanin now remembers everything that was his forgotten memories just a few moments ago. His hatred for his sisters returns, and he despises them so much that he wants to crush them and lavish on their broken and beaten bodies. He slowly calms himself and tries to remember what he did wrong, but he can see no wrong in his plan. He should have been able to destroy them because the dark is stronger than the Light. He can now feel the expanse of the crystal and thinks that it is more significant than he would have expected, but at the same time, he also feels confined, as if something were pressing him into a small insignificant corner. He tries to reach out, and as he does, he feels a small tendril of something touching his mind, and once there is contact, it is too late. Unfamiliar with what is about to happen, his mind is defenseless, and he feels more pain and suffering than he thought earlier. Through all the grief, he hears a voice, which tells him that he is weak, his mind is weak, and that he should not be allowed to exist. He tries to defend himself from whatever it is and finally pushes out what is causing him this unsurmountable pain and fear. Seconds pass, and then he finds some relief from its tormenting onslaught. He knows that what he has done has put him on the brink of using anything and everything he has and can call forth and let out a small sigh.

 He then hears a burst of sick laughter, and the tendril of terrifying pain he has come to fear rears back, smashing his defenses as though they did not exist. The pain, horror, and vileness once again saturate his being, and when he is on the verge of what he thinks is the brink of death, a calmness comes over him, unexpectedly.

He then hears a thought, asking, "Who are you?"

Tanin hesitates when suddenly he feels the excruciating pain shoot through his mind, and he screams. Sobbing, he projects his thoughts to whatever has attacked him and says, "I am Tanin, from the world of Chikyu, son of Kamiyobo and the Dark…

The entity cuts him off and projects the pain again into Tanin's mind as he hears the voice ask why he is lying to him. The voice asks, "Why do you smell of her?" and applies tremendous pain, though this time not as excruciating.

When the pain subsides and Tanin can cast his thoughts, he asks the voice, "What do you mean the smell of her? Who are you talking about? I have no idea who you say I smell of!"

Tanin feels the pain, and this time it is worse than the first time, his mind touches on the verge of exploding, and when he feels himself about to explode, it stops. Again, the voice asks him, "Who are you, and why do you smell of her?"

Tanin allows the now throbbing pain to fade, and it dawns on him as he now understands that when he came to be, the corruption from the Stain possessed the male God's body and that Stain became part of him. He now realizes what the voice in his head is asking. He answers, a little more sternly than he thought he could bring forth, "I am Tanin, a God from the planet "Chikyu" my existence came about from the union of the female and male Gods of our world. They created us. I reek of her because she was my mother, and as for my father, he was weak, and the "Stain" corrupted his body and consumed him. My brother and I have devoted ourselves to the Darkness and the God, Nimponin. We have been searching the lands to find the other pieces of Dark Crystal so that we can join them and release Nimpinon. The tendril releases him, and Tanin feels the pain slowly fade.

The voice demands, "Where are these other pieces you seek?" tell me.

"I do not know; my brother and I had in our possession one piece that was given to us by a set of Twins from the Dark Realm, and I think my brother found another one in a cave in the northwestern part of these lands.

"You say you already have one piece, and your brother may have found a second piece. Will he join them?"

"I am not sure, and I think that my sister might have stolen one of the pieces and the Tome that explains how to fuse the crystals and release the trapped essences."

"Where is this piece you speak of now, and who is this sister?" the voice demands, and as the tone of his thoughts increases, so does the pain in Tanin's mind, though just slightly.

"My sister is the one who entrapped me here, just like my mother did to you, millions of millennia ago. As for the piece of crystal, where it is now, I do not know!"

The voice mentally shouts, "You lie!" and inflicts another onslaught of pain. Tanin whimpers and tries to understand how he feels the pain. He knows he is a celestial entity, so why does he feel the pain. When he feels the tendril strike him a second time and then a third. Tanin has had enough and mentally shouts "STOP!" and lashes out with everything he can muster.

The tendril pulls back, and he hears the voice say, "How dare you defy me," and inflicts an exuberant amount of pain on his mind. Tanin feels his mind is on fire, and as he trembles with pain, a scene appears in his mind in explicit detail. He is now witnessing the creation of the heavens. Nimponin's imprisonment, the manifestation of the Black Hole, and how Void is a portal to the Dark Realm. The images end with pieces of the crystal shooting out into space and the "Void" drawing other pieces into its center. The images slowly fade, and consciousness becomes something more. He dares to reach out, and after what seems an endless expanse, he feels it, a pinpoint, and he lightly touches it. The horror explodes so fast that Tanin cannot react quickly enough. He is so overwhelmed by the evil that he finds himself torn to pieces, like when he was first imprisoned, and then everything stops, and Tanin knows he is no longer broken; he feels different, more alive than before. Any remnants of good within him are now gone. He immediately senses the Darkness more than ever; he feels it coursing through his celestial being. He embraces the hate, the evil, and the vileness to the point that whatever remnants of anything good within him are gone. He feels hatred for the Light and his sisters like the entity.

Tanin reaches out with his mind, and the entity touches him and says, "Now you understand, the powers you will be able to reap will be unsurmountable.

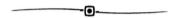

Tanin knows that this evil, this hatred, and vileness, is not an abomination but a solution to anything living. Tanin does not think of himself as once being broken, only misdirected. He has cast away anything associated with his Mother, sisters, and anything else that this world might embrace as good, and he knows that he must take his thoughts and his new beliefs and spread them throughout Chikyu.

The Darkness invades Tanin's mind, and though the pain is nothing compared to what it used to be, Tanin displays no emotion as he witnesses their creation. They are awake, and rage courses through his being as he sees his sisters and what his Mother instructs them in the world's ways. He continues to observe as Guichi, and himself go out into the world and touch the most deplorable and despicable souls they can find. He and Guichi are in the cavern, and they capture Jutsuk. He sees their fight unfold and assumes that his sisters have lost. Now beaten and bleeding, he drags Jutsuk over to Laki and drops her on the ground. He turns his back and now sees his mistake. He watches as his sisters make contact with his other. Then his sister Laki suddenly displays an exuberant amount of power, more than he could have anticipated. He sees himself on the altar and this Laki's lips moving, and he knows without hearing that she is chanting the entrapment incantation. He feels the pull of the crystal as his body dissolves into a whisp. The entity is disgusted by what it has just witnessed and cannot believe that this tiny insignificant being could be so weak and pathetic, and it releases him. Tanin cringes from his release. Nimponin reaches out to him once again, and Tanin can feel the distaste that he is emitting. He projects that he and Guichi were wrong in being sent out into the world to preach what they had interpreted as his will.

Tanin listens to its thoughts to project the vileness onto this world. Tanin listens to him with more enthusiasm than he ever listened to his Mother's lectures. The lectures continue and seem to go on endlessly, then at one point, because time does not exist in this crystal, the lessons stop. Tanin is taken back by the eerie silence and reaches out with his mind.

He seeks out the one, finds nothing, begins to panic, and realizes that he is alone, but how is that possible? And asks himself, "How could he be alone?" He extends his thought out farther and farther to only find nothing and continues to panic.

The vileness of the Dark One inundates him once again, and then his thoughts take form and speak to him and say, "You and your brother are weak and pathetic, and the two of you will never be able to defeat your sisters. Unlike your sisters who join together to fight, you and your brother fight separate battles, whereas your sisters fight these battles as one. That is how they were able to defeat you and entrap you in the crystal."

Tanin reaches out to him and, with anger in his thoughts, "What can I do? I need to destroy them, I need to humiliate them, and I need to crush...."

The Dark One lashes out, induce Tanin's mind with pain, and says, "You can do nothing!" The voice tells him, "You can do nothing because you and your brother are stupid and weak. But I will teach you, and when you leave this prison, you can prepare your brother for the true ways of the Dark Realm. Remember one thing: You will need to join four pieces of the crystal for me to escape this prison. Once free, the power I will generate will be enough to rain devastation on this world.

Chapter 18

Nova Meets Mia and Mae

Nova stands on the black diamond precipice and looks over her growing army. She sees her army growing daily as her Tashisans continue spreading the word about the Dark Scriptures. When they arrive, she has tasked General Picard Harris and General Buford T. Heath to recruit and train every man and woman into the Barrens. They are to train and categorize the new and place them within their ranks from Elite down to the skullduggery. Those who do not meet the requirements set forth by Harris are ordered to report to Colonel Tomas and Colonel Sayle. They will take them and initiate them into the ranks of the Zokotarumo, which consist of murderers, prostitutes, and thieves. Once they become a Zokotarumo, they believe that when one defiles oneself, a person demonstrates a commitment to all who participate in the self-mutilation and becomes one with the whole body of Zokotarumo. The markings and piercings also allow one to identify as a whole.

Colonel Sayle accepts the Zokotarumo, agreeing upon the nickname Freaks. The High Priestess has told Colonels Sayle and Tomas that she needs an unstoppable army, and if his small army of Zokotarumo or Freaks can help her fulfill her wishes, so be it. He will do anything, even die for her, so her dream comes true. Nova sees her army growing daily but knows she cannot move forward with her Master's plans until she has a well-disciplined army to command. An army that can wreak havoc and destruction on this world and be an unstoppable juggernaut so that she can fulfill her Master's wishes. She has set the standards for fulfilling her needs, and though they are not so far out there to be untouchable, she feels that she is missing an element to make her army that unstoppable juggernaut, a force to be reckoned with. Nova stands, walks back to her chambers frustrated, and tries to relax by drinking a glass of wine and lying on her bed. She sits up and starts flipping through the pages of the Tome of Dark Scriptures. She feels empty and craving something but can't pinpoint what she needs. Nova casually turns the pages looking but not looking, and as she flips past a few pages, she feels something. She goes back and stops, finds the page, runs her fingers over the words, and feels a sense of belonging. She looks at the strange shapes drawn on the pages, and they slowly start swirling and shifting on the page. She is mesmerized as the once written words, conditions, and letters on the page turn into something new and unimaginable. Slowly the swirling stops, and she sees an image, a circle, a dark hole with depth, and two rings of words slowly moving around the outside edge of the image. The outer ring of words moves clockwise, and the inner ring moves counter-clockwise. It is challenging to distinguish between the two rings as they constantly move.

    She sits up, places the book in her lap, and tries reading the outer ring of words around the edges of the image. She sits there trying to read as the words are constantly moving around the edge, and she finds herself losing her place, or she also finds herself repeating the exact words repeatedly. After an hour of getting nowhere, she decides to read the inner circle of words that traverse the page in the opposite direction as the outer layer, but as she reads the words out loud, she starts to get a severe headache, and the words blur. She closes the book; her headache disappears, and her vision becomes clear.

    She leaves the book open on the bed to refill her glass and contemplates her options for reading the words without getting a headache or blurry vision. She takes a sip of wine and thinks of maybe trying to read the words slowly, and as she reads them, she can write them down on parchment. It starts well; she can read and copy, read and copy, then a severe headache hits her, and she stops. She carefully closes the book, her headache subsides, and she looks down at the parchment and watches the words slowly fade. She is more frustrated, knowing she has just wasted the past two hours. It is late, and Nova falls asleep with the book open to the page. The morning comes, and Nova hears one of her servants bringing her some tea and a bowl of warm water to refresh herself. She gets out of bed to splash some water on her face. She dries her face, and as she leans on the dresser, she stares at herself in the mirror. She looks tired and can feel the frustration building again, and she hasn't even looked at the book this morning. She knows she is missing something and must solve this mystery lying before her.

NIMPONIN

She glances at the book on the bed in the mirror's reflection, and then she sees ii, as the book is open to the page with the black Void. She looks closely and sees that the words around the diagram are not moving and are legible but different. The words are backward, but she can read them. She walks over to the bed and picks up the book, and when she looks down, the words are spinning as they did. She carries it back to her dresser. She places the book on her dresser and holds it to the mirror. The words are not moving, and she can read them. She brings the book back to the bed and sends for a mirror. A young slave enters her chambers and hands Nova a mirror. Nova dismisses her and then holds it up to see the page in its reflection. She sees that the words are not spinning and that she can read them. When she finishes with the outer circle of words, it dawns on her that she does not have a headache or blurry vision. She starts reading the inner circle. When done, she recites the words and runs her fingers around the edges of the image of the dark Void and feels excitement in their touch, and the hair on her arms stands up. She reads the words several more times and soon has them memorized. She closes the book, walks over, and places it in an elaborate chest. She closes the lid and locks it with a key. She turns the key, says, "*Akappanasi*," and hears the distinct click to let her know that the locking mechanism is in place.

She remembers the words underneath the picture of the dark hole, "When the moon is at its fullest, a dark gateway will appear. Upon entering, the win will allow you back. If you fail, you shall be nevermore."

She walks out to the precipice and looks into the evening sky. The night sky is full of clouds; at first, she does not see the moon. The clouds slowly part, and she looks at an almost full moon. She says mostly to herself, "One more night," and returns to her chambers. The following day, Nova is excited, and as the day drags by, she starts to get restless. Nova sees one of the slave girls and tells her to get some wine. Then, a few moments later, the young slave carries her wine on a tray and places it on the table. She goes to leave. Nova stops her and tells her to tell everyone; under no circumstances will she be disturbed. The young slave says, "Yes, Mistress," and is gone and closes the doors behind her.

Nova slides some furniture, throws back a rug, and in the spot, she has just cleared, she can see the moon through the hole in her chamber's ceiling. She takes a deep breath and recites the words she memorized from the Scriptures. At first, there is uncertainty, but there could have been a shimmer. She stands in her chambers, and by the light of the torches, she again chants, "*Kurawafu Kuritomo Fuka Kyudoko,*" still nothing. She concentrates harder and repeats the spell once again. Then a tiny pinpoint of darkness appears before her and then disappears. She tries several times but can only muster a point of darkness. She walks over to her table, grabs the glass of wine, and takes a sip, wondering what she is doing wrong. Then she remembers the words, "When the moon is full… She throws back her chamber doors and walks out of her chambers to stand on the precipice of the cavern. She basks in the almost full moon's glow and repeats the chant, "*Kurawafu Kuritomo Fuka Kyudoko.*"

Suddenly a black fluctuating mass appears before her and then vanishes. She tries again and can keep it open a little longer this time. She walks to the very edge of the precipice and slowly and carefully brings her hands up, thinks about stepping into the black mass, and then thinks better of it. She has an enormous headache and decides not to step through because she wants to be aware and not be distracted. She closes the portal, steps back from the edge, and returns to her chambers. She walks over to the chest, opens it, and sees that the Dark Scriptures are safe.

The following day, she awakes, and though tired from lack of sleep, she realizes that her headache is gone. She walks over to the chest, unlocks it, and pulls out the Tome'. She sits cross-legged on her bed, takes a couple of deep breaths, opens the Tome', and flips through the pages. She comes across a passage that seems to be directed right at her, and she swears it was not there yesterday. She reads from the passage, "Through trials and tribulations, a woman will rise from the depths and come forth and become the anointed High Priestess of the sacred Dark Religion. She will fulfill the requirements of the Dark Scriptures that the very Gods wrote. She will go forth into the world to find the four. The four must be pure in heart and maidenhood, untouched and pristine. These four will assist the newly appointed High Priestess in her endeavors to fulfill the wishes of the Gods. These four will be the "Chosen" and swear complete devotion to her and her alone. They will answer to none but her. "So, say the Dark Scriptures, and so it will come to pass."

She is about to close the book when an additional passage reveals itself right before her eyes at the bottom of the page, and she continues reading.

Two will be brought forth as a pair. One is to become the fourth "Chosen," and the other will become a "*Sakuri*. "The Sakuri will fulfill the High Priestess' wishes at all costs. She will be a shadow in the night and a manifestation of death at the wishes of the High Priestess.

Nova stops reading, closes the book, and sits there trying to figure out how she will find the three "Chosen" so that they can find the fourth and the "Sakuri." Nova hears a soft knock on the door and says, "Enter," a young slave girl enters and informs her that the full moon is just beginning to rise. Nova looks at her, says, "Thank you," and dismisses her. The young slave smiles, bows, and goes to step back, but then Nova says, "Wait, come here." The young slave stops and walks over to stand before her. Nova pats the bed and tells her to sit down. The young girl sits down, and Nova can tell she is nervous.

"Is your maidenhood still intact? Nova asks,

The young slave says, "Yes."

Nova looks at her and asks her, "You look familiar. Have we met before?"

The young slave looks at her and says, "Yes."

Suddenly she brandishes a small knife from underneath her shift and lunges at Nova, aiming for her heart.

Nova is quick to deflect the blade away from her heart but not before it slices her upper arm. She punches the young slave, knocking her to the floor, and when she does, the young slave girl drops the knife. Nova yells, "Guards!" Two of her Elite rush into the room and see Nova bleeding. They immediately grab the young slave and stand her up. Nova picks up the small knife, walks up to her, places the blade against her throat, and calmly asks, "Why?"

The young slave looks at her and says, "You murdered my family."

Nova looks at her and asks, "Who was your family?"

The young slave tells her that her family was inside the house next door to the whorehouse, and when she burned down the whorehouse, her family's home also went up in flames, killing her father, mother, a younger sister, and her baby brother.

Nova looks at her and says, "That is too bad."

The young slave is hanging between the two guards, weeping, and Nova goes to walk away when she stops and turns back to the young slave and asks, "What is your name?"

The young slave stops crying, but she answers, "Erin."

In a stern voice, Nova asks, "Erin, what?"

The young girl looks at her and says, "Tally, Erin Tally, why?"

"Well, Erin Tally, why don't you join them!" and runs the knife across her throat. The look of surprise on Erin's face brings a smile to her own.

She nods to the guards, and as they drag her away, she leaves a trail of blood behind her.

Nova looks at her forearm and sees that she is still bleeding and covers the gash with her palm and chants, *"Byoki Go Saseru,"* she removes her hand, and other than the dried blood, the gash is gone.

She calls for a slave, and two enter her room. She orders one to summon her Elite Commander and tells the other to pass the word to all the slaves that any slave who enters her chambers will not be allowed to wear any pieces of top clothing. The slave bows and leaves. Her Elite Commander steps forward, comes to attention, and says, "Yes, my Kaisoshosuko." Nova tells her that she is not to be disturbed under any circumstances. Her commander bows and say, "Yes, my Kaisoshosuko," steps out of the room and closes the doors behind her. Nova then hears her giving orders that no one is to enter her chambers. Nova steps into the moonlight, beaming down through the hole in her chamber's ceiling. She looks up and stares at the full moon and feels elated. She starts the chant, *"Kurawafu Kuritomo Fuka Kyudoko".* A black portal appears, and it pulses and gradually grows in size, and soon it is large enough to walk through. She steps up to it, and the blackness fades, and she can now see a flowing river and what looks like rice paddies scattered throughout the region. Nova senses something pulling at her, and she is hesitant to step through when she realizes that the portal is slowly shrinking. She knows she cannot wait until another full moon to try again, so she takes a deep breath, holds it, then steps through, and as she does, Nova feels every hair on her body stand on end. Nova then hears a pop behind her, she turns, and the portal is gone. Nova is nervous and tries to summon a fireball and says, *"Moerutonoriko,"* and nothing happens. She tries again, and still nothing. She is getting nervous because she has no idea exactly where she is. She looks at the surrounding land,

and it does not look like anything that she has heard or seen on Chikyu. She continues down the brick path, and having no idea where it will take her; she keeps walking.

Nova comes around a sharp bend in the path, and she sees a tall multi-tiered pagoda-like building. She cautiously walks up, places her ear against the door, and listens. She hears two female voices with light accents. The doors open, and she is slightly overwhelmed with an array of aromas, with cinnamon being the strongest, but it is not overwhelming. She stands at the door, and the distinct aromas vanish, and then she hears, "High Priestess, please come forward."

Nova steps over the threshold, the doors close behind her, and the room becomes illuminated with soft light. She sees two young women sitting on plush cushions and notices that their faces are partially hidden in the shadows cast by the lights around the room. They gesture for her to sit on a pillow in front of them. Nova steps forward and sits down.

They offer Nova something to drink, and then one of them rings a small bell. Moments later, a young girl who looks to be around nineteen years of age enters the room carrying a tray, bows to the two women, lets them each take a cup, and then bows to Nova and hands her a cup of warm liquid. Nova is hesitant to drink and watches the two young women take a sip. She puts the cup down without sipping it and tries to look closer at the two young women.

The one on the right says, "Thank you, Isa."

The two of them lean forward, and she now sees that they are identical twins. She admires the physical looks of the two young women and cannot tell them apart, except that one has a small beauty mark on her right temple, and the other does not, but other than that, it would be as if one were looking in a mirror.

These two young women look no older than twenty-two, but she looks into their eyes and sees what seems like many years of experience. Though they are sitting down, they look slightly shorter than herself, and both have slender bodies. They are wearing form-fitting thin silk shifts that hug their slender bodies. She sees that their breasts are small but firm as their nipples poke slightly against the material. She then looks at their faces and sees that they have compelling, slightly smaller almond-shaped eyes, high cheekbones, prominent jawlines, button noses, and shapely thin lips. They both have long straight black shiny hair that entices their sensuality. The one thing that stands out is their flawlessly smooth fair complexions, and not a blemish, scar, anything on their entire bodies from what she can see, other than the tiny beauty mark just above the one temple.

One asks her, "Are you satisfied with what you see?"

Nova answers, "Yes."

The other says, "Good," Now, let us begin."

Nova asks, "Why am I here? Why have you summoned me here?"

The young girl Isa steps up to Nova, bows, takes her cup, and leaves.

The Twins stand, and then two other girls approach Nova, saying to her simultaneously, "Because you are the Kaisoshosuko."

"What is this place, and who are you?"

The Twins smile and say, "We are known as the Dark Twins. We are Mia and Mae, and you are in the Dark Realm, our Realm."

"What and where exactly is this Dark Realm?" Nova asks.

Mia says, "The Dark Realm is the Realm that at one time our God Nimponin lived and harbored much evil that coexisted with your Realm, which thrives on the good. When the celestial entities came into existence and created your Realm, they also created ours, making us the same but different. When the Gods in your Realm came about, our God Nimponin came into being in our Realm. Then your Gods created life; a strange phenomenon occurred between our Realms. A thin cosmic veil that kept our Realms separated and in balance prohibited anything from crossing over from one Realm to another. Unknown to how or why the cosmic imbalance occurred, it caused a rift to appear in the veil, though minuscule and undetectable. It began as a blemish on the veil, thus, in turn, allowing a rift to form. When the rift pulsed, it allowed the essence of good to enter our Realm, and the nature of our Dark God became determined to destroy all things good. The goodness he sensed on the other side of the rift called out to him, driving him mad with the desire to eradicate what his senses led him to believe. When the rift finally drew him in, he became a significant blemish in the heavens of your world.

Then Mia continues, "The Dark God's appetite was enormous, and his only desire was to spread evil and eradicate anything that went against his nature or wishes. He had not expected the defiance and fortitude of the two Gods in your Realm, and a catastrophic battle occurred. The battle between the Gods of your Realm and a manifestation of the God of our Dark Realm lasted thousands of millennia. After many millennia of fighting, your gods defeated and entrapped our Dark God Nimponin in the "*Shingakusha Hoseki*," a crystal of immense power. The "*Shingakusha Hoseki*" crystal imploded on itself, leaving a "*Kurosagasu*" in the fabric of both Realms and causing a ferocious vacuum. The "*Kurosagasu*" pulverized remnants of the crystals as they were drawn into the vortex's vacuum. Some escaped and landed throughout both our Realms. As the Keepers of the Dark Realm, we have fought against our Realm's destruction. What remains of the Dark Realm is what you see before your eyes, a minor sanction that we can keep safe from the onslaught of the Goddess Mother of your Realm. We need to find the lost crystals and rejoin them so that we can release our Dark God, Nimponin, and have him put a stop to this destruction of our world, our Realm, before it is too late.

Nova looks at them and asks, "What can I do?"

As overseers of the Dark Realm, we descended into your world by an oversight on our part; we were captured, drugged, and then held prisoners until Guichi and Tanin found us and rescued us. Since then, we have sworn our allegiance to them. We told them we would train anyone they chose if they could discover how to get here between the Realms. They asked us to instruct anyone who enters the Dark Realm to become something unimaginable in your world and beneficial to the goals of the Gods. As overseers, we can teach you and those you deem "The Chosen" the sacred teachings of fighting, weaponry, poisons, stealth, sorcery, magic, potions, and the fine art of erotic lovemaking, anything that will benefit you in your world.

"What about this Sakuri?" Nova asks.

The Twins look at her and tell her. "That discussion is for another day," and they clap their hands.

Nova looks at them, "Who are these "Chosen" you mention?"

We know you have questions, and they will be answered all in good time, but you must first complete your training.

Nova asks, "What training?"

"Why this, of course, and again they clap their hands.

Before Nova can do anything or say anything else, two other girls approach her from behind, grab her wrists, and bind them behind her back, and then she sees the girl Isa walking towards her with a glass bottle and a rag in her hands.

She asks the Twins, "What are you going to do?"

The Twins respond, "Training," just as Isa covers her mouth with a vile-smelling cloth, and as Nova stares at the Twins, her vision blurs, and she is soon unconscious.

Chapter 19

Nova's Training

Nova awakens in a small room with no windows and only one door. She has no idea how long she has been out. She lies on her bed and remembers the other three girls when the sound of footsteps comes down what she assumes is a hallway, and then they stop. Nova sits up and hears female voices talking on the other side and then the sound of a key being turned. The door to her cell opens, and as she sits there, she looks at Isa, the young girl who brought her tea, and the two other girls who look similar and remembers briefly seeing them when she first got here.

Isa tells Nova, "These two are Nydia and Octavia, and they will be assisting me in your training. Do you have any questions?"

Nova thinks she has many questions, but they probably will not answer them, so she shakes her head. "No"

Isa says, "Good, shall we begin!"

The four of them walk down a corridor when Nova asks Isa, "How long have I slept?"

Isa looks at her and says, "Three weeks, so your body becomes acclimated to the Air and temperatures in the Dark Realm.

They come to a large room, and Isa asks her, "Shall we get started?" and Nova nods yes.

The days turn into weeks, and the weeks pass slowly. The routine is the same every day. They wake her up, feed her, and put her through rigorous training all day, though once she has perfected something, they move on to the next.

They have instructed Nova on how to attack and defend with every type of weapon she could think of and some she didn't. She learned to fight with her hands and her body. Through all the training, fighting, the cuts, and the soreness and bruises that miraculously gone every morning,

One morning she was sitting at a low table on some pillows, drinking some tea with Isa waiting for Lydia and Octavia to show up when Isa tells her that she would be instructing her in her lessons today. Isa says, "Let's begin," and lays her hands on the table with her palms up and tells Nova to place her palms face down on top of hers. Nova does as she is told, and Isa says, "What I am about to teach you is probably two of the most difficult spells to master and be able to cast. These spells are for summoning, and to cast them correctly, you must not only understand the difference but must know the differences. The first will allow you to summon the rift, which is the passageway between our two Realms. Once you master this spell, you can pass between our two realms without having to wait for when the moon is full as you did when you first came here. The second is a portal spell that is just as difficult, but it will allow you or anyone to travel long distances in your world in seconds. The only drawback is that you need a clear, concise picture of where you want the portal to open. If you were to open a portal somewhere, there is no way of controlling where it might open up, and it could be fatal to both the caster and the ones traveling through it, do you understand."

Nova looks at her and tells Isa, "I understand."

Isa doesn't say anything and begins chanting, *"Guka Kachi Mi Dit La Ro Chiakobo,"* Nova feels her fingers moving. She hears the pop as the rift opens, and Nova finds herself staring at a valley scattered with breastplates, leggings, sword shields, and woman's attire, and then the rift closes. All Nova can say is, "That was amazing!"

Nova looks at Isa; she sees sadness in her eyes and knows it has something to do with small piles of equipment of broken leather uniforms. Isa smiles and begins chanting again, *"Guko Kachi Mi Dit La Ro Chiakoba,"* but this time she doesn't hear the pop but a ping, and then she sees the large section of the temple where she first met the Twins. Isa moves the portal slightly, and Nova sees two racks of draped cloths. Then the portal closes, and Nova looks at Isa and asks, "Can the passage be used at any time?"

Isa says, "Yes, as long as you have a clear picture of where you want to go."

Over the next four weeks, Isa continues to instruct Nova in the finger gestures needed to go along with the pronunciation of the spells and explains the difference in the similar words.

Nova is sitting at the table when Isa walks in, and she asks Nova to stand. Nova does, and Isa tells her to cast a spell to summon a passageway.

Nova does as she is asked and summons a passageway, and Isa can see that the other end is in Nova's room in the temple.

Isa tells her to close it and to open a rift in her Realm now. She hears the pop, opens a rift, and does it flawlessly. Isa can see that it is in her chambers in her Realm.

Isa asks her to close it, and she does. Nova asks Isa what would happen if one accidentally mixed the spells' pronunciations. Isa looks at her and says, "That should never happen because mixing the spells could be catastrophic to anyone standing next to the caster. Nova says, "I see," and tells Isa not to worry; with her teaching, there is no way for her to mix them up. She smiles at Isa, and Isa smiles back and says, "Good." Then tells her that she will continue with her lessons in the morning with Lydia and Octavia.

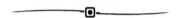

That night Nova lies in her cot and thinks about what Isa told her could happen if the two incantation spells were to get mixed up. Nova is soon asleep, and she dreams that she pictures herself doing just that when suddenly the very ground on the other side of the portal erupts in a massive explosion. The explosion blows back at her, and she feels stone and rock pelt her body. She sees a rock coming straight at her, and she wakes up, realizes that she is sweating, and swears to herself that she will never try that again.

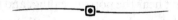

The following day, Octavia and Nydia, who she found out are considered sisters in their tribe, bring her to a small room. They tell her to remove her clothes and then step inside, and as she does, Octavia tells her, "Do not kill," and please wait. She steps into the room she finds herself standing in a massive room with a high ceiling. Nova looks around the room and sees a bed, a basin filled with water, and another door opposite her. She goes to ask Octavia what is happening when she hears the door behind her lock. The other door opens, and in walks a large man and a young woman almost her size; and sees that they are both naked. She then notices that the woman is wearing a collar and the man is holding a leash.

He jerks on the leash, causing the woman to fall to the floor, kicking her. The man then takes the leash, hangs it on a metal peg, and tells the young woman to stay.

He faces Nova, and she can see that he is starting to get aroused as he looks at her and says, "Bitch, you are mine!" and Nova sees his legs tense and knows he will come at her. He lunges, and she steps to his side, and just before he can grab her, she thrusts her fist directly into his crotch and hears him grunt. Her punch surprises him, and he swings his arm wide, hoping to catch her. She anticipates the move and drops down to kick him just behind his knee, and when she does, she hears something snap. The man screams out in pain and drops to one knee. Nova sees her advantage, and she gets up behind him and places her arms around her neck to choke him. She starts to squeeze, and the man tries desperately to break her grip on his neck. He is just about to pass out when suddenly Nova feels a cord around her neck, trying to cut off her Air. She releases the man, throwing her body backward against the bed. Nova hears a grunt, and the pressure on her neck is gone. She jumps up and sees that the young woman who came in with the man on the leash was the one trying to choke her. The young woman is trying to get up when Nova hits her, and as she begins to go down, Nova goes to strike her again, and just before she makes contact, something grabs her wrist, and she feels herself flying through the Air. Nova does a somersault in mid-Air and lands on the floor across the room in a three-point stance, on the balls of her feet, legs slightly spread, and one hand on the floor, resting on her fingertips. Her other hand is cocked and ready to strike. She looks up and sees the big man standing before the young woman as if protecting her. She can see that he favors his right leg and rubs his neck, and she remembers what Octavia said as she entered the room, "Do not kill."

He rushes her, and she remains still until she moves just about on top of her. She sweeps her leg around; while pivoting on her hand and catches the man on his ankle. His ankle swept out from beneath him, and with his bad knee, he cannot support his own weight and crashes to the floor. Nova sees her opportunity, leaps, bringing her knee down onto the back of his head, and knocks him out cold. Distracted from taking out the large man, she does not see that the young woman has gotten up and is now slowly twirling her leash. She hears a whistling sound as the leash begins spinning faster, and as she turns, she sees the steel blades at the end of the leash, and then she feels them as the young woman lashes out, and the steel blades catch Nova on her upper arm. The young woman pulls back the leash and reaches up to unclip the leash from her collar. Nova now watches the young woman start swinging the leash above her head, faster and faster, and the whistling gets louder. She can tell that the woman knows how to use it because of her training with whips. The woman lets loose with the leash, and Nova sees it coming, but the woman is quick and jerks the whip at the last second, and the tip of the leash catches her on her thigh. Nova feels it but does not cry out; all she does is rush the woman closing the gap between them. The woman sees this and drops the leash to bring up her blade to slash at Nova. The woman is quick, but Nova is just a hair quicker and throws a punch at the woman's face. The young woman lets out a horrific scream as Nova says, "Bitch!" and feels her fist connect with the woman's face and knows that she has broken her nose. The woman staggers back from the blow, and Nova performs a perfect roundhouse kick to the side of the woman's head. She follows through with an overhanded double punch to her stomach and chest. The woman collapses to the floor, with blood oozing out of her nose, and Nova sees she is unconscious.

Nova catches her breath when she senses something behind her, and then she feels two massive arms wrapped around her body, pinning her arms to her side and then lifted off the floor. She tries kicking with her legs and realizes it is futile. The man carries her over to the bed, and then he sees his companion lying on the floor, bloody and unconscious. He screams at her and says, "You fucking Bitch, what did you do to her?" Then he throws Nova like a rag doll across the room, and she lands against the wall hard. As she slides down the wall, she touches the back of her head, looks at her fingers, and sees blood, and she immediately becomes enraged; in two strides, she leaps in the Air and she lands perfectly on the big man's back, her positioning does not allow him to grab her, or throw her off. In a total rage, she starts to pummel him around his head and shoulders. She feels him drop to his knees, and though he has stopped struggling, she continues to bash him. Nova climbs off his back and kicks him square in the back, and he falls forward onto the young woman pinning her with his body. She remembers what Octavia told her and reaches over and checks that the two of them are still breathing. She sighs with relief, then she feels the pain in her thigh and upper thigh and remembers that the woman had cut her. She rips the sheet from the bed and cuts a strip to help stop the bleeding, and when she hears the door opening, she reaches down to grab the woman's leash. She turns to defend herself and sees Isa, Nydia, and Octavia standing behind them, two young slaves, holding some towels. Isa tells her she can drop the leash as her test is complete. Before Nova can ask, Isa tells her that, at times, looks can be deceiving, and sometimes it is better to incapacitate someone than to take a life, as she demonstrated today by following the instructions of "Do not kill,"

Isa snaps her fingers, and the two slave girls step up to Nova and proceed to clean her wounds. While they do that, several more slaves enter, pick up the male and female, and carry them from the room.

Nova is soon standing there with her thigh and upper arm wrapped, and she feels a few stitches on her scalp, she is feeling little discomfort when Isa tells her to enjoy her next training, and the three of them exit the room leaving the two young slaves alone with her.

They each grab Nova's hands and lead her back to the bed. She lies on the bed with one of the girls on each side.

Nova asks the two girls, "What training?"

The two girls giggle and remove what little clothing they are wearing, and one leans over and kisses Nova deeply on the lips while the other pulls off her top and then delicately kisses and bites her nipple. The one who kissed her on the lips is now kissing and biting her other nipple. Then they both start working their way down to her stomach and kissing and licking her inner thighs. Nova feels elated. The two young girls kiss, bite, lick, touch, suck, and blow on different parts of her body. She climaxes to the point of passing out, and when she awakens, she finds herself alone in her bed.

Over the next few weeks, Nova learns the finer points of erotic lovemaking. She prefers the sessions of eroticism with the two young slave girls, and she voices her opinion to Isa that she does not want anything to do with a man.

Isa asks her, "What if your Gods Guichi and Tanin demand something of you. Are you going to tell them "No?"

Nova shakes her head, No.

Isa explains that she needs to understand that there are other ways to satisfy a man, but it should only happen if the need outweighs the means. Nova learns to endure the times she has to perform certain aspects of eroticism with a man.

One morning, she walks to the room for another day of training when Nydia approaches her and tells her that she must appear before the Twins. She is a little disappointed because she looked forward to the fine art of erotic lovemaking as part of her training with the two young slaves. While walking, she remembers what she was taught about potions and poisons that by enduring small doses, she was able to build up an immunity slowly, so that no matter what part of her body these were applied, her neck, her breasts, her lips, they had no effect.

She walks into the main temple and sees the Twins Mae and Mia sitting on cushions. Nova walks over, bows to the two of them, and then kneels on one of the empty pillows. She also notices a large red square painted on the floor. She then watches Nydia and Octavia bring in two racks with the same weapons and place them inside the edge of the painted square.

Isa walks in with another young woman whom Nova has never seen before. The young woman is a pretty girl, a little shorter than Nova, with long blond hair, small breasts, and big brown eyes. The Twins tell her that the young woman is here to fight her and that if either of them steps out of the red square, they will forfeit their life. Nova hears a small bell, and as she gets up, the woman suddenly lunges at her, grabs her, and throws her across the floor; she slides almost out of the red square. She saves herself by spinning around to land on the balls of her feet, which stop her from going out. Caught off guard, Nova takes her favorite position in a three-point defensive stance, as she has done on many occasions while training.

The woman rushes her, and Nova dives forward, underneath the combination of punches and kicks that the young woman has thrown with tremendous speed and accuracy. The girl turns around, and just as Nova comes out of her role, she finds herself blocking more of her punches and kicks. Nova tries to take the offensive, but the young girl is relentless in her attacks, and then Nova notices that she is slowly being pushed back towards the redline.

The young woman continually throws punches and kicks at Nova. She blocks and dodges the woman's attacks relentlessly to gain the upper hand. She has endured worse and now realizes that she hasn't even worked up a good sweat with her training with the girl Isa, Lydia, and Octavia. She is just a few inches from being pushed back out of the square when she smiles at the woman. A punch is about to hit her face when she reaches up, grabs the woman's fist, and stops it. Nova looks the woman straight in the eyes and says, "My turn," then twists her wrist, blocks her second punch, and shoves her back with a tight kick to her chest. Nova lets loose with a barrage of punches and kicks that the woman has difficulty blocking. Nova grabs her wrist and arm, drops to her knee, and tosses her across the floor. The girl is saved from being thrown out of the square by the rack of weapons rolled in.

The woman quickly gets up, grabs some long knives off the rack, and comes at her. Nova grabs a couple of *Tonfu* short hardwood batons and is quickly blocking and deflecting the woman's knife attacks. The woman is good, but Nova knows she is better, and as the woman steps back, she smiles because she was able to give Nova a small scratch on her forearm. Nova immediately puts her lips on the cut, sucks, and spits the blood. She is a little dizzy, and she also feels the poison coursing through her veins, and though she was able to suck on the wound and spit it out, she knows there is a slight lingering effect. She shakes her head and sees the woman coming at her, this time with twice the enthusiasm as before. Though nauseated from the cut, her vision slightly blurry, she deflects everything thrown at her, but she also loses one of her Tonfu. Nova is now sweating and tired and knows it is from the poison. She sees that she has wholly disarmed the woman of her blades and that she still has one Tonfu. She also sees that the weapon racks are gone.

In a powerful roundhouse kick toward Nova's head, the woman brings up her left leg. Nova sees it, brings up her Tonfu, and holds it with two hands to block the kick. The force of her kick is so hard that she snaps the Tonfu in half, pushing Nova off balance and shattering her lower leg simultaneously. The woman falls, screaming in pain and holding her leg. Nova sees the bone sticking out through her skin as she tries to catch her breath. The woman struggles to get up, putting all her weight on one leg as she does. She tries to punch Nova, but she bashes it away with her remaining piece of the baton, and when she does, she hears the bones in the woman's wrist crack. Her assailant cries out in pain for a second time as Nova sees her wrist dandling and broken. With no weapons, a shattered leg, and a broken wrist, the woman throws a two-fingered jab at Nova's eyes to try to blind her. Nova tilts her head and feels the thrust go right by her. Nova grabs her wrist and drops down, and as before, she allows the forward momentum to bring the woman over her shoulder and slams her onto the floor, so she lands on her back. Nova puts the woman's head and neck in a chokehold and squeezes. The woman struggles desperately to break Nova's hold, but she has no strength left when she is about to pass out. Nova looks up at the Twins.

The Twins look at each other and then back to Nova and say, "Kill her!" That is what Nova does and snaps the girl's neck without hesitation. Nova immediately feels a sensation of purging through her heart, body, and soul, feeling stronger than ever.

Nova untangles herself from the woman's lifeless body, and before she lets it fall to the side, she looks into her eyes, feels no remorse, and then stands up. She walks over to the Twins and sees that they have placed their heads on the floor with their hands out and tells Nova, "Mistress, you have passed the test, and we are now yours to command."

She tells them to rise. They grab her hands and lead her to a comfortable chair. Nova sits down, and the Twins start to explain everything that she has gone through and why.

Mia is treating the scratch on Nova's forearm, and the remnants of nausea subside.

Nova is satisfied with their explanation, to make her understand and accept the Guichi-Tanin Religion, the Dark scriptures, and the Dark Realm. Most importantly, Guichi needed her to go through these trials and tribulations to ensure his choice was the right one.

She asks them, "How will I know how to find these "Chosen" you speak of?"

The Twins tell her, "Do not worry; we are here to serve you, Mistress. We will help you find them." The Twins open up a rift between the two Realms; all three walk through and are back in her chambers, she hears the distinct pop, and she knows the rift has closed.

Nova looks around and sees nothing has changed; everything is as she left it. She looks to the Twins, and they tell her that Time is different in the Dark Realm. In this world, she has only been gone a couple of hours. She walks over, opens the doors to her chambers, and tells a passing slave girl to bring some wine and three glasses. There is a knock on the door, and Nova tells who it is to enter. A young slave girl enters carrying a tray with a pitcher of wine and three glasses. She also notices that the young girl is not wearing a top. Nova dismisses the slave and tells her that she is not to be disturbed.

The three drink some wine, and Nova motions for the Twins towards the bed. They do it without argument. Nova walks over, gets on the bed, and says, "Let's see how well I learned what those girls taught me."

The Twins Mia and Mae welcome her with open arms.

It is now morning, and as Nova gets out of bed, she smiles at the Twins. The Twins are lying there in each other's arms with smiles. Nova thinks to herself. I guess I learned my lessons well

Chapter 20

Gustavo Heinz

Nova stands on the edge of the black diamond precipice with General Harris by her side. Nova thinks back to when the General approached her with his plans and told her General Health is committed to carrying them out. She knows that neither one cares for the Empire or its Emperor. The goal is to take the town of Shira to the northern part of the Empire, and after they do this, it will allow her dark army to establish a stronghold. When they complete that phase, they will have complete control over the northern Pass between the Empire of Ozake and the Kingdom of Basra and will be able to stop any support from the Empire to the north of the Kingdom when the time comes for her army to march.

She looks down at the contingent of her army comprised of Harris's regular army led by General Heath, and her Freaks, who Colonel Tomas will lead. She asks Harris if he is ready to go forward and build a stronghold for her. He bows and says, "Yes, my Kaisoshosuko."

Nova is excited but does not show it when she says, "So be it," and starts chanting, "*Guko Kachi Mi Dit La Ro Chiakoba,*" and moving her fingers. Suddenly, a portal opens in front of General Heath and his mount side steps. He gets it under control and orders his men forward through the portal. His scouts go first, and when they get to the other side, he sees them immediately spread out to check the surrounding lands. Colonel Tomas and his Freaks go through, and Heath can see Tomas quickly gathering his ranks, and then he sees Tomas pointing to the Pass and a small force of about a hundred Freaks head up into the Pass.

It takes the better part of a day to move the army through the portal, as they find themselves congregating in a large field on the western side of the Tammayaku Mountains, at the base of the Kassukoku Pass in the northern lands of Basra. Heath establishes a base camp after his scouts have all confirmed that the area is secure, and he is not to worry about prying eyes from locals.

The following day he orders his army to start moving up the Pass. They travel quickly up and through the Pass, and when they reach the summit, Heath finds a small group of travelers lying off to the side of the summit, with their throats cut and stripped of all their belongings. They move through the night and are almost down the other side when Heath calls a halt and patiently waits for sunrise.

Sunrise comes, and the army swarms out of the Pass and quickly overruns the town of Shira. Two hours later, General Heath, Commander of the Dark Army, has established its foothold in the Ozake Empire.

A young soldier in the bird sanctuary located in the barracks tower is cleaning out the cages and feeding the messenger birds when he hears the commotion below. He watches in shock as he sees his friends and comrades rounded up and placed in shackles. He then watches as some are trussed up on crosses for all to see. He continues watching as the townspeople are pulled from their homes and forced into the town square. A large man who looks to be in-charge steps onto a wooden platform, and he hears him tell the people of Shira, "You have a choice, convert to the worship of the Dark Scriptures and live, or if you do not convert, you can become like your militia over there. The townsfolk look and see a couple of the militia nailed to x-crosses. Some immediately choose to convert to the Dark Scriptures.

The young militiaman knows what he must do and makes his way over to the bird coop.

He quickly writes down what is happening on several pieces of parchment, places the notes into the small cases strapped to the bird's back, and then releases them.

No sooner does he release them when two filthy-looking men searching the barracks see the birds take flight and rush up the tower stairs. The young soldier draws his sword as the two men make their way onto the rooftop through the roof hatch. They rush him, and though he is young, the soldier holds his own and takes down one of them with a stab to his chest, but he cannot remove his blade quick enough as the other man screams and rushes him and knocks him down. The man is on top of him and is struggling to drive his sword down into the soldier's chest. The young soldier can grab his short knife, brings it up, and stabs the man in his side. He feels the blade slip through his ribs, and then his assailant stops pushing down, as the young soldier knows he has pierced his heart. He pushes the man off of him, and when he catches his breath, several more come up through the hatch, and as they look around and see the other two, they rush him and beat him to unconsciousness.

He starts to wake up as they throw him to the ground in front of the Colonel, and the Colonel asks if he is the one who released the birds. The young soldier tells the Colonel, "Yes," and the Colonel says, "So be it." The young soldier is dragged to where some of his friends are hanging. They do the same to him., but unlike his friends who are already dead, the young soldier is still alive as he is nailed to the x-cross, and his screams echo throughout the day and into the night.

It has been three years since receiving their Second Lieutenant commissions, and almost three years to the day, Samuel, Reiko, and Hikaru have been promoted to First Lieutenants. They are in the Officer's dining hall drinking tea and talking about their duties for the day when a young runner comes in and hands each of them a sealed envelope. Hikaru thanks the runner and tells him he may go. They open their orders simultaneously, and after reading them, they lay them on the table and look at each other. All three orders have their names on the top and orders to mobilize in twenty-four hours. That is all the orders say; there is nothing about the actual mission other than they are to travel north.

The three of them have heard the rumors circulating about how a large army came over the Tammayaku mountain range through the Kassukoku Pass, laid siege to a town in the Empire, and is now occupying it. The biggest argument was how an army that size supposedly could move through Basra without being seen or heard. Some of the prominent houses in the Empire who opposed the Emperor's rule, and favored his brother Tao to be Emperor, thought it a waste of time, money, and resources to send a large force to Shira. They demand that whoever sent these erroneous messages be flayed and displayed for all to see.

Samuel keeps reading and notices four other names as additional Second Lieutenants. The one that stands out the most on the list is Gustavo Heinz, the squire who was always trying to best Samuel when they were in the Squire Corps. Gustav Heinz was known as Squire Piss Pants because one day, Master Sargent Higgs laid into him and scared him so much that Heinz pissed in his pants, hence the nickname.

Once he became a Second Lieutenant, the name is not spoken out loud, but the nickname of Piss Pants had stuck with him when he was talked about behind closed doors. His attitude about the whole thing caused him to delay his graduation, and he graduated with the class right behind them. For some reason that is only known to Heinz, he has always blamed Samuel for the nickname and also blames him for being passed over for promotion to First Lieutenant this last time. He has remained and probably will stay a Second Lieutenant throughout his career.

Heinz loathes all three of them, but he hates Samuel the most. After their commissions, upon graduating, Samuel, Reiko, and Hikaru were kept very busy, and none of them crossed paths with Heinz until one day, the three of them had to draw supplies from the Quartermaster for a mission near Dart to quell a border dispute. Rumor was that the Commander of the base assigned Heinz to a position with the Quartermaster, and everyone knew it was a position that did not allow much advancement.

Samuel, Hikaru, and Reiko are walking to the warehouse when Hikaru says, "I hope we don't have to deal with Piss Pants." When they enter the supply office, low and behold do, they see sitting behind the desk in the office, Second Lieutenant Gustavo Heinz, and Hikaru mutters a very soft, "Shit."

They found Heinz sitting behind a desk and waited for him to look up from what he was doing. Hikaru stood there and then cleared his throat, and when Heinz looked up, he saw the three of them, and he had a smile that made him look like a ferret. He came over to the window and very politely asked, "Can I help you, Sirs?" and showed all disrespect to Reiko for not addressing her as Ma'am, and unseen by anyone, Hikaru squeezed Reiko's hand to calm her.

Samuel hands Heinz the paperwork and says, "Yes, you may, Lieutenant Heinz." He tells them just a minute and that he must verify the requisitions with the Senior Officer in Charge. Heinz returns after fifteen minutes, informing Samuel that he will have to wait for the OIC to come back, and says flatly, "Sorry." Four hours later, the three of them are picking up their supplies, and Hikaru tells the two of them that he wants to do an inventory. Samuel and Reiko agree, and when all is said and done, they find several discrepancies and report them to Heinz.

Heinz said he was sorry and blamed it on the workers because they have no pride in their work ethic and told Samuel that he would bring them up on dereliction of duties.

Samuel tells Heinz it is no big deal; if he would make things right with the requisitions, they will be on their way. Heinz personally brings them their missing items, tells them to have a nice say, and salutes them.

When Samuel finishes reading, he sees the looks on Reiko and Hikaru's faces as they also see who is going on a mission with them, a Quartermaster and an acting Field Lieutenant. In a very low voice, Hikaru says, "Fuck Piss Pants." Reiko starts laughing, not because of what Hikaru has said, but more because she rarely, if at all, hears him swear. Samuel is soon to join in, and all three are laughing. Their laughing slowly dies, and Reiko says, "Finally, we are on a mission together."

Twenty-four hours later, Colonel Frederick D. Bradley leads a large army of three Divisions with First Lieutenants Takahashi, Sato, Miro, and second lieutenants Heinz, Tombs, and Bradley, through the main gates of the Empire's capital city. Once they have lost sight of the Capital's gates, the Colonel orders the march to the northwest. Samuel, Hikaru, and Reiko do not ask where they are going because they know the Colonel will inform them when he is ready. They perform their duties and carry out their orders. On their fourth night from the Capital, the Colonel calls all his officers together for a meeting. He informs them that they are headed to the town of Shira, just east of the Tammayaku Mountains at the eastern base of the Kassukoku Pass.

Unknowing to anyone, but the Colonel, a half-day after their departure, a caravan of heavily loaded wagons leave the Capital.

Under cover of darkness, they follow in their wake of the advancing force. Every night for ten days, they rest and post sentries. A sentry comes to Colonel Bradley's tent on the eleventh night out and asks to speak to Lieutenants Miro, Takahashi, and Sato. The Colonel allows it, and after the sentry explains what has transpired, the Colonel dismisses them and tells them to return when they take care of this matter. Samuel, Reiko, and Hikaru say, "Yes, sir," and follow the runner to one of the outer sentry posts. When they get there, Samuel and Reiko find their old friend Barnaby Cook sitting on a rock, drinking from a flask with two armed soldiers standing on each side of him.

Barnaby sees them and stands up. The two guards grab the hilts of their swords—Samuel tells them to stand down.

"Barnaby, you're a little far away from your usual stomping grounds. What brings you way out here?" Samuel asks and extends his hand. Barnaby takes it and smiles. He nods to Reiko and asks Samuel, "How is the "Reaper of Souls" doing? Though Reiko cannot see, Samuel smiles and says, "She is doing just fine," then introduces Hikaru to him and tells him that Hikaru is their third group member. Hikaru nods at him.

Samuel asks, "So, Barnaby, What brings you way out here, or should I ask, what are you doing here?"

Barnaby tells him, "Well, I look at it this way. I could have stayed back east and grown bored and returned to my old ways, or I thought what better way to help my old friends Miro and Takahashi. then to send my men out to cover a greater area to establish, shall we say, an information network?" Barnaby pauses to take a swig from his flask. "That is when I learned about this little invasion into the Empire by an army of Dark Soldiers.

Reiko asks, "An army of what?"

Barnaby says, "An army of Dark Soldiers led by a former Empire officer, General Buford T. Heath," and takes another swig from his flask.

Reiko clears her throat and tells him, "Please, Barnaby, get on with it," Barnaby says, "Yes, Ma'am."

Barnaby hands Samuel a detailed hand-drawn map of some hills, valleys, and a layout of the town of Shira. Samuel sees some letters and numbers drawn on the map. Samuel asks, "What do these numbers and letters represent?" though he already has a good idea.

Barnaby looks at the map as if he had never seen it before and says, "That is the estimated number of troops presently in and around the Shira." The letter beside the number means what type of soldiers, for example, "The number two with the "Hm" means, "Two thousand horsemen," etc. The three of them and Barnaby talk for another thirty minutes when Barnaby tells them, "These are some sick people, my friends. The march to the town's valley is about three days." Barnaby says, "Oh! one of my men has reported that you have a shadow that keeps pace with you off to your west. My man thinks he is keeping track and taking count of your forces. When he has tried to approach him, the man runs off. "That is all I have; for now, if I hear anything else, I'll be sure to reach out to you."

Barnaby bows to the three of them. Samuel calls out to him and tosses him a purse of gold coins. Barnaby says, "Thank you, Samuel, and then he's gone into the darkness. The three of them are walking back to camp talking about what just transpired when a Second Lieutenant Tombs comes up to them and tells them the Colonel wants to see them, and they hurry to the Colonel's tent.

Samuel knocks on the tent post and waits for the Colonel to tell them to enter. They hear, "Enter," and as they walk in, the Colonel asks them what that was all about when Samuel places the detailed map on the Colonel's table. The Colonel asks, "What is this?" Samuel explains the map and that a former Empire officer is commanding these forces.

The Colonel asks, "Who did your friend Barnaby say was commanding these forces?"

Samuel tells him, "General Buford T. Heath."

The Colonel says, "Are you sure that is the name he gave you?"

Reiko speaks up and says, "Yes, sir, that is the name he told us."

The Colonel looks at the map, then at the three of them, and asks, "Can we trust him?"

Reiko answers, "Yes, Sir."

The Colonel says, "Lieutenant Sato."

Hikaru steps forward, salutes, and says, "Yes, Sir?'

The Colonel tells him to take Second Lieutenants Heinz and Tombs and a small detachment of eight men to scout out this valley and see if their friend is telling the truth. You will leave at dawn and then report back as soon as possible with your findings," and then he says, "Dismissed."

"Yes, Sir," and salutes the Colonel and departs to prepare to leave at dawn.

The Colonel says, "I am surprised to hear Heath's name come up, after all these years, seeing that he was found guilty of conspiring to overthrow Emperor Hojiko, and after he was court-martialed, he somehow escaped and then disappeared. We knew he had friends in the government, but no one knew where he went off to."

Samuel says, "I remember that. It was right before I entered the Stewards Corp. The military was up in arms about this. Wasn't there another high-ranking officer also court-martialed for being part of the conspiracy?"

The Colonel says, "Yes, another General by the name of General Picard Harris, and like Heath, he also disappeared without a trace."

Reiko sits there listening when she speaks up and asks, "Sir, if this General Heath was a high-ranking general in the Imperial Army, wouldn't it be safe to say that he would know our battle plans. I mean, once he saw our formations approaching, wouldn't he have the advantage of knowing what maneuvers we had planned."

"Dam! you are right, Takahashi; whatever formations and maneuvers we attack him with, he will know how to counter them, and this battle is over even before it gets started." The Colonel orders some wine and then says, "Now let's take a closer look at your friend's map and come up with a plan" They talk through most of the night, and just as the sun begins to rise, the Colonel agrees that it is an excellent plan and that Heath should be very surprised.

Lieutenant Bradley knocks, enters the tent carrying a tray with three cups of tea, and says, "I thought you might need this."

The three of them say thank you, and the Colonel tells the Lieutenant to get something to eat, and Second Lieutenant Bradley salutes and leaves. The Colonel looks at Samuel and Reiko and says, "Yes, he is my son. He is also an officer in the Empire's Imperial Army. His mother would," and then he changes it to "I would appreciate it if you could keep an eye out for him."

They both say, "No problem, Sir." The Colonel says, "Thank you, now go get something to eat; it has been a long night."

Samuel and Reiko walk to the mess tent and see Hikaru loading his pack onto his horse. They walk up and tell him they will see him in a couple of days. Samuel shakes his hand, gives each other a quick hug, and tells him to be careful.

Hikaru looks around, smiles, and says, "Who needs luck? I have Second Lieutenant Piss Pants with me," The three of them laugh.

Reiko does the same but gives him a quick peck on the cheek and tells him to be careful, and if anything were to happen to him, she would never forgive him."

"Come now, my little apricot, you know nothing can happen to me because who would keep your butt out of trouble," and he smiles at her.

Reiko punches him in his stomach, smiles, and says, "Just be careful."

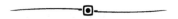

After two days of hard riding, and a cold camp the night before, Lieutenant Hikaru Sato and his small detachment reach the farthest outskirts of the town. They tie their horses in a clearing in a crop of trees and carefully make their way up to the ridge that overlooks the town.

Hikaru is pleased that the hill overlooks the town and gives Hikaru an observation advantage. His men stay low and join him on the hill. He sees the standard town layout along the base of the mountains, consisting of merchants' buildings and two-level houses built in the traditional block design, allowing the morning sun and setting of the late afternoon sun to allow total exposure to the town.

Hikaru pulls out his eye scope and scans the town to see a massive gathering in the town square. He observes several scantily clad women walking through the crowd offering drinks in whatever is in the buckets they are carrying. The small army of people in the town square is a mix of men and women who carry swords, shields, spears, and long knives. The other outstanding thing that he can see is that these men and women have piercings and carvings or tattoos on their skin. He places the count at just under one thousand, and with the way their bodies are scarred and marked, he decides to call the Crazies. He is about to move to the left when he sees something flash in the afternoon sun in the gap leading up to the passage of the mountain. Hikaru orders Heinz to wait with the others and takes Lieutenant Tombs and two other men to follow him and stay low. He moves through the trees, and as he gets into position, he sees the real threat, a large force hiding out in the mountain pass. Hikaru looks at the mountain pass through his eye-scope and sees riders in heavy armor and lances, longswords men, halberds, archers, maces, and light cavalry leather armor. He tells Tombs to pull out the map to write what he tells him. Hikaru starts adding the numbers, and when done, it puts the count of the force, counting the crazies, at about six thousand soldiers combined. He takes the map, checks the numbers and positions, and places a small indiscrete mark on the corner of the map. One of the other soldiers from the group he left behind with Heinz runs towards them and comes up to Hikaru, telling him to come quickly; something is happening in the town.

He moves quickly back to where he left his men, and even without his eye scope, he can tell that the gathering in the square has turned into a frenzy. He looks through his eye scope to see the commotion and can now see many cages hanging to the left of the town square.

He watches as one of the cages is lowered to the ground, and two robed figures pull a young woman from the cage and carry her kicking and screaming to what looks like a wooden altar placed at the top of the road that leads down into the valley. Hikaru watches as they pin her arms above her head and tie her hands to a large ring on the altar. They rip her clothes from her body as Hikaru momentarily puts down his eye scope and looks away. He sees Heinz looking through his eye scope, and Hikaru swears that he is drooling, and then he says, "Geez, will you look at the body on that girl? What a waste of a beautiful piece of flesh. What I wouldn't do to get some of that?" Hikaru tells Heinz to shut up, stop worrying about the girl, pay attention to what is going on, and then says, "That's an order, Lieutenant Heinz."

Hikaru is steaming because of the way Heinz was talking about the young lady and desperately wants to punch him in the mouth. Hikaru picks up his eye scope and zooms in to see what is happening. He tries not to stare as the young girl lays there naked, but he watches her continue to struggle, and he does see that she is an attractive woman.

He turns to see the crowd part and then sees a robed figure walk up to the head of the make-shift altar and stand there with a long-bladed knife in his hand. Two filthy-looking females come out of the gathered crowd and climb on the altar. They start groping the young woman's breasts, and he can see that while one is kissing her and seems to be forcing her tongue into her mouth, the other slowly works her way down the woman's body and licks her in different areas. The young woman starts pulling on her bonds and rubbing them back and forth through the ring, desperately trying to break them. Hikaru sees that the robed one has stepped back to watch to see if she can get herself free. He assumes it is some test. The robed one takes a step forward, and at that moment, the woman breaks her bonds, and the robed one lowers his knife. The young woman who has broken her bindings grabs the back of the filthy woman's head and holds her against her mouth. She then releases the woman, and the woman rears back, screaming as blood pours from her mouth. The young woman reaches out with her hands and grabs the screaming woman by her hair, and slams her face with what seems an ungodly strength straight down onto the altar. The young woman hears bone-breaking from the force that she drove the woman's face into the altar. Hikaru can almost hear the woman's facial bones shattering as she untangles her hand from the woman's hair and lets her roll off the altar to land on the ground at the feet of the gathered crazies. Hikaru sees the young woman spit something out and can only assume it was a piece of the woman's tongue.

It had happened so fast that the other woman had just now seen the other woman lying beside the altar, with a swollen face and half a tongue. She lunges at the young woman, grabs her by her throat, and pushes her onto her back; as she squeezes, she screams, "You fucking bitch! What did you do to my sister?" The robed one commands her to stop, and when she doesn't, he does not hesitate in the least and slashes the woman's throat with his long-bladed knife. The woman stops screaming, and she releases the young girl's throat. She reaches up to grab at her own throat, and as she does, her body starts to lean to one side, and as it does, the blood shoots out from the slash in her throat, and somehow the spray misses the young girl on the altar, but it covers the gathered crowd closest to the altar in blood. Some in the crowd grab the nearly beheaded body and fight among themselves to drink the still-warm blood. The robed one tells the others to return the woman to the cages and that she deserves to live another day. Two other robed ones cut the remaining bindings, roughly lift her off the altar, and start to drag her back to the cages. They throw her to the ground, and then she hears the robed leader tell them to rinse her off. They throw buckets of water on her to rinse off any of the woman's blood and then force her into the cage. Just before the cage door closes, someone tosses the remains of her clothing, and then she is hoisted back into the Air. She watches the robed leader walk through the crowd, and she thinks she sees a look of disgust on his face, and she smiles.

Hikaru has watched the whole thing take place, and just before he puts his eye scope away, he looks one more time at the young woman, who has beaten the odds, and sees a smile on her face.

Chapter 21

Tolland

Nova has spent what seems like an eternity in the Dark Realm training and honing her skills and needs to have a change of pace. She has opened a passageway to the Kassukoku Pass to allow a contingent of her army to seize the town of Shira in the northern part of the Empire and take control of the Pass. She needs something and decides to get away for a bit, and calls for her Senior Officer, Commander Nunes, of her Elite Guard and asks her to inquire if there are girls from any decent-sized towns.

A few minutes later, Commander Nunes is standing at her door, and Nova sees a pretty girl beside her. Nova tells them to enter and asks the young girl, "Where are you from?" The girl answers, "Mistress, I am from a town called Tolland, maybe a six-day ride once you are out of the barrens." Nova tells her to point to it on the map, and when she does, Nova sees that it is east of Sagawa Lake. Nova asks her if it is a large town. The young girl tells her, yes, explaining that the town has four quarters, the Upper Quarter, the Market Quarter, the Mid Quarter, and the Lower Quarter. Nova asks her to explain, and she does. "Mistress, the Upper quarter is for the richer people in town, where the Market Quarter is where you will find different items for sale from around the continent, the Mid Quarter is where the decent folks live and have the types of shops," and she pauses there. Nova looks at her and asks, "What about the Lower Quarter?" The young Elite is hesitant, but she says, "The Lower Quarter is where the worst of the worst dwell., from cutthroats, thieves, prostitutes, and the homeless. You will also find the whore houses, opium dens, the gambling houses, bars, taverns, and dancehalls." She looks at Nova and asks, "If I may, Mistress!" and Nova nods for her to continue, but before she does, Nova asks her, "What is your name? and the young girl says, "Jessica" Nova asks, "Jessica, are there any landmarks near the town, and please be specific. Jessica tells her about an old church in the woods just off the main road. Nova tells Jessica to picture the place in her mind, and as she does,

Nova places the palm of her hand softly on her cheek, and she immediately sees the rundown church in the woods.

Nova dismisses the two, but before Jessica leaves her room, Nova tells her, "When I get back, come see me, I would like to talk," and leaves it at that. Jessica gives her a big smile and says, "Yes, Mistress," and is gone.

Nova tells her slaves that she is not to be disturbed and that if any issue arises, bring them to Commander Nunes's attention. Then she changes into some traveling clothes and smears some dirt on her face to make it look like she has been traveling recently. Nova starts chanting, "*Guko Kachi Mi Dit La Ro Chiakoba*," while at the same time she moves her fingers, and then she hears the distinct ping, and Nova is walking through a passageway and is standing outside an old, rundown church. She walks out of the woods, finds herself on the main road, and wraps a scarf around her head to hide her hair and cover her face. She is soon walking through the gates of Tolland, which she assumes is the Mid Quarter by her surroundings, small shops, houses, and apartments.

She notices a young girl standing near the gates staring at her, and then she walks up to two of the local town militia. Nova sees the young girl press some coins in their palms, and the guards nod to the young lady and then look at Nova and start walking towards her. She sees them coming closer and blocking her way to the Mid Quarter. She doesn't have any papers or identification. She does not want the hassle of being questioned, and then she realizes that they are maneuvering her towards what she assumes is the Lower Quarter. She obliges them, turns down a fair-sized street, blends into the crowd quickly, and ducks into an alley. She watches as the patrol loses sight of her and heads back to the gates. Nova's heart is racing, not from being scared, but from the excitement, and then she sees the young girl again, but this time on the opposite side of the street, and sees her talking to two men about her age or a little older. One of them kisses her on her cheek, and then the two head down the street, and she, like the guards, loses sight of them.

She watches and can see that the young girl is involved with the two gentlemen, and her heart races as she can only anticipate how this will unfold. She smiles, steps from the alley, and deliberately crosses the street; as she walks past the young girl, she bumps into her and stops momentarily to turn to the girl and say, "Sorry." Like Nova, her face is partially hidden in shadows from the hat she is wearing, but she does see a slight movement of her lips as she is surprised. Nova turns to continue on her way and then smiles as she hears the young lady's footsteps following her. Nova continues walking along the sidewalk and comes to the shadiest part of the town as she recognizes the typical bars, opium dens, and the whorehouses that are always about in any town. Nova feels a slight pressure on her back and then a soft voice that says, "Keep walking, Bitch, or I will stab you right here." Nova does as she is told, and they keep walking, and she doesn't say or do anything.

She tells Nova to turn down an alley when she sees the two men the girl was talking to earlier. The two men grab her, and the young girl does not look back as she walks out of the alley and turns to continue on her way down the street. Nova didn't get a good look at the young girl's face, but she could tell by how she dressed that she would not be hard to find in a crowd wearing a bright pink dress like she was. Nova knows that if one dresses nice, they are less likely to be suspicious of any wrongdoing like kidnapping victims at knifepoint.

Nova knows that the girl is smart for not allowing her intended victims the opportunity to see her face as the two men pull her deeper into the alley, and she doesn't try to fight back. Once they are farther back in the alley, one holds her against the alley wall, with a blade against her throat. His accomplice reaches up and grabs the scarf wrapped around her head. He pulls the scarf off, and they are both surprised to see her flaming red hair come loose and cascade down past her shoulders.

The one with the blade against her throat says, "Hey, Tommy. We might have something here," He takes the cloth they put over his mouth and wets it with his tongue. He wipes the dirt from her face. Tommy says, "I think if we clean her up and dress her right, she could bring us some serious coin on one of the main corners or charge her out to the snobs in the Upper Quarter, "What do you think, Tommy?" "Sounds good to me, Mickey." Still holding the blade, Mickey says, "Now, little lady, let's have you remove some of that clothing so we can see what you are hiding underneath." Mickey steps back but is still pointing the blade at her. Nova smiles and says, "Mickey, is it? Why are we doing this out in the open? Why don't we go around the corner to the back alley for more privacy?" After all, we don't want to show the goods before we try selling them now, would we?" She unbuttons the two top buttons of her coat and walks farther into the alley. She looks at Tommy, sees that he is very nervous, and tells him to keep a look because she doesn't want to be disturbed, and not to worry, his time will come and smiles at him. She sees him blush, and he says, "Yes, Ma'am."

She turns the corner and coaxes Mickey to follow her with one hand while the other continues unbuttoning her full-length coat, and he follows her like a little puppy. She sees they will be out of sight from Tommy when she turns the corner and walks to the end of the short alley. She has her back to him as she lets the coat fall off her shoulders, but before it touches the ground, she catches it, walks over to a barrel, and places it on top. Unbeknownst to Mickey, she has pulled a straight-edged razor out of one of the pockets as she put her coat on the barrel. She turns and steps back to the middle of the alley and stands with her legs apart and hands on her hips, with the straight edge hidden in her hand. Mickey stands there staring as she reaches up and unbuttons the top button of her blouse. Mickey is almost drooling with anticipation as he looks at her face and sees her piercing green eyes. He is so mesmerized by her eyes that he does not see the straight-edged razor held in the palm of her right hand. She unbuttons another button and steps toward him, and she also calls out to Tommy and tells him to make sure the coast is clear because Mickey might be making some ungodly noises. Nova is now standing in front of Mickey at arm's length, and he sees that all her buttons are undone, except one that holds her blouse closed just below her breasts. Mickey sees what they were hoping for as she stands before him. Nova is a tall statuesque woman in a sheer top, with perfect full breasts and erect nipples from the cool Air, a toned stomach, long legs, and ahead of flaming red hair. She seductively looks Mickey in the eyes, and her body tells him that she wants it. He drops his knife as he steps closer to her while reaching out to grope one of her breasts.

When he gets half a step closer, Nova turns her body slightly, brings her arm up, and then holds it, raising her arm straight out from her side. Then she quickly gets her hand in horizontally, bending her arm at her elbow to allow her hand to pass in front of his throat, and as her hand makes contact with his throat, she steps back quickly. Tommy is around the corner and cannot see what is happening. Mickey throws his hands up to his throat, starts gurgling, and then drops to his knees as the blood saturates his clothes and the ground from his almost decapitated head.

She can hear Tommy calling, "Come on, hurry up, I want a turn!" She has severed his throat deep enough, so she takes the palm of her hand and pushes on his forehead. She hears the neck snap, and his head rolls backward, and then she hears Tommy approaching, and when he comes around the corner, he sees Mickey looking at him upside down. A look of terror crosses his face as he sees his best friend looking at him upside down and sees that the only thing holding his head on is some unsevered neck muscles. Nova tells him, "I told you to keep watch and wait your turn. Now I have to," and before she can finish what she was going to say, Tommy panics and runs. Nova picks up Mickey's blade, and right before Tommy reaches the street, she throws the knife and catches him at the base of his neck. She watches him stumble and then fall as he crashes sideways into a pile of wooden crates, and when he falls forward, she sees him hitting his head against the alley wall and rolling onto a pile of rotting garbage.

Tommy felt the prick as the blade penetrated the back of his neck, but he didn't feel any pain for some strange reason. He lies there and watches her come back around the corner, buttoning her blouse and then putting on her full-length coat. She adjusts it and then walks over to stand in front of him. He does not realize it, but he has pissed himself. She reaches down to retrieve the knife, and he hears a slight sucking sound as she pulls the knife from the back of his neck as he lays there. Tommy has a hard time understanding why he cannot feel anything.

With her partially buttoned blouse, she squats and pats him down, checking his pockets and avoiding the wet areas. She laughs and tells him, "When Mickey's knife stuck you in the base of your neck, it severed all your nerves, so now you are completely paralyzed and can feel nothing." Here, let me show you," she grabs his finger with the small diamond chip ring, and instead of wrestling with it to try and get it off, she just cuts his finger off. "See, I told you. You cannot move, talk, or feel pain. Now! all you have to do is ask me politely to end your life, and I will be happy to oblige, or I can let you live like this for the rest of your life as a pile of worthless shit."

She dumps a slop bucket on him and then turns it over to pile all his valuables. She places his severed finger with the ring down on the bucket, then unfolds a piece of paper and holds it up to the light, and she sees a sketch of an attractive young woman and two men. "Your wife?" she asks. She can tell she is by the look in his eyes, and he starts crying. She tells him to be a man and live up to his choices because he and Mickey brought this on themselves and then asks, "Who might this other gentleman be?" She looks toward Mickey, but Nova is skeptical until she turns her head slightly upside down and looks at Mickey. "Oh! Now I see it, he looks like her, is he your brother-in-law?" and she can tell by his eyes that it is yes, and she starts laughing, then says, "Excuse me, I'm sorry, I guess I should say, "Was he your brother-law?" and laughs even more. She rips the sketch into small pieces and sprinkles the torn pieces over his body.

She looks at him and says, "I am feeling generous today, so I will go to your ex-brother-in-law and see what he has in his pockets. When I come back, you can tell me what you decide. She walks over to Mickey, pats him down, checking for valuables, and then returns to the overturned bucket and places the items she found down with the others.

Nova looks at him and says, "Well, what will it be, live like this or end your miserable life?" Nova squats there and waits, and after a few minutes, she says, "If you can't tell me, then how the fuck am I supposed to know? I can't read your mind, dipshit!"

She then shows him the piece of paper she found in Mickey's pocket, reads it out loud, "Club Fanta," and says, "I wonder what I will find there?" She looks at him, and he looks back at her with pure hatred. She takes all the items from on top of the bucket and puts them in her pockets. She then stands and sees another bucket close by, knowing what it is by the smell. She picks it up and places it on a broken chair beside his body. She walks away, and as she reaches the street, she turns and says to him, "Enjoy!" and throws a brick at the broken chair, the brick hits the chair, and she watches as the bucket tips and its contents spill all over him. She walks towards the street laughing, leaving him covered in slop, piss, and shit.

Nova adjusts her coat, walks out of the alley, glances back, and says, "Let me see, how am I going to spend the evening. Why don't I go to Club Fanta and talk with your charming wife and see if she wants to have fun?" She hears a very faint gagging sound and walks away.

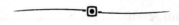

Nova finds a public bathhouse and takes a bath to get rid of the grime, blood, and stench of death. Two women join her, washing every part of her body and then some. She returns the favor, and soon both girls are quivering with pleasure as Nova demonstrates her training in the Dark Realm.

After her bath, she cleans her traveling clothes, and as she waits, she gets a massage from a pretty girl. Nova lies there as the young girl knows what she is doing as she slowly works out the knots in her upper and lower back. She starts to massage her legs when the young girl's fingers brush the insides of her thighs, and Nova lets out a soft moan. The young girl slowly gets on the table and straddles Nova's backside; Nova can tell that the girl is naked and continues to massage her back. She gently runs her fingers along the sides of her breasts. Nova turns herself over, so now the young girl is straddling her pelvis. With no words spoken, she leans forward and kisses her, and Nova feels her tongue part her lips and is receptive. The two of them are now in a state of heated passion, and before long, the young girl is lying on her back as Nova straddles her and gently returns the massage.

Nova notices that her clothes have been brought back clean and folded. She also realizes it is getting late and tells the young girl, thank you. Then she kisses the young girl on her cheek and gets dressed. She leaves the massage girl exhausted on the table. Nova leaves her with a smile, and like the two girls that washed her, she leaves an excellent tip. She thinks about the plan she came up with as she was getting her massage and now knows what she has planned for the girl on the sketch.

She stops at a local dress shop and picks a dress to display her figure without looking like a whore. She has the dress wrapped up, and as she leaves the dress shop, she sees the local town patrol and asks them where she could find a nice hotel, and they both agree that the Sakura Hotel would be her best choice.

Nova thanks them for the suggestion and heads to the Sakura Hotel. She walks into the Sakura Hotel and asks the clerk if the hotel has any rooms. The clerk tells her yes, the night is slow, so he has plenty of rooms. Nova places a small chip of black diamond on the counter and asks him if the three top floors are accessible. The clerk looks at the diamond and asks, "Is it real!" and Nova tells him, "It is real if the top three floors are vacant." The clerk smiles pockets the diamond, and says, "They will be if you would be so kind as to give me a few." She tells him she needs to do some shopping and should be back within the hour. Before she leaves, she asks him if that will be sufficient payment. He tells her, "yes," and she leaves. She stops at the apothecary, and like the hotel, she pays with a small chip of black diamond. She then stops at a store to buy some other items. One hour later, she is in her room. She prepares everything, sits at a window, and drinks a glass of wine as she watches the comings and goings of the Club Fanta. She decides to get ready, and after donning her dress, she heads downstairs and out into the street.

It is evening as she heads to Club Fanta to see what she can find. She checks her coat, then stands in the doorway, looking about the place. Several sets of eyes, both men and women, are staring at her. She ignores their stares, and then she sees her, the girl from the sketch. She sits at a table, calls the girl over, says, "Hello," and then asks her, "What do you recommend?" The young girl tells her to stay away from the meat, but the fish is delicious. Nova says, "Thank you, and what did you say your name was?" The young girl says, "I didn't say, but my name is Gertrude; my friends call me Gertie."

"Nice to meet you, Gertrude; my name is Nova," and she shakes her hand. Gertrude asks Nova, "Have we met before?"

Nova says, "My dear if we had met before, I would surely remember a beautiful young lady like yourself." Gertrude blushes and apologizes for her mistake and asks Nova what she would like to start with, and Nova asks her what she would suggest. Gertrude recommends a nice bottle of white wine to go with the fish.

Nova knows that Gertrude doesn't recognize her because the last time she saw her, she wore her traveling clothes, and a scarf covered her hair and partially hid her face.

Nova sits there in the restaurant sipping on her wine and having small talk with Gertrude. Several male patrons approach her, and she kindly tells them no thank you, and most bow slightly and leave. When Gertrude takes a break, she joins Nova, and they talk and giggle. Gertrude tells her it's time to go back to work, and Nova now sees that Gertrude is a charming girl and will make it more pleasurable to do what she must do. It is getting late, and she explains to Gertrude that she has just arrived in town and could she suggest a decent place to spend the night. Gertrude tells her to go to the Black Swan Hotel, probably the cleanest place in this part of town for the price. Nova says, "Thank you, and places a small stack of coins on the table. Then she says, "Gertrude, please stop by if you want to join me after you get out of here."

Gertrude says, "Maybe if it's not too late."

Nova winks at her, says, "It's never too late, my dear," and says, "See you later."

She grabs her coat, and just before she leaves, she turns one last time and waves to Gertrude. She sees Gertrude smile and wave, and she can tell by her body language that she will have a guest tonight in her room. Nova smiles back and then steps into the street.

Nova stands across the street in the shadows, and a few minutes later, she sees Gertrude come outside, write a note, and then give a coin and the message to a young boy, and she hears her say, Tommy and Mickey, now go and sends him off. Nova watches the young boy head down the street towards the ally.

Nova hopes she doesn't miss her with the bright lights from the bars, restaurants, and brothels illuminating the streets with their bright lights, to almost blinding. Forty minutes later, she sees young Gertrude walking up the road towards the Black Swan. She has already left a note with a runner, and she tells him that Gertrude is wearing a bright pink dress, and he can't miss her. Nova looks out the window, watching the runner give Gertrude the note. She opens it, reads it, and quickly pulls out a pencil, and Nova watches her scratch something out and then rewrites something. Nova can only guess that it is a change of hotels, and then she gives the note back to the boy and watches him take off down the street, just as Gertrude is walking towards Sakura Hotel.

A few minutes later, Nova hears a light tap on the door, and someone says, "Nova? It's me, Gertrude." Nova opens the door, and Gertrude stands there with a bottle of red wine. She can tell that Gertrude has had a few more drinks after leaving the club. Nova takes the wine, hugs Gertrude, and tells her to sit down. She sits on the couch as Nova opens the wine, and while her back is to Gertrude, she pours a little white powder from the apothecary into her glass of wine and watches it fizzle settle.

Nova walks back over to Gertrude and hands her the glass of wine. Nova tells her that she will go and throw something a little more comfortable on and be right back. While in her room, she yells out to Gertrude that there is an extra robe in the closet, and if she wants to change her clothes and get more comfortable, she is welcome to it.

Then she hears Gertrude say, "Thank you."

Nova walks back into the sitting area and sees that Gertrude took her advice and changed into the robe. She also notices that she has not touched her wine. Nova comes around, sits on the couch, and is about to say something when Gertrude leans into her, throws her arms around her neck, whispers her name, and says, "Nova, I'm sorry." Nova is sitting there slightly surprised, and she is about to ask Gertrude what when she starts kissing her neck and placing her hand inside Nova's robe. She gently cups the underside of her breast, and Nova moans softly. Gertrude then softly rakes her fingernails down her side and then gently runs her fingernails against the side of her breast. Nova breathes in, and then she feels her other hand untie her robe. Her robe comes open, and Gertrude takes one fingernail and places it at her throat, runs it down between her breasts, and then gently pinches her nipple between her forefinger and thumb, causing Nova to moan softly.

Nova puts her glass of wine down and returns the pleasure. She carefully undoes Gertrude's robe, pulls it off her shoulders, and brings it down to pin Gertrude's arms at her sides. Nova stares at her medium-sized breasts with dark areolas and erect nipples and licks her lips. She then pushes Gertrude onto her back, lowers her face, returns the favor, and gently bites her nipples, first one then the other. Gertrude starts moaning as Nova continues down from her breasts to her flat stomach, gently blows on her belly, and then kisses her, stopping just above her womanhood.

Nova can tell that Gertrude is ready, and as she tries to stand up, Nova stops and pushes her back onto the couch. Gertrude looks at her as if to ask what now when Nova carefully crawls over her body and gently straddles her.

At first, Gertrude is uncertain, but as Nova reaches back and touches her slowly and more vigorously, Nova has Gertrude exploding and quivering. Nova then stands in front of Gertrude, and as Gertrude goes to stand, Nova stops her again, reaches to the back of Gertrude's hair, undoes the hair clip, and lets her hair fall free around her shoulders. Nova carefully wraps Gertrude's hair around her fist and pulls her head back, exposing her neck. Nova leans in and starts kissing Gertrude's neck while sliding her tongue along her throat, pulling her hair a little harder; then, she sticks her tongue into her mouth.

Gertrude moans again in response to the hair pulling and the kiss. Nova releases her hair and pulls away just enough to hold Gertrude's wrists above her head, and Nova whispers, "Keep them there." Gertrude does as she is told, and then Nova places a black silk blindfold over her eyes and ties it. She can hear Gertrude's breaths getting quicker. Nova takes a silk cord and ties Gertrude's hands behind her head. She tries to look in the direction of Nova, and Nova jerks the cord tight, keeping her arms tied above her head.

Nova reaches down once again and gently penetrates her. Blindfolded, tied up, and breathing heavily, Gertrude manages to say in a whisper, "More, Nova, I want more!" Nova brings the glass of wine to her lips; and. Gertrude is so anxious and downs the wine in three gulps. Nova takes her hand and begins to work her fingers as Gertrude starts to buck slightly on the couch and begs Nova, "More, give me more, please!" Nova obliges her and pulls a wooden phallus, and when Nova touches her with it, Gertrude screams, "Yes!"

Nova hears her beg for more, and she obliges, but unknown to her, Nova carefully laces the wooden rod with the same drug she put in her wine, and Gertrude takes all of it. Moments later, Nova sits beside Gertrude, watching her body twitch and seeing that the drugs have worked. Between the drugs in her wine and the sprinkling of the drug on the wooden rod. Nova knows she will be out for a while and will not interfere with her plans.

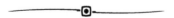

It is late as Nova is now sitting beside the bed in her robe; Gertrude first stirs and then starts to come around, and once she is coherent, she realizes that she is tied to the bed in a spread-eagle position. She immediately begins to struggle, and when she realizes that she cannot get herself loose, she asks Nova, "What is the meaning of this?" Nova replies, "My dear; we are going to play a little game." Gertrude can tell by her voice that it is not a sex game and starts to squirm on the bed.

Nova calmingly says, "Now, my sweet, you have to stop moving, or the knots will get tighter and cut your circulation."

Gertrude relaxes, and through gritted teeth, she asks, "What is this game?"

Before Nova can say anymore, Gertrude screams, but Nova is quick and shoves a cloth in her mouth, places her finger against her lips, and says, "My dear Gertrude, before you start screaming and making a fuss, let me tell you two things. One holds up a finger and says, The whole floor and the two floors below us are completely vacant, no one can hear you, and two, Nova holds up a second finger and says, "You picked the wrong Bitch to fuck with!" Now back to business, as for the game, It's called Truth, plain and simple." The rules are, I ask you a question, you tell me the Truth, but if I think you are lying, the consequences could be, shall we say, quite unbearable, shall we begin?"

Nova sits there looking at her and says, "Gertrude, I was thinking, you know, Gertrude is so formal, and after what we did tonight, I think if I called you Gertie, like your friends, it would make this so informal, wouldn't you agree, Gertie?"

"Now, shall we begin, Question number one, What did you say about me to the town guards at the gate?"

Nova removes the cloth from her mouth for her to answer.

Then she says, "I don't know what you are talking about."

"Wrong answer," and she shoves the cloth back into her mouth, takes her blade, slices off her pinky at the first knuckle, and immediately throws some white powder on the severed finger.

Gertrude screams, and after the powder takes effect, she feels no pain and is now whimpering.

Nova looks at her, "Shall we try this again? What did you say to the town guards?"

Nova pulls the cloth out of her mouth and, through her sobbing, she tells Nova that she had a scheme going with the town guards that if she saw someone who looked like they didn't have much but was pretty, they would coerce the person down the street towards her two friends. They, in turn, would follow you and force you to pay an entry tax to the city. They would then split the fee sixty-forty. ova says, "Good answer, I believe you."

"Question number two, who were those two men you talked to just before I was forced into the alley by you at knifepoint?"

Then it registers why Nova looked familiar.

She looks at her and says, "I'm sorry."

"Sorry, wrong answer." She cuts her next finger at its first knuckle, throws some white powder on the cut, and then tells her, "It is too late for sorry!"

Same thing, the scream, the whimpering, and then asks her again about the two men, and she does not say anything.

"Wrong answer," this time, she makes an incision with Mickey's blade on her forehead, throws some white powder on the cut, and says, "That one might leave a scar!"

She removes the rag as Gertrude continues to sob.

"Now, where was I? Who were those two men you were talking to just before they pulled me into the alley at knifepoint?"

Sobbing, Gertie says, "They were my husband and brother." Nova says. I believe you."

"Question number three, what plans did your husband and brother have for me?"

She says, "I don't know, honest."

"My dear sweet Gertie, your lips are moving, and do you know what I am hearing."

Gertie acts a little defiant and says, "What?" with a slight attitude, and she tells Nova, "You had better let me go, and I promise I won't have them hurt you."

Nova stands up, looks terrified, and says, "Who, my dear? Who are you going to tell not to hurt me?"

Gertie looks at her and says, "My husband and brother, I sent a boy after them with a note with the hotel's name where you're staying, and they should be here any minute."

Nova looks at her and says, "So, your husband and brother are coming here to this hotel to rescue you and rob me? Then what? Force me into a life of prostitution?"

She defiantly says, "Yes!"

"Lies, Gertie, all lies!" and shoves the cloth in her mouth and covers her nose with another wet cloth, and as she breaths, in the fumes, Gertie passes out. Nova looks at the sleeping girl and thinks if things were different, but then again, they are not, and starts to get to work.

Three hours later, just as the sun rises, Gertie wakes up and finds herself still tied to the bed and covered in white powder and bandages.

Nova comes back into the room and sees that she has changed into her traveling clothes and is drying her hands. Nova walks over and places something on her chest. Gertie looks down, blinks once, then twice, and starts crying again.

Nova says, "Such a cute little piece of glass," then, "Gertrude, please pay close attention. I will leave your brother's knife here, and you should be able to figure out how to cut yourself loose. I will also tell you that your adorable husband and brother are back in the alley where they tried to assault me. Please tell your husband I am sorry about his missing finger," and then says, "No wait, it is not missing, you have it," and she starts laughing. Nova walks to the door, opens it, turns, and says to her, "Don't worry about your beloved husband. I swear he is alive, but I can't say the same for your brother, other than he might look at the world a little differently, and "Please make yourself presentable before you go see them. They had been through a lot yesterday,"

Just as she closes the door, she says, "Thank you for an enjoyable evening, and Gertrude, always remember to smile," and again starts laughing as she closes the door. Before leaving the hotel, she stops at the desk and sees the clerk from yesterday. She tells him, "I had a delightful evening, and please forgive my mess," then places another small chip of black diamond on the counter then says, "My acquaintance is still sleeping. Please allow her to stay as long as she wants." All the clerk says is, "Yes, Ma'am,"

She leaves the hotel and heads to the city gates, but before she does, she decides to make a quick stop at the headquarters of the town militia. She enters the outer room, and several of the militia stand at once, and she asks to speak to the Commander of the Watch. He is very polite as she explains what a couple of his men are doing to people coming into the city through the South Gate. The Commander says, "Thank you, and escorts her out.

She stops at the apothecary and tells the proprietor to thank him for his powder and discretion. She leaves another small chip of black diamond on his counter. She walks up the street to the town gates when there is a commotion, and the two guards she encountered when she first arrived are being escorted towards the jail. She decides to stop and have a cold drink before she goes back. Nova sits at a little outdoor café and drinks some juice, enjoying the day.

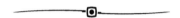

A little over an hour later, Gertrude finally figures out how to cut the bindings on one of her wrists and soon has the other three bindings cut. She gets off the bed, feels a pain in her chest, and looks down to see that her chest is wrapped tightly in a bandage. She reaches up and touches her face, and finds more bandages. She unsteadily walks over to the night table and sits down. and looks in the mirror and sees most of her head and face are wrapped in bandages.

She decides to remove the chest bandage first, and as she removes the last layer, she sees in the mirror's reflection that both her nipples are gone. She sits there crying into her hands and feels a little pain when she touches her face. She runs her hand over her head, and she sees that she has another bandage wrapped around her forehead. She finally removes the bandage and sees something in the mirror, and when she leans in to look closer, she sees the letters "FEIHT / EROHW," and it takes her a moment to realize that what she is looking at is the words "THIEF and WHORE" carved deep into her forehead. She breaks down crying again, and as she touches her face, she feels something is not quite right and proceeds to take the facial bandages off. She removes the last of them, and what she sees, she immediately starts screaming and then turns away from the mirror. She now knows that the white powder numbed her features where Nova cut her. She looks again and cries even harder. She regains her composure, reaches up, and removes the bandage around the top of her head. When she removes the last layer, she sees that her beautiful dark hair has been shaved off and is completely bald. She collapses on the bed and cries.

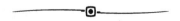

Gertrude has no more tears, and she replaces the bandages on her chest and wraps a scarf tightly around her head and face. She keeps her head down and her arm across her chest, making her way out of the hotel. She hurries down the street, then turns into the alley and sees no one. She walks farther down the alley, and as she turns the corner, she sees her brother staring at her, but something is wrong, and a rat crawls out of his mouth and scurries away. She brings a hand to her mouth to stifle a scream, steps back, turns to run, and then trips over a pile of rotting garbage and feces. She falls into the trash and hears a noise as an escape of breath. She realizes the trash is soft, and as she looks, she sees a pair of eyes staring at her. She immediately recognizes that it is her husband's eyes and tries to help him. She stares at him and sees the horror in his eyes. She realizes that her scarf has fallen away from her mouth, and she notices the disgust in his eyes. He now sees that the corners of her mouth are cut to make it look like she is smiling. She reaches up and removes the scarf covering her head, and he now sees that she is completely bald, and the words "THIEF / WHORE" are carved into her forehead. She sees the contempt in his eyes, and with tears in her own, she takes her brother's blade, and while laying on top of him, she slips the knife under his chin and pushes upward, driving the point of the blade into his brain. She lies on the heap that was once her husband and tries to cry, but realizes that she has no more tears and just lies there in the filth on top of her husband,

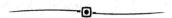

Nova is walking out through the town gates, and she notices two different guards standing at the entrance. She nods to them as she passes. One of the guards wishes her a wonderful day, and she smiles at the two of them. She has just gotten past the gates when she hears a woman screaming and comes running up to the two guards, saying, "There is a hideous monster down there in the ally, and it has killed two people."

Nova smiles and thinks, "Poor Gertie, I guess she figured out how to get free," then laughs. She walks up the road and turns onto the path that leads to the old church. Nova stands in front of the old church and chants, *"Guko Kachi Mi Dit La Ro Chiakoba,"* she hears the distinct ping, and a passageway opens and is just about to step through when she hears a commotion and then the whistles of an alarm. She steps in and turns to face the path. Through the trees, she sees a hooded figure come running out of the gates, being pursued by the two gate guards. Nova watches the hooded figure turn down the path to the church, and starts laughing. The hooded figure hears the laughing, and then she sees Nova and screams at her, "I'LL KILL YOU, YOU FUCKING BITCH!" Nova smiles blows her a kiss, and the passageway closes.

Chapter 22

The Traitor

Hikaru is disgusted by what he has witnessed but silently thanks the Goddesses for sparing her. He can now finish what he started and has a good count on the size of the enemy force and signals for his men to work their way back down the hill to their horses. They reach the clearing, and just when they mount their horses and are about to ride out, they hear a couple of other horses' whinny, causing theirs to whinny. A small force of about thirty men breaks through the brush into the clearing, and both parties are surprised and momentarily stare at each other. Hikaru quickly tosses the map bag with the enemy tally to one of his men and tells him to get it back to the Colonel no matter what happens.

He sees that they are outnumbered three to one and quickly draws his battle-ax, and with the rider still behind him, he orders the rider to go. The rider takes off at full gallop as the enemy force draws their swords and attack. Hikaru starts swinging his battle-ax, taking down a few of the enemy as his men fight diligently to allow the rider to escape so that he can get the information back to the Colonel. Weapons clash, men and horses scream, and the dying are quiet on both sides.

Hikaru swings his battle-ax, and he feels it as a flash of silver crosses his eyes and a state of euphoria courses through his body. Suddenly he is demolishing the enemy with his deadly ax. They come at him with swords slashing high and low but are killed, maimed, or forced back. Hikaru is holding his own and keeping the enemy away from his rider with the map and tally. He grabs a fallen sword, and using both hands, he makes a hole in the enemy formation and tells his rider to go. Hikaru sees the rider break free and gallops off. Thinking that he is in the clear, Hikaru concentrates on the enemy, blocks a spear aimed at his chest, and then sees Heinz break rank from the skirmish and gallops after the rider with the map bag. Hikaru is angry that Heinz would abandon them, but he thinks it would be better for two riders to ride back to the column and report what is happening and the enemy count.

Hikaru takes down another man and can keep the others back when he looks over the shoulder of one of his assailants and sees Heinz swinging his sword at the other rider; he sees Heinz slash him, and he draws blood. The other rider draws his sword and deflects Heinz's second swing. They are still galloping away but are now battling each other on horseback. He sees the rider lunge at Heinz and watches as Heinz is stabbed in his leg, and he hears Heinz scream out in pain and then start cussing. Just as the rider pulls back to try and stab Heinz again, Hikaru is surprised to see Heinz then take his sword and swing it wide and slightly down, and when he does, he catches the rider on the side of his neck, and the rider loses his head, as does Heinz loses his sword in the process. Hikaru sees the body of the dead rider start to lean away from him and then sees Heinz, while still the two horses are galloping beside each other, grab the strap of the map bag, and he somehow pulls the now headless rider back up straight. Heinz takes his long knife, reaches over to cut the bag strap, and lets the rider fall from his horse. Heinz kicks his horse in the flanks, and as he tries to gallop away from the skirmish, Hikaru hears and sees Heinz grab his thigh, then slumps forward in his saddle. Hikaru looks over and sees a Dark soldier with a short bow and knows he was the one who shot Heinz, and he can make out two arrows protruding from Heinz's body; one is in his leg, and the other in his shoulder.

Hikaru stops another sword thrust by taking the attacker's arm at the elbow, but he is distracted as he watches Heinz and what he did. He comes back and takes down two more of the enemy before they rush him and force him to the ground, and then he is struck in the head, and before he blacks out, he hears one of the soldiers say. "This fucker is going to the Arena," and then all goes dark.

He slowly stirs, and he finds himself on the back of his horse, and he can see that they are getting ready to leave and be escorted to the town. Sitting astride the horse, he thinks about how Samuel and Reiko's friend, Barnaby Cook, had betrayed them but did not quite understand why Heinz stabbed and killed the other rider if they were riding back to the column. Was it a mistake? Did Heinz panic? He sees that Tombs and the two others are stripped of their weapons and gear and tied like Hikaru is on their horses.

Hikaru now sees that Tombs has a small gash on his head while the other two remaining soldiers seem okay, other than some scrapes and bruises. They are getting ready to move out when he sees his other five men and the enemy's men staring up at the sky, unblinking. Though groggy, he does a quick count, and the odds are five of his for seventeen of theirs, and he knows he took down at least eleven of them.

One of the men riding beside Hikaru says, "You know that guy that was with you, the one who killed your man. Hikaru says, "You mean Lieutenant Piss Pants." The Dark Soldier starts laughing and asks Hikaru to explain.

Hikaru thinks, "What the fuck." and tells him the story. The soldier stops laughing long enough to tell Hikaru, "It almost wasn't worth the second arrow, but I will say it was gutsy for him to willingly take an arrow in the shoulder just to make it look real." The other one riding with them says, "That's why I put one in his leg, to make it more real. They both laugh, then the first one says, "Better Lieutenant Piss Pants than me, and they both start laughing. One of them says, "I never really liked that low-life bastard!" Hikaru now realizes it wasn't a mistake or Barnaby Cook but that Heinz betrayed them and that he needs to get word to the Colonel somehow that this is a trap.

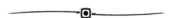

Hikaru is between the man who helped the others take him down and the other one that shot Heinz in the back and leg, to make it look good on his escape. Their hands are tied tight so that if any of them fell off their horses, they could choke, snap their necks, or hang themselves with the ropes around them. Their horses are led back through the same bushes they came through and are soon being led up a hill, and it takes everything Hikaru has to stay upright. The remaining soldiers are behind him when one is not so lucky as he loses his balance and falls from his horse. The enemy does not stop or try to help him but urges the fallen man's horse onward as Hikaru listens to the soldier slowly choke to death while dragged up the hill. They get to the top of the hill, stop, throw the body over his saddle, and secure it. Hikaru looks at them and says, "You bastards, why didn't you help him?" One of the soldiers moves his mount closer to Hikaru, hauls off, punches Hikaru right in the jaw, and says, "No one calls me a bastard," then laughs and then urges the horses forward. They make their way over some low hills and are soon heading up the main road to the town square; as they enter the town square, the one soldier still alive is dragged from his horse and carried over to the altar, and as they carry him, they strip his clothes. They place the body on the altar when they get to the altar. The one in the robes Hikaru saw earlier tells his men to throw Hikaru and Tombs in the cages. Both are placed in separate cages and then hoisted into the Air. They are raised high enough to have a clear view of the altar. They watch in horror the dirty and disgusting things performed on their comrade. Hikaru then sees two filthy-looking females with piercings and scars of self-mutilation start rubbing their naked bodies on his man. He sees them pull out some small blades and continually slice, cut, and mutilate the soldier's body.

Hikaru then notices splotches of red where the females have placed their blades and realize that they are cutting into his flesh.

The robed one who directed that Hikaru and Tombs be placed in the cages walks to the head of the altar, raises a knife, and plunges the knife into the soldier's chest without hesitation. Hikaru watches his body mutilated and drained of his blood. When there is no more to drain, the robed one slices open the soldier's chest, reaches in, and rips out his heart, holding it up for the crowd to see. The two females are now walking through the crowd and offering the followers sips of the soldier's still-warm blood from small cups. Hikaru realizes what the women were doing while walking through the crowd earlier, and all he says is, "Fucking crazies."

Second Lieutenant Tombs starts throwing up as he sees what they are doing to the body. The sun begins to set, and the woman beside Hikaru in the next cage says, "That is all for the day," Then she leans against her cage and goes to sleep. Besides Hikaru waking up occasionally and hearing Lieutenant Tombs crying, the night is quiet. As he sits in his cage, Hikaru wakes and notices that Tombs is now a nervous wreck. He can also see that he has not slept.

Hikaru sees three of the robed figures walking back toward the cages. Tombs looks at Hikaru and says, "Lieutenant, Please, I don't want to go like that. Do something, anything?" The next thing that he knows is Tomb's cage is being lowered, and Tombs starts screaming for Hikaru to help him. Hikaru watches and knows he can do nothing to help his fellow officer. He watches as Tombs puts up a good fight and swings his fist, and it sounds like he has broken the nose of one of the robed ones; and hears a voice cry out, and he thinks it is a woman's voice. One of the others stuns him with a savage blow to the head, and they drag him not to the altar as expected but towards a large stockade-type structure. He looks at the young woman, and all she says is, "The Arena."

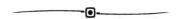

Heinz keeps riding for about an hour and then reigns in his mount to remove the arrow from his left thigh and wrap his leg. He is angry because that fool with the bow was supposed to shoot him once, not twice. Heinz swears to find out who those idiots were and make them pay for the second arrow. He can do nothing about the arrow on his shoulder, but he can make a copy of the map and change the positions and totals. Heinz grunts in pain as he does it, and when done, he praises himself for learning the skill of map-making before joining the military. He tries to get back on his mount, and the horse is skittish. After his second attempt, the horse rears and knocks Heinz to the ground, and the horse bolts and gallops back to the base camp, leaving Heinz sitting on his ass. A few hours later, the marching column sees a riderless horse galloping towards them. The Colonel orders the column to stop and make a cold camp until they get the report from Lieutenant Sato. The camp has just about settled when the sentry shouts out that someone is coming. Heinz staggers into the base camp, and when he gets to the sentry, he passes out and falls to the ground. Word quickly spreads that Second Lieutenant Heinz has returned to the camp with two severe leg wounds and one shoulder wound.

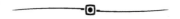

The Colonel is in his tent with Samuel, Reiko, and Second Lieutenants Bradley and Rumley, laying out the plan as discussed when the word is brought to the Colonel that Second Lieutenant Heinz is awake. He tells the two Second Lieutenants to stay here and asks Samuel and Reiko to join him. They get to Heinz's tent and see him sitting up, and he looks in extreme pain. The Colonel says, "Report Lieutenant Heinz. What did you see, and where are Lieutenants Sato, Tombs, and the other men? Heinz is looking at Samuel when he says, "Dead sir, All Dead!" and starts crying, saying to anyone who will listen, "I tried, Sir, but Lieutenant Sato ordered me to get his report back to you; no matter what the cost. I'm sorry, Sir." and then pulls the map from the pouch and hands it to the Colonel.

"That's okay, Lieutenant, you rest. I will be back later to debrief you. Don't mention this to anyone, and that's an order!" says the Colonel. The three of them exit the tent, and as Reiko steps through the tent flap, she looks back at Heinz to see a wicked evil smile cross his face, and as he moves, he seems to be in very little pain.

Reiko catches up to Samuel and tells him what she saw. He believes her knowing well enough that Reiko is neither paranoid nor an overimaginative person.

Reiko asks him, "Do you think I should say something to the Colonel?" and before you say anything, I don't believe that Hikaru is dead, or we would have felt something." Reiko and Samuel walk to the Colonel's tent and ask to speak with him. The three of them are alone when Reiko asks the Colonel if she can look at the map Heinz brought back with him. He hands her the map, and she examines it very closely and then gives it to Samuel as he does the same. The Colonel asks what this is all about when Reiko tells him that the map is a forgery, and Samuel agrees. The Colonel asks, "What do you mean a forgery? How do you know?" Samuel explains to the Colonel that when the three of them were training and living together, they became very close friends and devised a way to mark important documents, letters, and other things. They all agreed on a small symbol and placed it indiscriminately on anything they thought would be significant. The mark that only the three of them knew about, and this map is missing that mark. The Colonel asks, "Could Lieutenant Sato have forgotten to put this symbol on the map?" Both Samuel and Reiko say "No" at the same time.

Reiko says to the Colonel, "Hikaru, Excuse me, Lieutenant Sato knew how vital this map was, and he would not have forgotten to mark it. Sir, I think Second Lieutenant Heinz doctored that map to lead us into a trap with the enemy."

The Colonel looks at Lieutenant Takahashi and says, "Lieutenant, those are some serious charges against a fellow officer. If what you say is true, Heinz will be charged as a traitor, or if your accusations prove false, then there is a good chance that you will be court-martialed and discharged from the army. These are not for me to decide, but the military courts will need to investigate the matter, is that understood?"

Reiko says, "Yes, Sir," gives him a firm salute, and turns to leave.

The Colonel tells them," You are not to discuss this with anyone," and waves them off.

Samuel leaves the tent, and Reiko is just about to step outside when the Colonel says, "Reiko; she turns, and the Colonel says, "I believe something is not right, so keep a close eye on Heinz."

Reiko says, "Yes, Sir, she meets up with Samuel, and she quietly tells Samuel what the Colonel said.

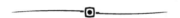

The following day, the Colonel gives the orders to break camp and move out within the hour. The bustle of the breakdown of the camp is like a well-greased wheel; with a few minutes to spare, the army is on the march toward the town of Shira, presently occupied by a Dark Army that has taken it over. Heinz tells the Colonel that he cannot ride a horse because of his leg, so the Colonel allows him to ride in the back of one of the supply wagons. Heinz chooses the wagon at the end of the column. He is sitting in the back of the wagon and knows he only has one more day before the Imperial Army makes its way into the valleys near the town. He needs to get this map to the General. Gradually the supply wagon falls behind and then stops. The driver gets down and checks the tie-downs on the wagon, and the driver, a Second Lieutenant like himself says, is standing near him when he says, "Go now, and warn the General, now hurry and may the Dark protect you." Heinz lowers himself out of the wagon and says, "Thank you," He runs off as best he can into the woods. He does not realize that the driver did not tell him the correct response or see the Lieutenant signal to let Samuel and Reiko know that the bird has flown the coop. They hurry up to the driver, and he smiles and says, "That was easy enough," and then points in the direction Heinz headed off.

Reiko says, "Thank you, Lieutenant Sips, and when we get back to the Capital, I owe you a drink for your fine performance."

Heinz knows he has to quickly meet up with his contact, hand him the map he drew of the Empire's battle plans, and make it back before the army stops one last night. He cusses at the archer, putting the second arrow in his leg because it is starting to hurt and slow him down.

Samuel and Reiko easily follow Heinz's trail by the broken branches and footprints he is leaving for them to follow. They realize that Heinz is not concerned with leaving a trail because he figures he will be back in his tent before they camp for the night. No one other than his fellow Dark friend, Lieutenant Sips, knows that he is gone, and he probably assumes Sips won't say anything unless he wants to incriminate himself.

Samuel and Reiko hear a whistle and stay back in the woods as they see Heinz in a clearing as if waiting for someone.

They listen as he gives the contact signal and then hear the required whistle in return. They watch a Dark soldier enter the clearing, and Heinz steps forward to meet him. They clasp hands and hear Heinz say, "May the Darkness watch over you," and the Dark Soldier replies, "May the Darkness protect you." Heinz hands him a rolled parchment and says, as his contact puts it in his pouch, "These are the numbers of the forces making their way to Shira; get them back to the General.

Heinz sees a movement out of his eye, feels the wisp of a breeze on his cheek, and then sees an arrow protruding from the Dark soldier's forehead. The man crumples to the ground. Heinz backs away when he hears, "Well, if it isn't Second Lieutenant Piss Pants! Fancy meeting you way out here. I rode to the back because I felt terrible. After all, you had to travel in the supply wagon." Reiko tells him.

Samuel walks up and asks, "Hey Gus! How's the leg?" He takes his boot and rolls the dead man over. "Strange looking uniform for an Imperial soldier, wouldn't you say so, Lieutenant Takahashi?"

"By all means, Lieutenant Miro, definitely strange-looking uniform for an Imperial soldier. Reiko places her foot on his neck and pulls her arrow out of his head. She then reaches down, cuts the pouch from his belt, and tosses it to Samuel.

"What do we have here, Gus?" Samuel reaches into the pouch and finds some coins and two rolled-up pieces of parchment.

Heinz grabs for his knife and lunges at Samuel. Samuel steps aside and grabs Heinz's wrist, twists it, and snaps it, causing Heinz to drop the knife. He falls to his knees, screaming and crying as he holds his broken wrist.

Reiko walks up to him and says, "That was pretty stupid Piss Pants." Samuel smiles when she calls him that because she knows he hates it. "Why would you think you could do any harm with that little pig sticker?" She picks up the knife and throws it so it sticks in a tree about three meters above the ground.

Samuel unties the string holding the parchment and unrolls it. Samuel starts reading it and walks over to sit down on a rock. He knows Heinz isn't going anywhere, especially with Reiko having her bow, and he calls her over and hands her the parchment.

Reiko finishes reading it, whistles, and says, "Hey, Piss Pants, what the fuck were you thinking?" All Heinz says is, "Fuck you, Bitch!"

She starts laughing and says, "Oh! Piss Pants. What a tangled web you weave. Do you know that the Colonel suspected something was wrong when we told him about our suspicions with the map? He knew you were not smart or talented enough to escape whatever you were supposed to escape from, so we set the stage, and guess what, you fell for it."

Samuel says, "Okay, Gus. Let's have a little chat, shall we," and then adds, "Lieutenant Takahashi would you be so kind as to help Gussy up and have him take a seat on that rock over there" and he smiles at Reiko.

Reiko smiles back and reaches down to help him up, and as he stands, Heinz decides to run for it and bolts towards the woods. Reiko shrugs her shoulders, notches an arrow, and draws back her bowstring. She then calls out, "Oh! Lieutenant Piss Pants," and just as Heinz is about to enter the tree line, he turns as if to laugh at them. He thinks he will get away when suddenly Heinz feels a sudden pain in his left thigh, just about the exact location as the wound on his right leg, and he falls to the ground screaming. Reiko casually walks up to him, places her boot on his thigh, says, "This is for abandoning our friend, and yanks the arrow out of his thigh. Heinz screams, writhing in pain, and all Reiko does is toss him a field bandage for him to dress it.

The two of them carry Heinz back to the rock they were sitting on just before Heinz tried to flee, and through the pain, Heinz tells Samuel and Reiko about what happened, and he does not know if Hikaru is alive. They look at each other and know he is still alive.

A half-hour later, Samuel and Reiko return to the camp with a rope around Heinz's neck and his good hand tied behind his back. They walk up to the Colonel's tent and ask permission to enter. The three of them enter the tent, and Reiko tells Heinz to stand where he is. The Colonel notices Heinz has bruises and scratches that he didn't have this morning and sees a bandage on his other leg. They hand the Colonel the written parchment with the Empire's numbers and resources. They leave Heinz standing where he is as they report to the Colonel how they found Heinz with the now-dead Dark soldier. They also show him the other map they found in Heinz's pouch that shows the estimated enemy count and their last positions. The Colonel compares the two maps, and then Reiko points out the mark on Hikaru's map and sees that it is very discreet and would never have noticed it unless he was looking for it.

The Colonel turns to Heinz and says, "Second Lieutenant Gustavo Heinz, you have been found guilty of treason to the Imperial Empire. You will immediately be stripped of your rank and executed per the Empire's Articles of War. Do you have anything to say?"

Heinz looks at the Colonel, Samuel, and Reiko and says, "You can't kill me; my father is Brigadier General Heinz; he will have your bars if you kill me."

The Colonel tells Heinz, "You're wrong. Under the articles of war, or engagement detrimental to the Imperial Empire, any individual, no matter their heritage or rank, can and will be executed if the actions they participate in are detrimental to the well-being or lives of their comrades in the Imperial Army. So, you see, Lieutenant, sorry, Mister Heinz, I have all right as the Commander of this mission to ensure my troops' well-being is safeguarded."

Heinz looks at them and says, "You fucking bastards, you don't know the first thing about dedication or understand the true meaning of faith. Sacrificing myself to the Dark Gods is the ultimate gratification that I can give. Kill me. I do not care because, in the end, the Dark will overcome Light," and starts laughing.

The Colonel orders one of his soldiers to take Heinz away and place him in shackles. Once Heinz is out of the tent, he calls Samuel and Reiko over to his table and asks, in a whisper, "Do you think he took the bait and got a good look?" Reiko answers, "Yes," and I know Heinz was involved in map-making when he was younger. The Colonel says, "Good, now if only my guard allows him to escape but not too easily or quickly.

Heinz is escorted to one of the wagons when his escort tells him to wait. Heinz sees an opportunity, and he doubles over as if in pain. The guard grabs him to stand him up, and then Heinz brings his head up, quickly catching the guard in his jaw, and shoves his whole body into him, making him hit his head against a tree. The guard buckles and falls to the ground unconscious. Heinz pulls his hand free and then grabs the guard's sword from its sheath, and thinks to himself that he must tell the Dark Commander of the Colonel's plans and what he saw on their map. Heinz quietly sneaks over to where the horses are and untie one. He leads it into the woods and uses an old tree stump to mount it. He then rides off in the direction of Shira.

Reiko and Samuel are watching from the shadows, and they see him heading into the woods with the horse in tow. Then they hear the horse gallop off towards Shira. A few minutes later, they help the guard and ask him how he feels. The guard responds, "My jaw is a little sore."

Chapter 23

The Keep

After her little excursion to Tolland, Nova walks out of the cavern, gazes skyward, and sees that the moon is half full. She feels invigorated and wants to do something, so she decides to visit one of the villages south of the Barrens and see how her Elite Guard performs. She summons them, and within the hour, Nova and her five-hundred Elite Guard are riding south out of the Barrens. Nova imagines the bottom of the gorge that leads to the Barrens and opens a passageway. She sees it has opened where she wanted it to and notices it is just before dawn.

After coming through the passageway, Nova and her Elite follow along the base of the mountains. They follow the baseline, and then she sees some structure set against the mountains in the distance. She removes her eye scope and sees an Elenni flag flapping in the morning breeze. She looks closer and sees that the stone structure is a Keep and a village surrounds the Keep. Vague pictures suddenly fill her mind, and she swoons slightly. Commander Nunes is there to balance her. Nova looks at her Commander and says, "I am alright; I just had a flood of memories that I have not thought of in a very long time. Nova smiles at her and says, "Shall we go?"

The sun is just rising, and the village is waking up. One villager is to the base of the mountains to gather his goats when he sees the Elite Guard coming along one of the roads that lead from the gorge. He drops his staff and runs back towards the village, shouting an alarm.

Five hundred strong, they slowly make their way to the village, and ten minutes later, she sees a lone rider galloping through the gates and heading south. She orders ten of her Elite to go after him and bring him back alive. She pictures a crossroads, opens up a passageway, and ten Elite enter without hesitation, and she then closes it. The Lord of the Keep unknowingly sent a falcon with a message tied to its leg just as the young rider departed.

The young rider is rounding a bend in the road that will bring him to a crossroad and straight to the Capital. He rounds the bend and almost crashes into ten soldiers wearing Dark uniforms. Before he can do anything, he feels himself unseated from his horse and sprawled out on the ground, winded. He gets up groggily and draws his long knife. One of the soldiers draws his sword and approaches the young rider. He swings his sword to knock the knife from his hands, but the young rider drops down and avoids the swing. The soldier is even more surprised as the young rider plunges his long knife into the throat. The other nine move quickly and subdue the young rider before he can withdraw his knife. They pummel him unconscious, then throw his body over his saddle, secure him, and ride towards the Keep.

The Kings Chamberlain is in his library researching something when the bell sounds that a messenger bird has arrived. He goes to the falcon perch and sees the bird perched on its stand and the message strapped to its back. The Chamberlain walks over to the bird, places some raw meat in its cup, and unties the message. He reads it and quickly heads to the throne room to meet with the King.

King Theo is in the middle of negotiating a Baron squabble when he sees the Chamberlain enter the throne room, and he holds up the message for the King to see. Theo tells the two Barons that he will have to think about this and dismisses the court. The Chamberlain quickly approaches, bows, and hands the King the message.

King Theo unfolds the parchment and reads:

My Son,

I hope everything is going well with you and Princess Danielle. Your mother and I have missed you and are still waiting to hear that we will be grandparents.

I am writing to you because I am concerned with activities in the Barrens. Some of the Keep guards have noticed men and women traveling north. I thought this strange because I had not heard of any events that would draw people so far north. People of all ages are making this journey north. Several weeks later, we saw people who seemed to be coming from the Barrens traveling east and south. They were all wearing red robes. I sent a small patrol north to investigate, and they returned with nothing to report.

Men and women have passed through the Keeps lands again and headed north for the past few weeks. I sent patrols to bring in all the people and supplies from their homes. I have also pulled back my men and placed sentries on the walls. Every day I receive reports from the sentries of people they have seen.

I have asked the villagers to stockpile and store goods inside the Keeps storage. I grow weary, and I fear for my people. I'm asking you to send a small force up north to investigate what is happening and stop it.

Sincerely your father,

Lord Theo I

P.S. Your mother and I miss you and hope to see you soon.

The King finishes the letter and knows that his father is not a man who would ask for help unless he thought the situation was severe. He tells the Chamberlain to call for a meeting with his War Counsel. When they have all gathered, he tells them to assemble a battalion of one thousand men to be ready to move within one day. His advisors start to protest, but the King slams his fist on the table and yells, "Now!"

The following day, a well-equipped battalion of Elenni soldiers is marching north to the village of Marion, where the old King and his Queen reside.

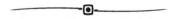

The Keeps militia continues urging the villagers to hurry as they start running for the safety of the Keep. The Elite Guard enters the village's outskirts and starts burning some of the houses. Men, women, and children who tried to hide in their homes perish as their homes become engulfed in flames, while others are pillaged for food, clothes, gold, jewelry, and anything of value. Doors that are locked and barred are battered open. Anyone who tries to hide in their cellars or attics is pulled from their home crying and screaming. Men and older boys are immediately put to death.

Those who are slow in trying to reach the safety of the Keep end up falling to the ground with arrows protruding from their backs. Most captured women and older girls are rounded up and forced to strip. The Elite gather them together, so they can watch their homes burn. The Elite troops, like their Priestess, are cold-hearted and show no feelings or remorse other than protecting their High Priestess.

They force the younger children to take babes from their mothers and march them into the Sacred Laki-Jutsuk Church across the square from the Keep. They seal the windows once the young children and babies are inside the church and place guards at the door. The guards on the walls protest and start shouting out how cruel they could be. The shouting stops as the Elite guard forms a path, and a woman with flaming red hair makes her way to the Keeps gates. She is surrounded by her Elite guard, with Commander Nunes by her side. She hears the portcullis lowering and the crossbar on the Keep doors set. Then the remainder of the Keeps soldiers joins their fellow soldiers on the wall. An older gentleman steps up to the parapets and says, "I am Lord of the Keep," then asks, "What do you want?"

Nova says, "We know that you in the Keep are unbelievers and practice the ways of the Laki-Jutsuk Religion," and she spits on the ground.

The Lord says, "Yes, we do, and what do you mean, unbelievers?"

Nova continues, "Do you not know or realize that a new day is coming, and the true Gods will sweep this land of unbelievers, and the Dark Scriptures will bring deliverance to the masses. You will need to throw down your arms and convert to the beliefs of the Dark Scriptures."

The Lord calls back, "Why would we want to do that? We believe in the Goddesses as the true Religion; they are more powerful and understanding than any Dark Gods, who seem to be no better than trash!" and spits from the wall on the ground in front of Nova.

Nova remains calm though she is boiling mad inside, particularly about what he said referring to her Gods.

The Lord gives the signal, and Captain Sims and one other stand in the shadows of the gatehouse. They raise their bows and aim. Sims has his arrow aimed at the red-headed woman, while the other has his aimed at the one they think is her First in Command. The Lord drops his hand, and two steel-tipped arrows fly from the shadows. Nova is lucky as one of her Elite female guards beside her reaches out and snatches the arrow out of the Air just before the point touches her armor and snaps it in her hand. Commander Nunes is not so lucky as the steel-tipped arrow slams into her chest, knocking her off her horse. The other Elite surround Nova so no other arrow or bolts can reach her.

Nova ignores the ones on the Keep wall and tells the young woman who snatched the arrow aimed at her, "Thank you, and what is your name?"

The Elite soldier bows her head and says, "Bernadette, my Kaisoshosuko."

Nova looks at Nunes on the ground and says, "Bernadette, you are now the First Commander of my Elite Guard; serve me well," Nova tells her.

Bernadette says, "Yes, my Kaisoshosuko" Then Nova says, "Remember Bernadette, I do not accept failure." She says, "Yes, Kaisoshosuko."

Nova orders her guard to part so that she can move just a little bit forward with Bernadette by her side, whose eyes are constantly searching for threats.

Nova looks back at the Keep and says, "My Lord, why would you want to go and spoil these negotiations? What you did was uncalled for and what I must do now is because of you," She chants, *"Moerutonoriko,"* and a ball of white flame appears in her hand. She throws it at the Keeps portcullis, and the steel melts like butter. The Lord feels the heat from the melted portcullis and orders the villagers cowering in the courtyard back into the Keep.

He is mortified by this woman's demeanor and orders his guards to fire on the woman and her soldiers. They shoot a volley of arrows at her and her soldiers, but the steel-pointed shafts never reach their intended targets. An unseen force protects her army, though some guards receive minor scrapes. The Lord orders his men to stop shooting and stares as he sees the woman conjuring another fireball and bouncing it in her hand.

He orders everyone to get off the wall and fall back into the Keep. He knows he can do nothing and orders the Keeps doors to be closed and barred. Just before they close, he sees the outer gates start to glow red, and he hears the outer gates explode inward, and the clang of what is left of the metal portcullis strike one of the inner courtyard walls.

The Elite Guard storm through the gates and automatically take up defensive positions in the courtyard. Nova rides through with Bernadette by her side and orders her guards to grab what is left of the gate's wooden iron-clad bar and bring it to the Keep's doors. Several of her Elite dismount and pick up the wooden crossbar, and she tells them to use the wooden bar as a battering ram against the Keep doors.

Nova hears a scream and sees one of her Elite go down with an arrow to her chest. Bernadette points to an archer's window in a tower above the doors. Nova reaches into her saddlebags and pulls out a small clay pot with a cloth wick like a candle. She tells Bernadette to light the wick, and as it comes to life, Nova watches the wick burn just about halfway down, and then she throws it straight through the window. Seconds later, they hear an explosion, and flames shoot out of the arrow slit. Moments later, two Keep guards come running out of the tower engulfed in fire and jump off the parapet, while the third throws himself off a balcony. Nova knows they are dead before hitting the ground, and she silently thanks Isa for teaching her the art of explosives.

Slowly the Keep's doors start to splinter, and then on one last bash, the doors shatter. Her Elite pour through the doors, and they find themselves in a large entryway and set up a defensive position.

Nova walks through the splintered doors and directs her Elite to knock down the Main Hall doors with the same ram. She orders others to spread out and search every room on the upper and lower levels. Her Elite immediately moves out through the Keep, Nova sits patiently on the steps that lead to the upstairs, and then she hears the screams of men, women, and some children as they are found and immediately put to the sword.

The main hall doors take two hits from the ram and are now buckling, and then on the third strike, the doors are split open. Her Elite draw their weapons, rush through the doors, and the first ones through the door, receive crossbow bolts to their chests and are down. Her Elite continues to pour into the room, and before the guards can get their crossbows reloaded, they are overwhelmed and put to death. Nova walks into the Main Hall, steps over her fallen without giving them a second thought, and sees the villagers cowering against the walls of the Great Hall. She leans into Bernadette and whispers something in her ear. Bernadette makes some hand gestures, and some of the Elite move towards villagers and forcefully separate the men and old ones from the group, and they escort them out of the Hall, leaving the woman behind. Nova is standing in the Great Hall when an Elite female approaches, bows, and tells her they have discovered an array of food stockpiles in the lower cold storage. Nova tells the female to gather the male villagers and to have them clear the storerooms. She bows and says, "Yes, Kaisoshosuko," and is gone.

Nova turns her attention to the Lord's men, standing in two groups, a large one and a smaller one, with their swords drawn and shields at the ready. She sees their determination to protect the Lord and Lady of the Keep. Nova steps forward, and the Lord sees her balancing another ball of white flame in her hand though this one is smaller.

He stands, addresses Nova, and asks, "Young lady, If there is no more resistance or bloodshed, will you spare my guards and these villagers."

Nova looks at the Lord of the Keeps men standing in two groups, one large as a main and two smaller ones to cover an assault from all sides, and they are ready to forfeit their lives to protect the Lord and Lady of the Keep. She also sees nervousness in their eyes and smiles. Nova looks at the Lord and says, "No more bloodshed," He now sees two balls of flame, and she throws both balls of fire directly at the two groups of swordmen. Two white-hot flames encompass the two groups, leaving several piles of smoldering ash in their wake when they go out. The Lord and everyone else in the Great Hall is shocked, and then Nova says, "Agreed, no more bloodshed, and she then whispers something in Bernadette's ear.

Bernadette takes two steps forward and tells the Lord that her Kaisoshosuko agrees, that there should be no more bloodshed, and will allow his remaining men to surrender and join the others.

Still shocked by what he just witnessed, the Lord commands his men to lay down their weapons and surrender. They do so reluctantly but do it because their Lord has commanded it. Once again, Bernadette makes some hand gestures, and several more Elite move in, surrounding the remaining Keep guards, and escort them from the Hall. All that remains are some of the villagers, a small group of pretty young ladies in fancy dresses, who Nova assumes is the Lady of the Keeps entourage, a Laki-Jutsuk Priest, a Captain in the Keeps uniform, and the Lord and Lady of the Keep.

The Lord has remained standing through everything that has just happened, and he looks at her and asks, "Why?" and Nova says, "Because they deserved it, they killed my Elite."

The Lord is shaken, but he remains to stand and asks, "May I ask your name?"

Nova says, "Yes, My name is Nova. I am the Kaisoshosuko of the Guichi-Tanin Religion and Speaker for the Dark Scriptures."

A Priest of the Laki-Jutsuk Order steps forward. He says, "This is blasphemy and preposterous because there is no such thing as a Kaisoshosuko or whatever you call yourself of a stupid Dark Scriptures Religion, and you are a heretic." Nova asks the Priest if he has finished. Then the Priest says, "NO DAMMIT! I demand you let these good people go, leave here immediately, and pray to the Goddesses for forgiveness."

Nova gestures with her hand, and Bernadette draws her sword. The Lady sees this, and then she realizes what will happen, and just before it does, and shouts "No!"

Nova nods; Bernadette swings her sword and removes the Priest's head from his shoulders. The women scream and cover their eyes. The Lord falls back into his seat, and everyone else watches in horror as his head hits the floor, bounces, and comes to a stop in front of the Lady. His lifeless eyes stare up at her while its lips still move to say something. The Lady falls to her knees, covers her eyes, and starts sobbing. Nova looks at her new Commander and says, "Thank you!" Bernadette wipes her sword on the Priest's clothing and then places it back in her sheath.

The villagers and young ladies are screaming and crying when Nova says, "Will you whining bitches please SHUT THE FUCK UP!" Suddenly, there is silence other than an occasional sniffle. Nova conjures another ball of flame and passes it across her fingers.

Nova says, "Thank you." and looks back at the Lord sitting there in total shock and says, "Now, that we have silenced that winded Airbag, and those whining women, who pray tell are the Lord and Lady of this Keep that I have the pleasure of speaking with?"

Lord Theo clears his throat and says, "My name is Lord Theo, once King of Elenni, and this is my wife, Lady Priscilla, the former Queen.

Nova almost drops the ball of flame in her hand, for she cannot believe what she is hearing. To find the two people she has always despised and hated for murdering her beloved mother. She had always hoped that one day she would see them again and get her revenge; now, it seems that day has finally arrived.

Lord Theo asks, "Kaisoshosuko" could you find it in your heart to let these innocent villagers go? They have done nothing wrong."

Nova replies, "I have no issues with that, my Lord, as long as they pledge loyalty to me, the High Priestess of Dark Scriptures Religion, and make a blood pact with the Dark Scriptures." Bernadette looks to Nova as if to ask, "blood pact," knowing very well that no such thing. Nova gives her a very sly smile.

Lord Theo asks, "May I?"

Nova bows slightly and sweeps her hand as a gesture for him to proceed.

Lord Theo stands, addresses the villagers, and says, "If you want to live, you will have to disavow the Laki-Jutsuk Religion and pledge your allegiance to the Dark Scriptures Religion and follow the words of the Gods, Guichi, and Tanin by performing a "Blood Pact."

Some villagers fall to their knees and start praying to Nova repeating the words. "Yes, we will convert!" While others remain loyal to the Laki-Jutsuk Religion.

She then orders her guards to escort the villagers who have pledged their devotion to her from the Great Hall. She has the non-believers escorted to the dungeons to decide their fate later. Only one soldier, the Captain, did not swear allegiance, and Nova admires his determination and dedication no matter how stupid it could be. Bernadette walks up to the Lord and his Lady, and she politely asks them to join the Captain on the floor. Nova takes the former Queen's throne and looks at the once most three influential people in the Keep standing before her.

While the last villagers are being ushered from the Hall in two groups, Nova shouts out, "My Elite, do not forget to perform the Blood Pact," One of her Elite shouts back, "Yes, My Kaisoshosuko."

Nova gestures for the former Queen's entourage to come closer, and as they do, Nova looks over the ones gathered before her and asks, "Now, what shall we do with the rest of you people?"

Bernadette leans forward and whispers in Nova's ear. "Oh! What a wonderful idea, especially seeing that all these young girls look like they want to have fun, "Isn't that right, ladies?" None of the young women answer.

Nova looks at the three of them and instructs two of her guards to tie the Lord and Captain's hands behind their backs. When she does not tie Pricilla's hands, Nova looks at her and says, "I not a barbarian," and forces them to sit on the steps below the thrones.

Nova then asks Lady Priscilla, "Are these beautiful young ladies' part of your court? Is one of them your Lady in waiting? Now, be honest. If I catch you lying, the consequences could be horrible?"

Lady Priscilla turns towards Nova and says, "Actually, Analisa is supposed to marry a Colonel in the King's Army."

Nova says, "Is that so, and which one is she?" but before Pricilla answers, Nova says, "No, don't tell me, let me guess, and then points to a beautiful blonde girl, and the Nova says, "How about we start with her?" She says to them, "Shall we begin?" and nods her head to three of the Elites in the room.

The three Elites walk over to the girls, and the one named Analisa is cringing and trying to hold onto one of the others. They struggle until she is grabbed by her hair and pulled away from the group. Two Elites hold her with her arms straight out from her sides. The third has stepped behind her and waits for instructions. Nova is about to say something when there is a commotion at the entrance to the Great Hall, and she sees nine of her Elite enter the Hall; four of them are carrying something that seems to be struggling. They unceremoniously dump what they were carrying at the base of the steps, and when they turn the body over, Lady Pricilla gasps and says Taro, and the boy moans at the mention of his name. Nova looks at the boy and sees that he looks like Lady Pricilla through the bruises.

Nova says, "Interesting," and orders him tied up like the rest. After the boy is secured, Nova looks back at Analise and says, "Now where were we, before the interruption." and says, "Oh, yes."

Nova looks at Lady Pricilla and asks, "Were you a good Queen? Did you look out for your friends and family?"

Pricilla looks at Nova and says, "Yes. I think I was"

Nova keeps staring at her, and all she says is, "Liar!" and nods her head. The one waiting for instructions reaches up, grabs the top of Analise's dress, and pulls it down, ripping her bodice and exposing her breasts and body. The guard then reaches down and tears away the rest of her clothes, and the three turn, looking at Nova. Nova dismisses them with a wave of her hand. The three guards pick her up and carry Analise from the throne room, kicking and screaming until one of the Elite shuts her up with a solid punch to her stomach. Nova can hear her whimper as they carry her out the door, and she sees them head up the stairs.

Pricilla says, "I thought you said you were not a barbarian."

Nova looks at Pricilla and says, "I'm not, but my soldiers might be, and after all, I'm just taking care of my troops, you know, moral and all that stuff."

Nova says, "Save some for the Colonel," and she hears them laughing as they continue up the stairs, and one of them yells back, "As you wish, Kaisoshosuko." Analisa seems to have caught her breath, and as she starts to scream, they hear a door slam shut. The remaining girls are trembling as Nova asks questions, Pricilla answers, and Nova calls her a liar. There is no prejudice as her Elite treats the girls all the same. They take the other young women of Lady Priscilla's court, strip them of their clothes and drag them out of the throne room screaming. Soon it sounds like the whole upstairs is crying and screaming. Nova sees no one else is left but the Lord and Lady of the Keep, their son Taro and the Captain of the Keep's Guard.

Bernadette sees the hate in the Lord's eyes, gets up from his throne, walks over to stand behind him, and slowly draws her sword without a sound.

Lord Theo can take no more and starts yelling, "How could you do this to those poor young girls? What did they ever do to you to deserve this type of treatment, you FUCKING CRAZY BITCH?"

Nova stands up, walks over to Lord Theo, and backhands him across the mouth. She then leans forward and whispers something in his ear, and just as the Lord says, "No, It can't be, you're supposed to be dead!" She nods, and Bernadette drives her sword up through his back and out the front of his chest. Lord Theo look's down, sees the tip of the sword blade protruding from his chest, and then looks at Nova; for a second, it seems that he does recognize her, and then falls forward as Bernadette removes her sword.

Nova says, "Thank you, Bernadette. You know how I hate being called a Bitch." Lady Priscilla screams and rushes to her slain husband. Captain

Sims has somehow gotten his hands free and lunges at Nova. Bernadette steps in and hits him on the side of his head with the hilt of her sword. His knees buckle, and he lands with his hands outstretched on the steps as he tries to pull himself up. Bernadette sees the small blade under his fingers, lays the edge of her sword across them, and cuts them off. He screams, grabbing hold of his fingerless hand, and as he goes to stand, he slips on the bloody floor and falls, bashing his fingerless hand against the steps. Over the painful screams of the Captain, Nova looks down and sees the small blade that he used to cut his bindings, mixed in with his severed fingers.

Bernadette kneels before Nova and begs for forgiveness. Nova tells Bernadette, "Please pick up the blade and hand it to me."

She does as she is asked and hands the small blade to Nova.

Nova takes the blade, places the blade's edge against Bernadette's cheek, and says, "Bernadette, my dear, please be more careful." She makes a small slice across her cheek, not deep but just enough to leave a scar as a reminder. She smiles and says, "Now please get up; the Commander of my Elite should not be kneeling."

Bernadette then clears her throat, bringing Nova's attention back to the three people remaining, including Lady Priscilla, who is still hugging her dead husband. The Captain is desperately trying to stop the bleeding from his severed fingers, and the young boy who doesn't look more than fourteen is just now waking up.

Nova says, "Excuse me, my Lady, there is a small matter I must attend to first. She then leans forward in the chair, placing her elbows on her knees and resting her chin in her hands, and asks in a very kind voice, "Who was the one responsible for searching these prisoners and checking them for weapons?" An Elite soldier steps forward, kneels before her, and says, "My Kaisoshosuko, please forgive my mistake."

She looks at him and says, "I forgive you," followed by "*Moerutonoriko*," The irresponsible guard is hit with a ball of flame and is immediately incinerated, where his ashes still hold his form, and he remains there kneeling and smoldering.

Nova looks to Bernadette and asks, "Commander, what do you think we should do?" She walks over and leans in to start whispering in Nova's ear, and a smile comes across her face as she says, "Why Bernadette, that is an excellent idea, but first, I think the young boy should not be here.

"Why don't we put him down in the cells with the others? After all, I am not a barbarian," and she laughs.

Two Elite step forward to take the boy, and Lady Pricilla tries to stop them. One of them slaps her across the face, and Nova yells, "That is enough. None of you will lay a hand on Lady Pricilla unless I deem it necessary do I make myself clear!"

The Elite drops to one knee and says, "Yes, my, Kaisoshosuko."

Nova says to Lady Pricilla, "I promise I will do nothing to the boy." Lady Pricilla looks into her eyes and can see that she is telling the truth, so she does not put up a fight anymore. The two guards pick up the boy and carry him from the Great Hall. When they get to the doorway, one looks back, and Nova nods her head slightly, and the boy is gone.

With tears, Pricilla looks back at Nova and asks, "Will you keep your promise?" and Nova says, "Yes."

Nova looks at the two of them and says, "It seems Lady Pricilla, that my new Commander of my Elite Guard has taken a liken to you, so why don't you and the Captain here remove your clothes so that she can have a better look. I suggest you get started or do I need to make an example out of one of you?"

Lady Priscilla unbuttons and removes her outer clothes and lets them drop to the floor, only to be standing in a light camisole that reaches mid-thigh. She reaches over to give Captain Sims some help. When Nova says, "who told you to help him? If he cannot undress, he might have to lose some more fingers, so maybe you could help him. Do I make myself clear, Captain?" The Captain struggles but finally has his clothes in a pile on the floor.

Lady Priscilla and the Captain are now standing there semi-nude when Bernadette leans in and whispers something in Nova's ear.

Nova looks at her, then Lady Priscilla and Captain Sims, saying, "Why you dirty little girl, Commander." She tells them that her new Commander likes one of them. Then she says, "Do not worry, Captain, it is not you," and gives Lady Priscilla a wink.

Bernadette walks over to Lady Priscilla, grabs her by her elbow, and escorts her out of the throne room. Minutes later, she hears Lady Priscilla screaming, which brings a smile to her face.

Smiling, Nova tells Captain Sims to follow her and not say anything under penalty of instant removal of other fingers. Though struggling and a little pale, he does as he is told and remains quiet. They walk through the Main Hall's doors, and when they reach the Keep's shattered outer doors and step outside, the Captain sees what is happening, calls her a bitch, and takes a swing at Nova with his good hand. He never had a chance as one of her guards cut off his arm at the elbow and watched his arm fall to the ground. His knees buckle as he desperately tries to hold his bleeding stump with his mutilated hand.

Nova says, "I warned you, Captain," as he continues to scream, Nova tells the guard, "Please shut him up." Without hesitation and with two hands, the guard drives his sword straight down and through the Captain's head into his upper body, killing him instantly. Nova looks to her guard and says," Thank you." the guard bows and removes his sword.

She looks over the courtyard to see that soldiers and villagers have not been spared even though they pledged themselves to the Dark Religion. The Keeps guards have been nailed up along the walls and riddled with arrows, knives, and spears. Some soldiers are dead, some are bleeding from their wounds, and some are still struggling and screaming.

Nova stares out over the carnage when Bernadette walks up with Lady Priscilla in tow. Nova sees that she is naked, with some new bruises, a cut lip, and blood trickling down her inner thighs. She also sees that the Lady of the Keep is wearing a collar, and Bernadette is holding a leash. Though humiliated, raped, and beaten, Lady Priscilla stands tall. Nova whispers and points to her subjects, "Look over there at your once devout proud Laki-Jutsuk villagers. Lady Priscilla wipes the tears from her eyes and focuses on seeing that the men and women are being raped, sodomized, and forced to do unnatural things with Nova's Elite guard. Lady Priscilla can no longer condone what is happening to her loyal subjects. She turns to Nova and asks, "Why?"

Nova holds out her hand, and Bernadette places the leash in her hand. Nova says, "Walk with me," pulling on the leash and leading Lady Priscilla slowly down the stairs and into the courtyard, amongst the carnage. Nova says, "Lady Priscilla, you should know why this is happening; it is all your fault." Lady Priscilla looks at her and asks in a slightly defiant tone, "How is all this my fault?"

Bernadette raises her hand to strike her when Nova waves it away.

Nova smiles and says, "Think back, Lady Priscilla or, should I say, Queen Priscilla. Eighteen years ago, you condemned your closest friend and confidant to be brought up on trumped-up charges against the kingdom and had her executed. Do you remember her?" Lady Pricilla nods her head yes.

Priscilla looks at Nova, and she can tell by the look in her eyes that she still does not know who she is.

Nova continues, "That woman had a daughter, and you sent that daughter away to an orphanage to rot and die. Do you remember her name?"

Priscilla says, "Yes, Sarah Priscilla Novasta, and after I found out what my maid had done several years later, I sent her to the dungeons. I searched everywhere to find Sarah. I heard rumors here and there but was never able to find her. Do you know where she is? Can you tell me? Is she alive?"

"Oh, I can tell you, she is still alive," Nova moves to stand behind Lady Priscilla.

"Where is she? Please tell me?" Priscilla asks.

Nova leans in close, reaches around to grab Pricilla's breast, puts her lips against Lady Priscilla's ear, says, "Right behind you, my Queen," and plunges her blade deep into the middle of Priscilla's back. Nova hands the leash to Bernadette, turns Lady Priscilla around, and says, "This is for my mother, you heartless fucking bitch!" and spits in her face and stabs her in the stomach.

Lady Priscilla's knees buckle, and she drops to the ground, she goes to fall forward, but Bernadette is holding her up by the leash, stopping her from falling forward. Nova takes her boot, places it on Pricilla's chest, and pushes her backward as Bernadette lets go of the leash. She walks over to Pricilla, squats down beside her, looks into her eyes, and says, "Do you know that little promise I made about your son." Priscilla's eyes widen at the mention of her son. Nova leans close to her, says, "I lied," and runs the blade across her throat. Nova stands up, stares at her, and says, "For you, mother." and orders that she be strung up naked with the others.

Her Elite has plundered the Keep, and most of the village is in flames. Nova is leading her army out of the village when Bernadette brings up the subject of the church. Nova turns it to go back, and when she gets close to the church, she can hear the crying and whimpering of the small children and babies inside. Nova sits astride her horse and hears Bernadette ride up beside her. Nova orders her Elite to go back into the Keep and bring out the young girls left upstairs and tells them to put the girls in the church with the children and reseal the doors. Nova sits there and thinks back to her years in the orphanage and what she endured to survive. Nova decides not to put these children through the same ordeal, and she softly says, "*Moerutonoriko,*" and a small white ball of intense flame appears in her hand. She throws it at the steeple, then turns her horse and rides out of the village. She is riding towards the Barrens when she conjures a passageway. She sits on her horse to its side, and Bernadette joins her. Nova watches her Elite enter the passageway, and as the last one goes through, she looks back and sees the church entirely engulfed in flames. Bernadette goes first, then Nova. Once on the other side, there is a distinct ping as the passageway disappears. She leaves the village a pile of rubble, with burning timbers and stone walls crumbling. The sweet smell of burnt flesh lingers in the Air.

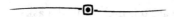

In the Kingdom of Elenni, King Theo II resides in a castle in the center of the capital city of Blanby. He is a well-loved King who has always been fAir and looks out for the well-being of his subjects. He did not take it seriously when he first received petitions from the Lords and Baronesses of the northern and western keeps and strongholds about people traveling through their lands heading farther northwest into the Barrens.

King Theo will regret his actions by not listening to his Lords and Barons, for his lineage will come to pass.

Chapter 24

The Battle of Shira

Hikaru has been hanging in the cage since his capture for two days and is furious at what these bastards have done to his men. He is worried about Tombs because he has not heard anything about him. Yesterday, they took him, and he has not come back. He catches himself looking at the young lady and remembers her as the one who fought back when she was on the altar, and when she looks at him, he blushes, making her smile. Hikaru sees that she has a friendly smile and says, "My name is First Lieutenant Hikaru Sato; pleased to meet you under the circumstances."

The young lady replies, "Hello, First Lieutenant Hikaru Sato, my name is Mrs. Carrie Ann Barnes, and I am also pleased to meet you under the circumstances."

Hikaru asks her, "Yesterday, you mentioned something about an "Arena" when they took my friend away. Can you tell me what did you mean by that?"

Carrie points to the stockade-style structure and says that is the Arena, and she tells him that she does not know what happens in there, only that she hears what sounds like ferocious beasts and screams. She also tells him that whoever goes there does not come back.

Hikaru says, "Okay," and then asks, "Can you tell me what happened?"

She tells him, "I don't know much, just that the army came down from the Pass, quickly rounded up the militia, slaughtered some of them, and hung them up for all to see. It took them about a week to build the Arena, and the dark soldiers took the remaining militia to the Arena. She tells him that is all she knows and that she was woken at first light by shouting and screaming. The soldiers kicked in our door, and my husband and I were dragged from our home. Soon, everyone in the town was standing in the town square.

"Any idea how they got here without being noticed?" he asks.

She tells him, "I heard a couple of the red-robed ones talking about coming through some sort of passageway, but from where they came from, I do not know."

Hikaru looks down and sees a small metal wire partially broken from the mesh on the cage. He pokes at it with his finger, and the metal wire moves. He starts working it gradually back and forth, and while he is doing this, he looks at the young woman across from him, and through all the dirt, blood, and grime, he sees that she is a beautiful young woman, and he is guessing around twenty-one years of age. Hikaru also notices that she has taken strips from her torn clothes and has wrapped her wounds. She has been able to take some pieces and fashion some covering for her waist. He would expect her to be embarrassed, but she isn't. Carrie tells Hikaru that the two women molesting her were women from the invading army. They were showing some of the local girls that converted to the Dark Scriptures what they had to do." then she smiles and says, "but I think I screwed up their training lesson." Hikaru smiles and says, "I think you did."

Carrie looks at him and says, "You saw!?" He tells her yes, just before they captured us.

Hikaru is just about to ask her when the Army of the Dark Scriptures arrived when they see three robed figures and a small contingent of soldiers walking towards the cages. One of the robed ones moves to the lowering mechanism while the soldiers stand in a circle, Hikaru feels his cage being lowered, and he looks at Carrie and says, "Don't worry, I will be back," and he hears one of the soldiers laugh, and say, "I don't think so!"

The cage touches the ground, and Hikaru can see that all of them have their swords drawn. One of the robed one's steps forward and tells Hikaru, "The Dark Commander has Chosen you to fight in the "Arena." Hikaru knows it is a woman under the hood, and with speed almost unheard of, Hikaru has one hand at her throat, squeezes just enough to make her cough, and then releases her. In a low, raspy voice, she grabs her own throat and tells the soldier to bind him. They do as they are told and march him towards the large round stockade fence.

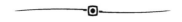

They arrive at the Arena, and right before they cut his ropes, the robed one says, "Survive the Arena, and you may live another day." Then she touches her throat and says, "I hope you die painfully!" The soldiers push him through the door, and he finds himself in a small room and another door. Hikaru hears the locked door behind him, so he reaches for the handle, opens the other door, and steps into the sunlight. He raises his hand to block the sun and can make out two men on the other side of the Arena. One is sitting on an oversized chair that overlooks the Arena, and the other is standing beside him. Hikaru assumes that the one in the chair is the Commander of the Dark Army, and the other man looks familiar, but Hikaru cannot make out his face due to the sun; he covers his eyes.

The Commander says, "Soldier of the Imperial Army, my men had informed me that you took the lives of eleven of my soldiers single-handedly before they captured you. The test is simple. If you pass, you live another day; if you fail, you die, and the Commander gives the signal to open the gate.

Hikaru looks around, and he sees many bodies that are nailed along the inside wall of the Arena. He looks closer, and he now knows why Lieutenant Tombs did not come back to the cages. He sees Tomb's mangled body nailed to the inside of the Arena's walls along with several militias in different decay stages. There is no discrimination as Hikaru sees that the hanging bodies consist of men, women, and older teenage boys and girls. He hears a door creak, watching as it starts to open, and then he hears a feral growl. Hikaru looks around, and all he sees are some broken batons and some articles of clothing. He runs over to pick up the clothing and then the broken batons. He sees that the door is almost open and quickly wraps his arms several times with the clothing, then grabs two pieces of the broken batons and waits.

The door opens, and there is some hesitation on whatever made that hideous growl, and then the creature bursts through the door and stands there sniffing the Air. Hikaru is taken a little back by what has just entered the Arena, but whatever it is, Hikaru plants his feet, brings up his arms wrapped in old clothing and waits. The beast has caught his scent, paws the ground in anticipation of a fresh kill, and then it charges him.

The beast is coming straight at him, and to the surprise of the Commander, Hikaru drops to one knee, takes a deep breath, and as he exhales, the Air around him becomes still, and the outside noises are gone. He senses the strange beast charging at him, and then the silver flash crosses his eyes, and the two broken batons become an extension of his body. Even before the beast gets close, Hikaru has already played the scenario in his mind. He charges the beast head-on, and when the beast leaps, Hikaru drops down and slides underneath it to drive one of the broken batons just under its front shoulder from underneath, and he hears the beast roar with pain. The beast lands wrong and falls to the arena grounds. Hikaru sees his chance and charges the beast, grabbing it around its neck, and as the beast roars, Hikaru jams the second broken baton into its mouth, locking its jaws open. Hikaru begins to apply pressure to its throat, and within minutes the beast is hanging limply in Hikaru's arms.

Hikaru, though slightly winded, takes the broken baton from its mouth when suddenly the beast lashes out with its massive paw, and its claws are fully extended. Hikaru's senses are heightened, and he steps into the creature's swipe and drives the broken baton into the creature's brain through its eye. The beast now lies on the ground, unmoving.

He turns to face the Commander and hears a very distinct voice yelling and complaining that Sato must die. Hikaru now recognizes the voice, and it is the voice of Gustavo Heinz.

Hikaru watches the Commander backhand Heinz, and as he falls to the floor, General Heath tells him to just shut the fuck up.

The Commander stands, leans on the railing, and says, "It seems that you have won; what was it, "Sato" yes, Sato."

Hikaru can hear Heinz go to say something when the Commander tells him, "Shut up."

The Commander asks Hikaru his full name and rank, and Hikaru obliges because Heinz has already told him, saying, "First Lieutenant Hikaru Sato of His Emperor's Imperial; Army, Sir."

The Commander clears his throat and says, "Lieutenant Sato, as I stated previously, you won the contest, so you get to live another day., and then motions for the detachment to take him away.

Before his escort gets to him, he yells to Heinz, "Hey! Second Lieutenant Piss Pants, sorry to disappoint you. Go fuck yourself!"

Curiosity has gotten the better of the Commander, and he asks, "Why did you call Lieutenant Heinz here, Lieutenant Piss Pants?". Heinz jumps up and yells at Sato to not say a fucking thing.

Hikaru smiles and tells the story to the Commander of how Squire Heinz, and now Lieutenant Heinz, had gotten the name of "Piss Pants."

The Commander starts laughing, and Hikaru hears Heinz yelling at him as he is escorted back to the cage, "YOU FUCKING BASTARD! I WILL KILL YOU!"

They take Hikaru back to the cages, and he hears the mutterings between his escort, and he hears the words, ferret face, and Piss Pants. Hikaru is smiling as he is brought back to the cages.

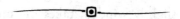

They push him inside and raise the cage into the Air. Once they secure the cage, he watches them walk off but hears them talking about what he had done and how Heinz, that ferret-looking Lieutenant, was nicknamed "Piss Pants," and they all start laughing.

He looks over at Carrie, says here, and tosses her the clothing he had wrapped around his arms. She says thank you and can get most of her body covered, and then she sits there looking at Hikaru.

He looks at her, and she smiles, which is charming under the circumstances. He then says, "Now, where did we leave off?' She looks at him and says, "That's it, you are not going to say anything about what happened over there!" She points to the Arena."

Hikaru tells her, "Mrs. Barnes, it is not something that should be discussed right now, trust me." She asks her again when did the Dark Army arrive.

She says, "Okay, and tells him about a month ago, and they came in fast. Before anyone knew it, they were entering people's houses and forcing them from their homes in the early morning light. They dragged everyone to the town square and offered them the choice to convert to the Dark Scriptures or be branded as nonbelievers, and you saw how they branded the nonbeliever. He looks at her, sees tears in her eyes, and says, "I'm sorry." She tells him how some of the sacrifices were her childhood friends. She wipes her nose and eyes and then tells him that those who stood fast in their allegiance to the Goddesses were stripped, assaulted sexually and physically, beaten numerous times, and then taken to the Arena or thrown onto the altar for sacrifice. The lucky ones were placed in these cages. Hikaru sees the expression on her face change from sadness to anger and then hate. She tells him of her husband, how weak and pathetic he was, that he converted to the Dark Scriptures practically without being asked, and she hates him for it.

Carrie tells him the traditions of Shira: when two people get married, they swear on the scriptures that they will defend and stand by each other's decisions no matter what happens. She found out the truth; when she was being molested and tortured on the altar. He just stood there looking at her, smiling, while he rubbed and grabbed another woman's breasts, and at the same time, one of the women, whom she thought was her friend, was on her knees with his manhood in her mouth.

Hikaru says, "I'm sorry, but you must believe and keep the faith. If nothing else, believe in me because we will get out of here."

She sits there in her cage and asks, "How?" Then she sees a smile cross his face, and at that moment, the small sliver of metal he was diligently working back and forth snaps. He holds up the sliver of metal for her to see, which is about two inches in length. She asked, "What are you smiling for?" Hikaru looks at her and says, "Be patient; we will be out of here soon, and I think it will get interesting."

After the incident with that Imperial soldier in the Arena, General Buford T. Heath, Commander of the Dark Armies, sits in his chair drinking wine when he starts looking over the map that "Piss Pants" brought with him. Heinz had explained in great detail what he saw regarding the Imperial Empire's battle plans. After Heinz finished his report, Heath realized that the Imperial Royal Army had not updated their tactics since he was court-martialed and escaped with his friend Harris. He shouts for his subcommanders to rally so they can begin to lay out his plans to counter the Empire's assault. He tells his subcommanders where to position their men and when he's finished, he orders them to prepare for battle.

Heath sits back down and calls for more wine. A young local girl brings him some wine, and as she bows, she spills some on the ground. The Commander looks at her, slaps her, and yells at her to get out.

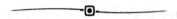

That afternoon Heinz finds the Commander astride his horse directing his forces. He places his commanders on the south and east of the town. Horns start blaring, foretelling of the advancing army. The General watches the Imperial Army approach, marching four abreast into the valley. Heinz sees Miro leading the swordsmen and starts to drool, knowing this will be his demise, but he also senses a change in Samuel's demeanor that tells him something is wrong.

Heath sees the standard formation of swordsmen and orders his heavy cavalry to attack the approaching ground forces in full charge to rout them and break them. Company flags are raised and flown, followed by others to signal the troops into battle. The Dark Force's heavy cavalry of two battalions of over sixteen hundred horse riders with lances start at a canter and are soon bearing down on Samuel's forces at full gallop. They are almost upon the Imperial Army when Samuel orders the pikemen, who were concealed within the ranks of the long swordsmen, to spread out two ranks deep and bring up and plant their long steel-tipped pikes in the dirt and hold them at an angle. The momentum is too much as the heavy cavalry is bearing down on a skirmish line with deadly pikes planted in the dirt. The calvary continues to bear down on the lines at a full gallop and are impaled onto the deadly pikes as the rear ranks push the forward ranks by the momentum, forcing the front lines into the line of sharpened spikes. Though the line holds, some of the Imperial pikemen are impaled or trampled by the Dark Armies' heavy calvary's lances. The pikemen stop the lancers from advancing, and soon, a half battalion of additional pikemen arrive and fill the gaps of the fallen. The other half of the division is halberd bearers who are soon stabbing and pulling the lancers from their horses, trampling them by their panic-stricken mounts.

Samuel's long swordsmen sweep around the ends of the skirmish line and flank both sides of the heavy calvary. The heavy cavalry, now caught in close combat, drop their lances and try to fend off the attackers outflanking them. The function of the heavy cavalry was to trample and rout the enemy so that they would split and run. In combat, with all their cumbersome armor, the heavy calvary is not made for close combat maneuvers. The General's heavy calvary is no match for the pikemen's skirmish line and the long swordsmen halberds combined. Heath signals for retreat and watches a third of his men trying to fall back and return to the town.

He orders a larger battalion of over two thousand five hundred long swordsmen to advance and route the pikemen's and swordmen's defenses. Heath watches his troops advance when they are met with a more significant number of Imperial swordsmen as the pikemen lay down their pikes and draw long swords. Heath hears a charge signal, watches a detachment of Imperial heavy cavalry charge into his swordsmen, hitting them in broadside maneuver, and begins to route them. The Imperial heavy cavalry pushes through, and as his men are in disarray, Heath hears another signal and looks up to see a rain of deadly arrows falling onto his men. He watches in disbelief as his swordsmen are like his heavy calvary impaled of steel-tipped shafts falling from the sky. Heath is infuriated that Heinz's plans are nothing compared to what the Imperial Army is doing. Once again, he signals for his troops to retreat. He watches many running back to town for cover and even sees some drop their weapons and surrender. He is surprised that the Imperial Army does not advance but forms a box formation with the pikemen on the outside and the swordsmen behind them and then sees the box formation start to pull back.

Heath brings up his remaining heavy cavalry in front, swordsmen on the flanks, and his archers three thousand strong in the middle to advance and prepare to fire. The archers move with the long-swordsmen and heavy cavalry for protection. They are almost within striking distance when Commander Heath and everyone else hears several dull thumping noises and gaze skyward to see what looks like a giant clay canister flying through the Air.

General Heath calls Heinz and asks him. "Why didn't you know about the catapults?" and then asks, "What are these things? Heath watches as more clay canisters hit the ground and explode on impact. He sees the contents of the exploding clay canisters saturate his archers, long swordsmen, and heavy cavalry in a sticky black substance. He watches as more canisters fly through the Air and, like the others, explode on impact.

One of the heavy calvaries comes galloping up and shows Heath that the substance is almost tar-like.

General Health is sitting on his horse, rubbing the tar-like substance between his thumb and forefinger, and then smells it, and he smells coal oil, a very flammable substance. He is just about to order a complete retreat when someone shouts and points to a lone figure on the opposite ridge. He pulls out his eye scope and sees someone standing on the edge of the opposite side of the valley, holding a longbow. Heath hears Heinz say, "Takahashi!". The Commander adjusts his eye scope and watches in silence as he sees this young woman, standing on the opposite ridge, slowly pulling back an arrow notched in her bow.

Reiko takes a deep breath, feels the euphoria, and then sees the stillness as the silver flash crosses her eyes, and the clay pot flying through the Air is but a few feet away. She releases the first arrow and watches it fly true, and then she takes the second arrow from her mouth, has Sargent Stell light it, and she notches and pulls back the string of her bow, and she releases the flaming arrow, and it is on the same course as the first one.

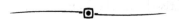

Hikaru hears the thumps, sees the canisters flying through the Air, and hears them smashing on the ground. He then sees a larger pot flying through the Air, followed by a single arrow, and right behind that one is a flaming arrow. Suddenly the fighting stops, and there is a deathly quiet as if the anticipation of seeing what will happen. Hikaru points towards the sky and tells Carrie to watch. At first, she doesn't see it, but then she does, as the arrow comes from the same direction, and a few seconds later, she sees a flaming arrow right behind it. She is surprised when the first arrow connects with the pot and shatters it, allowing its contents to scatter in the Air, and is more surprised as the second arrow, the flaming one, passes through the scattered remnants and ignites them. Blazing balls of burning tar explode as they fall to the ground and begin to ignite the previous splotches of tar splashed onto the Dark Forces.

The next thing Carrie hears is the screams of animals and humans alike as if on fire, and someone shouting and sounds like someone trying to give orders. She hears the commotion, and out of nowhere, she sees a man running by the cages, fully engulfed in flames; as he heads down the hill, she watches as he suddenly stops running and falls over. She looks at Hikaru, and all he says is, "Apricot," then smiles. Carrie can see love in his smile, not love as a lover, but love for a truly good friend. All Carrie can think about is, "I need to meet this friend!"

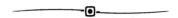

Heath watches through his eye scope as this girl stands on the hill opposite him and draws back an arrow with a longbow. He also sees that she has a second arrow between her teeth. He watches as the arrow tip points skyward, and then she pulls back the bow a bit more and nods her head. Heath hears a thump and watches as a large clay canister comes sailing through the Air. The canister is larger than the previous ones. When he looked back at the girl, he could have sworn that he saw a flash of silver cross her eyes right before she released the first arrow, and then she pulled an arrow from between her teeth and shot the second arrow, but this one is alight with flame. He is still watching as someone hands her a third arrow, notches it, turns the arrow points the arrow in his direction. She releases the arrow, and all Heath hears is a twang as the arrow embeds itself in the wooden post just inches from his head; and as he looks at her again, she is smiling.

He turns his attention to the arrow as it continues to streak forward. He thinks the chances of a single arrow striking an object that is now plummeting to the ground are impossible. He notices that his soldiers have stopped advancing to watch the canister fly over their heads. When it gets directly above them, the first arrow shatters the canister, releasing a massive shower of tiny balls that ignite immediately as the second arrow, the flaming one, passes through them.

The Dark forces realize what is happening, but it is too late. Panic sets in, and many drop their weapons and try to pull off their uniforms, which causes the others to break rank and formation. The small balls of flaming tar fall to the ground and immediately ignite the sticky tar covering the land and the men. Within seconds the whole area surrounding Commander

Heath's archers, long swordsmen, his heavy cavalry, and their horses are in flames. He hears the screams of his men, and Heath is furious; he draws his sword and looks at Heinz with pure hatred in his eyes and shouts, "YOU BASTARD!" YOU KNEW THIS WAS GOING TO HAPPEN! YOU PLAYED ME FUCKING PISS PANTS!" Heinz tries to draw his sword, but before it can clear its scabbard, Heath swings his sword and separates Heinz's head from his shoulders.

Heath orders an immediate retreat of his remaining forces to the Mountain Pass. Heath races to the Mountain Pass and is shocked to find that the Pass is blocked, and the men he left at the Pass to guard it are either dead or in shackles. A large force of pikemen and archers of the Imperial Army now controls the Pass. He wonders, "How the fuck did they get to the pass?" but doesn't worry about that now. His only concern is to escape. Suddenly a third of his light calvary is slaughtered under a volley of steel-tipped arrows.

Heath keeps moving and is soon back in the valley, galloping directly towards the Imperial Army's box formation, when they disperse and charge the town square. Distracted, he does not see a contingent of heavy cavalry with lances, led by a young Lieutenant, charging toward him. They crash right into his men performing the perfect broadside wedge maneuver. His remaining calvary is demolished, unhorsed, and trampled. He sees his men start throwing down their weapons and surrendering. Heath knows it is fruitless to continue this fight and only thinks of saving himself and trying to escape to safety and get back to the Barrens.

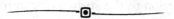

Reiko stands on the hill watching the Dark Commander fight through the battle and sees him break free, urging his mount into a full gallop. She sees that his concern is not for his men but for himself. Reiko nods to Sargent Stell, and he hands her two arrows; Reiko slowly notches one and places the second in her mouth. She begins to pull back the string ever so slowly; the stillness arrives, her eyes flash silver, and she feels the euphoria coursing through her body and then silence. She exhales just a bit, and she releases her arrow.

Commander Heath turns in his saddle to see his men surrendering as he rides hard. He does not hear it, but as he turns back around to escape his own men's demise and this accursed valley, he feels a sharp pain in his left side right below his shoulder as an arrow finds the spot where his shoulder armor and his backplate meet. A second later, he feels it pierce his heart. The Commander of the Dark Army, General Buford T. Heath, falls from his horse only to catch his foot in the stirrup. His body hits the ground, but his foot is caught, dragging him behind his horse. Eventually, the horse comes to a stop and starts to eat and does not even concern itself with the bloody, mangled body of its rider hanging from one of its stirrups.

The town square is in turmoil as the Imperial Army makes its way into town and clashes with the Freaks. Hikaru starts to play with the lock on the cage, and within a few minutes, he has the lock picked. He places the cage lock on the cage floor, carefully lifts the latch, and swings the cage door open. The noise from the ongoing battle covers the noise made by the cage door. Three robed figures are below them, and he looks at Carrie and places a finger against his lips. He lowers himself to hang for a split second and then drops silently to the ground. He sneaks up behind one of the robed guards, reaches up, and twists his neck, killing him instantly. Hikaru grabs his sword before he falls, making any noise, and as the dead one falls to the ground, the other turns only to find a sword blade protruding from his throat. Hikaru is just about to check the bodies for the keys when Carrie shouts, "Hikaru, look out!" Hikaru turns just in time to block a spear point from penetrating his back.

He bats the spear tip aside with his sword, thrusts his sword at his assailant, and feels the blade jab into his side. He drops the spear, and as Hikaru goes to end his life, Carrie shouts a warning again, "Hikaru," and he sees one of the crazies running directly at him with a battleax raised high. He kicks the robed body in the chest to push him out of the way and then brings his sword up to block the downward strike. He performs a spin sweep with his leg and knocks the legs out from under his attacker, and as he falls, Hikaru swings the small sword and decapitates him. A moment after Hikaru decapitates the Freak, a small group of Dark soldiers, heavily armed and wearing thick leather armor, appear and immediately charge

Hikaru. Hikaru reaches down, and as his hand comes in contact with the battleax, Carrie senses a change in his demeanor as the attacking Dark soldiers force him backward until he plants his back foot. Carrie looks at him from her cage and thinks she sees a silver flash across his eyes. He smiles at her, and she sees a change in him as the battleax seems to become an extension of his arm. The Dark soldiers come at Hikaru, and she sees him take a deep breath and, like a flowing, intricate detailed dance Hikaru quickly and what seems to be, with little effort, kills or maims anyone who comes close to his battleax. Carrie watches with fascination, and soon the area around Hikaru is littered with the dead bodies of the Dark soldiers. Carrie calls out to Hikaru, tells him the sect leader is escaping, and points in the direction she sees him running. Hikaru grabs a knife from the sheath of the fallen Dark Soldiers, holds it in his right hand, spins the blade as if feeling its weight, then pulls back his arm and throws it. Carrie sits in her cage and watches the knife flying true to imbed itself into the back of the black-robed leader and watches him fall forward dead. Hikaru picks up a sword from the ground and finishes anyone still alive.

When done, he notices that the third-robed one that came at him with a spear is gone and sees a blood trail on the ground. He assumes he dragged himself away to die. Carrie sits in her cage in disbelief. She looks down at him and sees that his eyes are back to normal, if you call a very deep blue normal. She also sees that he is smiling. She smiles back and thinks to herself, "I think I love this man!"

Chapter 25

William Meets Laki

It has been thirteen days since William left the comforts of Tokora, and he has been walking most of the day. He comes across the skeleton of an old stone building with half its roof caved in. He sees that it is getting late and decides to stop for the night and make camp. He finds a room of the structure with three walls still intact and starts a fire. Once he has a fire going, he places the last of the cooked meat he bought from the tavern on a flat stone and then places a small metal pot on a stone near the fire to heat water. While he waits for the cooked meat to heat up and the water to boil, he unwraps his tanbur and starts tuning it, and when he feels it is tuned, he smiles. He is just about to start playing when he hears it.

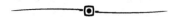

Laki walks, enjoying the lush grasses under her feet when she smells an aroma of spices and a hint of mint. She follows the scent and comes across a man sitting in an old rundown structure room with a fire going. She sees that he is tuning an instrument. Laki looks at him and feels something is different about him. He is a handsome-looking young man, and since he is sitting down, she can only guess that he is just about two meters tall and solidly built from what she can see. He has thick black hair that looks about shoulder length and is pulled back in a ponytail. His eyes are significantly almond-shaped, and his complexion has a weathered look about him as if he spent a significant amount of time near the water. Though his features are slightly weathered, it does not make him look old or take away from his youth. He leans over to sprinkle the leftover meat with some more spices and herbs, and she can sense that he is a man of integrity and honor. The one sure thing that she notices is the look in his eyes. She sees a calming, reassuring look deep within his dark sapphire blue with gold specks and a smile that immediately puts one at ease. She is about to shift from her *Spirit*ual form to her Earthly form when she hears the distinct pop. She watches the man rewrap his instrument and lean it against one of the walls, and then she is surprised to see him surround the instrument with a cushion of Air and Earth. He stands with his back to the fire, and that is when she sees a robed figure and four strange-looking beasts, with one of them missing a front paw, cautiously approaching the structure. She notices the man's hands are swirling with a red hue. She decides to remain in her *Spirit*ual form and watch.

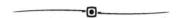

He hears the distinct pop a short distance away. He rewraps his tanbur, places it against the wall out of harm's way, and seals it in Air and Earth. He stands with the fire to his back and listens as the beasts slowly move towards the structure and his camp. He counts three of them and then thinks of four, as one of them seems to be walking with an uneven gait as if limping. Laki watches from above as she sees William's hands start to glow, and the hues change from blue to red, then to light brown, and finally white, and then the colors seem to meld together so that they swirl around one another. One of the beasts seems impatient and steps into the edges of the campfire light, and William sees that the creature's front leg is partially black, and its paw is missing. It dawns on him that this is the same creature that he and the four-town guards of Tokota, Joshua, Phillip, Jonas, and Peter, captured in a net, severed its front paw, and then released to lead them back to where they found the Sutaraukaji. The beast gives a guttural growl and leaps, and William sees that the beast's leap is off. William releases a tightly woven blast of Air from his hands and strikes the beast directly in the chest. The beast is dead before it hits the ground. He goes to take a step forward when he catches movement out of the corner of his eye and sees a Sutaraukaji standing in the shadows of the trees. William hears muttering, and the robed one shoots a fireball directly at William. He is caught off guard and manages to dive out of the way of the oncoming fireball. William shoots a blast of ice in the direction of where the Sutaraukaji is standing near a tree. He is surprised at its speed and watches the ice blast hit the tree but misses the Sutaraukaji. William comes out of the roll, and as he gets back on his feet, he has changed the metabolic structure of his manas, and he lashes out with a whip of Air directly at the Sutaraukaji, just as another fireball heads straight at him.

William manifests a wall of water just before the fireball hits him, and when it strikes the wall of water, it is gone. William sees the Sutaraukaji stumble, and he lashes out again with another attack of Air, and this time the whip hits the Sutaraukaji in the back and slams him to the ground.

William follows through with a mighty downward pour of Air, keeping it down and pinning it to the ground. Stunned, William manipulates the Air and binds the Sutaraukaji. He then picks up the Sutaraukaji and swings his arm so that the Sutaraukaji flies through the Air, and just before its body makes contact with a large tree, William freezes the Air and the creature just before it slams against the tree. There is a loud noise, similar to a block of ice shattering after being dropped from a great distance.

William hears the guttural growls of the two other beasts and is a little surprised when he hears the footsteps of another two-legged creature; and it is moving in slowly and circling the structure. He moves back towards the fire, drops to one knee, places the palm of his hand on the ground, and listens. William is surprised that these other three beasts have remained here after destroying the Sutaraukaji. He can now see their blood-red eyes peering at him from the shadows and their silhouetted forms, crouching slightly and ready to pounce. He remains calm, stays close to the fire, and begins to chant, allowing the four manas to spread out and encompass the structure.

The manas are pure, and as they touch the beasts, William can feel the darkness emanating from them. He releases the mana *Spirit*, and when it touches the beast's dark manas, the creatures begin to howl, a guttural bone-chilling howl, and then start to tremble uncontrollably and seem to remain where they are. William calls forth Earth, and one beast is skewered immediately and doesn't make a sound as a pointed spear of Earth penetrates its heart.

The other two shake off the sensation and move closer to the fire. William can see that the flames from the blaze make their eyes appear more blood red. William conjures two whips, one of flaming mana in his hand and the other of Air, as they both pulsate with power. He flicks his wrists to crack the whips, and they snap and reach their full potential in length and intensity.

The medium-sized one is the first to attack and comes straight for him, baring its fangs with its mouth open. William lashes out with the whip of

Fire in his left hand, and as the whip encircles the creature's neck, he flicks his wrist and pulls back his arm. There is no howl of pain from the beast as it no longer has its head. The creature's body falls at William's feet, and he senses the creature's heart is still pumping, not realizing that it is dead, as black blood continues to pour from the headless neck. William sees the black blood flowing from the creature's body and head, and they both burst into flames. The second larger one leaps into the camp and comes directly at him from his right. William sees its fully extended claws and tries to swipe at him. He dodges as the beast is in mid-Air and lets it flies past him, but as the beast passes him and the tips of its claws catch him, William feels the material of his jacket rip but knows the creature has not drawn blood. He quickly lashes out with the other whip in his right hand and catches the beast full-on, and he flicks his wrist and wraps the whip around the beast's body. The beast now captured, William brings forth the mana of water and sends it along the length of the Air whip, followed by a blast of sub-zero frigid Air. The beast is suddenly frozen solid. He can hear and feel the second two-footed creature circle the camp. He also knows it will only be a matter of time before it attacks, and he must prepare as quickly as possible. While holding onto the Fire and the water and Air whips, he now conjures the Earth and joins it with the Fire. The whips are unstable, and he brings forth *Spirit* to soothe them in their actions.

The creature has seen what this man has done to its companions and is cautious but has also learned. William knows where it is but does not know when it will attack. The creature moves, and then it launches itself directly at him. The creature comes running at him, swinging its black sword, and then body slams William knocking him to the ground. The creature turns to face him, and William quickly gets back up, but instead of standing, he faces the creature on one knee.

They now face each other, and as William stares directly at its face, he sees the blood-soaked white cloth and a hazy image of a woman for a fleeting moment. It releases a deep guttural growl and charges as William lashes out with the whips. The creature dodges the first whip of *Air* and water combined, as the tips of the whip just seem to sear the creature's robe.

William has misjudged the creatures' speed and agility and knows he has only one option: jam the creature up so it cannot swing its black sword. He does that but then finds himself flying through the Air to land on his back. Winded, he feels a weight on his chest, and as he tries to get up, he realizes that the creature is standing on him and pressing down on his chest. William can sense the edge of its black sword through the fabric of his clothes.

It stares William straight in the eyes, and William stares right back at the creature and says, "*Shuizumara Tamizou.*" *Earth* manas erupt from the ground to become solid stone spears that shoot upwards, lifting the creature off Williams's chest and high into the *Air*. The creature screams and thrashes with rage as *Earth's* slender shafts hold the creature aloft.

William rolls out from underneath the beast, gets up off the ground, and stands out of its reach. He returns to his campfire and finds the meat is just about heated through, and the water is boiling. William then sits down, puts the tea concoction into a small metal teapot, and adds the boiling water. He watches the creature struggling on the shafts of earth. William finishes his tea and places his cup down. He walks back over to the creature, binds its arms to its sides with *Air*, then grabs its head and sees and feels images of death and destruction. He learns that the vicious and evil beasts are called Chizobutsu. William has seen enough and steps back and calls forth fire, and bright red streams encompass William's hands. He then places his hands on the creature, says, "I'm sorry," and then the creature bursts into flames. Seconds later, the ashes of the creature float to the ground, and then a light breeze carries them away. William does the same to the creature near the rocks and watches the same light breeze carry the ashes off.

He places his palm on the ground, draws forth *Spirit*, and immediately feels where the cave and rift are. He walks to the cave's opening and sees the rift shimmering in the entrance. He conjures the four manas, brings forth the fifth to bind them, and blasts a stream of powerful energy into the rift. He hears the screams of pain in as many days, and then the rift collapses and is gone. He seals up the cave and heads back to his camp. He sits near the fire and throws some more wood on diminishing coals when he gets there. The fire flares up, casting a more extensive and brighter glow against the darkness.

He is tired but drinks more tea infused with "*Spirit*" and immediately feels better, stronger, and less tired. He removes the protective mana, unwraps his tanbur again, and starts to strum and adjust the strings. He starts playing a little melody that he has been working on for what seems like forever.

There is a new moon on this quiet night, and the sky is full of stars. Laki listens to the music he is playing and slowly descends into the shadows of the trees. A faint breeze and the fragrance of lavender float through the air, and as it reaches the young man, he looks up from his tanbur just as she steps into the light of his fire. She stands before him, only to have him stop strumming his instrument and stare at her.

At first, William thinks she is a mirage or some type of sorcery because he has never envisioned a more beautiful young woman in his life. Clad in thin sheer clothing, he can see the outlines of her perfectly proportioned body and realizes that with the evening air, she should be cold. William finds himself staring, then turns away, blushing. He offers her his cloak and asks her if she wants to join him. She says no to the cloak but sits beside him near the fire.

The cool evening temperature does not bother her. Laki looks at his tanbur and asks him to play something. He says, "Okay," but before he starts, he offers her what is left of his freshly cooked meat, and she politely declines with a shake of her head, and in a soft-spoken voice, she says, "No, Thank you." He then reaches into his bag and pulls a slightly ornate ceramic cup from his backpack. He pours some finely ground leaves into the teapot sitting close to the fire, and then he fills the teapot with the hot water from the metal pot. He then gently swirls the pot and sets it down near the fire. Laki watches the procedure intently, and after a few minutes, she smells the aroma of something sweet, followed by a very clean woodsy smell and then a hint of mint. She remembers that earlier smell, which brought her to this valley, and watched this man defeat those creatures. She has never smelled anything like this before. She watches as he picks up the pot, and swirls it to stir the contents inside. She immediately smells a more potent fragrance of mint as he begins to pour the liquid into the two cups. He holds out the cup of the warm mint tea for her to take it.

Laki hesitates, and then he smiles, assuring her, by the look in his eyes, that she has nothing to fear and that she will like it. She takes the cup, and he takes a sip of his tea and then places it near the hot stones. He picks up his tanbur and starts to play. The music enthralls Laki, and she subconsciously takes a sip of their mint tea. The aroma wafts up through her nose, and when she realizes what she has done, she looks at him, and he says, "Told you."

The light strumming of the music and the taste of the mint tea brings a smile to her face, and she begins to relax. When the young man stops playing, he takes a sip of his tea and wonders how a woman as beautiful as she is has enlightened him with her presence.

He asks, "My Lady, what brings you out in these trying times? It is dangerous for someone like yourself to be walking through the woods, especially at night. Some creatures are unnatural."

She thinks how adorable he is and thinks she is just a beautiful woman who is lost or separated from her group. She is just about to answer when William smiles at her and asks, "Would you like some more tea, my Goddess?"

Laki briefly chokes on her tea, looks at William, and asks, "How did you know?"

William looks at her and says, "I have traveled throughout these lands looking and searching for something, but not quite sure what it could be. I have met many beautiful women in my travels, but a beauty like yours could only belong to a Goddess, and I have seen the sketch posted here and there. I will take a chance and say, "Laki."

Laki softly laughs and starts to speak but changes her mind and asks, "May I have another cup?"

William pours her another, and they sit as Laki drinks her cup of mint tea, and William begins to strum on his tanbur again.

It is well into the night when Laki clears her throat, and as William stops playing, Laki tells him, "William, I am searching for a man, and then says, let me rephrase that, "A Champion" to lead our religion. One who could be a figure of strength and a liaison for the two of us. The people genuinely believe in the Laki-Jutsuk Religion but require something tangible to see and hear on this plane for *Spirit*uality. They need a *Spirit*ual Leader to know that this person is genuine and thoroughly understands the words and thoughts of the Goddesses.

William says nothing and sits quietly, sipping his tea.

Laki asks, "William would you consider being my Champion?"

She sees a hint of sadness in his eyes, and he says, "I'm sorry, my Goddess, but I cannot do what you ask of me." Before she can say anything, he holds up his hand so he can finish. He tells her that the moment he saw her, he knew she was one of the Goddesses and that she could be the one thing he has been searching for these past five years since he left his home. I wasn't sure which one you were, but I cannot do as you ask. Some things in my past will not allow me to fulfill your wishes. You are looking for someone pure of heart and willing to give some sacrifices to you, your sister, and to the Laki-Jutsuk Religion, and those I cannot do."

Laki looks into William's eyes to reach into his very soul and feels the pain and torment, and as she pulls back, she sees a single tear form and watches it roll down his cheek. She feels his pain but insists that William tell her why he cannot accept the position she is offering him.

William sighs and tells her of his Alexandria, beauty, love, devotion, and then of her defilement and murder. He did a tremendous wrong in breaking the laws of the very islands that he should have been protecting. How killing the man who took his beloved away from him, and how he tortured him in every hideous way possible. He tells her how he left his homeland, never able to return.

When he finishes, he sighs, looks at her with tears in his eyes, and says, "I am truly sorry, my Goddess."

Laki puts her cup down, slides closer to him, places her arms around him, and embraces him. She starts to glow softly, and as she gets brighter; William feels his burden slowly lifted off his heart and from his soul. He feels enlightenment that he could not think possible, and when she releases him, the pain and the turmoil are gone, though the memories are still there but without torment. He looks at her and wonders how he cannot love this beautiful woman the same way, if not more, than he loved his Alexandria.

Laki and William drink mint tea and talk well into the night. They realize that it is morning as the sun has cleared the peaks and sheds its morning light onto the valley. Laki asks William again if he would be her Champion. William remains silent as she waits in anticipation.

William says," I will agree to become your Champion and the appointed leader of the Laki-Jutsuk Religion under three conditions: One, you will always be honest with me. two, you tell me everything, whether good or bad, and three, that I can love you with all my heart, mind, and soul if it is at all possible."

Laki is happy knowing that she will receive this love from William, hopefully, more than he felt for his beloved Alexandria, but she will accept an equal love. She reaches out to embrace him and tells him, "Yes, I agree to these terms" He feels a gentle warmth throughout his body. She tells William that the next phase is a little unorthodox but asks William to remove his clothing and kneel on the grass. He removes everything but his loincloth and kneels in front of her on the grass. She kneels across from him and produces a small knife, and then an ornately decorated crystal chalice appears. Laki makes a small slice into the palm of her hand with the blade, and then she lets her blood flow into a chalice. When done, her incision heals itself, and then she asks William to do the same. He does without hesitation, and when finished, she kisses his hand, and his cut is gone, with only the remains of a thin line where he drew the blade across his palm. He gazes into the chalice and notices their blood swirling and mixing.

She takes a sip from the chalice and then places the palm of her hand on his upper chest just above his breast and tells him to drink. He drinks the warm blood, and Laki chants, "*Homerudo Torimaki* Sendoka *Kyu Ko Kyoja Ta-Da Chini Alde* Laki." Light from her palm glows on William's chest, and a feeling of euphoria spreads throughout his body. She pulls her hand away, and in its place, he notices a small scar of an ancient rune for Laki engraved into his flesh. He also understands the full beliefs and teachings of the Laki-Jutsuk Religion and immediately feels enlightened and stronger. He knows his name is William James, but that name only exists for a few. He is now the High Priest or Sendoka of the Order of the Laki & Jutsuk Religions.

Laki has found her Champion. She leans in, embraces him, and gives him a deep passionate kiss, and before the chalice comes close to touching the ground, it disappears along with the blade.

William holds her at arm's length and gives her that mischievous smile that she noticed earlier, and she blushes. She gazes downward and what she sees makes her blush even more, but she returns the smile. Laki's sheer garment disappears, and William sees her now, completely natural, leaving nothing to the imagination, and realizes that this young woman, no, this

Goddess is the most beautiful woman he has had the pleasure of seeing. Just looking at her makes him want her. William leans forward, places a sensuous kiss on her lips, and feels her reaching down and removing his undergarments. He puts his hand on her back between her shoulder blades, slides his hand up, gently grabs her hair into his fist, and slowly pulls her head back to expose her neck. William leans in and flicks his tongue on her neck to tease her, and then William places several soft, light kisses on her neck from her earlobe down to her collarbone, and she moans. He releases her hair, looks into her eyes, and softly brushes his lips against hers. She opens her mouth just enough, and he carefully slides his tongue between her lips and into her mouth. He tastes her sweetness, and she returns the kiss flicking her tongue over his. He feels a ripple run down her back as they continue to kiss and hold each other. He carefully lays her back on the grass, gently takes her hands, places them above her, and grabs her wrists. He slowly starts kissing her neck and throat. She shudders and goes to move her hands, but he holds them where they are, gently but firmly. He continues kissing her from her throat to her breasts, stopping just long enough to brush his lips across her nipples, playfully blowing his warm breath across them. Laki feels herself start to respond to his touch and gets very excited, as this is all new feelings to her.

William continues down along her stomach and softly flicks his tongue on her navel, and she moans again. He continues down and places soft, delicate kisses along her inner thighs. She breaks his grip, reaches up to entangle William's hair in her fingers, and tries to draw him in as she inhales profoundly and lets out a long, sensual moan. He pulls himself away under protest and as he stands, so does she along with him. He brings her in close to embrace her. She wraps her arms around his neck in response to his touch and feels him pressing against her. William reaches down and gently grabs her buttocks, and lifts her. Laki instinctively wraps her legs around his waist and whispers in William's ear, "I want you. I want you now!"

William grabs her and gently lifts her higher, and as he lowers her, she feels him. He looks into her eyes, and as she looks back, she gives him a nod, and then she feels pain and gasps, digs her fingers more into his back, and is then overcome with pleasure. Laki holds onto William as William squeezes her bottom with his hands. He stops and gently lowers her to the grass. He looks at her, and she softly says, "Please," and then Laki feels an emotion deep inside of her start to unfold. She wraps her legs tighter around his waist and pulls him in, and as she does, there is an explosion within her body. Emotion spreads entirely within her, causing her to shudder and tremble numerous times, and at the same time, she feels William's eruption.

She lies there, holding onto William tightly as her body quivers uncontrollably. William carefully moves her leg to lay beside her, and she is amazed by his touch alone. She inhales deeply and shudders with pleasure.

Now lying beside, her, William stares into her eyes, and she blushes. He realizes at this very moment that his commitment to this truly beautiful woman is unwavering and that he will love this Goddess for the rest of his life because he now feels complete.

She feels fulfilled as William lies on his side and reaches over to lightly draw small circles on her stomach with his finger, and she giggles. She smiles as she looks at him and knows she loves him, not as her Champion or Sendoka, but as a man named William James. She is almost to the point, as she has her way with William for a second time, and William does not fail her. She feels the eruption again, but this time it is more profound, so as she shudders, she remains sitting and breathing heavily. Laki takes in deep breaths and slowly exhales. William moves slightly, and she arches her back and lets out one final exhale.

Laki tries to stand, and William reaches up, grabs his wrists, and lets his hands drop to her sides. She bends over and whispers in William's ear, "*Watera Mutoku To Hogo Suru She.*" Then Laki places a beautiful rose diamond about the size of a qual's egg attached to a leather cord around his neck.

She places her hands on his chest, and though slightly unsteady, she stretches and is once again in her sheer clothing. She reaches out her hand to help William up. Once he is standing, she holds out her hand, and a leather-bound book and one-half of a parchment materialize in her hands. She hands it to him and says, "William, you are to travel north, and when my sister finds the Shikakin, her Champion, we will visit you both and give you more details, but for now, journey north towards the point of where the two great mountain ranges meet." She reaches out, lifts the diamond off his chest, and tells him that the man or woman he will be looking for will have a similar diamond in their possession. She then says, "In your travels, the diamond may be dormant, but as you get nearer to each other, it will begin to pulse, and then it will glow, the brighter the glow, the closer you will be to finding each other, and he will have in his possession the other half of this parchment.

When my sister finds him, she will instruct him to search for you. Together we think that the both of you can combine your talents and become a force that will surely benefit my sister, and me, against the dark times to come."

While William pulls on his boots, she tells him that the valley is far and that humankind has never laid eyes on this valley before. William and this one other will be the only two people who will see the map or be able to read the words in the book. There are instructions written in the book on what to do. Together they will need to recite the inscribed words in the book. Once in the valley, they will look for a pile of flat square obsidian stones, and underneath these stones, there will be a wooden box. They are to use the items in the box as instructed in the book. She leans forward, kisses him on the cheek, and says, "Thank you." The euphoria of true love envelopes his mind and body. He embraces her, then reaches down and gently squeezes her buttocks, and she moans ever so softly. William smiles at her as she steps away, and just before she disappears, she leans in and kisses him on the lips hard, then disappears, leaving the faint smell of lavender in the Air.

William packs up his belongings, puts out the remains of his fire, and then straps his cloak and tanbur to his backpack. He sets out on his new journey to discover this unknown valley, become the *Spirit*ual leader, the Sendoka for the Laki and Jutsuk Religious Order, and find one person in this world who has no idea what they could look like. William smiles and says to no one. "What the hell? I always liked a good challenge, and now after five years of wandering, it seems I have a purpose."

"Laki *reaches out to* Jutsuk *and tells her that she has found her Champion.*"

Chapter 26

Defeating the Enemy

A squad of twenty-five men carrying battle axes arrive at the cages and stop before Hikaru. Sargent Flack approaches Hikaru, salutes, and says, "Glad to see that you're still alive, Lieutenant!" Hikaru returns the salute and says, "So am I. How is it going?"

Flack answers, "As far as I know, Sir, the main force is suppressed and surrendering, and as we speak, Lieutenant Miro and his detachment of long swords are just entering the town square. We have heard that Lieutenant Takahashi took out the Commander of the Dark Army as he was trying to escape, but we cannot confirm this."

"Sargent Flack, leave five men here to get that young lady down and protect her at all costs, and will someone get me a bloody good ax?"

"Yes, Sir,"

Two men start to lower Carrie's cage, and when it is on the ground, Hikaru tosses them the set of keys he discovered on one of the robed bodies. When Carrie walks up, he is putting on a pair of stolen boots and notices that one of his men gave her one of the red robes to cover herself. Carrie tells him to be careful. Hikaru answers, "Yes, My Lady," and smiles.

Hikaru stands up and is immediately handed a battleax from one of his men. He swings it a couple of times to get the feel of a finely honed blade and loosen his shoulders, and he says to his men, "Let's go teach these Crazies a lesson!"

His men cheer, leading them towards the fight, wearing only pants and boots. She hears Sargent Flack tell him that the Dark Soldiers call the forces in the square are known as "Freaks."

Carrie realizes certain things about Hikaru: he is a solidly built man who swings a battleax effortlessly. He is a passionate man who cares for his men, and she thinks they would follow him into the pits of the underworld.

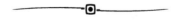

Colonel Tomas is trying to lead the Freaks, but they have no organization and try to rush the Imperial soldiers thinking of overwhelming them with sheer force. These deranged-looking men and women with weird markings and piercing on their bodies are like lambs to the slaughter. Colonel Tomas realizes that the fighting is useless and decides that it is time for him to leave. He deflects a sword, thrust at his stomach, and stabs his assailant in his arm, and he watches as the soldier drops his sword, his Freaks pounce on him and stab him multiple times. Tomas is thinking he is in the clear and escape when to his surprise, he runs into a detachment of Imperial battle axes, and as they try to push forward, they are pushed back by a greater force, led by a solidly built man with black curly hair, only wearing pants, boots, and a battleax. He watches as some of his Freaks throw down their weapons and beg for mercy, while others continue fighting.

Then Colonel Tomas is pushed back into the losing battle by the ax men that are led by the young curly-haired man, and he finds himself standing behind an Imperial officer, and he can see that officer is distracted. Tomas sees an opportunity and swings his blade to take the man's head off, and when he follows through with his swing, he is surprised that there is no resistance from the officer's head, and now realizes that he missed him. He stands there and thinks how could this possibly happen, he could not have missed, and then he looks down and sees the officer's sword sticking out of his chest, and he looks into the officer's eyes and not only sees a coldness, but he also feels it. The officer places his hand on Tomas's chest and pushes him back as he withdraws his sword. Tomas now realizes that the officer dropped below his swing and as he plays the scenario in his mind, he hears, "*Rinju Kitikorosu*, Death Slayer," and dies.

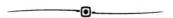

Samuel sees some Imperial soldiers, consisting of Hikaru's ax men, making their way into the battle and begin to push the Freaks back. Samuel then senses it, drops down, and drives his blade through the heart of a man wearing the insignia of a Colonel. He lets the body fall, and Samuels looks around and sees some of his detachment of long-swordsmen lying on the ground injured or dead, though the majority of bodies are Freaks, and then the battle is soon over. Any survivors are placed in shackles while the wounded are delivered a quick death. The injured Imperial soldiers are taken to a field hospital outside the town.

Samuel is on one knee looking at the body of a freak when he sees a small group of his men helping some of the injured, and he hears the talk, "His katana was a blur, and the bodies around him just seem to fall." Then he hears one of them say, *"Rinju Kitikorosu*, Death Slayer," and he shakes his head and resumes examining the bodies. He notices that some of them do not share in the same ritual of body mutilations or have freshly made tattoos and piercings. It dawns on him that these townsfolk have just converted to the Dark Scriptures.

He stands up and looks over the square to see Hikaru and his detachment of battleaxes. Samuel walks up to him and says, "About time you did something," Hikaru smiles and tells him, "I couldn't let you have all the fun." they shake hands. and then embrace.

Samuel asks him, "Are you okay?"

Hikaru tells him, "I'm fine, just a little sore from the beating they gave me when we got captured,"

Samuel turns and orders that every house in town be searched and cleared of any hostiles. If they find anyone in hiding, they are to escort them back to the square, if not willingly, then by force. Samuel turns around to speak with Hikaru and sees him heading towards some hanging cages.

Samuel is about to follow when he hears a horse approaching at a fast gallop. He instinctively places his hand on the hilt of his sword, and then he sees Reiko riding a beautiful black stallion. She dismounts and says, "Compliments of the Dark Commander." Then she asks, "Did you find him, and if you did, where is that big stupid lug?"

Samuel answers, "Yes, and starts to walk in the same direction as Hikaru towards the hanging cages.

Reiko follows Samuel with her new mount in tow.

Samuel and Reiko are about to reach the cages when Hikaru walks up with a young lady in a red robe.

In a somewhat loud voice, Reiko asks, "Samuel, if it was you, and you let yourself get captured and then placed in a cage, would you want to be rescued or stay in the cage?"

Hikaru says to Carrie just loud enough so Reiko and Samuel can hear, "Do not listen to that uneducated woman over there; she is nothing but trouble."

Hikaru walks up to them with Carrie and introduces them as he hears Reiko say, "Uneducated, why you crazy, deranged man, we should have…." But before she can finish her sentence, Hikaru grabs her and wraps her in his arms in a massive bear hug. He says, "It took you long enough," squeezes her tighter. She says, "I am glad you're okay," and kisses him on the cheek, saying, Now! put me down, what would the others think?"

Hikaru puts Reiko down and then asks Samuel, "How much trouble was she while I was gone?" Samuel responds, "Not too much," and Hikaru starts laughing.

Reiko rolls her eyes in exasperation and walks to her horse. She grabs a clean blanket and walks over to Carrie. She tells the two of them to turn around, removes the bloody robe, wraps the blanket around her shoulders, and asks, "Are you alright?"

Carrie answers, "Yes, other than some cuts and bruises."

Reiko says, "Let's see if we can get you cleaned up and find some decent clothes, seeing that these two idiots don't know how to deal with a lady!"

A while later, Reiko and Carrie meet up with Hikaru and Samuel. Hikaru is surprised by how Carrie looks, all clean and bathed and, in some clothes tailored for a young man, which she fills out very nicely in all the right places.

Reiko asks, "What about Heinz?"

Samuel says, "It looks like we won't be seeing him around anymore. The soldiers found a decapitated body in the Commander's tent and Heinz's head beside it." Hikaru details how Heinz broke from the skirmish, went after the one soldier that was able to get away, killed him, and took the pouch. He then took an arrow in the leg to his shoulder to make it look like he was telling the truth about his escape.

Samuel and Reiko explained to Hikaru what transpired back at the camp after Heinz returned, claiming that everyone who went on the mission was killed. They tell him how they followed him into the woods to meet up with the Dark soldier and how Reiko took him out. They got a confession from him, then allowed him to see the fake battle plans and planned his escape. Hikaru starts laughing and tells the two of them how he explained to the dark army commander how Heinz got the nickname "Piss Pants." Samuel starts laughing, and Reiko says. "No, you didn't." Carrie speaks up and says, That he did because she heard some of them call him that.

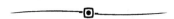

They are walking back to the square, and as Reiko and Carrie are walking in front of them, Hikaru tells Samuel about the Arena and what they will find inside. Samuel says, "Don't worry. I'll take care of it."

She was one of Carrie's friends, but unbeknownst to Carrie, she was one of the first to convert to the Dark Scriptures when they appeared over a month ago. Once she converted, she saw everything Carrie had as a threat and quickly turned to despise her. When she saw Carrie was on the altar about to be sacrificed to the Dark God, she was ecstatic, then suddenly filled with rage when the bitch had somehow saved herself from being sacrificed.

Then, they captured the Imperial soldiers and were taking one to the Arena when he got his arm free, punched her in the nose, and broke it.

She saw another opportunity to end Carrie's life, but that was taken away from her by an Imperial soldier who somehow escaped his cage, killed her friends, stabbed her in the side, and kicked her to the ground.

She was bleeding on the ground, and he was about to end her life when a Freak charged him. While fighting, she dragged herself away, finding herself in an alley. She knows she has to get out of Shira and make her way to Hokida, where there are fellow Dark friends.

She staunches her wound and applies a bandage, and just before she leaves, she sees Carrie, the Imperial Soldier, and two others laughing and embracing each other. She says to herself, "I will not forget you." and turns to leave Shira.

Samuel takes two squads and proceeds to the wooden stockade called the "Arena." They break down the doors and Samuel as well as his men are shocked at what they find. Samuel directs his men to start removing the bodies that are nailed along the walls. He tells his men to be careful with Lieutenant Tombs and the other Shira militia.

Samuel sees the beast that Hikaru mentioned and walks over to it to get a better look. He stands there looking at it, and he has never seen anything like this before. He takes his sword and pries open its mouth and sees the four-inch canines, that would have done serious damage to anything it might have latched onto. He then lifts one of its front paws and sees the black talons and he can tell that Hikaru was very lucky to not get bitten or clawed by this beast. He stands there for a few and thinks that in all his studies growing up, there has never been a beast like this mentioned.

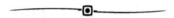

Colonel Frederick D. Bradley is standing in the town square speaking to the men and women of Shira, asking them if they want to stay and rebuild or to travel with the army to the Capital. The residents decide to stay and rebuild. The Major tells them that he will leave a small contingent of his soldiers to help rebuild and guard the town against further threats.

Carrie is standing with Hikaru, Samuel, and Reiko and listening to the Colonel when she hears her name being called, "Carrie, Carrie." She looks in the direction from where she hears her name and sees her husband pushing his way through the crowd. She immediately moves to stand closer to Reiko and slightly behind Hikaru.

When he gets within a few feet, Hikaru tells him, "Stop where you are and do not come any closer." The man says to Hikaru, "Like hell I won't, that is my wife, and I have come to take her home." Hikaru tells him, "Sir, for your protection, please go and get cleansed and when you are clean, we will discuss the arrangements for your wife to return home." Reiko holds her hand, and she feels Carrie squeeze her hand tightly. Samuel signals for three of his soldiers, and they approach and standby.

Carrie's husband says, "Fuck you, she is my wife, and I demand that you release her so I can take her home. As her husband, it is my job to protect her. Now release her!"

"Sir, as I have told you." Carrie places her hand on his forearm, takes a small step forward, and says, "You say that I'm your wife and that you are my husband and will protect me. When we wed, did we not swear, as our hands were bound, to love and protect each other no matter what may arise? According to our wedding ceremony, if either one were to break our bond under any circumstances, the marriage would be dissolved, and the one who broke that bond would lose all rights to properties and belongings. Was that not a vow we made to each other verbally in front of witnesses?"

Her husband said, "Yes, That is what we agreed to in our vows, and your point being, what?"

I will give you the benefit of the doubt but let me ask you this, husband, she says with malice. Where were you when they pushed me with the others to the cages? Where were you when I was held captive in those cages? Where were you when I was dragged to that altar and had my clothes ripped from my body? When those two filthy women were molesting me on the altar, did you come to my rescue, dear husband?"

Her husband stammered and said, "I did not know what was happening to you. I couldn't find you!"

Carrie looks at him now with hate in her eyes and says, "You say you could not find me and did not know what was happening to me. Why is that dear husband? Please tell me why? Carrie's husband stands there and doesn't say anything. Carrie then says, "I will tell you why, my dear husband, it is because you didn't give a fuck about me; while I was being dragged back to the cages naked and bleeding, I saw you grabbing and licking some woman's breasts. To make matters even worse, I saw Patricia, who I thought was my friend, on her knees sucking your cock, but the worst part was that you stood there, looked me in the eyes, and smiled at me. While they dragged me back to the cages. So, dear husband, our marriage is over, and you have nothing."

"Carrie! I made a mistake. Please forgive me!" He falls to his knees, pleading.

"You are not my husband. Nothing but a useless pile of shit who threw away everything to become a worshipper of the Dark Scriptures." Then she spat at him.

He is kneeling there, and his demeanor changes. He looks at Carrie straight in the eyes, with pure hate, and says, "Why you high and mighty useless bitch, I just want you to know that the greatest pleasure I have had in the few years that we have been together was seeing you up on that altar being molested, cut, and almost sacrificed." Hikaru places his arm around her shoulder and gently squeezes. The soldiers are ready to take him away when he jerks his arm free. In his hand is a knife, and he lunges at Carrie, saying, "This is for the Dark Gods!" Hikaru brings up his ax to block the lunge, and Samuel quickly pulls his short blade and slices off her husband's hand holding the knife. Carrie's husband falls to the ground screaming in pain as he grabs his now bleeding stump and sees his hand lying in the dirt, still twitching and holding the knife.

Samuel orders his men to wrap the wound and take him to the local jail to await trial. They drag him away as he is still screaming and crying.

Carrie looks at Hikaru and asks, "Please take me to the capital?"

Hikaru asks, "What of your belongings? We cannot take them with us."

She sees one of the town elders and says, "Give me a minute, and walks over to him." She talks with him, then they shake hands and bow to each other. Hikaru sees Carrie lean forward and kisses him on the cheek. She returns to the three of them and tells them, "The town elder will sell everything and send me half. The other half will go to the families who need it. So, when do we leave?"

Reiko steps up to Carrie, interlocks her arm with hers, says, "Not until I tell you everything there is to know about him, and points to Hikaru. I don't want you to realize too late your mistake."

They are walking off, and Reiko turns and sticks her tongue out at Hikaru and then smiles; the next thing Hikaru hears is them laughing.

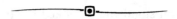

The next day, Carrie and Reiko walk through the town square and are talking when they hear a commotion. They check it out when they see Carrie's ex-husband and two women with their hands and feet locked in the stocks. She sees all three covered in garbage, rotting vegetables, and, in some cases, what seem to be animal feces. Carrie looks down at her husband, and when he sees her, he spits on the ground near her feet. Carrie slaps and tells him, "You brought this on yourself, and before I forget, I love another. She then looks over to the one woman she knew, pleasuring her husband as they dragged her back to the cages, and tells her, "You can have the bastard. Oh! and before I forget, he has nothing, Good Luck with your lives.

Reiko feels Carrie shaking, and she places her arm around her shoulders and says, "So, you love another!" When Carrie turns bright red, Reiko says, "Do not worry, this will be our little secret." Carrie says, "Thank you," they continue walking and are once out of the square. Carrie turns to Reiko and asks, "Please teach me how to fight and defend myself. Reiko does not question why but says, "Sure" So for the rest of the time they are in Shira, Reiko instructs Carrie in the finer arts of fighting and using a small deadly blade called a stiletto. Carrie is quick to learn, and Reiko finds herself pushing Carrie very hard, but she handles it all without complaint.

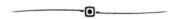

The Imperial Army has occupied Shira for over two months, and the city is clear of all Dark followers. Those Dark soldiers still alive are now in shackles and will be marched back to the Capital for trial. The townsfolk who converted will spend time in the stocks and then be sent to a remote monastery for prayer and reconditioning. The Colonel will send a detachment to escort them there. Colonel Frederick D. Bradley prepares to move out with his army and head back to the Capital by the tenth week. He leaves Orin, now a First Lieutenant, in charge of the military detail to remain in Shira. He has left a sizeable force with a couple of engineers to construct barracks, an outpost, and fortification gates to deter attacking forces, allowing the townsfolk to get to safety in the caves scattered throughout the mountain range.

He also decides to leave two of his catapults with an adequate supply of canisters if something arose that would call for defending the town. The people of Shira have started to rebuild their lives, and the Colonel knows it will be a long road to healing. He hopes that the people of Shira will heal quicker, knowing that the Imperial Empire is concerned for its citizens.

First Lieutenant Orin Bradley calls his men to attention and salutes Colonel Bradley and First Lieutenants Miro, Sato, and Takahashi as they pass. The Colonel notices that his son has removed the sling holding his injured arm for their departure. Samuel stops in front of him and says, "Lieutenant Bradley, once we are gone, you are to put your arm back in that sling and not remove it until the Army Doctor says so is that clear? And follows with, "That's an order," First Lieutenant Bradley."

Orin is beaming from his promotion, salutes Samuel, and says, "Yes, Sir!" Samuel says," Good, now make your father proud." and salutes him.

The first night after Shira, the Colonel has the four of them in his tent for dinner. The Colonel, Samuel, Hikaru, Reiko, and Miss Barnes are sitting at the table having dinner. The Colonel says, "I know this is not the best conversation over dinner, Miss Barnes, but I need to have a final tally for my reports." He looks at the three of them and says, "Please give me your reports on the loses." Samuel goes to stand, and the Colonel tells him to remain seated.

Samuel says, "Yes, sir," and continues. "Sir, we lost two hundred pikemen, one hundred fifty long swordsmen. Sir, Thank you, Lieutenant Miro."

"Lieutenant Takahashi, if you please." Reiko says, "Sir, we lost two hundred seventy-five longbowmen, and one-hundred-fifty crossbowmen, and one catapult that malfunctioned and caught on fire from a spilled canister." The Colonel says, "Thank you, Lieutenant Takahashi."

"Lieutenant Sato, if you please," He remains seated and says, Yes, Sir," We lost two hundred eighty axes and one hundred sixty-five halberds, and I lost Second Lieutenant Tombs and six other men."

The Major raises his hand for Hikaru to stop and says, "Lieutenant Sato, let me make myself perfectly clear. It was not your fault that you, no, let me rephrase that, Gustavo Heinz betrayed us. None of us saw it coming, and I am telling you that this was not your fault, but in reality, it is mine. Mine, for not seeing the deceit." With that said, "Thank you for your reports.

The Colonel clears his throat and says, Though the casualties are a little worse than I originally calculated, you three performed outstandingly. When you see your friend Mr. Cook, tell him, "Thank you and give him this as an appreciation from the Imperial Army. It could have been worse if Lieutenants Takahashi and Miro did not have their suspicions. We were up against a much larger force, and we obliterated them, and then the Colonel says, "A toast to our fallen comrades."

They have made camp many times since that first night, and the trip back to the Capital is taking longer with the wounded and the captured, but the *Spirit*s of the men and women are in good cheer. They reminisce about their fallen comrades now buried inside one of the mountain caves that has since become a tomb for them. Every morning, the Major sends out his hawks to deliver reports and get updates about Shira's progress.

One night at dinner, and still a week away from reaching the Capital, it is getting late, and the Colonel is talking about what will be in store for them when there is a knock on the tents post, and his steward walks in with three small boxes on a tray. The Colonel clears his throat and says, First, Lieutenants Miro, Sato, and Takahashi, please stand. The Colonel says, "By the powers authorized by his Royal Imperial Highness, I am proud to appoint the three of you to the rank of Captain. For your outstanding duties in these dark times and in destroying an attempt that would have been devastating to his Highnesses Royal Imperial Army, the citizens of Shira, and the Royal Empire." He steps forward and removes Samuel's first lieutenant bar and replaces them with a set of Captain's bars. He performs this ceremony with Hikaru and Reiko. He steps back, salutes them, then shakes their hands when finished. Carrie Barnes runs up to Hikaru and hugs him. The Major says, "Captain Hikaru, you've got a good woman there!" Though Carrie cannot see his face, Hikaru stands there smiling.

Captain Takahashi says, "She could probably do better," Hikaru blushes, and they all laugh.

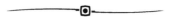

Three weeks later, they enter the Capital gates under the fanfare of citizens shouting out the Colonel's name and calling him The Dark Slayer. The Colonel takes it all in, sitting on his horse and waving to the people lining the streets. Flower petals are spread before him as Samuel, Hikaru, and Reiko follow right behind him. Hikaru tells them they will be doing this for us someday, and all three softly chuckle.

Chapter 27

The Investigation

King Theo, the II of Elenni, has ordered a mobilization of a battalion of Elenni's finest to be led by Colonel Horatio Smith to investigate and report any suspicious activities in the northwestern part of the kingdom just south; of the lands known as "The Barrens." Theo the I, the previous King of Elenni, sent a message to his son regarding his concerns at the influx of people heading into the Barrens. King Theo the II has informed Colonel Smith that they will set up outside the village and use the Keep as his father sees fit.

After the King retired to the Keep for health reasons, the town of Marion flourished. The old King, his wife Pricilla, the former Queen, and their son, Taro, the Present King's step-brother, reside in the Keep. Colonel Smith is excited about the trip; he will see some old friends and his fiancée Lady Analise Charbain. In court, she is the former Queens Lady-in-Waiting. Smith knows the old King and Queen from escorting then Prince Theo II up here to visit his parents on several occasions and was introduced to Analise by the former Queen at a party held for the visiting young Prince. He remembers the old King, now Lord of the estate, as a handsome man and Lady Priscilla being a very beautiful woman. A message arrived in Blanby from the old King, and Colonel Smith is now carrying out a forced march to the Lord's Keep only one day after the message was received.

It has been two weeks, but Colonel Smith has been here before and knows the route very well. He also knows that once they clear the woods and make the next large bend in the road, he should be able to make out the Elenni Flag flying from the Keep's gatehouse. They turn in the next bend, and Colonel Smith immediately knows something is wrong because the Elenni flags are not flying as they should be, and he can see carrion birds circling the town. He takes out his eye scope and can see several residual plumes of grey smoke rising from the village.

He stops the battalion and orders his scouts to advance and investigate. One hour later, one of the scouts is galloping back and tells Colonel Smith to come quick. Colonel Smith orders Captain Johns to take charge of the troops, proceed cautiously to the Keep, and set up an encampment in the fields outside the village.

He follows his man, and as he gets closer to the village, he is shocked to see that half the town is burnt to the ground. The Air shifts, and he can almost smell the odor of charred meat emanating throughout the village. He reigns in his horse, just inside the town's walls, and orders his men to search the town and not enter any buildings. They say, "Yes, Sir," and move out. They are soon back in the square, and the reports are the same. There is no one to be found in the village.

The Colonel sits astride his horse and orders one of his scouts to report to Captain Johns and have him send a twenty-five-man detail to meet him at the Keep, and he will wait for them there. He urges his steed forward as his remaining scouts join him and watch for any signs of trouble. He is coming into another open area just outside the Keeps gates and sees the burned and collapsed church on his right, and the gates to the Keep's compound are just barely hanging on by the hinges. He rides closer and notes that the sweet smell is strongest near the church and fears what they might find inside. He stays on his horse, waits for the detail, and thinks about his first assignment many years ago. Horatio Smith has been in the military since his young Second Lieutenant commission. He remembers his first assignment like it was yesterday: to lead detail to the edges of a ransacked village attacked by marauders and see if the marauders were still in the area. While Smith and his men were searching the town for marauders or survivors, the Air shifted direction, and he was surprised to smell the sweetness of cooked meat in the Air. He inquired about the sweetness of the charred meat to a Sargent, an older man who had been on many campaigns, who looked him straight in the eyes, and all he said was, "the villagers!" At first, it did not register, and then he caught it, and to this day, he has never forgotten the odor of charred human flesh, and he is smelling that same odor again.

While he sits on his horse, he realizes that the Keeps portcullis s missing, and as he rides a little closer; Smith sees the gates themselves are barely hanging on by their hinges and seem to have been blasted by something. His scouts return and report that they have seen no survivors, and many standing homes have been ransacked.

Soon, the twenty-five-man detail arrives, and Smith orders ten men to start a house-to-house sweep to look for survivors. The men take off, and the Colonel orders the remaining fifteen men to dismount and follow him into the Keep's courtyard. The men also notice that the portcullis is missing, and they proceed through the barbican, and they notice the twisted pile of metal lying inside the courtyard. Several of his men vomit when they walk through the gatehouse and enter the yard. The Colonel himself tastes bile in his mouth but keeps his last meal down. They find several Keep soldiers and one woman nailed against the courtyard walls. The carrion birds have already eaten away most of their delicate facial features. However, Colonel Smith can still make out the characteristics of the Lady of the Keep, the former Queen of Elenni, Lady Pricilla. He then orders two five-man teams to search the remainder of the surrounding areas around the courtyard. He keeps five men with him and tells them to find some ladders and cut the corpses down. They also find several bodies riddled with arrows and crossbow bolts lying at the wall's base, behind several hay bales. The two other teams search the courtyard and surrounding facilities, and they find a large group of men butchered on the other side of the courtyard near the stables. The second group heads into the stables, and the smell is horrendous as they find the bodies of more villages piled in the stalls. Colonel Smith hears more vomiting from his men, and a few come back to the courtyard with tears.

They follow the Colonel into the Keep and find the gatehouse's wooden iron-clad bar beside the splintered doors. Colonel Smith draws his sword, and the men follow suit. He orders two parties, one to search upstairs and the other group to explore the lower levels. The Colonel takes eight men with him and enters the Great Hall. They enter through the smashed doors, the room is very dark, and they can tell heavy tapestries are covering all the windows. The smell is more pungent here than outside due to a lack of circulation, so Colonel Smith tells two men to start removing the tapestries from the windows. They pull down the first two, and as the Colonel's eyes adjust, he looks around and finds piles of ripped and torn clothing strewn about the floor. His men continue to pull down the tapestries until they get to the last one and seem to have difficulty removing it. The Colonel sees something in the shadows but cannot quite tell what it is. He thinks it is someone sitting on one of the thrones. He cautiously walks forward and asks, "My Lord, is that you?" but gets no response. He is almost at the throne when his men finally rip the last tapestry down, and Smith is blinded momentarily by the sudden light. He allows his eyes time to adjust, and just as quickly, he takes a step backward, as he can now see that the old King is indeed sitting on his throne, and his arms are tied to allow him to hold his head out in front of him about chest high. The Colonel also sees that the King has been eviscerated and can make out maggots squirming around his insides. He now knows where the smell is coming from as he looks closer at the King's face and realizes that someone has cut the sides of his mouth to make it look like the old King is still smiling. One of his men gags, and when he looks at him, he sees his man pointing at something. The Colonel turns to look where the soldier is pointing and sees the headless body of the Laki-Jutsuk High Priest hanging upside down against the wall with his arms out behind the Keeps thrones. He immediately orders them out of the Hall of the Keep. The Colonel goes to leave himself when he inadvertently kicks something. He looks down and realizes that he has just kicked the head of the High Priest of the Order.

Colonel Smith is about to order two of his men to stand guard at the entrance when the four who went upstairs to search the rooms are now walking down the stairs, and all four are white-faced. He sees that one of them is carrying a white-wrapped bundle in his arms and that they have been crying. The one holding the bundle asks the Colonel how someone could be so cold to butcher children. The other soldier with him says, "We found him upstairs." The Colonel asks them if they know who he is, and when he sees their eyes, he knows it is the young Prince Taro. They then report that there is no one else in the Keep and that they found several ripped and bloody piles of clothing, but nothing more. He orders the three of them to place the young Prince inside the Great Hall's doors and tells them to go no further. Smith then orders two men to stand guard outside the Keeps doors and not let anyone pass.

He sees that the detachment has gotten bigger as more of his men are helping to wrap the bodies. He walks through the Keep's main gates, reaches his horse, and is about to mount up when he hears some men arguing. He leaves his horse tethered, walks over to the commotion, and sees several men standing outside the church with the doors unbarred and wide open. He calls Sargent Hopkins over and asks why all the shouting.

Sargent Hopkins looks at the Colonel and says, "Some of the men are scared and are refusing to remove any more boards. They don't want to see what might be inside." Smith places his hand on Hopkins's shoulder and says, "I will handle this." He walks to the church's doors and orders his men to stand down and stay back. He then tells Sargent Hopkins to get him a torch, and when Hopkins returns, he tells Hopkins he will go in alone. He hears Hopkins say, "Thank you, Colonel." Hopkins lights the makeshift torch and hands it to the Colonel. He takes the torch and tells Hopkins to wait outside.

The Colonel holds the torch high and cautiously steps inside. The memories returned from his first assignment many years ago. He remembers every detail because of the sweet charred smell and is now smelling the same sweet smell for the second time in his life. At first, the Colonel can see the burned-out pews, and then he starts walking down the aisle. He is about halfway into the church when he sees them and almost drops the torch. He raises the torch higher and can now make out several charred indiscriminate piles of different sizes. He squats down, lowers the torch to get a better look, and realizes that the charred piles are bodies. He counts several medium-size adult bodies surrounded by smaller ones, while others hold even smaller bundles in their arms. The Colonel takes a few more steps and realizes that these must have been the village's children. Tears well up in his eyes, and he says to no one, "Whoever did this will pay dearly."

He walks up to the altar and discovers several others laid out before the altar. He notices that these bodies are not as bad as the others. Smith then sees that they are all young females, and some look to have been beaten and mauled, He turns to leave, and a glint of something shiny catches his eye, he bends down to the body of a naked young girl, and like the others, she looks broken. He brings the torch closer and sees a small silver chain with an emblem of the Laki-Jutsuk Religion, a heart with a dove in its center. Smith cannot believe what he is seeing and prays that it isn't so. He reaches for the medallion and turns it over with shaking hands. Smith carefully removes the chain from her hand and rubs away the dried blood with his thumb, and he can make out the name "Analisa" engraved on the back in the flickering flame of the torch.

He clenches the emblem in his fist and says to his beloved, "I swear by all that is good in this world, I will avenge you, Analisa, my love, even if it kills me." The Colonel leans over, kisses the young girl on the forehead, and places the necklace in his top shirt pocket; he stands and walks out of the church. Sargent Hopkins meets him at the door, and before he can say anything, the Colonel holds up his hand to not ask questions, and he orders Sargent Hopkins to seal the doors and board up the windows.

"Yes, Sir!" and salutes the Colonel.

The Colonel walks over to his horse and leads it out of the village to meet with Captain Johns. They converse quietly, and soon Captain Johns orders the men to start digging the graves as another group is assigned to search through the rubble of the village. Another group has to remove the bodies from the Keeps courtyard and stables. Every day they discover more bodies, and after ten days, they believe they have found all the townsfolk.

Two weeks later, all the bodies are in unmarked graves in the fields outside the village. The Lord, Lady, and the young Prince are resting in the Keeps Great Hall with their guard. Colonel Smith has both the Keep doors and the throne room doors repaired and made stronger He takes one last look, then closes the doors to the hall and secures them with a heavy chain. He then has his men chain the Keeps gatehouse doors to secure them.

After two days of rest, the battalion is getting ready to depart as Colonel Horatio Smith sits astride his horse and waits for his detail to paint the words on the village walls. Minutes later, his men ride up to the Colonel, salute the Colonel takes out his eye scope, and reads the words painted on the walls, "No Trespassing - Punishable by Death."

A little over four weeks have passed since the battalion of soldiers had departed from the Capital, and the King is getting impatient, having not heard from Colonel Smith. He is about to send another half battalion when a courier arrives at the castle that afternoon and hands the King a sealed letter from the Colonel. King Theo is standing as he unseals the letter and starts reading, and then he falls backward onto his throne; the letter slips from his fingers and falls to the floor. The Chamberlain walks over and picks up the letter, and reads it. He is overwhelmed by the situation at the Keep and discovers that his old friends are gone.

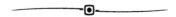

Nova feels good about herself as she sits in her chambers, drinking a glass of wine, and relishes that she has finally avenged her mother's murder after all these years. There is a knock on her door. When she says enter, Bernadette informs her that her scouts have reported that a military force of battalion size, which equals about one thousand soldiers, has just arrived at the Keep and started searching the village.

Nova says, "Wonderful!" and tells Bernadette to send for General Harris.

General Harris arrives, drops to one knee, bows, and replies, "Yes, My Kaisoshosuko, you sent for me?"

She asks, "General, are your troops ready for a little excursion?"

"Yes, My Kaisoshosuko," the General answers.

Nova knows they are; she had all the followers who were not her Elite but wanted to be part of something walk through the cavern entrance. Walking through the entrance to pledge their loyalty and devotion to the Dark Scriptures, and unbeknownst to them, actually determined their destinies. Some turned into "Zokotarumo" or Freaks, but most turned into soldiers. Whatever the outcome, intuition told them to take weapons and uniforms from the stockpiles that the tradesmen had made.

"Excellent, General Harris; my sources tell me that a military force of battalion size is presently investigating the Keep that my Elite and I raided a few weeks back. Take what you need and destroy them."

"As you command, "My Kaisoshosuko."

"General Harris, Do not fail me again."

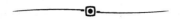

It is just a little over two weeks when General Harris informs Nova that his men are ready. She tells him where to meet her with his troops. It is early afternoon when General Harris meets Nova and bows before her. Nova tells him to wait as she pictures the place in her mind to the last detail, and then she chants, *"Guko Kachi Mi Dit La Ro Chiakoba,"*

he hears the distinct ping. General Harris watches as a passageway opens up, and he sees green hills on the other side. The General looks nervous because of what happened in Shira, and Nova tells him, "Do not worry, General, I am not sending you to the Dark Realm, just a day's march in front of the Elenni Army. General Harris goes to step through, but right before he does, Nova places her hand on his arm, and he feels the heat, and then she says, "General, do not fail me as you did in Shira; I will not be so forgiving; this time."

General Harris tells her, "Yes, my Priestess, I will not disappoint you this time, and thank you," He orders his men to start filing through, and as the horse-pulled war machines arrive, she makes the passageway larger. Once the war machines are through, Colonel Byron Sayle approaches, bows to her, and steps through without hesitation, and the "Freaks." follow. Nova estimates that she has just moved a combined force of over six thousand men and several war machines through a passageway and placed them strategically ahead of a battalion-size force. She watches through the passageway, and it looks like the General has the troops quickly organized and ready to move. General Harris does not look back but hears the ping sound of the passageway closing. Harris rides at the column's lead with Colonel Sayle at his side, and they formulate a battle strategy to squash the army of the Elenni kingdom. After about an hour, they agree on a plan, and Sayles gives a final suggestion that Harris accepts openly.

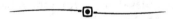

It has been three weeks since Colonel Smith sent a rider back to the Capital with his report. He can do no more and orders his men to mount up, to return to the Capital. He and his men are about three days from the Keep when one of his outriders comes galloping up and tells him a large force is marching onto the plains a half a day's ride ahead of them. The Colonel asks him, "How large a force?" The outrider reports that he estimates at least three battalions. The Colonel is quite surprised; two more outriders come galloping up and report that at least two battalions of soldiers are blocking the road leading south to the Capital. The two of them concur and decide to return to the Keep and hold up there. Colonel Smith is just about to order his troops to turn around when his last outrider comes galloping up and reports that a battalion-size force is marching towards them from the village of Marion. The Colonel thinks, then tells his outriders to find him an advantage point. An outrider tells him of seeing a stand of trees on a hill. The Colonel tells the rider to show him, and they gallop off. Smith then asks for some parchment, writes down his situation, and sends his fastest rider with the message requesting the King for reinforcements.

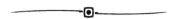

General Harris has strategically placed troops and barricades on all the routes leading south out of the lands below the Barrens. A battalion-size force at each of the two barriers blocking the roads south. Another five hundred men are strategically placed between the two battalions to reinforce any position the Elenni forces might attack. He has ordered a battalion to flank the Elenni troops and secure what was once the village of Marion. The more significant portion of his army is sitting right in the middle, below a low sloping ridge overlooking the valley, and on the opposite side of the valley is a large hill with a stand of trees. The General knows that the Elenni Commander should know by now that the roads leading south are blocked, giving him only two options. The first would be to turn around and head back to the Keep, but that would exhaust his foot soldiers in a forced march, and there would be no guarantee that with the number of troops blocking the roads south that there would not be a significant force blocking his way to the Keep. Harris assumes they will not try to move an entire battalion through the valleys, especially with superior force blocking the major thoroughfares. It would leave them out in the open, with no protection, and be a suicide march. If he were the officer in charge, he would find the tallest hill as a defense point and make a stand there.

Harris is looking through his eye scope when he sees two riders come riding up to the same hill that he was looking at, thinking that if he were in the enemy's position, that is where he would make a stand. Then he would have the advantage of being on higher ground and making fortifications out of the trees on the hill. As he surmised within the hour, the Elenni forces had arrived and diligently started cutting down the trees to fortify their position. Two days have passed, and General Harris is enjoying a glass of wine when a runner comes up and reports that Colonel Sayles says all activity in the enemy's camp has stopped. Harris finishes his wine, follows the runner up to the ridge, meets with Colonel Sayles, and checks on the enemies' fortifications. Harris is impressed with what he sees for only starting two days ago. Still, the only flaw is that the standard pentagon formation they built works well against cavalry assaults as long as the pentagon holds, and if one side were to collapse, then the strength of the pentagon would be lost. He also notices the tree branches are placed to protect his men from incoming arrows. The General orders his war machines to move up but stay below the ridge. He calls his commanders to his tent and points to a hill on the other side of the valley.

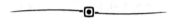

Colonel Smith looks out over the terrain and determines where he has set up his pentagon is the best possible location. His men have cut down the trees to make a defensive pentagon fortification, used the branches, and placed long sharpened spikes along the walls. He is looking through his eyescope when he sees a large man sitting astride his horse and watches him give a signal. Colonel Smith hears the distinct whooshing sound, knows what makes it, and knows that several catapults have launched their loads. He sees large stones flying through the Air and bearing down on his position, but before he can give any orders, the stones fall around him and his men. The stones pummel his fortification as both men and horses are slaughtered, and others receive broken bones, cuts, and bruises. Smith orders his men to hold to their positions as the stones rain from the sky and claim more of his men.

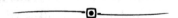

General Harris wants to destroy these Elenni troops, but sitting here and watching his catapults rain rocks down on them is not showing him what his troops are capable of doing. Harris orders another volley, but smaller stones to pepper the enemy this time.

Colonel Smith calls out to Captain Johns to get a status report when he sees the Captain lying under his mount and a hole the size of a grapefruit in his chest Runners come up to him and give reports from other officers and senior-ranking non-coms. Smith quickly counts and concludes that he has lost approximately two hundred and sixty men, or one-fourth of his battalion, killed or incapacitated with severe wounds and broken bones just after the first volley. Smith is trying to devise a plan and knows that his best bet would be to try and get back to the Keep and make a stand there; when he hears the shouts from his men as another volley of stones flies towards them. Smith is on the ground, as a stone that would have crushed him had it not been for his aide a young Lieutenant had not seen it coming. The young Lieutenant was not so lucky as the stone that would have taken out Smith ended up taking the Lieutenant's head instead. Smith cannot take anymore and knows what he must do. He orders his troops to rally, and anyone who cannot ride will be left behind. Smith looks to the ridge where the assault originated, then sees a mass of bodies starting to line the ridge, and he knows they are getting ready to charge.

Smith does not have enough horses to carry the wounded, so Smith orders the injured to be left behind and has the remains of his battalion move out over the pleas of the wounded and dying. Just as Smith reaches the next hill, he hears the war cries of the charging army, pull up his horse, and look back at the men he had to leave behind. The ones who can stand try and fight, but the odds are against them as they are soon overwhelmed. He watches as the enemy converges on his men and shows no mercy in slaughtering them and stripping the bodies of clothing and weapons as souvenirs. Smith spits on the ground, then turns his horse and gallops after his remaining men to join them.

Harris does not order his men to pursue the Commander and his remaining men; He watches them disappear over the next hill.

Harris thinks he would have done the same thing: "What is best for survival."

They have been driving their mounts to exhaustion as they continue along the valleys and try to make their way back to the Keep. Smith decides to head straight for the Keep, and they hit the road to the Keep at full gallop. When they clear the last bend in the road, the Keeps towers come into view, and Smith immediately sees that the enemy has formed a blockade, barring all access to the village and the Keep. He orders his men to slow down and stop their advance; He knows his men are tired, and the horses are lathered and breathing heavily.

He looks back to see another portion of the enemy's forces making their way to the top of the hills they had just come over and can see the dust from a large force coming up the road. Smith realizes he is blocked in with no means of escape. Smith orders his men to release their mounts; they will not be going any farther. The men remove all of their gear and then spook the horses. After the horses are gone or scattered, Smith keeps the mountains at his back and orders his men to form three skirmish lines, with the pikes and halberds in front, then the swordsmen, and finally the archers. They do as they are ordered and then wait.

General Harris and Colonel Sayles sit atop their mounts, and Harris sends several riders to gather the Elenni horses. He then looks to Sayles, and when Sayles nods, Harris gives the order. It is an all-out charge from four battalions of Dark soldiers to three-quarters of a battalion of Elenni Regulars.

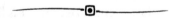

The enemy hits the pikes and halberds head-on, and soon the screams of the wounded and dying are barely audible over the clash of swords. Colonel Smith is proud of his men as they continue to hold off the enemy under the circumstances. He sees that this army is undisciplined, and all they have going for them is mass. Still, discipline or no discipline, the numbers alone of bodies charging them are overwhelming. Smith sees a portion of his wall of pikemen start to give, and he orders up half his reserves to reinforce the position.

Smith hears a horn sound, and suddenly, the attacking army withdraws, and the fighting stops. He looks over his men, and after the reports come in, he has lost another third of his men and is now down to half a battalion. He orders his men to stack the Elenni troops' bodies and the enemy's bodies to make a wall with the bodies. There are some protests, but they do as they are told, and by the time night falls, Colonel Smith has a mid-thigh high wall of dead bodies in front of him.

His men are tired, and the atmosphere in the camp is somber. Smith walks through the camp and tries to give words of encouragement, telling them all they have to do is hold out because he has sent a rider to the Capital for reinforcements.

Smith can catch a few minutes here and there for sleep, and he is sleeping when one of his soldiers shakes him to wake him up. Smith stands, rubs the sleep from his eyes, and asks the soldier, "What is it, Corporal?"

The Corporal answers, "A rider Sir, on the ridge."

Smith walks up to the wall and looks through his eye scope. He sees a rider and also sees that he is tired up and secured to a rack that keeps him on the horse. Smith also sees that the rider has been disemboweled to prolong his life. Smith looks closer and realizes it is the rider he sent to the Capital requesting reinforcements. Smith contemplates his options when he hears the whoop of the catapults and then watches as his men are tossed in the Air, and the boulders demolish his makeshift fortifications.

No sooner does the rain of boulders and pellet rocks stop than the enemy comes charging over the hill in full force and hits his skirmish lines. His men fall as they are gradually pushed in on themselves by the superior masses. Suddenly the attacking force breaks the ranks, and it is now more of a close combat fight; as his men are now divided, Smith blocks one sword thrust and sees that it is not a fight with honor but a massacre. He dodges another jab but is stabbed in his side by another attacker and falters. He has difficulty keeping his guard up and sees the massacre and horrors of his men dying. The enemy shows no mercy even to those who beg for mercy. He feels a blade penetrate his leg, and before he drops to one knee, he sees that most of his men are captured or dead.

Smith hears quiet, and he sees that the fighting has stopped. He now realizes that he is kneeling in the middle of a circle, surrounded by the enemy. He reaches into his shirt pocket and pulls out the necklace of his beloved Analisa. He looks at it, brings it to his lips, and says, "I'm sorry." Then the same large man he had seen on the hill steps into the circle, walks up to Smith, and says, "I am General Picard Harris, Commander of the Kaisoshosuko Dark Forces, and who am I addressing. Smith looks at him and says, Colonel Horatio Smith, Commander of the Elenni Battalion, that you massacred without honor. General Harris backhands Smith across the mouth and stands there smiling, Smith doesn't see the war mallet coming at his head, but he feels it.

Colone Smith regains consciousness and feels excruciating pain in his wrists and feet. He shakes his head to try and clear his vision and finds himself hanging in the Air and nailed to an X-brace. He looks up and sees General Harris sitting astride a horse, looking down at him.

"It's about time you woke up, Colonel Smith. I was getting ready to leave." Would you please take a moment to gaze upon your men?" and gestures with his hands for him to look left?

Smith looks to his left and sees his men are nailed to actual X-braces along the road like himself. He also sees that some are dead and others are dying. Smith watches the last of his men being raised like himself.

Harris holds up a small delicate necklace in his fingers, and Smith knows right away it is the necklace that he had given his betrothed Analisa and then took from her mutilated burnt body in the church.

Harris holds it up, looks at it, says, "Analisa, such a pretty name. She must have been a good-looking woman," and laughs. He lets the necklace slide from his fingers onto the ground. Smith watches as the General's horse steps on it, burying it in the mud.

The General says, "Farewell, Colonel Smith, enjoy your life or what's left of it," and rides off to join his army. Smith sees that Harris' army must have consisted of at least six battalions and now knows he never stood a chance. His only thought is, "Where did they come from?" Then he hears a distinct pop and looks to see the very Air open up. He hangs there staring as he watches the army that just massacred his men step into what looks like a hole in the Air.

Smith then looks down and can see her half-buried chain in the mud. He starts to say, "I'm sorry Anal…." and then hears a sharp whistle, and as he looks up, a crossbow bolt embeds itself in his right eye, killing him instantly.

General Harris hands the crossbow to one of his men and says, "no witnesses." The army of the Kaisoshosuko marches back through the passageway into the Barrens. Once they are all through, the passageway closes.

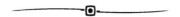

General Harris is on one knee in front of Nova, and Colonel Sayles is behind him. Nova asks, "Well, General, how did it go this time? I see you survived and did not end up like your friend General Heath."

Harris says, "My Kaisoshosuko, it went better than expected. We have approximately seven hundred wounded and only five hundred dead and have gathered over six hundred horses from the enemy.

Nova looks at him and asks, "What of the Elenni Army?

Colonel Sayles says, "My High Priestess, either dead or crucified, and those crucified will not be long for this world.

Nova says, "Very well, the two of you are dismissed, and as they bow and are about to leave, Nova says, "General Harris and Colonel Sayles, you did well. Thank you"

Chapter 28

Carrie Ann Barnes

After Samuel, Reiko and Hikaru return to the Capital, everything is back to normal and somewhat dull. The three of them are called upon to speak to the new recruits about their experiences with the Dark Army and what everyone is now calling the Freaks.

Their routines are the same practically every day when they decide to approach their old instructor, Sargent Higgs, and ask him if he could set up some sparring sessions with his friends. Higgs smiles and says he will ask. The following day they meet in the grotto, and all three remember Wiss, Nubbs, and Bruns, as do the three of them remember Samuel, Reiko, and Hikaru. After everyone is reintroduced, Bruns walks up to Samuel, shakes his hand, says, "Thank you," and then says, "Captain, I have been waiting for a rematch," and smiles. The seven of them agree to meet twice a week to practice and hone their skills. After the meeting, the four of them are at their favorite café and drinking tea. When they all agree to refrain from using their *Chirakas* and train normally if the way they handle their weapons is considered normal

Reiko continues to teach Carrie the art of hand-to-hand combat and how to defend herself. Then one day, Reiko decides to call on her old drill instructor Master-At-Arms Sargent Vernon Higgs. She sends him a note and asks him to meet her in town at a cafe. Higgs comes toward them, and when Carrie sees him, she says, "Oh My God, what mountain did they make him from?" Higgs steps up to their table, comes to attention, and salutes Captain Takahashi. Reiko returns his salute, shakes his hand, and offers him a seat. Reiko introduces Carrie, and then they go through the usual pleasantries, and finally, Higgs says, "Congratulations on your field promotion Captain Takahashi, May I ask why you called me here?"

Reiko looks at Higgs and says, "I would like to ask you a favor?"

Higgs answers, "What might that be, Ma'am?"

"Sargent Higgs, I would like you to teach Miss Carrie Ann Barnes here the finer points in fighting with concealed weapons and, if need be, to be able to incapacitate someone if the occasion should arise." What say you, Sargent Higgs, would you be willing to help out your favorite recruit?"

Higgs starts laughing, which makes both Reiko and Carrie smile. He clears his throat and says, "Ma'am, as a favor to you. I would be more than honored to teach Miss Barnes what I know, but only under two conditions."

"Two conditions Sargent Higgs, and what might those be?"

Higgs clears his throat again and says, "One, I can only teach Miss Barnes in my off time. /The reason for this is that I have a batch of recruits at the stages of defining what weapon they will favor, and two, I would like you, Ma'am, to stop by the field on occasion and demonstrate your finer talents in the longbow. Those are my two conditions. Ma'am."

Reiko laughs and says, "Sargent Higgs, I accept your offer, and as a future reference, you don't need to make bargains for me to stop by your training field to give a demonstration. Please feel free to call on me if I am not on assignment, is that understood, Master-At-Arms Sargent Vernon Higgs!"

Higgs smiles and then stands. He salutes her and says, "Yes, Ma'am," He turns to Carrie and says, "Miss Barnes, we'll meet tonight after dinner and wear something you won't mind if it gets dirty." He faces Reiko again, salutes, says, "Ma'am," and walks off.

Carrie looks at Reiko and says, "I thought we were friends," She smiles and then asks, "What did you get me into?"

Reiko smiles back and replies, "The best damn instructor in the Imperial Army, now finish your tea.

They finish their tea, and as Reiko walks with Carrie to where Sargent Higgs is instructing his recruits in the more delicate art of humiliation. She says, "Whatever Sargent Higgs asks you to do, no matter what it might be, do not hesitate. Higgs might seem unorthodox, but trust me, it will benefit you whatever he asks of you. Whatever you might have heard about Sargent Higgs, please do not give it a second thought because he is a professional, and one more thing, you never want to be late. Higgs continues to drill them, or as Reiko sees it, showing them their vulnerabilities, and she remembers her lessons, which brings a smile to her face. Sargent Higgs is finishing the lesson when he sees Reiko and Carrie standing off to the side. He yells at his troops to fall in, and when they see Reiko, they murmur. She hears a couple of them say, *Reaper of Souls*, and that is when Higgs tells them to shut up and yells, "Officer on the Field!" they all come to attention. He is about to dismiss them, but before he does, he says, "If I hear so much as a peep out of any of you, that will be a peep you and your squad will regret!" now dismissed. Higgs tosses the squad leader a clay pot and tells him what to do with it.

Higgs walks up to Reiko and Carrie; Higgs salutes her and says, "Ma'am." Reiko returns his salute and says, "Sargent Higgs." While they walk to Higgs' private training area, Higgs mentions to Reiko that the recruit rosters are filling up both as Squires and Field troops. Reiko is not surprised, seeing that the Dark Army invaded the Empire. They arrive at Higg's private training area, and Reiko takes the cue. She says to Sargent Higgs, "She is all yours," and looks at Carrie, "good luck," kisses her on the cheek, and she leaves.

The two of them enter the area, and without hesitation, he gently grabs her wrist and walks her to the middle of the training area, and then he asks her to remove her clothes except for her lower undergarments. Though a little embarrassed, she remembered what Reiko told her and does what she is asked. With her clothes gone, she stands perfectly still as Higgs walks around her several times and gently touches her in different places.

Satisfied, he stops facing her and asks her to stand to feel comfortable and try to be balanced. She does just that, and then he asks, "May I?" and she says, "Yes." Higgs takes a closed fist and places it against her chest between her breasts. He gently pushes, and she stumbles back and is a little surprised that she fell back so quickly. She again stands before him, and he asks, "May I?" She says, "By all means, Sargent Higgs."

He places his hand on her lower stomach and lower back and pushes with his hands but with more force than before. She feels her back crack, and the muscle aches slightly diminish. He steps behind her and tells her to wrap her arms across her chest. She does, and he wraps his arms around her upper body, lifts her into the Air, and then jerks her body. She feels her bones crack and most of her aches disappear. He puts her down, moves to stand in front of her, squats, and gently places one hand on her upper thigh and the other on her foot, moves her leg out a bit and turns her foot just so. He then does the same thing to her other leg and foot, standing back in front of her and saying, "Now, let's begin!" He shows her the basic techniques of standing and her legs and feet placement.

Over the next few months, Carrie religiously trains with Sargent Higgs in the grotto, and every night she comes home exhausted and with a few more bruises. Over time, her stamina increases, and she is no longer as tired as she used to be and is ending their sessions with fewer bruises. She has also become quite proficient and swift in her hand-to-hand combat training.

One night after training, she asks, "Sargent Higgs, I know I shouldn't ask you this, but when do you think I will be ready to use actual weapons in fighting."

Higgs smiles and tells her, "Don't worry, Miss Barnes. That training phase will be coming soon, so please be patient."

Two weeks later, she steps into the grotto and sees Higgs. She starts to remove her clothes when he tells her, "Leave your clothing on, Miss Barnes." For the next three months, they spar religiously. Higgs is impressed with her fortitude, and they quickly move from the usual wooden training weapons to the actual weapons. While they spar, Higgs never hurts her but would poke her intentionally with the tip of a knife enough to get her attention and explain how she left herself open. Higgs discovers that Carrie is the type of person who seldom forgets, so he decides to step up her training. He throws things at her that always surprise her, especially when she thinks she has figured something out; there is always something new.

One night after a vigorous sparring session, Higgs stands in front of her and says, Miss Barnes, we have been training together quite some time, and I would like to know if it would be okay to start calling you by your given name, of Carrie?" Carrie smiles and says, "Sargent Higgs, after what you have put me through over the last several months, I would be honored if you called me by my name," and she smiles.

Then Higgs says, "Yes, Ma'am. Carrie, and then asks her, "Do you trust me?"

She says, "Yes."

Higgs says to her, "Please stand and remove all her clothes, even your lower undergarments. She does as he asks, and he proceeds to show her, in great detail, the fundamentals and the advantages of hiding a concealed weapon on a woman's body and points out a few places for concealing a weapon. Higgs tells her to get dressed in one piece of clothing at a time and pay attention. She does, and he places certain small items on her body. Once she is fully dressed, he asks her to move around the grotto and then asks how the weapons feel, and she replies, "Comfortable like they are not even there."

Higgs says is, "Good," Now for phase two." Carrie looks at him and asks, "What is phase two?" and Higgs replies, "How to get at them and use them without having to remove all your clothes." Carrie laughs, which brings a smile to Higgs' face.

Over the next month, he teaches her how to conceal and use weapons. One night after sparring, he asks, "Carrie, what weapons are your favorites, and which ones do you feel more comfortable with?"

She tells him, "I have always liked the feel of the stilettos, the small throwing disks, and knives. I also like the straight edge, but I can't quite see how I would be able to conceal it."

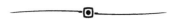

It was a day when Reiko went to Higgs' training session and demonstrated her skills with the longbow to his squires. They were in awe and were all asking her questions when Higgs called them to attention. He then asks her to stop by the grotto after dinner.

It was almost dusk when Reiko gets there, and when she enters, she sees Carrie quickly moving her hands and hearing small thuds and realizes she was throwing small killing disks and small but sharp blades into a training dummy. Higgs comes to attention when he sees Reiko and salutes her. She returns the salute and says, "Carry on." Higgs calls for a break. She stops what she is doing, runs over to Reiko, gives her a big hug, and whispers, "Thank you for introducing me to this beautiful man."

Sargent Higgs walks up to both of them and says to Reiko, "Captain Takahashi, and Reiko holds up her hand and says, Sargent Higgs, this grotto is your house, and as far as I'm concerned, you will call me Reiko when I visit your house especially socially." Higgs goes to say something, and then Reiko holds up her hand and says, "That is an order, Vernon!" Higgs clears his throat and says, Cap... Reiko, I just wanted to thank you and tell you that it has been my pleasure and an honor to instruct Carrie in the finer arts of hand-to-hand combat and the use of concealed weapons. I do not usually get a chance to train one-on-one with an individual, especially one so beautiful and talented as Carrie." He turns to her and says, "Miss Carrie Ann Barnes, please accept these tokens of my appreciation for allowing me the honor of training you." He hands her four wooden boxes, says, "Thank you, Vernon," and kisses Higgs on the cheek. He says to her, "If you ever need anything, do not hesitate," he then steps back, gives Reiko a salute, and says, "Captain, Duty calls, and again Carrie, thank you," and leaves the grotto. Higgs stops, turns, and says, "Captain Sato is fortunate to have you!" Higgs then leaves.

Carrie stands there with her mouth open, looks at Reiko, and says, "How did he know I never said anything." Reiko says, "Carrie, my dear sweet friend, you would be surprised at what our friend, Master Sargent Vernon Higgs, knows about what is happening around here." Then she says, Really, Vernon?" Carrie slaps her arm and tells her to stop it, and they both laugh. Reiko says to her, "So that, you know, that big man there never fails to surprise me. So, let's open those boxes!" They walk over to a bench and sit down. She opens the first one, containing a small delicate harness that fits around her waist and looks like a fancy belt with twelve razor-sharp and very pointed throwing knives. She hands one to Reiko, who can tell that the blade is perfectly balanced for a woman's hand. The next box has two perfectly matched stilettos with strap-on harnesses adjustable for her thigh, calf, or forearm. The third box is slightly heavier and contains another leather belt with several flapped pockets. When she opens one of the flaps, a throwing disk pops up so she can grab it without worrying about cutting herself. She also sees twelve detachable throwing disks attached to the belt to mimic a fancy silver belt. The fourth box is a mystery, and as she opens it, she sees that it contains a delicate handcrafted gold and silver necklace with a small pouch that has some weight. Carrie opens the pouch and lets a straight-edge razor slide into the palm of her hand.

Carrie says, "Now I see why he had me doing those at the time I thought were strange exercises," and puts the necklace on so that the pouch with the straight edge is right below the base of her neck, just above and between her shoulder blades. She then undoes her shirt and secures the chain underneath her breasts and around her back to stop the pouch from sliding down. She stands up and puts on the two leather belts, and then she sees that they can be connected so as not to interfere with grabbing the throwing disks or knives. She then straps one stiletto on her thigh, and Reiko helps her strap the other around her forearm; Carrie pulls her sleeve over it and then puts on the belt with the throwing disks, and the harness asks, "How do I look? Can you tell?" Reiko replies," You look sexy as hell, and unless I saw you put them on, I cannot tell that you are a walking arsenal other than the stiletto strapped to your thigh.

Samuel walks out of the Commander's Office, sees that it is late, and quickens his step to meet up with Reiko, Hikaru, and Carrie when a runner he does not recognize hands him a sealed envelope. He accepts it, dismisses the young runner, and heads over to a bench in the courtyard to read the letter. He turns it over and sees that it is a plain envelope with a smudged wax seal. He breaks the seal to find an elegantly handwritten note and starts to read:

> Samuel,
>
> I was hoping you could meet me later tonight to discuss something important. Would you please meet me at the far end of the warehouses, where the larger transports are kept? It has something to do with your father.
>
> Princess Asami

Samuel refolds the note, places it in his coat's hidden pocket, and heads out to meet with his friends. He finds them drinking tea at their favorite café, sits at the table, and orders a cup for himself. Reiko notices the look on Samuel's face and asks him, "Is anything wrong, Samuel?"

Samuel says, "It's nothing. We'll talk later," and smiles.

Reiko says, "Shall we go? We all know how Higgs can be if you are late."

It is now the four of them as Carrie is now included in sparring sessions, and she spars with Higgs. The four have come to enjoy these sessions with Higgs and his friends. Higgs always sets the rules, and the rules constantly change. Usually, before they start their sparring sessions, the four of them always meet here at their favorite cafe for a bit of hot tea and drinks.

Hikaru leaves money on the table, and they start walking to the grotto. Hikaru and Samuel talk as Reiko and Carrie walk ahead of them, arm in arm. The two of them have become very close friends since Hikaru rescued Carrie from the cages in Shira during the Dark Army occupation. They bonded even more on the journey back to the Capital. The four of them are walking when Samuel senses a call for help from the Princess, as do Reiko and Hikaru, and Samuel tells the others, "The Princess is in danger."

Samuel takes off at a run and heads to a different section of warehouses than where the note asked to meet. Hikaru, Reiko, and Carrie are right behind him, and as they are running, Carrie asks Reiko, "What is wrong?" Reiko tells her that the Princess is in danger. They turn a corner to go down an alley. They hear a scream, and when they reach the end of the alley, it opens up to a larger square, and they see nine hooded men surrounding a young woman in a hooded cloak and another woman holding a sword and keeping the assailants at bay. Samuel sees that the woman with the sword is bleeding. One of the attackers is on the ground and not moving as another attacker yells out, "Why you bitch?" he goes to lunge at the young woman, but he doesn't have a chance before he finds himself pinned against a warehouse wall with one of Reiko's arrows embedded in his head.

There is no hesitation as the four of them engage the hooded attackers, and Samuel says, "I want one of them alive," as he motions to Lenore to protect the Princess. Lenora nods, and he can see that she grimaces slightly but has the Princess behind her. Samuel runs his blade through one assailant and sees another go down, with arrows in his thigh, and his sword arm is pinned like the other to the warehouse wall. He sees Hikaru swinging his battleax while Carrie is at his back and has two stilettos in her hands. Samuel sees that she has taken out one assailant and has both her blades up, blocking and holding back a long knife from her attacker. Without a misstep, he hears Hikaru say, "Duck," and as Carrie does, Hikaru's battleax comes around and takes off the man's head as his body falls backward from the sudden push by Carrie's blades. One assailant sees Lenora's guard drop and charges the two of them. Samuel cannot get to her and sees the brute knock Lenora to the side. The attacker raises his blade and is about to bring it down on the Princess when two things simultaneously happen. He shouts out, "Reiko!" and sees the arrow hit the brute in his hand, piercing it, knocking the blade away, and then he sees the Princess's eyes turn a dark sapphire blue, and a powerful gust of Air comes from out of nowhere and slams the man against the warehouse wall breaking his neck. The fighting is over, and Samuel looks around and sees bodies wearing hoods and Capital Militia uniforms. He hears the Princess say Lenora's name, and Reiko and Carrie are beside her, and he sees Carrie wrapping her wound with torn pieces of fabric to stop the flow of blood while Reiko stays vigilant. Samuel and Hikaru remove the hood of one of the dead and see the piercings, scarring, and tattoos. Hikaru looks at Samuel, and all he says is, "Freaks," and they check the other bodies and discover that they are all Freaks. and that they are wearing the uniforms of the Capital Militia." They both look over at the only living assailant now leaning up against a wall with two arrows sticking out of him, and when they remove his hood, they see that he isn't a Freak but a regular soldier.

Samuel and Hikaru begin to interrogate the prisoner. At first, he doesn't say anything, but with a bit of persuasion, when Hikaru twists an arrow shaft, they discover that he did not know who gave the orders to attack and kidnap the Princess. He knows they were left Capital Militia uniforms at a warehouse, and they were to change them and come here to the Capital to kidnap the Princess and bring her back to Hokida. At that time, the local militia shows up, and a Captain leading the detachment sees the dead bodies strewn about the ground and asks, "What is going on here?" Samuel is about to say something when he feels a hand on his arm, and a feminine voice says, "Samuel, I will handle this."

The Princess walks up to the Captain and pulls back her hood. The Captain immediately recognizes her and drops to one knee, as do his men, and says, "Your Highness." Asami stands in front of the Captain and says, "Captain, would you be so kind as to have your men dispose of these bodies and escort the prisoner over there too, say one of the more undesirable locations. The Captain smiles and bows, says, "Yes, your Highness," and points to his men to grab the prisoner. The Captain's men pick up the other bodies, place them in a wagon, and haul them away. The Princess walks up to the Captain and says, "Captain, can we keep this between us?" The Captain stands straighter and then salutes. The Princess says, "Good, and stands on her tiptoes and places a kiss on the Captain's cheek. Samuel sees him blush slightly, then says, "Yes, your Highness," does an about-face, and goes after his men. In a whisper, Samuel leans down so only the Princess can hear, "Really, a kiss on the cheek, I thought those were just for me. What have they been teaching you in Princess school?" The Princess looks at him and says, "Why Samuel, what do you think?" and elbows him in his side. They go back to Lenora and see that she is up, though supported by Reiko and Carrie. The Princess tells them she must get Lenora back to the Palace. Through back alleys and then through a hidden door, they are soon back in the Princess's private rooms and place Lenora on a bed. Asami escorts the two of them out as Reiko and Carrie stay to help Lenora get out of her blood-stained clothes and lie down. The Princesses physician is now there to address her wounds. She bows to Reiko and Carrie, ushers them out of the room, and closes the door behind them. They are now standing in the outer room, waiting for the physician to tell them how Lenora is doing. Samuel looks at the Princess and asks, "Are you going to tell me what that was all about at the warehouses?" The Princess looks at the four of them and innocently says, "Why Samuel, what in the Goddesses name are you referring to?" Samuel says, "Oh! Let us say about your hazel eyes changing to a dark sapphire blue and then a torrent of Air so powerful that it can lift a man off his feet, slam him into a wall, and break his bones. The Princess looks at each one of them and says, "Oh! Did I not tell you that I can call forth the element of Air when I feel threatened, it must have slipped my mind?" At that moment, the doors open, and the physician tells the Princess that she can see her friend now. The Princess says, "Thank you," then tells the others that she will talk with them in a couple of days and closes the door.

Chapter 29

The Mission To Hokida

Samuel, Hikaru, Reiko, and Carrie return two days later to the Princess's chambers. Samuel knocks on the door, and when the door opens, he sees Lenore standing there. They ask her how she feels, and Lenora tells them she is still sore, but she will live and thanks, Reiko and Carrie. Lenora tells them their quick actions probably saved her life because she had lost a lot of blood from what the physician told her. Before Lenora knocks on the chamber's inner door, she turns and means the four of them, "Thank you."

She knocks twice, then once on the door. On the other side, they hear a feminine voice say, "Come in, please." Lenora opens the door for them, and as they step into the room, Lenora tells the woman standing in the room with her back to them, "I will be right outside, Asi," and she closes the door behind her.

Once in the room, the Princess looks at them, and Carrie sees Princess Asami for the first time, all cleaned up and in the daytime. She is wearing a form-fitting dress, no less, that hugs her slender waist and accentuates her long legs and small but firm bosom. Princess Asami is a beautiful young woman with long straight black hair that hangs a little past her waist. Her hair is pulled back in a braid and interwoven with small mother of pearl teardrops. Her complexion is flawless, and Carrie notices that the Princess does not wear makeup other than a small amount of pink gloss on her lips to highlight their sensual curve. She has a natural beauty that would make any woman jealous, and her eyes have a slight almond shape that is prominent in the Hojiko line. She wears a simple set of pearl earrings and a matching pearl on a gold chain.

The Princess quickly walks up to Samuel and gives him a very tight hug and a kiss on his cheek. Samuel returns the hug in kind and whispers something in her ear. The Princess giggles and takes a step back, then playfully smacks him and says, "Samuel Miro, if I weren't the royal Princess and a lady, I would kick your butt." She hears Hikaru snicker and tells him, "Behave yourself, Hikaru, or I will have Lenora teach you a lesson in swords once she feels better." She smiles again as Hikaru immediately stops snickering. Asami approaches Hikaru, embraces him, and kisses him on the cheek, and she says, "Thank you," Hikaru looks at her and says, "Princess," and does a slight bow. She slaps him on the shoulder and smiles. She steps to Reiko, embraces her a moment longer, kisses her on the cheek, and whispers something in her ear. Reiko laughs, and the Princess steps back and asks, "How in the world do you put up with the two of them?" Reiko says, "It takes many hours of special training." The Princess laughs, and as Hikaru starts to speak, Samuel quietly reminds him of the last time they were together. Hikaru immediately closes his mouth.

Carrie is unsure of what to do when the Princess steps toward her and asks, "You must be Carrie. Your description does not do you justice," and she hugs her. Carrie is surprised by the Princess's actions and feels connected with her. A connection that she has never felt before with anyone other than Reiko, but it also feels different.

Asami tells them to have a seat, and as they sit at a table, the Princess looks at the four friends and tells them that she has a mission and that the Advisor General himself has requested this. The Princess explains the situation when Samuel interrupts her and says, "Excuse me, Asa," and reaches in his jacket pocket, pulls out the letter delivered to him, and slides it across the table. The Princess opens it, reads it, and before she can say anything, Samuel says, "Asa, as long as we have known each other, you have never signed anything with your title or your name. The handwriting is close, and I think this was sent to try and get us as far away from you as possible on the night you were attacked" The Princess says, "I will look into this!"

Now back to the mission, she tells them, "I received this correspondence from one of my informants in Hokida three days ago. She opens the letter and begins to read its contents. When she finishes, she walks over to a brazier and lights the corner of the envelope, so it soon catches fire and is a pile of ash. She looks at the four of them, says, "For our Protection," and sits back down, takes a sip of water, and clears her throat. "Concerning my underground network of informants, only three people know of its existence; the Emperor, your father, Lenora, and now you four. What I am about to tell you must not leave this room. We must keep this to the utmost secrecy."

"Over the past few years, there has been a separation of the two factors of the royal family. When I say factors, I mean the Emperor's followers who supported him completely and his younger brother's followers who thought the Empire would be ruled better under his leadership. The issue that has arisen and the Princess has hinted at, but has no hard evidence, is that the Emperor's brother might have dealings with the Dark Scriptures and is trying to take power from his royal Highness and convert this country to the Guichi-Tanin Religion."

"You four had dealings with the followers of the Dark Scriptures up in Shira, and she looks to Carrie and says, I'm sorry, but I would like to ask you to investigate and, if possible, find evidence to expose the Emperor's brother and as many of his followers as possible. I am checking with my informants to see if they can find anything," She slides a piece of paper across the table and tells them that this is a hotel in Hokida where the Princess knows it is a safe house and will try to help you the best they can.

"If you decide to do this, you would be on your own until evidence is found and returned to me, your father, or the Emperor. Please think about it and let me know by tomorrow." Samuel looks at Hikaru and Reiko and already knows the answer. He looks at the Princess and says, "When do you want us to leave?"

She smiles, knowing he and his friends would not say no. "Let's say in two days now, would you four care to join me for dinner? I know just the place."

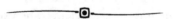

The six of them are finishing with dinner when Lenora excuses herself and leaves the room. She returns with a tray holding a rolled-up scroll, ink and quill, a candle, and red wax. The Princess takes the rolled-up scroll, opens it, signs its bottom, and places her royal signet ring in some melted wax on the bottom of the document. She then blows on the wax, says, "Carrie, if you would be so kind?" and hands the scroll to Carrie. She carefully unrolls it, reads it, and sits there staring at the letter. Reiko takes it from Carrie's hand and looks at it herself. She then clears her throat and starts to read. Reiko skips over the formalities of the letter. She says "that in regards to Carrie Ann Barnes's rigorous training with Master-at-Arms Sargent Vernon Higgs, she recognized and licensed as a Master in Small

Arms. Per the request from the Advisor General that Miss Carrie Ann Barnes is declared a Warrant Officer and that she will be reporting to the Royal Princess Asami's Royal Guard on this day in the year of his Royal Emperor Hisa Hojiko.

She then looks down at the bottom of the letter and sees two signatures, one of the Princess herself and the other of the Advisor General. Carrie looks up, and Asami calls for a toast to the newly appointed Warrant Officer Carrie Ann Barnes of the Royal Guard for the Royal Princess. "I must leave you now; duty calls, but please stay and enjoy the rest of the evening." The four of them start to rise when Asami waves them off and says, "Before you leave, stop by," She exits with Lenora leading the way, and they notice two others walking on each side of the Princess.

The four of them are walking through the west wing of the Royal Palace and the royal family's private quarters. They pass through numerous checkpoints until they come to a room where the Princess is waiting for them. They enter, and the doors are closed behind them.

The Princess greets all of them as friends, and then the Princess tells Samuel and Hikaru to find something to do, and she asks Reiko and Carrie to follow her. They go into another room and close the door behind them. Hikaru looks at Samuel and says, "A game, "They sit themselves down and begin a game of "Kudaki." Two and a half games later, the doors open, and the three women enter the room. Samuel and Hikaru both notice all three of them smiling.

Asami speaks first, "I made a wise choice in making Carrie a Warrant Officer in my Royal Guard. Samuel and Hikaru, Reiko will fill you in. Samuel takes the hint. He walks up to the Princess and places his forehead against hers, and she says, "Be careful, my Champion," and Samuel responds, "A champion always is, My Princess." They hug, and then the Princess hugs each of them individually and tells them to be wary that there are forces out there that will try to destroy them. "All of you, please return to me." Before they exit the room, the Princess calls out, "Captain Sato! Hikaru stops at the door and says, "Yes, Princess?" Asami asks him, "When will you make an honest woman of my newly appointed Warrant Officer?" Hikaru blushes deeply and starts to stammer; Princess

Asami giggles, and as Samuel reaches in to close the door, he sees the look of worry on the Princess' face. He smiles and mouths the words, "Don't worry," and sees her smile; then and only then does he close the door.

The Princess waits a minute, returns to her room, and calls for Lenora in a calm but cold tone. She says, "Lenora spread the word. I want every ear in the Empire on the ground listening for anything that pertains to my uncle."

Two days later, Samuel, Reiko, Hikaru, and Carrie are riding out of the Capital just before sunrise to begin their journey northeast to the city of Hokida, where the Emperor's brother, the appointed Governor of Hokida Prefecture, resides.

They make camp and talk about a game plan and their cover story. Reiko and Samuel agree that Carrie and Hikaru should appear as a married couple looking to establish a new supplier for their wares. Samuel and Reiko will do the same because two couples as business partners will help maintain their cover.

Ten days later, in the early evening, they arrive at the gates of Hokida and are immediately taken back by the conditions of the city. Filth and squaller are all around the gates, and as they head farther into the city, there is very little change. They find the inn the Princess had recommended to them in the Merchants Quarter and decide to begin in the morning. The innkeeper is an older man, and the four of them first notice the tattoos on his forearms of sea monsters and naked women with fishtails. He seems pleasant enough and is happy to have two young couples staying at his establishment. He shows them to their rooms and tells them the dining room will open in an hour. Before heading downstairs, Samuel asks, "Has Lenora stopped by here recently?" The innkeeper says, "Yes, she had just the other day." He gives a quick nod and heads downstairs.

They unpack, and an hour later, they go down for dinner and have an enjoyable meal of roasted duck, rice, and vegetables. They are having some tea and relaxing when a local militia walks in and starts talking with the proprietor. He points to them, and the militia walk over to their table, and the Sargent asks them, "What business do you have in Hokida?"

Samuels stands and answers for them, "Sir, we are up here visiting your fine city to acquire merchandise for my brother here and his wife. They want to establish a wholesaler for goods shipped to the Capital."

The Sargent asks, "Let me see your papers."

Samuel reaches into his inside shirt pocket, pulls out their papers, and hands them to the Sargent. The Sargent quickly looks at them and hands them back, saying. "Everything seems in order, as he hands back their papers. "Do not cause any problems in our fine city, understood?"

Samuel replies, "Yes. Sir"

After the militia leaves, the innkeeper comes to their table and apologizes, telling them, "I'm sorry, it's the law, and I have to report strangers to the local militia, or they could shut me down and make me pay a fine."

Samuel assures him it is not a problem as Samuel pays the bill. Then the four of them head up to their rooms while whispering. Reiko and Carrie are just about to head to the other room when Samuel clears his throat and says, "I know it is a little unorthodox, but wouldn't it look better, seeing that Hikaru and Carrie are married, should stay in the same room?" Hikaru starts to speak when Carrie grabs his hand, leads him into their room, and closes the door.

Samuel and Reiko go into the other room, and after talking for a bit, they decide to get some sleep. Reiko does not give it a second thought as she begins to undress. Samuel is sitting on the bed, removing his boots, when he looks at Reiko and sees how she has grown up. She has filled out in all the right places since she was a skinny little fourteen-year-old girl.

Samuel looks at Reiko, and with a smile, he jokingly asks, "Where did those come from?" She looks at him, realizes what he is talking about, and throws her pillow at him, saying, "I bought them at the Officers Cantina." Samuel laughs and finishes getting undressed, as does Reiko, and as she blows out the light, she says. "Good night, Samuel."

The following day the four of them are walking through the Merchants District looking at different wares when a mob of about fifteen men wearing hoods enter the district and start to harass some of the merchants. Vendors try and close their shutters before their wares are stolen or broken. The four see that the hooded mob is soon getting out of control when Samuel, Hikaru, Reiko, and Carrie step back into an alley to allow minimal access to the four of them. They hear a horn and a large militia force enter the Merchants District from both sides, and they immediately squash the mob and haul them away. The vendors in the marketplace start clapping and praising the militia's quick actions.

Samuel and the others are walking around admiring the other merchant's wares when Carrie thinks she sees an old friend from Shira, but when she looks again, the person is gone. Later that day, they head back to the inn just before dinner.

They walk in and find the innkeeper behind the bar polishing some glasses. Samuel asks the innkeeper to bring some hot water as Reiko checks the dining room, and then the four sit at a table away from the entrance and bar. They are all sitting when the hotel manager comes over with hot water. Samuel thanks him and asks, "Who were the militia wearing the strange-looking uniforms that dispersed the mob in the marketplace this morning?" The innkeeper tells them that the governor hired them about nine months ago to keep peace in the city. He tells them it is all for a show because he heard a couple of them talking one night about how they will be taking their turn as the angry mob." Samuel thanks him for the information. The innkeeper goes back to the bar and continues polishing glasses.

Reiko keeps an eye on the door as Samuel pours everyone some tea. Once everyone has a cup of tea, Carrie says, "Did you see those militias? What were they wearing? They almost looked like the military uniforms of the fucking Dark Army!" Hikaru places his hand around her shoulders to reassure and calm her trembling.

Samuel says, "Carrie, I know this is difficult, and if this is going to bother you, you can stay here at the inn while we continue our mission. Do you think you can keep it together?"

Carrie looks at all three and says, "I'm sorry, and yes." Then Carrie says, "I don't know if it was my imagination or the light was playing tricks on my eyes, but when the military started hauling the hooded ones out of the district, I could have sworn I saw a red robe just on the outside of the square hiding in the shadows. Hikaru says, "If that is the case, we will have to be careful and only go out in pairs." They all agree.

Beatrice is standing back in the shadows making sure everything goes according to plan, and then she sees someone familiar in the crowd and steps out of the shadows. She feels a slight pain in her side and pulls back her hood to look again to ensure that what she sees is real. Beatrice cannot believe that here in Hokida, the one who stabbed her and standing right next to him is the one bitch she has always despised, that bitch Carrie Barnes. She will never forget how she was about to kill her when that bastard Imperial soldier interfered and stabbed her. Beatrice continues to feel the ache in her side. She looks closer and wonders if the other two are the same ones she saw when she escaped Shira.

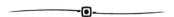

They have been at it for over a week, looking around and talking with the locals. Nothing unusual, life is good, the city's overseer Lord Tao is good to his people, etc. Hikaru and Carrie have been canvasing the upper-class residences all morning and are about to head back to the inn when a young boy approaches them. The boy tells them he has a friend that can give them the answers to their questions.

The young boy says, "Please follow me, and I will take you to my friend." They look at each other, and Hikaru shrugs his shoulders and says, "Can't hurt to check it out," They follow the boy back through some alleys and follow him to a large warehouse on the backside of some rich person's mansion. The young boy pulls back a loose panel and swings it out of the way. He motions for them to enter and that his friend is inside. Hikaru looks at Carrie and says, "Let's just take a quick look and then go back to the inn and tell Samuel and Reiko what we found." Carrie says, "Okay," and they enter the building. They hear voices and carefully move closer when they get inside and hide behind some crates. While they listen, they do not notice that the young boy has slid the panel back into place and secured it.

Hikaru and Carrie hear, "Sire, if we move too soon without having our forces in place, it could be disastrous."

"I don't care; as far as I'm concerned, the Emperor needs to be removed along with his Advisor General, and don't worry about our forces. The Dark Scriptures High Priest of Hokida has guaranteed my victory."

They listen to this exchange when they see the young boy who led them here walk up to Lord Tao and point to where they are hiding.

Hikaru looks at Carrie and tells her, "Let's get out of here." They move to the panel and realize that the exit is blocked. Then they hear, "Please don't leave so soon, Captain Sato and Miss Barnes. The party is just getting started."

Hikaru looks at Carrie and nods; they both stand and see men in Dark Army uniforms holding swords, battle axes, and spears.

The leader sees that they do not have weapons and asks them to come with him. They follow the leader when one of the Dark soldiers places his hand on Carrie's shoulder and pushes her. Hikaru turns and tells the man; I wouldn't do that again if you know what's good for you" The one soldier laughs and pushes her again. Hikaru tells him, "I warned you not to do that," turns and smashes the soldier, breaking his nose and jaw.

Before any of them know what is happening, Carrie moves quickly and pulls out one of her stilettos and, very quickly, stabs two of their guards in the neck, and as they go down, they drop their weapons. Hikaru snatches an axe and sword and swings them to take out two more. The warehouse breaks out in turmoil as Carrie moves with agility and speed, throws three razor-sharp knives, and imbeds them in the throats of three soldiers closest to her. She then flicks her wrist and a second stiletto is in her hand, stabbing two more.

Hikaru drops the sword and grabs another dropped battleax. Carrie sees the silver flash pass across his eyes, and he begins twirling the axes, as she witnessed before, and is immediately slicing off body parts and maiming others. The two battle axes become spinning blades of death. The bloodshed is fierce as they are forces to be reckoned with, and it seems that two more bodies take place for everyone that falls.

Hikaru is holding his own as the bodies continue to pile up near him and as he keeps moving to keep others at bay. Carrie is moving with him and defends his back. She silently thanks Sargent Higgs for his training, knowing she can help protect the one she loves. Suddenly, out of nowhere, a cross-bolt catches Carrie in her thigh, and she drops to one knee and falters. Though the pain is excruciating, Carrie stands back up, continues to fight, and realizes that she and Hikaru have separated. She throws two small knives and takes down two of the three soldiers coming at her. She then sees the crossbowman aiming at Hikaru, and she calls his name to warn him, "Hikaru!" just as the bolt is released. He sees it and turns his body while deflecting a sword-bearing down on him, but the turn of his body is not enough as the bolt catches him in his side. She sees the bolt hit him, throws her last blade with precision at the soldier with the crossbow, and catches him straight in the eye. She knows he is dead, and his finger spasms and involuntarily pulls the crossbow's trigger, releasing the loaded bolt. The third member of the three attacking her kicks out with his foot and drives the bolt deeper into her thigh; she screams in excruciating pain and drops one of her stilettos. She goes to pick it up when she sees her assailant is suddenly standing over her with his blade raised but is motionless. He falls forward, and she sees a crossbow bolt sticking out of the back of his head.

Hikaru sees what has just happened with Carrie, and he desperately tries to cut a path through the carnage to reach her. The wound in his side is bleeding severely and taking its toll. The blood loss causes him to stumble. Several men that were holding back see this and rush him at once. Two of them hit Hikaru low, binding up his legs, as the other two try to hit him high and disarm him. Hikaru's legs get entangled with the two who hit him low. He swings the ax and removes the arms of one of his attackers while the other desperately struggles and wrestles him to the ground. Hikaru goes down, and when he does, they quickly disarm him. Wounded, the soldiers kick and punch him into unconsciousness.

Carrie sees what is happening to her beloved and desperately tries to make her way to where he is now lying unconscious. She has lost her stilettos and is out of throwing blades, so she pulls out her straight edge and maims and disfigures anyone in her path as she tries desperately to get to Hikaru's side. Carrie swings her straight edge with precision and slices two more throats. Herself drenched in blood from her victims, she makes her way over to Hikaru, and just before she reaches him, her foot slips on the blood that has saturated the floor, and she goes down on one knee, and then she hears a voice yell out, "Stop that bitch!"

She feels at her belt and grabs her last three throwing disks as she drops to one knee. She throws all three razor disks at the man who shouted, and she hears him scream, knowing that one of them has hit its mark. She feels several hands grabbing at her and punches hitting her body. She lashes out with two hand jabs and kills two of her attackers with finger jabs to their eyes. She sees or feels the pommel of a sword or something bash the side of her head, and she falls to the floor.

Lord Tao holds a cloth to his cheek and reaches behind the bookcase to release a latch to a sliding bookcase that hides a stairway that leads down underneath the warehouse. Hikaru and Carrie are unceremoniously bound and carried down the stairway to the cavern below. When Carrie passes Tao, he says, "I want that bitch kept alive!" The bookcase is slid back into place, and the latch clicks.

Chapter 30

The First Chosen

Juliette Tate was born into slavery, as were her mother and grandmother. The lineage of the Tate name has never known any other type of life. Juliette was strapped to her mother's bosom to suckle at her breast while her mother worked long hours in the fields. When Juliette got older and could walk independently, she was required to help, whether taking water to the others while they worked in the fields or bringing them small snacks to help them keep up their strength throughout the day. In her early teens, she started to work beside her mother and grandmother.

One sweltering day, as Juliette was working the fields, her mother and grandmother noticed that Juliette was sweating, and her shift was clinging to her body, highlighting her figure. While everyone was moving along to start cultivating a new field, her mother and grandmother were tilling the soil and picking up missed or dropped crops. Juliette's mother tells her to leave the fields, go directly back to their hut, and not talk to anyone. If anyone asks why she is leaving the fields, she is to tell them that she has had too much sun. Juliette does as she is told and does not meet anyone on her way back to their hut.

The sun is just setting when Juliette's mother and grandmother return to the hut. While her grandmother prepares their evening meal. Juliette's mother sits down and explains that she must start wrapping her breasts to lay flat against her chest. She must also wear heavy cotton padding and strapping to stop the monthly blood flow when a young girl becomes a woman. Once she becomes a young woman, she is considered old enough to start childbearing. The landowners want to impregnate the young women because their slave stock will grow nine months later, and the cost is minimal other than room and board.

Juliette does not understand completely, but she does as her mother has requested. Days pass into months, and she sees her childhood friends disappear for weeks at a time. She asks her mother about it, and her mother tells her to be quiet and not concern herself with the other girls or families.

One night under a full moon, Juliette, her mother, and grandmother are at the estate hot springs bathhouse, one of the few luxuries the slaves are allowed only once every two weeks. Juliette is not wearing her bindings and is relaxing in the water of the springs when suddenly the door slides open, and one of the young nobles from the estate enters the bath. He was not expecting anyone to be here so late. Though Juliette is more surprised and she lowers herself deeper into the water. The young noble is twenty years old and one of the few masters who treat the field slaves fairly. Juliette slowly works her way back to the far end of the springs while staying covered up to her chin. The young nobleman stands in the doorway in only a loincloth and slightly sways. The three of them can tell that he has been drinking, and they know that a drunk lord is dangerous. He takes a few stumbling steps into the springs and walks towards Juliette.

He is close to her now and stares at her, and then he seems to remember her. He says he remembers seeing her working with her mother and grandmother in the fields. He always thought that she had a pretty face if you cleaned the mud and grime off and also felt that she was a little flat-chested for his liking. He finds himself staring at her. Juliette is no more than eighteen or so years, and she knows what he has in mind. He continues to stare and reaches out to grab her arm.

Juliette's mother approaches the young Lord and begs him not to harm her daughter. The young Lord tells her mother to shut up and says, "How dare you speak to me, slave. I am a lord, and I will take what I want!" and slaps her across the face and then shoves her aside. Juliette's mother falls against some of the stones, hitting her head. Juliette's grandmother rushes to her daughter's side.

The young Lord takes another step closer to Juliette, grabs her upper arm, and forces her to stand up. When she is standing out of the water, the young Lord is surprised, as he now sees a set of breasts he previously thought did not exist. He forces her to stand up completely, and as she stands there with the water below her waist, he is more surprised to see that she has a patch of hair down there.

He laughs and says, "All this time, I thought you were slow in maturing and probably stupid, but now I see that your mother was trying to deceive my father, the Lord of the Manor. I will be reporting this, but before I do, why don't we have some fun, and maybe, just maybe, I will ask my father to go easy on your mother and grandmother.

While holding her upper arm, he stands up completely. The water is just above mid-thigh on him, and he reaches down and pulls off his loincloth.

Juliette is surprised when she sees his manhood for the first time and notices it pointing at her. She remembers seeing the other little boys growing up, but they did not look like this. Juliette is scared and does not know what to do. She takes another step back and feels a medium-sized stone under the water with her foot. She tries to retain and maintain her modesty, and she sits back down as he still holds her arm.

The young Lord is getting very angry because this young girl, this slave, is defying him, and her being only a slave, should want to have this young Lord desiring her to bear his offspring. He applies pressure on her arm and forces her to stand up again. Before she stands, she reaches down to grab the stone.

The young Lord sees the stone in her hand and says, "Slave, how dare you raise your hand to me, do you dare to strike your Lord and master. I could have you flayed just for raising your hand to me; put down that rock NOW!" he demands

Juliette drops the rock, and the young Lord strikes out with his hand and slaps her across her face. Juliette tries to stagger back, but the young Lord still holds her upper arm. She tastes blood from her lip as the young Lord stands fully erect, admiring her breasts and body. The young Lord grabs her breasts and reaches down to force himself into her with his other hand to steal her virginity when she sees her grandmother approaching him with a large rock raised in her hands. The young Lord sees the look on Juliette's face and begins to turn to see what it is, and before he can say or do anything, her grandmother smashes the young Lord in the back of his head with the rock.

He releases Juliette as his knees buckle. He reaches up and touches the back of his head, and when he pulls his hand away, there is blood on his fingers. He sees Juliette's grandmother standing with the rock still in her hands, and then she drops it. He grabs her grandmother by the neck, choking her, forces her head underwater, and says, "You crazy fucking bitch, I will fucking kill you!"

Juliette sees her grandmother struggling desperately to breathe as her face begins to turn blue. Juliette tries to pull the young Lord off her grandmother, but he shoves her away and continues to strangle her grandmother. Juliette, now frantic, reaches into the water to pick up the large stone she held earlier, raises it as high as possible, and brings it down forcefully on the young Lord's head. She hears the stone crack his skull and feels the spray of blood on her face, hair, and upper body. The young Lord's hands are no longer around her grandmother's throat, and he is floating face down in the spring. Juliette rushes over to her grandmother, who is coughing, and spitting up water, as she helps her out of the spring and sits her down on its edge.

Juliette hears a moan, sees her mother slowly getting up while rubbing her head, and notices blood coming from her temple. Her mother looks at the young Lord floating in the water, Juliette, and asks, "What did you do?" Juliette looks at her mother and says, "Grandmother hit him with a rock so that he wouldn't hurt me!" He grabbed grandmother and was choking her, and he was killing her, and I could not stop him, so I hit him with a stone." Her mother is dumbfounded by the body of the young Lord, floating face down in the hot springs.

Juliette's grandmother gets up slowly and goes over to the young Lord's body. She turns him over, sees the blank stare in his lifeless eyes, and knows that the young Lord is dead. Juliette's mother is still sitting there trying to collect her thoughts, and her grandmother tells Juliette to give her a hand with the body. They push his body against the larger stones and lift him. They get the young Lord on the top of the larger rocks and position him such that when they roll him, his body should fall behind the stones. When they push, the body luckily falls into the crevasse between the rocks hiding it from sight. They walk back to the steps turning to check and look to see if there is any indication of the young Lord's body behind the larger stones. Neither can tell just by looking that a dead body is there. Juliette's mother, still groggy, starts cleaning up around the hot springs. Soon all three of them are working together, picking up the young Lord's clothes and personal items to make it look like he was never here.

They tell Juliette to get back in the springs, thoroughly bathe, wash her hair, and get all the blood off her body. Juliette does as she is told and steps out of the springs to dry off. Her mother and grandmother start rummaging through discarded clothes. Some clothes belong to other slaves, while some seem to have been left by lesser noblewomen. They take some decent items and know that getting caught with them is a severe violation and could subject them to ten lashings with the whip. Juliette quickly wraps her breasts to bind them and slips on her slave clothes. Her grandmother picks up the young Lord's clothes and wraps them tightly in one of their towels. While covering the clothes, she hears the clinking of metal, searches through the pockets, and finds a small leather purse with one gold, two silver, and eight copper coins. She rewraps the clothes, and the three leave the spring hurrying back to their slave hut, hiding the wrapped clothes between them.

Once there, Juliette's mother tells her to take off her slave shift and unbind her breasts. Her mother notices tiny droplets of blood on her bindings and tells her to throw them in the fire. She stands there naked and shivering, then moves closer to the fire. Her grandmother moves with lightning speed. Soon Juliette is putting on and taking off clothes at a fast rate. After several changes, the changing of stops. Her mother and grandmother are just standing there looking at her. They both smile and toss the rest of the clothes into the fire.

Her mother runs a stiff brush through her wet hair and pins it off her neck while her grandmother dabs her fingers in a small bowl containing the juice from berries and runs her fingers across her lips. They hold up a mirror, and Juliette sees herself transformed into a beautiful young woman. Her mother wraps a scarf around her head, and suddenly, Juliette is an upper-class lady rather than a lowly slave girl. Juliette finds herself staring at her reflection in the mirror.

Her mother sits her down and tells her they do not have much time and that Juliette must be far from the manor before sunrise. She starts quizzing her about the little secret sessions they had when her mother and grandmother taught her to read and write. They also told her that she could read and write if they knew and that being a slave was punishable by death. Her grandmother disappears from the room and returns a few minutes later. She takes Juliette's hand, places the small purse with coins they found in the Lord's clothes and puts it in her hand. Juliette somehow senses this is goodbye and embraces her grandmother in a tight hug. She then turns to her mother, and she embraces her as well. She asks her mother, "Do I have to go?" and her mother tells her that she must go and go now.

She explains to Juliette, "If you don't leave, and they find the body, and they will find it, hopefully, later than sooner, they will blame the three of us because we were the last ones on the designated roster for entering and using the springs. Your grandmother and I agree that this is the best thing for you, my darling daughter. We love you very much and pray to the Goddesses to watch over you. We love you, and now you must go." Her grandmother tells her, "My sweet, beautiful granddaughter, get as far away as possible, do not look back, and live your life. You are destined for greater things than to be a pregnant slave girl, bearing other slaves for our Lords. Your mother and I would not be able to live with ourselves if something happened to you."

The Overlord of the estates will want to make an example of your mother and me, blame the two of us, and hold us responsible for his son's death. Now, you must go before it gets too light outside. Her mother tells her that when you leave, you are to walk out of here with her face only slightly covered so that if anyone sees her, they will think you are a lesser noble lady leaving from a session with one of the male slaves.

Juliette steps out of the hut, looks around and doesn't see anyone. She gets to the end of the path, stopping to look back one last time. Her mother and grandmother stand in the doorway, smiling at her and then closing the door. She hears the sound of the lock latch clicking into place. Holding her head high, and just as the sun rises, she walks through the estate gates and does not look back, nor does she cry.

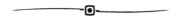

It had been four weeks since Juliette walked out of the estate, and one afternoon, while she was drinking some tea at an outdoor café, disaster struck. She hears a town crier shout out the news of a young nobleman found murdered. They found the body because the slaves who could use the springs smelled something, retched, and discovered the body.

Juliette sits there as the crier continues with how the Lord is offering a reward of one hundred gold pieces to return the young slave suspected of killing his son. Secondly, she hears him shout about two slaves, a grandmother and a mother who had worked the estates for many years will be charged with the murder. The authorities believe that the missing slave girl was responsible for his death. A massive search has begun to find the missing girl. The crowd looks at a sketch of the young girl, and Juliette sees that the drawing details slightly resemble her. She decides it is enough to raise suspicions if anyone were to compare the two of them together. She noticed that the drawing has of her with small breasts, which might be to her advantage.

Juliette is in her room that night crying softly over her mother's and grandmother's fate, and she knows that she must abandon them. Now, for the second time in her life, she has to leave quietly in the night and be quick about it. She prays to the Goddesses to protect her mother and grandmother.

She has completed packing the few belongings she now owns, climbs out her window to the house's roof next door, and is soon down on the ground. She quickly walks away but is not so quick as to draw attention. She has her bag, some coins, and a small stiletto that she purchased after being hired as a waitress. She walks through the city gates and does not look back.

The sun is rising, and she realizes that she has walked most of the night and decides to stop and rest. She is sitting on a roadside bench when she sees she is at a crossroads. She sits there and looks at the signs trying to decide which direction to take when she hears a soft voice say, "The Barrens," as if it floats in the Air. Her mind made up, she gets up and starts walking in a northerly direction. Soon weeks have passed, and any coin she might have had is gone. Occasionally, she can grab an occasional apple off a tree and water from a stream. It is not much, but it keeps her going. Though she might be hungry, she keeps doing the exercises her mother taught her before going to the fields every morning. These exercises help keep her toned and fit.

She follows a road, which keeps her traveling in a northwestern direction. She continues along the road and sees what she thinks are wooden crosses lining the sides of the road. When she gets closer, she sees that bodies are nailed to the x-braces and in different stages of decomposition. She walks up to the first one and sees a shaft sticking out of its eye. As she stands there, the clouds allow the sun through, and a quick flash of something in the dirt catches her eye. She looks down and sees a gold chain half-buried in the dried mud. She uses her knife and digs down, and it finally comes free. She looks at a gold locket, and when she opens it, she sees a picture of a beautiful young woman; when she wipes away the dirt, she sees the name "Analise." She puts the locket in her pocket and decides to get off the road and make her way across the open field. She is close to the remnants of a once smoldering village and reads the message painted on the outer wall, "No Trespassing - Punishable by Death." She decides not to enter the town and continues north to what looks like a gorge. She continues walking through the field, and then she trips and falls. She looks at what she might have tripped on, and then she sees a skull partially sticking out of the ground. She stands and then notices that the field has systematically placed mounds of dirt. She continues walking and then realizes she is walking through a mass gravesite. Startled at her discovery, she turns and decides to run and return to the village. She ignores the words painted on the walls and goes through the burned-out town. She finds herself in the town square, looks at the church, and sees that the steeple has collapsed onto the roof. She finds nothing of use and heads to the Keep.

The gates to the Keep are chained, and she finds a make-shift ladder and scales the walls. She gets over the top and walks along the parapets until she finds the stairs near the gatehouse. She heads down the stairs and into the courtyard and finds a faded red substance on the walls. She walks to the Keep; like the gates, the doors are chained and locked. She knows there is nothing here and turns to leave and sees a mangled pile of metal off to one side. She walks over to it, and as she places her hand on the cold metal, she suddenly gets an image of a beautiful red-headed woman who caused this massive metal gate to warp and bend, and then the image is gone. She feels invigorated and knows that she must find this woman no matter what it takes. She gets back over the wall and leaves the town, and as she walks away, she sees an old signpost leaning against a tree, and the sign on the post reads "Marion" she ignores it and walks between the walls of the village and the mass graves. By mid-day, she is walking along the base of the mountains towards a gorge. At the beginning of a ravine, she sees that the terrain could be treacherous and decides to rest for the night. She curls up under a stunted tree and falls asleep with the small stiletto in her hand. The following day she keeps moving north. Juliette knows something is out there for her because she needs a purpose; she needs a new beginning, and both of those can hopefully be found when she meets the red-headed woman.

She has been walking for three days, then she hears many voices and starts walking faster, almost running. The gorge opens to a wide valley, and she sees thousands of people. Some are milling about, and she sees a line going to what looks like an entrance to a cave. Then she smells the food and hears her stomach rumble. She walks through the crowd and sees men and women from all walks of life standing around and waiting patiently for something. She comes upon a cart with food and drink. The woman asks, "Are you here to pay allegiance to the Gods and their High Priestess?" If you are, then you may eat. If not, begone, and I will know if you're lying."

She tells the woman that she is unsure because she does not know what brought her here.

The woman asks her, "How did you hear of this place. Juliette tells her that she heard a voice in the wind that told her to come here. The woman stands there and looks at her and then smiles. Without saying a word, she hands her some food and some water. Juliette says, "Thank you," walks over to a good-sized rock, and sits down.

She is eating her food when she notices that the woman who gave her the food has called a younger girl over, and seconds later, the girl runs off through the crowd. She then sees the young girl running up the ramp to the black precipice and continues to watch as the young girl disappears into the entrance to a cavern. She is distracted and does not see a slightly older girl approach her and tells her that she wants her food. Juliette politely tells her to go away. The girl tells her again that she wants her food and threatens that she will take it if she doesn't hand it over. Juliette ignores her, and as she goes to grab her food, Juliette slaps her hand away, telling her again to go away for a second time. Juliette's clothes are loose-fitting, and the older girl is unaware of how toned and muscular Juliette is. Juliette politely tells her and her friends to go away and explains that she doesn't want to hurt them. The taller girl laughs and is about to grab her food when Juliette suddenly stands and punches the girl in the stomach, and when she does, her food falls to the ground. The girl drops to her knees and then falls forward onto her face in the dirt. The other girls are dumbfounded as they see their leader lying face-first on the ground, unsure if she is breathing. They hear her moan, and Juliette walks away.

She walks past the woman with the cart, and the woman says, "Nice one." She hands Juliette another helping of beef in a flour wrap. The woman tells her if she needs anything or has any questions to see her. She is here daily feeding the ones who come to pledge allegiance to the High Priestess and her Gods.

Juliette has been walking around the grounds, listening and watching, and all she hears about is this "Kaisoshosuko."

Juliette sees the ramp leading up to the cavern entrance and wants to go in, but she is unsure if what she hears is what she wants, even though the tickle at the base of her neck that she can never seem to scratch urges her to go in.

Later in the day, just before sunset, she contemplates what she must do when a robed figure approaches her. She has seen these robed ones talking with small groups of men and women throughout the day. He asks her if she wants to jump ahead of everyone else to see the High Priestess.

Juliette thinks about it for a minute and says, "Yes."

The man leads her up another path, and Juliette sees that this is not leading to the large cavern but past some smaller ones. She is about to say something when he grabs her and forces her into one of them. Juliette struggles, and the robed one is not expecting some girl to be so strong. He slaps her and tells her to stop struggling and that this will go a lot quicker and easier if she co-operates. She sees the man bring his arm back to punch her, and she tightens up her stomach muscles to lessen the impact of his punch. Even though the punch hurt, she is only slightly winded. Her assailant does not know this, and he grabs her top hoping to rip it open, when she headbutts him, causing him to bite his tongue. He yells, and as he stumbles back, he strikes her across the face, and she falls back onto the straw bed. He gets on top of her and slaps her hard across the face a second time, and she becomes slightly dazed as he tries to remove the rest of her blouse. The man tears the rest of her blouse off when he sees her breasts; he cuts away her pants with a knife. He gets anxious and tries to undo his pants underneath his robe as he straddles her. Juliette has a flashback of the young Lord, bringing back her fist and punching him in his manhood. He topples over, and she pushes him off her. She is half-naked, but she grabs the knife, walks behind him, and places the blade against his throat. Though he is in pain, he tells her, "Come on, baby, put down the knife.

I won't hurt you. I just want to have some fun. Why else would a pretty thing like yourself be here paying homage to the Gods?"

Juliette is about to say something when she hears, "Maybe because she wants to worship me and the Gods Guichi and Tanin and the study Dark Scriptures."

The man turns to see who said that, and his face turns white as fear enters his eyes.

Juliette looks up and sees that the woman who has entered the cave and spoken is the beautiful red-headed woman, whom she has never seen before but within a vision. She even finds herself blushing in her presence. The woman walks over to Juliette and places her hand on the same blade Juliette holds to the robed one's throat. She whispers in Juliette's ear, "Not yet," and takes that blade from his throat. The woman helps Juliette stand, and as the men walk past her, she nods her head. Two scary-looking soldiers quickly overpower the man and bind him. Juliette goes to pick up her clothes when the woman tells her, "Leave them; you will not need them anymore." The woman tells her to follow. Juliette looks back, and she sees a dark spot on the front of his robe, and then a black-robed one with a white cloth saturated in what looks like blood walks into the cave, bows to the woman, and then she sees a small black knife that seems to give off black smoke in his hand. She can hear the man screaming for forgiveness and that he is sorry, and then a gut-wrenching scream.

They walk up a different path, and Juliette finds herself heading deeper into the cavern. She then finds herself in a smaller cave lit by candles, and she sees two young women who are identical Twin girls sitting on pillows. They get up and say, "Mistress."

The red-head tells them to draw a bath and to wash the girl. She looks at Juliette and asks her name. She tells her, "Juliette."

"Juliette, the Twins, will take you to get cleaned up, and when you are ready, they will bring you to me, do not fret because you are under my protection." Juliette looks at the beautiful red-headed woman and asks, "Who are you?" Nova chuckles and says, "Why the "Kaisoshosuko," my silly girl, and you may call me Mistress."

Nova stands in front of a large stone throne covered in pillows when the Twins bring Juliette before her. Juliette immediately bows before Nova. "Stand," Nova commands. "Juliette, I am going to ask you some questions. Do you understand?" Juliette answers, "Yes, Mistress" Juliette starts fidgeting, and Nova covers her mouth to hide a smile.

"How did you come to be here?"

Without any hesitation, Juliette tells her about the voice on the wind.

Nova is intrigued and asks, "My Sweetness, do you want to have power"?

Juliette answers, "Yes."

"Do you want to be feared and have people fall before you?"

Juliette answers, "Yes."

Juliette, "Will you be devoted to me and only me?"

Without hesitation, Juliette answers, "Yes."

"My Sweetness, the training you will endure will be strenuous and hard; you may or may not survive. If you decide to accept me and survive the training, the rewards will be plentiful. Do you understand?"

Juliette answers, "Yes, I understand."

"What say, you sweet girl?"

Juliette looks deep into the High Priestess's eyes and sees a devotion, a love, that she has missed, and without any further thought, she says, "Yes."

Nova snaps her fingers, and the two young Twins that Juliette had met before and had washed her suddenly appear, and each of them takes a hand. Nova tells her that the Twins are named Mia and Mae, and they will train her in the arts of exotic pleasure and pain and open her mind to new sensations. They will teach you how to fight with weapons and by using your hands as weapons; and if you survive, you will become a "Chosen," and by becoming a "Chosen," you will be my very personal guard and will not have to answer to anyone but me. Again, I ask you, "What say you, Juliette?"

Juliette stands there, and without hesitation, she says, "Yes."

"Take her away," Nova orders. The Twins lead Juliette deeper into the cave, and Nova hears the distinct pop. She smiles and thinks, hopefully, one down and three to go.

Chapter 31

Exiled

Samuel and Reiko return to the hotel late, and as they walk past Hikaru and Carrie's room, they notice that the light is not on and assume they are probably sleeping. Samuel says, "Let's not wake them; we can talk in the morning."

The following day, Reiko is up, goes to their room, and knocks on the door. She doesn't hear anything, so she tries the door and finds it unlocked. Reiko slowly opens the door and softly calls out to Hikaru and Carrie. When there is no answer, and she doesn't hear anything, she calls out to Samuel. Together, they enter the room and see that Hikaru and Carrie are not in the room, and their beds are still made up. They leave the room and close the door.

Samuel has his katanas hidden underneath his cloak, while Reiko carries her longbow as a walking staff and two quivers holding approximately thirty arrows each inside a pack she has on her back. They have their weapons hidden, and within the hour, they're back on the streets quietly asking questions and making inquiries about their friends. By late, they are no better off and decide to take a break and rethink their plans. They are sitting at an outdoor café drinking tea when a pretty little girl approaches them and asks them if they are looking for their friends. Reiko says. "Yes," and asks, "Do you know where they are?" The little girl says, "Yes, but you must hurry. They are in great danger." The little girl starts walking away and then stops looking at them and waiting. Reiko looks at Samuel as he tosses some coins on the table for their tea, and they follow the little girl.

She leads them into the upper-class residences and then through some alleys until they find themselves in front of a large warehouse on the backside of a mansion. The little girl pulls back a loose panel and swings it back out of the way. She tells Samuel and Reiko, "Inside, you will see a bookcase on the far wall, reach behind the bookcase, and you will find a latch. Turn it, and behind the bookcase is an entrance to a stairway that will lead you down to a cavern, where you will find your friends. "Hurry now; the time is near."

Samuel holds back the panel for Reiko to go through, and when he looks back for the little girl, she is gone. Samuel enters the warehouse behind Reiko and lets the panel slide back into place. They are behind some crates when they hear two voices, and Reiko spots two Dark Army soldiers patrolling the warehouse.

She looks to Samuel and whispers, "How do you want to handle this?"

One guard is making his way over to the crates that Samuel and Reiko are hiding behind when the other guard calls out, "They are here!" He turns to head back over to the other guard. They watch both guards put on red robes, and soon several people are standing in the warehouse, all wearing red robes except one wearing a black robe. One guard reaches behind the bookcase, releases the latch, and swings the bookcase out of the way. The new arrivals are walking past the guards when Reiko hears one of them say to the one wearing the black robe, "Welcome, Lord Tao." The other guard welcomes several others by their names, "Master Merchants Naka and Lee, Chief of the Militia General Roger Wyman, and His Honorary High Priest of the Laki-Jutsuk Order Josef Midler. The men enter the opening in the wall and disappear down a stairway, followed by several more individuals. When the last robed one enters the opening, the two guards close the bookcase and are now standing on both sides of it.

Samuel nods to Reiko, and she pulls out two arrows. She places one in her mouth and notches the other. She stands and takes aim at the guard on the left and releases the deadly shaft, The arrow hits the guard in the middle of his forehead, and before the second guard can draw his sword or shout out an alarm, she drops the second guard the same way. Samuel and Reiko walk over to the two fallen guards and pull the arrows from their foreheads. Samuel wipes his arrow on the fallen guard's uniform, as does Reiko's on hers. Samuel then hands his arrow back to Reiko. Then they remove the robes, put them on, and drag the bodies behind some crates. Samuel goes to the back of the bookcase, reaches behind it, feels for the latch, finds it, and releases it. The two of them then slide the bookcase out of the way.

They cautiously head down the staircase with Samuel in the lead. They get to the bottom of the stairs and find themselves at the beginning of a long corridor. They continue down the corridor, and then they begin to hear chanting. They look at each other and sense that the chanting is ending. The chanting is unfamiliar, and when they get to the end of the corridor, the chanting stops. Then they both hear someone mention the Dark Scriptures and reference the Guichi-Tanin Religion. They step out of the corridor and find themselves in a sizeable underground cavern, and they see other people in the cavern dressed in the same red robes they are wearing. They also see several Dark Army soldiers scattered around the cavern. On the far side of the cavern, they see an altar, with Lord Tao standing on the side near the head of the altar, and behind him is a passage from what they both assume are the Dark Scriptures written in blood on a wooden wall. They now see the other men who arrived with him, the General, the High Priest, and a girl with her hood pulled back, holding a tray. They do not see the two merchants.

Samuel and Reiko are standing in the crowd when Lord Tao says, "Bring forth the unbelievers." Samuel and Reiko see four robed figures carrying a body and placing it on the altar; they take a step closer and see that it is Carrie. Reiko goes to move, but Samuel stops her when he sees a very long sharp knife sticking her in the back, and then he feels a second blade pricking him, and the voices say, "Watch." Samuel and Reiko stand there immobile as Hikaru is brought forth by six robed ones, laid on the ground, then hoisted into the Air by his ankles and suspended there. Bruises and cuts decorate his body, and his eyes are almost swollen shut. Reiko stands there bearing witness to what is happening to her friends. She tries to look away when she feels the blade shoved a little harder against her lower back, and then Reiko feels the knifepoint prick her skin, and the voice says, "I told you to Watch Bitch!" and she does as anger slowly builds up inside her.

Lord Tao speaks out, "Followers of the Guichi-Tanin and believers of the Dark Scriptures. I present to you two sacrifices that will allow us to overthrow the tyranny presently ruling this country of ours. Allow these two sacrifices to be the gateway for us to control this land and spread our Dark Lords' word. The young girl, standing to the side of Lord Tao and looking to be about Carrie's age, steps forward and offers the tray with two knives on it to Lord Tao. Lord Tao takes one of the knives from the tray, walks over to Hikaru, calls out, "Bear witness, and draws the knife horizontally across his chest. Reiko screams "NO!" and drops to the cavern floor, taking the one behind her by surprise. She immediately goes into action, grabs her captor's wrist, and snaps it. He screams in pain, causing him to drop the knife. She picks it up and rams the blade to the hilt into his throat. At that exact moment, the one behind Samuel is distracted by what Reiko has done, and Samuel moves with almost lightning speed, twists his body, grabs his captor's hand holding the knife, and makes him drive the knife into his own heart. They now see that their captors were the two Master Merchants, Naka and Lee.

Lord Tao sees what is happening and starts shouting orders to stop them as Samuel and Reiko throw off the robes. The dark army soldiers rush both Samuel and Reiko. Reiko throws the knife with her speed and agility and puts the blade into a dark archer's throat. She immediately grabs the archers bow, quivers, and drops five of the Dark Soldiers. Samuel uses his hands and kills two others in quick succession. The cavern is in turmoil as Reiko continues to draw and shoot arrows in a concise pattern at an incredible speed, and then she runs out.

In contrast, Samuel has drawn his katanas and becomes a living, breathing whirlwind that takes down anything that comes within reach of his deadly katanas, keeping Reiko protected as she strings her bow. Reiko now has her longbow strung, and Samuel tosses her the backpack. She pulls out the two quivers of arrows and straps them to her thighs. She then becomes just as deadly as Samuel. Lord Tao sees what is happening, starts to run over to Hikaru in the mayhem, and then falls to the cavern floor with an arrow protruding through his lower leg. Reiko sees another archer, turns to take him out, and sees Lord Tao trying to reach Hikaru. She sees the knife in his hand, and he has it raised to stab Hikaru, and Reiko knows the penalty for assaulting a member of the Royal Family, but shoots her arrow anyway, and hits the knife in the Lord's hand and sends it flying through the Air. She then shoots another, pierces his hand's palm, and nails him to a wooden timber.

She turns back to the fight and hears Lord Tao screaming in pain. Samuel and Reiko continue to rain death on anyone who comes at them. They have just about repelled the last of the Dark soldiers in the cavern when someone says, "HEY! you fucking bitch, this is for shooting a member of the royal family," and Reiko sees Lord Tao quickly draw a second blade across Hikaru's throat. Suddenly, Samuel and Reiko feel their friend's life force slowly leaving his body.

Back in the Empire, Princess Asami is writing out some instructions when she feels a pain in her chest, causing her to drop her writing quill. She sits there, and a single tear falls onto the paper, and all she says is, "*Hikaru.*" She calls for Lenora and tells her to dispatch a detachment to Hokida immediately.

Carrie is lying upon the altar and still paralyzed from a toxin they forced her to drink, but she can move her head just enough to see Lord Tao lying on the floor and screaming in pain, and she can barely see Hikaru as he hangs upside down. A shadow passes over her, and she rests her head back on the slab to stare at an old friend.

Carrie asks, "Beatrice, help me, please?" At that moment, a disruption breaks out, and she turns to see Samuel and Reiko start killing the Dark soldiers. Beatrice starts laughing, and Carrie looks back at her when Beatrice says, "Help you? Why should I do that? I have always hated you, Carrie. You took everything from me."

With tears in her eyes, Carrie asks, "What do you mean I took everything from you? We were friends, and our families were friends; you even dated Benji, my brother. Why would you think I took everything from you?"

"Oh! But you did. Your family destroyed mine, and you turned your brother against me. I loved him, and you took that away. That was the last straw, Carrie. I vowed to get my revenge and had my chance while you were in those cages, but that stupid man over there, pointing to Hikaru, stabbed me and took that away. So, Carrie, my time has come for revenge," and Beatrice raises the knife that was knocked out of Lord Tao's hand when that bitch shot him. She raises it into the Air and plunges it into Carrie's chest with two hands.

Reiko watches them and is just about to shoot an arrow at the woman who is about to plunge a knife into her friend's heart when she sees a Dark

Army soldier pointing a crossbow at Samuel out the corner of her eye. She quickly switches her aim and takes the brute out with a headshot. She already has another arrow drawn and aimed, but it is too late as she sees the knife penetrate Carrie's chest and watches her convulse. Reiko has her bow taut as could be allowed and releases the arrow. The force it travels catches Beatrice in the chest, lifting her straight off the ground and pinning her to the wooden wall with the Dark Scriptures written on them. Her blood runs down the wall smearing the words of the Dark Scriptures. Reiko looks over at Samuel and sees that he has finished up the remaining Dark soldiers and is tying up the High Priest and the General. He sees Lord Tao pinned to the wooden timber and sees him rip his hand free, and Lord Tao tries to escape. Samuel looks at Reiko and signals for her to stop Lord Tao from getting away. Without hesitation, Reiko quickly shoots an arrow into the Lord's other leg, causing him to fall to the ground screaming in pain.

Samuel runs to where Hikaru's body is hanging and cuts him down. He lays him gently on the ground, and with tears in his eyes, he covers him with a robe. He turns and slowly walks over to Lord Tao, lying on the ground holding his leg. Lord Tao starts shouting at Samuel, saying, "You will pay for this! Do you know who I am? I am the Governor of Hokida. I am a member of the Royal Family; my brother is the Emperor. When he hears of this and what you have done to me, he will have you and your girlfriend's head mounted on pikes decorating the main gate to the Capital. I am Lord Tao, the Emperor's brother next in line for the title of Emperor."

Samuel looks at him and says coldly, "Please shut the fuck up; I know who you are, Lord Tao. You are a creature of the sewers, a sub-being that does not even have the right to call himself human. Look around you. Your followers are finished, pointing to the two dead merchants, the General, and finally, the captured High Priest. Lord Tao." Samuel takes a minute for everything to sink in, then he continues. "I just want you to know that in your stupid plot of everything, you made four major mistakes, and I am going to enlighten you with what those mistakes were, right here and right now!" Samuel glances at Hikaru's covered body and says, "Your first mistake was plotting to overthrow your brother, the Emperor's regime. The second mistake you made was that you wanted to kill the Advisor-General, which was wrong because, you see, the Advisor-General is my father." Lord Tao's face turns deathly white. "Third, you ordered the attack on Princess

Asami and tried to have her kidnapped so you could use her as a bargaining chip against your brother." How am I doing? Are you getting all of this?

But do you know the most grievous mistake you made was, Is that young man over there, he was one of my best friends, and the young lady on the altar was his betrothed and also a dear and close friend of mine, so you see, Lord Tao, I don't give a fuck who your brother is or what you had planned for my friend and me?"

Samuel takes his short katana and places it directly over Lord Tao's heart, he looks at Reiko, and all she does is nod. Lord Tao starts screaming, "You can't do this to me. I am royalty!" Samuel takes a tight grip on his short sword and slowly pushes his blade into his chest, just before the blade pierces his heart. Samuel says, "This is for my friends Hikaru and Carrie," and drives the blade home.

Reiko sees Samuel talking with Lord Tao, rushes up to the altar, and finds Carrie alive and still breathing, but her breaths are very shallow. She takes her hand and tells Carrie that she is here. Carrie looks at her and says, "I'm sorry. Reiko, we should have never come in here without the two of you, and she coughs, and when she does, blood runs down her cheek. Reiko wipes her mouth. "Tell Hikaru that the first time I saw him, I knew he was my soulmate." and she starts coughing some more and spits up more blood; Reiko once again wipes her mouth and tells her, "Tell you what, my dear friend, when we get you fixed up, you can tell him yourself, How does that sound?" Carrie smiles and says, "Tell Hikaru that I lo…," and she never finishes the sentence as Reiko looks at her to see her staring straight at the cavern ceiling, unmoving. Reiko stands beside her, still holding her hand as tears fall onto Carrie's face, and they cause the blood to run in places. Reiko then bends over, kisses her forehead, and whispers to her, "You were one of us and will be greatly missed, and looks at her face, so beautiful and innocent. She then says, "This is from Hikaru," and places a soft kiss on her still warm lips. Reiko stands beside the altar and cries for one of her best friends. She stops crying, reaches over, and slides her hand over Carrie's face to close her eyes. She looks over at Samuel, sees his short sword over Lord Tao's heart, gives him a nod, and watches Samuel slowly push down on his sword as Lord Tao starts screaming that he can't do this.

She is still holding her friend's hand when she hears a cackle of laughter and looks over to see the woman who killed one of her best friends, still pinned against the wall with her arrow sticking out of her chest. Reiko does as Samuel did with Hikaru; she places a red robe over Carrie's body and then walks over to the woman hanging there and asks her, "Why did you do this to Carrie? What did she ever do to you?" The woman is in great pain and tells Reiko, "Because I hated her. All she did was wreck my life!"

Reiko says to her, "Is that so? I think Carrie told me about you; I bet you're one of her friends, Beatrice. Is that true?"

Beatrice looks at her and says, "Yes, I am Beatrice. Why do you ask?"

Carrie told me your story, "How your family lost all their money when the mine collapsed, how her brother broke it off with you when you became very bitter because your family went broke. Did you know that her brother didn't care about your dowery? How you ended up marrying a man who felt sorry for you, then raped you of your virginity and then told his friends about it, calling you a whore."

"Through it all, Carrie was the only one who defended you. She was the only one."

"Lies, all lies! That bitch hated me; she ruined my life!" she yells at Reiko, foaming at the mouth with specks of red.

Reiko looks at her and says, "What a stupid little girl," then turns and walks away, leaving Beatrice to hang there to slowly bleed out as she continues to shout out, "Lies, all lies."

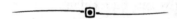

Reiko finds some shackles to chain the General and the High Priest to one of the columns in the warehouse. Samuel and Reiko carry Hikaru, then Carrie up from the cavern and place them on a couple of makeshift tables. Samuel finds a bucket and goes to the door. He checks that the coast is clear and finds a large rainwater-filled barrel. He fills the bucket, steps back inside, and secures the door. They remove their robes and wash them, carefully removing all traces of dried blood. Samuel and Reiko looked at the two of them all cleaned up and were able to find some clean white linens to wrap them in. Samuel reaches over and grabs Reiko's hand and softly squeezes it. Reiko places her arms around Samuel and hugs him tightly as she starts to cry again. Samuel holds her tight, and she squeezes tighter, Samuel squeezes back, and tears run down his cheek.

They go back to the bookcase and open it. Reiko still hears Beatrice laughing and shouting, "It's lies, all lies." They talk about bringing up the two bodies of the merchants and Lord Tao but decide against it, seeing that they were unsure when and if the forces from the Capital would arrive. It is much cooler in the cavern, and they walk over to Hikaru and Carrie, pick them up one at a time, and carry them back down to the cavern. They both agreed that it would be best to wait for the reinforcements, with the cavern being cooler. They head up the stairs when Reiko still hears Beatrice laughing and yelling. "It's all lies."

Reiko looks at Samuel; he smiles and turns to head back upstairs. Reiko notches an arrow and slowly pulls her bowstring back. Reiko takes a deep breath, lets it out slowly, and all she says is "Bitch" and releases the arrow. Reiko stands there and watches the arrow find its mark as Beatrice takes it in the middle of her forehead and pins her head against the wall. She feels little satisfaction in getting revenge for her friend Carrie and heads up the stairs. She sees Samuel waiting for her and steps into the warehouse. They check the General and High Priest shackles, gag them, and secure the warehouse. They stop at a Royal carrier shop to send two cryptic messages, one to the Advisor General and the other to the Princess. They tell of their findings and ask them to send troops.

They return to the hotel, collect their things, and pay their bill. They purchase supplies, return to the warehouse, and see that the priest and general are still here. The days pass without any further incidences. Reiko is washing her face in the bucket of water, and after eight days, they hear a knock on the door to the warehouse. Reiko immediately grabs her bow and notches an arrow as Samuel approaches the door with his sword drawn and asks who is there.

The response is, "Captain Miro; Lieutenant Parsons from the Advisor-General's office. Samuel opens the door and sees Lieutenant Parsons with fifty Imperial Army soldiers in the warehouse yard. Samuel allows the Lieutenant to enter and briefs him on what has happened. The only response the Lieutenant gives is, "I'm sorry to hear about Captain Sato and Miss Barnes; what are your orders, Sir?" Samuel tells him what they need and prepare for departure in the morning. Lieutenant Parsons assigns troops around the perimeter.

The following day the fifty Imperial troops march out of Hokida with two wagons; the first wagon holds the bodies of the Hikaru and Carrie. The second wagon has the General and the High Priest, who are still shackled and hooded beside the dead body of Lord Tao, who wears the black robes of the Guichi-Tanin Religion. They exit the city and are met by a more considerable detachment of Imperial soldiers consisting of fifty axe men, fifty swordsmen, fifty archers, and another fifty Imperial Soldiers. Reiko sees Sargent Stell among the archers and gives him a nod. A Second Lieutenant Lobe salutes Samuel and Reiko and says, "From the Princess," and then The axe men take control of the wagon holding Hikaru and Carrie.

They are about twenty leagues from Hokida when one of the outriders gallops up and reports a detachment of about two hundred-twenty-five soldiers dressed in the Hokida Militia and wearing hoods are riding parallel with them about three kilometers to the east. Samuel calls a halt to the march and quickly discusses it with Captain Takahashi and Lieutenants Parsons and Lobe. They all agree with the battle plan, and the Imperial army starts moving again, minus fifty longbowmen, thirty long swordsmen, and fifty battle ax men whom Samuel could not have kept back even if he wanted to.

The detachment moves out in an easterly direction, and it's about midafternoon when Lieutenant Parson leaves a detail with Lieutenant Lobe and the wagons and tells them to keep heading towards the Capital. He orders the remainder of his troops to turn in an easterly direction, and they come to a small hill that overlooks an open field. He tells his men to stay low and behind the hill.

The Dark Army Commander has temporarily lost sight of the enemy and orders the deployment of his troops in a battle line formation. He looks through an eye scope and is surprised at his opponent's numbers. His reports said that there were at least a hundred Imperial soldiers. He sees a small detachment of maybe fifty men through his eyes-scope but cannot see the wagons. He concludes that they must have gone ahead, and these troops have just signed their death warrant. He smiles, thinking this will be an easy slaughter, and orders his formation of soldiers to move forward slowly. They reach the base of the hill, and he sees that the Imperial soldiers have no archers and is just about to give the orders to charge up the hill when a hail of arrows hits his men from behind. The commander tries to shout out orders when his horse falls from underneath him. The commander kicks himself free and is now standing facing his attackers. He goes to shout out orders, but the words are unspoken, as an arrow embeds itself in his chest and pierces his heart.

Reiko lowers her bow and orders her archers to continue firing. The Dark Army is now in turmoil as they have no one to give them orders. They are trying to decide what to do when two groups of long swordsmen and battleax men attack their flanks, and soon with the advancing skirmish line, they find themselves boxed in with no escape. They continue to fight, knowing what awaits them. The battle is soon over, and the Imperial forces are triumphant other than some minor wounds. Samuel orders the bodies of the slain soldiers to be stripped and piled in the field and doused with coal oil.

As they leave the field, Samuel gives Reiko the honors. Still, before she has a chance to light the arrow, Sargent Stell is there, ready to light it for her. She looks at him and says, "Sargent Stell, we must stop making this a habit. If we continue like this, people will start talking." Stell says, "Let them, Captain, and I will personally see to it that it is stopped," and he smiles. Reiko nods, Stell lights an arrow, and once it catches, she shoots it into the pile of slain soldiers. Within minutes the pile is ablaze with burning bodies that send a plume of black smoke into the Air.

They reach the Capital without further incident, and as the two wagons enter the main gates, they split up. The wagon holding Hikaru and Carrie heads through the Capital. The other wagon heads through the back streets to the Imperial prison, where the General and the High Priest are thrown into separate cells, shackled to the wall, and they place Lord Tao's body in another cell.

Reiko thanks Lieutenant Parsons, tells him to dismiss the troops, and thank them for their exceptional performance. She meets up with Samuel, and they head over to the Advisor-Generals office to debrief him because a Royal was involved in the incident. Three hours later, Samuel and Reiko head to Hikaru and Carrie's apartment to gather Hikaru's dress uniform. Reiko goes through Carrie's things to find the appropriate clothes.

Samuel, Reiko, and Hikaru are promoted to the rank of Major. Carrie is promoted to Second Lieutenant for their diligence in stopping the spread of the Dark Scriptures in the city of Hokida, eliminating the contingent of Dark forces, and capturing two vital members of the Dark forces. Both the general and the former High Priest of the Laki-Jutsuk are found guilty of trying to corrupt the Empire's citizens and sentenced to be hanged by the neck until dead. The general, a military man, accepts his punishment. While the High Priest cries and pleads for his life. The General marches back to his cell, and the former high priest is dragged away, kicking and screaming.

A week has passed for others to pay their respects, and Hikaru Sato and Carrie Barnes are cremated in full military honors. Master-at-Arms Vernon carries Carrie's urn, and Princess Asami carries Hikaru's, as Samuel and Reiko are behind them as the parade makes its way to the Imperial Army mausoleum. Reiko looks down on the ground as the funeral march proceeds to the mausoleum, and she sees flower petals spread out before them. She looks at Samuel; he smiles and softly says, "Hikaru always wanted this."

They arrive at the mausoleum, Higgs and the Princess step forward, place the two urns inside the same vault, and then Samuel and Reiko place the bronze plaque and seal it. The bronze plaque reads Major Hikaru Hito Sato with crossed battle axes below his name and Second Lieutenant Carrie Ann Barnes, with crossed stilettos under hers. Everyone leaves after the services are complete, except Samuel and Reiko. Samuel places his arm around Reiko's shoulder and feels her body shake from crying.

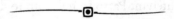

Three weeks after the executions of the General and the High Priest, Lord Tao's followers push for an inquiry to investigate the death of Lord

Tao, Governor of the City of Hokida, and a member of the royal family. They claimed that Lord Tao was not a member of the Dark Scriptures but took it upon himself to infiltrate the sect to determine if it had influential members ready to destroy the reigning monarchy. The Emperor could not ignore the outbursts of his brothers without stirring up unrest. Though the Emperor had the military's backing, he could not risk implementing martial law and possibly causing a civil war between the factions. Both Samuel and Reiko were called before the military board several times. After another four weeks, the military panel concluded and passed the judgment onto the Advisor-General, who informed the Emperor.

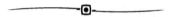

One week after the executions, Major Samuel Miro and Major Reiko Anzu Takahashi are standing before their commanding officers of the Military Justice Board. They call Samuel, and he steps forward. "Major Samuel Miro, you have been found guilty by a board of your peers in the killing of a Royal Family member Lord Tao. The Imperial Laws state that no one may harm or take a Royal Family member's life only if the Emperor himself so declares it and is present when the execution occurs. Major Samuel Miro, you have broken the Imperial Laws, and as punishment, you are to be stripped of the rank of Major and spend the rest of your days in prison until you die." Samuel says, "Yes, Sir." he salutes and steps back. The verdict is effective immediately. Samuel is stripped of his Major clusters and escorted out of the room.

They call Reiko next. "Major Reiko Anzu Takahashi as a co-conspirator in the death of Lord Tao, and though you did not outright assist Major Miro in his killing, you are guilty of assaulting a royal member with excessive force. You have been found guilty by a board of your peers and will be demoted to the rank of First Lieutenant, remain confined to base for six months, and be assigned to the Office of Supply". Unceremoniously, Reiko is stripped of her Major clusters, handed a set of First Lieutenant bars, and escorted from the room.

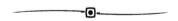

Every day she would visit Samuel in his cell, and they would talk. Six months pass slowly when First Lieutenant Reiko Takahashi finally resumes her role as a Junior Supply Officer. Reiko is just finishing up her duties in supply when she hears two officers talking that Samuel's sentence could be reduced by order of the Emperor himself.

One week after Reiko hears this, Samuel is in front of the Military Board for a second time and stands at attention in front of the presiding officer General Daniel W. West. He sees Major General Lucius Hinds sitting in the room and waits for the verdict.

Colonel West clears his throat and says, "Samuel Miro, your actions have been reviewed, and it is in the best interest and the suggestion of this tribunal that you, Samuel Miro, are to forfeit your citizenship of the Empire. You are to be exiled from the Empire's borders and never allowed to return upon penalty of death."

"Due to your meritorious service for the Empire, the tribunal will allow you one day to put your affAirs in order before you are escorted to the western border to start your banishment, "So says this Military Board, Dismissed." Samuel salutes, and right before he does an about-face, he sees the look in Major General Lucius Hind's eyes and can tell that he disagrees with the latest verdict.

Samuel visits his home and says goodbye to his mother, Aki, and his father, Hakimi, the Advisor-General. His father embraces Samuel and says, "I'm sorry, my Son, I might be the Emperor's Advisor-General, but I cannot go against Empire Law, and for the record, I would have done the same thing." Samuel looks at his father and says, "Please look after mother and the Princess." Samuel walks up to his little brother and tells him, "Take care of the young Prince; and gives his little brother a hug and whispers, "I'll miss you, and his brother says, "Me too." and then Samuel steps out the front door to the waiting arms of his detail led d by First Lieutenant Reiko Takahashi. He mounts his horse and rides out of the Capital heading west.

Chapter 32

Jutsuk Finds Samuel

A small contingent of ten swordsmen on horses arrives at a remote outpost used many years ago as a lookout to warn the Empire of any invasion coming from the west through the Insetsu Pass, as with several others along with the Tammayaku mountains range. During the great war with Basra, King Leopoff was mortally wounded, and his son, Prince heir, took over as ruler of Basra and became King. The new King conveyed to the Emperor that he wanted to call a truce and have peace between the two countries.

At first, there was disbelief, but the Basra troops pulled back beyond the mountain range, and peace finally came to the Kingdom and the Empire. Both parties signed the peace accords in the center of the Ga Taku Plateau, stating that the Insetsu Pass between the two Kingdom and the Empire be neutral territory. The two countries inscribed all the names of the fallen from both countries on the Plateau's walls.

The outpost is now considered a rest area for anyone entering or coming out of the Tammayaku Mountains. The Pass twists and turns, and with so many switchbacks, it could take a caravan a whole day to travel between the two countries. The only other landmark near the outpost is a four-meter-tall square monolith in the ground in the middle of the Pass marking the borders of the Great Imperial Empire.

Everyone dismounts; some take the horses to the trough to give them water, while others open the shutters and start a fire. Reiko walks with Samuel under the building's awning to get out of the afternoon sun. Reiko is not happy with having to escort her best friend to the Empire's borders to be banished. Most of the men in the escort feel the same way and have, on several occasions, expressed their thoughts about joining Samuel in his banishment.

Being the man he is, Samuel tells the men who have escorted him that when the time comes and after they have all served their allotted time in the military as proclaimed by the Imperial Laws, then and only then would he accept their service if the need were to arise. They eat, drink, and laugh that night, telling how Samuel became "*Rinju Kitikorosu*" and how they defeated the Dark Army soldiers twice.

In the morning, Samuel is getting ready to depart when Reiko approaches him, gives him a perfect salute, and hands him a backpack fully stuffed with the necessities for his journey and a field bedroll. One of the other men steps up behind Reiko, carrying a slender wooden box, and says something so only she can hear. Reiko takes the box, bows to Samuel, hands it to him, and says, "A gift for "*Rinju Kitikorosu*" from the men."

Samuel opens the box and finds a beautiful, handcrafted katana and a plain but highly polished black scabbard. He releases the blade testing its balance, checking the straightness, and the edge for sharpness. Samuel places the sword back in its sheath and tells Reiko to tell the men, "Thank you" Samuel holds out his hand to shake Reiko's hand when she slaps his hand away and embraces him in a tight hug. Samuel returns the embrace, and Reiko says, "Death Slayer," we love you, and he knows she is talking about the Princess. Samuel tells her, "You take care of yourself, "Reaper of Souls." They let each other go, and she then places a sealed letter in Samuel's hand, and he can tell at a glance that it is from the Princess, and says, "Asami says she is sorry." Reiko also places something else in his hand, feeling a little heavier. He looks in his hand and finds a set of Major Clusters. He starts to speak when Reiko says. "Shut up and just put them on." She helps him, then stands back and says, "Not bad." The detachment comes to full attention. Samuel does the same and gives First Lieutenant Reiko Takahashi and her men a very sharp salute. They return the salute, and he throws the pack over his shoulder and says, "Thank you," he turns and heads off into the Insetsu Pass that would lead him through the Tammayaku Mountains.

He is about to reach the first turn on the path and looks back to see Reiko Takahashi sitting astride the black horse she took from the Dark Armies Commander after the Battle of Shira. She waves, and he waves back, then she turns her mount and rides off to join her comrades, staying behind them, so they do not see the tears in her eyes.

Samuel readjusts his pack on his shoulder and continues the gradual climb up the Insetsu Pass into the Tammayaku mountains. His pace is steady, and he only stops briefly to quench his thirst. It is very late in the day, and he decides to make camp, for it will get darker in the mountains on this side of the Plateau than on the plains. He rifles through the backpack, finds what he was hoping for in the pack, and thanks, Reiko. He pulls out a couple of small game snares and moves back down the trail to set them. After setting the traps, he starts a fire, sits down, and places a small metal pot on the stones to heat some water for tea. As he is brewing some tea, he hears the sound of one of the snares tripping. He places his cup of tea near the rocks to keep it warm and walks down the trail to where he had set the snares. The first snare trap was sprung but had missed its prey. He picks it up and moves on to the next one. He finds a plump rabbit in the second one, unhooks it, picks the snare up, pulls out a small knife from his sleeve, and proceeds to field dress the rabbit. He takes the guts back down the trail and places them near some bushes for the scavengers.

He gets back to his camp and proceeds to skin the rabbit. Soon he has the rabbit on a skewer and roasting over the fire. He scrapes the skin and lays it out near the fire for drying. He sits on his bedroll, leans back against his pack, sips some tea, and waits for his dinner to cook. He is just about to pour himself another cup of tea when he hears some voices. Samuel places his cup of tea on the rocks, moves to squat beside the fire, and releases his katana from its sheath. He puts it beside him as two men come down the trail from the Basra side. They ask Samuel if he would not mind if they warmed themselves beside his fire. Samuel tells them to sit and notices that their clothing is remnants of Dark Army uniforms. The bigger one squats and starts to warm his hands. He asks Samuel for some tea and reaches for the pot while the smaller one remains to stand, looking very nervous.

Samuel says, "I offered you a place to warm your hands, but I didn't say anything about having some tea."

The one standing takes a small step forward, and Samuel politely says. "I wouldn't take another step, and I think you gentlemen have overstayed your welcome, now, if you would kindly be on your way."

The one standing has a look of frustration on his face, and Samuel can see that he is just about ready to move, waiting for his friend to say something. The bigger one squatting near the fire seems annoyed, especially since Samuel has asked them to leave and says, "Now, my friend, is that any way to treat your fellow travelers? We were polite and asked if we could join you. There is more than enough tea for us, and we wouldn't mind enjoying that roasted rabbit with you. So, why don't you be a good man and let us have some tea, rabbit, and any other valuables you might have, and maybe, just maybe, we might spare your life. How does that sound?"

Samuel replies, "I don't think so, and I can guarantee you will not like how this will turn out!"

The larger one stands and says, "So be it," and pulls a large dagger from behind his back and holds it as if to throw it, while the nervous one draws a short sword from a back scabbard. The big man throws the knife as Samuel had anticipated and rolls out of the way while snatching his sheath and katana. He comes out of the roll, pulls his katana, and raises it to block the short sword of the nervous one. The bigger guy is surprised at Samuel's speed and goes to grab his knife when Samuel hits him with the end of the sheath in just the right spot to knock the wind out of him. He immediately drops him to his knees, unable to breathe.

Samuel is on his feet, facing the one with the short sword. He does not concern himself with the bigger guy because he is now on all fours, unable to catch his breath. The man with the sword starts switching the short sword between his hands. Samuel bends down to pick up his scabbard, sheaths his katana, and then stands up straight. The nervous man with the short sword is slightly bewildered.

Samuel says to both men, "My dinner looks almost done, and I would hate for it to burn and lifts the skewered rabbit from the flames." I enjoyed this little game and would appreciate it if you took your friend there and were on your way."

The man with the short sword screams and charges Samuel, bringing his sword in high as if to take his head off. Samuel moves low under his swing, reaches up inside the man's arms, and jabs two fingers underneath his armpit. The man's arm immediately goes numb, and he drops his sword. Samuel grabs his wrist, twists his hand just enough, and hears the wrist snap. Samuel brings up his knee while simultaneously grabbing the back of his head and slamming his face into his knee. The man's head bounces off his knee, and as he almost stands upright, Samuel performs a perfectly executed roundhouse kick that catches the man on the side of his head and snaps his neck. Samuel follows through with a side thrust kick, catches the dead man in the chest, and propels his body over the cliff's edge. Samuel listens and hears the cracking of bones as the body tumbles down the side of the cliff.

The bigger man finally catches his breath, sees what this stranger has done to his friend, and charges at him. Samuel hears the man coming at him, and without turning, he drops down in a low crouch, performs a half spin with his leg straight out, and trips the charging man. The man starts to fall forward, and Samuel takes the short blade he used for gutting and skinning the rabbit, draws it horizontally across the man's stomach, and cuts him deep. The big man stumbles, but before he falls, he catches himself and now stands in front of Samuel. He stands there looking at Samuel and then feels wetness on his trousers. He looks down and realizes that the slash is more profound than he first thought. He does not move or say anything as he watches his insides slowly spill out. He drops to his knees and then looks up at Samuel as he desperately tries to hold any more of his insides from spilling out onto the ground. The big man realizes that all is lost, and he smiles and says, "I should have heeded your words." Samuel looks at him and says, "Yes, you should have." The big man falls backward onto his heels, and as he tries to catch his breath, he musters enough strength to ask, "Who are you?"

Samuel gives him the courtesy and says, "Samuel Miro, former Major in his Emperor's Imperial Royal Army."

The man looks at him and says, "*Rinju Kitikorosu.*"

Samuel always disliked being called "The Death Slayer."

He takes a step back and releases his katana from its sheath. He holds the blade firmly in two hands, brings it back to his ear with his elbows parallel with the ground, and says, "I will make this painless." he then swings the katana straight out at arm's length separating the man's head from his shoulders. The body falls to the side, his head bounces once, and then disappears over the Plateau's edge. He checks the man's clothes and finds a small bag of coins. He then bends down, grabs the headless body, drags it to the edge of the cliff, and throws it off, and as with the other one, he hears the body bounce and the bones snapping with every hit. Samuel walks back to his campfire, places the rabbit back over the flames to reheat it, and sits down to enjoy his tea and read the letter from the Princess.

My Dearest Samuel,

I am genuinely sorry for the situation and burden I have placed upon you. I did not mean this to happen, but the others wanted your head, and I suggested you be banished instead. I thought father would have fought for you, but his hands were politically tied, and I could not bear to see any harm come to you. You are banished from the Empire and never be allowed to return. I am fraught with unhappiness and pain because of what they did to you and what they have done to Reiko. I hope you will forgive me for the pain and humiliation I have put you through. I have talked with father, and he says that after everything has blown over and given time, the Empire will forget what happened, that he will speak with the military to have you reinstated and be allowed to return to the Empire, your home. Please take care, my Champion, and be careful.

I Will Love You Always,

Your Ward

He puts the letter away and finishes his meal. Samuel decides to check where the two men came from and soon finds their gear stashed behind bushes. He rummages through their bags and finds a few more coins, some cheap wine, a loaf of old bread, and dirty clothes, and under their packs, he discovers a crossbow wrapped in a thick cloth, and under the crossbow, a quiver of bolts. He picks up everything, walks over to the cliff's edge, and throws everything over except the coin, crossbow, and the quiver of bolts. He returns to his camp, sits on his bedroll near the fire, relaxes, and drinks some more tea. The rest of the evening is uneventful.

It is early morning, and Samuel awakens to find that the fire has almost burned itself out and douses the remaining embers. He wraps the remaining roasted rabbit in the dried rabbit skin, loads up his pack, grabs his new crossbow and quivers, and starts walking. Early in the day, he reaches the Ga Taku Plateau and walks over to the smooth polished wall.

Etched in the wall are the names of those who had fallen on both sides of the war. Samuel says a quick prayer and then walks to the path leading into Basra. He looks over the lands and is amazed by the beauty of what lies below him. He is almost halfway down when he comes across a smaller plateau just above the flatlands of the western Tammayaku mountains. He looks at the sun, and though some daylight is left, he decides to make camp. He places his leftover rabbit near the fire and hears running water. He walks through some bushes and finds a large pool of crystal-clear water fed by a small natural waterfall. He refills his canteen and notices how the pool's overflow drains into a type of cistern and then disappears through some rocks. He can only assume the water runs throughout the mountains. Samuel decides to wash and removes his clothes to wash them and lays them on the stones to dry as he bathes. When clean, he grabs his clothes, walks back to his campfire, and places his clothes near the fire to continue drying. He puts on a change of undergarments and then eats his warmed-up rabbit. While his clothes dry, he relaxes on his bedroll beside his fire, enjoying some tea. The hairs on the back of his neck stand up when he feels a soft breeze and the smell of lavender in the Air. He stands and ever so gently pushes on the hilt of his katana with his thumb to release it from its sheath.

Then out of nowhere and standing just out of reach of his sword is the most beautiful woman he has ever seen. The breeze dies down, but the smell of lavender lingers. This beautiful woman stands before him in a sheer outfit that leaves little to the imagination. He immediately drops to one knee and says, "My Lady."

She walks over to him, lifts his chin, and looks into his eyes. Samuel stares back at her and immediately feels joy that he did not even think could be possible, and with that feeling, he thinks back to a sketch he came across many years ago and remembers the artist saying that it was a sketch of the two Goddesses. He realizes now that this is one of the Goddesses standing before him.

Samuel says, "My Goddess forgive me, my apologies, the artists' renditions do not do you justice. Have I done something wrong to offend the Goddesses?"

Jutsuk laughs, "No, Samuel, you have done nothing wrong to offend my sister or me. I have come before you to ask for you to serve the Laki-Jutsuk Religion. I know of your past, Samuel. What happened to you was for others to decide. I can tell you that the Princess adores you and tried to intervene on your behalf because she loves you dearly. She considers you a true friend. Others wanted to incarcerate you in the deepest dungeon and let you die. At the same time, others cried out for blood and wanted your head on a pike for what you did to Lord Tao, a member of the Royal Family. Samuel Miro, you have been banished from the Ozeka Empire. My sister and I would like, and when she is about to ask him something, she is interrupted by laughter.

Samuel hears laughter coming down from the past, and then one of them says, "So, what do we have here? The infamous *"Rinju Kitikorosu"* doesn't have a home to return to, poor fucking baby!" The other two with him laugh as they all walk into his camp.

Samuel sees the three men wearing remnants of Dark Army uniforms, the same as the ones he encountered yesterday. Samuel knows they are deserters but does not know if they are from Shira or Hokida.

The one who spoke earlier tells Samuel to step away from his sword, and Samuel does.

The leader walks over to Samuel and says, "So this is the great Major Samuel Miro of the Ozeka Empire, Champion of the Empire, the infamous *"Rinju Kitikorosu"* and now a banished hero. The same man who murdered the Emperor's brother and then my brother and my friend just yesterday."

Samuel, "What do you mean murdered. Your brother and his friend tried to…."

The leader backhands Samuel across his mouth tells him to shut up, and says, "You killed my brother for sheer enjoyment, you bastard."

Samuel spits blood, and the other two laugh. Jutsuk steps forward, and Samuel gives a brief shake of his head. The leader notices and asks Samuel, "Is your little whore here going to step in and fight your battles for the great *"Rinju Kitikorosu?"* and he starts laughing.

"So, who is your little whore here?" The leader reaches out to touch Jutsuk; when he does that, Samuel notices that the man has dropped his guard.

Samuel is only half an arm's length away when he moves with lightning speed and seizes the opportunity by grabbing the leader by his throat and squeezing his throat like a vise. The leader reaches up with both hands and tries to remove Samuel's death grip from his throat. Samuel reaches over, grabs his sword from its sheath, and pushes the leader away. The leader falls to the ground and yells, "Kill him," and pulls a small dagger from his sleeve and goes to stab Jutsuk. Samuel swings the sword in one fluid motion and chops off the leader's hand, and the knife never touches her, but the man's severed hand sprays blood, and it covers Jutsuk as the knife comes within inches of cutting her. He falls to the ground, screaming and grasping his left arm to stop the blood flow from his missing hand, and starts yelling, "Kill him!" The other two are standing there dumbfounded at what just happened; when they hear their leader yell, "Kill him, you idiots, kill him!" for the third time, they move into action.

They rush at him swinging their swords. Samuel deflects the first one's sword, and the sword shatters, but Samuel pushes him backward and trips over their leader, who is holding his arm on the ground. He ducks under the second one's blade and dives out of the way to land near his katana. He snatches it up, and as the second assailant tries to rush Samuel again, Samuel swings his sword and releases the sheath and its belt from his katana with his thumb. The sheath flies through the Air, it catches the man around his ankles, and the man gets tangled in the sheath's belt. He starts to stumble and loses his balance, only to plunge into the campfire. He struggles to get up as his clothes and hair ignite. Screaming, he gets to his feet but falls back onto the fire and is now silent.

The other man sees what has happened to his friend and looks at Samuel, blaming him. He becomes furious over what has just happened, calls Samuel a bastard, and raises his sword, and before he attacks, they both hear a commotion coming from the campfire. The assailant stops and watches in horror as his friend rises from the campfire with pieces of clothing and charred flesh dripping from his body and then runs down the path towards Basra. They watch him fall to the ground, and he starts to tumble the rest of the way down the trail. The man's still burning body hits a switchback in the path and plummets over the edge. His body disappears except for a soft glow illuminating where the body finally came to rest.

The man points his sword at Samuel and says, "Damn you!" and then rushes at Samuel bringing his blade down with two hands to try and slash him. Samuel stands there and, at the last moment, raises his sword to block the assailant's downward slash, and then Samuel thrusts two fingers into the man's middle just below where his ribs meet. The man finds himself lying at Samuel's feet, clutching his stomach and coughing blood. Samuel squats down in front of the fallen man, puts his sword on the ground, and then grabs his head and snaps his neck. He starts to stand up when he hears a soft feminine voice say, "Samuel."

Samuel turns and sees the leader with the missing hand has somehow tied the stump off and now has Jutsuk in his grasp. He sees the point of the blade lying on her breast. He looks at the leader and says, "I wouldn't do that if I were you."

The leader laughs and says, "What will you do about it?"

"Me, nothing, but she might take offense to it'"

The leader yells, "You had better not move, or your whore here is going to get a permanent scar, then pushes the very tip of the blade into her breast, slicing through her sheer garment.

Samuel looks at him and says, "I would be very careful if I were you."

The leader is nervous and asks Samuel, "What the fuck are you talking about?

"Well, first of all, you don't know who you are holding there, and second I'm not going to do anything except stand here and watch."

The leader pushes on the blade's tip at her breast, and he draws blood, causing Jutsuk to very softly say, "Ouch!"

Samuel says, "I warned you!" The Dark Army deserter smells the fragrance of lavender in the Air, and then he realizes that the woman he was holding and threatening has somehow slipped from his grasp. The man is distracted as Samuel pulls the small skinning knife from the back of his loincloth. He palms the small knife, and just then, Jutsuk says, "Up here." The leader looks up and sees the woman slowly descending to the ground, and he falls to his knees, begging for forgiveness when Samuel throws the knife underhanded and lets it fly to catch the leader in his eye, causing him to drop his knife, screaming, and falls to his knees. Jutsuk lands near Samuel, and Samuel walks up to him and says, "I told you not to do that. He pulls the knife from his eye and immediately runs the blade across his throat. He then drags the body to the edge, tosses it over, and does the same to the other two men.

Samuel walks over to his pack, reaches into a side pocket, and takes out a small white cloth. He then walks back to Jutsuk, dabs delicately at the tiny drop of blood on her breast, and sees that she blushes.

Without missing a step, Samuel takes her hand and leads her through the bushes. She stares at a pool of water filled with a small waterfall.

Samuel looks her straight and says, "You were saying before we got rudely interrupted."

She notices how intensely Samuel is looking at her, and she gives him a half-smile but a smile and says, "Yes, as I was saying, my sister and I want you to pledge yourself to the Laki-Jutsuk Religious Order.

"Why me?" he asks.

Because you have to find a man who has accepted the position of the Sendoka of our Order, and when you have to find him, you are..."

Samuel raises two fingers and places them against her lips, and Jutsuk stops talking, and when she does, he asks her again, "Why me?"

Jutsuk looks at him, and as Samuel removes his fingers from her lips, she says, "Because Samuel Miro, I need you!"

Samuel does not say anything.

She looks back at him and asks, "What say you, Samuel Miro?" and before she can say anything else, Samuel steps forward, places one hand on her lower back, lifts her chin with the other, and gently pulls her close, and as he pulls her close, he kisses her. She goes to resist and then accepts it and returns the kiss.

He then pulls away, looks at her in her eyes, and says, "Yes."

He reaches out, places his hands on her shoulders, and hooks his thumbs under the straps. He slowly slides the straps of her gown off her shoulders and delicately brushes her arms with his fingertips.

Jutsuk starts to speak, and Samuel says, "Shhhh!" and lets her blood-soaked gown fall from her shoulders, and before it collects on the ground, the garment disappears. He takes her hand and leads her into the pool of water. He leans forward, kisses her softly, and brushes his thumb over the cut that is now beginning to fade. Her body quivers from his touch. He picks her up and starts to walk towards the waterfall.

She inhales slightly and asks, "What are you doing?"

He smiles and says, "Washing you off," and carries her into the waterfall; she just now realizes she is covered in her assailant's blood. Samuel puts her down, and as they stand together under the waterfall, he washes the dried blood from her hair and body. The water is vibrant and refreshing as Samuel washes the blood from her body. When she is clean, he picks her up, carries her back to the pool's edge, and sits her down. He cups her face in his hands and leans in gently to kiss her eyelids. When she opens her eyes, she sees him smiling and then feels his hand in the small of her back. He pulls her in close so that her legs are straddling him, and with his other hand, he softly runs it up her back to the base of her neck as she shivers in response. He gently bunches her hair in his fist, tilts her head back, and softly nibbles her earlobe. Jutsuk moans and does not know why but her body is soon warm and quivering. She instinctively wraps her legs around his waist and moves her pelvis close to his. She looks down and fumbles with the undergarment, and after a few moments of frustration, she finally gets it undone. She reaches down between them and touches it.

He nibbles on her neck and pulls her earlobe with his teeth, causing her to squeeze as he embraces her in a firm but not overbearing hug. Jutsuk places her palms on his shoulders and pushes herself away, and as she looks Samuel in the eyes, she feels it and that it is pure unadulterated love.

He brings her in close again, and she again reaches down with her hand to grasp it, and Samuel's body shudders. Jutsuk exhales heavily, and she now places one arm around his neck. She squeezes her legs tighter as she lifts herself, reaches down, takes hold of it, and guides him.

First, there is pain, then pleasure, as she holds onto him tightly and squeezes him hard with her legs. She stops and looks at Samuel with tears in her eyes. He asks if she is okay; she nods her head yes. Her endeavors allow her to move and not feel too much pain. She knows that he has given her everything, and she loves him for it. She is a little surprised by the sensation. It is beyond anything that she could ever have imagined. Samuel stands there, and soon the sensation is too great, then an eruption through her body that she was not ready for. She stops and holds onto him tightly as her body spasms, and she suddenly loses her grip around his neck and falls backward. She feels Samuel move his hands to her lower back to catch her as her body continues to have small quivers.

He lifts her and places her on a bed of soft grass. Samuel lays beside her and holds her close as she takes in intense breaths, and he feels her tears.

He asks, "What is wrong? Did I hurt you?"

Jutsuk answers, "No, Samuel, you did nothing wrong. You made me feel alive, and I love you more for it." She sits up, crosses her legs, and places her hands on her knees. Samuel remains prone and listens intently.

"Samuel, I want to offer you a home and a sovereign. I need you to help uphold and defend the Laki-Jutsuk Religion. As I have stated, my sister has found the one to be the Sendoka. Still, I am looking for a special kind of devoted man who can make calculated decisions under duress to protect and defend the newly appointed Sendoka.

Samuel goes to speak when Jutsuk asks him to let her finish.

"Samuel Miro, I am asking you to be my Champion and accept this position to fulfill both your destiny and ours. Will you accept what I am asking of you? Will you become my Champion, our Shikakin, the Sendoka's Defender?"

Samuel sits up, places his fist over his heart, and says, "Yes, my Goddess, I will do as you ask and accept this responsibility to you and Laki, the Sendoka, and the Order, but before I accept, I ask only two things in return."

She asks, "What are these things you ask of my sister and me?"

Samuel looks at her straight in the eyes and says, "The first is that you will never hold anything back from me because if I am going to do this, you will need to be honest and also trust me no matter what it might be, and second, that you love me as I will love you, do you agree to these terms" he asks,'

Jutsuk says, "Yes, I agree to your demands," and smiles.

Samuel smiles and says, "Then I will be your Shikakin, your Champion."

Jutsuk lunges forward and wraps her arms around him in a hug. She then sits back, and he sees that she has a chalice and a small blade in her hands. She cuts across her palm and allows her blood to drip into the chalice. She asks Samuel to do the same. He does and then watches their blood swirl in the chalice and blend. She lightly places her hand on the side of his upper chest and tells him to drink. He drinks the warm blood without hesitation as Jutsuk chants, *"Homerudo Torimaki* Shikakin *Kyu ko Kyoja Ta-Da Chini Alde"* a tiny pinpoint of light enters Samuel's chest. A feeling of euphoria spreads through his body, and like William, he also understands the complete beliefs and teachings of the Laki-Jutsuk Religion and immediately feels enlightened and stronger.

She pulls her hand away, and a small scar of an ancient rune for Jutsuk is etched into his chest. He immediately feels enlightened and strong; Samuel Miro no longer exists but for a name like the other. He is now the right arm and Defender of the Sendoka, Commander of the Order of the

Laki & Jutsuk Religion, and the Goddess Jutsuk's Champion. She places a beautiful rose-colored diamond about the size of a robin's egg attached to a leather cord around his neck.

She tells Samuel it is time for her to go and gives him a deep sensual kiss. She looks down, takes hold, and says, "I must go!"

Samuel looks at her and says, "Before you go, then she leans forward, kisses him deeply, places her hands on his shoulders, and pushes him back, so he is lying down. She doesn't have to go as slow this time, as she starts to rock back and forth slowly and then gradually faster. Jutsuk places her hands on his chest and throws her head back while he reaches around and caresses her backside. He sits up, allowing her to feel him slightly differently, and she wraps her arms around his neck and arches her body, and moans in response, and as she rocks faster, her moans get louder until they both explode at the same time for a second time today. She slumps forward and is shaking. He lays back down, and she lays on his chest as multiple aftershocks course through her body. She rolls off of him and regrets that she must leave but remains to lie next to him.

Samuel gets up and reaches out with a hand to help her up. He lifts her effortlessly, and they walk back to the pool to wash. They wash each other and then walk back to the campfire. Samuel goes to dry himself off and sees that Jutsuk is already dry.

Samuel reaches into his backpack, grabs a change of undergarments, and gets dressed. Jutsuk sits on the grass next to the campfire with her knees and arms around them. She looks at him when he is strapping on his sword belt and smiles. He reaches over and helps her up, and by the time she is standing, she is wearing her sheer garments again, which is now clean. A small parchment materializes in her hand, and she gives it to him and tells him to search for a man named William James, gives him a brief description, and tells him, as you travel, the diamonds be dormant. As you get nearer to each other, it will begin to pulse and glow. The brighter the glow, the closer you will be to finding him. He will have in his possession the other half of the parchment.

The man you seek will be traveling northeast, and you will need to meet up with him, accompany him, and protect him, but do not think he is helpless. He has abilities. Laki has explained everything to him, and he is searching for you as we speak. Together we believe both of you can combine your talents and become a force that will surely benefit my sister and me."

She leans forward, kisses him on the cheek, and says, "Thank you." He wraps his arm around her and gently caresses her backside while at the same time giving her a deep soulful kiss.

Jutsuk returns the kiss, pulls away, and says, "Next time" The euphoria of true love envelopes his mind and body; Jutsuk smiles, steps away, then disappears, leaving behind the smell of lavender in the Air.

Samuel puts out the remains of his fire and then straps his crossbow and quiver to his backpack. He pats down the two bodies and finds a few more coins. Samuel then starts his new journey to find this William James, the newly appointed Sendoka of the Laki-Jutsuk Religion. He will become his right arm and shield as the Sendoka, discover an unknown valley, and become the Commander of the Order of the Laki -Jutsuk Religions. Samuel throws his pack over his shoulder, says, Piece of cake," and heads northwest.

Jutsuk *reaches out to* Laki *and tells her that she has found her Champion.*

Chapter 33

William Meets Samuel

It has been six months since William and the Goddess formed their bond and two months since she last visited him, and that was in his dreams, telling him that her sister Jutsuk had found her Champion, and his name is Samuel Miro, and a description. He feels he is getting close to his destination as he has passed through many towns and villages. William has politely inquired about the gentleman in every town and village, and the answer is always no. No one has seen him or even close to the description he has been giving. William knows he has not crossed paths with this person, or the diamond around his neck would have let him know. So, he moves on, searching and asking. He knows that to discover the valley, this person, this other Champion, they need to be together. A large black obsidian wall guards the valley against the unwanted. William has tried to decipher the parchment, and the only thing he can tell is that the valley itself is shrouded in a heavy mist and that no one has ever seen this valley and from what he can tell now is, no one has ever heard of it.

Three days after leaving the last village, he comes across an old man with an ox-drawn wagon and can tell he is a tinkerer by all the noise his cart is making, and William sees that he is coming from the east. When the wagon gets closer, William holds up his hand, and it stops beside him. William wishes the man a good day, and the man seems to relax. William asks him if he has seen anyone with Samuel's description. The old man sits there and thinks for a bit, then tells him that maybe three weeks back, he was being hassled by four thugs who demanded his money and when he said no, they knocked him to the ground and started throwing his wares out on the road.

When a man about your size walks up and tells the thugs to put back all my things, they start laughing, but when they see the look in his eyes, they stop laughing and start to draw their weapons, which was a mistake. The young man, probably around your age, moved with such speed that the four thugs hadn't even fully cleared their weapons before all four men were on the ground. When they awoke, all four were hogtied and crying like babies.

The old man looks at him and says, "I thanked him and offered to pay him for his assistance, but he politely declined, telling me it was no problem. Do you want to know the most peculiar thing about that young man coming to my rescue? It wasn't that he would not take payment, but he asked me if I had seen a fellow traveler that seems to fit your description almost perfectly."

William asks the old man, "Did he by chance give his name?"

The old man thinks a bit longer and says, "Samuel Meelo, or Maro, no, that's not it."

William politely says, "Samuel Miro," and the old man says, "Yes, that's it!"

William thanks him, then places his hand on his arm and allows a bit of "*Spirit.*" to flow into him, and the old man doesn't look as tired as he did.

William asks him, "Could you kindly tell me what road he might have taken or in which direction he was traveling?" The old man tells William, "He wasn't taking any road but was heading southwesterly."

Willian thanks the old tinkerer, and William sees dark clouds roll in very quickly. Within minutes the clouds have blocked out the sun, and at that precise moment, William hears the distinct pop. William asks the old man if he has passed any close rock formations. The old man tells him that a large rock formation is on the other side of the hill and points. William says, "Thank you," and politely tells him to get inside his wagon and not come out until he says so. The old tinker looks bewildered but does as William asks and moves into his wagon, stepping over the seat and through a door. William reminds him, "Do not come out until I say so, is that understood?" He hears the man agree as he places a tightly fitting board over the opening to the wagon. William sets his pack, jacket, and tanbur near the wagon, moves off the road away from everything, and calls forth the elements as one hand glows a soft brown, almost beige, and the other becomes a pulsing blue and then he sees them just topping the rise. The three creatures come at him at a full run. William quickly shakes his wrists, and the elements in his hands extend to about four meters in length, and he snaps them so that he quickly recoils them in his hands.

The beasts are getting very close, and William lashes out with the whip of earth and hits the one closest to him in the shoulder, causing the beast to roar with pain and stumble as a shaft of sharp rock penetrates its shoulder. Though it struggles, it breaks free from the Earth shaft and keeps it coming at him. William softly speaks, "*Da Chik to Mu*," and the stone shaft that penetrated the creature's shoulder shatters, driving sharp pieces of stone throughout its body. The beast stumbles again, but this time it falls and slides along the ground, and when it comes to a stop, the beast is still. He immediately raises the other whip over his head and, with each turn, allows it to stretch out. He flicks his wrist and catches one of the other beasts directly in the face, and just like the other, it roars out with pain and falls to the ground. The beast slowly rises and shakes its massive head, trying to clear its vision, and then roars in rage as it realizes it is blind. The third leaps at William with a speed he had not anticipated or seen before, he rolls out of the way, and just when the beast passes him, he brings both whips together. Despite some resistance, they merge into a single lash, strike out, and wrap themselves around the beast's body. There is opposition, and without *Spirit* in place to calm them, the two manas split, and when they do, they pull themselves apart and the beast simultaneously. The remaining beast, now blind, is just out of the reach of his whips and begins sniffing the Air. William is distracted as he watches the beast and then notices a Sutaraukaji one with the bloody cloth covering its eyes standing at the top of the hill, and he seems to be weighing in the slaughter of the beasts before him. The robed one stands there, raises his arms into the Air, and chants something that William cannot discern, and at that moment, the beast seems to have captured his scent and takes a few steps forward, stops and sniffs the Air again. William drops to one knee and slaps the palm of his hand against the ground. The earth seems to tremble, and water flows up from the ground. The beast charged, and though it could not see, it came right at him. Then William touches the earth with tendrils of blue mana emanating from his fingertips. Suddenly the beast is lifted into the Air as its body is impaled by several large pointed and razor-sharp icicles protruding from the ground. William walks over to the creature and watches as its life essence drains from its body and dies.

William slowly builds up the elements in his hands as the Sutaraukaji pulls back its hood and raises its arms.

William sees the sleeves of its robe slide down, and when they do, he notices strange markings on its forearms, and then he hears chanting in an unknown language. Then the Sutaraukaji claps his hands together, and when it does, William hears another distinct pop and sees a second rift manifesting close to where the Sutaraukaji is standing. William watches as it manifests itself and notices that it is unstable, but something does not feel right. William continues to watch, and then it comes to him. The rift appears on the top of a hill without being in a cave, and two other Sutaraukaji steps through the second rift, both seeming disorientated. William takes the opportunity, lashes out with both coils of elemental whips, and hits the third-robed one; there is a silent scream as it disintegrates, and the unstable rift begins to fluctuate.

William coils the mana whips in his hands and starts running towards the rise, and as he gets closer, he lashes out with both whips with lightning speed and strikes the second-robed before it can react, and it bursts into flame from Williams conjured element of Fire.

The original Sutaraukaji lets out a scream and conjures a fireball, and throws it at William. He quickly deflects it with one of his whips and lashes out with the second elemental whip, and when they hit the Sutaraukaji, like its predecessor, it bursts into flames, and when it does, the fluctuating rift pops and is gone.

William releases the mana, and when he gets to the top of the hill, he sees the rock formation and walks down to it. When he gets to it, he walks around, and a look of worry crosses his brow because he cannot find a cave or anything that would be able to house a rift entrance. Then it hits him at what he sensed was off. His first experience with rifts was that they needed to materialize inside caves. He now sees that the rifts can open anywhere. He then walks back up the hill, contemplating what this could mean, asking himself, "Are the Dark Forces getting stronger? What has changed?" Then he remembers a rumor that some High Priestess of the Dark Scriptures can pass into something called the Dark Realm.

William returns to the tinker's wagon, knocks on the wagon door, and informs him it is safe for him to come out. The tinker can only see ashes floating on the Airs and sees no evidence of the battle that had taken place but knows he heard something outside his wagon. William thanks the tinker and apologizes for any inconvenience he might have caused him.

The tinker says, "Good Sir, there was no inconvenience. I'm just glad that you are okay." William bids him good day and heads off in a northeasterly direction.

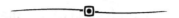

    Samuel walks through a large field when three riders come bearing down on him. He stops, lays his backpack and crossbow on the ground, places his hand on his katana, and releases the hilt while keeping his hand on the pommel. Three men pull up to him, and he sees that they are like the others he has had the pleasure of meeting, and they are wearing uniforms that resemble the Dark Army that he had fought in Shira or Hokida. One of them leans over to the leader and whispers something in his ear, and the reaction on his face tells Samuel everything. The Leader shouts, "You bastard! You were at Shira, and you slaughtered my friends," With that said, the leader charges Samuel on his horse. Samuel pulls out his katana and rolls out of the way of the charging horse. The leader turns his mount sharply, then jumps from it, landing on the ground, and runs directly at Samuel with his broadsword raised. Samuel brings up his katana, blocks the leaders' attack, and then turns his body and sweeps the man's legs from underneath him. The leader falls on his back spread eagle, and Samuel places the tip of his katana at the leader's throat. The other two sit on their horses and do not move when Samuel hears one of them say, "*Rinju Kitikorosu, Death Slayer*," and Samuel pushes the blade of his sword through the leader's throat. The leader tries to scream but cannot as the katana slices through his vocal cords, and with a twist, Samuel severs his jugular, and the man bleeds out in silence.

    The other two men watch what just happened when one charges Samuel while the other turns his horse and rides away. The charging horse is almost on top of him when Samuel steps to the opposite side of his assailant's weapon and swipes his katana along the horse's side. Samuel does not come close to hitting the horse but slices through the horse's belly strap and the man's leg right below his knee. The dark soldier and the saddle fall off the horse's back. The rider lands on his back and is screaming in pain as he struggles to hold his leg; Samuel walks by him, and with a quick downward swing of his katana, he slices the man's head off. The third rider slows, looks back on his two dead friends, and sees the Death

Slayer bending down to retrieve something from the grass. He is unsure what it is and does not pay attention to what it could be. The Dark soldier spurs his horse into a gallop, and as he reaches the base of a hill, he looks back and sees the Death Slayer holding a heavy-duty crossbow. The lone survivor kicks his horse's flanks, and just as he reaches the crest of the hill, a single crossbow bolt catches the rider in the middle of the back, right between his shoulder blades, and he falls from the horse, and lands on his back, pushing the bolt in deeper so that it is now protruding from chest.

Samuel walks up to the two horses and calms them; they are not skittish or shy away from him. He strips the leader's horse and the other horse of its saddle and bags, and he checks the bodies and unexpectedly finds a few coins and some crossbow bolts in the horse's saddlebags. Samuel checks each one and tosses the broken ones. Having scavenged the two dead men and the horses, he takes both the horse's reins and walks with them towards the direction of his third victim. He reaches the small hill and sees the third assailant lying on the ground, barely breathing. Samuel walks up to him and squats down beside him. The Dark Army soldier lies in the grass, gasping, and tries to catch his breath. Samuel smiles at him and says, "This is for my brothers at Shira," and places his hand over the soldier's nose and mouth and watches the soldier struggle briefly and then lie still.

Samuel checks his pockets, finds a few more coins, then goes over to the horse, checks the saddlebags, removes the saddles and bridles of all three horses, slaps them on the rump, and takes off running. Samuel takes a few minutes to clean his katana, sheath it, and is about to continue walking northwest, but something makes him turn southwest.

He started on this mission to find Major Samuel Miro and locate a hidden valley, and he feels that he is getting close to at least meeting this man. He walks along a well-traveled road when he sees a young woman sitting against her ox-drawn cart and notices that the cart is leaning at a peculiar angle. He gets closer and sees that the wheel has slipped off its axle. He walks up to her and sees that she is crying. His body blocks out the morning sun and casts her in his shadow. She looks up, and he asks if he can be of assistance. She slowly nods her head. William tells her not to worry and walks her to a nearby rock to sit down.

William removes his backpack, tanbur, and outer coat, placing them in a neat pile near the rock where the young lady is sitting. William rolls up his sleeves, picks up the wheel, and puts it near the cart. William knows he could use mana to lift the cart, but he thinks good old-fashioned muscle works almost as well. He looks on the ground for the hub pin and sees it under the cart. He gets lower and stretches out his arm to try and grab the pin. He can feel it between his fingers, and then he has it in his hand, and as he tries to pull his arm out, he realizes that the bracelet given to him by his first love, Alexandria, has gotten caught on something. He tries to release the bracelet without breaking it when he sees that the sun is partially blocked. He looks up, and the young woman is standing near the road, and until she steps somewhat down into the ditch, William does not notice that she has a large butcher knife in her hand. She raises it to strike him, and he sees the sun's glint flash off the blade. At that moment, he feels the pink diamond throb inside his shirt, and she starts to bring the knife down to drive it into him. William raises his free arm and brings forth the mana of Air to defend himself, and just as she gets the blade down, it stops within inches of cutting him. The woman draws back the knife to try and stab him once more, and then William hears a whistling sound, and the woman screams and drops the knife. He watches her grab at her shoulder, and as she turns, William can see a crossbow bolt sticking out of her back right between her shoulder blades. Her knees give out, and she crumbles to the ground sitting on the edge of the ditch, when she starts screaming at William, "You need to die; you are supposed to die!"

Though she looks in great pain, she somehow picks up the knife on the ground and tries to stab William again. She keeps screaming, "You must die!" Before she even gets a chance to, he hears the whistling sound once more, and the woman stops screaming; all William hears is a gurgling sound, and the woman looks down at him, and that is when William can now see that a second bolt has struck the woman from behind and is sticking out of her mouth. The woman slumps forward dead, only to land on William.

William realizes that he is lying in a ditch with his arm caught under a wagon, and sprawled across his legs is a dead woman, and he laughs at his predicament. He knows he could remove the woman with mana and probably do the same with getting unstuck, but he prefers not to take a chance on breaking the bracelet.

He lies quietly with the mana he had conjured to defend himself, in case whoever shot those crossbow bolts is in league with the woman lying across his legs. When the rose diamond around his neck begins to pulse, he can raise his head enough to see a lone figure walking towards him, carrying a crossbow nonchalantly over its shoulder. The figure gets closer, and William can see that he is a well-built man and about the same height as himself. The man is wearing light beige attire and is carrying an Empire-style katana on his hip. The man walks up, stands on the edge of the ditch, and then squats. William can feel the pink diamond throbbing faster, and he feels the warmth of its glow under his shirt. He looks at William and says, "You seem to have yourself in quite a predicament."

William cannot see his face as he is in shadow with the sun at his back but somehow senses that the man is smiling and answers, "That I do. If you do not mind, a little assistance would be greatly appreciated, if it is not too much trouble?"

He looks at him and says, "Would you mind answering a question?"

William lays there and answers, "Sure, why not? I am not going anywhere."

He hears the man laugh and says, "I guess you're not right now," Then he asks, "Are you, William James?"

William, at first, does not answer for anyone trying to kill him could ask that question, but once he mentions his name, William feels the crystal given to him by the Goddess Laki pulse even stronger, and he can feel it glowing. William notices a similar rose diamond around the stranger's neck, which also seems to be glowing. William says, "Yes, I am, and might you be Samuel Miro?" Like William, when Samuel hears his name, he feels his crystals pulse even stronger.

Samuel stands, places the crossbow on the ground, removes his belt and sword, carefully steps down into the ditch, quickly lifts the dead woman off of William, and tosses her onto the road. He then positions himself to lift the wagon enough so William can use his free hand to help him unhook his arm from under the wagon.

Samuel sees that William has pulled his arm and hand free and carefully lowers the wagon. He then steps out of the ditch and puts his hand out to help William. It wasn't a deep ditch, but William grasps his hand anyway, and Samuel pulls him onto the road. William brushes himself off as Samuel puts on his belt with the sword and then picks up the crossbow.

William continues to brush himself as he walks over to the rock where he left his belongings. William puts on his pack and watches Samuel walk over to the dead woman and pull the bolts from her body. He then searches the wagon and finds a hollowed-out gourd with some water. He takes the two bolts he removed from the dead woman and rinses off any traces of blood or gore.

When done, he looks at William and says directly, "Shall we go find this valley?"

William says, "Sure, why not, but let me properly introduce myself before we do." And extends his hand and says, "William James, thank you for your assistance." Samuel says, "Samuel Miro, a pleasure to give my assistance." and smiles. They both feel the small pink diamonds go cold, and when they pull them out, they see that they are dull in color and then crack with small fragments falling to the ground. William is surprised that the one man he was supposed to search for in this land appears from nowhere and saves his life. He mentions to Samuel that he is making his way north, and Samuel tells him the same until he felt the diamond and turned southwest.

Before they leave, William asks him to give him a minute, and he goes over to the young woman, rips her dress, and sees a small blood-red teardrop inside a pentacle burned into her shoulder.

Samuel says, "I had seen that before, when I was in the Battle of Shira, but not sure what it meant."

William tells him, "It is the sign of the followers of the Dark Scriptures." and lets her hair fall back to cover the mark.

William politely asks Samuel to step back.

Samuel does and hears William chant, *"Tenka Ti Iri Satai,"* and sees one of Williams's hands start to give off a red mist that seems to circle and caress his hand, and then he sees a flickering red flame appear in his palm. He throws it at the dead woman, watching as her body quickly burns and turns black, and within seconds the only thing remaining of the woman is a pile of dark ash promptly swept away by a gentle breeze. Samuel notices Williams's other hand has a white mist circling it. When done, William turns to Samuel and says, "Shall we go?"

Samuel says, "Nice trick."

William says, "Yes, it is, and I have a few more up my sleeves." and smiles.

Samuel notices that mischievous look in his eyes and says to William, "We are going to become very good friends," and smiles back.

They start on their journey to find the hidden valley.

William and Samuel travel the roads, meeting and chatting with strangers, or sometimes over and around small hills to try and reach their destination. They both know that the Goddesses must establish a beacon of salvation for the people of the lands, especially for the devoted followers of the Laki-Jutsuk Religious Order.

Within the first few days of walking, they discover that they have established a network of informants in their travels with William from the South and Samuel from the East. People to assist or call upon for favors and services. William finds out that the Goddess Jutsuk had visited Samuel, and they instructed him to search out William. The Goddess told Samuel that he and William were to make the journey to the hidden valley.

William tells Samuel everything he knows about the Dark Scriptures, the marks on the followers, the rifts, and the two creatures, one being a robed one and the other being a creature or beast.

William decided to be upfront while they were getting ready to enjoy a warm meal one evening. He tells Samuel about his ability to conjure the five manas or elements and to be able to use them. His younger sister is to become the next Queen of the Tatokai Archipelago when his mother passes on the necklace of royalty. His older brother, one of his best friends, and his fiancé Alexandria were murdered by a vicious little man, and how he had to leave the islands because he committed one of the most severe crimes and killed the bastard. He then tells how he left the islands and has traveled the continent.

Samuel says, "I'm sorry." and takes a sip of tea.

Samuel looks at him and says, "Well, as long as you are upfront, and for what the Goddesses have planned for us, I might as well be upfront myself. He tells William about his father being the Advisor General and the bond with Princess Asami. His training, his connection with his two best friends, how he can sense if anything were to happen to them, the battle of Shira, and fighting the Dark Army. Two of his best friends, Hikaru and Carrie, were murdered by Lord Tao, the Emperor's brother, and how he commanded Dark followers in the city of Hokida, his banishment, and why.

Samuel sits there for a moment in silence and quickly wonders about his friend, Reiko Takahashi, and how she is doing. He shakes his head and sees William sitting there quietly, knowing what Samuel might be going through because he has gone through it himself.

Then he says to William, "I almost forgot, earlier you mentioned some sort of beast that could be from what did you call it the Dark Realm?"

William says. "Yes, why do you ask?"

Samuel tells William what his friend Hikaru had to go up against when he was thrown into the Commander of the Dark Armies' Arena just before the battle. Samuel volunteered to help remove the bodies strung up along the inside walls of the "Arena," He remembers seeing some strange-looking beast that his friend Hikaru had killed and when he described it.

William tells him, What your friend fought was a "Chizobutsu," and it came from the Dark Realm."

All Samuel says is, "Good to know."

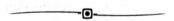

That night they make camp, and as in what has become a tradition, William cooks the meal, brews the tea, and plays his tanbur, while Samuel hunts for and usually finds the evening's meal. They both decided it would be in their best interest if William did the cooking. His experience working in the kitchen has been beneficial to both of them, and it seemed that no matter what Samuel might catch, William knew how to prepare it and make it taste good.

Another night as they were sitting in camp, waiting for the rabbit that Samuel caught to cook, he tells William that all he had to go on was a brief description and a name. When Samuel saw the woman going to stab him, he did what he did, whether William was the one he was looking for or just a person that was about to get murdered. Then he felt the crystal pulse and knew he was the one, so he did what he had to do.

William tells Samuel the same thing, other than the Goddess Laki appearing in his dreams and giving him a brief description and a name. They laugh, and Samuel says, "I guess they did not want to make it too easy!" They both laugh again.

William and Samuel travel the roads, sometimes following the fields and around small valleys but are always heading north to reach their destination. While they walk, Samuel tells William that Jutsuk said to him that he was the appointed Sendoka of the Laki-Jutsuk Religion, and it is his duty as the Shikakin to protect the Sendoka at all costs.

One night after they had made camp, William steps off to relieve himself, while Samuel sits at the campfire and carefully turns the rabbit that is on the spit off to the side to cool when he hears a twig snap, and then a woman says, "Be quiet you idiots!" not too far from their camp. William is coming back, and he sees Samuel raise his hand in the Air, followed by a few other hand and finger gestures. Silently, Samuel tells William to stay back because they have company and then holds up four fingers, telling him that four persons are approaching the camp and William needs to stay out of sight. William does so without argument, as he and Samuel discussed this. Samuel has taught William specific hand signals to communicate without words. William never takes offense when Samuel tells him to be quiet and knows it is for his safety and well-being.

A few minutes later, three men and a woman who all look in dire need of bathing walk into the camp. The woman steps forward, smiles at Samuel, and asks, "Who are you talking to?"

Samuel slowly places his hand on the pommel of his katana and says, "No one, "Now, what can I do for you, fine people?" He sits patiently and watches them as he gently pushes upon his sword guard with his thumb to unlock it, so he can draw his katana more quickly if it comes to that.

He sizes them up and sees that two men carry bastard swords and undoubtedly don't know how to use them. He knows how they hold them and use them more for intimidation. He knows these two are the least of his worries. The other man, who is quite large, has a mace on his belt, is probably the second biggest threat, and notices that he is quiet and just staring at him. The woman is the biggest threat, and he sees she has a small, short spear point blade tucked in her belt, and she looks to be the quickest of the four in the way she has her hand resting on the hilt of her blade.

The big guy grabs the spit with the cooled rabbit and takes a huge bite, ripping the meat from the carcass, and as the juices run down his chin, he smiles at Samuel and then tosses the rest of the rabbit into the fire. The rabbit's juices cause the fire's flames to flare up. The sudden flare-up causes everyone to move at once. The two men with the bastard swords hesitate slightly before their blades clear their scabbards. Samuel has drawn his katana and has finished nearly decapitating the two men with lightning speed.

After seeing his two friends disposed of so quickly, the big guy roars with anger, grabs for his mace, and then swings his mace in Samuel's head. Samuel sees it coming at him and drops down under the big man's swing, so it misses him and passes over his head. Samuel swings his sword, turns his wrist at the last second, and then flicks his wrist. The movement is so minute that he has chopped off the big man's hand holding the mace, and he has not yet realized that both his hand and the mace are gone. Samuel reverses his sword and drives it up through the man's chin and out through the top of his head, killing him instantly. Samuel quickly pulls back his sword and lets the big brute fall to the ground.

The woman doesn't move as she is shocked at seeing how quickly her partner and her two friends are dead, all within seconds of each other right before her eyes.

Samuel wipes the blood from his sword on the brute while keeping his eyes on the woman. The woman screams and starts shouting profanities and quickly lunges at him with the spear point blade in her hands. Samuel was waiting for it, but before she could take another step, she is held in place by something and could not move. The woman starts screaming as William walks back into the camp, and Samuel notices a white mist emanating from William's hands and sees the same mist encasing her body.

Like Samuel, William walks into the camp, flicks his wrist, and forcefully slams her down onto the ground. Her face and chest take the brunt of the impact, and she lies on the ground unconscious. Samuel walks over to her and takes her blade. He then goes around and checks the bodies of the three slain men. When the woman moans and begins to stir, he has found some coins and a few other items. William looks down at her and binds her with an Airflow. He looks beyond the black teeth and boils covering her body and the self-mutilations and sees that she was probably pretty in her younger life.

He has seen this in a few towns in his travels, the effects of the highly addictive drug *Yakukin*, and how the people become addicted very quickly. He has seen what happens after taking the drug; a euphoria like no other after smoking it for the first time. Then, one becomes highly addicted and chases that demon constantly to achieve that euphoria again but never can.

She is now wholly awake and immediately starts screaming profanities at Samuel and William. William has had enough, and he binds her mouth to stop her from shouting any more obscenities, though there is almost complete silence and even with her mouth muffled, she continues to rant and rave.

Samuel looks at William, smiles, and says, "Thank you."

William walks over to each body and looks for the burn mark on their shoulders. Only the big brute had the blood-red teardrop with the pentacle burned into his shoulder. He walks over to the woman, and as he looks at her shoulder, she stares at him with pure hate.

William and Samuel have encountered a few followers with the same burn marks at least every couple of weeks in their travels, and the outcome is always the same. William nods his head, and Samuel takes her spear point knife, looks the woman in her eyes, and says, "Sorry," then gently pierces the woman's side between the second and third ribs to drive the blade into her heart. Samuel picks up the four bodies, and like every other time, he watches, amazed as one of Williams's hands starts to encircle itself with a red mist, and then he sees a flame appear in the palm of his hand. William chants, "*Ite To Hidaku No Sensi*," and tosses the ball of flame onto the pile of bodies, and like before, Samuel watches as they slowly wither and turn black and then looks at four piles of ash. He hears William say, "*Mikamotosu Mewatisha*," and feels a gentle breeze blow through the camp and scatter the ashes.

They are back sitting around the fire, and Samuel reaches into his pack for some pieces of rabbit jerky to warm it over the fire as William starts making some tea.

William asks Samuel, "Does it bother you?"

Samuel nicely asks, "Can you be a little more specific?"

William says, "The killing, I understand that we have to protect ourselves because the Goddesses have plans for us, but don't you find it unsettling that someone or something is trying to stop us almost every time we turn around."

Samuel asks, "What exactly is your question? William."

William looks at him and says, "Do you get tired of it?"

Samuel looks at William and says calmly, "No, William, I don't. The Goddesses picked you and me out of everyone on this planet, and I'll be sure to do whatever it takes to protect you and the Goddesses. So be it if I have to kill one person or a thousand. Whatever these Dark Forces throw at us, I will make sure I give it back ten-fold."

William sits there smiling, and when Samuel asks him why he is smiling, William says, "I can hear it in your tone of voice that you have the same conviction as I do, and you said it yourself, the Goddesses picked us, knowing out histories and our flaws. I truly believe in them and what they have given us; whether it be a blessing now or a curse later, it doesn't matter. Like you, I have had the pleasure of meeting one of them and being embraced by her. I will do everything I can to see that their wishes are fulfilled. And like you said, "Whether it be one or a thousand, so be it."

William sits there and says, "The tea is ready." Samuel smiles back and says, "Good."

William hands him one of the cups of his mint tea and says, "Dinner might be a warm rabbit jerky, but we still have tea."

Samuel makes himself comfortable against his pack as William strums his tanbur. Samuel relaxes, listening to the music and drinking his tea. The remainder of the night is quiet and relaxing.

Chapter 34

The Sacred Valley

Since their encounter with the four bandits over two weeks ago, William and Samuel have not encountered any more hostiles and have continued on their journey north. They reached the southern edges of the Plains of Sayashi just over two weeks ago, and have stopped and rested, every night without incident. They are slowly getting to what they hope is their destination as the mountains loom ever closer.

After almost countless days of walking, they find themselves standing before a large black slab of obsidian stone that looks unnatural against the rough texture of the granite mountains. The black stone is smooth as glass with a mirror-like finish in some places and rough in others. The one thing that they both notice is that the slab of obsidian stone seems to divide the mountain range down the middle, and when they walk closer, they feel an ominous presence that appears to be generating from the other side of the stone. William and Samuel pull out their pieces of parchment, and they both notice s new phrase has appeared on the parchment. The sun is beginning to set, and they agree to make camp here tonight and journey on tomorrow at first light. They are relaxing and drinking some of William's tea, and Samuel remembers his history and recalls these are two separate mountain ranges, and that range from the West is one type of stone while the mountain range coming from the East is another type. They talk a while longer, and the night passes quietly.

The following day as the sun begins to rise, they break camp, and both stand before the slab of black obsidian stone. They look at their reflections, and William takes a deep breath and says, "Shall we?" They take out their pieces of parchment, place the two pieces side by side, and read from the parchment, *"Mato Kini Seto Darna Laro Obesut Chaptum."* They immediately hear a rumbling noise, and a line appears on the surface of the smooth black stone and runs from the Plains floor to disappear into the tops of the mountain. The line widens, and then the two halves of obsidian stone slowly separate and slide back into the sides of the mountains. The rumbling slows, and then stops, as the two stones are approximately ten meters apart. Samuel draws his katana as William allows the full spectrum of the mana colors to dance around his hands and through his fingers.

They cautiously enter the fissure and immediately feel something unseen break, like a seal or ward, and they know that what lies before them will soon be open to the world. They continue to walk through a large cavern of smooth black stone with various colors streaking through it. William runs his hand over the surface of the glass-like stone, and Samuel says to William, "Obsidian rock, formed through high volcanic temperatures." Though the fissure is broad, it is not long, and the light at the end is bright and blinding. They are about to exit the fissure and decide to stop momentarily so that their eyes can adjust to the bright light.

They step into the sunlight, gaze at what is before them, and are completely amazed. The magnitude and beauty of this gorge are genuinely breathtaking. William and Samuel cannot begin to imagine the source of power that carved out this gorge over the centuries. They find themselves looking up and around at the natural land bridges, and they even find some large and small caves with hollowed-out stones or large natural pools to catch the natural spring waters that run through the mountains. They continue their journey, and the next three days and nights pass uneventfully.

On the morning of the fourth day, William and Samuel are stepping out of the gorge and standing on a large plateau that gradually sweeps down into a luscious green valley. Two-hundred-meter-high canyon walls run the length of the valley on both sides. They walk to the plateau's edge and look over a vast, nearly flat expanse of land that looks to have been naturally created by the rivers and rains that made their way through the gorge. They see a stream that most likely carried nutrients from the Plains of Sayashi and can see that it was a great river at one time due to the water table lines that run along both sides of the valley's stone walls.

A natural path runs parallel with a small stream almost straight down the middle of the valley floor and curves here and there to meander around the outcropping of jagged obsidian stones that dot the valley floor. Though the rocks appear ominous, they add beauty to the backdrop of scattered patches of wildflowers blooming in every color imaginable. Small, rounded hills seem to have been pushed up from the earth and carefully smoothed over not to hinder one's view of what lies beyond them.

They walk down the plateau slope following the path and walk most of the day, and both know that due to the valley walls, the sun will set quicker here than on the plains. They decide to call it a day, and Samuel starts a small campfire when they find a suitable location. As the fire catches, he pulls from his pack some wrapped pieces of seasoned meat and a small carafe of wild berry wine he bought from a traveling caravan while they were on the Plains of Sayashi. He places the seasoned meat on a couple of skewers from his pack to cook them, then pours two cups of wine and hands one to William. William sits there, unwrapping his tanbur, and reaches for the wine for a quick sip. He places the cup on the ground beside him when they both feel the temperature quickly plummet a few degrees, and the sky becomes overcast with dark clouds.

Over the soft crackling noises of the fire and the sizzling of the meat on the skewers, they hear a distinct pop not far from where they are camping. William places his tanbur on the ground and looks at Samuel, and all he says is, "A rift," and Samuel nods, and without asking any questions, he stands and pushes up on the sword guard with his thumb to unlock his sword. They both sense something is charging them through the darkness, coming at them fast. They hear a guttural growl, and the running stops, and in that split second, they both know that the creature has leaped into the Air. Samuel has his sword fully drawn, grasping it with both hands with the blade placed close to his ear as a bluish-white mist encircles William's hands as he chants, "Kuri to Yuki."

The creature is in midair when Samuel takes four quick steps and brings his sword down in a slashing motion. The beast is severely wounded, and William immediately strikes out with two streams of cold blue mana, entrapping its body and then slamming it to the ground. Samuel walks up to the stunned beast, places his sword's tip on the creature's head, and drives his blade down through its head.

William releases the mana, and the ice melts from the creature's body, he then conjures Fire, and as his hands glow a deep fiery red, he blasts the pile of creature's parts, and they instantly disintegrate into ash. He then calls on the mana Air, and the ashes float away.

They leave the campfire and search for a cave where the rift should have appeared. William felt something, and he had felt this before, just before meeting Samuel. William motions for Samuel to follow him, and then William stands still and sees him point to a shimmering object in the middle of the Air. The shimmer is floating above the ground and is just over two meters high.

Samuel looks at William, already knowing the question, then puts a finger to his lips. William stares at the shimmer of the rift opening, looks at Samuel, and motions for him to be ready. Samuel does as he is asked and readies his sword.

William walks up to the rift, and when he gets within a few meters, he conjures the four manas and weaves them tightly together. The bond between William and Samuel has allowed Samuel to witness the weaving of the four manas. Samuel is always impressed at how William conjures the mana of *Spirit* and ties the four together. William looks into the shimmering rift and sees the same blackness he has seen before. Samuel stands near him with his katana ready when suddenly, one of the beasts jumps through the rift and knocks William to the ground extinguishing his elemental sphere, and he thinks he sees a flash of silver cross Samuels's eyes.

Samuel moves with extraordinary speed as his katana cuts and slices the beast in several places. William watches Samuel's katana move in one fluid motion with no hesitation, and then it is over as the beast lies on the ground in several pieces, unmoving. Samuel walks over to William, helps him up, and watches him conjure the four elements of Air, Earth, water, and Fire and weave them together for a second time. Samuel stands even closer to him, ready to defend William. William wraps the *Spirit* mana around the four to bind them and sends a blast of the five elements directly into the rift and blackness. Samuel feels the force of the explosion as it hits the blackness, and then he hears a loud painful shriek coming from the darkness, and the rift closes with a loud popping sound. William immediately places a ward around the rift to deter others from opening in the same spot. When the rift disappeared, so did the clouds, and the setting sun casts its evening glow over the valley. William then conjures a fireball and tosses it onto the beast, and seconds later, there is nothing but ash.

They are heading back to their camp when William places his hand on Samuel's shoulder. The same bond between them allows Samuel to sense what William is sensing, and Samuel immediately knows that someone or something is out in the darkness watching them. William takes to one knee, places his hand's palm on the ground, and chants, "*Kakeru Ni Tekihi To Na*." Blue light with silver sparkles quickly shoots out in every direction along the ground. Seconds later, they hear a throaty grunt, and a thud, as if someone was falling, not ten meters from where they are. William stands and walks with Samuel towards where they heard the grunt.

William tosses a small soft yellow flame into the Air, quickly illuminating the surrounding area. They see a Sutaraukaji lying on the ground in the fetal position, whimpering and holding his hands to his head. Samuel walks up to the robed figure and drives his katana through its heart. They step back as William conjures Fire that engulfs the Sutaraukaji, and a gentle breeze blows the ash away. They again search the area but can find no cave. William sends out a combination of mana and senses no more threats, but Samuel notices a look of concern on William's face as they walk.

They return to their camp, and Samuel asks him, "Was that a Sutaraukaji you told me about?"

William tells him, "Yes, that was a Sutaraukaji, and all Samuels says is, "Nasty fuckers."

"Yes, they are!" William says.

They eat and enjoy a glass of plum wine when Samuel still sees the concern on Williams's face and asks, "William, what is wrong?" William says, "Samuel, I have crossed paths with the Sutaraukaji and the Chizobutsu, and the one thing they always had in common was that when a rift appeared, it did so in a cave or cropping of rock. The cave or cropping of rock with an opening to harness the and refrain it from expanding too big, Samuel, as you know, we both saw that this particular rift was nowhere near a cave or cropping of rock. It seems to have manifested itself out in the open, and I know of only once of it happening, and that was right before we met, and the same thing happened. Dark clouds came in and blocked out the sun. Then a rift appeared just like tonight. Samuel asks, "Why do you think things are different now? What could have changed so drastically in this world to allow what has happened?" William tells

Samuel, "I think a catalyst has taken its place in this world, and I have heard rumors of a Dark Priestess and two others that can enter the Dark Realm where these creatures and beasts originate and return to ours. Somehow, if she or they have learned how to conjure these rifts without caves, it might have tipped the scales in their favor, but I also think that these rifts cannot appear in direct sunlight, per the dark clouds appearing.

Samuel looks at him and says, "I guess we will have to get rid of them." He raises his plum wine cup.

William smiles and asks, "Get rid of what?"

Samuel smiles and says, "Get rid of the clouds, of course!"

William answers, "The clouds, why didn't I think of that," and they both start laughing.

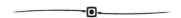

The following day, they continue their journey, and as they walk, Samuel asks, "William, why do you think these attacks by the what did you call them, oh yes, the Sutaraukaji and the Chizobutsu are becoming more frequent?"

William answers, "I think the Sutaraukaji, the Chizobutsu, and the Dark Forces are trying to upset the balance of good and evil in this world. I genuinely believe that the Dark powers want to release something so evil and corrupt that it could destroy everything we know and love in this world. The world we know will turn into chaos and darkness if that happens.

"William, you can't be serious. What or who would want or could do that?"

"Samuel, think about it. Why all these attacks, and even more since we met each other? If we find this valley and do as the Goddesses ask, it could make it more difficult for these unforeseen to do what they want. They are trying very hard to stop us from reaching the valley." Samuel thinks for a moment and says, "Do you think the "Gods Guichi and Tanin" are purposely trying to throw the world into chaos?"

William answers, "I think so, only because of what I have heard in my travels is that they want the chaos and darkness because, with those two things, they can release the God Nimponin and establish a new Dark Realm. I think they have someone in this world who can pass both ways through a rift from the Dark Realm, and whoever it might be is powerful or will become very powerful and is determined to help the two Gods to rule this world."

Samuel walks in silence.

William says, "My biggest concern is that if what we have seen in our travels is anything of what may come, there is a chance that Darkness will win, and that will make our battle worse than it is."

Samuel looks at William, smiles, and says, "I guess we need to find this valley."

Around mid-morning, on the fifth day, William and Samuel begin to see a dark horizontal shadow in the distance that seems to cross the canyon floor from one side to the other. By the afternoon of the sixth day, they find themselves standing before a monolithic wall that is black and as smooth as glass and looks to be over thirty meters high. There are no openings in the wall to go through or footholds or handholds to climb over. William and Samuel simultaneously touch the wall with the palms of their hands and feel a slight vibration. They step back, and William reaches into his pouch and pulls out the folded piece of parchment, as Samuel does the same. With both pieces combined, they recite "*Shintemo Toi Bokuta Yarakata Si*" from the parchment and then watch as a single pinpoint of white light appears about five meters up and in the middle, where the path stops at the wall. The pinpoint grows slightly more prominent and then separates into two white-hot flames, and the flames move in opposite directions cutting a horizontal line approximately ten meters across. The flames stop and then proceed down to the canyon floor, and when the two flames reach the canyon floor, they go out. William and Samuel then recite the following line, "*Kyoka No Sobika Issetsu.*" The ground vibrates as the freshly cut outline of stone slowly sinks into the earth to form a smooth walkway, and they now have a passage through the wall.

They walk through, noticing the ancient runes and glyphs carved into the tunnel's floor, walls, and ceiling. They estimate that the wall is over twenty meters thick, and as they exit the tunnel, they find themselves stepping into something. They feel the ground vibrate once again and hear a faint grinding noise. They turn to watch the cutout block slowly rise back into place, and the wall is again unblemished.

The land before them is shrouded in a lavender mist, and visibility is down to a meter. They take a step, and the mist melts away, showing the valley's width; as they journey farther into the valley, the mist continues to melt away until they find themselves staring at a massive mountain range on both sides with snowcapped peaks. The ranges progressively rise from the sides of the canyon walls and seem to reach even higher. They continue walking through the valley surrounded by the same mountain range on both sides except where they entered. After three days of walking in a westerly direction, they reach the base of a black obsidian sphere that rises high into the sky. They see that the peak of this single obsidian mountain rises far above the others, and it disappears into a cluster of low-hanging clouds. They move on and begin walking to the far eastern side of the valley, and as the mist clears, they discover a massive forest filled with various types of trees that neither one has seen before. They feel something in the woods and decide not to investigate it. William and Samuel turn north, and after another three days, they find what was foretold by the Goddesses. They come across a pile of flat, perfectly square obsidian stones stacked approximately one meter high.

The sun is setting, and they make camp; with very little wood lying about, William's hand glows a soft color of red and starts a campfire. Samuel takes a pot from his pack, fills it with water from his canteen, and places it near the fire. While waiting for the water to boil, Samuel reaches again into his pack, brings out some dried beef that is lightly seasoned with a range of spices, and hands some to William.

The pot of water begins to boil when William removes it from the fire and pours the water into a small ceramic teapot. He slowly swirls the water and tea around in the pot, and just when the aroma of delicate mint bursts from the pot, he knows it is ready and pours two cups.

While they are relaxing and sipping the sweet mint and earthy tea, Samuel asks him, "William, I have always been curious about how you came to know this particular blend of this tea. I have been drinking tea my whole life and never tasted or smelled anything like this. What is your secret, if I may ask?"

William says, "It is no secret, I learned the tea blend from a beautiful young woman named Freya, who was the owner and barmaid at a tavern in a little town called Tokora a few years back. I had helped the locals with a Sutaraukaji and a Chizobutsu problem. She was grateful and gave me the recipe for the blend of teas. William briefly thinks back, and a smile comes across his face.

Samuel sees this, says, "Just a recipe, okay," and smiles.

William looks at Samuel and says, "Now I have a question? When that beast came through the rift and knocked me down, I could have sworn that I saw a flash of silver cross over your eyes. Would you care to explain?"

Samuel looks at him and says, "It's called *Chikara*." My two friends, Reiko, Hikaru, and I have it. I cannot explain how I got it, but it somehow heightens my ability with my katana when it happens. It does the same for Reiko and her longbow; it did it for Hikaru, the battle-ax. It raises our proficiency levels many times higher than that of a Master's. Usually, it would take a Master practicing every day for twenty years, and he would still not even come close to achieving the level of proficiency that we are and were able to achieve."

William says, "Okay, because from what I saw, that beast didn't have a chance once you went into slice and dice mode."

Samuel laughs and says, "I like that slice and dice."

William says, Thank you."

"Don't worry about it; that is what friends are for," Samuel smiles.

Another night passes uneventfully, and as the sun spreads its morning light across the valley, William and Samuel are standing across from each other with the pile of flat obsidian stone between them.

Samuel looks at William and asks, "You want to go first?"

William says, "This should be interesting," and picks up the first flat stone.

They start lifting the stones one at a time, and when they lift the final stone, they discover a crate made from an ancient wood that neither of them has seen before. They carefully lift the crate out of the hole and place it between them.

When Samuel killed the woman and her friends, Samuel kept her spearpoint blade. Samuel now takes her spearpoint and uses it to pry open the lid. They look inside and see a large square object approximately the exact measurements of the crate's interior, and it is wrapped in a white linen cloth and tied with a leather cord.

William and Samuel carefully lift the wrapped object out of the crate and place it on the ground. Samuel puts the cover back on top of the crate, and then they pick up the box and place it on the crate's lid. William unties the cord and folds back the linen. Sitting before them is an intricately carved box made from the same type of wood as the crate, but this box is highly polished with ancient symbols and runes engraved on the sides and top of the box. William and Samuel both place their hands with their palms down on top of the box, and they repeat a single word, "*Hiraika*," and they hear a click. They lift the cover, and inside they find four smaller boxes and remove them. They close the lid and place the four smaller boxes and the cloth-wrapped object on top of the larger box. William picks up the cloth-wrapped thing and unwraps it to find a leatherbound book tied with a lavender ribbon. He unties the ribbon, opens the book, and then starts going through the book. He tells Samuel that the crate and boxes are hand-crafted and made from Bisham wood that grows only in this valley. While William reads, Samuel unties the cords and removes the linens wrapped around each box. He then takes the smallest of the three boxes, opens it, and discovers a pair of black stones engraved with glyphs and runes. The second box he picks has seven small Dark Obsidian stones, all engraved with ancient glyphs and runes and inscribed with strange symbols. He sees that there are three pairs and an odd seventh one. He closes the box and reaches for the following box. When he opens the lid, he lets out a whistle, and as William looks up from his reading, Samuel turns the box for William to see, and William says, "Wow!" Inside the box are six perfectly flawless multifaceted blue diamonds, all precisely the same size and weight, attached to a delicately crafted platinum chain. He closes the lid, takes out the last and largest rectangular box, and opens it. Inside he finds something wrapped in a soft lamb's wool. He takes out the object, carefully unfolds the lamb's wool, and discovers a monoclinic-shaped Black Obsidian Crystal with a highly polished mirror-like finish like the wall and ancient glyphs and runes exactly like the seven smaller ones.

William goes to turn another page when a letter falls from the book. He knows that the writing in the letter is the ancient script and language. He opens it and starts reading it out loud.

Our Champions,

Where you are now is the one place on Chikyu that man had never seen until you two stepped into the valley. The items necessary to protect this valley and establish a home for the Laki-Jutsuk Religion are in the crate. The book that you hold will guide you. In the small rectangular box, ancient runestones are placed throughout the valley and at its entrance to establish the protection wards.

The square box contains six perfectly faceted blue diamonds. You will each take one and place them around your necks. Through rigorous training, you will need to find four gifted individuals who distinguish themselves in your teachings, both in the manipulation of the manas and the art of fighting. When you deem them ready, you will present them with a blue diamond. The blue diamond will accept or reject them; there is no in-between. If the ones you choose have any doubt about accepting the honor of becoming one of the "Gifted," then the blue diamonds will reject them. We will meet you in the tallest tower when the temple is complete.

Our Love to you,

Laki and Jutsuk

Chapter 35

Gifts from the Goddesses

William finishes the letter while Samuel rewraps the crystal and places it on the crate. Samuel says, "I think the Goddesses enjoy these little excursions they send us on. We have to find four individuals with nothing to go on." Samuel smiles and says, "As I have said before, I love a good challenge." He then removes two diamonds from the box and hands one to William. They place them around their necks and immediately feel a dramatic level of awareness in their senses.

William asks, "Do we have everything?" Samuel says, "Yes," and pats his backpack.

William looks in the book and tells Samuel that we are to unwrap the stone, place it in the box and then put everything back to when we found

Samuel picks up the crystal, unwraps it, and places it in the box, and then the two of them replace the lid and set the box back in the crate. They lift the container, put it back in the hole, and cover it with the obsidian square flat stones.

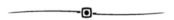

William opens the book and shows Samuel; they start to read aloud, "*Okiru No Shindin Dochu Hena.*" They can't see the crystal, but a pulsating glow begins to emanate from the hole's edges, encapsulating the pile of stones. The earth around the crate and crystal begins to tremble, and a small crack slowly opens, spewing a lavender mist. The crate slides down into the gap, and the once small crack now expands into a fissure.

The fissure starts to expand in-depth and width, and it slowly branches outwards in an east and west pattern to reach and touch the mountain ranges on both sides of the valley. Soon the trembling stops as the fissure can go no farther and begins to settle, causing a twenty-meter gap in the valley's floor. They feel a tremble beneath the valley's surface, and then a rumbling starts as they watch a wall of the same obsidian stone slowly rise along the edge of the fissure on the opposite side. It has reached a height of over ten meters when it finally stops. A heavy thick lavender mist rolls out of the fissure. It makes its way along the wall until it gradually moves over the top and is soon blanketing the entire region along and behind the wall. The lavender mist thickens, and the two of them cannot see anything, but they hear the constant grinding and movement of the stone. While they stand on the fissure's edge, a black obsidian slab appears on both sides and grows steadily to expand towards each other, and when the edges touch, they fuse. They glimpse a mass of black obsidian stone with grotesque misshapen spheres slowly rising on the fissure's other side and watch as the lavender mist encases them to hide them from view.

They can do no more, so Samuel and William leave the fissure and head back toward "*Kutosu Kyochi*. After walking most of the day, they decide to make camp, and as before, William brings forth the mana of fire and starts a fire, and as they wait for the water to boil, they settle against their packs. Samuel looks at William, and all he says is, "That was different," and William says, "Yes, it was." and then asks, "Samuel did you feel something when you put on the blue diamond?" Samuel says yes, and William says, "So did I." They sit and talk about the recent events that have transpired, and they can still feel, though minimal, the faint grinding and movements of the stones back at the fissure.

They are sitting and talking and drinking tea when they feel a warm breeze with the fragrance of lavender. William reaches in his pack to pull out two more cups, fills the two cups with mint tea, and places them on the stones to keep warm. Seconds later, Laki and Jutsuk are standing in their beauty and sheer clothing. William and Samuel go to rise, but the Goddesses gesture for them to remain as they are. The two walk over, kiss their cheeks, and sit between them.

Laki asks, "Is there enough of that delicious mint tea for the two of us?"

William hands them each a cup, and Laki says to Jutsuk, "Wait until you try this, and then says, "Where are my manners? William, I want to introduce you to my sister Jutsuk, and she looks over and says, "You must be Samuel?" Samuel says, "Pleased to meet you," and smiles.

William says, "Sisters, I don't see the resemblance," Laki slaps him, and they laugh.

William pours them each a cup, and as Jutsuk tastes it, all she says is, "Mmmmm!"

Laki says, "I told you."

She looks at Samuel and says, "Samuel, my sweet, why did you not give me this when we first met?" and punches him in the arm. Samuel looks at her and says, "Talk to William; it's his recipe." He rubs his arm as if it hurts, and Jutsuk smiles.

Laki speaks first, "You two have done well with what we have asked you to do." William and Samuel both say, "Thank you."

Jutsuk says, "Once you have completed your tasks here, you will need to send out the word to have our devoted followers and soldiers come to this valley to aid you. Something is happening in the world; we know it is happening because of what I found out when I questioned Tanin and before I impris......, Laki changes her choice of words and instead says before he tried to hurt us." William gives her a questionable look, and she says later with her eyes.

Jutsuk continues where Laki left off, "We know that Guichi and Tanin are behind all this, with the Dark Forces, and that they have Chosen a High Priestess as their leader, and she has close ties with the Dark Realm. We are told that two women can travel between the Dark Realm and our world, ironically calling themselves the "Dark Twins, and go by the names of Mia and Mae."

William tells them that their last encounter with the Sutaraukaji and Chizobutsu had been different.

Laki asks, "Why do you say that?"

William tells them, "Previously, the rifts always had to manifest inside a cave or large formations of rocks. It seems now that the rifts can appear anywhere, and I think that the skies need to be very dark because both times I have encountered this, dark clouds have blocked out the sun."

Jutsuk says, "We will need to check on this. If what you say is true, that could change everything."

"Samuel and I have discussed this many times, and there was always a missing key piece of the puzzle. You have told us about the High Priestess, and now that we know for sure that there is a High Priestess, we believe that she acts as a catalyst or focal point that allows the rifts to appear anywhere. We also think that Guichi and Tanin want to bring something so evil into this world that it will sweep through it and destroy everything we hold dear. Both William and Samuel notice Jutsuk's slight shudder, and Laki squeezes her hand to reassure her not to worry.

Samuel looks at Jutsuk and asks, "What is it?"

She answers. "Do not worry, I am fine."

William holds up his hand and tells Laki and Jutsuk, "When Samuel and I first met you, we both had conditions that both of you promised to keep no matter what it could be. One of those conditions was that if we both agreed to fulfill your desires by becoming your Champions and being appointed the Sendoka and Shikakin, there would be no secrets. How can you expect us to continue carrying out your wishes, especially when there are lies and mistrust between us?"

Laki tells William, "You are right, but not here and not tonight. When the temple is complete, we will meet in the tallest tower and tell you everything."

Samuel starts to disagree and tries pushing the subject, but Jutsuk pleads with him and asks him to be patient. They will answer all their questions and tell them everything.

William looks at Samuel, who nods, then looks back to the Goddesses and says, "We will agree, but we need to know everything. If we will fight and possibly die for you, we need the truth no matter how painful it might be."

Samuel looks at the two of them and says, "William and I have talked about this, and we love both of you, but we cannot move forward and help defend this world with lies and deceit. Do you both agree?"

Laki and Jutsuk both nod their heads and say, "Yes."

William asks, "Is there anything else?"

William looks at Laki and sees a look of worry in her eyes. He reaches over and takes her hand and squeezes it. She looks at him, and he smiles. When they hear Jutsuk say, "Yes."

"What is that?" asks Samuel

Jutsuk squeezes Samuel's arm and asks, "I would like some more mint tea and William to play his tanbur."

William tells them, "I think we can do both for you young ladies, and Laki and Jutsuk both laugh because, even though the four of them all look about the same age, the twins are a millennium older than the two of them.

Samuel pours more tea, and William unwraps his tanbur, performs a quick tune-up, and just before he starts playing, he and Samuel glance at each other, and then William starts strumming his tanbur.

In the morning, the Goddesses are gone, with only the light smell of lavender lingering in the Air. William asks Samuel to pull out the leather bag with the rune stones. Samuel unties the cord and opens the box to show William the obsidian stones with ancient rune markings. He sees seven stones, three pairs of rune stones, each pair identical in every way, but each pair is slightly different from the other pairs, and then a single stone utterly different from the other three pairs.

William says, "Thank you," Samuel closes the lid and ties the cord.

They reach the wall three days later and discover it is open. They walk through, and when they get to the other side, William opens the small leatherbound book and asks Samuel to pull out the pair of stones with the markings of "*Piptu*" engraved on them.

William reads the book and instructs Samuel to place the stones on the ground with one to each side of the opening and about five meters away.

Samuel places the stones and walks back to where William is standing, and they read from the book "*Fusega To Kekotu Sura Piptu*" the rune stones start to shake and then quickly sink into the earth. They feel a vibration, and then two five-meter tall, square-shaped obsidian obelisks approximately a meter in width erupt from the ground. Engraved on all four sides are ancient glyphs and runes. William feels a small piece of each mana drawn into the obelisks. He sways slightly, and Samuel stands beside him and grabs his arm to steady him.

Williams looks at Samuel and says, "Wow, I wasn't expecting that!"

Samuel asks, "What was it?"

When the obelisks finally settled, William tells him it felt like small pieces of all five manas were pulled from his being and absorbed into the stones.

Samuel asks, "Are you okay? Do you want to rest?"

William says, "No, I am okay. Let's continue."

They continue heading back towards the Gorge, walking during the day and resting at night. On the morning of the third day, William feels it, opens the book, and asks Samuel to pull out the pair of stones with the markings of "*Sefugu*" engraved on them. They perform the ritual for a second time, and like the first time, William sways, and Samuel is there.

On the sixth day, they reach the entrance to the valley and walk up onto the plateau. Samuel asks William if he wants to rest before performing the last ritual. William tells Samuel that he is okay and wants to continue. William opens the book and asks Samuel to pull out the single stone, marked *Mashin Ruta Toko*, and as he holds it, he feels that the weight is different. William tells him to place it to the left of the ramp that leads down to the valley floor. Samuel does, and then they recite the words together from the small leather book. They both see that this incantation is a little different. "*Fusega to Kekotu Sura Na Gatto Ni Contiya*," the ground trembles quite a bit more than the previous times. As with the others, an obelisk erupts from the ground. This one is in the shape of a triangle and stands about six meters tall. William feels a larger piece of himself drawn into the obelisk, and he is dizzy. Samuel is beside him to steady him when without warning, an energy pulse spreads out from the obelisk to flatten the ground throughout the plateau.

On the other side of the plateau opposite the obelisk, a section of earth opens up, and water bubbles up from the ground.

They watch as the water from the ground is encircled with perfectly placed stones to form a well, and on the stones are ancient runes. Clusters of trees start sprouting and growing at a dramatic pace. Soon different types of trees offer shade from the afternoon sun. Large patches of grass are growing exceptionally fast, as are other clusters of trees. Samuel walks with William over to one of the trees and tells him to rest in the shade. Samuel goes to the well, dips his hands in, cups water, and tastes it. The water is cool and tastes slightly sweet but not sugary. He fills his canteen and returns to where William is sitting under the shade of a tree, giving him some water. William takes a sip, and Samuel sees the color return to his face almost immediately but also sees that he looks tired and asks how he is.

William tells him, "Tired," and explains to Samuel the difference between this obelisk and the others as they erupted from the ground. Samuel sees that it is late in the afternoon and tells William to rest; they will depart in the morning. William agrees and is soon asleep. Samuel has never seen William like this before and is worried. He decides to stay awake to look over and protect his friend.

Samuel asks how he feels in the morning, and William says he is fine and feels much better. William notices circles under his eyes and asks him if he has slept. William then touches Samuels's arm and sends a wave of *Spirit* into him.

Samuel says, "Wow."

William tells him, "You look better; how do you feel?"

Samuel says, "I feel great like I slept for twelve hours."

William then looks around at the newly formed oasis on the plateau and asks, "All this happened while I was sleeping?" Samuel nods his head, and they stop at the well to top off their canteens. They take a drink and feel invigorated from the water. Three days later, they are back on the Plains of Sayashi, at the entrance to the Gorge. William asks Samuel to place the last pair of stones marked "*Koda Gichu*" about five meters from the opening as he did the others but set these a little farther apart. Together they say, "*Fusega To Kekotu Sura Koda Gichu*" As before, two obelisks identical to the others erupt from the ground, and William feels the pull. They feel the earth tremble, and then simultaneously, the two fantastic ranges of *Ishidosida Mountains* to the west and the *Tammayaku Mountains* to the east seem to open up and form two new gorges that open out onto the Plains of Sayashi. They both get a vision of the newly formed gorges farther south, and as they walk past the obelisks; they feel something.

A few days later, they find themselves back at the oasis, and as they walk past the obelisk, they feel a different sensation that neither can explain. The same happens to both William and Samuel again as they walk past the next pair of obelisks. The nights continue to pass without incident. They are still about one day from the wall when they hear thunder in the distance and see the dark clouds releasing their heavy rain. They know it is inevitable and make their way to an overhang of rock and decide to wait for the storm while underneath it.

William and Samuel are standing under the overhang talking when they both feel something break the tranquility of the valley. Then William feels something passing the second pair of obelisks in the valley and coming at them fast. Samuel also feels it and presses his thumb to unlock his sword as William mutters under his breath and his hands start to glow a warm orange color. They continue to stand under the overhang and wait.

The rains just let up when they see five Chizobutsu bearing down on them. William notices that these are larger and almost twice the size of their previous encounters. They seem more determined and run straight for him with claws extended and snarling ferociously. Samuel steps in front of William in a defensive stance. William speaks very softly, *"Kuri to Yuki,"* and the warm orange glow turns into a light blue, and as it changes to a bright blue, he unfurls two ice whips and then snaps them. Just as William cracks the whips, he sees the flash of a brilliant silver cross, Samuels, eyes, and William knows that he has reached *"Chiraka."*

The five beasts attack, and Samuel takes two steps forward and swings his sword at the first beast separating its head from its body. The second takes a wide swing at Samuel's shoulder, but he holds up his sword in a defensive stance that the beast drives its paw through the blade and severs it. The beast rolls to the side, roaring in pain, and then William lashes out with his ice whips, and the beast freezes where it landed. The momentum does not stop as Samuel spins his body one way while his blade seems to be glowing ever so intensely, and it seems to be doing its own thing, but the two of them together are like watching two professional dancers in sync that they appear as one. William strikes out at another maimed creature as it turns towards Samuel, and the beast turns into ice and is frozen solid. William looks back at Samuel and finds himself highly impressed by what he is witnessing. Samuel's sword seems to sing, and as William watches, he finds himself mesmerized by the exquisite dance that Samuel is performing. It is over as all five creatures are dead or dismembered and lying about the ground not more than two meters from where Samuel encountered the first one and the two that William took out with his ice whips. Samuel brings his sword down, flicks it, wipes the excess blood on the beast's fur, and then sheaths his sword. Samuel looks at William, and all he says is, "Shall we go?"

William notices that the rains stopped after Samuel killed the last beast, and the clouds dispersed as the sun bathed the valley again. They both hear the distinctive pop as the rift closes. William conjures a red flame that engulfs the creatures and incinerates them into piles of ash. He then calls for a breeze to disperse the ashes.

They are walking down the path, and as they walk, William says, "That thing you did with the sword was amazing; I have never seen anything like it before!"

Samuel smiles and says, "It was amazing, wasn't it?"

William laughs. "Now, you'll probably be intolerable to be friends with, aren't you?" Samuel smiles and says, "Probably."

William laughs harder and slaps Samuel on the back as they walk through the valley towards the wall.

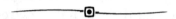

It is midday when they reach the wall, and they are just about to head down the path when they feel the warm breeze and smell lavender alerting them that the Goddesses are nearby. The Goddesses float down from the wall to stand in front of them. Jutsuk walks up to Samuel, embraces him with a hug, and kisses him. Laki does the same to William.

Jutsuk says, "Samuel, you have demonstrated skills with the sword that cannot be measured or surpassed and have proven yourself a true Champion. She stands before him, and a beautifully crafted sword materializes in her hands. She holds it to him with her palms up and says, "Take it." Samuel takes the sword and feels a bond between himself and the sword. Jutsuk smiles and says, "I present to you "*Shikei Narasu*" she is a handmade katana styled after your own country's blades. She has a power that a true "*Genkakuna Kyukyoku Shenshi*" or "Ultimate Dragon Warrior." Can wield. "*Shikei Narasu*" is a temperamental girl who will protect and grow with you, but when she senses anything that threatens you, she will let you know, but when unsheathed, she will require the taste of blood."

Samuel kneels before Jutsuk and says, "Thank you." Jutsuk says to him, "*My Genkakuna Kyukyoku Shenshi*, need not bow before me when we are among friends." Samuel says, "As you wish, My Goddess." and removes the sword his men gave him to his back and then straps on "*Shikei Narasu*" to his hip. He unsheathes her, and he hears a delicate females voice that only he can listen to and she says, "You are my Dragon, and I will be your flame," and then Samuel runs his thumb on the blade to draw blood and can feel the bond immediately grow stronger between them. He sheathes her, and just before the blade clicks into place, he hears, "Thank you." Once again, Jutsuk steps in to embrace him with a hug, kisses him but this time on his lips, and then steps back. Laki steps forward and kisses him on the cheek.

Laki looks at William and says, "William, you have done everything we have asked of you and genuinely demonstrated your devotion to us. No one since your great grandmother, the Matriarch of the James Clan who united the Tatokai Islands, has ever been able to bring forth the four manas or elements of Chikyu, let alone be able to bind them with the mana of *Spirit*. The elements of Earth, Fire, Air, water, and *Spirit* are the lifeblood of Chikyu. One like yourself who can unleash that power, harness it, and then control it with the element of *Spirit* can only be a *"Sukaimohotai,"* an Imperial Master of the Elementals. William, as my Champion, "I give you *"Nakeshidoka,"* Laki e brings forth a long wooden staff carved from a single Bisham tree and is over two meters tall. On the shaft are etched ancient runes and glyphs, and a huge multifaceted Dark Blue Sapphire sits on the top. She holds it out to him, and when he takes it, he can feel all five elements saturate the staff and watches as the Blue Sapphire takes on an even darker blue, almost black, until the sun hits it and the rich blue color emanates from the jewel.

Laki embraces him with a hug and plants a kiss on his lips, then Jutsuk moves forward and places a kiss on his cheek. Jutsuk and Laki address both of them and say, "We will talk soon," The Goddesses disappear, leaving William and Samuel standing there with the smell of lavender lingering in the Air.

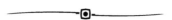

Samuel and William arrive back at the fissure and are mesmerized by what is standing before them. They walk up to the bridge, and William asks Samuel to take out the last two rune stones. Samuel hands one to William. William then opens the leatherbound book and shows Samuel. William then places his stone to the left of the entrance to the bridge, while Samuel places his stone on the right. They both step back, and together they recite the words from the book, *"Fusega to Kekotu Sura Na Gatto Ni Contiya Okiru No Shindin Dochu Hena To Kekotu Sura."* They see the lavender mist come out of the fissure and watch it spiral around the two rune stones, and they see the runestones turn into pedestals, and now those are shrouded in the thick lavender mist. Moments later, a slight breeze passes over them, and the lavender mist is gone. They see standing on top of the pedestals are two perfectly detailed statues of the Goddesses Laki and Jutsuk. They both feel the rune scars on their chests pulse. Then they both feel pieces of their essence drawn into the two statues and merge with the essences of the Goddesses.

When this happens, they both feel several pulses, tremendous power radiates from the two statues, and they feel the valley come alive through the Gorge and out to the two farthest obelisks.

Samuel and William feel the obelisks throughout the valley, generating the protection wards of the Goddesses.

Chapter 36

The Temple and the City

Once William and Samuel activated the statues of the Goddesses that triggered the protection wards of the obelisks throughout the valley, they could sense the valley teeming with life. They made camp on the side of the path leading from the wall to the fissure. They are drinking some tea and discussing what the Goddesses had written in the letter about finding and training the four Gifted. Samuel asks, "How will we know which ones will be picked, trained, and hopefully given a blue diamond without going crazy. William says, "I don't know, but hopefully the Goddesses will be a little more forthcoming when we meet them in the tallest tower once...., but before William can finish what he was saying, the mist on the other side of the fissure begins to dissipate. They break camp, walk over to the two statues of the Goddesses and watch as the mist continues to roll back into the fissure. They see two massive wooden gates made from ironwood embedded into the walls and a heavy metal portcullis barring the doors at the end of the obsidian bridge.

They are standing just before the stone bridge, with the statues of the Goddesses on each side of them. They hear a noise across the fissure and see that the portcullis is rising, and when it has raised itself all the way, the gates swing inward, allowing them access to the far side. They proceed across the bridge and see that the lavender mist is still shrouding everything inside the wall. They walk through the gates, and as they step into what they think is a small walkway, then more of the mist rolls back. When the last of the mist passes over them, they realize that they are standing in a massive courtyard with several fountains and an enormous stairway leading up to a structure beyond one's imagination.

The mass of black obsidian stone with grotesque misshapen spheres they had seen previously is now a magnificent-looking piece of architecture. Sculptured flowing lines, with fine delicate details of flowers and animals, decorate the exterior as the smooth edges sweep back to and blend with the coarse surfaces of the surrounding mountains that circumvent the valley.

Towards the back of the large courtyard is an elegant-looking five-sided structure with walls fused into the mountains behind them and each turn in the wall houses a watchtower. The watchtowers have pointed roof peaks and balconies around the towers about halfway up their height. The walls slope upwards from the ground to a height of five meters. The central and tallest sphere still reaches skyward but is now a smooth circular tower with an almost glass-like sheen, and unlike the smaller buildings, the central tower has a circular roof that looks open to the sky. They hear the voices of the Goddesses telling them of numerous tunnels that branch out through the mountains. Some will lead out of the valley to the other side of the mountains, while others will bring you into one of the Four Kingdoms. Others end in large storage rooms holding freshwater, and some tunnels will lead down into the bowels of the Temple into what will be catacombs.

William and Samuel walk around the courtyard and admire the design of the defenses of the outer castle. Beautifully engraved on both sides of the temple doors are depictions of the Goddesses down to the smallest detail. The stairs that lead up to the doors are wide and smooth as glass but are not slippery. The main temple doors themselves are the epitome of sculpturing and design. It seems like delicate strands of black obsidian intertwining and adorned with miniature roses in full bloom that run along the intertwining strands. Embedded into the wood of the doors are other sculptured flora and fauna from the same obsidian stone. The doors themselves are massive and made from interwoven blocks of what they both recognize as Bisham wood. When opened, one walks into another large open courtyard with well-manicured lawns and stone paths that lead to other parts of the building and annexes of the Temple.

Though the Temple is the main structure behind the wall, the other buildings are imperative to the sacred Temple's well-being and function. Watchtowers are placed along the outer temple walls and joined by covered battements. The gatehouse is large with a metal portcullis that opens out into the lower bailey where the weapons, armorers, tanners, and medicinal shops are situated. Though the castle and Temple join to resemble one structure, neither one takes away the beauty of the other. With its hard masculine angles and straight lines, the castle blends well with the temples flowing feminine curves and graceful turns. They see the architectural design of the fortress from the standpoint of defending it to the detail for its beauty. What was once a grotesque mass of stone with rough and misshaped spheres now resembles an epitome of beauty and elegance, with a single tower rising higher than everything and looking out over the valley's expanse.

William and Samuel are sitting in one of the larger rooms of the castle and relaxing, having just finished eating some roasted quail that Samuel had caught earlier in the day. They are enjoying a cup of tea, and Samuel tells William that he has outdone himself with the quail when they both hear, "Come to the tower."

William and Samuel look at each other, get up from their chairs, and walk out to the back garden. They walk through an arbor of blooming lavender flowers and then follow a path that ends at the base of the central tower. They get to the bottom of the central tower and see a door they know was not there previously. Samuel goes to open the door when it opens by itself. They step in, and the door closes behind them. They take a couple of steps up the spiral staircase and find themselves in front of another closed door. William goes to touch the door when it gently swings open. The room is dark, and light fills the room as they both step inside. They see the "*Shingakusha Hoseki*," a beautifully handcrafted flawless multi-faceted crystal hovering above a table in the middle of the room. When William and Samuel approach the table, a faint blue flame appears, and as they get closer, the flame begins to pulse. William stands on one side of the crystal while Samuel stands on the other. They place their hands gently on the *Shingakusha Hoseki* and immediately feel the pulse of the blue flame course through their bodies. William and Samuel remember the Goddesses' words bestowed upon them when they appointed William Samuel as their Champions—now blessed with the titles of the Sendoka and the Shikakin.

William stands opposite Samuel, and together, William says, "water*a Mutoku to Hogo Suru She.*" While at the same time, Samuel recites, "*Totaki Zasera to Hogo Suru She,*" they repeat the incantations several times. *Soon, the two incantations flow together until it sounds like one,* "water*a Totaki Mutoku Zasera to Hogo Suru She.*"

The blue flame inside the crystal glows brighter with each passage spoken; when the whole crystal is pulsating and looks about to explode, the two of them recite the final phase, *"Kuneru Shingakusha Hoseki Dikashimeta Natuki Mokodo* Laki *To* Jutsuk."

With the final phase spoken, the blue pulsing flame inside the crystal shoots a light straight out of the top. They watch it travel upward through a circular opening in the tower's roof, then the blue light hits the stratosphere, lights up the sky above the Temple, and rolls outward to cover all parts of Chikyu. Samuel and William leave the room, and as they step outside the room, the door disappears, and they find themselves standing in front of one another. Samuel opens it, and they are standing in the garden.

William looks at Samuel and says, "Tea?"

Samuel looks at William and says, "Why not." They head back into the castle.

Guichi feels the power that has just encompassed the lands. He curses his sisters for disrupting their plans, especially Laki, for imprisoning his brother in a piece of Dark Crystal that she stole along with the Tome' that the Twins from the Dark Realm gave them. He sits on the altar and flexes the wings that now protrude from his back. He extends them fully, and with a thought, they close up and disappear. He swears to use everything in his power, including the Dark Realm, to rescue his brother, destroy his sisters, and release the Dark God Nimponin into this world. He takes the glass of blood wine he was drinking and throws the glass against the wall shattering the glass. He watches the wine run down the wall and smiles as he imagines that it is his sisters' heads smashed against this very wall.

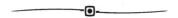

It has been a little over six weeks since they released the power of the *Shingakusha Hoseki* released its essence out into the lands, and it has been quiet. William and Samuel now have access to the tower, and when they returned, the crystal was gone, and a note was left in its place, saying, "Do not worry, it is safe." One day William and Samuel are sitting at a table drinking some tea when William feels something passing the first set of markers out beyond the Gorge. He looks up at Samuel and says, "We have visitors."

Fifteen days pass, and the two of them are standing on the rampart of the main gates when they see a few small groups of people making their way towards the two statues and stopping. William and Samuel come through the gates, walk across the bridge, and approach the people standing before the statues. Samuel approaches them slightly in front of William with his hand on his sword and asks, "What can we do for you, and why are you here?" The consensus is the same, they felt or heard something in the Air and felt they had to journey to this valley. William places his hand on Samuel's shoulder and asks, "Do you believe in the Laki-Jutsuk Religion and its beliefs.?" Everyone who has made the journey is standing before the statues of Laki, and Jutsuk bows, places an open hand over their heart and pledges fidelity to the Goddesses, and William says, "Welcome."

Each day, William feels the people coming into the Gorge and through the valley, and fifteen days later, he asks the same question and welcomes the new arrivals. Some want to join the military ranks, while others have made the journey to join the classes to become priests. The ones who wish to become priests carry the blessing of the Goddesses. After the "*Shigakushu Hoseko*" released its essence into the world, a faded crescent-shaped moon tattoo reappeared on many chests. The selected have journeyed to the valley and pledged fealty before the statues of the two Goddesses. The crescent-moon tattoo becomes prominent upon completing fealty, allowing those to enter Order. Once in the Order, one becomes a novice who will study the ways and beliefs of the Goddesses Laki and Jutsuk. The Temple comprises three factors, the Sendoka, the priests and novices, and the priests, the Shikakin, and the military. No one wants anything, and as more people come to the valley, the ranks swell with followers as the City slowly expands with people, and as it expands, more true believers come to the valley.

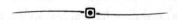

Once the *Shingakusha Hoseki* spread its essence into the night sky, the call went out to the people of Chikyu, and many felt it in their hearts and decided to set out to make the journey to the valley. The pilgrimage of the masses is spectacular, as people from all walks of life who believe in the Goddesses are welcome. Most can pass the obelisks at the entrance to the Gorge and journey to the valley and make their way to the "*Kutosu Kyochi*" gateway.

Some cannot step through the obelisks or come close to them. The protection wards do not let non-followers enter, and they are turned away, not through force, but by a constant ringing in one's ear that diminishes when one steps away from the obelisks. Only one way to the Temple and City is through the "*Meware Sukotai*," or opening where the two mountain ranges converge.

Upon completing a three-day journey through the breath-taking Busamoriku Gorge, the Gorge opens onto the "*Hinsayna Goken Plateau*," where a lone obelisk stands and an oasis flows with life. The path leading to *Kyosushinta, the Sacred Temple of the* Laki-Jutsuk *Religion and Order*, is majestic, as one can admire the natural beauty of the valley. What lies before one's eyes is a lush green valley that sweeps outward to blend in with its high walls that end with jagged snow-capped peaks on some. Small rounded hills seem to have been pushed up from the very earth and are ever so carefully smoothed over to not hinder one's view of what lies beyond them. Areas of the valley display small and large scattered outcroppings of rock and large patches of wildflowers sprawling in every direction. The farther they journey into the lush green canyon, the more abundant the fauna, with patches of the wildflowers blooming from bright pinks to soft lavenders and every color in-between. Clusters of sharp spiked black obsidian rock break through the valley floor; imposing as they may be, they do not interfere with the valley's natural beauty of the surrounding windswept grasslands. Bright flowers, crops of trees consisting of birch, cherry blossoms, ash, maple, oaks, and other varieties of fauna grow throughout the valley.

After six days of traveling on the hard-packed road, through this luscious valley and around the different types of outcroppings, lies the outline of "*Kutosu Kyochi*" in the distance. A Great Wall formed from a solid black obsidian stone rises from the valley floor to over thirty meters high. The wall seems natural in its formation and spans the width of the valley. Stories say the Supreme Mother Goddess Kamiyobo created the wall, then the daughters of Kamiyobo, Laki, *and* Jutsuk, raised the wall higher in ancient times.

Stories have been told and retold throughout the generations of a sacred valley. These stories tell of a spot in the secluded valley where a male God once rested. An unnamed god succumbed to a painful death, and to seal the valley, the God Mother created a wall, the "*Kutosu Kyochi*."

A black stone was created from the very bowels of Chikyu's core and forced to the surface thousands of millennia ago. The same black stone now forms the basis of The Sacred Temple of the Laki-Jutsuk Order itself. In color with a glass-like-sheen, the deep black Temple is not cold but offers a warm, comforting feeling, not in appearance but one's heart. The exterior of the Temple is etched with floral designs of flowers and fauna; scattered throughout the methods are vivid lavender flowers. The lavender flowers against the black stone make them seem vibrant, almost luminous. Upon entering the Temple, one can see that the interior walls are the teachings and beliefs of the Laki-Jutsuk Religion's written words so etched into the very walls themselves. They say that what transpired in the Goddess' lives was carved into the walls; indeed, even the Goddesses could not change the written words. One panel of their written story is challenging to decipher, and only four individuals know the real story.

The influx of people has allowed the City of Shinjukosuk to expand. Slowly at first, and as the merchants, tradespeople, entrepreneurs, and artisans arrived to try and establish themselves, the population quickly grew, and the City itself was soon expanding. Men and women who wanted to serve volunteered to join the ranks of the military to uphold the religious beliefs of the Order. The Order established the military, and soon the blacksmiths, armorers, weapon makers, fletchers, and tanners who made the journey soon set up their shops inside the walls to support the soldiers and became known for their superior skills.

On the valley side of the Great fissure, small businesses of other blacksmiths, thatchers, stonemasons, carpenters, weavers, and their families flourished and allowed the City to expand.

As the City grew, so did the Commerce, and when people saw this, the City erupted into a focal point of world trade, and Shinjukosuk established itself as an economic hub for all of the Continent. No other structure in the world comes close to comparison with the Temple of the Order, nor any other city in the world has the international trades of the four major kingdoms and the other smaller countries.

After the last two obelisks erupted from the earth, two smaller gorges opened a little farther south on the Plains of Sayashi up that, allowing other caravans from the kingdoms to reach the City quicker to trade goods that would continually flow in and out of the City. The City of Shinjukosuk has grown at an exuberant rate in a short time. Small single-family dwellings and businesses established themselves along the chasm, eventually working their way out onto the valley. Away from the abyss, multi-family houses, inns, taverns, craft shops, mills, and warehouses like the homes and small businesses expanded into the valley. An architect's dream was to build above three floors and some with four, five, and six floors. Facilities of this height were never considered, let alone built. Once completed, businesses of all types immediately filled the empty spaces. The best of the best swarmed to *Shinjukosuk*, and the City welcomed them. The crime rate was non-existent, other than some petty thievery.

Artisans and craftsmen always traveled to the City to sell their wares at the city trade markets. They knew that to get their wares distributed out into lands; it would be quicker to sell in the City and let the merchants buy and spread their wares. Most never leave and end up staying to live and prosper in *Shinjukosuk*. Once they have mastered their craft, they would need to present their arts before a Certified Craftsmen Board, and if approved, they would receive a Masters Seal, which allows the acquiring of an allotment of metals mined from the surrounding mountains. Some metals are rare and are not found anywhere else in the world. The valley and mountains are plentiful with rare metals and gems and are extensively regulated to offset the balance of Commerce in the other lands.

On the outskirts of the City lies the very valley itself. Fertile lands for growing selected crops and other vegetation. The one crop the local farmers excel in is always in demand, and the most popular are the bags of flour made from the harvested wheat that grows in the valley. The minerals in the soils and other conditions in the valley allow the wheat and other grains to grow exceptionally well. The grains have a savory flavor that can't be grown anywhere else on Chikyu due to the same weather year-round. The bags of flour are shipped to agents, who monitor the distribution to the bakeries all over the Continent. The one stipulation that *Shinjukosuk* enforces is that everyone gets their allotted portion no matter how small the establishment. The City is always full of energy, and the one thing that draws the people in is not only the Temple of the Order but also the City.

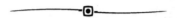

The temple guards of the *Temple of Kyosushinta* are not just guards but are actual priests of the Order. They have sworn to protect their fellow priests, novices, the Temple, and above all else, the Sendoka. They are responsible for guarding and defending the Temple and are a well-disciplined core of men and women willing to give their lives for the Sendoka, the priests, the novices, and the Temple. They have been trained by the best in the military, and there are about one thousand Temple guards. In comparison, the contingent of the Laki-Jutsuk army is approximately forty-five thousand strong and growing and considered one of the largest private armies in the world because they answer to no sovereign or king.

The Laki-Jutsuk Army consists of several battalions and the Third battalion with over eight-thousand five hundred horse lancers who Captain Roland Saito leads. His men consider him a hard man but fair, and he never asks anything of them that he would not do himself, and his men respect him for that.

The most significant battalion, the First, consists of the archers and the crossbowmen of nine-thousand strong, and they are currently without a Commander. The Second battalion is fifteen thousand battle-ax men, pikemen, and halberds, which First Lieutenant Yuichi Nakamori commands. The Fifth and final battalion is over eight thousand strong and are long swordsmen that First Lieutenant Takashi Kame commands. Finally, two archers and long swordsmen companies, approximately three thousand men, commanded by First Lieutenant Sagami, are responsible for patrolling along the valley and the men along "*Kutosu Kyochi.*"

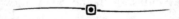

William and Samuel have been back to the room in the central tower many times, and after the first time, they noticed that the crystal was gone. The Goddesses informed them that the crystal was safe and that they would bring it back when and if the time came. On the several occasions of visiting the room, William and Samuel have brought specific items with them, for the space itself is not overly furnished, but for a table, four comfortable chairs, and a dresser. Usually, the teapot, the iron tripod, and four cups are on the dresser. There are three shelves in the room; one is an Imperial katana that is just as sharp the day it was crafted, though the sheath has seen better days. Another shelf is a beautifully carved figurine of the Eternal God Mother, Kamiyobo. On the third shelf are a small betrothal bracelet and a stiletto blade with a worn Royal Crest of the islands. The smell of lavender fills the room, and the Goddesses appear; they walk up to William and Samuel, place a kiss on their cheeks, and they find their chairs. The mood in the room is somber. No one speaks as they wait patiently for the tea. William mixes the tea by swirling the pot, and as he does, the aroma of an earthy mint fills the room, and the Goddesses smile.

William pours four cups, hands their favorite drink of mint tea to them, and then sits back in his chair. Samuel takes a sip, clears his throat, places his tea on the table, and tells the Goddesses what is happening in the valley and the Temple. He takes another sip and continues with the City, the military, and the ongoing preparations to be ready to defend the valley. Laki and Jutsuk listen, and Samuel picks up his drink from the table and says, "William."

William inhales quietly, lets it out, looks at both Goddesses, and says, "Recently, we have heard rumors that those practicing the Dark Scriptures have innocent women bearing the crescent moon mark abducted and brought to where the rituals occur. The High Priest selects devoted followers to stand around the altar and physically maul the woman while others rape her numerous times. The chanting starts, and several followers hold the woman down as the High Priest plunges a knife into the woman's chest, cuts it open, pulls out her beating heart, and raises it to the crowd for all to see. The followers continue chanting, bring themselves to a heightened frenzy, and then start to remove their clothes and participate in an orgy. Everything stops when the High Priest shouts, "All Praise the Dark Scriptures and our Gods Guichi and Tanin," everything stops. Then gathered followers disappear into the night. The remains of the young woman are left on the altar to rot.

Samuel takes a sip of tea, and William continues, "We think, sooner than later, this High Priestess is going to stop these false leaders and either do away with them or recruit them. Either way, it will swell her ranks threefold when she does this. Once she has all of them reined in and under her control, we think that is when she will make a move." William pauses to take a sip of tea and continues, "We also know that the woman appointed as their High Priestess, as you have told us, can cross over into the Dark Realm. We assume that she is the catalyst between the two Realms and has possibly acquired the ability to read one's mind to allow the rifts to appear without caves. However, we cannot confirm this last one."

William places his cup on the table, and Samuel follows suit and looks at the two of them as the sisters sit quietly, and both William and Samuel wait patiently.

Laki speaks first, "We must go," and goes to stand when William asks her to please remain seated; there is one more thing to discuss/. William looks at Samuel, and he nods his head to continue.

William says, "Laki *and* Jutsuk, as we had told you before when Samuel and I accepted the positions to become your Sendoka and your Shikakin, we promised to never lie to each other or keep secrets and tell the truth. The last time we met, you Laki started to say something and then changed the subject or your words at the last moment, we asked what you changed your mind about, and you told us that it would have to wait for the completion of the Temple and after the calling went out. The Temple is complete, and the call has gone out. We have met in this very room a few times, and neither of you has been forthcoming on the matter. Samuel and I love the two of you more than you could imagine, but now you must tell us what you are hiding. If you still want us to remain as your Champions.

Jutsuk looks at Laki and says to her, "We need to tell them, please, Laki."

Laki nods to her sister and then looks at William and Samuel and says, "What we are about to tell will hopefully not change your love of us or send you away, and have you abandoned us, But if you decide to go, so be it, and we will always love you?"

She takes a sip of tea and says, "We are not what you perceive us to be. In this world, we are revered as Goddesses, and our brothers as Gods, but we are neither." William and Samuel look at each other, and

Laki continues, "As you know, we have the power to shift between the *Spirit*ual and Earthly Domains, and we can draw power from both planes to attack or defend ourselves." Laki pauses to take a sip of tea and then continues, "Before Jutsuk and I met the two of you, we searched out our two brothers to persuade them to forget this farce of trying to release the Dark God Nimponin from the dark crystals." William interrupts and says, "Guichi and Tanin are actually trying to release the Dark God? I had my suspicions, but I never thought it could happen?"

Laki looks at William and says, "Yes, they know, and they are doing this because the Stain, essence of the Dark God, is in them and has corrupted both of them!" She explains how there is the possibility that it could have happened.

Samuel clears his throat and asks, "Before you mentioned that the four of you are not Gods, and if you four are not Gods, then what are you?"

Jutsuk says, "In the ancient language, we are called *Tendaishi*, which translates into something just below a God, but not quite a god, and we did not know this until Guichi and Tanin captured Jutsuk.

Samuel asks, and the two girls can hear the concern in his voice. "What do you mean that Guichi and Tanin captured Jutsuk?"

Jutsuk starts telling them about her capture, how Tanin tortured her, and how she was about to be beaten and have her essence absorbed by a piece of Dark Crystal. He was still torturing me, and that is when Laki appeared, and we fought him together.

Laki takes a sip of tea and continues the story. "When I found her, Jutsuk was on the altar, and these women were doing terrible things to her. I had not expected the power that Tanin could conjure, and he soon had me beaten down, trapped under some debris falling from the cavern ceiling, and placed some binding around me. I lay there with cuts and bruises of my own, and that's when I saw him throw Jutsuk down, and I saw her bruises, cuts, scratches, and welts, and then something inside me, something I never felt before, started to grow, and it consumed me, and I realized that this feeling I felt was hate. Jutsuk lay close to me, and I reached out to her, and with both of us on the verge of total exhaustion, we were finally able to touch, and our essences joined and blossomed. This new feeling bloomed and allowed me to break the bindings Tanin placed on me, and I felt rejuvenated and powerful and realized that Jutsuk and I were "Reborn," as Mother said."

They both stand, and William and Samuel are both surprised to see them standing there wearing pure white feathered wings, and then they are gone. "Our rebirth gave us these, and we can harness power far beyond anything imaginable, but we do not know to what extent. We are hesitant about using this power because if our brothers somehow succeed in releasing the Dark Lord Nimponin, then it will be up to us to fight him and put him back in the crystal."

Laki takes another sip of tea and continues, "When we fought, he hurt Jutsuk, and a pure unadulterated rage came over me, and then I beat him, and I beat him bad while this rage-fueled me on. After knocking him unconscious, I placed a binding on him as he did us, and I left with Jutsuk."

Laki sits down, takes another sip of tea, and then goes into detail about finding the Tome of Unholy Scriptures and the piece of Dark Crystal. I interrogated Tanin, and after a bit of persuasion, I found out everything that I needed to know about their plans and how he would imprison the two of us inside the piece of Dark Crystal."

Laki looks at Jutsuk, and Jutsuk nods her head to go ahead and tell them they have a right to know. Laki sighs and says, "I performed the ritual and transferred Tanin's essence into the piece of Dark Crystal. After I had completed the ritual, I knew that the crystal had the essence of the Dark God Nimponin, already trapped inside." she looks at William and says, "Please forgive me!" she sits down and bows her head as if in shame and begins to weep.

William and Samuel sit there and say nothing. William stands, walks over to Laki, and places a finger under her chin. He lifts her chin to look into her eyes, smiles, and says, "What is there to forgive? You know my history, what I did for a loved one, and what you did was protect your sister. After all, I know that Samuel is pleased you did."

Laki looks at Samuel, as does Jutsuk, and sees him nod; then, he smiles at the two of them. Laki asks, "What about the beliefs that we preach of honesty, morality, virtue? Did I not openly disregard what we have been preaching by feeling the hate and anger and then purposely imprison

Tanin in the crystal that already had the Dark God imprisoned? Does it not go against our teachings or beliefs of forgiving?

William looks at her and sternly says, NO! what you did was protect a loved one, and if that isn't honesty, morality, virtue, and love, then I don't know what it is." Laki stands up, and William embraces her very tightly, and she says, "Thank you." Jutsuk does the same and also tells William. "Thank you." She steps over to Samuel and embraces him, and then he whispers something in her ear, and Jutsuk laughs.

The two of them sit back down, and William fills their cups; Laki tells them that all they know about "Chosen" is that the High Priestess supposedly has found one and is looking for the other three with the help of the Dark Twins, Mia, and Mae.

William asks, "If that is the case, how are we supposed to battle this because Samuel and I have seen what the Dark Realm can bring into our world. Don't get me wrong, I am willing to give up my life for the two of you and Samuel, but even I don't know to what extent her powers go, especially if she can somehow draw what she needs from the Dark Realm."

Jutsuk tells him, "After Laki brought the Tome back with her, I studied it in-depth and from what I can gather, If she finds all four of these Chosen, as stated in the Tome' these four. "Chosen" will become a formidable enemy. These four Chosen will be able to manifest and channel power directly from the Dark Realm and use it themselves to fight beside the High Priestess or transfer their drawn power straight to the High. If she is the catalyst, this could give her more power. We don't know if it came down to a head-to-head battle between William, manipulating the five manas of Chikyu, and the High Priestess drawing on the sources from the Dark Realm, who would not only win but who would survive." Laki looks at William and softly says, "Sorry."

Jutsuk says to them, "We have a plan to help you with High Priestesses' four "Chosen." You remember in the letter when you first came to the valley. How you two will need to venture out into the world and find these four, or as we call them, the "Gifted." When you do find them, your biggest challenge will be to convince them of their roles, and if they accept, and after they have received the proper training and you are both satisfied, you will then give them one of the blue diamonds that Samuel you have in your possession."

Laki continues," These four Gifted already have the power to harness the mamas of Chikyu; it will be up to you two to train them."

Samuel nods his head yes. Laki says good and then walks up to William and says something in his ear, and all he says is, "Really, I did not think that was possible, but it is good to know. Jutsuk and Laki stand near the window and then are gone, leaving the smell of lavender in their wake.

Samuel looks at William and asks, "What was that whisper with Laki just before they left. William explains to him what she said, and now all Samuel can say is, "Really!"

They put everything back as it should be, and just before they leave the room, Samuel checks the room one more time and then closes the door. They both hear it lock, and as they head down the stairs, Samuel asks William, "Do you think they will be okay?"

William says, "Honestly, Samuel, I don't know, but it feels like a tremendous burden has been lifted off the both of them. Regarding this mission, how should we find these "Gifted" who and wherever they might be!"

Samuel laughs and says to William, "You know William, you and I are too much alike."

William asks, "And how is that pray tell."

Samuel says, "We both know we love a challenge!"

William laughs now and says, "That we do, my friend, that we do."

CHAPTER 37

ALIVIA RUTH CASRONE

Alivia Ruth Casrone came from a middle-class family and was an only child. She did not have any sisters or brothers because her mother passed away from the sickness when she was two years old. Her father was devastated by her mother's death and threw himself into his work, but he always found time to spend with Alivia no matter what he was doing. He was known for his talents and was the only blacksmith in the local area, and he lived in the town of Pell's River.

Edward Casrone always seemed to keep his conversations straight and to the point. The townsfolk admired his honesty; because of this, anyone who did not know him would get the impression of him as a cold, hard man. He was neither cold nor hard, but he was very protective of his daughter. From years of being a blacksmith, he was a big, solidly built man, and he could forge a shoe for a horse to fit perfectly or fix an old farmer's plow or his tools to almost brand new. He had clients all over the region and some as far as three or four counties away, and a few in other kingdoms. Thomas Casrone was content doing what he did and living with his daughter Alivia.

Alivia had just turned seven when she found an old sketchbook tucked away in a box and recognized her mother's drawings. She was sitting in a chair looking through her mother's old sketchbook when her father asked her what she was reading. She shows her father the sketches and asks him why he stopped making things, like the jewelry in the pictures. At first, her father was hesitant, but Alivia said, "I think Mother would have liked it!" The following day, he sat at his workbench and asked Alivia to pick something simple. She did, and as he unwrapped his tools, she saw the spark return to his eyes and thought she felt her mother standing beside him, guiding him. Time passed, and using his wife's sketches, he made the most exquisite pieces, and soon word spread that Edward Casrone, the blacksmith from Pell's River, was making fine jewelry again.

She remembers one warm sunny day when she walked into the back of his blacksmith shop and found him hunched over his workbench, holding a tiny hammer and other tools that seemed too small for his large hands. He turned to look at her, and she noticed that he had been crying. She went to him, wrapped her arms around his chest as best she could, gave him a tight hug and kiss on the cheek, and asked what was wrong. He picked her up and hugged her back, and she started laughing because his beard tickled her. He explained that Mother was an exceptional artist and that she had drawn all these beautiful sketches for different types of jewelry and promised her that he would still make them after she was gone. He looks at her and says, "Alivia, my sweet, I am keeping my promise, and hugs her. She laughs because his beard tickles her, and Edward Casrone laughs with her.

Edward Carson was already known as a talented blacksmith with his exceptional work in bending and forming metals. After he took back up making the jewelry from his wife's sketches, his name and reputation spread like wildfire throughout the four Kingdoms. People from all over came to admire his talents and the exquisite fine jewelry he produced. He was known to take any piece of metal and, with the dexterity of a small child, fabricate and engrave fine jewelry or whatever the customer requested.

One night Edward was in his workshop working on a small delicate silver locket for her thirteenth birthday and was putting the final touches on the piece. It was late when he finally finished, and he sat there admiring his work, thinking Alivia was on her way to becoming a beautiful young lady. He is happy to be making this locket from a sketch his wife had drawn, and it was the only sketch with Alivia's name on it. He was sitting there putting away his tools when he heard a distinct pop coming from the front of the house.

He thought it might have been Alivia and called out to her. He got up from his bench and placed the locket in his pocket without thinking, and just when he was going to blow out the light, he suddenly heard

Alivia scream. He instinctively grabbed his largest smithy hammer and rushed from his workroom into the central part of the house where Alivia's bedroom was. When he got to the living room, he saw a strange man wearing a black robe standing in the doorway of Alivia's bedroom. He also notices that ice or something has formed all around the opening, blocking the black-robed one from entering her room. He calls out to the stranger, "Get away from my daughter, you Bastard!"

Forgetting about Alivia, the robed one turns, and Edward immediately sees a white cloth that looks soaked in blood covering its eyes. He then sees the figure wave his hand, and something enters his peripheral vision, and it is coming at him fast. Without thinking, he brings up his hammer and swings it, striking a strange-looking beast on the side of its head. The creature goes down with his hammer embedded in its a smashed skull. He hears a hissing sound coming from the robed one and sees another one of those beasts pacing around the room. Edward tries to pull his hammer from the first creature's skull and finds it stuck fast.

The second beast runs directly at him, and Edward does the only thing he can, and being a big man himself, he rushes the beast. Right before they collide, the beast leaps and is caught off guard as Edward lowers his shoulder and catches it in its chest. He feels its claws rake across his back but ignores the pain. Edward quickly brings his head up fast and catches the beast right under its jaw, and though he might have stunned the beast, the beast has the weight advantage and knocks Edward backward on the floor. Before he was knocked back, he had grabbed the beast by its throat and somehow was able to keep his hands around the creature's throat and its jaws away from his face. He feels the beast's claws tear through the thick leather apron he is wearing, but he holds fast and keeps squeezing its throat. With all those years of blacksmithing, of holding and swinging a hammer, Edward squeezes the beast's throat and squeezes hard. The beast begins to panic and is snarling viciously as it tries to break free, but Edward holds fast. The beast kicks out with its hind legs, knocks over an oil lamp, and shatters. The oil from the lamp spreads quickly across the floor. The beast tries to gain footing, slips in the oil, and falls to the floor.

Edward moves quickly for a big man and somehow maneuvers himself so he is now on the beast's back and wraps his legs around the beast's body. The beast tries to jump and throw Edward off, but the beast slips a second time in the oil and falls to the floor. Edward then grabs the beast's upper and lower jaws and, using all of his upper body and arm strength; he pulls the beast's jaws apart; and when both its jaws snap, he sees the robed one turn to swing a black smoking sword at him and then he sees that the creature is frozen where it stands and cannot move.

The beast howls in pain as both its jaws are broken, and then Edward, unconcerned with the robed one, at this point, places his forearm under the beast's throat; the other hand grabs its snout, and he pulls upward with all his might. The beast struggles desperately to break itself free, but Edward is not letting go, and soon Edward is straining every muscle in his body when suddenly he hears a snap, and the beast goes limp. Edward is exhausted and remains on the creature's back, trying to catch his breath. He is not too exhausted to notice that the ice has worked its way up to its torso and is slowly encasing its arms, and for some reason, it stops at the thing's neck, leaving its head unfrozen. He now looks at the robed one and sees that it is now a frozen statue.

The robed one cannot move as Edward walks over to the first beast and struggles just a bit to remove his hammer. He finally yanks his hammer from the beast's head, and walks back over to the robed one, stands in front of him, looks at the creature in what he assumes is its eyes, and says, "How dare you go after my daughter!" and takes a massive swing with his hammer and brings it down on top of the creature's head. The blow from the hammer caves in his head, and the rest of its body shatters, and the black blade goes flying.

Edward calls out Alivia's name, hears, "Daddy!" hurries to her room, and notices the ice around the doorway. He rushes through the door, picks her up, and hugs her tightly. Unbeknownst to either of them is that the black blade struck the metal on the broken oil lamp, which caused a spark, and the spark ignited the oil almost immediately. Edward is in Alivia's room when she asks, "Daddy, what's burning?" Edward rushes to her bedroom door and finds the house is now ablaze in several places. He rushes over to Alivia, scoops her up, and uses his own body to protect her, he tries to make his way to the front door, but several falling obstacles block his path.

He is standing there trying to figure out what to do when ice crystals suddenly begin forming, and then ice columns somehow appear and divert or hold back the flames. Edward makes his way through, and as he gets to the front door, one of the main support beams comes crashing down and lands on his back; he collapses under the weight of the beam, but he is still holding onto Alivia with one arm close to his chest, while the other holds himself off the floor. Edward struggles with the weight and the fire, but he is determined to protect his daughter. Edward carefully lowers her to the floor to allow his other arm to help support the massive weight across his back when he hears her softly cry out, and he sees that she has a burn mark on her back between her shoulder blade and the shoulder from a falling cinder. He looks at her, tells her everything will be alright, and that she is brave because he loves her very much.

He hears his name and a loud kick at the front door. On the second kick, the door comes flying off its hinges, and he sees his friend, Ted Barnes, standing there and then reaching in to take Alivia from beneath his body. Ted grabs Alivia, and as he pulls her to safety, he is shocked to feel that her nightgown is wet and ice-cold while her body is warm. He sees his friend Edward trapped under one of the support beams, and Ted thinks he sees deep blue columns of ice holding up the burning timbers.

Edward somehow manages to reach into his pocket and then holds out his hand. Ted reaches in, and Edward places a beautifully engraved locket in the palm of his hand and says, "For her birthday." Edward then says, "Please take care of her and tell her I love her, and Ted, Thank y...." his arm gives out before he can finish as the beam, along with the rest of the house, comes crashing down, and engulfs the blacksmith shop, his workshop, and Edward Casrone in flames. Ted grabs Alivia and holds her tight as she lays in his arms, crying, and he hears her call out, "Daddy."

Ted stands there holding on to Alivia and is heartbroken, not only for his Godchild but also for watching his best friend's demise, and he cries.

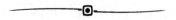

Just outside the town of Pell's River, in a densely wooded area, a humming sound is barely audible, and the Air seems to spiral inward on itself and then gradually expand. Seconds later, Samuel steps out of the spiraling Air and takes a defensive position, saying, "Okay." William steps through once Samuel tells him it's safe. Once through, William releases the mana on his hand, the spiraling Air is gone, and the humming slowly fades.

Samuel asks William where they are, and William tells him they should be on the outskirts of a small town called Pell's River, southwest of the city of Weyport. They walk out of the woods, and as they walk along the road towards town. Samuel says, "I understand that your element of *Spirit* somehow can find these "Gifted" by the aura that was planted in them by the "*Kachirano*," when they were newborns, but is that for anyone that has an inkling of power or for the actual four "Gifted?"

William tells him, "Honestly, Samuel, I am about as much in the dark as you are, but I felt as well as you did, through the element *Spirit* that someone has a strong affinity in this part of the lands, and when I conjured the passageway, opened up where we are."

They are walking along when Samuel stops and tells William, "company!" Six unsavory-looking characters step from the brush when he says it, and they all have their weapons drawn. One of them says, "Hand over your valuables, and maybe we will let you live."

Samuel flicks his thumb and releases "*Shikei Narasu*" but does not draw her yet; he feels her wants and smiles. Samuel then takes a step forward and tells the man who demanded their money, "Look here, my friend, we do not want any trouble, and it would be best if the six of you let us pass so no one gets hurt. My lady friend here, and Samuel gently pats the hilt of "*Shikei Narasu*" is a temperamental woman, and like all women, she is very demanding.

The group's supposed leader stares at Samuel and says, "What are you talking about? There is no lady here. Are you fucking crazy?"

While all this has been going on, William casually steps over to a fallen tree when the leader asks him, "Where the fuck do you think you are going?"

William points to the tree and says, "Right over here to sit down and watch how this little gathering will end, and just to let you know, my money is on my friend and his young lady friend."

The leader angrily shouts, "What the fuck? Are you both crazy? There is no fucking bitch here!"

Samuel says, "Excuse me, why did you have to go and call her that name? She is highly insulted as well as I, and Samuel slowly draws "*Shikei*

Narasu," a very feminine but young voice that only Samuel can hear says, "Thank you."

William watches Samuel take a deep breath, and when he almost feels the flash of silver cross his eyes, and with speed unheard of, he is in front of the leader at a sword's length and flicks his wrist. The other five bandits watch their leader's head wobble, and as if in slow motion, its slides off his shoulders and bounces on the ground.

William sits casually on the log, looks through the small leather-bound book for any new entries that tend to appear without notice, and finds a new entry about the Gifted.

Samuel flicks his sword to remove any access blood when the five bandits seem to rush him at once. He notices they are coming at him close together, hindering their attacks. He brings *"Shikei Narasu"* up close to the side of his head and very softly says to her, "Let's dance," and Samuel hears, "With pleasure, my Dragon," and Samuel strikes first with a diagonal downward stroke that opens up the chest of the closest bandit, and he falls to the ground. He then drops to one knee, spins, and with his katana extended, he takes out two more bandits by severing their legs below their knees, and they go down screaming. He sees a sword coming at his head, deflecting it and pushing his blade through his attacker's chest. Samuel sees that the remaining bandit has not entered the fray, and as Samuel stands, he flicks his blade of any excess blood and then wipes the edge on one of the bodies. He brings *"Shikei Narasu"* up to his face and watches as any few droplets of remaining blood are absorbed into the blade itself. After the blood is gone, he places a soft kiss on the metal and says, "Thank you, My Lady," and just before he puts her in her sheath, he hears, "My Dragon, and then she is quiet.

The last bandit stands there, and when Samuel looks at him, he drops his sword, then falls to his knees and begs forgiveness. Samuel walks up to him, takes his short katana, and smacks him on the side of his head, knocking him out. He then drags him over to a tree and ties him to the tree.

Samuel then stands, clears his throat, and William looks up from his reading and says, "Done already, that was quick?"

William watches Samuel check all their pockets, and when he is done, William brings forth fire. Samuel watches as five separate strands of a flame jump from his hand and onto the dead bodies, and within seconds there are only five piles of ash, and when the breeze blows away the ashes.

William asks, "What about him?"

"Maybe there is a militia or someone in town, and we can let them know he is out here, and I found some trinkets and coin. Hopefully, someone will know who these belong to."

They walk for another thirty minutes, and as they enter the outskirts of the town, they notice a building that appears to have been gutted by fire. The fire looks to have happened a few years back, and fresh flowers are tied with a purple ribbon around one of the charred timbers.

They continue walking into town, and as they pass several locals, the men nod, and the ladies smile at them. Though they are strangers, the people feel something about them, a warmth that puts them at ease. They politely ask a man and his young daughter for an establishment with food and drink and inquire about a militia or someone in authority. The man tells them to go to the Sakura Bistro; they have the coldest ale in town, and the food is good and reasonably priced. It is one of the locals' favorite eateries, and he also mentions Ted Barnes, the proprietor. They thank the man and his daughter for the information and continue on their way. They walk on and then see the sign and the large doors open to allow fresh Air to enter the room. They sit at one of the tables near the doors, giving the bar a more extensive look. They see one other customer in the place hunkered down over his food and drinking ale.

Samuel signals to the man standing behind the bar, and he gestures for them to wait just a moment. They hear him call to someone in the back, and after the dull clash of pots, a young girl of about fifteen comes out of the backroom drying her hands.

She comes to their table and asks what they want to order. Samuel politely asks her if there is any law enforcement or militia in town. The young girl tells them, "A militia comes around once every month and stays a couple of days to settle any local disputes, and that they have a store room in the basement here in the Bistro that they place people who cause trouble, but you will have to talk to Ted about that. May I ask, "Why?"

Samuel tells her, "We ran into some bandits on the road into own, and that they captured one, and he had all this on him," Samuel places the trinkets on the table. The young girl looks at them, points to a couple of items, and says, "That ring there is Mrs. Torts, and the other two rings belong to Mrs. Taft; as for the other things, Ted might know who the owners might be.

William says, "Now that that is settled, could you send over Mr. Barnes, and then asks, "What would you recommend, young lady?" She smiles and tells them to try the stew with fresh venison and a loaf of the tavern's freshly baked dark bread and that she made it herself. William says, "How can we pass up freshly baked bread, and Samuel agrees.

They order the stew, the fresh bread, and two draughts of cold ale. The young girl tells them she'll be right back with their drinks. William and Samuel are sitting and waiting, and Samuel asks William, "That was a neat trick with the fire element earlier," and is about to say something else when they both sense a change in the Air. They look around and see no one other than the serving girl. William releases *Spirit* and watches it head straight to the young girl. Then he sees the auras of light blue, bright white, and an unmistakable aura of *Spirit* emanating from her. He feels her turning with two mugs of ale, ice-cold, and then it is gone as he places them on a tray, walks back around the bar and to their table, and says, "I'll be right back with your stew and dark bread. She turns and heads back to the kitchen when she stops and asks the other customer if everything is okay with his meal. He immediately reaches out, grabs her wrist, and starts complaining loudly about his food being cold and his ale being warm.

Samuel is about to stand up when William places his hand on his arm and motions to wait and remain seated. The young girl asks, "Sir, please remove your hand from my arm, and I will be more than happy to get the tavern owner to discuss your complaints." The customer sits there with his hand still on her arm and says, "I don't want to talk to the owner, you were the one who brought me my food and drink, and I think you should be the one to compensate me for this lousy service." William and Samuel both notice the tavern owner standing in the doorway with a bludgeon hanging from his belt and are ready to use it if need be, but he remains leaning in the door with his arms crossed.

The young girl smiles very sweetly at the customer. "Sir, I asked very politely for you to remove your hand. Now! I am telling you to remove your hand from my arm." The customer starts laughing and asks her, "What will you do about it if I don't remove my hand? Call your Daddy?"

The young girl's face gets a little red with anger and, in an ice-cold voice, says, "No, Sir! I can handle a small piece of shit like you all by myself!"

The customer says, "Why you, snot-nosed little bit..."

Samuel stands up, and as he does, William watches as the young waitress places her hand on the customer's wrist; he sees the light blue aura turn dark, and they both see a look of concentration on her face. The customer screams, "Ouch!" and quickly pulls his hand away from the girl's arm and starts rubbing the spot where she touched him.

"What did you do, you little bitch?" the customer shouts and tries to stand up, but he cannot, as he feels something on his shoulder and sees Samuel standing beside him with his hand on his shoulder. Samuel asks, "Do we have a problem here?" as Samuel tightens his grip.

The belligerent customer winces and says, "No, I do not have a problem.

Samuel then leans forward and very quietly tells the customer, "Why don't you leave the young lady alone and apologize to her, and while you're at it, why don't you pay your bill like a good man, give her a little extra for your trouble, and then leave. Do we have an understanding here?" and Samuel squeezes the man's shoulder a little harder.

The man winces and says, "Yes!" Samuel releases his shoulder, and as he stands up, he throws some coins on the table and is about to leave when Samuel clears his throat and places his other hand on his sword hilt. The man yells, "Sorry!" and quickly leaves the tavern.

The young girl says, "Thank you, Sir, have a good day and then laughs. She looks at Samuel and says, "Sir, you should not have troubled yourself."

Samuel responds, "It was no trouble, young lady. Could my friend and I get two more ales when you get a chance?" She smiles and says, "Yes, Sir!" She heads for the bar, and Samuel sees her talking with the owner. William brings forth a small funnel of Air and propels it towards the man and the young girl, and he hears the man ask her if she is okay. The young girl answers yes, and then the man tells her, "Alivia, please be careful with your "Gift," you know how the townsfolk are with things they do not understand. Samuel walks back to his seat and sits down. A few minutes later, she brings over two more cold draughts of ale and hurries off. She returns with their venison stew and black bread and tells them to enjoy.

Samuel says to William as the young girl walks away. "Did you feel it?"

William says," Yes, and it's raw. She has an affiliation with water and Ice. Still, I also felt some slight traces of Air, a purely natural affiliation, and a connection with *Spirit*, and with the proper training, she could be very powerful."

Samuel says, "I agree. Now let's eat before our stew gets cold!"

They finish eating and enjoy the last drinks when the young waitress comes over to clear their plates. William thanks her for her recommendation about the food and then asks if she can join them to chat. The young lady sees the empty tavern and tells them she will be right back.

Moments later, she sits with a tray holding three cups of tea. William and Samuel look at her.

She said, "I had a feeling that you two enjoy a cup of tea after a meal." She smiles at both of them. William and Samuel say. "Thank you"

Samuel asks, "What is your name, young lady?"

She replies, "Alivia Ruth Casrone."

William says, "Well, Alivia, would you mind if I asked you a few questions?"

Alivia looks at him and says, "No, not at all, but we might not have too much time before the evening folks start making their way in for dinner."

William says, "I'll try to be quick and get straight to the point. We both noticed that when that customer placed his hand on your arm, you did something, and then the man pulled his hand away as if he got burned. May I ask what you did?"

Alivia is surprised and quickly stands up and says, "I'm sorry, Sir, I do not know what you are talking about, and if you would be so kind as to pay your bill and leave, I have to get back to work." She is about to walk away when William gently grabs her wrist. The second he touches her, she feels a slight tingle, followed by cold racing up her arm, and a soft breeze blows through the Bistro, and then she feels something raw that stops the cold and blocks the breeze. Alivia pulls her wrist from William's hand, rubs it, stares at him, slowly sits back down, looks at William and then Samuel, and sees Samuel smiling.

"How did you do that?" she asks.

"Do what?" William asks.

"Do what you just did when you grabbed my wrist," she says.

William sits there as if waiting for something.

Alivia asks, "Can you teach me?"

That was what he was waiting for, her wanting it. William says, "Before I agree to anything, could you answer some questions for me?" Before Alivia can answer. Samuel stands and pushes with his thumb on the hilt guard of his katana to release "*Shikei Narasu*," Dark clouds roll in very quickly; a distinct pop is heard not far away.

William tells Alivia to go into the kitchen, take the man with her, and lock the door. She sees Samuel's face and hurries to the kitchen. She then hears William say, "Alivia, do not come out until either Samuel or myself come and get you, is that understood?"

Alivia answers, "Yes," and quickly talks to the man, and he sees her pulling him into the kitchen. Just as she is closing the door, she hears screaming.

Chapter 38

Failure is Not an Option

Captain Reiko Anzu Takahashi is in her small office writing her daily supply reports when she hears a knock on the door and says, "Come in." The door opens, and a young Second Lieutenant Brandy Sulliban steps in, walks up to her desk, salutes, and hands Reiko a sealed envelope. Reiko opens the sealed envelope, and inside she finds orders for a mission. She skims through them and sees Dark forces, the Leader of an Army, and something about a High Priest. She sees that Major General Lucius Hind has signed the orders. She looks at an attached note and sees a list of soldiers by name that are supposed to go with her, and the last name on the list is Second Lieutenant Sulliban. At the bottom of the list of names is a handwritten note, and all it says is, *Failure is <u>Not</u> an Option*!

She knows that he has hated and despised her, Samuel, and their late friend Hikaru since the battle of Shira. The three discovered the plot by his nephew, Gustavo Heinz, who was trying to destroy the Imperial Army in Shira and set up a stronghold for the Dark Army. His brother, a Brigadier General in the Imperial Army, was disgraced with the official report, and with his name dishonored, the General killed his family and committed suicide. Hinds could never accept this because he knew his nephew was innocent, and the three of them plotted against Gustavo because of jealousy towards him. After being promoted to Major General, Hinds ended up in charge of the Imperial Army, and he despised Reiko and the others, either dead or banished, who were close friends to the Princess. The idea of an Imperial Princess having relations with a mere Captain in the Imperial Army was preposterous. He took that as a pinnacle of insubordination.

Reiko thinks but for a second and puts the note to flame and burns it. She tells Second Lieutenant Brandy Sulliban to gather the squad on the list and pull enough rations from the quartermaster for at least three months. She sees the look on her face and says, "Don't worry, you are coming." The Lieutenant gives Reiko a sharp salute and turns to leave the room when

Reiko tells her, "Brandy, tell the squad, civilian attire, and pull coin for the three kingdoms from the military coffer." Reiko listens as the Lieutenant walks quickly down the hall. Reiko remains at her desk and thinks about Samuel and then the mission.

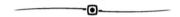

Two days later, Captain Reiko Takahashi, Second Lieutenant Brandy Sulliban, and a squad of twenty men ride out of the Capital city under night's darkness and towards the Insetsu Pass in the Tammayaku Mountains. They reach the outpost just before sunrise, prepare a morning meal and wait for their mission brief. After eating, they sit around a small fire in the main room; Reiko clears her throat to get their attention, and all small chatter stops, and everyone looks at her.

She says, "Men, it is time for you to learn of our mission. You have heard rumors that an army of men, and women, consisting of degenerates and other factors, are massing somewhere, presumably in the northern part of Elenni, known as the Barrens. Other rumors are surfacing that strange creatures and beasts are also massing beside them. These reports say that this is the same force that killed the old King and Queen of Elenni, butchered every man, woman, and child in the village of Marion, and then burnt the village to the ground. It is a known fact that the Old King's son King Theo the II, sent a battalion of seasoned Elenni troops to investigate, and they were discovered to all have been killed and crucified. We now hear that this army has grown to over sixty-five thousand strong. Some say this is part of the same army that attacked Shira and controlled Hokida under the late Lord Tao's rule. Both factions were defeated, while others say it is two different factors because there is no way an army of that size that attacked Shira could cross the three Kingdoms without being noticed. We know they are massing, and the suspicions are that this army will soon make its way into the three Kingdoms."

There are immediate murmurings amongst her squad. She raises her hand for silence, and the murmurings stop. As I have said, "The Kingdom of Elenni is in turmoil over what they call, "The Massacre of Marion," and the citizens want the King to do something about it before this mysterious army supposedly comes down from the Barrens and starts razing the lands. The opposition against the King is saying that this is just a hoax and that no army of that size could survive in the Barrens, so they are delaying the coin that the King would use to raise an army. All the Kingdoms are nervous due to the rumors surfacing about this army. As I speak, the Empire is mustering men and war machines to march into the three Kingdoms and assist in destroying this army if need be.

Murmurings start again, letting her squad vent and taking it all in. After a few minutes, the murmurings die down, and she continues. "Our mission is simple, get in close enough to the leader or Priest of this army, assassinate him, and then get out. Are there any questions?" Several hands go up, and Reiko answers each question best.

She then says, "If there are no more questions, please pay attention to the map on the wall, which shows the three Kingdoms, and I will explain what we plan to do. After telling them her plan, she tells the squad to rest because this will be a hard ride. Reiko goes over to take the map off the wall, and as she folds it up, she hears, "Ma'am," and turns around to find Lieutenant Sulliban standing there.

"Yes. Lieutenant, what is it?

"Captain Takahashi, I know this is my last chance to be allowed to stay in the military as an officer because of my service record, and I wanted to thank you."

"Lieutenant Sulliban, no need to thank me. Just do what you should do, act as an officer in His Emperor's Imperial Army, and tell her, "Now, go get some rest. We have a long hard ride later today, "Dismissed!"

Brandy gives Reiko a sharp salute and leaves. After she leaves, Reiko contemplates if it was the right thing not to tell the men that this mission that Failure is not an option, and decides to keep it to herself.

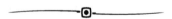

Reiko and her squad leave the outpost just as the sun is hitting its zenith, and they head into the Insetsu Pass, taking them through the Tammayaku mountains into Basra. They have ridden hard and decide to camp about twenty kilometers into Basra to give the horses a rest. While the men make camp, Reiko watches Lieutenant Sulliban walk outside the perimeter and start performing a *Kata* with her weapon of choice, the sickles. Reiko had tried the sickles, which have a short handle made from hardwood, usually a hickory or oak, and on one end is a twelve-inch double-sided curved blade with razor-sharp edges on both sides. The other end of the handle is a lightweight titanium chain attached to a person's forearms with pads to avoid placing a large amount of strain on the wrists. When one of Higg's men was training her on how to use and benefit from them, she became proficient enough to use them if she had to but didn't take to them. Reiko had seen Brandy wield them before, but she was always surprised to see her invent a slight deviation in throwing the sickles that made them twice as deadly. Reiko is amazed at her fluidity and how she can throw them out about three meters and hit her target, and her target is a small maple tree, and she is causing severe damage to her opponent. Reiko continues to watch as Brandy can stop them at any distance from her. With the attached chains, spin them so that when she pulls them back, the inside curve of the razor-sharp blade causes more damage or can even decapitate someone. Reiko notices that the forearm pads are not standard and look custom-made. Reiko knows that these two melee weapons are deadly in her hands. Reiko thinks that Brandy could be a fine officer if she could control her temper. The one thing is that Brandy herself knows this, and she needs to work on that.

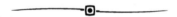

They have been riding for over fifteen weeks and have just passed the outskirts of Springfield in Toma. They are about halfway through the "Great Basin Lake Forrest" when Lieutenant Sulliban notices the border marker partially hidden, and informs Reiko, they are now in Elenni.

Reiko orders a halt, instructs her team to make camp and tells them that now they have to wait until the Elenni representative arrives.

The next day, Reiko is having a cup of tea with Brandy when one of her team shouts out that a rider is approaching. As the rider gets closer, Reiko can make out her insignias and that she is a soldier of the Elenni military, wearing the tunic of a scout unit and hopefully her representative.

She stops her horse inside the camp, dismounts, walks over to Reiko, salutes, and says, "Corporal Corrine Flagg, of the Elenni Scout Unit, Ma am." Reiko returns the salute and says, "Captain Reiko Takahashi," on Special Assignment from Ozake, and this is my second Lieutenant Sulliban. Reiko sees it is late in the afternoon and tells the Corporal that they are making an early camp, and asks the Corporal to join her and

Lieutenant Sulliban for dinner. The three are sitting, and Reiko asks the Corporal if she would not mind mixing dinner and business. Corporal Flagg has no issues, and Reiko asks her to point out where this leader and the horde might be on the map. The Corporal pulls a folded paper from her pouch and places it beside hers. Reiko sees it as a very detailed map, far more complex than her own.

The Corporal looks at both maps and places a finger on Reiko's map.

Reiko asks her, "Corporal, how well do you know this area?"

The Corporal answers, "Pretty well, Ma'am. I grew up just south of the Barrens, in a town called Tolland, and the King of Elenni hired my father to survey the lands around the Barrens and the lands leading up into the Barrens. He had been able to map out the lower two-thirds, but for some unexplainable reason, when he tried to head farther north, he and his surveyors were overwhelmed by headaches and other ailments. The Corporal places her finger on the map, traces it across the Barrens, and says, "This is as far north as anyone can go without getting the ailments. Reiko looks at the map and realizes that this will not do. If that is the case, they would have to wait until the army was on the move before she had a chance to take out the leader. Reiko looks at the Corporal and asks, "Corporal, In your opinion, where is the leader of this horde as we speak?"

The Corporal looks at both maps and places her finger on her map showing a large gorge near the very top of the Barrens, surrounded by high peaks and riddled with caves. Reiko looks at her map and sees that the area where the Corporal is pointing is labeled "Undiscovered."

"So, Corrine, may I call you Corrine?" The Corporal answers, "Yes."

"Corrine, based on your knowledge of the Barrens, where do you think the best location and position would be if, let's say, we were going to try and take out this leader, for example, from above?"

Corrine looks at Reiko and then closer at the map and points to two locations, "The first is here," she says, puts her finger on a spot, and explains that the side of the gorge is not too high. It is a shorter distance to the floor of the valley., but she is unsure being higher will counter the effects of nausea and vomiting. The climb is accessible on the backside, but she thinks the front is also easily accessible. She moves her finger a little higher up on the map and says, "The front access is nearly impossible while the climb up and down on the backside is treacherous but doable.

Reiko looks at the two locations and estimates that the first one puts her about three hundred fifty meters from her intended target and almost on the same plane. In contrast, the second one puts her at a little over nine hundred meters, but she is higher up, and there could be some severe crosswinds coursing through the gorge, not to mention the possible side effects.

She then asks the Corporal, "How long will it take us to get from here to say here?"

Corrine looks at the map and says, "Ten weeks at a good pace."

"Corrine, have you seen the leader of this horde?"

"No, Ma'am, but talking with a captive, he says she is a beautiful woman. Reiko interrupts her and asks, "Their High Priest is a Priestess?" Corrine looks at her and says, "Yes, a woman with fiery red hair, and then Corrine says, "We found this out after we arrested one of her Tashisan, and he told us all about her'."

Reiko interrupts her again and asks, "You arrested one of her what?

Corrine says, "Sorry, Captain, we arrested one of her Tashisans'. We found out that those who preach the word of the Dark Scriptures call themselves, *Tashisan*."

Reiko apologizes for interrupting her and asks her to please continue.

We arrested one for blasphemy against the Goddesses and preaching the word of the Dark Scriptures. Through extensive interrogation, he was shall we say, forthcoming with the information. He not only gave us the information we asked for but also a little more."

Reiko asks her, "Like what kind of information, and Corrine, any small details can help?"

Corrine starts explaining as much as she knows about the High Priestess. She is a very charismatic woman who is also about as cold as they come. The Priestess has five hundred hand-picked Elite Guard commanded by another woman who is almost as cold as she is hard. The Commander and her Elite are entirely devoted to the Priestess and would sacrifice their lives to protect her. She has a woman who is almost as beautiful but a bit younger. This woman is always by the Priestess's side and is untouchable as she is considered one of her "Chosen."

Reiko sits quietly, tapping her finger against her lips. Then she asks, "Do you know if she can wield magic?"

Corrine tells her of three things that she has no information on. The first is whether the Priestess can use magic. The second is rumors about a set of Twins and a Dark Realm, and the third, supposedly the Priestess, has a direct connection with the Gods Guchi and Tanin.

The interrogators could not find out anymore because the Tashisan somehow got free and threw himself out a window of one of our towers.

Reiko remains quiet, thinks about everything she has just been told, and says, "Well, Corporal, I think I have a plan, and puts her finger on the second location on the map. Corrine looks and asks, "Are you sure, Reiko? That is quite a shot, and you need to be an expert with a longbow?" Reiko smiles and says, "Let me worry about that, and you are more than welcome to join us unless your duties are required elsewhere; if they are, please take some rations and depart after you have rested."

The Corporal looks at Reiko and says, "Captain, if it is all right with you, I would like to stay and see this through. I have performed my assigned duties and given you, my report. I will gladly guide you to the point on the map, plus I want to see that Bitch pay for what she did to the folks in Marion."

"Excellent, Corrine; get some rest; we depart first thing in the morning."

"Yes, Ma'am, Corinne salutes and walks away.

Reiko stands looking at the map and the two spots the Corporal pointed out, and after a little more thought, she will stick with option B. The shot is farther, but she needs to look after her squad now that she is not sure if magic is involved

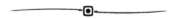

The following day, they move out quickly to make the twelve-week trek. They ride north between Omuso Lake and the Great Basin Lake and keep riding north until they reach the Great Forrest, and when they are a few days ride from the point on the map, they turn west and follow the base of the mountains. They have made good time and are within a day or two from their destination. Corrine points to a portion of sheared-off mountain tops. Reiko sees that they are close to the spot on the map. Three days later, as the mountains loom above them, her team pulls into a crop of trees, and she orders her men to secure their horses and loosen their sinches but leave them saddled.

She tells them to make a cold camp and be ready to ride out quickly if needed. Of the twenty men that came with her, she takes Lt. Sulliban, Corporal Flagg, six other men, and Sargent Wallos, who is an expert mountaineer. It is midday when they start climbing, and though the climb is treacherous in spots, they make it to the top; as they are about to climb onto the plateau, Sargent Wallos, who was the lead, motions for them to stop and remain quiet. He holds up one finger, saying there is a lookout at the far end of the plateau. The six of them stay perfectly still as Wallos makes his way over the edge, and a few minutes later, he motions for them to come on up. They climb over the edge and see an individual staring at them, lying in a pool of blood with his throat cut. Wallos immediately dons his outer clothes and stands to see the horde below. He says, "Wow!" and watches other sentries on lower cliffs, then signals that all is clear. He does the same, and the scene remains with no alarm going out. He steps back and tells Reiko everything is all clear.

Reiko tells her men to stay low and secure the ropes so that they can repel down if they need to get down quickly. She tells them to relax and have some cold rations and water. She asks Brandy and Corrine to come with her, and they remain low and make their way to the plateau's northern edge. All three pull out their eyescopes, and Brandy guesses that they are about sixty-five thousand strong and not the initially reported forty-five. The three move away from the edge, and Brandy tells Reiko that the guess is on what she can see and does not know how many could be inside the caves. They are talking about setting up a schedule when they hear a commotion from below. They return to the plateau's edge, pull out their eyescopes, and see a stunning-looking redhead coming out of the cave and walking to the edge of an immense black diamond precipice. Corrine says, wow, and everyone realizes the precipice in one large black diamond. Reiko moves her eye scope and sees another woman looking a few years younger and beautiful standing next to the Priestess. They see another attractive woman standing on her other side, wearing all black, and they notice that she has a small elongated scar on her cheek, but it does not take away from her looks. Surrounding the three is an entourage of women and men also wearing black. The one with a small scar on her cheek turns and says something, and they immediately take a defensive position around the three of them. Reiko guesses that she is the Commander of these women and men. Brandy takes a guess and tells Reiko that the reports about Priestess's entourage being about five hundred strong are accurate. The redhead starts preaching to the masses, and as the words reach where Reiko and the others are watching, they see a frenzy spreading through the horde.

Reiko believes this is her chance, and she snaps her fingers, signaling for her longbow and a quiver of arrows. Sargent Wallos continues to stand as one of the others stays low and brings them to her. The three of them step away from the edge, and Reiko puts her eyescope away, removes her belt, and then hands them to Lieutenant Sulliban. Corrine stands watching as Reiko carefully unwraps her bow and pulls a bowstring from her pocket. She uncoils the bowstring and carefully ties one end of the string to the bow. Reiko slowly bends the bow to attach the string loop to the other end and secures it. She pulls back the bowstring and is satisfied. Reiko inspects each arrow, picks the two she wants, stays low, and returns to the plateau's edge. Brandy and Corrine are right behind her. Reiko places one arrow in her mouth near the feathers, between her teeth, and notches the other. She looks at Wallos, and she sees him nod. Reiko then stands and slowly pulls the string as far back as possible. Brandy is watching the redhead while Corrine watches Reiko.

Reiko's arm quivers slightly and then steadies when the bowstring is taut to the breaking point. Flagg does not understand what Reiko is doing, primarily pointing the arrow up and to the left of her intended target, and the distance alone is virtually impossible. Still, she brings her scope to her eye and watches the redhead as Brandy does.

Perspiration slowly beads on Reiko's forehead, and she takes a deep breath and holds it; then it happens. The Air around her becomes; still, all outside noises stop, and the red-headed woman comes into sharp focus as if she is standing two meters away from the arrow's tip. Her concentration is so acute that she feels it slowly building, and then she sees it. A silver flash crosses her vision, and she releases the arrow a second later; the second arrow follows the first. She quickly squats down below the edge, carefully unties her bowstring, coils it up so as not to get tangled, and then puts it in her pocket. She then lays down beside Brandy and watches through her eye scope.

The two arrows soar into the rays of the afternoon sun, and as they reach their peak, the arrows arc and then streak downward toward their intended prey. Flagg is amazed to see the arrows slowly line up on the Priestess. All three of them are watching through her eye scopes and anxiously holding their breaths. They watch as her arrows are just about to hit their mark and hopefully, if not stop this horde, at least delay it for a little bit.

Just a breath away from taking out the redhead, the unforeseeable happens. The beautiful young girl standing beside the redhead throws her body directly in front of the first arrow as Reiko now watches her take the shot in her chest. Reiko sees her first attempt failed, then she watches the second arrow, and right before it reaches its target, the woman with the small scar on her cheek grabs the arrow in flight and then, with one hand, breaks it in two. Reiko watches her point to the plateau that they are on. She looks back at the redhead and notices that just now, the woman seems to realize what has just happened; she screams out, "NO!" and sees the young woman's body fall off the edge of the precipice and then hit the ground below. Lieutenant Sulliban and Corporal Flagg are shocked to witness that a young woman gave up her life for this Priestess. Reiko is more surprised that both arrows failed and missed their intended target.

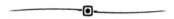

Nova stares down and sees Juliette lying on the ground with an arrow protruding from her chest. Her first "Chosen," her beautiful girl, is dead on the ground below her. She rages with pure hate and chants *"Moerutoniko,"* conjures a ball of white-hot flame, and hurls it in the general direction of where Bernadette is now pointing. It strikes just below the top of the plateau. The impact causes the plateau to shake and stones to tumble down its sides. She hurls another ball of flame, and this time, the plateau cracks, causing Sargent Wallos to lose his footing and fall over the edge. Just as Reiko shouts, "NOOO!" and rushes toward him, she sees a blur, and then one of the repelling ropes is flying over her head to Wallos. She realizes that Brandy somehow was able to grab one of the ropes and toss it to Wallos. Reiko sees Wallos go over the edge and then sees that he has reattached himself to the line that Brandy threw at him. He is still several meters above the valley floor when he gets everything under control. A pack of strange and fierce-looking beasts rush over to the plateau's base and try desperately to grab at Sargent Wallos. She remembers seeing these beasts before, but Hikaru killed the one she saw in the Dark Commander's Arena in Shira. Reiko watches him trying to pull himself back up, but some rocks break free, and one hits him in the head, stunning him, causing him to lose his grip, and she watches him fall back into the pack of strange beasts. Reiko hears his screams as the creatures begin mauling and pulling at his body, ripping it to shreds.

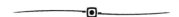

Nova stops momentarily to look down at Juliette and sees two of her Elite gently picking up her body and bringing her back up to the precipice. Nova brushes back her hair, kisses her forehead, and tells the two to take her into the cavern. Nova screams for something, and the woman with the scar on her cheek hands her a mirror. Nova chants "*Sasara Moketeka*," and Nova briefly sees her reflection in the mirror, and then the mirror starts swirling when she sees the man who shot the arrow that took Juliette. Nova sees the person standing with the bow pulled back, releasing the two arrows and watching them travel through the Air. When they are just about to hit her, Nova sees Juliette jump in front of the first one, and she watches the arrow hit her in the chest, and then she sees Bernadette snatch the second arrow just before that one hits her. Nova looks closer at her assailant and screams, realizing that it wasn't a man that took her "Chosen" from her. Disgusted and enraged, she throws the mirror to the ground shattering it, and shouts, "GET THEM AND BRING ME THAT FUCKING BITCH ALIVE!"

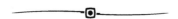

Reiko sees her screaming and throws the object she was holding to the ground, and Reiko says, to Sulliban and Flagg, "I think the Bitch is pissed!"

She watches as her squad leader is torn to pieces and orders her men to get off the plateau NOW! They get down safely except for one, the fireballs that the woman threw at the plateau must have somehow dislodged the tie-off point to his line, and when he was halfway down, the anchor came loose, and he fell to his death. The others get down quickly to the base, and she orders them to mount up. She sees that her men are mounted and ready; when six of them go to retrieve their fallen comrade, Reiko runs to her horse and tells them to leave him. They start to protest about a decent burial when she hears a distant ping coming from the top of the plateau, and then out of nowhere; she sees a red fireball coming at them from the plateau and watches it explode on the ground. The six men that were going to retrieve their fallen comrade are close to where the fireball hits the ground. The six of them are saturated by flames, as are their horses. The horses themselves rear up, trying to throw their riders from their saddles. Some riders are thrown to the ground while others stay on their horses, and then suddenly, they bolt, taking off at full gallop. Reiko sees that the faster they run, the more the flames consume riders and horses.

A couple of her men were thrown to the ground when their horses bolted. They are now lying on the ground, screaming in pain as their flesh burns and blisters. Lieutenant Sulliban runs over to the men, slides a thin-bladed knife through their third and fourth rib, pierces their hearts, and puts them out of their misery.

Reiko looks up with her eye scope and sees a robed man standing on the edge of the plateau, and she sees a blood-soaked white cloth wrapped around his eyes. She lets the eye scope go and grabs a bow from one of her men, and as she does, he hands her an arrow. Reiko has the arrow notched and slowly pulls back the bow's string. Reiko doesn't require the calm, and she releases the shaft before whatever it is can conjure another fireball. She watches as the arrow hits its mark, and the robed one falls off the plateau and plummets to the ground bouncing off outcroppings of rock on its way down.

She runs to her horse, grabs the pommel, and hauls herself into the saddle. She is about to urge her mount forward when she hears the ping again, but this time closer; then, she sees a hole or something of that effect shimmering in the Air. She watches it expand, and once it looks large enough, she sees the same type of creatures that killed Wallos emerge from the other side. Her mount does a quick sidestep, and as she gets him under control.

Reiko yells to her squad, "Ride Now!" She takes off at full gallop with the rest of her team close behind. Two of her men are having difficulty getting their horses moving, and as she looks back to check on them, she sees that those creatures are almost upon them.

The two men regain control of their mounts, and one seems to break free, and she stares in horror as the other rider and horse are brought down quickly as two of the beasts with elongated sharp teeth and claws come out of nowhere and hit the one rider and his horse from the side. She continues to watch as the second rider is about to get away when he is suddenly set ablaze by a fireball thrown by one of the creatures she just killed on the plateau.

She hears the screams of her men over the cries of the horses and knows she can do nothing for them, so she urges her mount to gallop faster to catch up with the remainder of her squad.

They continue to ride at full gallop and soon see that the creatures have stopped pursuing them, but they continue riding hard, and she urges her men and horses onward. Her horse has started lather, and she signals her men to slow their stride. She assumes they have put some distance between them and those disgusting-looking beasts. She orders her men to slow their mounts gradually, and then twenty minutes later, she tells them to dismount and walk with their horses and loosen the saddle cinches so the horses can breathe better. They have been walking their horses for a few hours, and though they look better, she knows they will need more rest. Reiko and her men stumble across a small mountain cave, and as luck is on her side, a small brook runs through the cove. She orders her squad to water and feed their mounts, leaving the horses saddled and making a cold camp. Reiko herself tends to her horse, and as she combs him down, she looks out over the makeshift camp and is shocked by what she sees. Her men look like a ragtag band of misfits who are exhausted, worn out, and ready to give in.

Chapter 39

The Gifted

William checks to see that Alivia is secure in the kitchen, and they place their packs and other items behind the bar. Samuel steps out into the street and releases *"Shikei Narasu,"* and he feels her awaken. Unexpectedly, a dense fog slowly rolls in from the south and starts covering the main road into town and some buildings along the road. Samuel and William can hear several screams through the fog as William brings forth the element of Wind and has it sweep aside the fog. They now see several Chizobutsu standing in the middle of the road, and a few of them are chewing on different body parts of some misfortunate person. The beasts see them standing in the street, and several of them let out vicious snarls and immediately charge both of them.

Samuel takes *"Shikei Narasu"* and holds it so that the edge is just touching his cheek. Samuel feels the bond between himself and the blade as William has drawn forth *Nakeshidoka,* a two-meter staff topped with a Dark Sapphire in his hand. William feels the manas coursing through his body, and a coiled red fire whip flickers with flame and appears in his other hand. He starts to chant, and the Dark Sapphire on his staff begins to glow. Soon the dense fog is completely gone, and William and Samuel now see six Sutaraukaji standing behind eight Chizobutsu, and they order them to attack.

Samuel rushes into the Chizobutsu and immediately drives his blade through one of the beast's hearts, only to spin away from it to slice at two others that are now decapitated. Three are charging toward William when he uncoils his Fire whip and lashes out at the three beasts. With great precision, he dances the tip of the whip to touch each of the beasts in some way or form, whether it be the head, shoulder, or any part of their body, and as the tip touches them, they suddenly burst into flames, and all that is left, is ashes.

William then raises his staff into the Air and drives the end onto the ground. Ice crystals begin to form around the Sapphire, and then several separate streams of ice shoot out from the Sapphire. With precision like the whip, the streams hit the seven Sutaraukaji in their chests, and they are immediately frozen. Samuel rushes the frozen Sutaraukaji, and with three quick sweeps of his blade, he shatters all of them. William sees movement in the shadows as one of them conjures a fireball and is getting ready to throw it at Samuel when the dark blue sapphire atop *Nakeshidoka* glows. There is an explosion as the Sutaraukaji finds himself engulfed in the very flames that it conjured. Samuel looks to William and nods. William sees another of the beasts struggling disparately to break free when Samuel steps up beside it and, like the previous one, drives his blade through its heart.

William steps backward and very calmly tells Samuel to duck. When he does, William quickly throws up his hands and shoots a blast of ice spikes in two different directions at once. Samuel counts the loud grunts and the sounds of eight bodies falling to the ground with a distinct thud. Samuel moves swiftly with his sword slicing through the Air and spinning just as another threat enters *Shikei Narasu's* field of destruction. The unseen beasts find death or dismemberment and soon cease to exist by Samuel's blade. William is doing the same as the beasts bear down on him. He slaughters them immediately, showing no mercy. The beasts continue to come out of the rifts and only find death as they feel the wrath of Samuels's blade and William's destructive elements. Then, as quickly as the attacks started, they stop, and Samuel and William are soon walking among the injured and maimed, swiftly putting an end to their lives.

William chants a few words, and the remaining dense fog starts swirling and dissipates. Samuel had his suspicions and now sees that he is right, as sixteen Sutaraukaji and twenty-four Chizobutsu are lying on the ground.

Samuel asks William, "Do you see it?"

William looks out over the carnage, and after a few seconds, he does. The attacks seem to have some organization compared to the times they have dealt with them. In the past, the attacks were haphazard, and they primarily tried using brute force and strength to try and kill them. Samuel points to the larger group in the middle of the road and tells William, "This group here was the main assault, and the other two groups were flank units," and points to the two groups on each side.

They hear a scream from the Bistro and simultaneously say, "Alivia," and run towards the Bistro; They both now think that the attacks were a ploy to draw them away from their real target, which is Alivia. William immediately throws up a wall of Air as several pieces of splintered wood and some ice shards fly through the Air. William sees a mix of three groups between Sutaraukaji and Chizobutsu standing in what remains of the Bistro. They are throwing fireballs at Alivia's ice shield. William sees that whatever damage the fireballs might do to her shield, the fireballs fizzle out on contact, and any damage they might have caused is quickly repaired.

Samuel quietly makes his way around to the three on the left and then nods as William concentrates on the three on the right. Just as Samuel steps up behind the three, William lashes out with his beige whip, and as he had done previously, with the Fire whip, he allows the whip's tip to touch the two Chizobutsu on their bodies, and it touches the Sutaraukaji on its shoulder. Before the others notice, all three crumbles to the floor, leaving small piles of stone dust. Samuel brings his katana down in a sweeping motion and decapitates the two beasts, and before the robed one can turn to see what has happened, he feels *Shikei Narasu* entering the back of his head to come out of his mouth. Without warning, the very foundation of the building itself starts shaking, and as fast as it started, it stops. There is a slight reprieve until geysers of hot steam burst from the Bistro floor exactly where the remaining three Sutaraukaji are standing. The Chizobutsu one goes to leap out of the way, but Samuel swings *"Shikei Narasu,"* and the beast falls to the floor through death convulsions. William casts a barrier of Air around the three of them so that they cannot move. The steam intensifies and rapidly gets hotter and hotter until it becomes so hot that the three Sutaraukaji melt where they stand. In their wake are three melted piles of flesh, three red robes, and three smoldering black blades.

William casts a shield in front of Samuel for protection and then calls out Alivia's name several times. She calls, "William! Samuel, is that you?" William says. "Yes. It is okay; they are gone; it is safe to come out now." The steam geysers slowly subside, and they can see her standing there surrounded by a wall of clear impenetrable ice, and beside her on the floor is Ted, the man she took into the kitchen with her. The ice wall melts, and Samuel rushers to his side and sees that the man is severely wounded. Samuel lifts his shirt and sees the black pulsing wound from the Sutaraukaji black sword.

William cautiously approaches Alivia and sees that the raw power is still swirling about her and the pupils of her eyes are almost entirely white. William softly calls her name, and he stands still and waits for her to regain her senses. The pure energy slowly subsides, and William can see that Alivia is exhausted and grabs her before she collapses. William asks her, "Are you okay?" She answers, "Yes, just a little tired." Samuel is beside Ted, and Alivia asks him, "Will he be alright?" Samuel looks at William, and William tells her, "We will do everything we can."

Alivia gets up, goes over to Ted, and sits beside him.

Alivia asks him, "Please help Ted, he is my father, and he is all I have left."

William walks over to where Ted and Alivia are and kneels beside Ted. He examines the wound, and Ted sees it in his eyes as bad. William asks Alivia to get some towels and hot water so he can clean his wound. When she leaves, William sees that the cut is already discoloring and turning black, and he places his hands just above the injury; and can feel the taint's black poison slowing, but he knows that it will last only so long. William whispers with Ted, explaining what will happen now that the injury has infected him from the black sword. William looks him straight in the eyes, and Ted can tell that William is telling the truth. He then says, "Take care of her, she has been through a lot for such a young girl, and he asks Samuel to fetch the metal box behind the bar. Samuel fetches the box, and when he returns, he places it on the floor. Ted reaches into his shirt, pulls out a key, hands it to William, and then asks him to open the box. William unlocks the box and pulls out a small pouch made from silk. He tells William, "This was the last piece that her father worked on before he died. I was going to give it to her when she turned sixteen, but I will leave it to you now."

William places the silk pouch in his pocket and tells him, "Do not worry, we will care for her." William stands and sees Samuel standing near what used to be the double doors. Samuel asks him to join him, and when he does, Samuel tells him to look carefully over his right shoulder. William does, and he sees a shimmering rift in the middle of the east road; then, he hears two feminine voices laugh, and the rift closes. William quietly says, "Shit," and Samuel says, "My sentiments exactly."

While the two of them talk to the side, Alivia returns with the hot water and towels and wipes Ted's forehead because he is sweating. They talk quietly, and he coughs once and spits up some blood. Alivia kneels there, wipes his mouth, and holds onto him. William comes back and tells Alivia we need to go. It is not safe here. Alivia makes Ted as comfortable as possible, kisses him on the cheek, and tells him that she loves him like her father. Ted smiles, and as tears fill his eyes, he tells her, "You be a good girl and go with these two nice men, and listen to them because they are your family now."

Alivia hugs him once more and says, "Yes, Father."

Ted says, "That's my sweet girl; now you go and learn everything you can, and do the best you can."

William nods to Samuel, and he leads Alivia out of the Bistro. Samuel stays behind and asks Alivia where the herbalist shop is.

Samuel kneels next to Ted and places his hand over his heart. He looks at Ted, and Ted says, "Make me a promise that you will take care of her and protect her with your own life in need be?"

Samuel looks at him and says, "I promise, as he carefully slides a small thin blade between his ribs and pierces his heart.

Samuel hears Ted say, "Thank you," and then he reaches up and closes his eyes.

The townsfolk start to come out of their homes and businesses as Samuel walks over to one of the men, hands him a small coin purse, and says, "Make sure he is taken care of properly!"

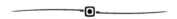

Alivia and William sit on the wall at the crossroads, making small talk when Alivia asks, "What was that shimmering, in the middle of the road. William is just about to answer when Samuel walks up to them and gives William a slight nod.

Alivia asks him, "Is Ted going to be, okay?"

Samuel tells her, "Don't worry about Ted. The townsfolk are going to take good care of him." He smiles.

Alivia looks at Samuel and says, "Thank you."

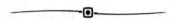

While they walk, William explains a little about these powers that she has and also a little about the rifts and the unknown Dark Realm. They did not know much about the Realm themselves, only that it exists and you should never crossover, or you could be lost in that Realm forever because getting back to this world would be impossible.

They continue walking, and while Alivia asks questions, William answers them. The sun starts to set, and they decide to camp for the evening. Alivia quickly gathers firewood as Samuel sets up some snares, and William begins to prepare a mixture of some herbs and other ingredients, along with a couple of blends of tea he bought in town before they left.

Alivia is piling the wood and setting up the spit when she asks, "William, why do I have these powers? I've felt like an outcast all my life because I was younger, and up until today, I was afraid that I would hurt someone?"

William stops preparing the herbs and tea blend and says, "Alivia, my dear, I will try to explain. Everyone in this world has an affinity to one of the manas or elements of Chikyu. These manas inhabit and circulate throughout the world. Some like myself, and he raises his hand and shows Alivia a multitude of colors dancing around his hand, and then they are gone. They can manifest the mana or elements and learn to control them, while others never realize they have them. The ones that don't know, and if the mana lays dormant, the mana will slowly fade.

William looks at her and asks, "This is a lot to take in. Are you sure you want me to continue?" She tells him, "Yes." William continues, "The Goddesses decided to work out a plan, so the Goddesses placed small statues of the Eternal God Mother throughout the world.

Alivia tells him, "William, there were never any statues of the God Mother anywhere in town.

William tells her that that was not the case and that the statues were imbued with the "*Kachirano*," a celestial *Spirit* that would seek out individuals with a strong connection with the manas. Many years ago, the

Goddesses created the "*Kachirano*" when Samuel and I were eight or nine. Samuel returns with a plump rabbit at that moment and says, "I think closer to nine." William continues, "Many have been touched, but only four can be accepted and have a conviction like no one else."

Alivia reaches out, takes the rabbit, and starts to prepare it for this evening's meal.

Samuel says, "I hate to tell you, but the "*Kachirano*" had you marked as a Gifted probably farther back than you realize it. Once the protection wards of the sacred valley were activated, it triggered something because of William's affinity with *Spirit*; it made finding you a little simpler. So, you know three other individuals in this world, like yourself, who have a solid association for specific mana or manas."

"That is all you will hear from me; please continue." and leans back against his pack and pulls *Shikei Narasu* out to wipe her down and hone her edge. When finished, he nicks his thumb with the blade, hears a soft "Thank you," and then sheathes his blade.

"Alivia, as I was saying before, I was rudely interrupted, "The Goddesses decided to bestow on certain individuals the powers you have felt inside you and used this morning. Samuel and I realized your power in the Bistro and thought, no, let me rephrase that, we know that you could be a very powerful individual with the proper training."

The Goddesses knew of this evil, and Samuel and I would need help fighting it."

William asks her, "Alivia, do you remember a feeling of something deep within you."

Alivia ignores William's question and asks, "What do you mean, you and Samuel?"

William politely ignores her question and continues talking. Alivia starts basting the rabbit with the spices William gave her while he explains to Alivia why she has what she has and what her destiny could be or should be. She checks the rabbit for doneness and removes it from the fire to allow the juices to settle and the rabbit to cool.

William asks, "Are there questions?"

Alivia tells him, not right now, as she cuts off pieces of rabbit and hands them to the both of them on large, broad leaves that they use as plates.

While they are eating, Alivia asks, "William, If the Laki-Jutsuk Religion is strong, why can it not just destroy these Dark Scriptures, its evil, and its followers.

Samuel answers for him, "If the Goddesses destroyed all the evil in this world, the fabric of life would cease to exist. The most we can accomplish is to subdue the influence of the evil, and that is where you and hopefully your three other cohorts come in."

Alivia laughs and says cohorts; I like it. Then she gets serious and asks, "I have never heard of the Goddesses appearing before the people, but the biggest rumor is that someone traveling the lands is supposedly a priest or something representing the Laki-Jutsuk Religious Order."

Samuel clears his throat and says, "I did not know it was considered an Order, but you are correct, Alivia. The Goddesses have Chosen a person as there, and I wouldn't say, High Priest. I would say more of a figurehead, and in the old language, he is known as "The Sendoka."

"The Sendoka does not necessarily go around preaching the words of the Religion as would a regular priest because he was Chosen for another matter, which I cannot get into right now. He is more of an earthly entity for the actual priest and novices of the Religion, and to welcome the followers into the Religion."

"I have heard stories, along with the rumors, she tells the two of them with excitement in her voice.

Samuel smiles and asks, "May I ask what stories or rumors you have heard?"

Alivia says, "That this, what did you call him, the Sendoka, is very wise and ancient, maybe over a hundred years old, and he can fly."

Samuel bursts out laughing and nearly chokes on his rabbit.

Alivia asks, "What is so funny?" looking at Samuel.

Samuel stops long enough to catch his breath, looks at her, then at William, and then back to her and laughs.

Alivia asks again, "Please, what is so funny?"

Samuel takes a deep breath, wipes the tears from his eyes, and in a heartfelt voice, he says, "Alivia, sweet child, l would like to introduce you to William James formally."

Alivia says, "Yes, I know he is William James; we have already met."

Then Samuel says, "My sweet child, you have not just met William James, but what or should I say, you have just been introduced to is the Sendoka of the Laki-Jutsuk Religious NIMPONIN

Alivia sits by the fire with her mouth open, then says, "You already to be over one hundred years old." She smiles at him.

Samuel laughs even harder, and William gives him a dirty look and throws a rabbit bone at him.

William looks at her and says, "No, my dear, I am not quite that old!"

Alivia immediately apologizes, and William smiles at her and says, "Go receive your lessons, and Alivia, kick his butt!" Alivia smiles and says, "I'll try my best."

Samuel stands and says, "Well, young lady. Now that you have made this old man here laugh, it is time I give you your first lesson in sword fighting while that hundred-year-old bag of bones sits there." Samuel laughs again.

Samuel walks away from the fire, and Alivia follows. They stand maybe twenty meters from the fire, and Samuel smiles and asks, "Do you trust me?" and she answers, "Yes."

"Please remove all your clothing except for your undergarments." and says, "I will be right back."

She sits down on a log, does as asked, and folds her clothes; when he returns, she sees he has removed his outer jacket and is holding a long, almost perfectly straight piece of wood and hands it to her. She takes it, and Samuel says, "Shall we begin?" and shows her how to hold the stick as if it were a sword and then place his hands on her body here and there to move afoot, hand, arm, and a leg here or there. He touches spots to show her from standing to balancing while holding a skinny stick as a sword and how to use it for attacking and defending. Three hours of practice later, her shift is drenched in sweat and clings to her body, while Samuel does not even seem to have broken a sweat. She is standing with her feet apart like Samuel has shown her when he says, "That is enough for one night. Let's go back to the fire to dry you out and get some rest."

Samuel reaches into his pack and tosses her a small tin, and when she opens it, the smell wrinkles her nose, and she says, "It smells!"

"I know." Samuel replies, "Rub a little on your sore areas, and I promise you will feel better. I used the same ointment on my sore muscles when I me when I say a very wise soldier gave me that and the recipe.

"Now let's enjoy some of that old man's tea," and then they hear William call out, "I heard that manservant." Samuel whispers to her, it is the best, but don't tell him I said that."

When they return to the camp, Alivia immediately smells hot tea, but something is different in the aroma.

William asks her, "Alivia, how are you feeling?"

She says, "A little sore, some bruises, and my body is unaccustomed to bend and stand in ways Samuel asked me to do,"

William reaches into his pack and pulls out a shirt. He tells her, "Change out of your wet shift," and tosses her one of his nightshirts. Then tells her, "Put this on, and dry your shift near the fire."

Alivia turns her back to them and removes her wet shift. William and Samuel both notice the burn scar on her shoulder. She turns back around to place her undergarments near the fire to dry. William tells her that tomorrow, we will begin your lessons in controlling this "Gift" bestowed upon you, and you need to get some rest."

William grabs his tanbur and softly starts strumming a lovely little melody that soon has Alivia sleeping. Samuel walks over, covers her with a blanket, rinses her cup in a small canvas bucket, and hands it back to William.

William is still softly strumming his tanbur when he asks, "What do you think?"

Samuel answers, "Well, she is a quick learner and seems to have the stamina and fortitude to learn. She might be an excellent candidate to be one of the four we need to find, from what Laki and Jutsuk have told us of the High Priestess's plans to find her four "Chosen."

"I agree. I feel the raw power, and once she learns how to release and control it, Alivia will be a formidable opponent in the greater picture of what the Goddesses have planned."

William continues to play his tanbur, and soon Samuel himself is sleeping. William sits there strumming his tanbur and stares at Alivia. He hears her softly call out Ted's name and is quiet once again. He hopes she can control her gifts to be an advantage in the coming war.

Chapter 40

Pawjuck

Nova is furious as she looks down upon her beautiful Juliette lying on the stone altar. Her slaves have washed her body of all blood, brushed out her hair, and dressed her in her Chosen attire. Nova orders everyone from the cavern, and while holding Juliette's hand, she kneels beside the altar and softly cries.

The Twins enter the cavern and walk up behind Nova, and each places a hand on her shoulders, and then she feels it, cleansed or purging of her heart, body, soul, her very being. The Twins say she has earned the right to be the High Priestess of the Dark Religion and the bearer of the Dark Scriptures. They also tell her that they have felt her cleansing, and now she will be even more powerful. She will become their beacon to allow passage between their worlds.

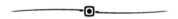

Reiko's men move around the makeshift camp and tend to the horses. Reiko notes that she has only nine of her twenty-man squad remaining. She walks over to a large shaded tree, sits on the ground, leans against the tree, and begins writing up her report, including her unexpected failure.

Corporal Flagg approaches Reiko and says, "Reiko, I need to get back to my detachment and give my report."

Reiko says, "I understand, Corrine, stay aware, and safe travels." and gives her a salute and a sealed envelope. Corrine looks down at it, and Reiko says, "A fully detailed report of what occurred during the mission."

Corrine says, "Thank you, Reiko, and take care." She returns the salute and heads to her horse. She mounts her horse and trots past the sentry and is out of sight and not gone for more than five minutes when everyone hears a high-pitched painful scream from a horse and then a woman. The next thing Reiko sees is one of those creatures crashing into the camp. Reiko grabs her bow, and before she can notch an arrow, the creature leaps.

Brandy Sulliban sees what is happening and lashes out with her double sickles taking the beast down in mid-leap, landing a couple of meters from Reiko's feet. Reiko immediately orders her remaining men to set up a warning line. Though tensions are high, the night is quiet.

The following day, Reiko and her men break camp and ride out of the cove; they come across Corporal Flagg's horse when they make the first bend and see that it has been ripped open by the beast. Reiko orders her men to search for Corrine's body. Ten minutes later, one of her men calls out, and when they reach him, he is on all fours and is throwing up. He points up, and when they look, they find Corrine's body up in a tree, wholly disemboweled, and lifeless eyes staring down at them. They get her down and lay her body to rest. They cover her with stones to keep the predators away. As they finish covering her and one of the men says a prayer. Lieutenant Sulliban happens to look behind her, and she sees a small column of dust coming toward them. and says, "Lieutenant, We got company!"

Reiko quickly looks through her eye scope and sees the small cloud of dust coming their way. She asks Brandy, "How long?" and Brandy tells her, "Maybe three hours!" She orders her men to mount up; They do as they are told and ride. Four hours later, they see a small rundown town, and as they get close, they come up to a sign, and Reiko tells her men to stop. Brandy pulls up beside her and reads the sign, "Welcome to Pawjuck," Below it reads," Enter the gauntlet, make it across; your life is spared, if not! you die!" Brandy tells her that Corrine had mentioned this village of Pawjuck and some others in the area. The occupants are sick fanatics who do not worship anyone or anything and are possibly cannibals. Reiko pulls out her eyescope, looks back from where they just came and sees that the cloud of dust has gotten bigger and closer. "Corrine also told me they are insane and to try and go around the villages.

Reiko looks at her and asks, "Did Corrine mention any other ways across the ravine?"

Brandy answers, "There are other bridges, but she said that they are probably the same way as this one, and it's about a one-day ride to get to the next one, and the other thing is we will be heading back into what is ever chasing us."

Reiko again looks through her eyescope at the approaching cloud of dust and says to Brandy, "The horses won't make it, so we will have to go through!" She tells her men to stay close and stay sharp." They ride up, and as they get closer to the town square, they hear a woman crying. When they enter the town square, they see a woman half-naked, with a cloth sack over her head. Reiko notices that her hands are around the post and look to be tied. She has her head down and is crying. Reiko feels something is wrong with this half-naked woman and is about to order her men forward when one of her men jumps off his horse and runs up to the crying woman, and as he does, he draws his knife to cut her bindings.

Reiko yells, "Wait!" but it is too late; as the soldier reaches her, Reiko and the others hear him ask her, "Are you alright? How could they do this to you?" The soldier removes the sack, and though her head is still down, he sees that her hair hangs down and covers her face. She slowly raises her head, and the soldier is horrified by what he sees as he tries to step back. Reiko and the others cannot see the woman, but Reiko sees the glint of steel in her hand and watches as the woman swings her arm and buries a meat cleaver into the side of the soldier's neck. The soldier falls to the ground, and that is when Reiko realizes what is strange about the woman is that her breasts are heavily scared, and she has no nipples, which immediately brings back the memory of the "Freaks."

Reiko and the others are horrified after seeing her mouth cut to resemble a hideous-looking smile. The woman ignores the others as she straddles the downed soldier and continually butchers him with the cleaver. Reiko can now see something carved into her forehead. The woman starts laughing uncontrollably as the soldier lies on the ground in pieces. She raises the cleaver again, and before she can do any more harm, Reiko takes the woman out with an arrow to her head, right between the two words of "Thief and Whore," and nails her head to the post.

Reiko tells her men to get moving and not stop for anything as they hear the hoots and hollers of more men and women, and soon the townsfolk are coming out of buildings, trying to surround them. She sees an older man with pointed teeth shouting out orders and profanities, assuming he is the town leader. She hears Brandy call out to her and tells her that a bridge is across the ravine. Reiko needs to quickly get her men across the bridge to the other side of the ravine. The horses are skittish, and Reiko has had enough, passing the word to everyone to follow her. She clutches her bow and a quiver of arrows and starts firing off the deadly shafts in rapid succession without hesitation, and within seconds, fifteen men and women are dead on the ground or impaled against a wall or a tree. Reiko has done what she set out to do and makes an opening for escape through the square. Brandy urges her steed forward, swinging her sickles in her hands as she keeps the space from closing, and yells to Reiko to get across the bridge.

Reiko urges her men to push through the gap. As she encourages them, one of her men tosses her another quiver of arrows, and she immediately takes up where she left off, dropping more town crazies one after another, and then she shouts out for Brandy to hurry.

She sees Brandy struggling with her sickles and slowly making her way through the gap that Reiko was able to create and towards the bridge, but she also sees Brandy is getting tired but is still able to keep the villagers at bay. Reiko shouts,

Let's go!" She makes her way to the other side but stays on her horse to take advantage of the height and continues firing arrows. A couple of the men come across with horses. While the townsfolk fall from Reiko's deadly rain of arrows, others quickly fill the once empty spaces, and she hears the scream of horses. She sees some of her men are now on foot and begin to make their way across and are almost to this side when she sees Brandy and realizes she is the last one and is still on the far side holding back the maniacs with her sickles, that allowed her men to escape. Reiko shouts out, "NOW!" and Brandy breaks for the bridge, but her horse refuses to step onto the bridge and turns to the side. Brandy grabs her pack, jumps from the horse, and hits the ground, rolling. She is now crouching on the bridge and has two clay pots in her hands filled with oil for starting campfires. She hits the bridge running, smashes the two pots against the bridge supports, and comes running across. She hears her horse scream and assumes the crazed townsfolk have taken it down. Reiko is watching from the top of her horse and stands up in her stirrups. She orders one of her men to wrap two arrows and soak them in oil. She places one arrow in her mouth between her teeth and notches the second one. She slowly pulls the notched arrow back, and when the bowstring is taut, she asks one of her men to light the arrow. She aims and sees that Brandy has just gotten on the bridge, and through clenched teeth, she says, "Come on; Brandy, move it," and then she sees Brandy trying to make a run for it, with her attackers right on her heels, while at the same time trying to fight them off, but she can't use her sickles like she wants to. Reiko thinks she will make it, and then she sees Brandy take a gash across her thigh and watches her go down. Reiko cannot wait any longer and releases the flaming arrow. It hits its mark, and one of the bridges supports flares up immediately and starts to burn. Reiko does the same with the second arrow, and the second bridge support is now engulfed in flames. Both supports are burning liberally, and the flames seem to have stopped anyone else from coming onto the bridge. She sees some townsfolk running up to the bridge with buckets of water, and she takes them out, spilling the contents onto the ground.

She is about to give up when she sees Brandy standing and running across the bridge. Reiko calls out, "Lieutenant Sulliban, move your ass!" when two villagers jump through the flames and tackle her to the bridge slats. Brandy kicks one of her attackers in the face, which allows her a moment of reprieve from her assailants. She tries to run, and before Reiko can take out her attackers, one of them drives a knife into her leg, and she falls again, but this time she doesn't get up. Reiko takes out her two assailants quickly. The far side of the bridge is now completely engulfed in flames. Brandy tries to stand, and as she does, the left side rope railing gives way, and she falls back down. She continues to drag herself across the bridge. The men want to help her, but Reiko orders them to stand fast, knowing it is too dangerous. Reiko climbs down from her horse, walks to the ravine's edge, and urges Brandy to hurry. She is within two meters of where Reiko is standing with an outstretched hand when the anchor points on the other side can no longer hold the bridge's weight, and they snap. Reiko looks Brandy in the eyes and sees her say, "Thank you," as she plummets with the bridge into the ravine below.

Reiko stands there for a few minutes and then orders her men to move out. Reiko looks down one more time and is about to say, "Thank you!" when she hears, "A little help would be nice!" Reiko has one of her men hold her as she looks over the edge a little more and sees Brandy hanging with one of her sickles entangled in the ropes from the bridge. The men work their way down and help pull her up, and when she is on solid ground, she tells them, "Thank you" They get off the main trail and decide to make camp. Reiko is bandaging Brandy's leg and is about to say something when they hear an explosion coming from the other side of the ravine, and with Reiko's support, they go back to the ravine. She looks through her eyescope, and as she adjusts the focus, she sees movement and can now see the woman with a scar on her cheek, the Commander of the High Priests guard, fighting with her soldiers and trying to get out of the village, but in her case, she needs to turn back. Reiko is still watching as she sees the woman finally make it out of the square. She then refocuses her eyescope to see the villagers attacking a soldier and his mount, pulling them to the ground and butchering both. She focuses back on the Commander and watches as she is ripping her sword from some woman's head and then reaches inside her saddlebag and sees her pull out a small clay pot like Brandy's. These are slightly different as she watches her light it and then toss it onto the pile of bodies that are butchering her comrade. Reiko sees and hears an explosion as the pile of cannibals is now in flames. Reiko watches and then notches an arrow, pulls it back, and holds it. The Commander seems to sense her and looks in her direction. Their eyes meet, and the Commander with a scar looks directly at her as if looking into her soul.

Reiko releases the arrow, and as it flies true, the Commander feels the feathers brush her cheek and then hears a thud. She turns to see the town leader kneeling on the ground with an arrow in his head. She also considers the long thin blade he was within moments of stabbing her. The Commander looks at Reiko, nods, and then salutes her. Reiko salutes back, and she sees the Commander smile as if saying, "We will meet again, and you will die." then she urges her mount back in the direction of her troops. Then Brandy says, "I hope we don't run into the bitch again!"

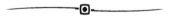

The following day, just after the sun rises, they mount up with Brandy sitting behind Reiko and cautiously enter the Great Forrest. Three days pass, and they do not encounter more priests, creatures, or local crazies. Reiko and her men are walking with their horses at a slow pace, and Reiko is thinking about the High Priestess's Commander when her horse shakes its head and snorts. Reiko immediately calls a halt and tells one of her men to check ahead and do it quietly. He returns and reports several carts and belongings along the road and some bodies. She asks Brandy how her leg is and if she feels up to it, to go with him and checking it out. Fifteen minutes later, Brandy reports there are no survivors. Reiko sees they have another hour before sunset and tells her men to make a cold camp. The mood is somber, and the night passes uneventfully.

They move out with no signs of trouble, and it is just about mid-day when they hear a loud commotion of shouting, screaming, and laughing. Reiko orders a couple of her men to check it out, and when they return, they tell her that there are some old ruins just through the trees, and there are about thirty bandits who have attacked a small caravan. She takes an arrow count and realizes that she has twenty-five arrows. Reiko decides to keep half of them, and she asks Brandy if she is up to it, and all Brandy does is smile. Reiko and her men tie their horses and work through the trees. They get to the tree line, and she can see the ruins or what left of them, and sees the bandits standing in a circle and pushing and shoving a young girl and an older woman at each other, urging one of them to pick up a knife. Reiko looks at the two women and can tell immediately that it is a mother and daughter. The daughter seems to be about sixteen, while the mother is in her mid-thirties.

Reiko hears laughing, and when she hears one of them say, "Come on now, one of you has to pick up the knife. We told you all you have to do is decide who wants to go free and who wants to die?"

She quickly looks around and sees some of the older men are dead, and then she sees something that makes her skin crawl as she sees two men off to the side. The taller one looks like the bandits' leader, and the other looks like a caravan guard. She sees the leader handing the guard a pouch and assumes it is filled with coins. The guard then shakes his hand and mounts his horse. The guard turns his mount and says, "Until next time." He nudges his horse towards the circle of men, and as the laughing dies down, she hears the guard say to the older woman, "If you had just given me your daughter, maybe none of this would be happening." Then he says, "Don't misunderstand, and sweeps his arm over the carnage; what is happening now was inevitable." The older woman spits at him, and he laughs, but before he leaves, he tells the others, "Don't be too rough; we still have to get a reasonable price for her; as for the mother, have your way." and then he once again nudges his horse and starts to ride off.

Reiko is disgusted, and without realizing it, she has strung her bow and notched an arrow. Reiko takes a deep breath, feels the euphoria, and sees the stillness as the silver flash crosses her eyes. His back comes into view as though he was standing a foot away, and she releases the arrow and watches it fly true and hit the departing guard in the back of his head. She watches as he keeps riding until the horse goes to jump a small stream, and as it jumps, the guard falls from the horse, and the bandits are none the wiser as her next shot takes out their leader with an arrow through his throat to silence him. She then starts firing arrows into the group. Every one of her deadly arrows finds its mark as the bandits begin to fall to the ground. One of them turns and sees Reiko firing her arrows with precision, and then Reiko realizes that she is out of arrows and places her bow on her saddle Three of the bandits are coming at her and quickly, when she sees Brandy run past her and directly at them with her sickles spinning, and soon the three bandits are quickly incapacitated or dead as her sickles continue to rain death. Reiko realizes that she is in battle mode and continues to kill or maim anyone who comes within the reach of her sickles. Reiko draws her saber, follows Brandy into the ruins, and together they rain devastation on the bandits. Reiko takes down two more bandits and then watches Brandy's sickles lash out to kill, decapitate, and dismember anyone in their path. She is amazed to see her perform a slightly unusual Kata, and then Reiko recognizes it as "The Kiss of Death," which is a battle, Kata taught to all junior officers. Still, Brandy has changed it up to suit her purposes, and Reiko admires some deviations to the form, which work well with Brandy's tactics to allow a more dangerous maneuver with her flying sickles.

The five remaining bandits surrender while their comrades lie dead on the ground. Reiko's men tie them to a turned-over wagon as the others walk through the slaughter and check the bodies. Brandy is sitting on the ground and leaning against the wagons, taking deep breaths as she keeps an eye on the prisoners.

She hears them talking, and one of them says, "Did you see that one who was shooting the arrows? Every shot was a dead shot, and she never missed, like she was possessed."

One of the captives says, "I have never seen anyone shooting arrows like she was, but that other one with the sickles, she had no emotion, and I think she was the one actually possessed."

Another says, "Yeah, the one with the sickles seemed to be possessed, but the one who shot the arrows, and then did you see her with her saber, she was like a she-demon.

One of the other bandits says, "Someone told me about a woman from the Empire who could shoot an apple hanging from a tree at three hundred meters."

Another marauder says, "I heard it was almost four hundred meters."

Brandy is sitting there listening when she says, "I was there, and it was six hundred meters, and she shot two arrows, the first one cut the apple stem on the tree as it swayed in the breeze, and the second hit the apple, dead center, about halfway before it hit the ground."

The first marauder says, "No fucking way!"

Then the other says, "Yes, that was it, and she had some strange nickname, something like "Keeper of Soils, or something like that.

Brandy shakes her head and tells them, "The Reaper of Souls."

One of her men brings up the horses, and as she grabs the reins of her mount, she sees the mother and daughter walking toward her.

Reiko looks at Brandy and feels sorrow because she has proved herself personally and professionally in all ways of becoming a fine officer. Her grief is that she has never told her or her remaining men that they can't go back to the Empire and that this was a one-way mission if they failed, and they would be like her friend Samuel, without a home. She asks how they are doing when she hears Brandy say, "The Reaper of Souls." she gives Brandy a quizzical look, and Brandy smiles at her and smiles back. Reiko asks the mother and daughter what happened when one of the bandits calls out to her and says, "Shut up Bitch! Don't you say a fucking word!" Brandy moves quickly and has the point of one of her sickles at his throat and tells him, "Not another word, asshole, or from any of you." The man leans into the point of her sickle and lets it cut him. His blood runs down his neck, and he looks at Brandy, says, "Bitch, I will fucking kill you!" and smiles.

Brandy tells him to shut up when suddenly, the bandit's hands are free, and he has a knife in his hand; before Brandy can react, the man plunges the knife into her chest and tells her, "I told you bitch!" and then pushes her away and gets up and starts running towards the woods.

Reiko sees Brandy slump forward and watches the man running into the woods. Reiko reaches to grab an arrow, sees that the quiver is empty, and says, "Dammit!" One of her men throws her a quiver with a couple of arrows, and she quickly notches one but cannot see the man. Reiko orders one of her men to go after him and runs over to a slumped-over Brandy. When she goes to help her sit up, she knows it is too late, as she can see that her life has gone out of her eyes. Reiko carefully lays her down and closes them. Reiko is standing when she sees her man returning empty-handed. He rides up to her and says, "I'm sorry, Captain, the woods got too dense, and I lost him." She tells him to carry on and get some men to dig a grave for Lieutenant Sulliban.

One of her other men approaches her and sees Lieutenant Sulliban lying prone on the ground, and Reiko hears him say "Dam," and then reports that they have found nine survivors, mostly women. Reiko decides to make camp in the ruins so that the survivors can try and gather their things. They do that, and a couple of her men help the women rummage through the remainder of the thrown-about caravans' belongings for food, and she sends out four of her nine men to set some snares and see if they can catch any small game.

An hour later, she is brushing her mount when she hears a commotion and sees five strangers enter the camp and unceremoniously dump her men on the ground with their hands tied behind their backs. Reiko grabs her bow, notches an arrow, and has it trained on who she thinks is the leader's chest in one fluid motion.

Though not a big man, he looks solid, confidently carries himself, and walks into the camp. He has a commanding appearance about him, and he raises his hands as if to surrender but instead says, "Now, let us not get overly excited!" He looks straight at Reiko and then asks, "Excuse me, are you the one in charge? I would guess from how everyone is looking at you."

Reiko slightly relaxes the tension on her bow, steps forward, and asks, "Yes, Sir, and who might you be?"

He looks at her and says, "Let's just say that I am speaking for an individual who is highly interested in the person known as the "Reaper of Souls," and she is paying a hefty price to have you; brought to her."

Reiko realizes right away who that individual might be, and she has flaming red hair, and then she thinks that she never cared for that name, even though she came up with it herself, but more as a jest to Samuel and scare Barnaby Cook. She knew that others might have heard her, but somehow it stuck when the stories spread about her mastery of the bow on her first mission with Samuel.

She asks, "Why would I want to have anything to do with this person of interest, and what is to stop me from killing you?" She pulls the bow's string a little more and keeps her arrow on his chest.

The man says, "Because my dear, there are several crossbows trained on your men, and that if you did kill me, then all your comrades here would surely die, including yourself."

Reiko responds. "What makes you so sure? Say we kill you, and we come to find out this is all a ruse?"

The gentleman stares at Reiko and asks, "If you don't mind, may I?" He raises his hand and holds up four fingers. Out of nowhere, four crossbow bolts hit the ground near the men presently tied up and lying on the ground.

He speaks again, "Now, as I was going to say, please surrender your weapons. There is no need for bloodshed!"

Reiko reluctantly orders her men to lower their weapons, but she is beside her horse, unstrings her bow, and straps her bow to the saddle.

The leader asks her, "What are you doing?"

Reiko says, "I am just putting my bow away." Soon several more riders show up and strip them of their gear. They are all kneeling with their hands tied behind their backs as a large caged wagon pulls into the camp, drawn by three teams of horses. She sees the man who killed Brandy sitting beside a massive man when it comes to a stop, and he starts shouting and pointing at Reiko that she was the one who killed most of his friends. The big man steps down off the wagon, and the whole wagon creaks and tilts considerably under his weight. The skinny man stays on the wagon and says, That bitch deserved to die."

Reiko spits at him and says, "Bastard!" then she watches the big man walk up to the other man, and she hears him ask, "What was the thing with the horse?" and the slender man starts talking in low tones with the big man. Reiko hears "Reaper of Souls" as the slender man gestures to Reiko, kneeling with her hands tied behind her back.

The big man walks up to Reiko, looks down at her, and says, "How the fuck could a little girl like you be the fucking "Reaper of Souls?"

Reiko looks up at the big man and says, "Why don't you untie me and let me show you?" and smiles, which sends a shiver down the big man's spine. He shakes it off and says, Maybe I will!" and waves his hand for the other man to come over.

The slender man walks over to her, cuts her bindings, hands her a bow, and points to a tree about two-hundred meters away.

Reiko laughs and goes to hand the bow back to him.

He asks, "What is wrong, too far a shot?" and she hears his men laughing.

Reiko looks at him and says, "No, it is not too far, just a waste of time."

He asks, "What would you suggest?"

Reiko smiles and says, "How about the main trunk just below the branches on that little white birch sitting all by itself.

The man says, "That must be six hundred meters!" That is impossible. No one can make that shot, not even a Master!"

Reiko smiles and says, "It's more like seven hundred, and how about if I make the shot, you let my men go free, or at least allow them the choice to join your marauders."

Reiko notices the slender man, who she assumed was the leader, looks at the big man and sees him nod his head.

The slender man agrees, and Reiko asks for a quiver of arrows.

The man hands her a quiver and tells her, "Don't get any ideas because I would hate to have something happen to your men."

Reiko sees that a marauder now has a blade to each of her men's throats. She takes the quiver and proceeds to examine every arrow shaft in the quiver. She picks two of them, places one in her mouth, and then notches the other. Reiko slowly pulls back the string on the bow to its maximum tensile strength and raises the arrow's tip in the Air. She takes a deep breath, and while exhaling, she feels a calmness overcome her where all outside noise is gone, the weapon in her hand becomes an extension of her own body, and her heart rate becomes one with her breathing. Reiko can see the soft breeze blowing, and then the Air around her becomes still. She sees the leaves blowing in the wind, then they slow, and then come to a complete stop as if just hanging there. Suddenly, the trunk of the birch tree comes into focus as if it were a meter away. Her concentration is so acute that she pictures the arrow striking the tree's trunk. She now feels the slight breeze and unconsciously adjusts her aim to the left of the target. The slender man is almost sure that she will miss, primarily where she points the arrow. A flash of silver crosses her eyes, and she releases the arrow. The slender man looks at her and then at the tree. He hears the twang of the bow and a woosh of an arrow taking flight, and a few seconds later, the same sound again. Both men wait in anticipation, and when they hear it, they also see it. The first arrow embeds itself dead center in the tree's white trunk right below the bifurcation, and the second arrow splits the first arrow right down its middle. Reiko walks over and hands them the bow, as both men stand there in awe.

The big man smiles back at her and says, "I didn't think it could be done, but a deal is a deal, and a marauder's word is sacred. He then orders his men to release her men, and once free of their bindings, none of them move. The big man is escorting Reiko to the wagon. She hears her men tell the other man, "We would like to stay with our Captain if you don't mind." The slender man says, "So be it." and signals for his men to take her men to one of the wagons.

Reiko then sees her horse paw the ground, and as one of the marauders tries to grab his harness, the horse rears and knocks the marauder to the ground and steps on his arm, breaking it. She lets out a high-toned whistle, and her horse gallops off. She hears the slender man say, "That was one fine-looking stallion; too bad you had to let him go!"

Reiko says, "I know, I took it off of a Dark Army General," and then leans back, closes her eyes, and is asleep. The slender man walks off and says, "That was a fine dam horse."

Chapter 41

Mijikuna Inkinjo

After breakfast the three of them are walking. William says, "Alivia, can I ask you a question?"

Alivia says, "Yes, anything."

"How did you come about that burn mark on your shoulder?" he asks.

At first Alivia doesn't say anything, and then he hears her sigh, and when she looks at him her eyes are moist, and she says "Sorry," and wipes her eyes.

William says, "No, Alivia, I am truly sorry for asking? Please forgive me.

Alivia tells him, "It is alright, but when I was twelve, one of those robed ones and two of the beasts came to our home, and I think they wanted to kill me. My father fought all three of them with one of his hammers, bashed two of them, and choked the third. Ted tells me that the house had caught on fire, and my father was protecting me from the burning timbers when I guess one of the burning embers fell on my shoulder, giving me this scar.

William very nicely says, "I'm sorry."

She looks at him and says, "Do you know what the funny thing is? I don't remember getting burned, and I don't remember the monsters. Still, I remember my father handing me to Ted, and right before the ceiling came crashing down, I do remember seeing blue columns holding up the roof until I was safely out."

"Tell you what, let's not talk about that, and let's start from the beginning, shall we.

Alivia says, "Okay."

William asks, "Do you believe in the teachings of Goddesses?"

Alivia says, "Yes,"

Samuel will train you in fighting and defending yourself with every style of weapon, to using your body, and I will teach and train you in the arts of manipulation of the elements. Do you swear to follow those teachings and use the training and power you have to use to fight the Dark forces?"

Alivia says, "Yes."

"Do you believe in the Goddesses Laki and Jutsuk?"

Alivia answers, "Yes."

"Will you devote and commit yourself to this training?"

William holds up a finger to wait before she gives her answer.

"Before you answer, I want you to know that I will ask much of you in learning your lessons and training. I will ask you many things that you may find hurtful, but you must always be honest. The training will be hard and frustrating at times. You might feel like giving up, but you will need to persevere and overcome any obstacles cross your path. I will teach you how to harness, control, and wield this power you have. Samuel will teach you all aspects of fighting with weapons for attacking and defending yourself mentally and physically. He will also teach you to use your hands and body as weapons. Alivia Ruth Casrone, this is the way it will be, and Alivia, if you have any doubt about this, and decide not to fulfill this destiny, your destiny, do not worry, for Samuel, and I will not abandon you,"

"Let me know your answer in the morning."

Samuel, as usual, catches the night's dinner, William seasons it, and Alivia cooks it. Alivia sits there after eating and seems to be in deep thought. She looks at William, and he smiles. She then looks at Samuel, and he tells her, "No training tonight, get some sleep, and give us your answer in the morning."

It's morning, and they are all enjoying some leftover rabbit and tea. William notices that Alivia is very quiet, holding her cup with two hands, and seems to be staring into it as if looking for answers.

William clears his throat, and he needs to know what she has decided. He is about to ask her when she looks up from her tea and says, "Please, teach me."

William smiles and says, "So be it," Alivia feels a veil wash over her and cleansed. William then tells Alivia that he will explain the fundamentals of controlling and manifesting this power she has inside her. Alivia smiles back at him and then rinses the cups, Samuel douses the fire, and William puts the cups in his pack and picks up his tanbur, and they walk east.

About midday, William calls for a break, and Samuel tells them he will check things out. William tells Alivia to come with him to a small clearing. William is maybe three strides in front of her, and as she tries to step into the clearing, she bumps into a soft barrier and almost falls back on her butt. She reaches out with her hand and touches a wall of Air, and then it is gone.

She asks, "How did you do that?"

William says, "All in good time, my dear. All in good time."

They sit in the clearing, and William continues explaining the fundamentals of the five natural manas or elements. All people have an affinity for them; some can call them forth though minimal, as you might see in traveling shows and magicians. When the God Mother statues appeared throughout the lands, the *"Kachirano"* lay dormant but still reached out until it found those with a strong affinity. Over the years, the seeds planted in the four of you have remained semi-dormant but allowed small trickles to come forth as you have experienced yourself by making the ale at the tavern cold or what you did to that customer's wrist when we met you. The seed or seeds have yet to open themselves up, to spread their roots.

When the Temple of Kyosushinta protection wards were activated, this somehow started the seed or seeds in you to germinate and began to spread its roots. That is why when they attacked you at the Bistro that day, you defended yourself the only way you knew, but it was draining your mind and soul.

William asks her, "Alivia, Remember when I asked you if you ever saw the statues of the God Mother, and you told me no."

Alivia says, "Yes, I remember.

William says, "This is just a theory, but I think you and the other three were all touched by the *"Kachirano"* when you were all newborn babes; this also tells me that you had a very powerful connection to the elements before you were born.

Alivia seems to be lost, and then she says, "I was thinking back, and I remember my mother telling me a story about how one time right after I was born, she was walking in town when she felt something good. She somehow felt she had a bond with three other mothers, but she never met them or knew who they were."

William tells her, "That would make sense, seeing that you were a newborn. As I have mentioned, the *"Kachirano"* had Chosen individuals with a high affinity for manas or elements. I think it chose you because you seem to connect to at least two of them. We know of the water as your dominant mana. I also sensed Air as a second, and you might have a third." Alivia says, "Really!" William looks at her, sees her smiling, and says, "Yes, let's get your lessons started.

Alivia asks, "William, before we start, why do you call them sometimes manas and sometimes elements.

William looks at her and says, "No reason in particular, other than if you are speaking the ancient language, you will use the term mana mostly out of respect for the language. The term element because times change, but other than that, there is no difference between the two. Do you understand?"

"Yes," she says, and William says, "Good, now let's begin.

The lessons William teaches her are always what to do and how to do it, but she cannot bring it forth no matter how hard she tries. Alivia is frustrated because she knows deep within there is something there. She can sense it, has used it, and wants to come out. She knows if she can sense it, then she should be able to embrace it, and if she can embrace it, she knows she can use it. She knows if she can learn how to do that, she will be able to learn how to release and control it. She trains with William and Samuel daily, week after week. William can sense it inside her like a flower with its petals closed tight. It wants to bloom and is ready to bloom, but something prevents the petals from opening, and he can feel Alivia's frustration. William knows that he can help her, but if he does, she will not experience the euphoria of accomplishing it herself. She would never be a hundred percent unless she did it alone.

That night after dinner, when Samuel gets up, so does Alivia. Samuel tosses her what she thinks is a wooden branch and catches it when she is standing. Alivia looks at it and sees that she is holding a wooden replica of the sword he carries. He explains that this is your sword, your weapon and that she has to take care of it. He tells her that she will be required to eat, bathe, sleep, and keep this sword within arm's reach. She is under no circumstances to relinquish her sword to anyone other than himself or William.

Samuel finally says, "Do you understand?"

Alivia answers, "Yes, Samuel."

"Good, Now please hand it to William, and I will wait for you over there and points to the clearing."

She walks over to William, kneels, and offers her sword with both hands and palms up and open. William takes her sword and says something that she cannot quite hear. Then she sees his hands softly glow with a mixture of colors and watches intently as the colors seem to flow and dance along the length of the wooden sword, and then watches as the dancing shades of color are drawn into the wooden sword.

She looks up at William and sees him smiling, and then he tells her, "Hurry now, you don't want to keep Samuel waiting." She takes her wooden sword, and she immediately feels the five elements infused in the wood. She runs up to Samuel and shows him, and he tells her, "Remember that is your sword; cherish it, and then he says, "That wood is ancient and can only be found in one variety of trees on Chikyu. You can almost say that it is a present from the Goddesses; as for the elements, those are all William, and your wooden sword is just as strong as the finest steel, as long as you take care of it."

Her lessons continue during the day, and her frustrations are vented every night.

Samuel has learned that the first ten or fifteen minutes of the lesson is a venting session to release her frustration. When that is gone, she takes a deep breath and relaxes. Then the lessons continue as usual. One night, after her frustrations have been vented, Samuel tells her to pay attention because he is going to show her something new, and that is when Samuel changes his sword to his other hand. He proceeds to attack Alivia in ways she is not used to, and she soon finds herself sitting on her backside with no sword in her hand.

Samuel helps her up, and she is at a loss as to how he did it because he made the same moves as always. Samuel tells her to sit, explaining that all sword fighters, whether left-handed or right-handed, learn the same basics for using a sword. The secret is that the blade position is always slightly different because they are taught the same technique in delivery and execution, consisting of slashes, jabs, sweeps, or whatever. It would be best to recognize these differences whether your opponent is left-handed or right-handed. He asks if she understands, and Alivia thinks for a minute as if turning different scenarios in her head and then says. "Yes."

Samuel has come to recognize these lapses when training because he has realized that Alivia has taken it all in and processed it, and just like everything else, within a month, she has learned to master it.

One night after their lessons, where Alivia is capable of using her sword in either hand, they are drinking some water, and Alivia asks Samuel, "Why?"

Samuel knows what she is asking but answers her question with a question, "Why, what?"

"Why can't I learn to bring forth this great power supposedly inside me?"

"Alivia, I have taught you the skills of fighting with a sword, and you are an exceptional student. You have fine-tuned your sword skills to the point so that it looks natural, and the sword looks like an extension of your arm. You have toned your body and mind, both physically and mentally. You adapt and learn from your mistakes with the situations I've thrown at you, and you remember your mistakes so that they don't happen again. I have taught you to anticipate most moves simply by the way I am standing or holding my sword. You see, with your eyes, the little things that would normally go unnoticed by any simpleton who thinks he can use a sword. I could probably stand here well into the night and explain why you cannot touch the *"Mijikuna Inkinjo,"* but before you ask, I will not say anything more; that is something William will have to explain."

Soon the weeks turn into months, and her sword skills are impeccable. Samuel is impressed with her adaptation of the fundamentals. She asks questions and tries different techniques that have surprised him once or twice. She could hold her own and beat some of the older and more experienced swordsmen he has known, and he thinks back for a moment and would love for her to experience and standoff with either Bruns or even Higgs, and he smiles.

Alivia is surprised to see Samuel smiling during their lessons, thinks he is not paying attention, and tries to take advantage. She throws a volley of sweeps, stabs, over-handed and under-handed attacks at Samuel, and he deflects every one of them, and he still does not give her his full attention. She gets frustrated and over-extends her thrust, and suddenly Samuel is there and sweeping her feet out from underneath her, and he has his practice sword at her throat. She gulps, and then Samuel reaches out with his hand, and she grabs it, and when he has pulled her up, he says, "Never underestimate your opponent, because while you might think one way, he is thinking the other." He then flicks his finger at her forehead, not hard, to get her attention, and says, "That was for over-extending your thrust!"

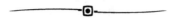

As with every lesson, Alivia is already a little frustrated because William will go on about her inner self in the morning. She is ready to hear it when William says, "We will try something different today," and asks her, "Do you trust me?"

Alivia says, "Yes."

William steps behind her and places one hand on the side of her face with two fingers on her temple and his other hand with his palm flat against her lower stomach just above her womanhood. He softly whispers "*Mijikuna Inkinjo*" into her ear. Alivia repeats the exact words. She feels the warmth in her loins and hidden emotions that she has never felt. William says, "It is alright, my dear, to feel this way. Nothing is going to hurt you. I promise that I will not allow anything to hurt you."

William asks her, "What do you feel?" She feels a warmth deep inside her loins, slowly expanding and running through her veins, saturating her body. She replies, "Different."

William says, "Good," and asks her, "What do you want?" Alivia thinks back to the night her father died saving her and how the monsters injured Ted, and then she feels the burn scar on the back of her shoulder resonate and tells William a single word, "*Revenge*." The warmth in her loins explodes, and a raw power emanates from within her. The hairs on her body start to tingle, and then she feels the coolness of the water, the chill of ice, and the earth vibrating under her feet. She then feels something unique that she has only felt once in her life, and that was the night her father died. It is a power that wants to caress her, and as it starts to caress her, it begins to blossom, growing ever more significant. She likes it, and she needs to feel it. She is about to reach its pinnacle when she sees them, the same creatures that were the cause of the burn on her back and her father's death. The same ones attacked her before she started on this adventure and injured Ted, her second-father. Four snarling and bearing large fangs with their claws extended to rip and mangle.

She panics and feels the blossom closing, fading, followed by the disappearance of the feel of the earth, then the chill of the ice, the coursing Air, and then nothing, as everything finally stops. She can feel nothing, and the creatures are still coming at her.

She feels William standing beside her and looks at him. He tells her, "Do not look at me; look at your enemy!" She sees that they have stopped coming at her. He leans forward to whisper in her ear, "Do not be afraid, do not panic, you are the power, you are the one who controls it. You and only you command it. It loves you; it wants to do your bidding, let it do your bidding, but mostly let it do your killing."

The creatures move slowly towards her once more.

Alivia feels the hate for these creatures, and then she feels the sensations slowly returning. The smell of Earth fills her nostrils, and she raises her hands and watches shards of earthen spikes erupt from the ground impaling one of the creatures. Then the feel of water and Ice. She brings her arms up straight and then slowly brings the palms of her hands closer together. When they are about to touch, she manifests pointed razor-sharp shards of ice in front of her, and then she claps her hands together, and the pointed ice shards shoot towards the beasts. She watches as the beasts are ripped to shreds, and she smiles. She sees one beast remaining, calls for Air and watches as a funnel appears above the beast. The wind funnel turns faster and faster; as it does, she draws in other streams of Air and combines them inside the funnel. Suddenly the beast is lifted into the funnel. Alivia watches as the beast begins to spin faster and faster, and then the image of Ted enters her mind, and she causes the winds to tug and pull at the beast in different directions until the beast explodes as the turning winds rip it apart. She releases the turbulent winds and feels the sensation slowly fade. Then she hears a shrill scream, one she has not heard for many years, and then she sees it. Standing before her is the creature that has haunted her dreams and given her nightmares. The creature wears a black robe and a blood-soaked white cloth over its eyes. She remembers the night when she awoke and saw this creature standing in her doorway, and Alivia knows that it was this creature that took away her father, her home, and her life, and she starts to panic.

William is at her side and softly whispers in her ear. "Breath, relax, concentrate; this creature before you is nothing compared to the power inside you. Let that power caress you, allow it to wrap itself around you and in you, and feel it blossom and grow. You want this; all you have to do is reach inside and touch it."

She takes a breath, and everything seems to settle as she reaches down inside her, more profound than she ever thought possible, and then she touches something. She feels a pure raw power, nothing like she could ever imagine, and she knows it is her "*Mijikuna Inkinjo.*" She accepts it into her body and caresses it with her mind, though not hard, for fear of losing it. She feels it, and it welcomes her. She touches it, and it touches her back. She feels a slight tingle, and this time she feels it deep in her loins, deeper than she has ever felt, and she quivers slightly, as she has never felt anything like this before. It is entirely different from anything she has ever experienced, and she loves it. She smiles as the black-robed one raises its hands, and she sees it muttering when she binds his arms beside him with Air and lifts him off the ground using one hand as if counting on her fingers. The black-robed one snarls and struggles, trying to break free. William asks her in a whisper, "Do you feel it? Do you know where it is coming from? Do you know how to call it forth?"

Alivia speaks softly and says, "Yes," and it starts to blossom, and she now knows where it is and knows that it will never wilt or die.

William says, "Good. Now, what do you need to do? Let me ask a different way. What do you want to do?"

Alivia looks at the robed one and calmly says, "I want to destroy it, and the once tightly closed flower opens up and comes into full bloom. William feels the power Alivia now possesses with her mind, body, and soul. He knows she has finally touched and accepted "*Mijikuna Inkinjo*" or "the *Virtual True Spirit*," and just as calm as can be, in a soft voice, he says, "Do it!"

Alivia slowly closes her hand to make a fist and crushes the black-robed one, and when she opens her fist again, she sees a blood-soaked white cloth drift to the ground. The cloth hits the ground and immediately starts to vaporize and soon is gone. The other creatures she has fought and killed do the same, and soon nothing remains except the earth spikes protruding from the ground and pools of melted ice, and then they are gone.

She looks at William, sees a look in his eyes, and asks him, "What has just happened?"

In a very calm voice, William says, "They were never here."

"What do you mean? They were never here. I saw them!"

"Alivia, please understand that I needed to see how you would do under pressure. The ways I thought would work were not working. I felt the block, but it was up to you to release it. I knew you had the elemental fortitude, but as I said, your *"Mijikuna Inkinjo."* was blocked, and I hoped this would be a way to unblock it. I needed you to remember, to see what was stopping you from touching *"Mijikuna Inkinjo"* to have you feel the pain of what these creatures did to you. You needed to see what it would take for you to manifest that pure raw power. I was unsure what you could do, but I had to see how you would do if it came down to a life and death situation."

Alivia is angry about what William just put her through by bringing back all those hurtful memories that she buried deep so that they would not hurt her, memories that she had locked away in the room. Then here William goes and releases them all. She storms off, leaving William where he is standing.

She returns to the camp, and Samuel does not say anything as he leans against his pack. She proceeds to butcher the rabbit, which Samuel had caught earlier, and then he asks if she plans to skin it or feed it to the scavengers. She is frustrated, puts down the rabbit, throws her knife, hits a tree center, a perfect throw, and then storms out of the camp. William returns, and Samuel nods in the direction Alivia took off. William takes his time approaching her and is almost behind her when he hears her crying. He stands behind her, places his arms around her, and says, "I'm sorry." Then he hears her say, "Me too, and Thank you."

Chapter 42

Reunion

Over the next few weeks, William teaches Alivia how to draw and control her *"Mijikuna Inkinjo"* a little bit more and to be able to bring forth her elementals without draining herself both mentally and physically. Samuel's training progresses, and Alivia is becoming highly proficient with her wooded sword.

They were walking one afternoon after their break, and William notices a group of horses approaching. William tells Alivia that she will have to deal with the situation as William and Samuel sit on a fallen tree trunk next to a stream and look to be carrying on a conversation. Alivia is asking them why when she hears the horses approaching behind her.

She hears someone clear their throat, and William says, "Alivia, dear niece, please don't be rude; we have guests waiting."

She turns to see about twenty-five riders sitting astride their horses. One man, who she assumes is the leader, urges his horse forward and stops within a few meters of the three of them,

He wasn't big, but he was a solid, muscular, slender-looking man with a commanding presence.

"What do we have here?" he asks.

"Nothing much, just two old senile uncles and their loving niece taking them out for a walk."

"Is that so, and why be told are you walking out here, especially on my property?"

"I'm sorry, Sir. We did not know this was your property. My two uncles are very old and had to rest their delicate bones." Alivia looks at William and Samuel, gives them a big smile, and sticks her tongue out at them.

"Please excuse us. We will be on our way," and Alivia goes to step around the bandit leader's horse. The bandit leader moves his horse in front of Alivia, and he hears his men laughing behind him. The man gets down from his horse and approaches Alivia.

He stands in front of her and asks, "Who is going to pay the fee for walking on my property?"

Alivia says, "I am sorry, Sir, but we are poor and have no money other than a few coppers for maybe a loaf of day-old bread in the next town."

The man says, "Well, young lady, that certainly won't do; how about if you give me that pretty locket around your neck, and maybe, just maybe, I'll let the three of you be on your way? How does that sound?"

Alivia looks at the man standing before her and asks, "May I ask a question?"

The man doesn't see anything wrong with a question, so he says, "Sure."

"May I ask your name, kind sir?"

The leader smiles and says, "Ronaldo Silva, the Marauder," May I ask why you want to know?

"I just wanted to know the name of the man whose fucking ass I'm going to kick."

His men start laughing as he hears one of them say, "Be careful, Ronaldo, she looks mean!" All the men start laughing again.

Samuel calls Alivia, "I have told you about your words; please apologize to the nice man."

"Sorry, uncle," and says, "I'm sorry, Sir, for my language, please forgive me," and quietly says so only he can hear, "I'm still going to kick your fucking ass!"

Ronaldo "Starts laughing and tells Alivia. "I like you!"

Alivia carefully draws her wooden sword, and Ronaldo asks her, "What is that stick for?"

She says, "My little friend here is the one going who will kick your…," and she hears Samuel clear his throat, and she says "butt" and whacks Ronaldo on his knuckles, and he yells out and says, "Why, you little bitch!" and draws his sword. Then Alivia says, "Please, Sir, watch your language," and his men start laughing.

They start circling Alivia with her wooden sword and Ronaldo with his sword.

"What are the rules in challenging the leader of marauders and slavers?"

Ronaldo says, "The laws require that the defeated leader relinquish his leadership to the winner.

"Why? Does one of your old teachers want to challenge me for leadership, or perhaps even you?"

Alivia says very calmly, "As a matter of fact, I would like to try it."

Ronaldo starts laughing, turns to his men, and tells them what Alivia just told him. His men start laughing along with him, and then he stops and sees the look in her eyes and can see that the girl is serious.

"Well, little lady, let's make this interesting then?"

"What would that be if you don't mind me asking?"

"If I win, I get to have my way with you," says Ronaldo

"And if I win, I get to do with you what I want, and I get the leadership of your band of men, agreed?"

Ronaldo says, "Yes, I agree!"

"Would you mind if I borrowed one of your men's swords because you see all I have is this stick, and I wouldn't want to embarrass you when I beat you with a stick in front of your men?"

Ronaldo laughs and says, "Sorry little lady, this is a come as you are affair."

Alivia says, "So be it," holds her wooden stick precisely like a sword, and takes her stance to face off against Ronaldo.

Ronaldo walks up to Alivia, takes his stance, looks back at his men, and smiles as his men start laughing.

Alivia feigns a step forward and swiftly brings her training sword down hard on Ronaldo's knuckles, causing him to yell out in pain and drop his sword. He looks at Alivia, surprised, and as he massages his knuckles, she reaches down, grabs his sword, hands it back to him hilt first, and then says, "I'm sorry."

He takes it, and no sooner does he have it in his hands is when she swiftly spins and hits his hand for a second time, causing him to lose his sword again.

There is grumbling from the band of men, and she hears, "Come on, Ronaldo, quit fooling around and teach that bitch a lesson, and let's get this over with, or are you going to let her beat you?" Once again, she picks up his sword and hands it to him, and she sees that he grabs it with his other hand; and she remembers Samuel telling her about ambidextrous sword fighters and how sometimes they make the same moves but are opposite.

Ronaldo sees that she is going to make the same move again, but this time he is ready for it, and as he goes to block it, she does not follow through as she did before, and at the last second, she drops to the ground and bashes his knee. Ronaldo howls in pain, and as he falls forward, Alivia brings her practice sword up, and with an all-out single-handed swing, she connects with the side of Ronaldo's head, and he is now unconscious and doesn't feel the ground smash his face.

Alivia stands back up, and she is feeling a bit invigorated; she turns to the other marauders while placing her wood sword on her back and says, "As your new leader,"

That is all she can get out before some men start laughing and one of them tells Alivia, "Fuck off, bitch!".

The men continue to laugh, but unbeknownst to them, Alivia brings forth the mana of Air, gently wraps it around the saddle cinch, and buckle on the saddle of the marauder who told her to "Fuck off" and releases it. He suddenly falls from his horse, saddle and all. The others start laughing at him. He kicks himself free of his saddle, jumps up, and looks around to see who did it. The others laugh even harder, and one of them tells her she is not the new leader of the marauders because she didn't beat the actual leader; she only beat the second.

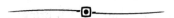

Samuel and William look up as a wagon pulls up, drawn by three teams of horses, stops behind the marauders, and then two more wagons pull up behind that one. They sit there and watch as the driver tries to understand the situation. They see him look down at Ronaldo lying face first in the dirt, and he raises an eyebrow. Samuel motions for William to look at the occupants, seeing that they are slave wagons, with one wagon holding males and the other with females.

The huge man sits in the driver's seat with the reins in his hands while a slender man with a cut on his throat sits beside him. The big man does not seem very happy to see his second unconscious and sprawled face-first in the dirt. He calls out, "What is the meaning of this?" The marauder that fell off his horse runs over to the wagon, and as the big man leans over, the wagon tilts slightly, and the man explains what has happened.

Everyone hears him, "Are you telling me that that little girl beat and knocked the shit out of Ronaldo?"

He steps off the wagon as it tilts precariously to one side, and the springs on the wagon protest. He steps down to the ground, and the wagon rights itself. He walks over to Ronaldo, lying face-first on the ground, grabs his hair, and lifts his head. He sees that Ronaldo is still breathing and lets his head drop back to the ground.

He walks over to Alivia, stands in front of her placing his hands on his hips and looks down at her, and says, "So you're the sweet little girl who beat my second, and it is my understanding that you want to take over as leader of my marauders?" and then he laughs. "If you want to control my men, you will have to fight me, seeing that I am the true leader of this band of cutthroats. So, are we going to do this, little lady?"

Alivia asks politely, "Whom do I have the pleasure of speaking with, Sir."

The big man is surprised by her question and looks at Alivia and says, "Ben, Big Ben Wallis, to be more exact!"

Alivia says, "Well, Mr. Big Ben Wallis; she holds out her hand and says, "My name is Alivia Ruth Casrone, pleased to meet you."

Big Ben takes her hand, shakes it, and says, "Likewise......"

Alivia glances at Samuel and William and sees that they are still having a conversation and does not even pay attention to her or the big guy.

Big Ben looks over at them and then looks back at Alivia and asks, "Were you any relation to that blacksmith in Pell's River who made the fine jewelry?"

Alivia says," Yes, he was my father."

Big Ben looks at her and says, "Sorry for your loss; our paths crossed a few times, and he was a good man and was never overly concerned for my lime of work, as long as whatever I asked him to do was legal, and he got paid, and I have to tell you he was very talented."

Alivia says, "Thank you."

"Now, let's get back to the business at hand, shall we," Big Ben smiles.

Alivia says, "It looks like it's just you and me, Mister Wallis," and she smiles back at him.

Without warning, he takes a massive swing at Alivia's head. She sees it coming from his body language and drops underneath his swing. She pulls her wooden sword from her back and then rolls out of the way. She stands about two meters from him. She has her wooden sword out in front of her and takes a defensive stance holding her wooden sword in both hands.

Big Ben looks at her and says, "Well, I'll be dammed, you are a quick little thing, I'll give you that" He smiles at her and says, "Looks like I'll have to get serious," and lunges at her. Alivia is slightly surprised at how quickly he moves for such a large man, and he tries to grab her in both his hands and misses. She quickly ducks under his grasp, spins around and comes up behind him. She then swings her wooden sword as an unexpected smack catches him behind his ear and causes him to stagger forward. She hears an "Ow!" making her smile as she follows through with several quicker hits to specific areas along his back and shoulders.

Wallis is furious as he turns on her and rubs the side of his head where she had hit him with her wooden sword. He fakes a motion to lunge at her again when she takes two quick steps backward. He gives her a sly smile as she plants her foot firmly and then takes a deep breath. She watches him closely, and in the back of her mind, she thanks Samuel for his training and diligence in the art of body language when fighting an opponent. She thought it was a waste of time, but she now sees what he was talking about since they started training these past months.

She keeps her defensive stance and pays attention to the big man as he distributes his massive weight, and now she sees that he is standing on the balls of his feet. He steps forward and punches out with his left fist, and she brings up her wooden sword to block the punch. When his left fist connects with her wooden sword, she feels the vibration through her body. Silently, she thanks Samuel for teaching her foot placement; otherwise, she could have probably been knocked off balance or over. He brings his right fist in an uppercut to smack this little girl who has become an annoying gnat and is very surprised as she grabs his left wrist. She has her hands on his wrist and pulls his arm straight toward her using his forward momentum. She steps to his right at the last moment, which causes his own body to block his uppercut.

She has hindered the effect of his uppercut as she continues to pull on his arm, and when he is past the point of no return, Alivia lets go with one of her hands and snatches her wooden sword, and when she has a firm grip, she bashes him on the side of his head.

Big Ben screams in pain as Alivia squats, launches herself into the Air, uses his knee as a springboard, and performs a half twist. She lands on Big Ben's back and brings her wooden sword down on his head. He reaches back to try and grab her when she pushes herself off, lands in front of him and brings her knee up to catch him in the face. She hears something crack and knows that she broke his nose. She quickly steps aside to allow him to continue his journey so that, like Ronaldo, he lands face-first into the ground. She hears Big Ben moan and knows he is not out quite yet. She starts to finish him when the other man, who has been sitting in the wagon the whole time, has been watching the fight unfold and does not like it. Especially when this little girl just took down both of his bosses and will be dammed that he will work for a little girl.

He jumps down from the wagon and walks over to the girl squatting near Wallis. He is about to reach her when he stops and allows a long thin blade to slide down his sleeve into his hand. He goes to take another step and realizes he cannot. He then tries to raise the thin blade and discovers that he cannot lift his arm or move. He now sees the young girl standing before him, and he starts sweating. Alivia reaches over and removes the slender blade from his hand. She presses the point of it on his cheek just below his eye and asks him, "May I ask what you had planned on doing with this?" then she throws the knife, and it embeds itself into a tree trunk by almost half the length of the blade, and she is now standing in front of the marauders.

The marauders jump from their horses and rush Alivia swinging their swords. Samuel starts to get up from the log when Alivia looks at him and smiles. Samuel sits back down with his hand on the hilt of his katana.

Alivia assumes a stance, and Samuel notices that it is the stance that manipulates a kata for taking on many enemies at once. They rush her, and she drops, sweeps, lunges, whacks, and swings her wooden sword with precision. Alivia stands back up after performing a forward roll and is now facing the marauders again. Still, this time she is only facing half of them, as the other half is sprawled out on the ground, incapacitated, and they are not getting up anytime soon. Alivia feels the warmth of the *Mijikuna Inkinjo* and raises her hand, and the remaining bandits are soon encased in individual bindings of Air and are unable to move. She puts her sword away on her back and waves her hand so they all fall to the ground.

Alivia walks up to each of them and asks them to surrender and accept her as their new leader. Some surrender while a couple still resists. The ones that still fight call her a "bitch and whore" she calls forth a cold wind, and the ones still not surrendering begin to feel ice slowly crawling up their legs. One of them is just about to call her a "cu," she freezes his mouth shut, and then his whole body. She's angry and speeds up the process on the others, and within seconds the remaining five marauders are frozen in ice up to their necks. She pulls out her wooden sword and walks over to the one marauder frozen in ice, smacks him, and the others watch him shatter into tiny pieces.

Just as she whacks the frozen statue, another wagon comes up behind the first and stops. She sees that this wagon is also full of females. She releases one of the marauders from his bindings, grabs the keys off Wallis's belt, and tosses them to him. She tells him to go and unlock the wagon and release the prisoners. He does as he is told and runs over to the wagons, and with shaking hands, he finally opens the cage doors and then begins unlocking their shackles. After the prisoners are released, she watches them go to a large in the first wagon and collect their weapons and gear. Alivia turns back to the five frozen marauders and asks them again to accept her as their new leader per marauder law. Though still frozen, only two accept her, and she releases them from their incarceration of ice. She calls two of the former prisoners over, who are now well-armed, and asks them to escort the captured marauders over to the wagons. The soldiers order the marauders to remove all their valuables and empty their pockets, some start to protest, and Alivia walks over and asks, "Do we have a problem here?" The captured marauders immediately shut up and do as they are told.

Alivia releases six of the marauders, still held captive by the bindings of Air, and tells them to follow her.

She walks up to the still unconscious Big Ben and Ronaldo and tells them to carry both of them to the wagons. It takes four of them to move Big Ben, and they place both inside the first wagon. All those who surrendered are locked up in the second wagon.

The ones who refused to surrender, along with the one that tried to stab her, are placed in shackles and loaded into the third wagon.

Alivia is sanding there and looks at the first wagon and counting Wallis and Silva; there are twelve marauders. She looks at the other and counts five marauders.

While standing there, one of the released prisoners walks up to Alivia and asks if she knows the man standing there talking with the other man. Alivia tells her that they are her uncles.

The woman has a look of surprise on her face and then says, "Thank you."

She excuses herself and walks towards William and Samuel, and Alivia tells the released prisoners to watch them, catches up to the woman, and walks closely behind her with her hand on her wooden sword.

Samuel looks up, smiles and says, "Captain Takahashi, "Nice to see you again,"

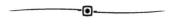

Princess Asami is in her room reading reports when she feels a slight tickle on the back of her neck; she smiles, then goes back to reading her reports and starts humming.

The End Book I

Pronunciations

Nimponin – Nim-po-nin – Dark God from the Dark Realm

Kamiyobo – Kam-e-yo-bo – Eternal Goddess / Mother to the Twins Laki / Jutsuk & Guichi / Tanin

Shingakusha Hoseki – Shin-ga-koo-sha / Ho-se-key – The Sacred Crystal of the Heavens

Kurosagasu – Koo-row-sa-ga-sue – The black hole that is the gateway to the Dark Realm

Kinoumi Gotenku - Kee-no-u me / Go-ten-cue – The Spiritual Leader in the Ancient Language for the Tatokai

Tendaishi – Ten-die-she – Neither Gods or Demi-Gods, but Celestial beings Laki, Jutsuk, & Guichi, Tanin

Sendoka – Sen-doe-ka – The High Priest or Leader of the Laki-Jutsuk Religion

Chiraka – Chee-ra-ka – The ability to achieve a heightened awareness of a proficiency well above a Seventh Level Master

Chikyu – Chick-you – The World

Laki – La-key – Female Twin to Jutsuk

Jutsuk – Jute-sook – Female Twin to Laki

Guichi – Goo-chi – Male Twin to Tanin

Tanin – Ta-nin – Male Twin to Guichi

Kachirano – Ka-chee-ra-no – The seed implanted in some to allow the Mijikuna Inkinjo to flourish

Choobachi – Chew-ba-chi – Queen in the Ancient Language for the Tatokai

Boturoka Tomoni – Bow-two-row-ka / Two-moe-knee – The words spoken by Samuel to establish a bond with the Princess Asami

Sutaraukaji – Sue-tar-a-ca-gee – The Eyeless Priests from the Dark Realm who control the Chizobutsu

Chizobutsu – Chee-zoe-boot-sue – The Savage flesh eating beasts from the Dark Realm

Chikashinmizawa – Chee-ka-shin-me-zawa – The manifestation when all five elements are combined

Kaisoshosuko – Kie-so-show-su-ko – The High Priestess for the Dark Ream, and Leader of the Dark Realm Army

Zokotarumo – Zoe-co-ta-rue-mo (Freaks) – Human beings that have taken to self-mutilation, piercings and tattoos, who thrive for the kill

Moerutonoriko – Moe-rue-toe-nor-ee-co – The Ancient language from the Dark Realm for conjuring fire balls

Rinju Kitikorosu – Rin-ju / Key-te-ko-row-sue – The ancient language for "Death Slayer"

Shikakin – She-ka-kin – The Ancient Language for the Title for a Defender of the Sendoka

Shikei Narasu – She-kay / Na-ra-sue – The blood sword of the Ultimate Dragon Warrior

Nakeshidoka – Na-kay-she-doe-ka – The Staff of the Imperial Master of the Elements

Sukaimohotai – Sue-ki- moe-hoe-tie – The Ancient language for the element / mana of Spirit

Temple of Kyosushinta – Kyo-sue-shin-ta – The Sacred temple where the second Crystal of the Heavens is kept

City of Shinjukosuk – Shin-ju-koe-suck – The City that has grown and expanded because of the Temple

Kutosu Kyochi – Ku-toe-sue / Kyo-chee – The black obsidian wall that protects the sacred valley

Mijikuna Inkinjo – Mee-jee-ku-na / In-kin-jo – The self-awareness that the Gifted bring forth from their inner cores to harness the elementents

Sadenkiwa – Sa-den-key-wa – The lands of Chikyu

Nangoku Tairi Kuare – Nan-go-coo / Tar-ree / Coo-ar-ree – The Great Plains of the Southern continent

Kari Dokegi – Car-ee / Doe-keg-he – The sea that separates the southern continent from the Land of the Clans

Hinashi – Hin-na-shi / Similar to Heaven

Tusukam – Two-sue-calm / Similar to Hell

Author's Note: The ancient language depicted throughout this book is a language that has only recently been rediscovered in a small fortress on the northeast coast of New Beige. The words are an ancient text, and any form of decipher is presently unknown, but the words seem to carry their own meaning.

Acknowledgements

To my son, William, who inspired me to write this book, and to my wife Akiko who has been patient throughout this whole experience.

I travel and spend many hours on the road. I would like to thank Isa B. for transcribing my earlier writings to a functioning word format, and also for urging me to take up the writing of this book after it had been on hold for a long time.

To all the others who might have read bits and pieces of the manuscript, at different stages to make sure the story stayed on track.

B⊕⊕K II / The Approaching St⊕rm

A nefarious darkness has come into this world and is sweeping across the continent. Kingdoms both great and small are decimated and left on the verge of extinction. Small isolated villages and towns are set ablaze, men, woman, and children horrible butchered or impaled on wooden stakes and placed along the roads that this darkness is traversing, while others are hacked to pieces and their body parts are roasted and eaten.

Horrible stories and rumors run wild of men and woman who wear black robes and blood-soaked cloths to cover their sightless eyes and have neither noses or ears and are known as, *"The Sutaraukaji"* once prominent priests of the Guichi-Tanin Religion. Stories tell of these priests having fallen from grace in their High Priestesses eyes, that as a punishment they are converted into *Sutaraukaji* and are imprinted with a lavish dedication to the High Priestess herself, and any deception is met with excruciating pain and death. The advantages of becoming a *Sutaraukaji* is that they themselves can change once loving, decent human beings, whether they be male or female into creatures that seem to be spawn of evil. These creatures have the characteristics of something human but also resemble some unknown species of beast. These creatures walk and run on all fours. They have a superior sense of smell, along with vicious fangs, and sharp claws, and prefer hunting and killing in small groups of three or four. Though they have a mentality of a carnivorous beast, they are cunning. They also have a hierarchy of an Alpha leader in each small group. Whether it be male or female that Alpha along with its pack have a great affection and dedication for their masters the *Sutaraukaji*.

The *Sutaraukaji"* or Dead Eyes control these creatures that are known as the *Chizobutsu*, by using words of a long-lost dialect, or straight out of the Guichi-Tanin Scriptures that are embedded in their minds once they are transformed into *Sutaraukaji*. They carry short handled leather whips that have steel barbs woven into the ends. One would think that these whips are used to control the *Chizobutsu* but in fact the *Sutaraukaji* use the whips to inflict pain on themselves for devotion and penitence, and on any captured woman for their own sexual gratification, and sweet taste of human flesh.

Another group of this massive army is human though to look at them one would have to think twice. Most are considered freaks due to the men and women are marred with grotesque scars and meaningless tattoos and piercings covering their bodies. Those unfortunates who are captured and who do not want to become a follower are beaten, and raped and end up usually impaled on long wooden stakes still alive and placed in the centers of towns and villages as the fire of the villages rage around them. The young ones are slaughtered and tossed to the *Chizobutsu* for food. The elder children are forced into slavery carrying the heavy burden of this non-stoppable army.

CPSIA information can be obtained
at www.ICGtesting.com
Printed in the USA
BVHW032103150722
642263BV00016B/385